HER FORBIDDEN PROTECTOR

COMPLETE SAVAGE SERIES COLLECTION

MILA YOUNG

DEDICATION

To everyone who loves wolves as much as I do, who will never stop dreaming, and who are certain soul mates exist.

COMPLETE SAVAGE SECTOR SERIES

Lost Wolf
Broken Wolf
Fated Wolf
Cursed Wolf

LOST WOLF

SAVAGE SERIES

LOST WOLF

My fated mate sent me to my death

But I can't be killed easily.

Especially when four Viking Wolves awaken a passion within me that ignites fire through my veins and heat into my bones. They see my potential. See me despite my unique blend of darkness.

With me at their side, they want to conquer our broken wolf world.

But it's a deadly game, one I won't play without a few demands of my own--

Help me get revenge against my fated mate, no matter the cost.

PROLOGUE

Narah

I wish I could say that my life will have a happy ending, but I've long ago accepted that's not my path. My status as an Omega has always drawn Alphas to claim me as their own. I've known this my whole life, had it drilled into me from the moment I could speak. I've had years to prepare for my mating ritual. But now that the night has arrived, all I want is to run away.

Does that make me weak?

Maybe… but I prefer to think it makes me a survivor. After all, we live in a broken world ravaged by a virus and ruled by wolf packs, where Omegas like my sisters and I are apparently only good for rutting and impregnating. But what's the alternative? Live outside the Storm Wolves' pack at the mercy of rogue wolf shifters who will kill us? No thanks. So we make do, even if that means lying and wearing fake smiles to ensure we keep our heads on our shoulders.

We grew up here, and this is where we are safest.

You do whatever it takes, my father used to tell us. *Just never let them see what you really are.*

"Are you nervous?" Kaira asks, distracting me from my thoughts. She combs my long hair as I sit in the middle of our small stone hut. To say I'm nervous would be an understatement, and I look up at my sister, the panic on her face mirroring my knotted insides. Like me, she has a narrow face, a thin nose, and full lips. But while her eyes are the color of the bluest sky, mine remind me of a burning sunset. My father said I must have been born from fire to have such bright amber eyes.

For my two little sisters' sake, I put on a brave face to reassure them. Even if a ripple of fear plunges into my gut that I'll somehow ruin the ritual tonight.

I ought to be bouncing on my toes and be grateful I found my fated mate in this pack. Otherwise, I'd be given to another wolf shifter for rutting since more than half the pack is made up of Alphas who haven't found their mates. The rest are a combination of Betas and Omegas at the mercy of these Alphas.

That's why I need a strong man by my side, so I can protect my sisters from the others in this pack. It will give me time to help find their true fated mates.

I breathe deeply and sit back as Kaira keeps combing my hair.

My stomach hurts the more I think about what's coming. *Moon goddess, forgive me should I end up vomiting all over my mate from nerves.* That would be the exact opposite of a perfect night.

"Do you think he will treat us well when we all move in together?" my sister continues. I hear the trepidation in her voice, only adding to my nerves. We've seen the atrocities taking place in the Storm Wolves' pack, a clan once run by our father. We watched him get defeated and killed by the current Alpha after our mother vanished in the woods. They called her a traitor for leaving the pack, and our father paid the price.

"How could he not," I answer. Martell is a new addition to our pack, and electricity sizzled through my body at our first and only meet, my body craving him instantly. Secretly, my reaction scared me, as there's something unfathomable about already feeling connected to someone I barely know. I am guessing with time I will grow more affectionate toward my mate, feel emotion beyond the jarring desire that ignites in my body around him.

"I'd be nervous," Jae butts in from across the room, sitting cross-legged on her blankets, plaiting a floral arrangement. She scrunches up her face in our direction. "Did you see the size of Martell, and his nose? How are you meant to kiss him around that?"

Kaira and I both laugh. Jae is the youngest of us at only fourteen, so she hasn't quite reached the stage of finding boys interesting. And it's better she stays that way for as long as possible.

Kaira leans in to whisper over my shoulder. "Mother told me that kissing was the *mildest* thing you need to worry about on your first night, sister. Are you ready for this?"

My stomach clenches at the thought, but it's what finding your soulmate is all about, right? Consummating your connection.

"How hard can it be?" I reply with more confidence than I feel. Mother told us the basics after we each experienced our first wolf transformation. *Let the man take control as he mounts you. It will hurt,* she said, *but that will pass.*

Kaira comes around to face me, pulling long strands of my dark hair over one of my shoulders, where it tumbles down to my stomach. Like Jae, she has shorter hair, the color of acorns, with a slight wave in it. She keeps it always tucked behind her ears, showcasing her face covered in freckles. She is beautiful, and even at sixteen years old—three years younger than me—she's already caught the eye of so many Alphas in this pack. The top Alpha who runs the Storm Wolves' pack is the only thing that has stopped the wolves from claiming us until now.

I lick my dry lips and try to push aside the thought of what's coming tonight. I'll deal with it when it happens.

"Done." Jae rushes over to help Kaira pin the flower arrangements through my hair.

A heavy knock comes from our front door.

"He is ready for you," a male's voice calls out from outside our hut, and suddenly I'm sweating and forget how to stay calm.

I'm on my feet, and my long, deep blue dress falls to my ankles. It's a simple garment, cinched at my waist with elastic, the sweeping V-neck decorated with dried flowers my sisters helped me create. The dress once belonged to my mother, and wearing it makes me feel like she's still with me.

I shift my weight from one foot to another, trying my hardest not to overthink this. *Just go and smile. He will mount me, then show proof to the top Alpha that I bled to confirm my virginity.*

I physically curl in on myself at the thought. Do I just lie there and let the others watch? Sweat trickles down my spine as a tremor shakes me.

There's no way I can do this.

"Take deep breaths. You look beautiful," Kaira says quickly, eyeing me from head to toe. "Now go, don't keep him waiting."

Jae just hugs me, and I embrace her back, holding her tight, wishing to stay with them instead.

"That's enough, or you'll have Narah changing her mind," Kaira interrupts. "It's just us tonight, so how about we play some games?"

The bang at the door comes again, and I flinch in my own skin, missing what Jae says.

"I'm coming," I call out.

With quick steps, I head to the door, fiddling with the ends of my hair, curling it around my finger, not sure I'm ready to do this. With it, a faint spark of golden energy leaps across my knuckles. It always happens when I'm nervous or scared, though it's not like I can do anything else with it. Mother never taught us how.

Kaira slaps my hand. "Don't show him your magic," she whispers angrily. "Do you want to be found out? First bond with him, and once he's smitten, then maybe he'll accept you as a Cursed."

Cursed.

I hate the word they used for half-breeds like us. Half-wolf, half-witch. Mother warned us as children, told us she had hidden her cursed side her whole life and we had to do the same to belong with the wolves. *No side would accept you,* she'd say. *You're neither a pure witch nor pure wolf. So you must pretend to be one to not become an outcast. Let the wolves believe you are one of them.*

I nod to my sister and hug her. "I know, and I'll be fine." Wolves aren't meant to possess magic, but Kaira and I do. Jae was fortunate enough to be spared.

Being an Omega is a disadvantage already in this ravaged world, but to be a Cursed is a death sentence.

"Go now." Kaira ushers me with a small nudge at my back.

I open the door and the cool breeze sweeps over me, but it does nothing to take away the fire swallowing me.

A guard with short-trimmed hair and tiny eyes greets me with a wry grin. His gaze slides down my body, leaving my skin itching. "Took your time, Omega," he snarls as he swings away from me.

I exchange glances with Kaira, who waves for me to follow him.

Wasting no time, I take quick steps after him over the broken stones that lead from our hut and down the middle of our pack village. Small huts dot the land covered in grass, smoke curling from their chimneys. Our pack territory is enclosed by barbed wire fences just in case zombies make it this far up north. Rumors speak of them swarming the south of Romania, and they have more recently been seen heading this way for food.

The moon shines brightly, and only the hoot of an owl rings in the air. Often on nights like this, Kaira and I sneak out to hunt for food in our wolf forms in the woods beyond the barbed wire fence. It's when critters are out, and we're fast and silent. Guess that might be a thing of the past if I am now paired with a mate who will provide for us.

It isn't long before we turn down the front yard of a stone house at least three times the size of mine. Curtains cover the windows, and there are no cracks or holes in the walls like many of the other homes. Two guards stand by the door, chatting with the Storm Wolves' head Alpha, Lovis. The man who killed my father yet kept my sisters and I protected under his command. I loathe him but would never show him those feelings.

He studies me with dark eyes. Hardness washes over his wrinkled face, and his tight grin deepens the healed scars across his cheek and neck.

I lower my head on approach for respect. It's the way I've been brought up. Show loyalty to all Alphas.

"Narah." He grips my chin and forces my head up to meet his gaze. "You look pretty tonight in that dress."

I can't even bring myself to smile with how much my throat tightens.

His guards sneer and whisper nearby, their eyes lingering over me. It's not the first time they've leered at me, which is another reason this mating is necessary. Most days it burns me up, the way they stare with hunger like it takes everything in their resolve to not attack me. I'm no fool and know Lovis's time as head Alpha is close to ending. There are so many who wait in the shadows for their moment to replace him. I need to make sure my sisters and I are protected before that happens.

"You look more and more like your mother every day," Lovis mutters, a heaviness sliding behind his gaze, then he clears his throat. He always speaks of her fondly, though I don't remember seeing them talk often when she was alive. "Martell is a lucky man." A hint of jealousy paints his voice, then he releases my chin and steps aside before pushing open the door to the house.

Head high, I walk inside, sensing the guards' eyes on me and hating how they see Omegas as good for only one thing. Hating that in order to protect myself, I have to give myself to another Alpha. I hate this so much I can barely breathe.

I pull the door shut behind me and sweep my gaze across an open living area. There's a small table and chairs to my right with a bowl overflowing with apples and oranges. My mouth salivates because fruit is hard to come by and is sparingly distributed among the pack members. A bookcase sits in the corner, the shelves decorated with a collection of animal skulls, not a book in sight.

Martell stands in the doorway to the bedroom, watching me, his eyes narrowing, but he wears no expression of happiness at seeing me. He's tall and at least two times my width, with short, combed hair parted at the side. His arms are by his sides, one hand gripping the neck of a bottle, and he watches me with the same hunger as the men outside. Thick stubble coats his jawline, his mouth thin, and his sneer reveals a line of white teeth. Everything about him screams power. He isn't the handsomest of men, but I'm looking for someone who will protect us. And my wolf picked him, so I need to keep reminding myself of that.

His dark eyes intensify, and I swallow past the dryness of my throat. Suddenly, I'm frozen on my feet, forgetting completely how to speak.

A wave of uncertainty mingles with so many other feelings… mostly desire sliding over me like invisible hands running up my legs and under my dress. My wolf lingers just below the surface too, calling to him. I still struggle with how my body has a mind of its own around him... my fated mate.

He stumbles on his feet suddenly, then catches himself. How much has he had to drink? This isn't the man I encountered at the gathering a week ago. Sure, he'd been quiet most of the time, but I assumed he was nervous. Now he wears a loose shirt over his large frame, his black pants stained at the knees, and he's barefoot. I can't even tell if he can walk a straight line.

"Come. Join me," he demands, the look on his face a mix of hardness and arousal.

Unease curls in my stomach at the way he beckons me, but my Omega wolf sparks at his command, and I unwillingly step forward. The reality of what's coming slams into me. I can't do this. My earlier bravado is now an illusion, even as I move closer to him.

Outside the house, I hear the men talking, and the room seems to close in around me. They're waiting for the proof that will confirm Martell is my first. The proof that he's claimed me and no other man can dare touch me.

"Hurry up," he yells.

I stiffen, my throat thickening.

"Tell me a bit about yourself," I say with a strong voice, forcing myself to stop several feet away from him.

He snorts. "What for?" He takes a long swig from his bottle, alcohol splashing onto his shirt, before setting it down on the floor. Behind him waits a large bed covered in fur throws.

Bile climbs up to my throat. This is happening too fast.

"We should get to know each other if we are soulmates." I recoil a bit, my voice cracking. "What is your favorite meal, where were you before you joined this pack, those kinds of things?"

He barks a laugh as though I made a joke and takes long strides to reach me. His hand lashes out toward me.

Instinct has me jutting my arm out to block him. He narrows his eyes in response.

"You're a fighter." He growls, and in his presence, my wolf comes to life even more. A single damn touch, and she's there, pining for him. Heat flushes my skin at being so close.

"Good. I like someone who can keep up with me," he announces, and my chest automatically sticks out for his attention at the small compliment.

Martell studies me, the corners of his eyes crinkling as he grins. Then his hand falls to my shoulder. In seconds, he tears the fabric down my arm, material ripping, ruining my dress... Mother's dress.

I gasp and shove him away. "Stop!"

The need to run away drills into my skull. He's triggered a button in my head, one where I suddenly see myself abused by this man, used like I've seen others treat females.

I've been wrong and so stupid to think he was anything but a brute. Fear grips my spine, while a fire bursts between my thighs. My wolf completely betrays me. I recoil, not wanting to cry and seem weaker than he already sees me.

But with meaty hands, he snatches me by the waist and swoops me off my feet, then walks us into his bedroom. A small whimper falls past my lips from the sudden move, my heart pounding against my chest for escape.

"If you want to play hard to get, that works for me." He growls and tosses me onto his bed. "I prefer a fighter over someone who will just lay there."

I bounce on the mattress and rush to frantically scramble off the other side of his bed.

But he's too fast and snatches my arm, then hauls me back toward him. His hands wrench at my skirt, tearing more of the fabric.

A scream wedges in my throat, and I fight him, throwing a punch. "Don't touch me."

He catches my fist with his hand and makes a *tsking* sound. "You better hope that when I knot inside you, your body bears me many children, or..."

The way he leaves his sentence unfinished scares the hell out of me at what lays in store for me. His hand grabs the back of my neck and wrenches me toward him, his breath stinking of Țuică, a local spirit made from plums, and I almost vomit at the stench.

"Can you feel our wolves? They are calling each other. You aren't going anywhere, soulmate. I smell your arousal. You want me, and I will fuck you for a week straight."

My fingers grasp onto his arm, digging fingernails into his flesh, but it makes no difference against someone this strong.

My wolf rises as if beckoned, and there's no denying we're paired by the universe. But this isn't who I want. I always thought the man my wolf would pick would be someone I found myself attracted to, not just my instincts drawn to him. But everything about him repulses me. He is meant to be our savior, my beacon in this dark world, but now I fear I've walked into the demon's den.

"I can taste your slick on the back of my throat. You have no idea how insane you make me." He releases me, and I drop back onto the bed, my breath jammed in my throat. I clamp my legs shut and pull at the fabric to cover my exposed breast. This isn't how I pictured this. Not like this.

Martell pulls his shirt up and over his head before tossing it behind him, revealing a hairy body covered in cuts and bruises. The bulge in his pants makes me dizzy.

I shudder. "Please, can we take this slower?"

His laughter is like claws dragging down my back.

"Strip," he demands, his voice holding no tenderness.

I curl my knees up to my chest and hug them harder while scanning for the nearest window, which I find at the back of the room. It looks big enough for me to climb through, if I'm fast enough. Except, then what?

This is for my future and my sisters' safety, but I don't know if I can go through with it. Sobs catch in my throat as I stare wildly at this monster. My arms shake as I hug my bent knees, fear spreading quickly.

He kneels on the bed, the whole side of the mattress indenting from his sheer mass, and he snatches my ankle. He drags me closer, my dress riding all the way up to my waist. I whimper, wriggling to scramble out of his reach. He breathes heavily like a wild boar, his gaze falling to my underwear. He hastily slides a hand up between my legs.

Fire floods my skin from that single touch. My insides are at war between panic telling me to run for my life, and my wolf whimpering for him. Primal instinct claims me, and all I can think is how he'll rut me, bite me, hit me, hurt me. I hate my body and wolf for wanting this.

"Please, no." I push him away, but in response, the bastard backhands me across the face.

The strike has me flinging back down on the bed, and I clutch the side of my face, tasting blood. My face burns like someone's pressed fire to my skin, and tears spring to my eyes.

This isn't how it should be with a soulmate. Mother and Father never fought. Never.

Martell's hand once again shoves up my legs, rougher this time, before I can clench them shut. He fists my underwear and rips them off me. I scream in response at his aggression and scramble to get away from him.

Rage jolts through me. With it comes sparks of power racing down my arms, lifting the hairs on my nape. Power rushes through me so fast I don't react in time.

Yellow threads of my magic suddenly snap over my fingers and strike outward, biting his hand like vipers.

He shouts from the shock and jerks backward, wrenching his hand back so fast it startles me. He stares at the dark burn marks crawling up his hand, the color from his face draining.

"Goddess, no!" I cry out, frozen in the bed, staring at his hand, at his panic-stricken face.

He's going to report me. He's going kill me.

Wolves don't possess magic.

Cursed are feared and loathed and butchered.

"What the fuck are you?" He scrambles to his feet, unable to get away from me quick enough.

I wrench my gaze to the dark stains on his hands as he tries to rub them clean, the pain clear on his face. I've just burned him, and those marks will never come off. Shit! "It's nothing. Please, let's try again. I'll cooperate."

He stares at me with an empty gaze, like he no longer sees me as his soulmate, but as a stranger. "I asked you a question," he barks, squaring his shoulders, his good hand curling into a fist.

I don't have a clue why I have messed-up magic. I hurry off the bed on the other side, putting something between Martell and me. My hands tremble as I tug the torn fabric of my sleeve back up my arm.

"I'm a wolf. Your soulmate," I answer, unsure of what else to say. My parents always told me to hide this part of myself, to not tell anyone, but with time, it feels as though the power in me has billowed. It has been sparking of its own accord lately.

"Like fuck you are," he snaps, snatching his shirt off the floor and rubbing his fingers on the fabric. "I don't want no freak as my mate. You're a filthy witch! A Cursed, aren't you?"

I hurry to his side, well aware that if Lovis finds out, he'll kill me and my sisters. Nothing with magic is accepted. "It's just me, a wolf," I insist, fear closing in around my throat. "There's nothing unusual about me. Please, I want to make this work. I'll behave, I promise." My voice cracks with desperation.

I reach for his hand, but he flinches from my touch, his lips twisting with disgust. "Don't fucking touch me. You are not my mate. I reject you." He turns and marches to the front door.

He's rejecting me? Is that possible?

Coldness sinks right through me, tearing me to shreds, my wolf whimpering at his words. An ache gouges my chest, like my heart is splitting in two, while my shoulders slump and my knees hit the ground.

"No, no, this can't be." I rock back and forth.

My soulmate rejected me. My wolf will never bond. I will be an outcast forever. And I can no longer stay in this pack.

There is nothing outside our pack fence but wilderness, rogue Alphas who will rut me to death, and zombies if I escape the wolves.

His thumping steps are like a drumbeat to my demise. I can't think of anything but what's coming for me.

Death.

My sisters! Fuck!

I'm on my feet, my heart colliding into my ribcage, then I dart over to the rear window and shove it open. Glancing back, I see Martell swing open the front door. Dread of what I've done cuts me deep, at how horrible tonight has gone.

I hop up and throw myself out of the window in a rush.

I land on my back in a shrub, which stings badly, but there's no time to waste or wipe my tears.

Why the fuck should I care if he rejected me? He's an asshole who'll beat and rape me. But that's not what I mourn. It's my wolf who pines for the soulmate connection. Her agony splinters through me, and my legs feel ready to collapse out from under me at the pain. Soulmates meet only once, and I've just been pushed aside by mine. Banished.

Fear collides into me. I stumble into a shrub, but I can't lose myself. Not now...

Sticking to the shadows, I sprint around the rear of the houses, in and out of yards until I reach my small, dark hut. I burst in through the rear door, startling both Jae and Kaira, who are on the blanket playing cards.

"Narah?" Kaira's panicked voice adds to my fear. She's on her feet, as is Jae, both of them eyeing my torn dress. "What happened?"

"We need to leave the pack right now," I say quickly. "He saw my magic and rejected me as his mate." The words taste sour on my tongue, and a wave of unbreakable sorrow crashes into me. The pain wears me down, slamming into me over and over.

"He *what*?" Kaira's eyes bulge, drawing my attention, and I hurry toward them.

"Are we going to be in trouble?" Jae squeaks. Her hand, still holding a card, is quivering.

"Baby, we need to leave the pack immediately," I persist, taking her by the hand. "Quickly, get your coat and your boots. I will tell you everything later, but we are no longer safe here."

"But this is Father's pack!" Tears roll down Jae's face, and I drag her into my arms. I wish I didn't have to expose her to this, that I could keep her protected from how ugly our world is, how dangerous it is for Omegas like us. My breaths hiccup, but I need to be strong for her sake so we can get away.

I pull back and cup her wet cheeks. "Listen to me, Jae. You are so much stronger than you know. And now you need to be a fast runner for me. Don't stop, no matter what, okay? Can you do that for me?" My skin itches with urgency, and I keep glancing at the front door.

"We should go," Kaira says, her voice frantic, quickly sprinting around the house to collect clothes and food and shoving them into her bag.

Jae's face pales. "W-where are we running to?"

I lick my lips, my mind whirring. "Remember when we once went fishing with the other women in the pack by the river farther up north?"

She's nodding fast.

"If we cross the river, I've heard there are safe places." I hate lying to Jae, but she's so young and already looks terrified. I need to give her hope, anything to keep going. Once we escape the pack, I can come up with our next action plan. But right now, all I can think about is surviving.

"The river by the giant pines?" she asks, her chin quivering.

"Yes, that's the place. And if we ever get separated, we always meet there. I'll wait there for you both for weeks, months, years. However long it takes. Now we need to move fast."

We sprint around the house, putting on coats and heavy boots, taking with us a bag with minimal supplies and a blanket. My mind is too busy racing with fear to really make sense of what we should take. I quickly collect the firestarter from the table and hurry to the pantry where I collect my hunting knives and slide them into my boots. That's when I spot Mother's golden bird-shaped brooch with a large emerald. It might come in handy for bartering, so I take that as well.

The moment we slip out the back into the darkness, there's a pounding on the wooden front door.

I'm shaking, my mind numb from how quickly our life has slipped out of control, but I won't let them catch and hurt us.

Cold seeps into my bones, and I'm trembling. I stay at Jae's back while Kaira takes the lead. Night conceals us as an icy wind sweeps past. This isn't how the ritual was meant to end, and I keep going over the incident in my mind. It's all my fault. I fought Martell too much, which then unleashed my magic. And if I had been a true witch, then I'd have known how to use it to shut him up. But I don't even have the ability to do that. Maybe I really am cursed. Maybe I deserve this punishment.

But my sisters don't.

Kaira reaches the wire fence behind our house, night concealing her and Jae. She tugs at the cut wire to reveal a small opening, and Jae slips through. I grab Kaira's hand before she follows. "Take Jae and run. Don't you dare stop. I'm going to try to distract them in a different direction."

"Narah, no," she gasps, her eyes wide and glistening beneath the moon. Her body trembles beneath my touch, and I hug her fast before my resolve dissolves. "Take care of her. We will meet by the river, alright?" I reach for my boot, pull out a blade, and place it into her hand. "Go quickly." I push her when she doesn't move.

She stumbles, but she never stops staring at me as a loose tear escapes from the corner of her eye. My heart has already shattered into hundreds of shards from the pure fear of what's waiting for us out in the wilderness. But first we need to survive the Storm Wolves.

"I love you, Narah," she whispers, then turns and slips into the hole, vanishing into the night.

Voices from farther in the pack territory reach me. They're searching for me, coming this way.

Desperately, I throw myself into the gap in the wire fence.

Someone seizes my arm from behind me, pulling me back into the darkness behind my hut.

Fear punches me in the gut as I stumble back around, tripping over my own feet. I jerk my head up to a dark form standing over me, a snarl slipping past his lips.

Martell.

Shit!

"You fucking bitch!" The punch comes out of nowhere, and I don't see it until it collides with the side of my face. My legs crumble under me, and I'm screaming with agony as I fall over. Pain spreads up the side of my head, and my vision blurs in and out. I land on my side and stare out through the wire fence and to my sisters sprinting away. They are just two shadows vanishing, blending into the dark, already so far that I doubt anyone's noticed them leaving.

Don't you dare stop.

He grabs me by the arm and drags me across the ground, my head still spinning, my vision painted in stars.

Terror is razor-sharp, cutting into me at how I've made everything so bad tonight. I push myself to get to my feet, but I only keep tripping over myself from how fast Martell is moving.

"Please, it's not what you think," I plead between muffled cries, my throat splintering from holding back the choking sobs.

"You're pathetic," he growls over his shoulder at me, never relenting in dragging me over the ground, rocks and twigs tearing at my skin. "I can't believe I wanted to fuck you."

I thrust against him, my legs dangling behind me, and I'm swallowed by terror. Yet my wolf still whines for him, my body buzzing with need that makes no sense to me.

When he finally does come to a stop, I'm crying and gasping for air.

We're at the main gates leading into the pack territory. Two guards stand nearby, flaming torches throwing shadows over their scowling faces. I know them, have seen them around, but now they look at me like I'm dirt. Martell meets my gaze, and a ruthless smile spreads over his mouth.

His grip eases and I drop to the ground. I glance up, my gaze swinging to Lovis, who steps out of the shadows, and I count at least six other Alphas from the pack surrounding me. All I can picture is my own death, how much they will make me suffer.

"Please." I turn back toward Lovis, still on my hands and knees. "You knew my parents. This was my father's pack."

"She's a fucking Cursed," Martell bellows, resulting in the other men repeating the word. "How could you not know she was in your pack?" His words are venom.

Lovis shakes his head, lowering it like my very presence has humiliated him and put his position as Alpha in question.

My throat clogs, and I can barely breathe. There is no hint of sympathy or endearment in Lovis's expression. All that remains is pure anger, his eyes erupting with wild fury.

"You are nothing to me," he spits the words at me. "Your father knew you were a Cursed and lied to all of us. And just like him, you will pay the ultimate price. As will your vermin sisters." He waves his hand at one of his men. "Bring them."

"Stop!" I bellow, rage striking me right in the core. A spark of electricity zaps down my arms, crackling like fire across my fingertips.

Yellow lightning shoots outward but fizzles just as quickly. This is my fault for always suppressing my power, and now when I need it, it's dead.

"Cursed!" the men shout, keeping their distance. They stare at me with contempt, while Martell's face darkens. His shoulders curve forward like he might transform into a wolf and tear me apart on his own this very moment.

My lungs pump furiously for air. The world spins around me too fast as dread sparks down my back. I call to my power again and fist my hands, but not a damn thing happens.

No spark.

No magic.

Nothing.

"Kill her," one Alpha commands.

I shudder at their hatred. These men are unsympathetic, savages, monsters.

Lovis jerks his attention toward Martell. "She is your soulmate, so the decision is yours to make."

"We're soulmates for life. You can't do this," I plead. More men shout for my death. I scramble to my feet, but someone kicks the back of my knees and I fall back onto the ground. Deep down, I know where this is going, and I need to escape.

In seconds, I'm wrenched to my feet again by Martell and thrown over his shoulder, my mind paralyzed with fear.

I pummel his back with my fists and try to kick my legs out, but his arm is clamped over the back of them like iron. "You don't need to do this."

He's moving fast now through the opening gates, almost running. Darkness swallows us, and I jut my hands out, imploring my power to emerge. Anything so I can strike Martell with it so hard, it breaks him.

Please work, please.

My teeth are chattering while I'm bouncing on his shoulder, screaming. Hot tears flow down my face and neck.

"M-m-martell, I'm not dangerous. You are my soulmate." My voice shatters, and I feel like I'm trapped in quicksand.

"You will never have anything I want. You are filth," he croaks, then abruptly shoves me off his shoulder.

The next thing I know, I'm flying.

I expect to hit the ground, except I'm still falling. And reality tugs me into every direction. He's thrown me off the edge of the cliff that runs alongside our pack territory.

He vanishes from my sight as I descend with speed, and I'm stolen by the night.

I scream, flinging my arms and legs out. My heart is bursting in my chest when a spark of light flares over my hands, and my power ignites.

Suddenly, my back slams into something, hard and fast. Darkness sweeps in and steals away my magic, my hope, my life.

CHAPTER

ONE

ONE DAY LATER

Narah

My eyelids flip open so fast they hurt. Orange lines streak the sky like it's on fire, like the whole damn world is burning. It's only when I attempt to lift my head that every inch of me screams as if someone is dragging blades down my body. I swallow past my dry throat and whimper at how much it hurts to do just that. My mouth tastes metallic and pasty. I flick my tongue out, running it over cracked lips.

I moan as my stomach quivers, and I hurt so bad that I can't move again without feeling sick. Crying, I lay there, remembering being thrown off the cliff. I have no idea how I survived. Though with my body screaming like I'm on death's door, I'm not sure I'd call this survival.

Martell rejected me, and I'm replaying the night in my mind, how badly it ended, how the agony on the outside of my body is nothing compared to the heartache of missing him. My heart lunges faster while my wolf throws herself at my insides, blaming me for losing our soulmate.

I want to scream that I crave such a monster, so I scrunch my eyes tighter to stop the tears. "I don't need him," I croak.

When I finally open my eyes and twist my head to take in more of my surroundings, blinding pain shoots across my skull. The world tilts on its axis, and I stiffen until it settles.

I'm lying on the bottom of the cliff, surrounded by jagged rocks. Beyond them lies a dense forest of wild trees and grass, leaves blowing in the breeze. I have no idea by what miracle I didn't land on the sharp rocks and get impaled.

With a groan, I bite down on my lip to rid the harrowing agony as I pull myself to sit up. I take it slow, sucking in shallow breaths with each move.

Glancing all the way up the rock face, I can't believe how far I fell and that I'm still alive.

Patting my body for broken bones, I gasp at the sight of my fingers and lift them in front of my face.

The top half are black, stained as though I've plunged them into ink. Except this is magic, like the kind I used on Martell. And I remember the fall, the spark of power, then I passed out. Magic is the only explanation of why I survived such a fall, and why I now wear the mark of a Cursed.

My power saved me... somehow.

Like Martell had done, I rub my fingers, but it won't come off. Mother had two black fingers also singed from her magic backfiring, always covering them up by wearing gloves. She had no control over her magic either, which is why she told us not to use ours.

The magic in your blood is unstable, it's wild and can hurt you or kill you just as easily as it does others. So she only ever taught Kaira and me one ability: to detect other magic so we could avoid witches.

I wiggle my toes and slowly rub feeling back into my legs. Somehow my magic saved me, and now I have to get out of here before Martell returns.

When I roll over to get up, fire lashes my sides, and I stop. I have to go slow. I fill my lungs, firm my muscles and get to my hands and knees, then push myself up onto my heels.

I climb to my feet, and my knees wobble. A throbbing ache bites into the back of my head, and I cringe, reaching my hand up. My fingers graze over dried blood matted into my hair, and I search over my skin for the wound but find nothing. All that remains is the mess of what should have killed me. And the pain. My eyes widen, and I'm unsure how to feel after losing so much to survive.

I stand tall and take my first step on unsteady feet, then I stumble into the woods.

There, I press my back to a tree and catch my breath, waiting for the ache in my body to lessen. I look back up at the cliff, still unable to believe what happened. My mind and heart are a battleground of anger and longing, but no matter what, I will never return to Martell's side.

What I need is to focus... and to find my sisters.

Two Months Later

I FAN out the set of cards face down across the table with a gloved hand, then glance up to meet Finn's eager gaze. He's a regular customer, a younger Beta who's never found his fated mate and is determined to discover where she is. Every week it's the same question. But who am I to complain when his payment gives me a place to sleep at the tavern and puts food in my belly?

Raucous laughter spills into the small room I rent in the tavern, but Finn doesn't seem to notice. He's concentrating on the cards. I make it very clear to the clientele that I'm not a witch. Whether they believe me or not is their choice.

We're in a town with no name because it doesn't exist, supposedly. Only the deadliest wolf shifters pass through, those who carry secrets, and others who don't want to be found. No one asks questions. It's a safe zone, run by a self-appointed sheriff, an outcast Alpha who is not afraid to use his rifle to take out anyone who challenges him.

Something I've witnessed a few times. When the man says to follow his town rules, you damn well better follow them.

I've been in this town for two months, waiting for my sisters to turn up at the nearby river, so I sell fortunes people want to hear to make a living. And as long as I keep my predictions vague, those who believe in fortune tellings will make my words fit their circumstances.

I stay cloaked when in public and never get close to anyone should someone from the Storm Wolves travel into town.

The candle on the table suddenly flickers despite there being no windows, and the scent of sandalwood is stronger today for some reason.

"Pick a card," I instruct Finn.

He reaches over, and his hand hovers in the air over the line of cards, waiting for his instinct to select one. His finger falls on one, and he pushes it across the table toward me.

I flip it over to the image of a man lying on a bed with nine swords in his back.

Finn hisses and leans back into his chair, nervously running a hand through his short, golden hair. "That's bad, isn't it?"

"No card is ever good or bad. This card represents fear, so that's stopping you from finding what you really want."

He studies me, then gives me a slow nod. "What else? Can you look deeper?"

"Of course," I answer, knowing when he asks me that question, he wants to hear the words about finding the woman of his dreams. I mean, don't we all want the answers to the universe? I want to find my sisters and not stay up most nights worrying so much about them that I can't sleep. But no cards in the world will give me that answer.

My fingers dance over the card, and I close my eyes, taking a deep inhale to give him the impression of meditating. I should feel guilty for cheating these men out of money, but I don't. Not when I know that none would stop at anything to hurt me if given the chance. In this town, there is a "no fighting" rule. Break it, and you're leaving in a body bag. Since arriving here, I've started to discover so many things about the world no one ever told me. Like not all Alphas outside the Storm Wolves' pack are rogue. That the northern part of Romania is a mecca for all kinds of packs from around Europe, with no one Alpha in charge of the whole territory. Part of the reason has a lot to do with the fact that witches live in these lands too. They are feared by all.

Another deep inhale, and I shuffle in my seat to find comfort.

The air feels thick, like mud, and a little sticky. Or it might be from me having a restless night, or crying by the river this morning, worrying that the worst has happened to Kaira and Jae.

That's why last month I hired someone to search for them. I figured if I'm mingling with monsters, I might as well hire one to work for me. Ragnar, an Alpha from up in Denmark, insisted he has ways to find lost people. Of course he didn't elaborate, just like I didn't expand on how I could help get him through the Poisonous Woods as he requested. If he finds and returns my sisters, I will guide him into the enchanted forest layered with magic traps, which I can detect. It's good to know the only ability my mother taught me will come in handy.

A whisper comes from my left.

I stiffen and crack open an eye, seeing nothing but the empty room with Finn and I sitting at the small table.

"Did you see something?" he asks.

"Yes," I lie, which perhaps is my new secret power, seeing as I excel at telling fibs.

His breath catches, but I close my eyes for a bit longer to authenticate the experience.

A growl slips into my right ear, coming with a blur over my mind, and suddenly I'm lost to darkness, lost to images that collide into my thoughts.

Something is very wrong, and the hairs on my arms lift.

In a sliver of a second, I'm ripped away from the room and now stand in the middle of the woods surrounded by lofty firs heavily ladened with leaves. Something trickles along my arm, and when I look down, I'm clutching a blade stuck in the soft flesh of my chest. I do a double-take, and as if reality catches up, so does the agonizing pain, and my panic. I scream, but my voice strains, and my body stiffens, as every move is hell. I stumble back into a tree, barely able to draw a breath. Blood rolls down my arm, covering my clothes.

What is going on?

A snarl comes from somewhere in the thick woods, the sound deepening.

I jerk my head up just as Kaira emerges from the shadows, cloaked in furs. She studies me, her eyes almost white, and on her forehead she has four white dots trailing from her hairline to the bridge of her nose. More dots sit over her eyebrows. I don't recognize the painted look or where it comes from.

Jae steps out of the darkness too, her skin and eyes normal.

"Help," I plead.

Kaira doesn't move, but Jae's rushing toward me, her eyes wide. "Narah," she bellows.

Movement comes from my right and I wrench my head in that direction, but it's so fast I'm unable to make sense of what I'm seeing at first.

Next thing I know, the biggest gray wolf I've ever seen slams into Jae and pins her to the ground. The animal unleashes a thunderous growl that seems to shake the ground beneath me.

Jae screams, shoving her hands against the beast, kicking its belly.

Kaira only laughs, and I don't understand what's going on.

"Jae," I scream, trying to move, but I only stumble to my knees.

The wolf bites down on her neck, so ferocious, so fast, that the sound of torn flesh sickens me. Her cries turn to gargled sounds. He pulls away with her throat in his mouth, and blood sprays all over Kaira, who keeps laughing.

"Jae," I murmur. My heart clenches.

She can't be dead... she can't be.

I hit the ground on my side, my chest seizing, and the last thing I see is Kaira, who crouches in front of me, tilting her head to the side.

"You chose the wrong side, sister," she says.

My eyelids flip open, and I'm back in the tavern room. Involuntarily, a scream rushes past my lips. Startled, I push away from the table and Finn. The chair under me swings backward, taking me with it, and I fall over, my legs catching under the table, bringing that down with me too. Tarot cards are tossed into the air, the candle thrown across the room. Everything happens so slow, yet my heart is galloping, my throat squeezing shut.

Jae's death.

My death.

Kaira....

No, no no! She wouldn't.

I scramble to escape the tangle of the table and chair while Finn puts out the small fire that caught on the fabric covering the walls to give the room a more soothsayer look.

Tears blur my vision, unsure what I just saw. I've never had visions before... never. That can't be what I experienced.

Finn is there, lifting the chair off me, then he grabs my arm and hauls me to my feet. "What the hell was that? You kept screaming Jae's name. Is that who you see as my future mate?"

I blink at him, unable to think straight. My teeth gnash as part of the vision still holds onto me, sliding over my mind. Yanking my hand free from his grip, I turn away.

"I've got to go," I murmur.

Jae's death is all I can picture, all I can focus on. I stumble toward the door, terror bleeding right into me.

"I paid you, so I want my reading," Finn demands, slapping his hand down on my shoulder, fingers digging into me. They're like steel, forcing me to stop.

Turning toward him, I shake off his grip, my lips curling at his command. Anger burrows through me as his disgusted gaze settles on me, at the way his nostrils flare.

I dig my hands into my pocket, taking out his payment and tossing the coins at him. The words slip from my mouth. "Take it, because you will never find your fated mate."

"You fucking witch," he snarls, and his calloused hand grabs me by the throat, hauling me toward him, his response cold and merciless.

Maybe it's the fear of what I've just seen, but a new bravery comes over me, and I jab my fists at his chest. "Get the hell off me."

But my attack is weak and unsteady, managing to do nothing but anger him further.

The bastard roars and releases me, after which he grabs me by the hair. He hauls me across the room to the overturned table. "Let me show you how you will pay me back."

I throw punch after punch into his arm to let me go as I stumble after him. Something suddenly rushes right past me, an explosion of air buffeting against my side.

Finn's grip slackens, and I recoil from his reach. It's only then that I realize someone else has entered the room. Someone big and moving like a storm. They slam into Finn with such speed that Finn is shoved right through the wooden wall. But the attacker, a man big enough to be a bear, goes right after him and wrenches him back before snatching his neck and snapping it.

The break of bone is loud and precise. It all happens so fast.

I can't help but gasp as Finn's body crumbles to the ground, dead.

I tremble, stepping back as the assailant turns toward me, dusting his hands and grinning proudly. The man is over six-foot, muscles everywhere, and smiling like a madman. Deep blond hair sweeps over his brow, and his piercing hazel eyes meet mine. I shouldn't stare, but he is beyond beautiful with such strong features. Except he just killed Finn.

If I wasn't already terrified, I might have fainted before this wolf shifter I stood no chance against. I sense the energy from his body, the ripples of electricity that always dance down my spine when I stand in the company of an Alpha.

"Is this her?" he asks, smiling. His question confuses me further.

"You killed him! W-who the hell are you?" Goosebumps race up my arms.

"Wrong question," a deep male's voice replies from behind me. I whip around on the spot to come face-to-face with three men. Each just as big as the next, they are a wall of muscle with strong features and looks that tell me they aren't from this country. But one of these Alphas I recognize instantly.

Everything melts away, leaving behind just the hope that maybe the sonofabitch in front of me has found my sisters.

"Ragnar!"

TWO

Ragnar

I've been standing in the messed up room, studying Narah from the moment the dead-wolf-walking thought it was okay to drag her across the room to make her pay. I'm familiar with the drill. Wolf doesn't get what he wants, and he takes something else from an Omega. Yeah, it's the fucking circle of life. But today, that bullshit has frustration pinching across my brow.

So I asked Crius to fix the problem. I don't order kills on just anyone, but when it comes to a bastard in my way, I believe in cutting straight through to get what I want. In this case, Narah.

"Ragnar," she repeats my name as though I hadn't heard her the first time. The little fox stands with shock on her gorgeous face, those amber eyes almost alight, her full lips parted, and I can't help but wonder what they would taste like. Her scent mingles with the smell of fire in the room. I could easily let myself fall prey to the girl with a heart-shaped face and eyes of fire. They glance down my body and back up, her fascination in me clear.

Since meeting Narah, she's captivated my thoughts beyond the normal lustful ones. There's something about her I can't quite put my finger on, and it's not the cascade of hair the color of ravens running perfectly down to her waist, or how much I can't stop watching the rise and fall of her chest.

My insides tighten each time I see the vulnerability in her expression and in those big doe eyes. It's like the whole world has done so wrong by her that she's already accepted things will be fucked up until the end.

How long has it been since I cared about why an Omega was upset? Years?

It doesn't stop me from admiring the curve of her porcelain white throat that dips down to her breasts pushing up against her laced-up bodice with each rushed breath, or the way her black pants hug her ass and thighs. Fuck, I'd prefer her bare and wrapped around me. Whatever it is about her, she has me enamored beyond the usual second glance I give Omegas as potential ruts.

"Hello, Narah. I'm here to collect your part of the deal."

She steps forward like my words alone connect to her with an invisible cord. "So you found my sisters?" The eagerness in her voice has me drawing in a sharp breath, my mind whirling with the truth I know she'll not accept well.

"Walk with me and we can talk."

Her nose wrinkles, and she squares her shoulders. "No, tell me now. Did you find my sisters or not? It's not a hard question." There's sharpness in her voice, but I hear the brittleness beneath the words.

"We will talk in private," I repeat.

She stares at me incredulously, then at my three men and to the lump of a wolf shifter by the smashed-up wall. Her brow furrows.

"What's going on, Ragnar? Who are the men with you? And why did you kill Finn? Shit, he was my best paying customer."

"Which question do you want me to answer first?" She's grown braver since I last saw her weeks ago, which is rather refreshing in a world where most females are timid and fall to their knees to obey Alphas. Maybe living in a lawless town agrees with her. Me, I like a challenge, and I wonder if she's up for the task.

She glances over to the dead man.

"What is one less Beta in this world?" I answer. "And these are my men, Crius,"—I point to him behind her, then turn my attention to my left and right—"Nikos, and Stone."

Crius steps around her, studying her like a vulture inspects his prey. The guy likes to taunt anyone he can, and it offers me great distraction. "We did you a favor." He rubs his hand, decorated with rune-engraved rings, over his jawline and down his chin to his beard. "You ought to thank us." He sweeps behind her and lifts a lock of her dark hair, drawing a quick inhale.

"Yeah, right." She swings away from him, her hair slipping from his grip, her glare promising retribution as she turns away from him.

"I can think of a few ways," he continues, regardless. He is nothing if not persistent.

She doesn't tremble in his presence, which I admire, though it's a foolish decision to turn her back on Crius. But she must also know that while we have an unfinished deal, I won't let anything happen to her. From the moment we struck a conversation in this very tavern weeks ago, after she listened in on me talking with the bartender about the deadly Poisonous Woods, I suspected she was no ordinary Omega. No one enters that forest unless they want to die, but she offered me a chance to travel within the woods, and that I took seriously.

She slouches on one leg, turning her sneer from Crius to me. "It's a bad idea to kill Finn. Sheriff in town is a trigger-happy loony and hates fights, but don't let me stop you from getting shot by him. Be my guest."

"Ragnar, did you hear that? She's worried about us." He places a hand to his chest, feigning shock, and Stone next to me chuckles. "Can we keep her? She's so adorable," Crius coos, while my other sentinel by my side, Nikos, groans. Then again, he is short of patience on many things.

"Narah, come with me," I command. "My men will clean up this mess like it never happened."

"Not until you tell me about my sisters." She doesn't move to join me, so I grab her by the arm and haul her outside into the main tavern, the door shutting behind us.

"Let me go," she hisses, tugging against my hold, but I'm not ready to let her go just yet.

Alphas and Betas are in every direction in the tavern, most drunk, others with females in their laps, so no one pays us any attention.

A few quick steps and we're outside in the afternoon sun, the wind stirring the dust on the road. Old wooden buildings sit around us. It isn't a big town, but enough for a rest, food, and fuck for passers-by. We have a few of these places back in Denmark too.

"Let me go." Narah yanks her arm from me, her wry expression ready to skin me alive. "Did you find my sisters or not? Otherwise, give me back my brooch, and we're done with you wasting my time." She speaks so freely, like she's never felt the command of an Alpha, but her voice shakes, and her gaze constantly scans the area around us.

I lean forward and retake her arm, drawing her to me so we stand a breath apart. She is so much shorter than me this close, the top of her head reaching my nose, and if it was anyone else speaking to me this way, their body would have been tossed into a river already. Except she has something I very much need. Magic. A wolf with magic intrigues me, as they are an oddity. Plus, I am rather fond of her scent, breathing it in, rousing my wolf, giving him something to crave.

I clear my throat and remind her, "You and I made a deal, and that means two things. One, I always keep my end of the bargain. Two, you signed yourself over to be under my protection until we finish our transaction. So until then, I can make your life hell, or we can pretend to get along. Up to you, but I'm sure you won't be a problem, right?"

She stiffens against me, tugging her arm while giving a deadpan stare. "Where are my sisters?" she hisses, then twists free from my hold.

I lash out and snatch her wrist, then lift her gloved hand between us. "Is this where you keep your magic, wolf girl?"

Her eyes widen, and she rips free from my hold, coaxing a laugh out of me. There is something enigmatic about her, and the more we spar, the more I want to keep pushing and pushing her. I shouldn't bother, but to say she doesn't intrigue me would be a blatant lie.

"Seeing how you keep changing the topic, it tells me two things," she counters with a smirk. "One, you failed at finding my sisters. Two, you're hoping to distract me, as I must be an idiot who should be grateful for the scraps of your help."

"Touché, little fox, but let's clarify a few things, shall we?" I reply in a calm and steady tone. I lift my attention to the three-story inn across the road from the tavern, and she follows my gaze to the window on the top floor. The curtain is drawn back, and behind the shut window is Jae, waving crazily, hitting her other fist on the window to draw our attention. Next to her lingers one of my men, looking bored as shit.

"Jae," she gasps, her body trembling, and when she looks back at me, there are tears rolling down her cheeks. I'm not surprised often, but this reaction takes me utterly off guard. It's rare to see such emotional connections in this world. Back home, I had never seen my parents shed a tear, not even when my sister was taken by force and given to the enemy as part of a treaty between our clans.

When my grip slackens, Narah's lips twitch into a smile, and the next thing I know, she's pulled free and is sprinting toward the front entrance of the inn. She vanishes inside.

I push forward and follow her into the building and head upstairs. The thumping of her rapid footfalls on the steps above brings a deepening pinch in my chest. I doubt my family would ever show such enthusiasm to see me. But fuck them. They're the reason I'm in Romania to stake claim of my own territory, to find a way to save my sister because my parents are doing fuck all in the name of not angering the enemy wolf clan.

With the small pack of followers I've gained, it's enough to establish my own territory, seeing as no particular pack owns the whole northern part of Romania, the Savage Sector. I set my sights high and won't back down, and from what I can see, the only thing between me and my goals lies in the Poisonous Woods.

That's where my little fox comes in.

When I reach the room we rented for her sister, Jae, I walk in on Narah bounding forward and pulling her sister into her arms. They're both in a tight hug, the sniffling sounds filling the room.

Rai meets my gaze, and I wave my hand for him to wait outside the room.

Narah releases Jae from her embrace. She wipes her tears away and pushes the hair out of her face. "I missed you like mad. I've been so worried."

Jae blinks fast. "The things I've been through, Narah, will make your head spin. There are so many zombies in the South, it's terrifying, but I met a girl, Meira, in the Shadowlands Sector, and she's immune to them. Can you believe that?" She's talking so fast, smiling and crying. "It's so good to be home." She throws herself into Narah's arms again.

Last I saw, the Shadowlands Sector pack was in deep shit between the zombies and a betrayal from someone within their ranks. I had made their Alpha, Dušan, a promise because I am not heartless. He cleans up his territory, otherwise, when I pay him another visit, I'll be claiming his sector as well and rule over the whole country of Romania. Plus, I also told him I was the Alpha of the Savage Sector, the northern part of Romania. And I don't want to make a liar of myself.

"Please tell me you didn't get bitten?" Narah's holding Jae's arms out, studying them for injuries.

Jae shakes her head.

I clear my throat to catch their attention. "We are heading out at first light. Jae will remain here under my men's protection until we return. No harm will come to her. You will spend the night here with Jae." I turn to leave when footsteps tap the wooden floorboards behind me.

"Ragnar," Narah calls me.

I turn to her.

"Thank you." She throws her arms around my neck, her body soft against mine, her breasts pressed to my chest. My pulse kick-starts like an old motor, my cock twitching. Her alluring, seductive, sweet honey scent swirls around again, infiltrating every inch of me. In my head and nostrils... in my veins and cock.

"It's fine," I say as she slides away. I step away from her and leave the room, heat crawling up my spine.

The thing is, Alphas and Omegas are made to come together, our bodies chemically drawn for the act of rutting. It's as primal and raw as that, but I made a promise to myself since the first time I met her that I'd focus on the mission until I got what I wanted. I am under no illusion that we can be fated mates. That beast is off the table, seeing I'd met mine back in Denmark and the bitch betrayed me. What I feel with Narah is animalistic, pure lust.

A soft touch prods at my back, and I turn in the hallway outside the rented room. It's Narah. She shuts the door so her sister can't listen.

"What about Kaira?" She holds herself tall. Of course she'd insist on finding out now.

"Like I said, I always keep my word." I dig my hand into my pocket and retrieve the brooch, then hand the jewelry back to her as it had come in handy to show Jae so she could trust me when I had found her in the Shadowlands Sector. I did everything in my power to find Kaira, but I came up short.

She takes the piece with a shaky hand like she knows I have hard news to deliver.

"Here's the thing," I begin. "Jae was all the way south in the Transylvanian woods, and she'd made friends with the Shadowland Sector's pack Omega, so I can only guess your other sister was in the vicinity too." I pause, trying to find words that might be easier for her to swallow.

She stares up at me with a heartfelt look in her eyes that rips right through me. How long has she been in this fucked-up world looking after her sisters more than herself?

I ignore the drumming of my heart and say, "We found someone who might or might not have been Kaira."

Her eyes narrow. "What does that mean?" Her words quiver. I fucking hate delivering such news to her, yet I don't blink at killing. But I have no reason to hold back the information from her, and if she insists, then the truth is hers.

"The southern part of Romania is swarming with zombies, and the girl we saw had been half eaten by the infected, so like I said, it was hard to see her identity. She seemed young and had chestnut-colored hair." I shrug. "Could be anyone."

"So." Her face blanches, and the wheels behind her eyes are spinning. Even the small mannerism of lowering her eyes, her shoulders curving forward, shows she's trying to convince herself it's not real.

"So?" I ask. Her hope, even in this shitty world, floors me.

Her head lifts. "Doesn't mean it was Kaira."

"No, it doesn't, but I wanted to mention it, as we couldn't find her."

Something flashes in her eyes as they hold onto mine, but she never says a word. Instead, she draws her bottom lip between her teeth, gnawing on the flesh gently like she's suddenly miles away. Narah silently steps away from me and opens the door before going inside, shutting me out.

I stand there for a few moments, staring at the door, not needing to make this my problem. I'm no fool. I know she will go and search for her other sister herself, and she's welcome to, but not before she completes my end of the bargain. I hate half completing jobs myself, but one of my men has an ability to track down people, and Kaira was non-existent in our search. Most likely she is dead, but I won't push that point with Narah and take away what hope she has left.

The sound of whispers and muffled cries reaches me from inside the room. I've got enough trouble in my own life to drown the world in, yet I struggle to get her scent out of my nostrils or to step away. *I've got to get her out of my system. Now.*

I move down the stairs, needing fresh air and a big night of drinks and food to prepare for our mission. Rai is downstairs at the main entrance, keeping guard.

"Neither of them are to leave until I come to collect Narah in the morning."

He nods.

I march across the dusty road and back into the tavern, needing to get Narah out of my fucking mind before I decide she is mine to keep, mine to hide from the world, mine to rut until I lose myself completely.

Stone

"Can we trust Narah?" Nikos asks, lounging in the chair in the tavern. His gaze travels around the table from me to Ragnar, finally landing on Crius. There's a darkness behind his green eyes like there always is, and I hate how I can never tell what he's thinking by his expression. I've always felt he wears a broody demeanor as a guise, appearing content, his words and smile just a mask. But who am I to question Ragnar's second in command?

"The way I see it," he continues, "she's got her sister back, so what's to stop her from leading us into a trap?"

"Are you afraid of a little girl?" Crius mutters before taking another swig of the beer from his flask. "Last time I looked, she wasn't a full witch, she was one against us, and hmm, let me see, she's still looking for her other sister, which we can say we'll continue searching for after our mission."

"Or better yet," Ragnar adds, "if she returns to collect Jae without us during our mission, Rai will slice both their throats. She is not leaving our side until we complete our task."

"That's fair." I raise my flask, because no matter how much I want to bend the Omega over and fuck her, she is a vessel for us to use for our benefit. "Skål," I repeat three times.

They all chant with cheer and we smash our cups together, beer sloshing over the rims and running down our hands. I drink back the whole cup in a few mouthfuls, then bang it on the table. "More."

I catch Nikos's twisted expression like he hasn't finished his point, and he proves me right when he says, "We've all heard tales of witches, of the lives they've stolen with their magic. All I'm saying is we must be cautious since we don't know the full extent of her ability."

"Good point," Ragnar admits. "But the little fox isn't the only one with abilities among us." He glances my way, and I steel myself. The small power I hold is not even comparable to that of a witch, or even a Cursed. "And she will be the least of our worries once we reach the real danger in the forest. If anything, maybe she'll make a good ally." He smirks and finishes his beer.

Crius leans forward, pressing his stomach to the edge of the table. "Tell me you're talking about winning her over, because I'm up for a five-way fuck with her."

Nikos groans. "I'll cut your heart out before I fuck anyone at the same time as you."

The corners of Crius's mouth tug upward with sinister intentions, his hand reaching down and groping his cock over his pants. "You're doing that weird shit with your eye, Nikos, where it twitches. Are you going to have a fit from thinking of sliding into her sweet pussy?"

"Fuck you," Nikos barks, squaring his shoulders, looking ready to dive over the table. Wouldn't be the first time these two started a fight that led to a whole tavern breaking into battle. Warfare and anger have a way of spreading like wildfire.

Ragnar watches them, smirking with amusement, and while I would normally enjoy the show, tonight I feel unease curling over my spine. My muscles stiffen at what's coming, and it has nothing to do with the Cursed girl, but where we're going.

The Poisonous Woods are synonymous with death. No one goes in and walks back out unscathed... and that's if they survive. One tale talks of a dozen Alphas wandering inside and only one of them making it out, barely clinging to life. He spoke of the others left behind as nothing more than piles of ash left by an unseen assailant.

I shake away the dread that rises through me quicker than the frozen wind back home. Fear is a path to the dark side, and I won't let it in. After all, fear makes the wolf bigger than he is. I've seen this too many times growing up in the Ulv pack, where the leaders painted a scarier picture of their warriors to terrify the enemy. Half the time it worked. The other half we fought like the devils they believed us to be.

"Are you ready for tomorrow?" Ragnar asks me.

"Of course, cousin. You know I'll travel into Niflheimr by your side if needed."

He laughs boisterously and claps a hand to my shoulder. "That's why you're on my team, Stone. We've been through so much together. Faced endless battles."

"And bedded countless Omegas." I laugh. Some days I'd be happy if it were just him and me in the pack like it used to be when we grew up back in Denmark.

Ragnar's father and mine are brothers, and to me, Ragnar is like the brother I never had.

A shadow falls over us, and I twist my head around to find the owner of the tavern carrying a large platter of food to our table. The aromas of roasts and vegetables have me salivating. Our table fills with plates of food quickly.

"There is more where this comes from," he tells us. His red, round cheeks and big belly speak of a man who finds his pleasure in food.

"You are too generous," Ragnar answers.

Crius dives in, and we all eat straight from the platters. The bartender soon returns with more beer.

Ragnar collects a plate with a full roast chicken surrounded by helpings of bread and potatoes, and when he gets up, I know exactly where he's going. Our Alpha may be a ruthless bastard, but when it comes to those under his protection, his loyalty has no boundaries. Cross him, and he'll become the demon coming to collect your soul.

I get to my feet and reach for the platter in his grasp. "I'll take it to the girls. You eat. Just don't let those two eat the whole suckling pig."

We both look over to Nikos and Crius gorging on the tender meat, not even noticing we've gotten up from the table.

"Might be too late," Ragnar jokes and hands me the platter. I grab a couple of the forks, and I'm out of there.

The two guards outside the inn are sitting on the front steps, enjoying their own plate of food. Ragnar always makes sure everyone under his command is fed. It's one trait he picked up from his father back in Denmark. A place Ragnar wants to leave behind. The country is split in two, in fact, ruled by two very different Alphas. The north is controlled by Ludvig, the Norse Sector Alpha from the X-Clan pack, while the south falls under Frode's jurisdiction, the Viking Alpha of the Ulv wolves and Ragnar's father.

Upstairs, I knock on the door, and Narah opens it immediately. She's wearing a loose-fitting blue shirt with tight pants, her hair wet and slicked off her face. She's still wearing black gloves. Her eyes fall to the plate of food, while Jae rushes over from across the room.

"About time, we're starving. Hand that over."

I offer Jae the platter, which she greedily accepts, and when Narah retreats into the room, not endeavoring to shut the door in my face, I take that as an invitation to enter. I straighten the collar of my coat and step inside.

Jae is on the bed, legs crossed, the plate in front of her, already tearing at the meat with her bare hands. Her brown hair sits in a braid over one shoulder, the freckles on her nose and cheeks deeper in color under the flickering candlelight. "Stone, are you joining us?"

I smile back. After traveling with her for the past couple of weeks, she's grown on me, in the way an annoying sister might. "It's all yours."

She shrugs. "Your loss, but don't complain that I never offer you any food." Sarcasm threads her words that stem from the small incident in the woods during our travels from South to North. One evening, while we'd been hunting for our shared meal, Jae caught herself a rabbit, cooked it, and ate it, all before we even got back to the cave with our catch. Then she wanted her fair share of our meal. She didn't get it, out of principle. She's a cunning young girl who's learned the hard way how to survive in this treacherous land, but I can't hate her. She reminds me too much of Hel, Ragnar's young sister. Over-opinionated, brash, and a fighter, even when facing an opponent three times her size.

The memory of Hel being sold off grates on me. Even after all these years, I haven't found peace with the lead Alpha's decisions back home.

Narah studies me cautiously, and the longer she does so, the more I tell myself I should walk out of her room. Even in her loose-fitting clothes, I can't forget the curve of her ass from earlier in the day, the perkiness of her breasts, and that gorgeous, long, pitch-black hair.

When an Omega, who is hot as fuck even dressed like this and can still get my cock hard, then I'm lying to myself if I think there's nothing happening here.

Except I need to get it through my thick skull that she's our key into the woods. Ragnar would cut my head clean off with an ax for ruining his chance to claim the northern part of Romania.

After the deal's done, she's fair game to claim, seeing as she will no longer be under Ragnar's protection.

"I've been hearing a lot about you four taking care of my sister," Narah says, her amber eyes slicing through me as if she knows more about our journey from the South than I do.

"I didn't think she'd last long on her own."

"Hey," she calls out from the bed. "I had my friend Meira."

I lift my chin in her direction. "And last time we saw them, Meira and the three Alphas in her company had been locked out of their own pack compound, which doesn't bode well for their survival."

She wipes her greasy lips. "You're wrong. I have no doubt they'll have claimed their home back."

Some days I wonder how much easier life would be if I believed in the good of others as much as Jae does.

"I better leave you both to enjoy your meal and a comfortable night's sleep," I say to Narah.

She sits at the end of the bed, eyeing the knife at my belt. "What do you know of the Poisonous Woods?" Something in the way she asks me transcends her standoffish attitude, sounding more like concern.

"That going in might be a suicide mission. But that's where you come in."

She blinks, her expression blank, which partly worries me. I expected a cocky response about it being easy, except her silence is a dead giveaway that the mission scares her too.

"You are prepared for the forest, right?" I ask.

She drops her gaze to her gloved hands in her lap, then drags her gaze to mine. "Being prepared and being ready are two very different things. Yes, I have the ability for what Ragnar asked of me, but I have never ventured into those particular woods to know for sure that my ability is enough to guide us away from danger."

I sigh, my muscles bunching up across my shoulder blades. That's not what I want to hear, but Ragnar won't back down. Once he's set his mind on something, he'll insist we barge through hell itself. "Get a good night's rest, Narah. You will definitely need it tomorrow."

Crius

I stride across the tavern, Stone at my side, leaving Nikos and Ragnar at the table. I'm used to them planning together—it's what an Alpha and his second in command should do. Doesn't mean Nikos still won't piss me off. And it has nothing to do with who he is, but the way he carries himself. Since he arrived to live with us in the Ulv pack in Denmark, he's never truly opened up and has always remained by the sidelines. I'm not one to believe he is against us; the bastard is just angry with the whole fucking world. I just wish he'd find a way to deal with that dark shit and move the fuck on already.

Stone stumbles on his next step and I snatch his arm, steadying him before he face-plants into the front door. "You trying to kiss the wall?" I chuckle as he finds his feet.

"What the fuck was that?" he glances back around to see what he tripped over.

"It's called your feet." I wrench open the door to the tavern, and a burst of cool air rushes inside and curls around us. "Let's take you back to your room."

Stone straightens and heads outside. We've both had too much beer and food, but after our recent trip down south, I've missed a decent feed. Not to mention, if I never see another zombie, it'll be too soon.

"What do you think we'll find in the Poisonous Woods?" Stone asks.

I briefly glance at him, the breeze blowing through his blond hair and tossing it over his face. "Fuck, man, are you freaking out about it?"

Sure, I've heard scary shit about the forest, but I don't go into battle with fear. Whatever the hell comes at us, we'll destroy it.

He snorts a partial laugh. "You know me, I want to go in prepared. I hate going into battle blind. I'm trying, but damn, I've heard too many stories about the place to not worry."

I wish I could clue him in on something, anything, to put his mind at rest, but we're all going into this completely blind and with the Cursed girl as our eyes. That means having our crap together and not being a damn pussy about being scared.

Stone suddenly jerks his head toward the woodland pressing up against the inn like he saw something. "For fuck's sake," he grumbles, staring at the darkness in disbelief.

I scan the area and spot two figures sprinting away from the building. They look mighty thin and small, like two females.

"Are you kidding me?" I lift my head to the window on the third floor, seeing a light flickering, which I assume is a decoy for us. "It's them, isn't it?"

"Narah's good and sly. She may prove a problem for us on the mission," Stone says. "But for now, feel like a round of hunting?"

"I'm always up for it. Narah is mine. You get Jae."

He cuts me a side glance filled with bane. "Why do you get her?"

"I called it first. Now, are we darting after them or are you going to fuck around as they escape? Ragnar will hang us by our balls if they do."

Stone cracks his neck, and he launches himself after his prize.

Adrenaline thumps through me at the chase, everything inside me demanding I rush after her and claim her.

I'm running in an instant, my feet pounding the earth as I burst into the woodland. The cold air is crisp with forest scents, but on the breeze, I catch her sugary scent tinted with a sprinkle of fresh meadow and wolf... a smell unique to her.

It shouldn't excite me to pursue her, but fuck, it does. Stone is ahead of me, and even from a distance, I spot the girls looking back at us. Alarm tightens their expressions, and I smile.

In their panic, they abruptly spear outward in different directions. Yeah, fear confuses people in times of high tension. I swing left after Narah, while Stone bears right.

Narah sprints away, dodging around trees and under low-hanging branches. She's small and nimble, but she won't get away from me. My wolf is in my chest pounding for release, for escape, but then what? I already know I'm faster, more powerful than her, and a chase is only fun if there's a challenge.

She darts out of my sight, bleeding into the darkness, but I have her scent, and that leads me dead ahead through the wilderness. My feet punch the ground with speed, wind blowing through my hair, adrenaline spiking.

It's only when I hear a cry that my heart slams into the back of my throat. The sound comes from the direction I'm headed. I leap forward quicker than before, thundering like a bullet until I finally come across Narah forced face-first against a tree. Some fucker has her pinned in place while he tugs down on her pants.

Why the hell hasn't she used her magic against that bastard?

But fury burns those thoughts aside and delivers me to the point of no return. Where the fuck had he come from, anyway?

Her cries and writhing to escape only fuel my rage. I throw myself toward them, the crunch of foliage under my feet revealing my approach.

The asshole Alpha twists his head to look over his shoulder at me. His eyes widen with shock, his shoulders rising, lips peeling back as he growls his threat. "Fuck off."

But that's not going to happen, now is it?

I slam into his side furiously, and we're both off our feet and flying toward the ground, leaving Narah unscathed.

"She's not yours to touch," I snarl in his ear. Swiftly, I roll off him, snatch him by the throat, and wrench him to his feet in one move.

The fucker has no idea what's coming at him. All I see in his eyes is lust, and his goddamn tented pants from his dick, which I want nowhere near me.

"She's not yours either," he gasps, throwing a punch directly in my gut, which I take. "Omegas are for all to rut." He sweeps his gaze to Narah behind me.

"Wrong thing to say." My fingers around his neck squeeze tighter. He may be built like a tank, but I am convinced he's never experienced the number of battles I've endured or faced the monsters that live up in the North. The kind that rip your head off with one swipe for looking at them the wrong way. And yet Ragnar's father sent his only daughter to them in exchange for peace between their two packs. But I shake those thoughts away. They have no place in this moment.

The dickhead in front of me is swiping at my arm, his face turning blue.

Narah comes into view from my side, and I look at her, at the welt mark across her cheek from where the bastard slapped her. "How much did he hurt you?" I snarl.

She's breathing heavy, furious and so scared. Her words never come, but they don't need to. She gives me the answer, whether she knows it or not.

"You will never touch another Omega again," I promise the man. As I turn toward Narah, all I spy is her shadow slicing through the darkness away from me. "Fuck!" I place another hand on the man's neck and snap it sideways so violently, the crack of bone pierces the silence. It's rather rewarding to hear that final sound. And while I would have preferred to take my time with him, make him suffer, time isn't on my side.

He drops to the ground, and I grab the ax from my belt. Gripping the handle with two hands, I lift the weapon and come down fast, the sharp blade biting into the man's neck, making it a clean cut. Warm blood splatters up my arm, a few speckles across my cheeks. I do love the feel of an enemy's lifeblood on my skin. But I probably showed him more mercy than he deserved by decapitating him after he died. He can count himself lucky.

Dropping the blood-stained ax, I swivel on my heels and dart after the minx who is going to be sorry she ran from me after I did her a favor.

Adrenaline soars through me once more from the chase, and this time I won't give her the satisfaction of slipping away from me. I swing around the back of the inn where I'd seen her vanish, following that addictive, sugary scent. Branches whack into my head, and I growl my annoyance, but I'm closing in. All I see is her small, curved body swerving right and left around trees, her dark hair whipping across her back like a flag.

My cock throbs at the pursuit, at the sight before me. I'm well aware she isn't mine to take... at least not yet, anyway, but who says playing with your food isn't permitted?

I quicken my pace and use a fallen log to catapult myself over a cluster of shrubs. My feet hit the soft earth just as she whips back around a nearby tree and comes at me so fast I can't react quick enough. By the time I notice she's grasping a branch, she's already whacking it wildly at my side. The ache spirals up my back, but it's nothing compared to real pain in warfare, so I swallow back the sting. I turn toward her and snatch the weapon, then toss it aside.

"What the hell are you doing?" I growl.

She blinks at me, giving no response. Her cheeks are still red, one more so than the other, her dark hair speckled with leaves. Then she comes at me and rams her shoulder into my gut. That I don't expect, and I groan as I bend over. She got me good.

She pants and breaks free from my grasp as I reach for her. Then she's gone again.

Shit, she's a slippery thing, and very well versed in escaping capture. She is definitely not like all the other Omegas I've encountered, who crumble and accept their fate. That's so much easier, but then again, I can't remember the last time I enjoyed a chase this much.

I throw myself after her, my legs pumping, my pulse racing. My wolf is in my throat, his hot breath rushing past my lips.

This time I come up on her quicker than she expects, and when she looks over her shoulder, finding me on her heels, a small whimper spills past her throat.

I'm addicted to that sound.

I seize her by the waist and rip her off the ground, then tuck her up against my waist.

"Put me the hell down," she roars. To show her I'm not a monster like the other Alpha, I do just that. But just as she jumps to flee, I snatch her forearm and force her to stand in front of me.

"Enough!" I growl. "Is this the respect you show Ragnar after he saved your sister?"

She throws her fist to my face, her punch clipping me just below the eye. She has little strength behind her punch, but the sharpness of her knuckle hits a soft spot, and shots of sharp pain spear across my face.

I shake my head and haul her behind me back to the inn. If I were dealing with anyone else, they'd be bleeding into the soil by now. But I'm trying my best not to harm this wild girl.

She punches my arm. "I can't go with you into the woods, you need to let me go." The desperation in her voice almost gets to me... almost.

Reaching the back of the stone building, I spin her around and press her back flush to the wall, then I plant my arms on either side of her shoulders and lean into her. "And why is that?"

But being so close to her, all I can see are her huge fiery eyes, her jaw clenched with determination. Her chest rises and falls quickly with each breath. Beneath me, she's so small, so absolutely sexy, it takes everything in me to not taste her here and now. My cock hardens in my pants as I take in her scent, and arousal suffocates me.

"I'm not going anywhere until I find Kaira."

"That's not going to work with our plans," I answer, my mind on a rampage with the need to run my tongue down her body.

"Get off me." Her brow furrows as her chest thrusts out despite her words, clearly eager for my touch, her Omega side craving me as much as I do her. I watch the war on her face as she fights her impulse, and damn, she's cute trying to go against her primal instincts. I press my body against hers, brushing my erection against her stomach. She gasps, and a hint of slick taints the air, driving me utterly insane with desire. My balls tighten, and for those few moments, I can't see straight beyond the hunger pulsing into me.

She sets my body on fire. Here I intended to punish her, but now I can't get the idea of fucking her out of my mind. Finding a sliver of control, I say, "We backtracked several times looking for Kaira, trust me. We couldn't find her anywhere, so where will you go to track her down?"

She stares at me as reality sinks in, and with it, her eyes glisten.

"Hell." I don't do crying, and I pull away from her, then grab her hand. "Let's get you back to Jae. Ragnar doesn't have to know about this."

Her gaze widens. "What would he do if found out?"

"Make you pay. He's rather fond of hanging people by their toes." I shrug, and we begin our hike back around the building.

She stares at me as if I'm making crap up. If only I were.

The weight of her resisting me continues, but staying out here with her any longer will end up with me ripping her clothes off. And well, I'd prefer not to face Ragnar's wrath and end up with broken ribs and slow torture by compromising our one ticket into the Poisonous Woods. No matter how delicious and fuckable she is.

I haul her through the woods alongside the inn just as movement catches my attention from up ahead. I raise my gaze to Stone dragging Jae toward the main road in town. The fighting spirit is high in these sisters.

Narah is off-limits for now, but that doesn't mean I won't show her the power of an Alpha. We may be holding back on claiming her for now, but that's only a temporary arrangement.

A squeal comes from above, and for a split second, I swear it comes from Stone. Once I saw him freak out over a rat in his bed, so it wouldn't surprise me. Except the way he and Jae retreat in our direction quickly, with him pushing Jae ahead of him, tells me something else has happened.

My grip tightens around Narah, my muscles taut as I bring us to a halt. For a change, she's not trying to pull away from me. She is just as curious as me as to what the hell is going on.

I tilt my head to the side to see past the duo. Two figures are coming this way behind them, staggering, lurching through the woods. My stomach freezes up, which doesn't happen often, but I know exactly what I'm looking at. I've seen them back home and in the Shadowlands Sector. Those abominations are everywhere, except for some reason they haven't overrun the Savage Sector yet.

Part of me can't help but wonder if that has anything to do with the witches also living here.

Fucking zombies!

"Shit, shit, shit." Jae is freaking out, her expression falling, her shoulders curving forward. She instantly huddles up against her sister as she reaches us, while Stone snarls under his breath.

"You take care of the girls, and I'll fix this," Stone instructs.

Something about the way he says that irks me. Maybe it's the competitive side of me, or that he says it with such cockiness in front of Narah, that it rubs me the wrong way.

"Don't think so." I shove Narah right into his arms. "She gets away and it's all on you."

Before he can even respond, I strip my shirt off and toss it behind me, kicking off my shoes and unzipping my pants. I'm rather fond of these clothes, and I don't want them destroyed. The warm breeze rushes over my naked body, and just as fast, the change erupts through me like a tornado, tearing me to shreds as my wolf pours out of me like lava. The agony stings, my body shuddering. In seconds, my large, white paws hit the ground, and the surrounding smells intensify. Dew, the stench of earth, and the promise of rain in the distance flood my nostrils. But with it comes the putrid stink of death.

Two dead are lurching toward us, the tall guy sporting only one arm, both seemingly missing lips. Their yellow, broken teeth chatter with their desperate need to eat. Torn and filthy clothes hang off their frail forms. Pasty, gaunt faces make their eyes look bigger. They are ugly things.

I've fought so many of these filthy creatures on our retrieval mission to find Jae, it's second nature to me now. Though I can't deny that zombies are one of the few things that send shivers up my spine because where there's one, there are others. And I don't want them here if this sector will be my new home.

I lunge at the one on the right for the single reason that he has two arms... always take out the more powerful so when your back is turned, it's only the weaker one you have left to contend with.

My teeth scrape into his neck, digging into flesh, and I rip off his bulbous head with ease. Zombies are barely held together when they haven't fed, their bodies feeble and easily torn. No blood pours from his rotten body either, meaning it's been a long time since he ate. The real danger with them is all about the sheer number, and I hope with everything in me that more aren't coming.

Something slams into my back, the sharp stab of teeth sinking into my back leg. I buck my weight into the bastard, hurling him into a nearby trunk. I'm on him in seconds, slashing my jaws across his throat. After all, decapitation is the best way to ensure they don't get back up.

His head tumbles to the ground and into a nearby shrub.

I spit out the rancid taste on my tongue, my throat closing up, gagging at the smell. My fear isn't that I'll get sick with their virus. From what I learned down in Shadowlands, most of us wolves are not resilient to the disease, while other wolf packs like the X-Clan are immune. But us normal wolves are carriers. The moment we die, we'll become a fucking zombie, so the trick is to not die anytime soon and ensure our heads come right off.

Heaving for breath, I sweep the area with my gaze, past the two undead who aren't moving. Let's hope they are all that made it up here, because these bastards congregate like the great river of death coming from the underworld. Been there, done that. Prefer to never encounter it again.

I head back to Stone and the girls, transforming into my human form on my way. I wipe my mouth with the back of my hand. My attention homes in on Narah. The way she's checking me out is not missed, nor the way her gaze dips to my groin. Yeah, it's hard to miss it, and I'm not even erect to truly give her the full show, but even at my relaxed state, I'm damn big.

"That wasn't so bad, now was it? You three butterflies all okay?"

Stone gives me the death glare, then nudges Narah back at me, and I gladly seize her arm. In that same moment, a gargled groan cuts through the early morning from deeper in the woods. We all turn in that direction to find another damn brain muncher hunched over the dead Alpha who attacked Narah, tearing at his intestines.

"Eww." Jae looks away and Narah takes her into her arms, protective of her sister, which I can respect.

Stone doesn't say a word and heads across the woods to finish the zombie.

"Well, you girls picked a great time to head into the woods," I say, gaining myself no response. But glares are in abundance.

"You know you have no choice," I remind Narah. "No one breaks a deal with Ragnar."

"He never completed his end of the bargain. I have two sisters," she reminds me, but even as she rebels, I watch the dread slide behind her gaze, recalling the chat she and Ragnar had about Kaira.

It doesn't take Stone long to return. Without a word, he hands my bloody ax back to me, takes Jae by the arm, and starts dragging her toward the front of the building. "I'm ready to get out of these fucking woods."

I turn toward my witch girl. "Did you enjoy my show?"

She eyes me with a narrowing gaze. "Do you mean killing two dead things that could barely stand on their own feet?" She tugs against my grip, though her bravery is just an illusion, seeing how she's trembling and how her gaze keeps darting around us like a scared little sheep. "And I can walk on my own."

"You lost that privilege with the shit you pulled earlier. Plus, I'm talking about my strip show for you, my sweet sparrow."

That time she laughs, all fake of course, but I bet I'll be in her thoughts tonight.

FIVE

Narah

The morning sunlight spills out over the horizon, bruising the sky with reds and oranges. I stare out of the bathroom window over the town and beyond, my gaze grazing over the landscape for anything. But it's dead. Not a soul in sight.

A haunting breeze sweeps through my hair, cooling the sweat collecting at my nape. I stirred most of the night, getting no more than an hour's sleep after Crius and Stone caught us escaping. I'm still burning up that we could have gotten away if we'd left earlier. But then what?

Face off with zombies?

Hellish, walking corpses who are now up in the North. I've heard rumors of them, like most, but to see one left me shaking. I might have peed my pants in terror a bit, too, because everything about them is wrong. Yet Crius didn't blink an eye as he ripped their heads off with his mouth. And here I'd let myself dream of what it might feel like to kiss him when he had me pinned to the wall.

How am I meant to be comfortable in the Poisonous Woods with those things about? But maybe there aren't others? Please don't let there be more.

Stories talk of a powerful witch coven living in the middle of the forest, and to find them means entering a woodland littered with protective spells and hexes. So to add zombies on top of that will only exacerbate the situation.

And I'm no fool to think Ragnar wants to visit them for the sole purpose of seeking their help or for any other peaceful reason. Despite trying to get out of it last night, at the end of the day, I made a deal to find my sisters, and I won't feel guilty for helping get these wolves to the witches' doorstep. No one likes Cursed, so I don't have allegiances to either side. That means what happens between them is none of my business. All I want is my sisters, and I'll use the one ability my mother taught me to get the wolves through the woods, then I'll step away before anyone turns on me.

I worry about Jae being left behind. She can't come with us. I support this, but my chest tightens at knowing she's under the protection of Alphas. Like me, she's an Omega, but while she's still young, some Alphas won't care about her age.

My mind also keeps going to Kaira and what Ragnar told me. I refuse to believe the body he found in the woods is her. Jae said last night that soon after she and Kaira ran from the Storm Wolves, they encountered a small cluster of rogue wolf shifters near our pack home. They were split up in their escape, and the last time Jae saw Kaira was up here in the Savage Sector of Romania. Jae found herself running from one danger to the next, which eventually led her to the Shadowlands Sector down south. This is why I need to find Kaira myself before I believe anything.

I thread my arms through the leather corset and tug it down over my head before pulling at the cords to tighten the fabric around my chest. The white, long sleeve shirt bunches up underneath it, but who cares when the corset holds my breasts firmly in place. I tuck the shirt into the black pants that are a tad on the tight side, but I feel comfortable in these fresh new clothes that were left just outside our room. I'm unsure if I should be more impressed by the fact that the men found these pristine clothes in this town or that they knew my size perfectly.

Brushing those thoughts aside, along with the hair off my face, I head out of the bathroom, well aware that as much as I hate going on this mission, I don't have much of a choice.

In the bedroom, Ragnar's hardened face greets me from where he stands by the main open door to the hall.

Shock freezes me in the doorway to see him waiting for me, as I didn't expect him to *actually* arrive this early.

He's broad-shouldered and somehow appears taller in his full-length black coat. It's zipped from the base of his throat to just above his groin, where the rest of the fabric falls loosely around his black pants that are bunched up over his dark combat boots.

The way his eyes rake down my body leaves a fire in their wake. He runs his hand over his dark hair, which is shorter around the edges and the back and long across the top. He still wears those tiny silver rings tied into his hair, and it suits him. My mind yells at me to pull myself together before it's too late and he thinks of me as nothing more than an Omega who lusts over any Alpha I cross paths with.

"Morning," he says. This beautiful man in my room knows exactly the impact he has on me. I see it in his grin.

"Umm, you were serious when you meant early?" To conceal how much he affects me, I sweep my attention to the rest of the room, finding no sign of my sister.

"Where's Jae?" I ask, straightening my shoulders. I eye my boots by the table. I grab them and sit down on a chair as I tug them onto my feet, then tie up the laces. "Is she having breakfast at the tavern?"

"No," he answers abruptly. "She's safe."

My head jerks up. "What does that mean?" A shiver races down my spine, and I'm on my feet.

"My guards have taken her to a secure location. Three of my strongest will ensure nothing happens to her until we all return in one piece." His intentions are clear. He doesn't trust that I won't ditch them, or worse yet, set them up for failure.

My heart no longer thumps like a drum. Instead, it's squeezing like someone is trying to wring out the last drops of blood.

"That wasn't part of our deal," I say loudly, raising my head higher to stare Ragnar right in those pale blue eyes that look ghostly against his dark hair.

"What exactly did you think your payment was for us risking our lives and traveling into the South to find your sisters?"

I stiffen, and my shoulders curve forward. "You only found one sister, so already the deal is incomplete. Plus, you initially said I was only to ensure safe travel for you *into* the Poisonous Woods, not back out again. Now you're holding my sister hostage to ensure I deliver more than we bargained for."

He raises an eyebrow as if I've spoken out of line. "You have a wickedly sharp tongue, Narah, and now you want to renegotiate our deal? That's fine, but you may not like the outcome."

A quiver grips my spine, and I hold myself still, refusing to back down.

He steps toward me and seizes my hand quickly, his hold solid. The rational part of my brain tells me to step back and not let him invade my space, but instead I lose myself in his gaze, in the tingle that starts in the pit of my gut and rouses my wolf at Ragnar's touch.

I've been disciplined to smile, to go along with Alphas and not show them my real intention until I am out of harm's way, but I suspect if I show weakness to this wolf, he'll rip my throat out.

My voice comes out clear and crisp, even if my nerves are jumping under my skin. "You don't scare me."

I draw my hand from his and move away from him, knowing I shouldn't turn my back to a predator. But I want him to see my bravery, despite the vulnerability twisting my insides into knots.

Suddenly, the warmth of his breath ghosts over my shoulder and ear. "Are you sure of that?"

His arm skates around the front of my shoulders, pulling me backward to collide into his solid chest, leaving me breathless. I frantically grab at his arm, my fingernails digging into flesh, but he doesn't so much as flinch. "We can do this your way. Your sister's freedom for yours. How does that sound? We release your sister now, she's free from my men, but you become mine forever. And to show I can be kind, I will send my men to keep searching for Kaira, after which we will free her too, if she's still alive."

My veins turn to ice as my mind chokes on the fear of Jae being alone. And what if he'd been right about Kaira the first time and she isn't alive? A shutter coils around my heart because I'm not ready to accept such a fate. She's not dead. No, I refuse to believe it until I see it with my own eyes. And he wants to own me? Fuck that.

"I promise to take very good care of you," he whispers.

"No." My voice comes out shaky.

Just as quickly, he releases me, and I stumble to catch my footing, my hand reaching for the bed to keep from falling. He turns his back on me and strides out into the hallway, throwing his words over his shoulder. "That's what I thought. Get your stuff. We're leaving."

I'm shaking.

Bastard.

My heart is close to exploding as a feeling of doom cloaks me. "Fucking bastard," I mumble under my breath, furious that he just took Jae without letting me give her a farewell. Now more than ever, I am determined to find a way back to my sister. Then we'll find Kaira. I pray with everything that Ragnar's insistence on this insane mission is something I won't regret.

It seems every Alpha I meet always finds a way to destroy things for me, and the single thought of Martell brings with it a deep, wrenching sting under my breastbone, one where my pulse pounds loudly in my ears, where the heartache of losing him slices into me. That feeling of loneliness, of abandonment and betrayal simmers within me, and despite it all, my wolf still pines for Martell. Maybe it's not this world that is broken, but me...

My wolf and soul crave a monster who tried to kill me.

My body desires a Viking Alpha who sees me as a pawn.

And me... all I want is freedom, but it seems fate has no intention of playing nice with me.

Knowing time is against me, I hurry through the room to grab my knife, which I tuck into my boot, then I collect a long coat, figuring it will make a good blanket at night. Our mission will take days through the Poisonous Woods, which are enormous, and under no circumstance will the witch coven make it easy for any wolf to reach them.

These Northern Alphas don't seem to be bothered that I am Cursed as long as they get what they want.

If Ragnar has any thoughts that somehow I will be a force on their side against the witches, he's in for a rude awakening. I won't risk my life to anger the witches. They loathe wolves, and I'm sure that includes half-breeds. Plus, what could I do to help Ragnar when my magic is untapped, broken, and lost in my veins?

Narah

Ipull the coat tighter around my throat, my bag hanging across my back as we head down the dusty road out of town. Ragnar and Stone take the lead, Nikos at our rear, and Crius strolls alongside me, hands deep in the pockets of his black pants like nothing in the world can touch him.

His V-neck Henley top hangs loosely on him, but there's no hiding his muscles. Out of the four men, he is the largest. He killed Finn with such ease, and with zero remorse too. I should feel more guilt as well, but he was going to hurt me... just as Martell had wanted. And after last night's incident, now when I watch Crius, a strange explosion of butterflies flutters through my gut. Of course, they shouldn't, but staring at him, all I can picture is him pressed against me, feel how my body flared to life. All I can think about is how he protected me after I've been looking out for myself for so long. I hate to admit it, but to have someone else stand up for me brings an unexpected relief.

Still, everything about Crius is complicated and terrifying.

I mean, the guy has a small throwing ax on his belt, and hell only knows what else tucked on his body. And this is before he even transforms into his monstrous white wolf form.

Crius glances over to me, catching me staring at him, and winks. I find myself caught in that moment under his gaze. The breeze sweeping through his deep blond hair that blows wildly over his shoulders. Stubble graces his jawline, while the longer beard at his chin has been formed into two short braids, each with a silver ring at the end. It should look ridiculous, but on him... goddess forgive me, but on him, it makes my knees tremble. He is the living epitome of what I've pictured Viking warriors to look like from books I read. Vikings, men who fight with berserker tendencies, who are rugged, who are scared by nothing. And the one walking beside me is drop-dead gorgeous. Muscled, tall, sharp cheekbones, healed war scars. His piercing hazel eyes crowned by thick eyebrows are still on me.

"You good?" he asks.

I force a nod while my brain struggles to find something to say. My initial instinct is to admit I changed my mind about this trip, but then what? These Alphas won't just hand over my sister. Already I miss her. Being with her again was hypnotizing, just listening to her telling me about everything she went through before Ragnar found her. It also scared me to learn how close her encounters with zombies had been, the dangers she faced down in the Shadowlands Sector. We had been apart for a short period, but she seemed to have matured so much over that time. Gone is the carefree younger sister I once knew. If I ever meet the Omega from that region, Meira, who helped my sister several times, I will give her the biggest hug ever.

One night catching up with Jae isn't enough when I've been missing my sisters terribly for the past two months. I twist to look behind me and up to the room in the inn I'd spent the night in with Jae, my chest hurting.

I clench my teeth. I've come this far and survived; I can't let the fear paralyze me now.

Jae, please stay safe until I return. And Kaira, wherever you are, stay alive so I can find you.

When I turn back around, Crius straightens and lifts his chin back toward the town we're leaving behind. "Your sister will be safe."

"I guess," I murmur. He shrugs, and soon only the crunch of foliage and grass accompanies our footfalls.

The silence between us adds to the trepidation building inside me. Except I shake those emotions away. To survive, I need to be on my game. Ragnar most likely thinks I possess lots of magic and that I will be their savior, but I can't let them find out I am not the powerful witch they suspect. What they don't know right now is what will keep me alive.

I've lived with lies my entire life, telling them to the Alphas of our pack. Sure, my undoing was my own ability coming to the surface in front of Martell, but that's not going to be an issue here, now is it?

The farther we stride from town, the narrower the dirt road becomes, swallowed by overgrown wild grass and oaks with overarching branches flanking our path. We are alone out here with only a few birds chirping around us. I allow myself to believe there is still beauty in this world amid the chaos.

"Is there anything we should know about your magic, wolf girl?" Crius asks, pulling me from my thoughts. I give him a side glance, studying his face for sarcasm. Except he's serious.

"That's kind of a weird question," I answer.

He raises a thick eyebrow. "I get it. You want to know about us first before you'll open up." He gives me a lopsided grin. "Okay, I'm game to play along."

"That's not really wha—"

"What you see in me is what you get. I'll always be honest whether you like it or not, and well, not to blare my own horn, but I am amazing on the battlefield and in bed." He smirks as his hand reaches down his body and gropes his groin.

Yeah, I can see who I'm dealing with when it comes to Crius.

Nikos fake coughs from behind us, murmuring under his breath, "You forget being fucking crazy, unpredictable, and a death trap for us."

My breath catches in my throat at his words. Death trap?

Crius chokes out a laugh. "Ah yes, and next we have Nikos, the black sheep among us. He's prone to jealousy and can't get his dick up."

"Fuck you," Nikos hisses, his shoulders rising, fists curling. He drops the bag from over his shoulder to the ground, ready for war. The sides of his head are shaved, a tattooed pattern covering the skin on one side. The swirls match the ink running out from under his short sleeved top and crawling over his bulging biceps. His Mohawk is a deep chestnut brown and drawn into several thick braids, all tangled together into one big dreadlock reaching halfway down his back. Everything about him screams *warrior*, including those intense green eyes. He is someone that would terrify me if we crossed paths on a dark night, yet there's something behind his gaze that intrigues me. A vulnerability, which has to be wrong.

Though I have no idea why Crius called him a black sheep. To me, it seems Crius is better suited to that title than the others.

I quickly step away from them, trampling through the knee-length grass, as neither seems to be backing down.

Crius holds his position, chest out. I'm pretty sure these two will kill each other before the witches get a chance. Fine by me, but I'd rather not be harmed in the process.

The air thickens, their chests furiously rising and falling with fast breaths. I grip the straps of my bag over my shoulders, unable to look away from the wreckage about to happen.

"Save it," Ragnar barks, his words like a knife slicing through the air.

Both men fall back instantly, Nikos lowering his gaze, shadows gathering over his face as he collects his dropped pack. Crius looks around, making sure to catch everyone's gazes, like there's an unspoken understanding between them.

What is going on between these four? Am I making a huge mistake teaming up with them?

Crius clears his throat and turns to me, wearing a grin, then steps into the grass after me and takes my hand. His touch is softer than I expected, sending shivers up my arm, and he draws me back onto the path. "Now, where were we? Ah yes, Stone."

We are back on our brisk walk forward, the rising sun brightening the landscape, the altercation that felt like the world would erupt a thing of the past. Yet my head is still whiplashing from what I just witnessed.

"Save your breath," Stone snaps. This blond Viking looks calmer than he probably is, powerful and captivating with dark blue eyes. He hasn't left my thoughts after his visit to our room last night, delivering our dinner. And the way he stared at me told me he was trying to work me out. His question about whether I was prepared for the Poisonous Woods has been playing on my mind since he asked it. Just like these Alphas, this is my first time in that forest as well, but my response to him seemed to make him uneasy.

Maybe I had too quickly made the deal with Ragnar weeks ago, but in truth, I never gave my offer much contemplation. I wanted my sisters and would have promised him my soul to have them back. So I guess me being stuck in this situation is my fault for blindly promising Ragnar safe passage.

"Stone is Ragnar's cousin," Crius continues. "Not the most chatty among us, but what's that saying again?" He taps his chin. "The quiet ones are the most deadly." He smiles at me like somehow that's meant to soften his ominous description of Stone.

"You suck at introductions," Stone adds, while Nikos groans under his breath behind us.

They aren't wrong.

Crius doesn't seem to care and continues. "And you've met our Alpha in command, the most dangerous of us all, Ragnar. The man we'd all die for."

Die for? The Storm Wolves were loyal to Lovis, but I'd never heard them declare they would die for him or even my father when he ran the pack.

"You're all from Denmark, right?" I ask, figuring things must be very different up north. "From the same pack?"

"Yes and no," Crius answers quickly, but then goes no further to explain. And neither do the rest of them.

"And what about you, little fox?" Ragnar asks, twisting his head to look at me from over his shoulder, his words laced with curiosity.

Now I can't help but wonder if Crius's questioning wasn't pre-planned.

"Ah, you know, the usual Omega story. Growing up in a pack, then doing everything in my ability to evade Alphas who are incapable of thinking straight beyond their dicks." I laugh, but it turns into a strange choking sound when no one finds my response funny. "Well, not you four, of course," I gasp, and this time, they all glance my way, even Nikos. "What? Geez, that was a joke."

That wasn't completely a joke, but I have no intention of telling them anything about me beyond the necessities.

We live in an unfair world, one where Omegas are things to be claimed and broken over and over by brutes. Yes, Ragnar offered me immunity while completing our deal, but what happens afterward? I'll be just another Omega for them to take, and as far as I'm concerned, I want them to think of me as a dangerous wolf with powers who can freeze their balls right off if they anger me.

"Try again," Ragnar insists, and I scrub my face with one hand as we all keep marching onward through an open field covered in tiny white flowers. Beyond them lies a wall of woods. Darker, bigger than any I've seen, and I tighten my grip on my bag straps as we move closer.

"Don't think she's listening to you," Crius says.

"I heard him," I respond. "But I'm not sure what to tell you that you can't work out for yourselves. I'm a nobody. I don't fit in with wolves or witches, so I've spent my life hiding who I am. It's why my sisters and I left the pack we grew up in, because we were no longer safe there. That's who I am. A lost girl trying to hold onto the last fragments of family I have left in this world. My two sisters." My breaths are coming quickly now. I said more than I wanted, and there's not a lie in sight.

I shift my gaze on the woods ahead of us, on anything but the faces looking my way. Let them think what they want, let them feel pity. As long as it keeps me safe. Never mind the fact that my chest tightens each time I think of not having a home to go to when we return, or that when I remember my fated mate, Martell, I forget how to breathe. The longing sits inside me constantly, but the hardest part is the loneliness my wolf drowns in. It seeps into my body like venom, the emotions breaking me slowly.

When I look over at Crius, he's still staring my way. "What?" I ask.

He shrugs. "Nothing." Then he refocuses on our walk, which is all that I ask for... to be left alone and to get this trip over with. Secretly, I also thank him for keeping his word and not telling Ragnar about my attempted escape this morning. I can only guess if Ragnar knew, he'd insist on the new deal he'd proposed back in the inn. I shudder at the thought of being owned by anyone.

I don't need to get to know my companions that well. Right now, I've learned everything I need. One needs attention, another broods over a dark secret, then there's the peacekeeper with has own mysteries, and finally the one who loves to be worshipped.

In the distance, two figures burst out from the dark woods, racing wildly, bounding away so fast I expect something to emerge out of the line of trees behind them. But nothing gives chase.

My pulse thumps in my veins, dread rising to the surface like an oncoming tide as they get closer.

We all pause, Crius stepping forward, while Stone falls back alongside me, his arm jutting out across my stomach. It's a strange sensation to keep having these Alphas look out for me. I've been the protector of my sisters for so long, I'd forgotten how it feels to be protected.

I stare ahead, now clearly seeing two gray wolves darting across the field. They bound forward with terrifying speed, their mouths open, tongues out, and the fur running down their spines standing on end.

They're petrified of something in those woods.

A shiver grips me, but I can't let fear get to me.

We watch the wolves dart right past us without a glance our way, then they're gone.

No one says a word, but the men are exchanging worried looks because I'm certain we are all thinking the same thing. We're about to walk into the devil's den.

"Narah, you're up front with me," Ragnar demands, waving for me to join him. I do, showing no hesitation. "You detect anything, you let us know instantly, understand?" He watches me like a predator, and he's got his guard up. His unsaid words are the focus here. *Or else...*

"Of course."

We're on the move again, and footsteps from the other three close in behind us. I remind myself that my detection of magic will keep me safe, but I can't seem to shake off the worry that I've bitten off more than I can chew.

"Once we're inside, you know how to track down the witches, right?" I ask.

"It's been said there's a small track that intertwines through the woods. Follow that and it will take us to them," Ragnar confirms.

All I can think is how most of the hexes and death traps will be placed along that path, and it won't be the direction we take if we want to avoid death.

Dark clouds gather with the promise of rain. My breaths speed as I scan the woods up ahead for any movement. Upon reaching the forest, the men stop and look at me.

"Alright, that's my cue." Squaring my shoulders, I turn and set my sights on the dense woodland, the shadows. I take one step, then another, and enter the Poisonous Woods. A chill closes in around me the moment I step over the threshold, wrapping around me, digging its claws into my flesh. My wolf stirs, suddenly alert, and she's pushing against me, hating this place.

"It's just for a little while," I whisper.

I look around to the trees that give way to a strange darkness, like somehow the sunlight struggles to breach the canopy.

Breathing deeply, I take another step, then a couple more, my attention falling to the worn path Ragnar mentioned snaking through the landscape and vanishing into the shadows. Behind me, the morning light beams brightly, and four Alphas are waiting for me to call them inside. Facing the forest once more, I exhale slowly, and with it the first sparks of magic tingle through me as though I'm getting the feeling back to my body. *Power always hums under my skin,* my mother would tell me, *and a single concentrated breath will ignite it to life.*

The landscape before me sharpens, colors brighten, and I scan the area for the sparks of magic. Those indicate a spell, yet there's nothing here. Not in this location, anyway. Just the oppressive sensation like something is pushing down on my shoulders. I glance down at my hands and remove the gloves for full effect. Tiny white lines of magic leap across my fingers, and I smile at how pretty they look.

I sigh at the burned magic on my fingers, but there's nothing to be done about those, and it's not like I have to keep concealing them from the Viking wolves. They know what I am. Ragnar guessed it when we first met, something I've been meaning to ask him about. But that's not important... not now.

On quick steps, I reach the edge of the woods and wave for them to join me. "It looks all clear. Let's start."

They don't move. "You sure?" Ragnar asks, staring into the forest behind me like he expects a monster to leap out at him.

"Would I really risk never seeing my sister again?" I reply quickly, not wanting to make this trip any longer than it needs to be.

Ragnar scrutinizes me for a long, hard moment.

"Or are you getting cold feet?" I ask.

He huffs, shoulders springing back, and he looks back to his men. "Are you all ready?"

They nod almost in unison, then the four of them stride into the woods alongside me.

"We need to keep our distance from the path," I tell them. No one protests, though they are studying the terrain, the path, the shadows in the distance with uncertainty. "Spells would be more likely near the path. Us staying away means we are hopefully safer from any hexes."

"Are you sure you know what you're doing?" Nikos asks.

While I'd like to admit that I really don't and I'm doing my damn best, I lift my chin in his direction, remembering I need to come across as a strong witch. "Of course I do. I can detect where magic has been used before we walk into its snare."

He looks at me like I've just told the world's biggest lie, except that part is pretty accurate. The fact that I've never encountered a lot of magic up to now is something he doesn't need to know. As long as I follow my mother's instructions and keep an eye out for enchantments, we should be safe.

"Just remember, you trick us and I won't hesitate to leave your body in these woods," he threatens.

I swallow the lump forming in my throat, never lowering my gaze from his.

"You heard the girl, let's move," Crius mutters and brushes past Nikos.

"After you then," Stone says, waving an arm for me to take the lead.

Striding over shrubs, fallen logs, under low-hanging branches, we move swiftly. The deeper we progress, the heavier that earlier sensation tightens around me, except I spy no sign of magic.

Stone groans as if in pain, and I turn to him, scanning him from head to toe. His face is twisted in agony, and he's gripping his middle, looking like he might topple over any second.

Panic drags through me that I missed something obvious. "What's wrong?"

The moment he drops to his knees, an ear-shattering howl breaks the silence from behind me. I whip around, only to see Ragnar stumbling into a tree while Nikos trembles as if he's about to transform and is fighting the urge. Crius is breathing heavily... too heavily.

That's when a sharp pain strikes me in the pit of my stomach, and my wolf shoves against my insides like she's trying to rip out through my rib cage.

I scream, the pain like burning water poured over my skin. My knees hit the ground as my wolf starts erupting out of me. She's scared... so scared that if I let her emerge, she'll bolt out of here just like those two other wolves we saw.

Someone's whining, another growling, but I can't focus on them when I feel like my body is splitting in two as I fight to hold back my wolf. She's never hurt so much or tried to get out this fast before. I stiffen, my muscles rigid, knowing what I'm feeling is her fear.

Goddess, my wolf is petrified of these woods. If I let her out, there's no way I'll be able to re-enter without her fighting me to death. I can't let her win.

"Whatever you do, don't let your wolf come out," I cry out, bending forward as I grit my teeth, my body trembling furiously.

Pain beats into me, scratching and gouging at my insides, while my heart breaks for my wolf, who's whining in fear. I'm on hands and knees, my body convulsing. Blocking a wolf from emerging shouldn't be such a problem, except right now she's so out of her mind with terror, she doesn't know anything but the primal desperation to flee. This isn't my wolf normally...

A strangled cry rushes past my lips, followed by her threatening growl. It's what cornered animals do—they strike back—and mine feels abandoned.

Tears squeeze out of my shut eyes as I'm torn from the pain pummeling into my sides.

You don't need to be afraid, please, I plead with her, trying to connect with her, but she's not hearing me. Or perhaps she's choosing to ignore me. It feels like there's a wall between us, and I hate this so much.

She stirs inside me, shoving for escape, her emotions like a rope strangling me until I can barely breathe.

A ravenous snarl spears through the air, stealing my attention. I snap open my eyes and jerk my head to the right where three of the Alphas are on the ground just like me, writhing in agony.

But it's Crius my sights set upon. He's on his feet, breaking into a song. It's in another language, but the tune... oh, the tune is a powerful war song. It glides into my mind, slides over my body like a silk ribbon. My wolf quiets down as if drawn to his music, and with it, the sharpness cutting through me starts to ease.

Crius's voice booms, the song on his lips boisterous and fast, each word punched out like an arrow fired to hit its target. His chant reminds me of the battle hymns the Storm Wolves would sing before marching out to face an enemy clan.

He comes to me in two long strides and scoops his hands under my armpits, then wrenches me to my feet with ease.

I turn to face him, his hand sweeping from his mouth to mine, never stopping his song. For a man who has only shown an arrogant side of himself, his voice seems to have a way of stealing all that is wrong with the world.

It's only when Ragnar breaks into the same hymn, on the same beat as Crius, that I understand. He wants me to join him in the music. I don't know the language, but I've got the melody stuck in my head, so I begin to hum. From the moment I do, a spark of energy rushes down my body. It's as if the music has single-handedly stripped the pain from my body and calmed my wolf.

I don't question it but hum louder, even if my throat starts to sting. Stone and Nikos are also on their feet, bellowing out the melody, and I would be blind and deaf to not be utterly mesmerized by these four men harmonizing together. All we're missing is the tavern and beers in their hands.

The sound brings with it deep-felt emotions where moments earlier there was nothing but agony. With it, I feel a vibration buzzing through me. Is it strange to feel a sense of envy at wishing I knew the words?

Ragnar looks at me, his chest pumping in and out as he delivers the loud chorus, his fist punching into the air. There's so much pride in his face, the corners of his mouth close to breaking into a smile. And here I thought the guy had no idea how to experience pure happiness. Except it's staring me in the face. He is so proud of his Northern heritage... they all are.

Which then begs the question, *Why does he want to take over the Savage Sector if his heart belongs in Denmark?*

Crius falls silent first, and the others follow. I do the same, swallowing past my dry throat and hugging my middle, my wolf settled.

"How did you do that?" I croak. "My wolf hasn't been this calm in months."

His lips turn upward in a prideful grin. "Music calms the beast. Plus, it's our war hymn to prepare our wolves for battle and be focused."

"So if needed again, we break into a unified song?" I ask.

He nods. "At our core, we are blood-hungry animals, and such music should help."

But when Nikos brings his attention my way, his wry expression has me stiffening, completely ignoring Crius's happy moment.

"What the fuck just happened? Why didn't you detect that spell?" Nikos growls. "You said you saw *all* magic, yet we're barely a few steps into the woods before we're attacked." The fury on his face has me recoiling, and unease bleeds into my veins.

"Nikos has a point," Stone adds. "If you couldn't detect whatever in the world that was, what else is lying in wait for us deeper in the woods?"

I square my shoulders, needing to stand up to them or this mission will end with me dead. "It's not a specific spell that caused our wolves to react that way, it was the air filled with magic, with each of our fears," I snap, failing miserably at holding back the anger in my voice. "It's your natural instinct, your wolf knowing when it's in so much danger that running is the only option. So how could I have detected it when it's not a spell? The whole damn forest is tainted with different enchantments."

My arms are rigid by my side, and I'm trembling. I don't even know why I'm arguing with them on this point when I did nothing wrong. They are just looking for someone to blame instead of admitting they were scared. "And if you're going to all freak out so quickly over something without a spell targeted on us, then we are all just wasting our time. Give me back my sister and we'll part ways now." I follow their gazes as they all turn to Ragnar.

I'm furious at how quickly they turn on me, and now alarm bells ring in my head that these men—these animals—will become my enemy the moment I fail. Maybe that's how they see me now, as having failed. It bugs me more than it should, because who cares what they think?

"We continue," Ragnar answers abruptly, and I deflate on the inside, partly wanting them to keep blaming me and take the easy way out. "I'm giving Narah the benefit of the doubt."

He looks at me sharply, and I'm shaking, more with fury than anything, because he's saying indirectly he doesn't believe I did enough either. Fuck him.

"First and only chance," he adds, then looks over to Crius. "And quick thinking. Now, let's not turn on each other after one test, as there will be many others."

I'm seething, burning up.

Nikos doesn't say a word but studies me, then gives me a nod of acknowledgment, which I didn't expect. I can't help but suspect it's more about pleasing his Alpha than me. As far as I'm concerned, he's the last person I can trust. Even if he happens to have the face of an angel, cheekbones cut sharply with a knife. He's a demon lurking behind that mask, getting ready to finish me.

If he doesn't stay out of my way, there'll be a showdown between us.

I give him a ghost of a smile and slip back to where I dropped my bag, unable to stop thinking that this trip might be my demise. If not by the witches and their spells, definitely by the hands of these wolves.

A shadow falls over me, and I twist around, expecting Nikos, but it's Crius. "I don't blame you, by the way," he reassures me while his attention slides down to my hands. Thin yellow lines of magic crackle and snap between my fingers, which leaves behind a slight tingle across my arms. Right now, I'm myself, open to detecting magic.

"Would it hurt if I touched them?" he asks.

"While I'm concentrating to detect other spells, it would hurt."

He keeps studying my hands, and I know what he's thinking. He wants to know why the top half of my fingers are stained black, which then fades as it reaches my knuckles. So I give him the answer before he asks.

"It's magic I used months ago, and it came with consequences," I tell him, then swing my bag over my shoulder and tuck my hands into my pockets.

"You don't have to hide them from me," Crius says, drawing my attention back to him. "I'm a collector of scars myself." Before I can respond, he drags his shirt up to his armpit, where my gaze instantly inhales the sight of his ripped stomach muscles, the way he wears his pants low on his hips revealing that wicked V-dip hunks like him possess. Then I lift my head to the huge, scar curling around from his back, over his ribs and across his abs. Whatever did that could have cut him in half. I gasp at the sight, coaxing a laugh out of him. "It hurt like a fucking bitch. Never get in a fight with someone wielding a chain whip."

"Hell, Crius, do you ever stop braggin' about yourself?" Nikos states. Stone chuckles, while Crius doesn't seem to give a shit. He goes back to grab his backpack, talking crap back to them. But I'm not listening.

I'm staring at my hands and can't help but wonder if that's how he sees the mark... as a scar. I guess, in a way, it is. What else can it be called? I still have no idea why it happened after I was thrown off the cliff or how my magic saved me that day.

It isn't long before we're moving again, and the deeper we travel, the more the atmosphere changes. It's like this place has its own weather system. Each breath I take grows easier, the air less stuffy, but the light is dimmer. Sunlight barely reaches through the canopy overhead. Down here, it's shadows and barely enough light to not trip over our own feet.

"Is it strange that there are no animal or bird sounds?" Stone asks.

"They probably all ran for their lives like our wolves tried," Ragnar responds with a dark mirth in his tone. I'm not sure if I should take that as *ha-ha, let's take another stab at Narah,* or admitting they were actually scared, which caused their wolves to go into panic?

Ragnar strolls alongside me, both of us taking the lead. I keep glancing over to the dirt path farther to our right. As long as we follow that, we shouldn't get lost. Though now I keep frantically double scanning everything around us for any traces of magic, for anything I feel that might be a spell.

I'm certain we've walked for half a day so far, though it might have only been an hour. It's impossible to tell in here. There's been minimal chatter, which is fine with me. I can only guess the way our wolves reacted has spooked everyone.

The farther we travel, the more the woods change. Gone are the tall pines and firs, replaced with twisted and bent trunks, their branches stripped bare of leaves and bark, like we're walking through a graveyard of skeletons. While earlier the canopy concealed the sunlight, now a murky cloud covers the tops of the trees.

Foliage crunches under our shoes, dried like it hasn't seen water for months.

"Is it just me, or does it look like we've entered a new part of the woods?" Stone asks.

"Keep an eye out for anything." Ragnar states the obvious, and I'm scanning the surrounding land. Not a spark, nothing magical here.

"I don't pick up on anything," I say, stepping over a rock and bumping into Ragnar. He looks over to me as if I did that on purpose or out of fear.

He steps away from me, and at first I assume it's to avoid me walking into him again, but he's veering to the right, away from all of us.

"Ragnar?" I say, a shiver running up my spine that he's been affected again somehow.

When he stops and looks down at something, we all join him, only to find him standing near the remains of someone. Bones are all that's left, really, but by the skull with a jagged hole in the side of the head, and a rib cage, it's obvious it's a person and not an animal.

I turn quickly on the spot, staring in every direction, feeling like I missed something obvious and that we've just walked into another trap. There's nothing around us, magic or otherwise, only broken trees and shrubs. Everything seems bleak and gray... not to mention it's getting dark really fast.

"This sucker died from dehydration," Stone says with confidence. Maybe he's right.

"Doubt it," Nikos adds.

My mind runs wild with thoughts that I underestimated how hard this mission might be. Doubts that I might not be up for the task especially when my magic is broken, and it's not like I can use it for anything aside from detecting spells. Plus, what do I really know about witches aside from what my mother told me? And she went and died on us.

My thoughts race with how she used to tell us that she'd always protect us, and the memory brings with it a pain that burns across my chest. Grief washes over me like it hasn't done in a long time. What I wouldn't give to have my parents still alive, for my mother to have trained me to use my magic instead of just forcing me to hide it.

I look down to my hands. There's no longer the dance of magic over my dark fingers, which isn't right. It should flare in these woods, as I am still open to detecting enchantments.

Magic can burn, Mother would tell me. *Not just the witches or victims, but what's nearby as well.*

I sweep my gaze across the landscape once more, up and down the charred trees, following the upward slant of the earth, and finally across to where we're keeping the path as far from us as possible. The woods are darker there, almost greener, and I take several steps toward it for a better look.

Someone grabs my arms and tugs me back, pausing me on my feet. "You told us to steer clear of the path," Stone reminds me.

I don't look at him, but keep staring at the leaves on the trees back in the direction we came from. "There's no magic in this section of the woods," I murmur. "It's burned, the ground barren. Just look at the path over there." I point to it. "It's green and even a wind stirs, while where we stand, it doesn't reach us, and we're only what, fifty feet away?"

"Are you sure?" Ragnar asks, his words stretched out almost like he thinks I'm blowing smoke up his ass. He doesn't believe me.

"Well, when magic is overused in a place for too long, it can physically burn anything it touches. This is an example of the Poisonous Woods not being as strong as many think. Plus, there's no spark of magic on my fingers. There should be when I'm open to this much power. Magic has a way of igniting anything similar. Think of it as a magnetic pull."

Crius strolls over to a thick tree. The bark is dark brown in color, and it's hard to tell if it's burned or worn. But he tears away a strip of the outer layer with ease, and it simply disintegrates in his hand like dust. The inside trunk is also dark and burnt. Even from where we're standing several feet away, an acrid smell finds us. It carries an electric stench, just like magic.

When I glance at Ragnar, he's blinking as he takes in our surroundings, like he's viewing it for the first time. "So no magic means this is a safe zone."

"No guarantees, but I'd feel better resting here than over by the path," I say, not loving the idea of sleeping in these woods at all, but I knew we wouldn't be able to make this trip in under one day.

"Then we camp here," Nikos states, and instantly, three of them set on collecting wood for a fire. Ragnar heads over to a small area near a dead log that would be a perfect place to stay. I don't know how much sleep I'll get, but being off my feet will be good.

I help collect more branches, as I prefer not to have the blaze go out at all tonight, but not large enough that we accidently set the place on fire. These woods give me the creeps during the day, so I can only imagine night will be ten times worse.

Night comes quicker than any of us expected. The faint crackle of the fire echoes around us, while its flames lick at the darkness crowding in at our backs. "This place is beyond eerie," I say.

Stone acknowledges me with a blank stare while Ragnar remains deep in thought, sitting with his back to a tree, legs stretched out toward the fire, not seeming to have heard what I said. Crius lounges on the log, legs parted, arms resting against his thighs. In one hand he holds a paring knife, and in the other is a red apple he cuts and eats in slices.

"What do you think would happen if zombies came in here?" he asks. "Not like spells can kill them, so what if they made it all the way to the witches and killed them?"

"Not sure I want to picture that right now, seeing as we are sleeping out in the open," I respond.

"Are you hatching another scheme?" Nikos asks as he strolls into camp and drops down on his ass in front of the fire, legs bent and arms draped over them.

"Heads up, Narah," Stone says.

I lift my gaze as he tosses me an apple. Instinct has me ducking my head while throwing my arm out to catch it. It hits my palm dead on, and I'm rather proud of the small feat of impossibility. No one seems to notice, so I bite into the fleshy fruit, juice filling my mouth. Stone is sharing the food from his backpack, which is mainly dried meat and fruit, along with a large flask of water and a bottle of wine.

Everyone takes their portions and passes the rest around as the five of us sit around the fire. I have my bag on the ground behind me, my large coat underneath me as a blanket as I cross my legs. I lift the bottle and uncork it, then take several mouthfuls, not realizing how thirsty I am until then.

"So, Narah," Stone begins. "You're very different from another Cursed I met back home." His observation draws everyone's attention to me.

They've known other Cursed? I meet Stone's eyes, which seem to glint against the fire. "How so?" I'm curious to hear more about half-breeds, as I've never met another aside from my mother and sister.

"She would constantly threaten to turn all men into rodents if they didn't do as she asked. It worked at first, as people were scared, you see, but she made one fatal mistake."

I'm hanging off his every word. "What's that?"

"She assumed no one would harm her because she started fucking the pack Alpha. But in the end, the second in command killed her with his bare hands when she insisted she was untouchable." He takes a swig of wine from the bottle near his feet. "But you don't even show us the extent of your powers, so what are we to assume? That you are being modest?"

I swallow and collect myself enough to wonder if this whole time he was setting me up, while my mind swirls on what he's told me. This Cursed was sleeping with Ragnar's father? I refocus on Stone. "So what you're saying is that no one is untouchable. Not Cursed and not Alphas, right? And you're right about me being different. If I lived in a place where Cursed were not hated, I might be more open about it, so my decisions have nothing to do with modesty and everything to do with survival."

Stone stares at me, lost for words, it seems, and when I look over to Ragnar, a smile tugs at the corners of his mouth as he just sits back, observing us.

I lower my attention to my meal and start eating while the three men fall into a conversation about zombies. Mostly it revolves around the method with which they would kill them. I tune out after Crius says, "I'll chop mine up then watch it squirm on the ground."

I can't tell if he's serious or just trying to have the grossest answer. Instead, I let the fire warm me and stay quiet, just like Ragnar. He's sitting to the side of me, his hands deep in the pockets of his pants. He's built and solid, towering over me, taller than his men, but something about him now makes him seem normal. Not a warring Viking, but someone reserved and deep in thought.

What's strange is that a tingle erupts in the pit of my stomach when I look at him. As if sensing me, he turns his head in my direction and the fire reflects in his eyes, along with indecision warring on his face.

I'm not sure I want to find out what bothers him so much, so instead I shuffle to get comfortable on the hard ground. I tuck my bag under my head as a pillow and pull my coat over me. Closing my eyes, I block out the men's chatter while my instincts have me listening for strange sounds. For anything sneaking up on us. Of course, there's only the crackle of fire, but I can't shake off the unease.

Exhaustion sweeps over me, the warmth relaxing, and my eyes slide close as I fade away.

When twigs snap, I flip open my eyelids and find Ragnar, Stone, and Crius lying by the fire, fast asleep.

Had I passed out that quickly? The fire still burns brightly when another crunch of a branch comes, and I lift my head to see a figure walking away from camp and going deeper into the woods.

Nikos?

EIGHT

Narah

My sight sets on Nikos, who walks away from our camp and blends into the shadows of the night. I don't move from the fire, listening for any sounds, figuring he's going to pee. All I hear is the other three Alphas snoring. Beyond that, the night in the Poisonous Woods is deathly silent.

I'm not completely awake yet, but I sit up and reach for the flask of water, then take several mouthfuls, the lukewarm water rushing down my dry throat.

Back in the Storm Wolves' pack, I'd often stay alone in our back yard on the garden bench, staring out toward the back fence, listening to my heartbeat amid the breeze. I've always liked the darkness, the night. Its tranquility brought me joy after a chaotic day.

But here, I don't feel that serenity or the warmth the night brings me. Instead, I focus on the lack of life, the dead trees. I should be happy that the land is barren of magic, but I come to the conclusion that I hate these woods.

I glance over to Crius, who's twitching in his sleep. Stone is dead to the world, while Ragnar remains slouched against the tree, his chin tucked into his chest. First day of the trip, and it started off shitty. I don't owe these Viking Alphas anything but safe delivery through the woods. They haven't died yet, so that's a win, regardless of how we got here.

I don't remember how much time has passed, but Nikos hasn't returned to camp. The longer I wait, the more my nerves tighten. It's pitch black out there, so he could easily stumble onto hexed land and walk straight into danger. Sight at night is a strength for wolves, but this place has no moon or stars to give a hue of light. It's just black.

I shouldn't care.

I don't care.

Yet I get to my feet and stretch my arms into the air to crack my back, then, before I can stop myself, I grab the end of a branch sticking out of the flames and use it as a torch. Curiosity hammers into me, wanting to make sure Nikos isn't in trouble. I chase away the darkness with the small flame I carry. It's enough to carve a path for myself through the woodland.

I shouldn't be out here, but then, neither should Nikos, and I refuse to be blamed again for something else I have no control over.

Raising the torch in front of me, I travel farther through the quiet, eerie woods. There are no smells out here, and any calm I carried earlier is now completely dissolved, taken over by the insistence that I should turn back.

Just as I decide to do just that, I spy a figure standing against a tree several feet away. That earlier sense of danger now skyrockets through me. Something feels wrong here. My heart thumps loudly.

I squint through the dark, easily making it out to be Nikos by his hairstyle, the dreadlocks that are entwined to run along the top of his head like a Mohawk and fall down his back. What is he doing just standing out here?

"Nikos," I whisper loud enough for him to hear me, and he lifts his head to face me, the light catching his bright green eyes. My attention dips down his body, but he's not rushing to zip himself up, so he wasn't peeing.

"Can't sleep either?" he asks me, striding in my direction.

"Actually, I think you woke me up when you stepped on twigs."

He grins like that had been his intention all along, which I struggle to believe, as that would mean the other three slept like bears. When I turn my head in their direction, spying them through the trees, none of them have stirred.

Suddenly, Nikos stands in front of me, so close and unexpectedly, that I flinch and the flaming branch slips from my grasp.

He tsks and hastily steps on the flames, putting it out, throwing us into darkness.

I back up until I hit a tree. He follows and pins me to the trunk with his sheer presence alone, his eyes glinting in the flames from the campfire behind me. He hasn't touched me, but we're standing a breath's distance apart, and I instinctively press my hand to his chest. He grabs me by the wrist but doesn't push me away.

Warmth rushes up my arm from where we're touching, and he's staring down at me like he sees right through me. Yet the way he keeps studying me, the way his thumb runs in small circles across my wrist, fills me with an unexpected desire.

This is very wrong. I shouldn't feel this way when he's been nothing but a danger to me.

"What are you doing out here?" I ask, trying to shake off the fire spewing from his hand and engulfing me.

"I wanted you to follow me."

I study his face, trying to find the truth, but with so many shadows, there's nothing but the beating of his heart against my touch.

"That doesn't sound like me." I'm breathless, downplaying how him being this close to me has even my wolf stirring.

He laughs softly, his other hand going to the side of my face, cupping my cheek, his thumb dragging across my lower lip.

Something feels off with me as I just stand there, barely knowing this Alpha, clenching my thighs together from the way he plays with me. I shouldn't let him touch me, not after his earlier rudeness.

"If you didn't want to follow me, you would have stayed in camp," he tells me, and just like Crius, he's full of ego. But when he leans in and his breath whispers on my cheek, I lose all ability to think logically. The warmth of his proximity is a toxicity that swallows me. He whispers in my ear, "I have a proposition for you."

My free hand grips the tree behind me as I brace to hold myself up, my back against the trunk, unsure why he makes me feel like I've lost all ability to think straight.

"What do you mean?" My question comes out sounding sultry even though I hadn't meant it to.

His fingers trace across my jawline and dip over the front of my throat, soft, yet I sense the power in them. How one small twist of his wrist and he'd choke the life out of me. Still, I can't move my legs to get out of his way. The chaos that is Nikos consumes me, his presence like a poison seeping into my veins.

He presses in close to me once more, our chests smothered together, and my breath catches in my throat.

His cheek brushes against mine, his mouth on my earlobe, and a moan escapes my lips.

"You and I go to find the witch coven alone. We ditch the rest of them, and that way we're quicker. No drama, and we get out of these woods faster. How does that sound?" His words are hot against my neck, and it takes me a few moments for their meaning to sink in.

I push against his chest to separate us, but he doesn't budge, only brings his face up in front of mine. What he's saying scares me, because here I thought the four of them were a unit and trusting, yet Nikos offers to leave them behind. What am I missing?

"What do you get out of this?"

I have no loyalty to any of these men, but I also want to know the devil I'm playing with.

He shrugs nonchalantly, as if he wants to make me think this is a topic he just thought of, except that's not the case at all. "It's the right thing to do, and I'm not doing it to trick you. Once we're out, I will get your sister back to you."

I blink at him, so lost, so confused.

"I thought you and them were loyal to each other." I twist my head back to the camp, then back at Nikos.

"We're friends, yes, and they may not know it, but I'm doing this for them. They will kill each other before we reach the coven with their bickering and competitiveness, so I want to help get this done for them."

He wants to impress Ragnar by being the hero? Is that what this is all about? His hand reaches over and lands on my shoulder, distracting me for a moment.

"What exactly is your intention with the witches? What does Ragnar want? To negotiate with them? To kill them?"

"You're a kind Omega—maybe too kind for this world, Narah—and I'm offering you a way out of dealing with wild Alphas. Have you not seen the way they look at you?"

"I've seen the way you look at me too." I realize then his trick to distract me from my question worked.

His mouth splits into a wicked grin that should scare me, but when his hand combs through the back of my hair, fisting it and tilting my head back, I can only look at his lips and the promise of what they offer.

My head demands I push him away and remember who the Alpha in front of me is. I shouldn't let him touch me like this, except I seem to be stuck in a frozen state of mind where the rest of the world has vanished and all that remains is us two. I know it's in my head, but he's not backing away either, so maybe he feels something between us too.

For all I know, these Alphas are killers, just like Crius took out Finn back in town. So why aren't I more fearful of Nikos? Why does my body buzz with anticipation when I can just imagine he's been with dozens of women? Why is my wolf stirring, suddenly more interested in him than she should be?

He kisses me suddenly, and another moan slips past my throat. My body softens against him, my chest pushing into his like it has a mind of its own. Maybe I've been wrong to think that only one man will drive me this insane, except whatever is happening between us is all attraction.

His mouth is wicked and on fire, kissing me insatiably, licking and tasting all of me. I have never been kissed this way in my life. Goddess, he is making me rethink every emotion I've ever felt except for the hunger thumping through my veins, collecting between my thighs. He grips my chin with his other hand and leaves a trail of pecks down to my neck. "Consider my offer, Omega."

Next thing I know, he pulls away, drawing his hand from my hair, from my jaw, and studies me for a long moment. "Your lips are beautiful when they are full and red from my kiss." His gaze dips down my body, pausing right on the apex between my legs, and he smirks. As quickly as he came to me, he steps into the shadows and makes his way back to camp.

I collapse against the tree, my heart thundering in my chest, my mouth bruised from how hard he kissed me.

What the hell did I just do? He's not a guy to get close to. He's the enemy, a man who will walk over me. Not to mention, it sounded very clear to me that he either wants to betray his pack or is so desperate for Ragnar's approval, he's willing to risk angering him to complete this mission on his own. Even if it means risking both our lives by going alone.

He is insane if he thinks I will get in the middle of whatever the hell is going on between them. My sisters are my priorities, not the Alphas.

I can still taste him on my mouth, still feel the pressure of his body against mine, and that thought alone sends a jolt right through me. My eyes close, and I try to calm my raging arousal. I dig my fingers into my arm to eliminate the excitement, to wake up from what I've just let myself fall into.

Each time I remember his lips on my neck, his whisper, I shudder with excitement and my wolf rubs her fur against my insides, approving of him. Heat flushes through me, and now I'm more lost than before.

I don't intend to betray Ragnar, as I doubt he would forgive me, even if he would forgive Nikos. My deal is with the leader to save my sisters, and that's the way it's going to stay... for now.

Even if in my mind's eye I can't stop picturing Nikos's insatiable grin, or the fact that he's left me panting from a single kiss that never should have happened.

Nikos

SHE IS like nothing I've had before, nothing I've tasted. Fuck, that kiss wasn't meant to happen. I'd made sounds on purpose when leaving camp to ensure she heard me. The Omega's weakness is her curiosity, but it seems I have one of my own... her.

I lay on the ground on my back, my coat rolled up into a pillow, legs crossed at the ankles and hands behind my head. The sky is black, not a star in sight. Not even the lofty tree branches are visible. Whatever fucked-up place this forest is, nothing here is normal. It makes my skin crawl to be in here, so my offer to Narah had been genuine. Get this shit done fast and get the fuck out of Death-ville.

Ragnar would never agree to my plan, of course. The guy's a control freak and needs to be involved in everything, needs to ensure he gets the glory. The other two carry their own baggage, enough to slow us down, so if I work on Narah, maybe she'll see sense and accept my offer.

The kiss. That was unexpected, and fuck me but she is delicious. I hate to admit it, but I might be addicted to that small touch. She's not someone I intended to bring into my already shitty life, but after this mission, anything is possible with her. Sure, there's the complication of her sisters, but that's a problem for later.

For now, I bathe in her scent, her sweetness on my tongue, her softness still marked on my hands where I held her. Her body was so responsive to mine, while her cheeks burned with shame, as it was clear she couldn't control herself. Seeing her that way only makes me want her more.

The crunch of foliage has me cracking open an eye to see her sneaking back into camp. She gives me a fleeting look before quickly lowering her head. But my mind is already racing as I eye her chest breathing faster, her breasts pushing against her tight top, straining against the fabric. To pause my mind now would be impossible. All I can picture is me ripping the material off, freeing her breasts. How I'd take her hardened nipples into my mouth and slip two fingers into her pussy.

My cock twitches. Fuck. I'm going to strangle myself if I don't jerk off.

I turn on my side, thinking of the dead on the battleground instead, the many I've slain, the blood spilled. But tonight, that imagery does fuck-all to put out the flames.

The memory of my family comes to mind so easily that I hate

them for it. The time when they gave me away to the enemy pack without a second thought to achieve peace between two warring clans. Ragnar's sister went to my family pack. Fair exchange, everyone agreed... everyone but us. Assholes, the lot of them. If there is something to fuck up your life, it's your family selling you off. That shit twists inside me like barbed wire, ripping me to shreds every time I remember how I have no real family anymore.

Coldness swims through me at the painful memories.

Yeah, that does the trick, and now my veins are back to their normal raging, furious selves.

Narah settles down across the fire from me, and I shut my eyes, taking a deep breath, and am reminded that what I felt in the woods with her had been a ravenous desire. Nothing else.

Omegas are made for Alphas. They're drawn together by irresistible urges, and I shouldn't fool myself to think she'll want anything beyond that. But that doesn't change the fact that I may just keep her anyway.

CHAPTER

NINE

I wake to the delicious smell of coffee, and for those few moments, I'm back in the family hut in the Storm Wolves pack. My sisters are trying to wake me while I pull the blanket over my head, desperate for a few extra minutes of sleep before starting my routine of going to collect water from the well and helping the women in the kitchen and with their sewing. We were exhausted with all the things we had to do, even when we were sick, to keep our place in the pack.

But when Ragnar's deep voice sounds nearby, I'm ripped out of my past and brought back to reality. To where I'm sleeping in the Poisonous Woods along with four Viking Alphas who I know still doubt my abilities. To where I kissed Nikos last night.

Yeah, if I thought living with the Storm Wolves was complicated, I'm starting to think that it was nothing compared to this.

Cranking my head up, my stiff muscles strain from the hard ground, and I open my eyes to a morning light that floods the woods around us. It's brighter than yesterday, warmer, but murky clouds still hover overhead.

A small pot is sitting near the low fire, the smell of coffee wafting from inside. I figured these men had come prepared with pots and coffee and enough water for the trip. The four of them are farther away, chatting casually by the looks of Ragnar leaning against a tree, Stone standing with hands in his pockets, and Crius talking with his hands animated like he's telling a grand old tale.

I rub the sleep out of my eyes and crawl over to the pot, grabbing one of the previously used metal cups nearby and filling it with the nutty ambrosia. Sitting back on my heels, I take a deep inhale and smile. It's funny how a small thing like a familiar smell can make the worst day seem manageable.

It's not burning hot in my hands, but I still take a sip to test the temperature. When it doesn't scald my tongue, I take two mouthfuls. Slightly on the bitter side, but it's still amazing.

A shadow falls over the pot, and I glance up to see Nikos standing there, watching me with his spectacular green eyes. Butterflies burst in my stomach, beating their wings wildly as I remember his kiss, and my lips tingle in memory of our encounter in the woods. The truth is, if I had known he'd kiss me, I would have *still* followed him.

And that's why I have a problem. That's why I have to keep my distance and pretend last night never happened. Not to mention, his cryptic offer to have me go off with him to reach the witch coven first was ludicrous. That kind of conspiring will lead to my death at the hands of these Viking wolves. Plus, there's a greater chance of us getting killed without more of us to help each other out. Like, who would have thought Crius's singing would have aided our wolves in their time of panic?

"What's going on?" I ask casually, like nothing happened between us.

"That's my cup," he states, and gone is the man who pinned me to a tree last night. Instead, he's back to his normal grouchy, dickhead self. It's definitely for the best.

The expression on his face is patronizing, and I am starting to really hate the way he tries to intimidate me with that expression.

Unable to help myself, I lift the cup to my mouth. "Do you mean this one?" I sweep my tongue along the rim, making sure to not leave a single section unmarked, then I proceed to drink the whole cup of coffee in one go. I stick my finger in, too, for good measure, and run it along the inside before sticking it into my mouth. Then I get to my feet and hand him back his cup. "Here you go."

I smirk while he eyes me with what I can only imagine is shock. The fact that he didn't expect that from me makes me smile.

He accepts the vessel and bends over to proceed to pour himself the rest of what's left in the pot. Then, as if to prove his point, he stands so close to me, I can feel the warmth from the coffee in his hands on my cheeks. He stares at me with a challenge in his eyes.

"Do you think you can intimidate me, Omega?" He lifts the metal cup to his lips and downs the caffeine in one go, then licks his lips hungrily. "If you keep pushing me, I can promise that you'll soon find me buried deep inside you, knotting in you, and you'll beg me for more."

My throat grows tight, and I have to look away to stop him from seeing me blush. He laughs and grabs the pot before dispensing any last drops onto the dried soil.

"Asshole," I mumble under my breath.

"Your sweet words only make me harder," he mocks.

Why did I think antagonizing him would end well for me? New rule: don't engage Nikos in anything, possibly ever again.

It takes me several long minutes to settle myself down, and by then, Nikos has put out the fire and is kicking loose soil over the remains.

Stone is beside him, his sandy blond hair windblown and messy like he didn't bother to even pat it down after waking up.

"Morning, Narah," Crius says, joining them. "Hope you slept well. Today we are going to reach the coven. It can't be that far now."

Stone laughs and slaps him on the shoulder. "Just because you say something doesn't make it so."

I turn my attention away from them as Ragnar approaches, and instantly my stomach twirls with nerves. I catch the way he glances over to Nikos, who is packing the pot and cup into his bag. Then the leader returns his gaze to me.

Did Ragnar see us talking in the woods last night? A shiver zips up my spine that he might think I conspired to backstab him... or did I completely misunderstand Nikos's purpose? Maybe it had zilch to do with me taking his side but was a test to see if I would jump at the first better offer.

I eye Ragnar, unsure how to feel. It shouldn't surprise me that he doesn't trust me when I don't think I trust any of them.

He picks up his bag and flashes me a grin. "It seems like a good day for a walk."

I don't know what to think... is he trying to confuse me because he knows something? Or am I being completely paranoid now?

Stone and Crius stand ready, both so different, yet they share a similarity. Their obedience to Ragnar, the way they wait for his order, how they look at him with determination, is admirable. So what is Nikos's story, then? He's got his back to us, staring out into the woods as if determining the best direction for us to take.

"Let's go," Ragnar orders, then glances out in the woods.

"Yep, almost there," I respond and move to slip into my shoes and roll my coat into my bag. Once I'm all packed and ready to go, Stone comes over and hands me a kitchen towel wrapped up around something.

"Saved you some," Stone announces.

I quickly unwrap the gift to find a slice of salted fish on bread, along with an apple. It's more than I'd eat most mornings back home, and it's ridiculous to get excited over a meal, but he saved me some when he didn't need to. When I lift my head, he's back over with Crius, and I catch his eyes, smiling my thanks.

With everyone waiting on me, I quickly wrap it back up and tuck it into my pocket to eat as soon as we get moving.

"Alright, we follow the path from a distance like yesterday." I step up in front of them and take the lead, only this time Ragnar isn't following me. When I steal a peek over my shoulder, I notice he's walking alongside Nikos, and now I am more confident than ever that last night was a test after all. Perhaps the kiss was too, to trick me into taking his offer. And the thought leaves a sour taste in my mouth because I enjoyed the kiss a bit too much to discover it was a game.

Something in me insists on playing by the rules, to show them I want the same as them. To get this mission over and done with to get my sisters back. It's tearing me apart on the inside to think of Jae closed in a room, to know Kaira is somewhere out there alone.

There are too many things going on in my head, not to mention that my power consists of only detecting magic and nothing beyond that. Unless I include the possibility of having my ability go haywire and accidentally burning one of the Viking Alphas. Yeah, I can see that going down well.

That single thought alone brings back a wave of memories of Martell, and I loathe that each time he comes to mind, my chest feels like it might crack open. My wolf growls in protest that I left him, that I now associate with these Alphas.

Yep, my wolf hates me even more as she pines deep inside me. She doesn't understand that I left for our survival.

I refocus my attention, as it's the only way to ease the longing that strangles me.

The burned woods extends out a lot farther than any of us anticipated, and all the while in the distance to our right, the greenery by the path rustles in the breeze.

Sweat drips down my back, and I long for a single movement of air through my hair, something to take away the stuffiness choking me. Despite the danger, the temptation to take that risk grows by the minute as more perspiration collects along the back of my neck.

Behind me, the four men keep up easily, though by their red cheeks and perspiration, it's clear they are no less affected.

Dark, charred trees surround us, the ground crisp and dry, and I am starting to wonder if the landscape is another means of discouraging anyone from leaving the path. When I sweep my attention straight in front of us, the gray of the forest blends into colors of deep greens and browns. I almost squeak out loud to see we're finally out of this deadland.

When the ghostly fingers of a warm wind wash over my face, a surge of excitement bubbles inside me. "Did you feel that? It's a breeze!"

In that same moment, a spark of energy bubbles in my chest, and I know what that means. We are in a part of the woods where the witches' magic is now detectable. I take in a deep breath and call to my power to see spells, just as Mother taught me. The sensation of a feather flows down my arms and across my fingers. We're back on track, thank goodness.

"Fuck me, but tell me that's a river," Crius states, and before I can even scan the woodland to find what he's talking about, he charges ahead of me like a mad bull. "This walking so slow is rubbish," he growls. "I'm fucking bored out of my brains."

My heart leaps in my throat at the web of magic lines I spot right in his pathway. Thin threads sparkle beneath the light right in front of the river that comes into view. Of course, no one else will see it, but to me, it's golden and sways in the breeze like a temptress waiting for her victim.

Crius is rushing right toward the water and into the trap.

Ice floods my veins.

"Stop!" I bellow, chasing after him before I can think straight. I drop my bag, my heart banging in my chest. "Crius!" I scream. "It's a spell, stop before it's too late!"

My feet pound the earth to reach him, and the others rush forward with me.

Crius is fast, so caught up in the freedom the glistening river offers, he's insane with the sense of escaping this gray world.

I snatch the back of his top, trying to get him to pay attention to me. Not that I actually bring him to a standstill, but my weight dragging after him has him finally pausing. He pushes my hand away.

"What the fuck?" he snarls.

"Which part of *stop* don't you understand?" I snap.

"Shit, man, are you fucking deaf?!" Nikos roars, and well, I can't help but appreciate him taking my side for a change.

"I didn't hear you," Crius admits, and I believe him. We are in a place where nothing can be trusted.

"Well, you were just about to walk into a massive magical snare."

The guys are all looking in the direction of the enormous web, but they are looking right past it, Stone's nose creased as though confused.

"There's a magical net between us and the river. As much as I'd love to know what it will do to us if we touch it, I promised to keep you four safe, so we can't go that way."

"Alright, so which direction then?" Ragnar asks, and I notice he's carrying my bag over his shoulder.

I scan the landscape and point away from both the spell and the path. "You all wait here and I'll go check how far it stretches out."

Crius gives me a deadpan expression, and well, he may not like it, but I won't be blamed for one of them dying.

"Agreed," Ragnar adds. It surprises me that he conceded so quickly.

With quick steps, I hurry beside the net that intrigues me in how truly beautifully it has been crafted. When the light hits it from different angles, it shimmers with a rainbow of colors, but what's stranger is that it appears to be bending in my direction, as if sensing me.

My hands are also buzzing, and when I glance down at them, the magic lines are arching outward as if attempting to reach for the spell. The notion of them connecting terrifies me, so I take a few more steps to put some distance between me and the net.

I work my jaw back and forth, toying with the idea that maybe going to the path would be an option if I can't find a way to pass.

Up ahead, I spot where the net abruptly ends, and I'm practically jumping up and down on my toes. I don't even care if the men see me, but I'm speeding up my pace now. "I think we've found the end," I shout to them over my shoulder.

The shrubs are densely clustered in this part of the depressing woods, skeletal things that tear at my pants and snap with each step I take. I swing to where several dense trees huddle together. This is where the net halts, and beyond lingers the gray mist that chokes the light out of this whole damn place. I breathe heavily, hating how sorrowful the depleted forest is.

Not missing a beat, I move hastily past the trunks, only to have strong hands snap around my waist and draw me back against a solid chest.

I flinch, shuddering in my own skin.

"Don't take another step," Stone whispers in my ear.

I freeze, my head spinning with confusion. "Where did you come from?" I ask, twisting my head around to face him. Even in this moment of pure panic and uncertainty, this Alpha is dead sexy, and with me pressed against him, the earlier heat now swallows me.

"You really think Ragnar would let you go alone?" he muses. "Now, look down in front of you."

When I follow his gaze, my attention falls upon a fissure in the earth, split open and wide enough to inhale me if I blindly stepped into it. Only blackness yawns back at us from within it.

"Shit. How could I not have seen that?"

My eyes have been high up on the net and not on what lay at my feet. How deep was it really? It's like the ground opened up to devour any unsuspecting visitors. Or was this just another addition to the witches' scheme to ensure no one passed through their lands? While I'm still trembling from having almost become a victim, part of me can't help but hold a sense of admiration for the witches in thinking so thoroughly about their spells. It seems there is so much more to casting, which is information I tuck into my mind for later.

"It looks like a pit trap to me," he whispers.

"How did you see it when I didn't?" I ask him, my back still cradled against his chest.

"Observation," he answers, but when he steps back with me still in his arms, I break from his hold and turn around. A glint of blue catches my attention from just under his collar. It's the edge of what looks like a circular tattoo, except it's glowing.

"Maybe it makes more sense if we both take the lead together." He adjusts his shirt to cover the marking, clearly noticing I've been staring.

"What is that?" I ask, because I was under the impression these wolves were just that... wolves. Is Stone a Cursed like me? Is it strange that excitement rises through me at sharing something with him that I have feared my whole life?

"Nothing for you to worry about," he answers. "Now, I suggest we head back toward the path as you said earlier." He gives me an easy smile, which must be a code for leaving this topic of conversation alone.

Of course, my mind is now racing with what this all means. If he wants to keep it to himself, that's fine for now. But later, he needs to come clean.

We trample over the bushes and squeeze between two trees to emerge back to where the other three wait for us.

"Well?" Crius asks, pacing like a trapped wolf. "I don't know how much longer I can walk in a place that looks like we're going in circles."

"It's a dead end," I respond, half expecting Stone to tell them how I almost died, but he doesn't. "We'll need to take our chance on the path to pass this spell. We'll have to move slowly, because I can only suspect there'll be something waiting for us there."

My entire body is shaking just thinking back to how I almost fell into the gaping hole. The reality hits me harder now that I've settled down.

Stone is at my side, his hand on my back. "Let's go." He nudges me to move, and I do just that before I freak out.

"You'll be okay," he reassures me.

I nod. I want to take a moment to catch my breath and slow my beating heart, but that will make me seem weak, and I can't fall apart. I've faced danger my whole life, so I can do this too. I swallow back the thickness in my throat. One step in front of the other, we keep going.

When we reach the section with the river, my gaze traces its blue surface. It's like somehow the sun has made its way to this part of the forest.

"It really does look inviting," Stone says.

I look over to him and whisper, "Thank you for before."

His hand runs along his short, golden beard, and his eyes soften. "You can trust me, Narah."

But do they trust me?

We wander forward, and soon the harsh ground softens beneath our shoes, and the dull, lifeless land blossoms with life. A cool breeze swishes past, and I moan with the satisfaction of finally finding some comfort.

The men groan with their own relief, but the closer we get to the dirt track, the more my skin crawls. Around us, branches rustle like out-of-tune songs.

Then I pause right beside the dirt path. I flick my gaze to the other side of the path where a rocky mountain juts upward, blocking any possible new routes for us to take.

Studying my hands, the spark of magic dances about furiously. Something is wrong here.

"Is everything okay?" Stone asks, staring at me with narrowing eyes.

Lowering my voice, I say, "I'm not sure. I can't see any spells, but my magic is bouncing about inside me like it detects something. Can *you* sense anything?" I ask, my gaze shifting to his collarbone where the top of his tattoo no longer glows.

He shakes his head.

"What's going on?" Crius asks, his impatience grating on my nerves.

"Just hold your horses," I say, glancing over my shoulder. Nikos and Ragnar wait patiently, while Crius is acting all jumpy, his arms folded over his chest, then he drops them by his sides. His feet never stop moving, even if it's to pace in a tight circle. What the hell is going on with him?

"Trust your instinct," Stone tells me. "Where does it tell us to go?"

I look back at him. "It tells me to get the hell off this path, except this is the only way forward."

Stone

Narah stares down at her hands, looking so lost and confused, and my insides constrict to see her this way. Despite her bravery and strong words, I can't help but wonder if she's new to magic. She's extremely timid when it comes to using her ability… or maybe I'm used to everyone boasting about themselves at every opportunity.

But she's also all we've got. Ragnar has been searching for a witch to help us for months, but they aren't exactly just wandering around freely. Most wolves despise and fear them, so they are killed on sight. But a Cursed is very different… half-wolf, half-witch, and from what I've seen, they have limitations on both their powers and the strength of their wolves, but they still wield it at every chance they get. They straddle both worlds, never really fitting into one completely. And I see that struggle on Narah's face. She knows very well the world would spit her out, so she lives on the fringes.

Hell, I shouldn't feel pity for her, but I do. The way she looks around for an answer, the way her hands shake... yet the power that comes off them has so much potential.

A tingle flares over the runes on my body. They were inked on my flesh when I turned five, a ritual on my mother's side. Her family carries the ability to tap into the power of runes, and the best way to hold onto the skill is to have them marked on my skin. A talent that took me years to learn, and even then, it's minuscule in comparison to the power of a Cursed, let alone a witch.

It's the part of me Father detests. He calls it a woman's power and scoffs in my presence. At the age of eight, I found my mother's rune stones, and the moment I touched them, I called for a tree to sprout up in the middle of our home, tearing it apart at the foundations. Yeah, it was fucked up, and then my father fucked me up. He broke two ribs, fractured my skull, and physically threw me out of his house. That's when I went to live with Ragnar's family.

My father is a piece of trash, and it's one of the many reasons I jumped at the chance to claim new territory with Ragnar and leave Denmark.

The gods gave you the power for a reason, Mother would tell me, but that didn't change a damn thing, now did it?

I exhale loudly, letting go of the past, and instead, I refocus on Narah.

Her shoulders curl forward in concentration, then she jerks her head up toward me with a newfound confidence. "We have no choice but to take the path." Without waiting, she steps onto the dirt road and starts ahead of us.

If nothing else, I will say the girl has balls of steel... and she does have a curvy, gorgeous ass too, from this view.

"That river better be over this hill or I'll fucking dig into the ground and make my own river," Crius goes on while Nikos laughs at him.

"I'd like to see you do that."

Ragnar is especially quiet, like he's worried too that perhaps we jumped the gun too quickly to rush in here with Narah. I fall back a step so he catches up to me.

"Is this going to work?" I ask him quietly.

He shrugs and swallows, his gaze locked on Narah. "It has to.

She's rusty and lacks confidence, but if she can just keep steering us around the spells, it should be fine."

"Do you think the witches will allow us so easily to pass through their land?" I whisper, not wanting others to hear my concern.

"From what I've heard, they rarely leave their coven. Maybe they've become complacent that no one will ever make it through their maze."

The thought brings a twist of hope in my chest that our plan of surprise will work.

Ragnar continues, "I intend to blindside them with our arrival, then we'll take them out." The way he looks at me comes with darkness and a reminder of the plan we've worked out. Our own magical secret weapon. "Until then, we need to keep a close eye on her," he whispers. "Make sure she feels safe and is on our side."

We walk for a few moments with only the sound of Nikos and Crius arguing, something I learned to block out long ago. "What do we do with her afterward?" I ask, curious if the possibility of keeping her for myself is even an option.

Ragnar hesitates to answer at first, and shadows cloud under his eyes as he considers my question. "She will be my problem to deal with," he finally answers.

"Sure." I have no idea what he means, considering it isn't his usual response when we deal with an outsider. His go-to tends to be *kill them*. So this is new, and also leaves a bitter taste on my tongue that he is showing such interest in her this early.

Silence follows us along the path, flanked by a mountain on one side and a cluster of trees on the other with the web.

"Don't move," Narah suddenly cries out, and I walk right into Nikos, who growls from me knocking into him.

"What is it?" Crius asks, already grasping his ax in one hand. The guy has been dying to fight anything from the moment we left Denmark.

"A spell just appeared out of the blue across the path." She points to the ground, which looks pretty ordinary to me, then looks up at Crius, who's ahead of her.

"Wait, I tripped the invisible spell?" he barks, picking up on her cues instantly.

"Well, you rushed in front of me again," she snaps back.

"Then it's my fault?" He's standing tall, his brow lifting with sarcasm.

Abruptly, Nikos falls over right in front of me and is yanked sideways by his legs.

His yelling pierces the silent woods as a dark serpent wraps around his ankle, hauling him to fuck knows where. His terrified shouting hits me square in the chest where cold fear claws at my insides.

My hand flinches to my belt, and I raise my blade as I leap after Nikos. He's dragged so fast across the ground, I can barely keep up, so I lunge for the beast that's taken him. Mid-movement, I reach down and seize the thing that is hard as rock in my grip. I'm still half running, feeling awkward as fuck. Except the rough bark beneath my hand tells me this isn't a snake.

It's a damn tree root.

I swing my blade down against the wooden limb in a chopping action and hack my knife across its surface.

We come to an abrupt stop, and I fall to my knees to make quick work of sawing the root in two. The thing shudders and fights my grip to escape.

Nikos is kicking it off his leg, his hands frantically pulling at the limb around his ankle.

"Sonofabitch," he snarls.

Once my blade slices all the way through, I snatch Nikos by his shirt and haul him to his feet.

"What the fuck was that?" he asks.

"Hell if I know."

But as we retreat, the root I'd chopped rears up in front of us like a viper. I touch my collarbone, igniting the buzz of power across my chest, then I jut out my other arm, a pale blue glow emitting from my hand.

"Return peacefully to the ground," I mutter, my body humming with energy.

But nothing happens.

The tree root stands upright before us, and I can't stop staring at the hacked part of the wood, which is just as dark as the bark on the outside. Gods, is it growing another limb? If it's going to attack, it needs to do it all-fucking-ready.

"You need to touch it," Nikos tells me.

"Like hell I do," I answer.

"Well, this isn't working," Nikos insists.

"Fine, just stop fucking nagging me." I march forward just as the limb strikes right at my face.

I duck, dodging the attack, and instantly grab it with both hands as the blue power ripples over the dark bark like relentless waves. The thing vibrates violently in my grip, then swings left, my arms jutting in that direction. I tense my muscles and hold it back as it tries to escape. "You little shitty piece of wood."

Yet my power does nothing to calm the attack. My ability has an affinity with nature, and I've never been unable to perform. What the fuck?!

Nikos throws himself at the root at my feet and chops it off with his blade.

Its strength has my arms shaking, and I hiss, "It won't listen to me." When I glance across the grounds, the rest of our pack are wrestling with tree branches and roots as well. Narah uses a dead branch to swat away the slithering roots across the ground. Crius madly swings his ax so fast, he'd just as easily cut one of our heads off. Ragnar is already in his white wolf form, his clothes somewhere behind him, and he lunges into one of the attacking trees, his teeth tearing at the branches, ripping it to shreds.

Where one moment we were discussing a potential spell, we're now thrown into pandemonium.

We race toward them, Nikos by my side, and we join the battle of wooden limbs lashing at us. Narah is in the middle, protected from the attack. And that's when I realize we are being attacked by just one tree, the ambush coming from one direction.

Frantically, I grab a swinging branch coming right for me and shove it downward before whacking it right over my knee, snapping it in half. A whining sound comes from the thing like it feels pain. Like I should feel pity.

Fuck that.

Another branch madly swings at me, and I duck to avoid being knocked out.

"Stone!" Nikos calls from behind me.

"Already saved you once today." I throw the words over my shoulder as I leap over a root lashing for my legs. I land on my knees and mince the damn thing with my huge knife.

"Stone!" he snarls again.

I snap around. "What the fuc—" My voice flatlines.

He and Narah are facing another tree that seems to have animated... right out of the ground. My stomach twists with terror at what I'm seeing. It's completely out of the ground, balanced on folded roots, reminding me of an octopus. The knotty trunk stands at least eight feet tall, branches falling toward the ground like snakes wriggling across the earth in our direction. And for the life of me, I can't help but see a resemblance to a woman standing before us.

When it unleashes a screeching sound no plant should ever make, I know exactly what we're dealing with. All those years of being forced to read old texts on history and mythologies by Ragnar's tutors have finally served a purpose. No wonder my runes did nothing around them.

These aren't normal trees.

Something whacks me across the back of my head, and I'm suddenly seeing stars, stumbling forward. I rub my head and look over to Crius, who's pulling at a branch, trying to dislocate it from the trunk. I sprint over to him and grab it, both of us wrenching at it like madmen.

"The witches' spell has summoned *Muma Pădurii*," I tell him. "A patron of evil spirits in the woods. A goddess, some say."

"Who gives a fuck! I'll kill it still the same," he roars when the branch suddenly snaps and we both scramble backward to catch ourselves, shrubs slowing our fall.

Back on the path, Narah is murmuring to herself, shaking her head, looking down at her hands where her golden magic lines hop from one finger to the next. I sure hope she plans to do something, and soon.

In a flash, the ground shakes beneath my feet, sending me stumbling about. Ragnar leaps off the tree, and that's when I notice that the thing is dragging itself out of the soil as well. Along with three other trees... five of them now surround us.

We are so fucked.

I can't even wrap my head around what I'm seeing, but I also don't intend to die today at the hands of goddamn oversized shrubs.

Next to me, Nikos's expression falls. A stuttered breath rattles deep in my chest as I back up and regroup with everyone.

"When I meet those witches, I'm going to choke them with one of these damn vines," Crius mutters, his cheeks and neck scratched and bleeding, his arms mottled with welts from where he's been struck. Ragnar isn't faring any better, blood spotting his pure white pelt.

I turn to Narah. "What do we do, witch girl?"

That gets everyone, including Ragnar, looking at her for a moment.

Her mouth opens with a response when a thin branch lashes around her throat and yanks her backward so fast, she's taken from us in a heartbeat.

Terror grips her face as she reaches out for us.

I lunge after her when the sharp bite of a whip strikes me across the back, sudden and vicious. I hiss and drop to my knees with the pain. Before I can recover, vines snake around me, sliding under my clothes, over them. I tug at them, my heart pounding.

Suddenly, I'm ripped off my knees and hauled across the ground.

I buck and thrust against my attacker with only our screams ringing through the forest.

Narah

I CHOKE, and I'm clawing at the vine strangling me, squeezing tighter around my neck.

Panic flashes across my mind, as all I can think about is death... my death. Being dragged backward, my legs peddle to keep up as I'm drawn farther from the men. But like me, they are each fighting their own battle against damn magical trees.

I refuse to go down like this because Crius tripped a spell. I grabbed his arm to stop him, but he brushed me off and charged ahead. Now I'm going to die because of his stubborn ass. That only makes me angrier and more determined to escape so I can make him suffer at my hands.

My heart slams into my ribcage as I gasp for air, my lungs straining. Stars dance in my vision, and it's just happening too fast. I buck my body and fight, but the limbs are so strong. Each passing moment stings like the lash of a whip to my chest, to my head. Knees buckling, I open myself up to magic, not caring what comes out. No more holding back my power.

And in an instant, a zap of electricity runs up my spine, every hair on my body standing on end. Sparks race from my fingers, and an explosion erupts in front of my face.

Golden light pops.

My skin crawls.

I'm shoved forward to the ground from a great force at my back, the noose around my neck unravelling. A terrifying screech pierces the air, but I don't care about anything except feeding my lungs. Each inhale hurts so much.

Unbearable heat licks across my back, so excruciatingly hot that I finally flinch around.

All I can see at first is a golden explosion, but then the image comes more into focus. My fire magic bites across the warring tree, burning it, devouring the leaves and limbs. A screeching cry floods my ears from its suffering, and I cringe, recoiling, doubt crawling over my mind at the agony I've caused it. Except, it's just an animated tree, right?

The thing shudders and stumbles about for freedom like a lost soul. It bumps into other trees, but the flames never leap anywhere else.

A chill runs up my spine.

The tree disintegrates before my eyes, turning to ash, becoming nothing. But the sounds of pain are relentless, and it hurts my ears, my heart.

In a final burst of light, the magical fire fizzles to nothing, and I don't know how to feel... happy, devastated, confused.

Screams come from behind me and distract me from falling apart. I whip around to find the four Alphas battered and bleeding, fighting regardless. Breaking branches, ducking them, wrapped in vines. They are losing.

Stone is on his knees when Ragnar catapults in front of him, taking the brunt of a whipping branch. He falls, growling with pain, and blood collects quickly around him on the ground. But he's on his feet again, and I'm running to them before I can think straight.

Anger laps against my insides, rousing more magic, bringing forth whatever I called to earlier.

Power bursts from my body like a ruptured dam, rushing outward in a tremendous wave. Rage embraces me, and I let my magic roar. It streams from my hands, pushing right past the men, and like a hungry zombie, the power slams into the four attackers.

Starved.

Vicious.

Ravenous.

Golden flames swallow our enemy, twisting and entangling around every limb, every root.

I barely catch my breath as my body rocks on the spot as more and more energy rushes from me, draining me. "Stop," I murmur under my voice.

Nothing.

Fear floats to the surface, and the more I flick my hands to end the expulsion of magic, the faster it rushes out of me. I'm quivering terribly, and I note the Alphas are now staring at me, their faces bloody, their clothes torn, but the look behind their eyes is one of trepidation... toward me.

"Fucking stop already," I scream with fright, shaking my hands, which only sends the energy out in wider waves, and yet it still swirls in the air like a light show and funnels back to the four trees. It doesn't so much as touch the men.

A pop echoes.

And the power halts as abruptly as it started, taking with it every inch of strength I held onto.

My knees buckle out from under me, and I collapse on the ground, completely spent, hurting so much I whimper. A tremor shoots through me as the stench of burning wood fills the space, black tendrils curling into the foggy sky.

I know I stopped them, but why does it feel so wrong?

Exhaustion tugs at me and flashes of light dance behind my eyes, but I never lift my gaze from the animated trees who cry out for salvation. But they are too far gone now—I made sure of that—and in moments, they wither into piles of ash.

And just as their flames extinguish, darkness feathers at the corners of my eyes and steals me from this world too.

CHAPTER

ELEVEN

Ragnar

The cold water laps up to my abs, and I walk deeper into the river, Narah cradled in my arms. Her head is nestled against my chest while her body is burning up. I need to lower her temperature, hoping it will wake her up. Her wet clothes stick to her body, and I can't ignore the way her shirt clings to her breasts, revealing the circular pink-colored area of skin surrounding her tight nipples. The sight drives my pulse.

But so do the images of her assault on the sentinel trees and the extravagant ability she's been hiding all this time. I expected power from her, being a Cursed and all, but the show she put on back in the woods is beyond startling.

Coldness seeps up my spine at the thought.

This girl in my arms saved us, but there's so much more to her. I've encountered witches in Denmark, and a memory hovers at the edges of my mind. Tora, a witch who lived on the fringes of our village, was known for her terrifying power. The thing about her was that she often lost control of her power and would regularly set into motion dangerous chains of events she never intended. Like calling animals from the woods, putting them into such a panicked trance that they charged through our town in a wild stampede, killing so many. My father kept her alive regardless, with the hope that he could help her control her ability and utilize her magic for his own deeds. Though we all knew he had fallen for her charm and called her to his bed often.

Then, one day, Tora brought to our world a massive trembling of the earth, our homes crumbling, the foundations cracking as a great crack split down the middle of our village. Father's second-in-command had enough. He took several of his men and slayed the witch.

Father bellowed with fury and had him killed the next day for an act of betrayal. My father had always been an angry bastard. But while Tora didn't deserve to die, she had to be dealt with, as she was a danger to everyone. We all knew it, but Father refused to listen to reason. It was my men and I who cleaned up the dead bodies, who took them into the woods and burned them for the families to have their final farewell.

Inwardly shaking, I can still smell the stench of death now at the memory.

Glancing down at Narah with her eyes closed, her small nose sprayed with black soot, and her lips parted as she breathes softly, I can't ignore how beautiful she is... or that she may be just as dangerous as Tora.

I step deeper into the river and lower myself, the cold water greedily rushing over Narah's body. I hiss against the sting across my back where the trees whipped me. But I'll heal in no time, even if I'm fucking exhausted. Narah passing out worries me, though.

The sound of splashing water has me turning my head back to Crius and Stone, who dive into the river for a wash. Nikos sits on a rock, arms draped over bent knees, watching. I see the way they all study Narah, how she's captured their attention whether she tries or not, but that's the thing about my little fox. She has an alluring aura that draws us to her like a bug to a flame... and whether the other three have noticed or not yet, there is something between us and her that is beyond a sexual connection.

A spark flares in my chest when her eyelids flicker open. Fire burns in her round eyes, akin to the flames that erupted from her hands.

She is quiet for a long time, the water brushing around the edges of her face, and she blinks up at me as if finding her thoughts.

"Did I die?" she asks so innocently, I can't stop my lips from curling upward.

"If you had, then it would mean you've joined me in Valhalla, little fox."

It takes her a few moments to respond, but it doesn't come in the form of words. Tears glisten at the edges of her eyes and roll down the sides of her face to merge into the river.

"Did I hurt anyone?" she murmurs, not making any signs of moving out of my arms. She reaches up and runs a hand under a deep cut across my cheek. "You're hurt."

"Yes, but I'm alive."

Her gaze roams over my face as she wriggles in my arms to be let down, and I release her to her feet. Water washes up to her shoulders, and she looks around, taking in where she is, where the rest of my pack are.

"You passed out," I tell her. "How are you feeling after..." I glance over my shoulder to the woods we emerged from. "After what happened?"

She swallows hard and her hands emerge from the water, the top half of her fingers still black, tendrils fading as they reach down to her knuckles. She murmurs something under her breath I don't catch. I try not to pry and don't ask her, but when she looks up at me, there's something worrying behind her striking amber eyes.

"Are you alright?" I ask.

She bites the inside of her cheek and dips her hands back under the water, her clothes clinging to her small body.

"What happened after I passed out?"

"Stone picked you up and we got the fuck out of the woods."

She glances up into the sky instinctively, as if trying to work out the time of the day based on the position of the sun. It's past noon, and we're staying here until tomorrow morning, by which time we should be healed. She then glances around us and says, "How did you know the river was safe to enter?"

"I didn't," I say. "We took a risk, as I needed to cool you down."

She blinks a few times. "You're looking at me strange, like you're waiting to blame me for what we encountered in the forest," she admits. "Just so you know, I noticed the spell the moment Crius triggered it. The witches are smarter than I anticipated, concealing their curses."

"Narah, I'm not blaming you, but I want to know what exactly happened back there with your magic."

She shrugs, her gaze sliding to the rippling water between us, avoiding mine. "Things went bad quickly, and I protected you like I said I would."

Instead of continuing, she dips into the water to her neck and twists away from me, avoiding my question, and that's just not going to work. There is no more hiding behind caring words. My pack's lives and future depend on her, and I'm not going to back down because she's scared.

"Narah," I state sternly, my voice rising, and my ears tune in on the lack of splashing behind me. The other three are still, listening in on our conversation.

When she doesn't turn back around to face me but pushes into a swim toward the bank, I catch her arm underwater and pull her toward me. "I asked you a question."

"Leave me alone." She looks put-off and tugs her arm back. "And what's the big deal? I'm a damn Cursed, so of course, I did what I had to. What is your problem?"

"What's going on, Narah? I've seen the powers of Cursed in the past, but what you did back in the woods shouldn't be possible. I know you're not a full witch, which begs the question—what are you, exactly?"

Her jawline clenches, and I expect her to argue, but she doesn't. Things are just not adding up.

She starts to drift away from me in the water again, and it takes all my inner strength to not grab her and throttle the answer out of her. I know that won't work with her.

"Narah, if you insist on playing these games, I will tie you to me until you respond to my question. Or would you rather I chase you down... it's something I hear you quite enjoy."

Her eyes widen at my words as her attention swings over to Crius closer to the shore. What she doesn't seem to understand is that my men and I are a unit, and there are no secrets between us.

"Why do you know so much about magic? Most Alphas hate witches," she counters, and the corner of my mouth curls at her clever tactic. Distraction is the key. Smart move, but it won't work on me.

"If I have to ask you one more time to answer my question, you aren't going to like the way I do it."

On impulse, her head jerks up, her eyes burning with fury. "What do you want me to say? We made a deal where I'd detect and guard you from magic, and I did that. Why are you now insisting I'm something other than a Cursed?"

I don't expect the deadly tone in her voice but am also suddenly turned on by her fiery temperament. Her chest rises and falls quickly beneath the surface of the water, and now I wish more than ever that I had stripped her down before bringing her into the river. But my concern at the time had been to cool down her burning body. Now... well now, my interest has shifted gears.

She whips away from me and pushes herself into a frantic swim toward the shore. A laugh escapes past my throat, and I take my time going after her because she's not going to get far. The thought of going after her has my cock twitching, and I reach down and stroke it once. I hiss with the hunger growing for my little fox. She has no idea what she's doing to me.

When Stone and Crius slosh through the water to block off her path, she pauses and frantically looks from them to the other end of the shore for her escape.

"Are you in the mood to chase down an Omega?" Crius nudges Stone, his voice filled with sarcasm, loud enough for Narah to have heard.

I use that moment to my advantage. I dive under the surface, kicking fiercely, my sights set on her through the murky water. Her legs are paddling in the water, as she no longer reaches the sandy bottom of the river.

I sweep right up behind her and grab her waist, then dunk her under with me. She bucks and splashes crazily as I pivot her to face me.

Her eyes are wide, and underwater, they are like fiery flames come alight. Air bubbles slip from her mouth and float upward as she desperately thrusts against me to free herself. She scowls at me, then throws a hand to my shoulder as she pushes against me to get to the surface. But I hold onto her waist tighter just a while longer, just until trepidation sets in her eyes.

There is something magnificently beautiful about the fear in her eyes, the panic on her warped lips, the way she fights me. My cock hardens further at the sight, and I find such allure in her as we teeter on the edge of death.

My heart soars in my chest, and my skin pricks with a strange excitement. I want to claim her as mine, dismiss every hesitation.

I grab the back of her neck and pull her to me, then drive us upward in an explosive burst. Our heads break the surface, and she gasps for air, splashing about as I hold her against me, facing me.

"What the fuck? Were you trying to kill me?" She shoves her hands against me, but she isn't going anywhere.

"Are you ready to talk?"

Her eyebrows shoot up. "Are you mad? You're torturing me to answer your stupid questions?"

"If you prefer to call it that. I think it's nothing more than me swimming with you."

"Ha, you're hilarious." Her fury is intoxicating, and fuck, she's gorgeous. Her lips are full, and all I can picture is them wrapped around my cock.

I understand now what Crius meant when he said the chase awoke something inside him that he hasn't felt in years.

I draw her face closer to me and my mouth ghosts over hers. She softens against me, eager for my lips on hers, and I know she craves me. Fuck, I consider stripping her and fucking her here and now, my hardening cock a painful reminder that with any other female, I wouldn't have hesitated as much as I do with Narah.

Her lips part, and as my erection twitches against her stomach, her breathing hitches. Such a perfect sound.

And this here is why I've kept my distance. Mixing pleasure and business never works out... first I get what I want from this mission, then I'll take what I've longed for from her. I can't let my thoughts go there just yet.

She watches me with worry, with lust... her emotions are all over the place.

"Trust me, Narah, when I'm torturing you, you will be very aware of it."

Her breasts are pressed against my chest, and it's hard to focus on anything else but her unspoken need for my torture... my cock, more precisely. I feel the pounding of her heart, watch the fear in her eyes, sense the desire in her trembling body. Everything about her riles me up, awakening my wolf, and it takes more effort than it should to stop from making her mine.

A snarl breaks from my chest, and as if that gives her the wake-up call she needs, she drives her hands against my bare chest. Heat pours from her and across my skin.

"I don't know what you want me to tell you. I'm a Cursed, nothing freaking more."

"Then how did you kill the tree goddesses?"

She stiffens in my arms, and my cock twitches at the most inappropriate time. "No, they were just animated trees," she rebuts. "Controlled like puppets by the witches."

"Those were not mere trees, my little fox, and deep inside you must know that. The only person I've heard capable of using fire magic was a witch coven elder. So, who exactly are you? I don't take well to being lied to."

She holds her head high, water dripping down her nose and cheeks from her wet hair. She is stunning, and I curse her beauty.

"I never lied, because we never spoke about my ability. All you cared about was that I could take you through the woods with magic. That's it. Now get the hell off me."

My grip tightens, and a frustrated growl rolls past my lips. I'm torn between wanting to force her to tell me the truth, knowing she will hate me for it, and letting this go, trusting her. But how can I do that when there is so much at risk?

Her gaze floods with fury, and already the fire to her body intensifies. My pulse picks up at the notion of what she is capable of, but I won't back down.

"You so much as touch me with your magic, little fox, and we will have a big problem on our hands."

The blaze between us remains, like she is provoking me on purpose, and I love her tenacity.

I grab her jaw and hold her close to me, our bodies plastered. "While on this mission, you are mine. Now, talk."

She looks me in the eyes, and beneath the anger, I sense her trepidation. She's scared of what she's done but insists on putting on a brave face, on not letting down her guard. Her small body shakes against me, and I scoop an arm across her back, holding her still.

"What do you want to hear?" Her voice grows brittle, and I soften my hold. "My father was a wolf, and my mother a Cursed. They're dead now, and that's all I know of my family line. So how can I tell you what I am when I have not a fucking clue myself? And you want to know the truth? What happened back in the woods scared the hell out of me too. I've never done that before."

She trembles harshly now, her lips paling from the cold water, and any self-control I had evaporates. My mind swims with her response, and it seems my earlier observation was accurate. She's still working her way around magic, except what she carries in her veins is a lot more dangerous than any of us could have guessed.

"We will work on this together, and I give you my word, Narah, that I will help you uncover your abilities safely." I release her to show her I am a man of my word, and she rears back as if I've struck her.

"You have a brutish way of getting your way, don't you?" she throws at me.

I don't have the heart to tell her I've been soft on her compared to my normal approach, but I smile in response. "Let's get you warmed up."

She isn't moving.

Instead, she lowers her head, her hands playing with the water.

"Were they really goddesses?" Her voice is tender, and when she finally lifts her glistening gaze, her expression is one of disbelief.

It takes me a moment to realize she is talking about the sentinel trees. "Stone said they were part goddess and keepers of the forest, but were also of evil origin and most likely easily swayed by the witches to do their bidding."

She tugs her lower lip between her teeth, chewing on the corner of it, and my earlier fighting spirit has spiraled into one of concern.

"It was us or them; there is nothing to regret or pity. There was no hesitation about what they wanted to do to us," I say and head toward the shore, noting that she joins me.

She rubs away the water running down her face from her messy hair. "I know, but it doesn't make it any easier. Until a couple months ago I'd never met anyone other than my own pack of wolves I grew up with, and now I just killed five tree goddesses. I'm a monster." She gasps, and I can't help but laugh at how adorable she is.

"It's not funny."

"Actually, it is," I say. "You mourn those who would have you killed? Where is the sense in that?"

She looks at me for a long pause, her tense shoulders physically drooping as the realization sinks in. "I get what you're saying, but I'm not sure I completely agree. A death is still a death. But then again, I did react in self-defense."

"That's right."

In her presence, my mind weakens, and I let her get away with so much more than I'd ever permit anyone else with.

As we move through the water, Crius and Stone emerge, stark naked, while Nikos takes this chance to dive off the rock he's been sitting on and plunge into the river.

Narah doesn't seem to notice, as she's looking at me as we step out of the river, her gaze trailing down my body to my erection.

"What made you behave this way?" she asks.

Her question takes me aback. It's not something I've ever had anyone ask me. I can only assume she's talking about me pushing her, not my hard-on in response to being so close to her.

But she keeps talking before I can respond. "Everyone has history that makes them who they are. You know mine, which isn't much, but what made you who you are today?"

I wonder just how much interaction she's truly had with the pack she grew up in to ask me such a question. I also doubt I know her full story, but I've pushed her enough for now. "It's expected of me. I take charge or I will get walked over. *Never show fear* is how my father brought me up. And when I did get scared, he beat the hell out of me until I feared nothing but him and his strap."

"That's horrible," she says, and I realize then how naive she is. Wherever she has been living, they have kept her hidden from the real world.

"Not really," I say. "I hated him then as I do now, but he made me who I am."

Confusion crosses her face, but she lowers her head. Narah is a complex woman who I am only starting to understand. This is just the beginning with getting her to open up, as far as I'm concerned.

I gesture for her to walk over to where we set up camp just on the edge of the woods, while I stride over to Crius and Stone.

"Change into dry clothes," I tell her. "We're going fishing for our meal."

She nods and doesn't say another word as she hurries across the pebbly shore with conviction in her eyes. Her clothes are dripping and plastered to her body, following every curve of her ass, her toned legs, her tiny waist.

My heart pounds in my chest, and I try my damn hardest to not let my instincts make my decision when it comes to Narah. But that may be a battle I'm happy to lose.

TWELVE

Narah

I take another bite of the fire-cooked fish while the rest of the pack also enjoy the freshly caught meal. Chatter crowds in around the blaze from Ragnar, Stone, and Crius comparing notes on a hunting game, Stone passing the wineskin to Crius, who gulps down several mouthfuls.

Nikos sits next to me, eating his meal, staring out at the others as well. I've gotten used to him seeming to be the outsider to this group, but I don't understand why. In fact, I'm in the dark about many things when it comes to these Alphas.

I swallow the food in my mouth and twist my head toward Nikos. "Why are you with those three when you seem so different to them?"

Nikos's green eyes are dark like a storm when he gazes at me, and there are so many emotions behind them I can't read. Maybe I shouldn't have asked such a personal question, but I'm curious to understand who I'm fighting alongside. Sure, his kiss, his hot and cold reaction confuses me, but when I look at him, I feel myself drawn to him. I don't even try to make sense of my ridiculous logic or the way my heart pounds faster. How my wolf stirs uncomfortably inside me, reminding me Martell is my soulmate. Or the torture curling around my heart like I might break out crying at how harshly my body hurts for him.

Drawing in a deep breath, I drive away the feeling of my body being torn apart from all the feelings battling inside me. It's ridiculous I should feel this way, and I don't want these Alphas to know about it. It's none of their business.

"I don't belong with them, and yet I am one of them," he answers.

I look at him with a narrowing gaze. "Is that meant to be a cryptic response I have to decipher? I can tell you now my guesses might be pretty out there."

His lopsided grin makes me smile, somehow softening the tension that's always between us. "My father is the Alpha of the Balor Wolves from Denmark, mortal enemies of the Ulv Wolves."

"Ragnar's family, right?" I say quietly.

He nods. "To end the brutal wars between our clans, I was given to the Ulv pack as payment, and Ragnar's sister was sent to my family." He speaks softly as his gaze wanders over to Ragnar, who doesn't seem to be listening to us but telling his own tale to the other two.

It takes me a moment to truly understand what Nikos just revealed and how horrific it must have been for them to be taken from their families and sold off like cattle. "Shit, so you had no choice?"

"There's always a choice. Death or follow the rules."

There's no sarcasm when he answers, but a deadly serious tone, and at hearing the hardness in his voice, a chill curls around my spine. Suddenly, things are making more sense. Why Nikos is the black sheep, as Crius called him.

I huff. "That's not a choice. How long is the arrangement?"

His jaw tightens as he stares into the flames, lost in his own thoughts. I figured he hadn't heard me, so I let it go, when he finally says, "Forever. We break the truce and blood will spill from both packs. We are the payment, and I was taken in by Ragnar's father. He calls me 'son,' but that's the farthest from the truth. Ragnar has been the kindest to me since my arrival a year ago, and he has sworn me into his pack. He may be my enemy by family association, but I now hold allegiance to him, even over my own flesh and blood."

I'm trying to wrap my mind around everything, to understand how Ragnar feels about losing a sister. I wonder about how Nikos has been fitting into a world that spat him out... maybe he and I have a lot more in common than I ever suspected. When I sneak a look back at Nikos, his face is crowded in shadows. The sharp angle of his jaw, and the ink on the side of his shaved head catches my attention as it flows down to the nape of his neck. Up close, I can clearly see the tattoos are of two snakes circling and biting the tail of the other.

Silence hangs between us while question after question tumbles around in my head, and I leave them unasked and unanswered. He told me more than I ever expected, and maybe he needed to share it with someone rather than hold onto it.

We both continue eating, and I'm left drowning in so many thoughts, especially after a second day in the Poisonous Woods that seemed to be worse than the first. Then I zero in on my magic and stare down at my hands.

I closed my connection to magic tonight after having checked the area. I need my body to rest after everything that happened. Everything crazy, that is.

The magic that came from me today shouldn't have been possible, and I can't shake the dread of what I've done, what Ragnar told me about the tree goddesses. I lose my breath, and a coldness sweeps through me at the thought. So I push it aside with the rest of my messed-up life, refusing to think about it when I have no answers.

I hate not knowing anything about myself or thinking that maybe whatever is inside my veins is something other than witch powers. And if that is the case, why wouldn't my mother have told me about it?

Ragnar's expression back in the river was one of terror, and I'm too scared to ask him what he thinks I am. Whoever said ignorance was bliss was onto something, because sometimes not dealing with a problem is the best way to make it through another day.

I'm stuck out here with these Alphas, and I can't fall apart. I *won't* fall apart when I'm doing this for my sisters and our freedom.

I set my empty plate on the ground near my feet and tuck my hands into my lap. My fingers curl, knuckles whitening with how hard I tighten my fists. A jolt of power shoots right into my bones, then instantaneously fades to nothing once more. Heat flares over me and goes just as quickly. My ability simmers just below the surface, so much wilder than before, as if these woods call to my magic.

It's just power, I say to myself. I can't fear what's inside me or what's waiting for me. I shouldn't, yet the uncertainty seizes me, melts into me.

I feel broken, and for an instant, I ponder just walking away from this all, telling Ragnar I can't do it. I can't deal with what's inside me.

It's a foolish, fearful thought that comes and goes just as quick, leaving me unnerved.

"Trust in yourself," Nikos whispers, leaning in closer, his warm breath brushing my cheek just as it did back in the woods when he kissed me.

My body pulses with an instant need, my mouth parting as I picture him against me, his lips on mine. His masculine and woodsy smell swirls around me as his gaze pierces into me, sending a shooting throb to the pit of my stomach, to the apex between my thighs.

I try to focus on his words. *Trust.* The same word Stone had said to me earlier, yet that's something I find the hardest to do.

Nikos's fingers are on my neck, and he strokes down the curve of my collarbone.

My heart beats in my ears louder and louder.

"You shiver so beautifully under my touch," he says, giving a dark laugh from deep in his chest. He pulls his hand away too soon, and I look over to see Ragnar watching us from across the fire. There's darkness in his expression, and I'm no fool to know the way he stares at me is that of an Alpha wanting to claim me all for himself. Two days ago, I would have hated the idea. Now? I'm lost in confusion about what I am, who these men are, and how they bring out something in me I've never experienced before.

"If you can't trust anyone else around you," Nikos says, "at least have the faith of trusting yourself."

His words close in around me, and I'm trembling at the thought that I don't even have that.

"Those are wise words," I respond. "Are they yours?"

He shakes his head. "My brother is much older than me, and every now and then he used to surprise me with such sayings."

"Do you miss your family?"

"Yes and no. My family aren't exactly the loving kind, but they were all I had growing up."

My chest clenches at hearing of his loss, at remembering how much I miss my parents. There isn't a day that passes when I don't think of them.

"At least your parents are alive," I say, regretting my words. His parents may be alive, but if he can't visit them, what good is that? Nikos and I are nothing alike, our futures unaligned, even if I do have to admit that I am beginning to enjoy his company a bit too much.

"Sorry, I shouldn't have said that."

"How long has it been since your parents passed?" He deftly responds, like he's used to dealing with comments about his family.

"I want to say eternity because it feels like it." I know I sound crazy, and I swallow the thickness that forms in my throat against the memories that insist on pushing forward. I hate how every time I think of my past, it only comes with sorrow and agony. Maybe one day I'll look back on things and smile about them.

But who am I fooling?

I don't know how long we sit in front of the fire, listening to the men talking about a battle they shared where Crius got stuck in a tree. I missed the part of how he got up there, but they were all howling with laughter. If I feel out of place among them, I can only imagine how hard it must be for Nikos.

Part of me is trying to work out if this is why he asked me to go off with him to the witches alone last night. "Why did you ask me that question last night?"

If he is nervous about my question, he doesn't show it or even look over to the others. "Have you made up your mind?"

"No, but I'm curious."

He studies my face, his expression morphing into something blank, something distant. He's climbing to his feet.

I narrow my gaze at him in question, unsure what that's all about.

"You should get some sleep," he tells me. Next thing I know, he strolls away from the guys and across the dark shore to the water's calm edge.

A twinge jabs in my stomach. All I can picture are his green eyes filled with so much emotion that it lulls me into believing he cared about me. I cut my gaze to the three men who all stroll out to their friend by the water, and I study the way they bring him into their conversation, taking their wineskin to him. I truly believe they don't see him as the outcast as much as he probably does himself. Nikos may feel like a bit of an outsider, but the Alphas make an effort to include him.

My thoughts drift to Jae, and my chest tightens at how much I miss her and Kaira, and suddenly memories resurface of the times after we lost our parents. How after Lovis brutally killed our father and took his place as pack Alpha, he came to tell us they finally found our mother in the woods. How she was naked and broken. I can't wipe from my memory the softness in his eyes at announcing she was dead like he cared... yet there is no doubt in my mind he was the one who murdered her. And then he watched Martell try to do the same to me.

I tremble with how much I detest him. I loathe all of those spineless assholes, and yet I lived under their command for years, put on a smile every day to keep my sisters safe from the man who took everything from us. Part of me wonders if doing that—seeing him every day and being reminded of what he took from us, while I did nothing—has broken something inside of me.

I suck in a deep breath, my eyes pricking, a shot of adrenaline driving through my veins. But I won't cry... not for those bastards. My wolf simmers just below the surface, still whimpering for a connection with Martell, and an emptiness billows in my chest. I straighten my spine, needing to find a way to make my wolf see we are never going back to that murderer.

My throat and eyes burn with that pressing ache that always reminds me I'm not good enough, that I don't know what I'm doing. Most days I don't let it bother me, but others, like today, the pain comes quickly and leaves me in ruins.

I hold myself tight, then grab my coat and drag it over me as a cool breeze blows past, sending the flames into a wild sway. That's when I notice Ragnar strolling back into camp, his gaze finding me. I blink my eyes to drive away the tears.

I crane my head back, staring at him, while my mind swirls on the past, on losing my sisters, on being so alone it threatens to suffocate me.

He's barefooted, wearing black pants and a loose-fitting sandy-colored shirt. The fabric is crumpled yet still shows the outline of his muscles. He is a powerful Alpha, his shoulders like boulders, biceps that strain against his sleeves. His dark hair blows in the wind as his blue eyes trace up and down my body. I can't help but admire how sexy this man is, and I clear my throat, nudging away the monsters in my thoughts.

On the way, he pauses and grabs something from his bag and comes by my side. He hands me a folded blanket.

I flash him a smile and take it greedily, then cover my legs.

"How are you feeling?" he asks.

My skin flushes at being this close to him, and my breath catches. His effect on me still surprises me. I hate to admit that I seem to have such little control of my body, how all over the place I am. From holding back tears to my body betraying me and craving him, I'm a hot mess.

"A week's worth of sleep would help. Though I put my exhaustion down to someone almost drowning me." I give him a sarcastic grin as I arch an eyebrow.

He settles down, and when he looks at me, our gazes clash, the sides of our arms touching. A buzz zips up my body, and a warm sensation engulfs me, just as it had back in the river with him naked, forcing us together, his large cock pressed against my stomach. He roused my wolf to the surface, something that scared the hell out of me, as she's never been that close to coming out for another Alpha since Martell.

"So you're not tired from battling the tree goddesses who almost killed us?" he asks, his deep voice slicing through my thoughts.

"Nope," I lie, which has me involuntarily smiling, and he catches it.

The way he looks at me leaves me covered in excited goosebumps. Earlier today I wanted to kill him for almost drowning me, and now those feelings remain, yet there is a headier sensation crawling over my mind. How could I ignore four gorgeous men who make my knees weak? Except, I know all about Alphas. About what they want, what they are capable of. Still, my body responds so easily to Ragnar being this close to me.

"While you are with us, you will always be protected. I wouldn't have let you die," he admits. His hand moves and settles over mine in my lap, and his touch is all I can think about, all that my lust-driven mind can focus on.

"You could have fooled me." My gaze drops to how large his hand is over mine, to the healed scars on his knuckles from what I can only imagine are too many battles to count. "There are other ways to get information from people," I mutter.

"True, but they are lengthy and not as effective." He pulls his hand back, and I feel the coldness instantly.

"My mother once told me that Alphas are born fighters and females are born to bear children," I say. "I hated her for a long time for telling me that, but then I realized that her words had the desired effect. She made me detest the idea of what is expected of females so much that I decided I would never mate with anyone. But the universe really did have a way of punching me in the gut once I grew up."

I can't help but think of how quickly I accepted Martell as my soulmate, how I went to him for the mating night. Of course, I did it for my sisters, for my wolf... but not for me. I lost part of myself long ago, and it's scary how easily I've accepted that too.

"From the age I could walk, my father threw me into fighting pits to train, to become his warrior, so your mother wasn't too wrong."

His admission has me curious. "Is that common in Denmark?"

"In the Ulv pack, yes. We lived close to a dangerous pack who killed our men and stole our women, so it was fight or die."

Nikos's words come to me about him being exchanged with Ragnar's sister... Was his family pack that vicious?

"In the pack I grew up in, the Alphas rarely trained, but they went out to fight other packs all the time," I say.

He licks his lips and asks, "Is there a reason your Alpha never claimed the Savage Sector, then?"

"For a long time, I thought he had," I admit, realizing how stupid I must sound. "Then I left the pack and realized how small-minded I'd been in my thinking and how much bigger the world is. Along with how petty and backward the pack Alpha was. I doubt he had it in him to challenge the witches."

Ragnar stares straight into the flames, lost in his own thoughts, shadows gathering under his eyes. Everything about him screams *Alpha*, from the determination in his expression to the energy he gives off, the impression that he'll never back down if challenged.

"Have you seen any of the witches from this sector in the flesh?" I ask.

He nods. "Upon our arrival in Romania, we saw two of them destroy a small wolf pack's village. They were ruthless. I watched from a distance how they called to the elements, cracked open the land that swallowed everyone. Then the ground closed up as if the village never existed. That's when we learned that the Alphas in this region feared them, and for good reason."

"So what are you going to do when you meet them? Aren't you afraid they will kill you just as quickly as they killed that other pack?"

I tell myself I shouldn't ask or care because I don't want to take sides, that this is just a job for me to get my sisters back. Yet I sit there, waiting for his response, dying to find out.

"Are you always this curious?"

"When it comes to survival I am," I say. "I prefer not to be surprised at the last minute."

A smile cracks his mouth, but he says nothing, holding onto his secrets. Of course, I shouldn't have expected him to share his plans with me, but I had hoped for a small hint, at least.

I search his face for anything to tell me what he's thinking, while he stares right into me like he always does, alert and focused, fully aware he is in control of the situation.

He reaches over and skims his hand across my cheek before threading his fingers through my hair, his other arm wrapping around my waist and drawing me closer. He brings his face close to mine and says, "Why do you look scared?"

I sit breathless, staring at this beautiful man, drawn by his touch. Up close, his pale blue eyes are like a summer's day, calling me closer, while his chiseled cheekbones and strong jaw remind me how out of my league I am with him. His fingers move lower down my back until they find bare skin beneath my shirt, and a small moan slips past my lips.

"I'm not scared," I murmur.

He smiles again, making me weak in his arms.

I want to push him away, but I don't. Maybe I'm just another woman who falls insatiably easily for such powerful Alphas. Or maybe I've longed to know what a man's touch feels like.

When his hand glides farther up under my shirt, his touch grows feather-soft across my skin, and I find it harder to speak.

His gaze lowers to my lips, and all I can think is *please kiss me*. He leans in as if reading my mind, but his mouth presses to the corner of my lips, then sweeps down to my neck, where he nuzzles and takes a deep inhale.

My heart races.

His lips trace the length of my neck, taking mock bites out of me. My hands slide over his shoulders as he raises his head and claims my mouth. We come together quickly, our mouths mashed together as he stakes a claim on me.

There is nothing soft or sweet about the way Ragnar kisses. He's rough and dominating. His tongue presses into my mouth, tasting me, exploring, taking what he wants.

I press myself closer to him, my breasts up against his chest, my nipples tight with a roaring desire that takes me by surprise. My wolf doesn't miss a beat and makes herself known, her whimpering sounds the opposite of the wolf that wanted to submit to another. She doesn't make any sense to me, but as Ragnar takes my lower lip into his mouth, gnawing gently on it, holding me in place, I release my own moans of pleasure. Noises I can't help but make as fire burns between my thighs so intensely, it heats me up in moments.

His hand cups my breast, a thumb brushing over my tight nipple. I press my fingers into his shoulders, pulling closer, and all the while, electricity buzzes through me. No man has ever touched me this way, and I draw in each breath from excitement and fear of the unknown.

He runs his tongue over my lips and whispers, "Are you feeling more relaxed now?"

His mouth trails to my neck once more, and he takes my earlobe between his teeth as he pinches my nipple harder. He licks my neck, tickling me.

Instead of responding, a moan escapes my mouth.

Every nerve in my body is alight. I quiver as his hand slides from my breast, down my stomach, to the buttons of my pants, popping them open.

A sliver of panic tangles with my breathlessness, and my hand instinctively falls to his, stopping him. We're out in the open and in view of the others by the river.

"Someone will see," I gasp.

"Let them," he answers.

My heart beats so fast, I have a hard time focusing on anything but his hand dipping under my pants and underwear.

I barely know this man, and I'm letting him put his hand down my pants. I peer over my shoulder to where the others still stand by the river, not looking this way. In that same moment, Ragnar's fingers slide deeper, skimming where I'm burning up and so wet. Instantly, I feel pressure building deep in the pit of my stomach.

I'm holding onto his shirt and kissing him again, hiding my groans of desire. *Goddess, what am I doing?*

He slides a finger up and down my slit, my legs falling wider under the blanket, and he starts swirling in one spot that drives me completely insane with arousal. He moves faster, and my heart beats quicker, my pulse throbbing between my thighs.

"You smell so sweet, so fucking delicious," he growls against my mouth.

Our gazes meet as he inserts a finger into me.

I flinch in response, not expecting that so suddenly.

"Fuck, Narah, you're so tight." His eyes light up with hunger, and he pushes in and out of me with speed, leaving me gasping for air. I've never felt this way before, ready to burst into a thousand shards from a touch alone.

He watches me while I moan.

I'm drowning, sensing him every time he slides into me, stretching me. He moves faster now, and I'm lost to him, forgetting where we are.

"I want to taste you," he tells me. "I want you naked, spread, and to eat you so you will never forget me."

His words are like a trigger, wrapping around me, and suddenly my core tightens and I shudder, falling apart at the seams. I clench my thighs as an explosion rips through me, but Ragnar never stops plunging his finger into me. His mouth steals my loud moans as I shake against him. I tremble violently as the orgasm claims me, crashing over me in waves. My cries grow wilder, and he takes them, holding me close to him. I don't want him to ever let me go.

"Narah," he says as I quiet down. He pulls his finger out of me, and I notice the spotting of blood on the ends of his glistening fingertips. He notices them too.

The grin he flashes me is full of possessiveness, of wickedness, while my cheeks burn up with him seeing I have never been with a man before.

"I'm not sure I can ever let you go now, little fox," he promises me.

THIRTEEN

Narah

Last night I had a dream of the woods, of shadows circling me. The wind blew ferociously, and blood ran across the forest ground. But my eyes were focused on the dark figure embracing Kaira. There was something beautifully disturbing about how happy she looked. Yet I couldn't stop the tears from running down my cheeks, stop my chest from feeling like it had split in half, when finally a whisper found me.

Time to wake up, sweet Narah.

My skin crawls each time I remember the dream despite us having already walked most of the morning away from camp, but I can't get the image out of my head, along with the dread that I'm too late for Kaira. My chest squeezes as I remember Ragnar's words of the girl he found dead.

It can't be too late. I will find you, Kaira.

With each step, I put the dream behind me. There's nothing I can do to help Kaira yet... not until I finish this mission.

Heat burns me up as I think of what I let Ragnar do to me last night, how easily I gave in to him.

I blush just thinking of it while a shot of euphoria zips down my spine. All I can remember is his fingers in my pants, his kisses, the way he quickly brought me to orgasm.

Now, when I glance over to him behind me, fire creeps up the back of my neck. Last night never should have happened.

Strangely, Nikos and Crius have kept their distance from me this morning, walking behind me with Ragnar. As usual, my panic insists that they saw what Ragnar and I were doing by the fire. Were they jealous? Upset? Should I even care? Of course not. They are going to be in my life for a fleeting moment, and once we complete this mission, I'll be putting distance between us.

Yet my chest stings.

I kick a pebble, and it goes skimming right into a tree I pass.

"Everything alright?" Stone asks, stepping up alongside me, his hands gripping the strap of his bag slung over his shoulder.

I shake my head, then nod. "Not too sure," I answer truthfully. "Didn't sleep the best."

He offers me a warm smile, and despite everything we've gone through since coming into these damned woods, he seems to be nice to me.

"Well, I'm here for you. You need something, I'm your go-to."

The morning light brings out the deep blue of his eyes, the small bend in his nose, the softness of his expression as he looks at me, the same expression he had on the night he brought Jae and I dinner back at the inn. Today, he's got his blond hair pulled back into a man-bun, and it's almost impossible to find a fault with him.

"Thank you," I say, knowing it sounds lame. But the more time I spend with them, the more I lose my direction.

With Stone by my side, I'm heating up, so how can I stay away? I mean, even with the slight bend in his nose, he's gorgeous, and that makes him a temptation I promised myself not to fall for. After last night, I realized how easily I am led by the promise of desire, how these Alphas won't say no, and that means I need to be the strong one.

His gaze searches mine, and paranoia pushes forward. I can't help but wonder if he saw me with Ragnar too. It shouldn't bother me, but it does.

The breeze washes over me, bringing with it his enticing pine and wolf scent. He's wearing a black shirt with the sleeves pushed up to his elbows, deep blue jeans, and heavy combat boots. The whole look works so well on him, and when he winks at me, my cheeks flush.

I'm playing on shaky ground with my body reacting so intensely to him. I don't need distractions, but what do I really know about these Alphas anyway? Well, aside from a few snippets of information they've shared.

My pounding heart warns me this will turn out badly, and the more I think about me kissing both Nikos and Ragnar, the more I worry about the can of worms I've opened.

"You know you talk in your sleep," he says out of the blue.

I literally stop mid-stride and cut him a sharp stare as coldness washes over me. Had I said something in my sleep about Ragnar?

"I do?"

"What's going on?" Ragnar asks, stepping alongside me, as do Crius and Nikos. Four sets of eyes land on me, and if I was nervous before, now I'm buried under a damn mountain of pressure.

"It's nothing," I respond instantly, fiddling with the strap of the bag on my back. Since waking up, I've been avoiding Ragnar for the simple reason that I'm not sure what to say to him.

Oh, good morning, loved our kiss last night and how you fingered me until I came where most likely everyone else saw us. That comment can only go two ways with him. Either he gets turned on and decides that I'm asking for more, or he'll laugh at me. Neither are options I want to pursue.

"It's something," Stone adds, smirking.

"I want to know," Ragnar says.

"Why are you blushing?" Crius stares at me, wearing a perpetual smirk that pulls on the corners of his mouth.

Oh shit! He knows, doesn't he? I feel it in my bones. What else could they be talking about? I hate how much that affects me when it shouldn't. But I'm clearly stupid and let my attraction to these men actually blindside me. Except, I'm an Omega, and that's what I am to them... a rut.

"I'm pretty sure she's scared we're going to mention her and Ragnar making out last night," Nikos growls.

His jealous words turn my veins to ice. To have all four watching me, Nikos's voice echoing in my head, I'm ready to curl under a rock and hide for eternity.

"Leave her alone," Ragnar states. "What's a bit of pussy play between us, right?"

My mouth falls open. The other three go silent. It's clear they didn't know that part... until now. I glare at Ragnar, and he laughs. "It's not a big deal."

"Yes, it is!" I shoot back. I want to murder him, to run from them all.

"Actually, all I was going to say is that you kept calling out for Kaira in your dream," Stone says. "But *this* is more interesting. I want details."

"No! No details," I stammer as a growl from my wolf rumbles in my chest. I'm upset that I've been put into this situation, that my face feels like it's on fire, that Ragnar has turned a moment I enjoyed into a nightmare.

Damn the lot of them.

They ask questions, but their voices are lost to the banging of my heartbeat in my ears. I whip around and march ahead, needing so much distance between myself and them that I want to be on the moon.

I'm trembling, hating that a moment that was special to me is being aired for their amusement.

Before I take two steps, a strong hand grabs my arm, and the next thing I know, I'm being hauled into the nearby woods by Ragnar. He pauses about ten feet away from the others like somehow this gives us any sort of privacy.

"What's going on?" he asks sharply, his gaze glued on me with a fierce look.

I'm still reeling with shock, and when my mouth opens, nothing comes at first. When I try again, anger spews from my voice. "How could you mock me like that in front of them?"

His brow pinches across his forehead, his hand squeezing tighter around my wrist. "There is no mocking, little fox. What you gave me last night I will always cherish, but I don't keep secrets from my men. You think they didn't see or smell what we were doing? And while you are under my protection, you are mine."

I stiffen and wrangle free from his grip, furious at his revelation, angry at how I can't help but seem like a joke to them. "You don't own me." I curl my hands into fists.

"That's where you're very wrong, Omega." He takes me by my arms and forces me back to him. I let out a groan, shoving against him, but his grasp tightens, and he kisses me so deeply, my knees weaken beneath me. My body completely betrays me in a moment I should be fighting back. Instead, he takes what he wants.

My belly quivers at how quickly my wolf awakens, how my body bows toward him. I dig my nails into his arms while I drown in his masculine scent, in the delicious way he tastes. My pulse flutters, and I'm lost under him, my head spinning.

I shouldn't be enjoying this, yet I find myself pressing closer, liquid building between my thighs. No, this can't be happening. I hate him, I hate my wolf, I hate how weak I am as an Omega.

When he breaks from my lips, I sway closer, unable to stop the purr on my lips from coming out.

"You see, Omega. We are meant to come together, so what is there to be embarrassed about?"

The way he calls me that grates on my nerves, but I should have known that dealing with four Alphas would come with repercussions. And now, suddenly, the offer from Nikos grows more enticing by the second.

Ragnar

She looks at me with so much hatred, it hardens my cock. She shivers, and that only makes me want to bend her over and claim her now. To show her that there is nothing to hide from my men.

My little fox has no idea what she's gotten herself into. I've instructed the men to give her space, to let her acclimatize to us, but it seems that time has come and gone. Along with a truth I've been ignoring since we first met.

She yanks against my hold, her whole body jerking. Her chin raises toward me with her threat. "Release me."

Those amber eyes brighten to a flame while the corners of her mouth tighten. I can still taste her, and I'm ravenous for her, starved to have those pouty lips wrapped around my cock, fucking hungry to sink into her. My need for her grows, and it's growing harder each day to ignore my attraction toward her. My wolf howls in my head, eager to take her.

"This wasn't part of the deal. Once this is over, you will never see me again," she tells me as she looks over her shoulder at my men chatting amongst themselves.

I hook my fingers under her chin, turning those gorgeous eyes to meet mine, long lashes raised, and fuck, she's gorgeous. "Nothing is set in stone, little fox, so let's focus on our mission before you make other plans."

She glares at me, her entire body going stiff, while desire twists inside me. My wolf pushes to make a connection, wanting to eat her up. Now this is something new he's never done before.

"You don't know what you're talking about," she says, her voice harsh, her cheeks stained red. "You don't get to decide what happens to me."

I adore her fighting spirit and laugh, more sure about what I want from her now than I have been over the last few days.

"Here's the thing," I say to her, while the sparks in her amber eyes light up. "I told myself that nothing would happen between us, but I've changed my mind."

Her gaze widens, and the reality of my words sinks in as awareness flares over her expression. In truth, my "stay away" policy had everything to do with completing our mission first, but now I'm not sure making myself wait will change anything.

"You must sense the connection between us," I urge as she pulls free from my hold.

Her lips tighten. "I get that with all four of you, so it's nothing special. Just the usual Alphas thinking of nothing but their dicks."

My cock tightens at the way she says that... seeing her riled up turns me on. Little does she know how deep she's in. "Tonight, you will be mine, and I will be your first."

Her mouth parts with no response, but the look behind her eyes is either shock or murder. *Fuck she's hot.*

"I'll drive a blade into your heart before that happens." She grips her hips, anger bleeding into her voice.

"I'll hold you to that." I reach for her just as an ear-piercing growl rips through the air.

The hairs on my nape rise while Narah shivers, glancing around.

"Oh, fuck!" she calls out and runs back to where my men are.

I jerk my attention to them, seeing nothing at first. My feet hit the ground with my hurried steps. "What the hell did you see?"

But something else catches my attention.

The air in front of Narah and the men ripples like heat waves, and instantly a monstrous bear materializes before us.

At least ten feet tall, the creature stands on hind legs, towering over us like a mountain. Brown fur sways in the breeze, and behind the creature, a trail of black fog disappears into the woods. It's watching us with bright yellow eyes, back feet firmly on the ground, front paws by its sides, sharp claws extended. Its chest pumps in and out, hot breath flaring from wide nostrils.

My men and I step forward as they nudge Narah behind them.

"Find a tree and climb it, Narah," I tell her, never taking my eyes off the animal. Except he's not just any beast, now is he, having come from magic, from the witch's intention to destroy anyone who crosses this land.

It raises its enormous head, and a tremendous roar bellows past his throat, spittle flinging in every direction. The woods tremble. My fingers curl over the hilt on my belt, and a spear of terror jolts through me. It races in my veins, yanking at my chest, but what would a battle be without the anticipation?

"Who's ready for a new fur blanket?" I ask, but when no one responds, I glance at my men, who are too captivated by the sight. Suddenly, Crius sprints to the right, Stone to the left, and Nikos backs away.

A shudder consumes me.

The ground beneath my feet quivers so suddenly, so fast, I forget what I was saying.

I snap my attention straight ahead.

Coming right for me is the creature on all fours, thundering toward me, eyes burning as if on fire. Large paws pound the ground as the animal throws itself into each leap to reach me faster.

Those eyes... they pierce into me as though he sees only me.

Adrenaline floods me from how quickly things have turned sour. I don't understand what my men are doing, but they must have a reason for backing away.

I grab my blade from my belt and rush forward, a war cry on my lips. My wolf is just below the surface, ready to emerge and spill blood, but first I need to slow down this beast.

My heartbeat bangs loudly in my ears.

I dart at lightning speed and throw myself into a forward roll, skewing to the left to miss the bear. Air buffets across my back from the creature's paw slicing through the air.

I leap to my feet and pivot back around, then hurl myself onto its back. We've taken down bears so many times back home. The beasts come down from the mountains when they run out of food.

I scramble up the creature's back, the blade between my teeth, my hands clutching at fur to reach its head.

Sudden movement snags my attention from my right, and I half expect it to be Crius. Instead, a savage swipe of a large paw crashes into me so unexpectedly, there's no time to duck. Claws scrape the side of my face, and I'm thrust off the bear's back. I slam to the ground, my blade flings away, and my body rolls from the momentum until I crash into a tree.

I groan from the impact, a sharp pain cramping my back, searing pain from the claws, while my head spins. But I don't have time to rest. I shove myself off the ground, the woods tilting around me, my face burning from the bear's scratch.

My gaze settles on the animal who's not paying me any attention anymore.

It's facing someone else... someone that has my stomach dropping.

"Hel?" I call out, staring incredulously at my sister standing in the small clearing. A tremble curls under my heart. The last time I saw her, tears streamed down her cheeks as Father's men dragged her out of our home in exchange for Nikos.

My gut twists in on itself, and an invisible hand grabs my heart, ripping it apart. Memories gouge my mind, and the past resurfaces.

"Send me instead," I shout from across the room to Father, the sting of anger piercing through my chest.

He stands with his back to me, peering out the window at the field outside, in the direction the Balor Wolves took Hel. He's a large man, bigger than me. I've only seen one person stand up to him, and they didn't live to see the next day.

"Say something," I bellow, my hands curling into fists, loathing the cold-hearted bastard. Mother's cries echo from the hallway, and my heart thunders.

Father turns to me and looks at me with hurt-filled resignation in his eyes.

Rage fills every inch of me, and not even his regretful agony can dampen my need to shove my fist into someone's face.

"Ragnar, son," he begins, but I've had enough and march up to him.

"Did you not hear me? I'll take her place. Bring her back."

I expect him to react, to grab my throat, to strike. Anything but lower his head and turn back to the window.

"We are outnumbered by them, you know this." The edge of his voice carries a warning.

"So what? Hel pays the cost? She's the sacrifice for all our lives?" Heat tears through me like a storm.

"If I could, I'd send you in a heartbeat," he admits, his words despondent, and I realize then he means it. He'd get rid of me without hesitation. "But it's not you they want," he mutters. "The Alpha came to me with a deal. He wants to claim Hel, and that buys us our safety."

I growl. "You sold her to that fucking old pig?"

His arms fall by his sides, but he doesn't respond or even pay me any attention. My gaze tumbles to the ring on his finger, dark and blood-stained, worn by his father and grandfather, all Alphas of the Ulv pack before him. But what good is being a powerful Alpha if you let others rip the soul out of your chest?

I wrench my gaze back to reality, from Hel to the other men who are fighting something I can't see... what the fuck is going on? I look back quickly to find Narah behind a tree, her expression one of horror.

"Bear got your tongue, brother?" Hel teases. "Will you fight alongside me, or have you lost your spine in the Romanian lands?" She cuts me a hard stare, her blue eyes sparkling in the light, and she wears the mischievous grin she always did when she challenged me during our battle training.

I shake my head to clear my vision, convinced I'm hallucinating.

Long brown hair hangs down her back, untouched by the wind beating into me. She's in her battle gear: leather pants, heavy boots, and a close-fitted dress that falls halfway down her thighs. They are blue as midnight, her favorite color, and in her hand she grips her short dagger, the one Mother gifted her before she was sent to the Balor Wolves.

The bear rises on hind legs once more, growling its threat, promising to rip us apart.

Hel smirks my way, and I almost crumble at seeing her... Gods, I've missed my sister so much.

"You being a pussy, Brother?"

This isn't right... she can't be in the fucking Poisonous Woods. Yet my grasp tightens around my knife.

The bear suddenly barrels toward my sister, and terror slams into me.

I hurl myself toward them. "Watch out," I yell, rushing toward her madly, dropping my blade, and my wolf tears out of me, shredding my clothes, my skin.

Air rushes in, doing nothing to put out the angry flames flooding my insides.

I don't stop... never stop. I lost my sister once for being too gutless to save her, to stand up to the enemy wolves. But no fucking way will that happen again.

FOURTEEN

Nikos

"Bear," I shout, my eyes never leaving the black monstrosity that emerges out of the woods. Yellow eyes find me, a growl rolling from the newcomer's huge chest. I'm recoiling from the animal that seems set on making me its prey.

"Fuck! Crius, Stone!"

I swipe a look over my shoulder when no one responds, but they aren't even remotely near me. Stone's across the clearing doing fuck knows what, while Crius is darting in and out of the woods, ducking and rolling about like a lunatic. He's finally lost his mind. I knew he would one day, but why now of all damn times?

Of course no one comes when I ask for help. It's the story of my life, isn't it?

Fuck every single one of them. I didn't need them when my family sold me out, and I sure as hell don't need them now. Instead, I lower my gaze on the approaching bear, his fur black as a raven's feathers. There's nothing normal about him, with his flaming eyes and the dark fog trailing behind him. It coils around his legs like somehow I'm in a terrible dream.

Head back, it roars, the sound piercing my ears, and fuck me but that sounds pretty real to me.

Grabbing my blades from my boots, one in each hand, I'm ready to skin this fucker. It's not my first time dancing with these giant furballs.

I lift my head and stare into the promised death of the animal's face, waiting for it to make a move, to lunge.

Seconds tick past.

Then it suddenly bursts forward.

The ground shudders, my sights set on the beast. I try to swallow the lump in my throat.

My brother's words come to me at this moment. *Let the enemy think they've won until the very last second. Then you strike.*

My heart lurches to my throat. Every inch of me is thundering with the adrenaline of battle, responding to the hunger in this animal's eyes. It wants my blood, and I'll finish him off.

The creature lunges, mouth gaping with razor-sharp teeth, extended claws reaching for me.

I throw myself sideways, the animal lurching after me, but momentum makes him slow and clumsy. I pitch my attack directly at the animal's side and thrust my knife upward into the softer hide of the underbelly, the blade sinking into flesh.

An ear-splitting growl comes from the bear's mouth as it swings around, sweeping a paw the size of my head. I duck and hurl myself toward its chest.

Watch the mouth, always watch it, my brother's voice sings in my ears.

In haste, I thrust the blade upward as the creature bends down, mouth gaping.

My knife pierces him under the chin and goes straight through. Abandoning the weapon, I dart out of striking range and whip back around.

Heart pounding, I expect to find it collapsed on the ground. Instead, its snarl blazes like thunder, the blade under its chin doing nothing.

What the fuck?

That's when I realize there's no blood coming from this beast. Not a single drop, and reality catches up to me that I'm dealing with magic, with something that's maybe already dead.

How the hell am I meant to eliminate that?

"Narah," I bellow, but when I glance back, she's nowhere in sight. Hell!

Fear crawls up my spine as the animal prepares to attack again, showing no sign of slowing down.

I turn my head, scanning the ground for the others. Ragnar is the closest, edging into the shadowy woods, his attention on something inside the forest.

"Ragnar," I yell. "I need backup." The words swell in my throat as he doesn't even acknowledge my call. He darts into the woods instead, leaving me behind.

Dread buckles through me, anger punching me in the gut. He left me, the fucking asshole.

I jerk my head to the other two. "Crius, Stone, I need your help here."

Nothing. Not a damn response or even a glance my way.

Cold hatred flares over me and it strikes me in the heart, reminding me I am not one of them, but an outsider. The one they can use as prey.

Taking a fleeting look behind me, I watch Narah darting into the woods after Ragnar, and I ball my hands into fists.

The sting of rejection tears through me, and that's when the bear makes his move, coming for me relentlessly.

I'm alone to face death. My stomach tightens, and I can taste fury on the back of my tongue.

In my mind, there is only emptiness, a void I've become used to. Clarity drives fear through my veins.

Just like my family abandoned me, so will everyone else.

So I accept my fate of being alone.

A roar drives from deep in my gut, and I lunge into battle, ready to fight to the end.

Crius

PUNCH AFTER PUNCH, I drive my fists into the white beast's side, my feet moving fast. I dodge a swinging arm and leap out of reach of snapping jaws.

It comes at me so fast, so wild, my adrenaline soars. I'm in my element, facing off with the animal. Both of us move with lightning speed, and at every chance, I drive punches into him, but it doesn't even slow him down.

Fuck!

I'm gasping for air, but I'll die before I give up.

The great monster swiftly twists and throws itself at me, so large it blots out the light overhead. I laugh and rush at it, ducking its swinging claws as I grab the ax from my belt and drive it into its gut. It stumbles back suddenly, losing its balance from the attack.

I take that moment to madly swing my weapon at the animal. The sharp edge of the ax carves into his side, fur falling away, but where the hell is the blood?

Not a drop stains the perfectly white fur.

I cling to the ax's handle and keep chopping, yelling, "Die, you fucking bear, die!"

A paw smacks into my side so sudden and unexpectedly that I'm thrown across the forest clearing. I tumble and hit the ground hard, my sides screaming with searing pain. When I touch my ribs and pull back my hand, red stains my fingers.

"You fucker!" I groan as I draw myself to my feet, a sharp ache lashing over me. I hiss, clenching my teeth. This scratch is going to hurt badly before it heals.

For the first time in too long, doubt creeps into my head that this might be a battle I can't win, that death has finally come for me. That I've taken on too much.

My head pulses with the excruciating ache at my side, while my heart beats to keep fighting. I didn't come this far to fall before my time. This is not my fate... not yet, and not here.

The bear blurs before me, and I shake my head, dropping my ax. With a single thought, my wolf rushes out of me like a storm, tearing my body. I cry out from the pain in my ribs, from the blood I'm losing.

Around me, the other men are darting about, fucking around as usual, but I don't need them. Never did in battle.

On all fours, I sprint forward and attack the bear, my teeth bared. Nothing will stop me.

Speed is on my side, and I careen around the beast, then come at him from the back before he even spins. I bite into his leg, teeth sinking in, the taste on my tongue like dirt.

I rip away flesh and fur, burning up with rage. Recoiling out of reach, I spit out the chunk of the bear and it turns to dust before it even hits the ground, vanishing from sight.

I flinch and jerk my head up as the monster whips toward me, the fury of hell in his eyes. Nose creased, the thing bellows a deafening growl.

Rage catapults within me while a flicker of fear lights in my chest, because no matter what I do, I'm not going to be good enough to take down this bear.

Stone

"Ragnar," I shout. He's standing ten feet from me, his back to me while a massive brown bear scratches at the earth in the distance, his gaze locked on me. It's like Ragnar can't feel the animal's presence or even see the damn thing.

"Deal with your own shit," he suddenly barks, and when he glances over to me, there's a fiery yellow glow in his eyes. I stiffen, taken aback, as something's wrong with his eyes.

Yet his response consumes me, sends a dull ache over my mind. He's never spoken to me like that before. "What the hell is your problem?"

I collect the blades from my belt. Around me, the trees shake from the wild wind, branches swaying and rustling. There's no sign of Crius or Nikos... and behind me, Narah is gone. She was there earlier, which is why I took this position to block anything from coming toward her.

A shiver snakes up my spine, and the runes on my chest glow blue from the magic tainting the air. Hairs on my nape lift, and the glint of fire in the bear's eyes looks too similar to what I'd seen in Ragnar's.

I glance over my shoulder once more for Narah, fear dripping down my spine at not seeing a sign of her.

An earth-shattering growl has me snapping my attention back around to the bear, who's now barrelling my way. Front paws slam to the ground, hind legs propelling him closer and closer.

"We got company," I yell to the team. "Someone, flank it from the side, and I'll take it head on."

The heavy thundering whips through the air, and I study my opponent, the thunderous way he travels.

When no one gives a response, I tense up.

"What the fuck, man?" Rage burns me.

"For hell's sake!" I toss my knives down, having had enough. I'm seething, my jaw clenching.

The storm of the bear is almost on me. I fall to my knees and slap my open palms to the soil. A surge erupts across my chest, and in seconds it sears across my runes as power zips down my arms and into the ground.

I call to the elemental energy to do my bidding against the encroaching danger.

Instantly, the world shudders beneath me, quivering, and at once a great fissure splits open the earth right under the bear's paws.

He's so close I can feel his hot breath when suddenly he drops down into the dark cavern. His whimpering terror echoes as he frantically scratches at the walls, trying desperately to claw his way back up.

My heartbeat thunders in my chest, my pulse racing at how fucking pissed I am at Ragnar, fueling my energy as I pour more and more of my power into the ground, so exhausted of this witch crap.

"Close." My whisper catches on the breeze.

The land trembles, trees swaying heavily, nature seeming to come to life, and the crack in the earth closes hastily with a final thump. It comes so fast, the monster stands no chance.

And he's gone.

No more cries or threats.

Fuck, yeah.

On my feet, I shake my hands of the power, the flare over my chest dwindling, and I'm proud of myself. Now where the fuck is Ragnar?

Around me, there isn't a soul in sight. Turning on the spot, I glance through the woods when abruptly, another bear pummels out of the shadows, coming at me faster than the previous one, mouth gaping, spittle flinging on the wind.

I flinch, and I'm yanked to the cold, hard reality of the situation.

No matter what I do, the magic in this land won't let me win, now will it?

Then I'll burn the whole fucking forest down to finish this.

FIFTEEN

Narah

Like the half a dozen times I've already tried, I hurl my hands outward, aimed at the clearing in the woods where the Alphas are battling four bears. Sounds of war flood the woods, growls and the terrifying thundering of massive paws on the ground. The men are tossed about like dolls, but they never stay down, not even once. I am starting to wonder if they are indestructible.

Short, golden sparks of magic splutter out from my fingertips, flatlining with each of my attempts. I want to scream. Of course it chooses now not to work, and a shiver jolts up my spine at how hopeless I feel.

"Shit!" I shake my arms, sensing the energy pricking down my flesh, and try again.

Fucking nothing.

"Come on, already."

Monsters and terrifying things linger in the woods, and I can't do a damn thing about them.

A spell is attacking the men. That's the only way to describe what

I'm seeing and why the bears aren't going down, why each of them leaves behind a black trail of feathery smoke.

I lick my dry lips, panic tearing me apart. I'm pacing, gnawing on my cheek.

These bears aren't real animals... not at all. They're magic, illusions made to kill.

"Stone," I call out for the tenth time as he's closest to me, but he doesn't respond, and when he does look my way, he seems to stare right through me.

I swallow hard, my breaths racing. I need to understand how in the world to help them before it's too late.

The shouting and growls flood the air with anger, with a poison that taints nature.

Illusions... my mind goes over the scene where each one combats his own bear. The fights spill into each other. A bear whacks a paw into Ragnar's side, sending him flying across the ground. He crashes right through the white bear Crius fights like it's not really there. No one seems to notice each other.

It's fake... the whole damn thing is smoke and mirrors, yet the men bleed from the attacks. They are big and strong enough to look after themselves, yet worry drums over my thoughts that this is no ordinary enemy they face.

Fear paints their expressions like they know there is no way they can win this war, yet they don't dare stop. It's stupid, but I admire their tenacity. It's like nothing scares them... except everyone fears something.

The quickest way to be defeated is to let fear into your soul, Father would tell me. *It's how many on the battlefield fall. They let terror defeat them.*

I wrack my brain for answers on how to help them, while faint magic skips over my fingers, then completely vanishes.

Rules, Mother told me. *Magic exists by rules, and everything happens for a reason. A cause and effect, a positive and negative to nullify an attack.*

Movement draws my attention to Stone, who makes the whole forest shudder. His power astounds me with how he splits open the ground with such ease to swallow the bears attacking him, again and again. Yet, I know that for a witch to crack open the ground like this is the tip of the iceberg of their ability... something I am still to learn. The whole thing leaves me a bit intimidated.

But for all of us right now, there's an urgency that completely consumes me, and I breathe deeply. I have to do something.

My gaze lifts to the shadows surrounding the clearing in the woods, how they darken as if additional bears are manifesting to jump in and attack the Alphas, to kill them.

I shouldn't care, because if I wanted a way away from these Alphas, this is my moment, my chance to escape. Yet I can't get my feet to move, and my frantic thoughts are out of control. I struggle to make sense of anything but the raw emotions that demand I protect these wild men.

I must be going out of my mind. I may regret it later, but I can't walk away from them when I can possibly help.

Quickly, I rush over to Stone on quick strides, my skin crawling with dread, my gaze zipping across the four battles going on at the same time. Spells to affect the men... but they don't impact me, which makes no sense either.

Crius's eyes fill with terror from across the field, blood drenching his body as he drags his clothes back on after his shift, and my chest tightens. The bears are all of various sizes and colors, but the wisps of black mist that linger around each of them are the same. It has to be the key that connects them, and the idea consumes me.

The ground swallows up yet another bear as I reach Stone, his power impressive, but this spell won't relent until exhaustion makes him sloppy and he makes a mistake that will end his life.

"Stone," I call to him and set my hand on his arm.

He flinches around at my touch, his shoulders and head rearing back as if expecting me to be a bear.

The moment his gaze lands on me, softness washes over his gaze, and he shakes his head as if seeing me clearly. "Narah, where the fuck did you go?" His attention sweeps back over his shoulder to the surrounding woods and back at me. The next bear will appear any moment now, so we don't have time.

Hope beams in my chest that this will work, that I'll make a difference. "I think I know how to stop this."

He turns his attention to me, his hand grabbing mine, squeezing. "Well, do it already."

Adrenaline pumping, all my senses are on high alert, so taut they are going to burst.

"Everything here is an illusion. It can hurt you and even kill you, but you will never destroy the bears. They are energy, nothing more."

He's shaking his head. "That's fucking great. So use your magic then."

I swallow hard, feeling the pressure to perform. "This isn't about me," I explain, thinking of how badly my attempts went. "You need to counteract the spell. It's an illusion, a lie, so only you can stop this. You need to reveal the truth of what you truly fear."

The opposite of their bravery.

He stares at me, bewildered, then scans the area, and a flash of worry wrinkling the bridge of his nose. "That makes no sense."

"Yes, it does," I insist, my shoulders tense.

Without missing a beat, a roar bellows from behind Stone, and we both glance at the gigantic bear steamrolling toward us from across the open land. My mouth goes dry, and my hope dwindles.

Stone drops to the ground, his hands flat on the soil. My skin pricks instantly at his power as a blue energy zips down his arms and into the soil.

"How long will you keep doing this? Until you collapse from exhaustion and the bear kills you?" I say as frustration digs into my chest.

"I don't understand what you want me to do, Narah," he barks, his attention never leaving the bear.

The earth quivers beneath my feet from the oncoming animal charging at us. I can't help but recoil at the intimidating sight.

"The spell is a phantom. How do you combat a lie? You tell the truth of something you've been hiding. Of what scares you. Magic is about positive and negative energy, about balancing the power. It's not that hard to understand." Irritation laces my words, as I just want him to do it already.

An explosive cracking sound shudders through the air, and I jump in my skin. I glance up just as the attacking animal is swallowed by the earth. I look away, not wanting to see it suffer, even if it's not real. Its whimpering sounds are bad enough.

Stone is on his feet in moments and looking at me strangely. "So I just tell you the truth? That's it? About what?"

My pulse spikes, as this is theory only, but it's all I've got right now.

"Say something you've been lying to yourself about, something you fear. Then tell it to the energy encasing you. A secret you haven't told a soul. Like, I contemplated for a few seconds leaving you four here to die as I escaped." My cheeks are on fire at admitting that directly to his face, but I don't have the patience for tact at the moment.

His expression falls, then he shrugs. "Yeah, I'd probably do the same."

When I look over to Crius, he's bleeding severely from his side, and I keep thinking about Father's words about how letting fear in will lead to failure, and maybe my strategy of getting them to admit their fear is wrong, but then what else can it be? The element of fear has to be what holds them back, what applies here.

"Each of you are fighting your own war. Maybe the bears represent each of your fears, so you need to confront them with the truth of what scares you."

Despite his brow furrowing, he closes his eyes for a moment, saying, "This is ridiculous, but I'll play along." He growls under his breath, then his voice comes out soft. "I tell everyone I'm fine when really I'm terrified that I'll never be taken seriously and remain the joke to every Alpha." He pauses, and I'm hanging off his words, my heart drumming louder to hear him admit something I'd never expect from him. Then he opens his eyes. "Something like that?" His voice darkens, his expression twisting like he suddenly wants to take back what he's said.

I reach for his arm, but he pulls away from me, and my stomach twists that I've hurt him. "Stone, it's not—"

Suddenly, his eyes widen with surprise, and his legs give out from under him in a heartbeat. He collapses to the ground. Eyes shut, he lays half on his side, an arm across his stomach. He's passed out.

A coldness strikes me in the chest, and panic has me falling to my knees by his side.

"Stone!"

Hastily, I check his pulse. He's still alive... but his heartbeat is slowing down.

"Wake up!" I shake him frantically.

There's no response.

What have I done? Cold seeps into my veins, and I stare down at him, waiting for him to wake, for something.

But there is nothing.

No sudden waking up to laugh that he's joking.

Not a damn thing.

"Shit. Shit. Shit." I shake Stone by his shoulders. "Please get up."

Still nothing, and I pull back onto my heels, my eyes pricking with dread that I've somehow made things worse. That I will cause his death.

When I lift my head, there's no bear coming for him. With him passed out, there is nothing for the creature to attack. Regardless, the other three Alphas never relent in their battles, but their moves grow sluggish, more exhausted.

There's a tremble in my hands that races up my arms, and a soft whimper spills past my throat.

What do I do?

Running my fingers through my hair over and over, I get to my feet and lower my gaze back to Stone. I'm shaking and I hug myself, my breathing ragged. My mind fills with images of Stone's death, of all the Alphas' deaths. When I look down at my hands, the tips of my fingers will no longer be black, but covered in their blood, because this will be all my fault.

Everything is my fault.

My sisters were lost because I couldn't control my magic.

Kaira is still out there somewhere.

Tears prick my eyes, and I want to collapse, to cry at the unfairness, to wish I was stronger. I want to be in the inn room I've been living in for weeks, except I am nowhere near safety, am I? Out here, I'm in a wilderness where death waits in the shadows, where even animals don't dare to tread.

Instead, it feels like a terrible storm is coming... one I can't escape if I don't turn back now.

I am quiet for a long moment, hating myself for letting my parents down, for not being what they wanted me to be.

The muffled grunts from the men and growls have me lifting my gaze. They fight an unwinnable battle, regardless.

"Get your shit together, Narah. Think. Stone's bear isn't returning, and he's alive for now. All the men are under the same spell. So that means one thing. They are connected under the one spell. Of course they are."

I don't even wait for the thought to settle before I'm sprinting toward Crius, following the one possibility of saving them.

The sheer display of his savage masculinity as he leaps out of the bear's reach catches my attention. Crius pivots and throws himself at the animal, leaving me practically frozen with awe. Everything about Crius is seductive and powerful, particularly the way he moves with such swiftness and prowess.

"Crius." I reach out and touch his arm.

He looks at me, his cheeks and forehead streaked with blood, and I cringe. "Get the hell out of here," he snaps, then whips back to the creature charging for him. He catapults at the white furred monster so easily that I can't look away.

He slams into the bear's shoulder, and at lightning speed, spears his ax into the back of his head before being thrown off. His grip slips from his weapon still wedged into the animal's neck, and he's tossed across the clearing before crashing into a tree.

He groans and hits the ground hard.

I sprint across to him, terrified of him dying. The bear doesn't even notice me, but it snarls furiously as he tries to reach for the ax embedded in his neck.

"The spell's an illusion, and you can stop it by saying out loud the truth of what scares you."

He cocks an eyebrow at me. "Is this some kind of trick to get to know me? You don't need to try so hard, gorgeous. Just ask and I'm yours."

I may have just swooned on my feet, but this isn't the moment to get gushy. "Just shut the hell up and listen. You can't win this battle with your strength. You need to counteract the spell."

He's dusting himself as the bear roars, rearing itself up on hind legs, batting at the weapon still wedged in his flesh.

"Will you hurry the hell up?" I snap, staring at the blood dripping down his hip and soaking into his pants. I don't even know how he's still standing from so much blood loss. He towers over me with a slight slant from an injured leg, and the scratch marks on his neck look so deep it scares me.

He shrugs, then makes a moan as his lips tighten from the clear agony he's feeling.

"You want to know something, right?" he begins with an edge in his voice. "Something about why I'm so fucked up... I once made a deal with the neighboring pack Alphas who challenged me, and I agreed to take them all on my own. It's fucked up and I knew it, but I couldn't back down. Ragnar stopped it before it started, or I wouldn't be standing here with you." He half-grins like it pains him to admit this to me of all people.

"I don't judge you," I admit, while he glances at the bear falling to all fours and pushing into a run toward us.

"I am scared shitless of failing, or not winning a battle, of getting others killed. And strangely, I'm not worried about dying."

Just as the last word leaves his lips, his eyes roll into the back of his head and he drops to the ground as a shadow crests over us.

My heart thumps loudly in my ears, my mind caught on what he's just revealed.

A shower of dark mist abruptly cascades over us, and I duck out of pure instinct, my hands covering my head. The vanishing bear darkens the world for a moment, creating an ominous feeling in an already terrifying forest.

Crius lies by my feet, sprawled on his back, arms stretched out on either side of him, his legs bent... and he's unconscious, just like Stone. I want to believe what I'm doing is going to work. Please work.

Except part of me is still rocking on my heels at his revelation about death... for me, dying scares me more than anything. To leave my sisters behind alone is my worst nightmare, and yet Crius embraces that? He's more afraid of not succeeding.

But I shake those thoughts away, needing to get to the last two Alphas.

Without pausing, I swing around and run at full speed, yelling before I even reach him across the clearing. "Nikos!"

When I lay my hand on his back, he whips around and frowns at me, then turns back to the bear. What is it with him... he's so hot and cold all the time?

"Please, Nikos, hurry." I grab his hand, imploring him to open up, explaining what he has to do. His brow furrows like I've done him an injustice to show him I cared. He turns, ripping his hand out of mine, charging for the bear.

His response carries on the wind. "I lied to Ragnar when I told him I had no intention of leaving his pack." He ducks the bear's swinging paw and jumps into battle, his blades slashing across the beast's underside. "In the end, it's easier if I leave before I'm tossed out."

His words carry as much punch as the ones he delivers to the animal, but in seconds, he crumbles to the ground while the bear morphs into a floating mist, evaporating on the breeze.

Yet I can't move and instead drown in Nikos's secret, to hear the defeat of already accepting that he'll be pushed aside. Hell, these men are tough as mountains, but on the inside they are just as broken and twisted as me.

As much as I want to shake him awake and make him talk about this shit, I tear away from him and swing toward Ragnar in his white wolf form, clashing with a huge brown bear. It still amazes me how massive he is... he's unlike any Alpha I've seen before. But he is the last I need to fix, and I hurry to him, not sure if I want to hear his secret, in all honesty, when my mind is hurting with what I've just learned from the other three.

I close in on him as he rushes in for an attack. There's a long, painful-looking wound ripped down the back of his arm, blood dripping behind him. He's limping and sluggish in his movements. I ache on the inside, struggling with seeing how beaten these Alphas are, how they keep battling an impossible fight.

"Ragnar," I yell, doubting he can hear me, so I rush to him, my arm reaching out for his back.

Suddenly, Ragnar's knocked in the face by the bear's swinging head. He groans with agony and reels backward so fast that I don't have time to get out of his path.

Panic captures me as I cry out, and he whips around so quickly that his huge wolf head slams into me with the force of a mountain. Next thing I know, I've hit the ground with a tremendous sharp pain zigzagging across my nose and eyes. Stars blot in and out of my vision, along with a deepening darkness coming for me.

SIXTEEN

Ragnar

Confusion blinds me momentarily as I slam into Narah. She's falling to the ground from my impact, her eyes fluttering, then closing finally.

Where did she come from? One minute my sister, Hel had been by my side, then she vanished. Now Narah appears out of thin air.

The deafening roar of the bear is right there, and terror seizes me that Narah's now in mortal danger. And why hadn't she just zapped this fucking bear out of existence?

Fuck! I rip my gaze from her limp body, my chest tightening, and twist around just as the bear throws itself toward us.

The world darkens for moments as the dark mass looks ready to swallow the world. It should terrify me, but right now I'm burning with fury that Narah's life is at risk. A newfound adrenaline soars in me, thumping through my veins.

I throw myself at the beast in my wolf form to destroy him, having had enough of his bullshit.

We collide, and all I see is savagery, dark fur, and anger driving me wild. Nothing matters but eliminating the foe, protecting Narah. My wolf is in charge, and he demands that we save her and then finally claim her as ours. He's damn pissed with me for dragging my feet, for not rutting her already, as he insists we keep her as our own.

Uncertainty blurs my emotions on this... I'd lost a fated mate and promised myself I wouldn't take any other female aside from fucking. And Narah... well, she is here for our mission. That's why I kept my distance.

My wolf laughs in my mind, insisting I'm not fooling anyone.

Fuck! That's not what I want to hear.

I keep tearing into the bear, over and over, my teeth sinking into soft fur and flesh, ripping away chunks. No blood, which is wrong. The whole thing is horribly wrong.

A sharp burn races up my back, and I howl with agony from the bear's scratch, tearing up my skin.

I leap out of the way of his next swing, duck another blow and curve away from him. It's only then that the full extent of my attack on him is shown. Bite marks and missing chunks of flesh dot his chest and underbelly. He staggers, but the wounds are healing from the dark sparks sizzling across them.

I swallow, wobbling on my own feet. How am I meant to defeat the unbeatable? But it does me no good letting that shit into my mind.

"I am invincible," I tell myself.

Then I turn and sprint back to Narah, knowing we need to run. I have no shame in turning away from a fight when someone's in danger.

This is our small window to escape.

Skidding by Narah's side, my wolf retracts, and my limbs stretch, bones cracking. Scorching pain digs into my body, tearing me apart from my injuries. Fire flares across my back and chest from the bear scratches, my head dizzy. I wince through the agony and shake my head to clear my vision.

"I am invincible."

My wolf is my armor, but right now I need to carry Narah out of here, and I bite back the horrendous pain engulfing me.

A quick scan of the clearing shows no signs of my men, and I'm too fucking exhausted and in pain to even be furious that they've vanished. They would have their reasons, as we are one and would never abandon one another. With that a new concern rises through me, one that maybe they are in worse peril than me.

I crouch and sweep Narah into my arms. On fast steps, I carry her out of there. Behind me, the bear still stumbles about, but he'll be healed quick enough and give chase. And I'm not waiting around to give him the chance.

Narah lays limp against my chest, a big red bruise forming across her brow where our heads collided. Shit! I want to shake her for being so stupid to come to me during the battle, or perhaps she had a magical solution?

Fuck knows, but I am the one protecting her, and that's how it should be.

"Shit, Narah," I growl under my breath. My feet pound the ground, and I keep checking over my shoulder, but each time my gaze falls to Narah, my wolf growls his intentions to claim her.

Except I'm still angry she put herself in harm's way and never listens to reason. "Next time I say to stay back, you listen!"

No response. Not that I expected one, but the whole situation is fucked up. "I don't know how you did it, but I don't appreciate you crawling under my skin and into my thoughts. I can't get your scent out of my nose, the softness of your body out of my head, and the hunger to take you grows by the day."

Behind me, the bear rises on hind legs, completely healed, and my heart almost stops as the creature stares at me with full intention to charge after us. I need a place to hide Narah, to get her out of harm's way.

"You want to know the truth," I say and sprint forward, holding her tight against me as she bounces in my arms. "I don't want to like you or take you as mine. I promised myself I wouldn't. Not with how complicated and shitty my life is. But everything about you makes me question myself, and whatever you've done to bewitch me needs to end. Because right now, I'm going to take you as mine and keep you for eternity. And that right there scares the fuck out of me more than the monster coming for my blood."

The ground shudders behind me, and I face the charging animal.

In that same split second, my knees suddenly give out beneath me as a strange sensation envelops me. One of exhaustion, of utter weakness, and with it the world around me wavers.

What the fuck?

My arms slacken, and Narah slips from my grasp. She falls to the ground as everything around me tilts.

Terror grips me. What's happening to me? With my last bit of strength, I wrench my head up to the bear just as his body starts dissolving into black mist. The creature vanishes just as fast as darkness sweeps over my mind and steals me from this world.

Narah

SOMETHING SOFT STROKES MY CHEEK, and it takes moments for my thoughts to snap back to reality, to remind myself of the spell with the bears and what a dangerous situation we're all in.

I flip open my eyes at once with that thought, and Crius is looking down at me, smirking.

"How are you feeling, gorgeous?" he asks and pushes loose strands of hair from my brow, and I wince from the touch. "You've earned yourself a massive bruise." He reaches down and pokes me in the brow.

"Ouch." I bat his hand away and push myself up. Crius doesn't miss a beat and takes my hand, then I'm on my feet in a flash. At first, the land around me sways, and I grasp onto his strong arm until I find my balance.

Crius's embrace constricts, not letting me fall. I grip his shirt.

The place is so quiet, and I can feel the rush of cool air against my face, hear the thud of my heart in my ears. We are no longer in the clearing, but by the river's water once more. A fire burns nearby, while in the distance Ragnar, Nikos, and Stone are strolling toward us along the water's edge.

"You've healed," I say, staring down at Crius's body. "You were bleeding terribly from the bear's attack."

"My wound has closed up, and it won't take long to completely heal. You've been unconscious for a couple of hours now."

"I have?" Echoes of what we recently went through ripple over my mind, while the trees sway in the cool breeze and the river glistens beneath the sunlight. I glance up, because I've missed the sun.

"You saved us," Crius tells me, his hand sweeping more hair off my face, and at his touch, I melt. "Very clever way of doing it, too. Though I will warn you... not everyone is particularly happy about being forced to share their secrets with you."

I blink at him, at his sharp jawline and cheekbones, at those brilliant hazel eyes with green flecks. "I was trying to save your lives." I think back to Crius admitting he wasn't afraid of dying but cared more about impressing others.

"The way I see it, I've told you something intimate, and you helped save me. You didn't need to, but I appreciate it," he mutters.

"Do you really not care about dying?" The words slip past my lips in a whisper, and I regret them at once.

He stares at me for a long pause, his expression turning impassive. "I should have died long ago for my actions, Narah, and no, that's not a secret you will ever pry out of me."' His jaw clenches while a flare of pain crosses his gaze. The tragedy in his eyes squeezes around me, and now I wish I never asked the question. What could have happened so that he now wishes for death?

I reach up to cup the side of his face, still unable to believe this is real and we all survived the last spell. He leans into my touch gently and closes his eyes momentarily as if the reality still hasn't fully found him either. He doesn't move, and I want to lean in and taste his lips. I take in the beautiful structure of his face, his throat, his powerful body, and I sway forward in response. I'm half tempted to reach over and smooth out the pinched wrinkles across the bridge of his nose.

His eyes slide open. "Narah, why don't you have injuries from a bear attack?" He swiftly changes the topic, and I don't push him on it either.

"One never came for me. Only for you four." As the response leaves my mouth, I can't help but wonder if the witches are playing games with us. Did they want to see how I'd react, how I'd use my power to help the men?

My fingers curl tighter around Crius's shirt. The thought races and brings with it a terrifying revelation that we are walking into a bigger trap none of us will be able to escape from.

A tremble races up my spine, and I glance up to meet his gaze. "Maybe it'd be wise if we turned back and forgot this mission."

His eyes narrow in response, but it's someone else's voice that distracts us.

"She's awake," Stone declares, stealing the chance for Crius to answer. Stone's voice is dark, and when I face him, there are shadows painted across his expression. His secret of not being taken seriously by anyone flutters to the forefront of my mind, and I can tell he thinks I'm not worthy to see this part of him. But he couldn't be more wrong.

Crius unfurls his arms from around me, and I turn to the other three approaching.

Nikos stares at me with the same unsettling stare as Stone, the one that reminds me how he intends to leave Ragnar's pack, worried he'll be thrown out as he had out of his own family. He lowers his gaze from me, and my chest constricts. This isn't what I want... for them to pull away, to feel less of themselves.

These men can rip me apart, yet they withdraw over secrets they hold onto like their lives depend on it.

It's only Ragnar who stares at me with a look of dominance... of course, he has nothing to hate me for, but would he if he had revealed his deepest secret?

"How did you survive?" I ask him. "I never got the chance to tell you how to break the spell."

He shrugs and tilts back his head, his lips tightening, yet his gaze never leaves me. "I was going to ask you the same question. I ran with you in my arms from the bear, and next thing I knew, I passed out and the bear dissolved into nothing."

His pale blue eyes study me, and it leaves me covered in shivers. He's not a man who'll be gentle if he thinks I'm hiding something from him.

"Pretty sure Narah made you spill your darkest secret like she did with us, as that is what had us passing out," Nikos says bitterly.

My posture bristles, and I can't stop myself. "Don't blame me. I saved your lives. I'm sorry you had to share something with me, but I am not judging you for it, and I won't be sharing it with anyone else, so take your hatred somewhere else."

I want to punch Nikos in the face for standing there, dark and formidable, clear he has no intention of forgiving me. Except I did nothing wrong, and my arms tremble by my sides.

"No one is upset because you saved us," Crius adds, trying to be the peacekeeper. "You've got to understand, our backgrounds are fucked up and beyond broken. Why do you think the four of us have bonded so well? And what we shared is a small insight into our weakness. It's not something anyone wants to share. That shit makes you soft and vulnerable. So give it time and we'll all deal with this crap our own way."

My muscles across my shoulder blades tense. "Fine, I get that, but don't take it out on me or look at me like I'm the devil when I just tried to help everyone."

Standing before them, my anger and frustration continue to billow, and my mind fires up with furious words I want to throw at them. With it comes the devastating longing for Martell from my wolf, and how she insists it would be so much easier if I had just controlled my magic with him. Except I wasn't good enough, or he wouldn't have rejected me. All I can remember is the hatred and fear in his eyes when he looked at me... and now a similar expression crosses these Alphas' faces.

When no one speaks, I continue. "As I said to Crius, I recommend we all turn back and forget this mission. It's a damn waste of time, and I think we're walking into a bigger trap."

I don't wait to hear their responses because I'm shaking with anger. Instead, I turn and march away from them... to be anywhere but in their presence. How could they be so ungrateful?

The woods swallow me as I enter them, and I'm breathing heavily, my eyes tearing up, hating that they make me feel this way. The things they told me tear me apart at how horribly sad their pasts are. I wish I could sweep it all away for them, but they won't even let me be there for them. And they aren't the only ones with ugly upbringings.

"Narah," Ragnar calls from behind me.

But I hurry forward, not looking back, not ready to deal with this or have him see my crying because of them.

They don't deserve it.

SEVENTEEN

Narah

I wipe my teary eyes, racing past trees, hating how quickly the Alphas have seemed to turn against me.

Ragnar is right behind me, his footfalls hitting the ground rapidly, announcing his approach.

"Narah," he shouts, his temper darkening his voice.

"Leave me alone," I throw over my shoulder.

But his hand clasps around my wrist, and before I know it, I'm swinging back around and colliding right against his stone chest. "Why are you running? Where are you going to go?"

I keep my head low, hating these Alphas with every fiber of my being for making me attracted to them and caring about them. This isn't why I came into these damned woods.

"Talk to me," he persists, his tone firm.

His blue eyes blaze at me when I look up, and I expected them to be cold and empty, except there is warmth etched in them. I pull against his hold, wanting to put distance between us, but his grip squeezes.

I lift my chin higher, blinking away the tears, and speak to him directly. "Did you know I was actually contemplating leaving you four behind with the bears? And let me say, the idea was ridiculously tempting."

He touches my shoulder with his free hand, and a longing stretches out across the pit of my stomach. Confusion batters within me about my feelings, about my wolf insisting Martell will come for us while all I crave is these men. So the answer is to run away from everyone until I work out what in the cursed world I want.

"Why didn't you?" he asks like it would have been an easy decision for him.

"What would you have done in my position?" I retort.

"For my pack, I would have saved them in a heartbeat. For my enemy, I wouldn't have wasted a breath on them and let them die."

My mouth might have fallen open to hear him so brazenly admit that he thinks I made the wrong decision. "I'm sorry, but let me get this right—you would have left me to die?"

I'm shaking as he stands over me, staring at me with his over-inflated Alpha ego, and yet I've shed tears for them. The bastard. He's got me so upset, I can't even remember why I cried for them.

"Well, clearly that is where we differ," I snap and wrench my wrist free from his grasp, then retreat from him backward. "I have a heart and could never let anyone die... not even my enemy, it seems."

He watches me from behind hooded eyes and doesn't move to come after me.

"But I get it," I say. "I'm weak for having feelings, for caring, but at least I'm not drowning in the darkness swallowing your men out there. Their secrets will eat them alive until they destroy them." I turn from him and hurry away.

Only the faint voices of the others by the river's edge fill the void. My head spins with everything we've gone through, with remembering what each Alpha confessed. It shouldn't bother me. They aren't my problem, yet my stomach lurches when I think of their agony.

I swivel around and run in the opposite direction, having had enough. I no longer want to be part of this mission. Not after I've been foolish enough to let these Viking Alphas get under my skin and make me desire them. When the heck did that happen, anyway?

With a single breath, my magic awakens, the woods sharpening under my gaze, and lines of energy skip across the tips of my darkened fingers.

There are no spells around me, and up ahead lies bright light from where the woods thin. I hurry forward and burst into a meadow that sways with green grass and yellow flowers. I might even be forgiven for believing this place is beautiful, except it's poisonous with everything it touches. I see that now.

I keep running, the long grass brushing against my knees.

When I look back, Ragnar suddenly bursts out from the woods, hot on my heels, and my heart jams in my throat at seeing the ferocity on his face, the fury in his eyes.

I barely have time to react when he's on me, larger than life. Strong hands snatch me around the waist, and he wrenches me backward. He turns me to face him, and anger lunges through me.

I shove a hand to his chest, my words loud and shaky. "No, you don't get to stop me from leaving."

He draws me closer to him regardless and with pain in his eyes, a wincing pain rolling from his throat.

The stringent smell of burning has me looking down to where my hand rests on his chest. My touch is still fueled with magic, and it burns right through the fabric of his shirt and marks his flesh with my power.

Fear strikes me, and I shut down the magic instantly with a single thought, but before I can even remove my hand, his mouth is on mine.

His mouth is powerful and his kisses dominate me, his tongue plunging into my mouth. My lips hurt from his forcefulness, but I don't draw away.

I groan with pleasure. My body melts against him, and the whole world dissolves around us. I really don't want to acknowledge the influence Ragnar has over me, how his Alpha side suffocates me with his presence, or that I crave so much more.

My wolf rises in me, growling against him to back away, but she gains a throaty snarl in response from Ragnar's wolf.

Perhaps my body knows more about what I want than my wolf

who is threatening him. I don't let go of Ragnar, and instead, I kiss him back just as passionately. I wrap my hands around his neck and push myself on my tippy toes to better reach him. As if sensing my eagerness, he grabs my waist and lifts me up against his body.

Instinct has me looping my legs around him, and that earlier hollow space in my chest begins to fill. Every inch of me aches for him, and I tell myself to not show him how much he affects me, but I'm failing miserably.

He breaks from our kiss, and our raspy breaths tangle.

"You never let me finish explaining," he says. "You are not my enemy, Narah. I told you before, you are under my protection, so I will fight to the end to save you."

"You don't need to say that. After this mission, I will be gone from your life, so don't pretend I mean anything."

He sighs with frustration. "Open up your eyes about what's going on between you and I... between us all." His gaze sweeps over my face, searching for my response, for my reaction.

How dare he bring this back to the way they've all made me care, how much I've desired them. The thought has me clutching onto him stronger when I should be shoving him farther from me. But in truth I don't know if I can... or if I want to.

My gaze falls to his chest to where my handprint is now a black brand marred into his flesh. "I hurt you."

"Yeah, it fucking stings, but I'll survive." His hands squeeze my ass as he presses his groin against me, his large erection fitting so perfectly between my legs. My primal hunger has me rocking my hips to rub myself against him, a move that feels natural.

My cheeks blush that I react so easily and openly. A moan spills past my lips, and he smiles, approving of my reaction. My mind swings back to Martell, to how he denied me because of my magic and called me an abomination, yet Ragnar doesn't bat an eye that I just burned him.

Except, I'm falling so quickly for his charm when my priority should be finding my sisters, not taking over territory with a pack of Viking Alphas. And in response, my wolf bristles inside me with disapproval that I would even consider another Alpha when we have

Martell. I clench my teeth at how nothing I do will make her understand that he's not ours.

"Maybe we shouldn't be doing this." I push against his chest, needing to clear my mind and not let the heady emotions control me. "My wolf has already found her mate, and she longs for him. Did you hear her earlier growling at you?" Even in my head, my lame excuse sounds like just that. I'm scared to let myself feel the things I do for Ragnar.

One of his eyebrows arches. "Where is your mate now?"

"Hopefully as far from me as possible."

"Then what's the problem? It's not your wolf I want to fuck. You must be feeling the pull between us, Narah."

My skin flushes at his words. "But I also feel my wolf rejecting you." I push against his shoulders, straining to get down to my feet. Fire fills my lungs that my instincts so easily lead me.

Ragnar licks his lips. "There's only one way to retrain your wolf and make her forget your fated mate. We realign her."

I offer him a narrowing gaze in response. "What are you talking about?"

"Our wolves are primal animals who long for one thing—rutting with their mate." Ragnar's arms squeeze around me, his muscles tense as he drops down to his knees in the field with me still clinging to him.

My breath wedges in my chest as he lowers me to the ground on my back, and he follows, covering me with his body. I keep my legs wrapped around him as I quiver at what he's proposing.

The grass tickles the side of my face while Ragnar kisses my cheek and makes a path to my neck. I cry out with pleasure, my spine curving in response, pressing my breasts against him with a growing need coming over me.

"So, to help your wolf," he whispers in my ear, "I will mark you as mine."

His words have me stiffening beneath him, then I tremble to hear he will take me as his own.

"Wait! What? Don't you dare. And is that even possible?" My stomach heaves from my wolf's protesting snarl, her anger leaching through my veins, while my whole body burns with heat. I'm at two extremes, feeling like I'm coming apart at the seams between two overbearing needs.

He pulls back to look down at me, grinning wickedly. "What scares you, little fox? That you'll enjoy it or that you have to finally admit the truth of what you want from me?"

"I don't understand. You're going to make me your mate?" My mind fires up all kinds of scenarios where he'll leave me, because I wasn't good enough for Martell, so how can I be good enough for him? And what now? I need to be forced into a being with a mate?

"Think of it as a distraction to stop your wolf from pining for your fated mate. Unless, of course, you have every intention of returning to him." His hand slides over my shoulder and down my chest, cupping my breast.

A moan rolls over my throat, and I'm attuned to every single touch, every movement of his body against mine. He angles his hips to fit perfectly between my legs and presses his hard cock to the apex of my thighs. The warmth of his body on mine reminds me how tiny I am compared to him, how I know exactly what I'm doing, and yet I still blush.

Finding my voice, I ask, "What does marking me as yours really mean then?"

"That I'll allow your wolf to believe I am your fated mate, but there will be no painful longing, no agony for your soulmate. You will rarely find another fated mate. I'm giving you a gift, Narah. You ran from your soulmate, and now I'm going to make you forget him."

"I didn't run," I admit, unsure why I even told him, but the words rush past my lips regardless. "The bastard rejected me then he tried to kill me by throwing me off a cliff." I'm gasping hard at saying those words out loud as they awaken the agony of being thrown aside like I was nothing. The memory stings horribly.

But Ragnar doesn't react.

I turn my head from him, tears burning in my eyes, and suddenly a scorching embarrassment encases me, just as it must have done for the men revealing their secrets. I don't want to see the pity in his eyes, or worse yet, have him think of me as so unworthy that my own fated mate didn't want me. But there's nowhere for me to run when he's got me pinned under him.

He lowers himself closer and his mouth claims mine once more. Instead of hunger, this time he kisses me softly across my lips, luring me to him as sweetly as honey. A tear slides from the corner of my eye from the emotions burning inside me. His breathing intensifies and his fingers sliding across my jawline and holding me there as he breaks our kiss.

"I promise you, little fox, that I will destroy that fucking asshole for hurting you. I will make him endure unbearable suffering." The intensity of his stare comes with sincerity and he means every damn word. Instead of making me feel humiliated for uncovering my secret, he promises me retribution, he stands up for me.

He runs a finger under an eye, catching my loose tear. Despite his huge size and dominating demeanour, he is a man whose values are deeply seeped in loyalty to those close to him.

I shouldn't be excited by his promise, but it ignites a blaze deep within me. His desire is laced with mine, and feelings I shouldn't experience lurk under the surface. I don't want to think about what happens when we go our separate ways, or that I might pine for someone else like my wolf has been doing.

When he kisses me with promises of what he'll offer me, with giving me what Martell never could, a glimmer of hope chases away the worry.

My heart stutters at how easily I'm falling over the edge for Ragnar.

Every inch of my body seems to wake up, vying for his attention.

He licks my neck in long strokes as his hand tugs up my shirt, his actions rough and fast. Inching down my body, he pulls back the fabric of my bra and smiles at my exposed breasts.

I'm trembling, half tempted to cover myself, but there's something incredibly rewarding to have such a powerful Alpha study me like he'll destroy the world if anyone gets between us.

"You want to know my secret," he whispers, then runs his mouth between the valley of my breasts.

A humming sound is all I can manage as his tongue teases my breasts, making his way up to my nipples. "My fated mate rejected me too."

His mouth instantly falls onto my nipple and he suckles on me, while his hand glides down my stomach and opens the buttons of my pants.

I'm hit by a powerful arousal at the flick of his tongue. A simple touch ignites the fire of desire intensifying in the pit of my gut, and I don't think I could stop even if I wanted to.

Yet his words circle on my mind as his fingers circle my other nipple, and my wolf is there, reminding me I am making a huge mistake.

"Wait... is that true?" His soulmate rejected him too? What could have happened between them? And now, when I stare into his eyes, I see so much more than a powerful Alpha. He wears the scars of his past as protection. I wonder how long it will take me to be like him.

He groans a yes, then tugs on my nipple gently. I cry out with pleasure, easily forgetting what I'd just been thinking about. Before I can even get my bearings of what comes next, he lifts my legs and rests my ankles against his shoulders.

"I want to see all of you, if you're going to be mine." He smirks, and I'm breathing too hard to truly make sense of his words. He'd said this was a fake mating, right? To confuse my wolf.

His fingers curl under the band of my pants and underwear, then he tugs them over my hips and pulls them down my legs, then yanks them off past my boots.

I gasp at how quickly we're moving now, at how much I'm drowning under him that my mind can't catch up.

I don't see where he throws my clothes, because he's lying over me once more, and the heat from his chest flares over me, his scorching breath heating me up. He takes my mouth in his, and I grasp onto his strong shoulders, my fingers digging into muscles. I lift my head to kiss him back, needing this more than I need air.

"Are you sure this will work?" I whisper against the seam of his mouth. It has to work.

"How do you think I've dealt with losing my fated mate?" he answers as he pulls back to study me. My body flushes, which is the best way to describe the impulse to cover myself, to drag my clothes back on, terrified he'll hate what he sees.

He leaves a line of kisses down my stomach, and his tenderness chases away all thoughts. His broad shoulders spread open my legs the lower he drifts. Then he tilts his head up, wearing the most seductive smile. Goosebumps of excitement skim over my skin. How am I supposed to ever say no to him... yet the prominent thought on my mind is why would anyone leave a man like Ragnar? If he was mine, I'd destroy the world to hold onto him, to have him look at me like nothing else matters but me.

This is what I expected to feel and experience with Martell. I cringe internally as my thoughts rouse my wolf to whimper deep in my chest, and I curse myself for even thinking of that bastard in this perfect moment.

Ragnar shuffles lower and is now positioned with his face right between my legs, his strong hands on my inner thighs spreading me wider. Gently, he blows a breath on my exposed area, and I can't stop myself. I slide my hand quickly to cover myself, my cheeks burning.

"You expect me to help you like this?" he asks sarcastically, one of his eyebrows arching. I never thought I'd ever see a man down between my legs, let alone one that resembles a god, one who is so beautiful I might faint. I lose myself to Ragnar too easily.

Then he leans in, and his long tongue strokes across my fingers, tickling me, and I flinch my hand back. It's a split-second moment, and his mouth is on my pussy.

I cry out, my back arching with him taking me so hungrily. I don't know what to expect, but this... oh my fucking god, this is incredible. My experience with men has been nonexistent when it came to anything sexual. I've heard women talk about their experiences, seen the men stare at me, grope themselves, but none of that compares to the real thing.

To have a strong Alpha kneeling between my legs is reassuring in the best possible way, his face pushing closer to where I need him the most.

"You are fucking beautiful," he whispers, then runs his tongue in long strokes over nerve endings that come to life.

I shudder with each touch, my body on fire, and I need him to put out the flames. My pelvis lifts to meet every attentive lick while he slides a finger into me, teasing me just as he had back by the campfire.

It's hard to believe I'm outdoors being devoured by Ragnar. What stops the other men from coming and finding us? And the witches?

But that concern evaporates as quickly as it rises, leaving me utterly at the Alpha's mercy.

His tongue flicks faster, and we fall into a rhythm. A whimper rolls over my throat, my whole body squirming. I never expected Ragnar to go down on me, and I sure didn't expect my body to sing in response to his mouth.

The more he eats me, the harder he fingers me, the more intense the arousal crests within me.

"Please, go quicker." I moan, and he pulls away, gaining himself a loud, protesting snarl.

"Did you say something, little fox?" He licks his glistening lips, then presses two fingers into me.

My eyes widen, and I respond with my legs widening even more, excitement rending me a shivering mess.

"Good girl. I need you ready for me," he says.

I have questions about exactly how big he is to make such a statement, but when his mouth is on me again, I lose all logical sense. I flop down onto my back in the grassy field, floating on elation. This time he changes it up between licking me and suckling on my sensitive lips, sending jolts of excitement through my entire body.

The wet sounds his fingers make are deplorable and so sexy. So it's not a surprise when waves of euphoria crash through me so fast, I scream.

My knees squeeze around his head and I fist the grass, but he doesn't release me, only takes his fingers out and puts his tongue in me, never unleashing me from the precipice.

Toes curled, I shut my eyes and float on my climax, never wanting the moment to end. This is where I'd happily live for the rest of my life.

Ragnar finally releases his hold and gets to his feet, while I clench my thighs together, moaning with the last threads of pleasure tearing through me.

Collapsing onto my back, spent and breathing heavily, I stare up at Ragnar, who's managed to remove his clothes while I wasn't looking. And right now I can't stop staring at his erection, at how incredibly well-endowed he is, and I swallow hard.

"Don't worry, little fox, it will fit," he tells me while palming his cock a few times, hissing his anticipation.

That's when I take in all of him, all the hard and sharp lines of muscles, the strength he exudes. I shuffle to get up and kneel before him, then lift my head.

A savagery captures his gaze, and I reach over to clasp his large erection, the skin like silk, but beneath it's iron. In front of me is a man made of muscles, and his heavy cock sits in my hand. Yet my attention is drawn to the black handprint on his chest, his skin charred and blushing red around the edges. I did that to him, and guilt curls in my chest because there is no way to undo that damage.

He growls when I stroke him back and forth softly. His tip glistens with pre-cum, and I lean forward, my mouth parting, wanting him to know I have no intention of hurting him.

"No," he says and steps from my reach, his dick slipping from my grasp. "As much as I've fantasized about having those sweet cherry lips around my cock, today I will fuck you. I will give you what you've desired, what's driven me insane with lust. Lie down for me, little fox, and spread those gorgeous legs. Show me how wet you are for me." His voice is deep and full of lust, his eyes filled with a sexual haze.

I follow his instructions, not even blinking at obeying him, though lying on the flattened grass and him lowering himself on top of me brings a sense of trepidation. It's one thing to be fingered, but to take his size into me, to know that fucking an Alpha who is anything but normal slightly scares me.

My breathing grows ragged as he presses himself over me, caging me in, his erection nestled against the length of my wet pussy. I flinch at how big, how hot he feels, and I'm not so sure about doing this now. He knows it's my first time, and a small whimper spills past my lips, followed by my wolf growling, a deep, guttural sound in my chest. She's thrashing inside me for a way out, to escape, to stop me.

But Ragnar is right about breaking off the connection with Martell, even if it means confusing my wolf. I hate the notion that part of me yearns for a monster who tried to kill me. Everything is wrong with that, so despite my fear, I need to do this.

"Don't be afraid," he reassures me and covers my face with kisses so soft I lean toward him, longing to be in his arms. The strange lure he has over me is unexpected, as are his touches, which calm me.

I try not to think about what's coming and instead focus on the attention he pours over me. His hand slides between us and he adjusts himself, running the tip of his cock along my slick length.

My muscles tense, yet the longer he teases, the more I crave what he has to offer. There is something so dangerously delicious about him that my heart beats faster as he presses his tip into me.

I yelp at first as if I expect it to hurt, except it's the opposite.

"Take a deep breath," he explains, and the tendons in his throat move with his words. I want to lean in and lick his neck, to give him as much pleasure as he offered me.

Being honest with myself, I have been attracted to Ragnar since we first met, and when I'm nervous, I talk. "You want to know something?" I say.

"Of course." He inches into me, stretching my opening, going slow.

I clutch onto his strong arms, bracing myself for what he's about to deliver, and I wince at the slight ache. "I've also fantasized about you taking me." The words rush from my mouth.

He laughs, making a kind sound, not something to be ridiculed. "I know."

"No, you don't."

He drives deeper into me, and I groan louder. My thoughts center on the way he stretches me to the point of unbelievable arousal, to how the pain blends in with the desire, except I don't think he can make it all the way inside me. I'm not made for someone as big as him. And fear tugs at my chest.

"You're not going to fit."

He leans down and kisses me, sucking on my tongue, rousing the fire within me. "You will find greater pleasure with a touch of pain," he whispers, then he pushes deeper into me. "I am going slow, as this is your first time."

My eyes flicker upward, and my whole body jolts from the strange way my muscles relax around him, my inner walls embracing him, accommodating him.

"I meant what I said earlier," he says. "You will be mine after today."

"You mean for my wolf—" I cry out as he pulls out and plunges back into me so hungrily, my entire body shudders.

There's excitement in his eyes and his mouth claims mine again, stealing my screams, crushing my lips, all while being gentle.

I swallow past the fiery passion rising through me, and Ragnar starts going in and out of me faster, the friction between us electrifying. I want more.

"Are you okay?" he asks, but I can't answer. I'm shuddering with a desire that engulfs me, that feels like he's tearing me apart and putting me back together. Everything about the way he steals me from reality is like I'm smashed into a million pieces.

I nod my head and fall into the pattern of movement with him as he dives all the way into me, and I lift my pelvis to meet each of his thrusts. He growls deeply, the sound sexy as fuck and so demanding.

"Fuck, Narah," he snarls with satisfaction, dragging his cock in and out of me, stroking me, filling me, tilting his hips in such a way that he reaches deeper into a spot inside me he hasn't found yet.

Shivers race over me, triggering a sudden, unexpected orgasm. My stomach flutters and I growl, arching against him.

Ragnar also roars suddenly, being fully inside me, he stills and hisses. My pussy clamps down on his erection while my wolf awakens, surging forward, growling at Ragnar to back off. But I'm too busy moaning like whatever is bursting between us is magical.

He slides his mouth down to my neck, nibbling on the soft flesh between my neck and shoulder. Sharp teeth break skin, and he bites down into the flesh.

"Ow!" I whimper, while my pussy convulses from the orgasm. Ragnar slurps on my blood, burying his teeth into me, still pumping his seed into me like it's an endless supply. And I feel him then thickening inside me, growing.

My wolf groans and thrashes inside me, fighting against the bite, against Ragnar. And I don't know where to focus, as so much is happening at once.

Unbelievable pleasure.

Sharp, slicing pain.

And my wolf attempting to claw her way out of me.

Panic flares because on top of all that, Ragnar's knotting inside me. I know this, I've heard about how an Alpha's tip swells and my pussy tightens around him, keeping him stuck within me, unable to come out until we settle down, but to experience it scares the hell out of me. It's a strange sensation to have something expanding inside me.

I thrash against him while the pain in my neck stings. It's too much... everything is too much.

"Ragnar, I can't do this. Let me go, please."

He pulls back from my neck, licking his bloodied lips. "Take a deep breath, little fox. You will be okay." He groans, and I sense him still flooding me with his seed. "How does your wolf feel now?"

It takes me a moment to make sense of his words and to ignore the fear ripping me apart. I dig deep within myself to find her, and she's there, whining for Ragnar's connection. My thoughts automatically go to Martell, to see her reaction, but there's nothing.

I blink at him. "I think it worked."

"Of course it did." He smiles and tucks a hand against my back, the other pushing us up and off the ground. He's kneeling and I'm straddling him, his huge cock still embedded in me.

The pulse between my thighs throbs with having him buried deep.

"I will always keep my promises," he says and kisses my chin. "I won't hurt you, and your wolf will soften in her yearning for your fated mate. For now, we are locked together, but fuck me, Narah, you are so tight, I might go again."

Licking my lips, I can barely breathe, and my body tingles as he runs his fingers down my spine. His hand curls around my waist and up to my breast where he cups me in his large palm.

"How long does knotting take?" I whisper, not realizing until now that moving about stirs up unfathomable desires deep inside me. My focus dives to the fire between us, and a low growl rumbles in his chest.

"You are so fucking responsive to my touch." He breathes heavily before answering my question. "It all depends on how many more times I'll make you come while I'm inside you."

My mouth dries. "I'm going to climax from just this? And seeing where we are, that should be zero more times, right?"

He smirks, and I'm shaking my head, hating that we're out here so vulnerable, yet it doesn't seem to worry Ragnar.

"Rest against me, little fox. Let your body relax, as that will help."

I do as he asks and swing my arms around him, then nestle my face against the curve of his neck. His skin is soft against my lips, and everything about him smells inviting—musky and sexy—like it belongs to me. I don't feel shame for what we did. I felt adored and worshipped. Ragnar is a mesmerizing lover, but I worry if giving myself to him shows him my weakness for him. Every touch he delivers ignites all my nerve endings.

He is magnificent, and I can't deny that he calls to me. But he can't be my mate. Not when I'm trying to escape from one.

His hand strokes my back gently, which soothes away the tension. "You were perfect today." He kisses my shoulder tenderly.

We held each other for a length of time until he went down enough to slip from me, then with the both of us utterly exhausted, he picks me up and carries me back to where the other men have set up camp. They're by the river fishing and with my eyes closing, Ragnar lays me down by the fire and covers me with a blanket.

He brushes hair off my brow, and I'm on the verge of passing out when the last words I hear are, "We might just keep you after all."

CHAPTER
EIGHTEEN

Narah

Ragnar's words are all I've been thinking about all night and most of the morning after we had amazing sex yesterday.

We may just keep you after all.

That wasn't part of our deal, and as a result, I barely slept from confusion, from anger, from battling my own emotions that drew me to him... while he dozed off like a bear. All the while, my insides fought between hating him for thinking he gets to make such a call, and me buzzing with untameable desire each time I remember our time together.

His lips.

His touch.

His cock inside me.

Fuck!

I should have known it was a bad idea, but the thing is, I doubt I'd change anything if I had the chance.

That's why I'm furious... more at myself that his mere presence calls to me. The only other person who's ever done that to me was

Martell, so whatever is going on with Ragnar and me is hurting my head. Not to mention how I felt so calm against him after our sex that I fell asleep in his arms.

Of course it had been a terrible idea to have sex with him, and of course I knew better, but I succumbed to weakness. And in my defense, ignoring an Alpha like Ragnar is close to impossible. Whether it's his irresistible body, his scent, the way he touches me, or just that he gives me no choice with his temptation.

But I'm not fooling anyone. I went into that bonding with him with my eyes wide open, knowing exactly what I was walking into, and I hate myself for loving every single moment of it. I did it to eradicate a monster from my life, but have I made it worse?

My wolf has finally calmed down about her addiction to Martell, so that is something, right?

I push the strap of my bag up my shoulder, causing a sharp pain to dig into my arm. I wince and readjust it over the bite mark Ragnar gave me. The thing is, the wound is healed, except it's left behind dark teeth marks where he'd damned bitten me.

My hand grazes over the spot under my shirt, still tender under the pad of my fingers.

It was the only way to tame back my wolf, by showing her dominance. Except now, I worry that I've led my wolf astray. And that frustration and concern has me teetering on the edge of tears. I escaped the pack to save my sisters and me, and here I am being the problem, as I can't stop being drawn to these Alphas who seem to think I belong to them.

I glance over to Ragnar strolling through the woods several feet to my right, his shoulders back, and when his gaze meets mine, the wink he gives me melts me on the spot.

"You doing alright?" he asks.

I nod and offer him a soft smile. My wolf awakens instantly at his attention, whining for me to move closer, to reconnect, to claim what is ours. Ragnar insisted the mark would distract her from Martell and I'd no longer feel the lure he held over her.

But then why does the ache in my chest intensify for him, why does my desire grow to have him rip my clothes off and fuck me?

Those emotions overwhelm me and remind me a lot of the longing I experienced for Martell.

What I don't regret is losing my virginity to Ragnar, because I'd rather him than some other Alpha who'd hurt me... because beneath all the dominance, there is softness in Ragnar's soul. Something he keeps closely guarded from everyone.

Like me, his fated mate rejected him, and maybe that's what draws me to him. That we both share similar agony and embarrassment. While I'd like to ask him questions about what happened to him, I already pushed my luck with the other men, so I figure he can share with me what he wants when he's ready.

I lower my head, having noticed I've unconsciously swayed to walk closer by Ragnar's side, and I shuffle a few steps away again.

Crius strolls on my other side, and he breaks into a whistle, while behind me Stone and Nikos haven't said a word. In fact, they've been avoiding me since this morning. I can't tell if they are still annoyed with me over the whole secret reveal or whether they actually saw Ragnar and me in the field.

I don't care. I shouldn't care.

Taking a deep inhale, I push aside my mixed emotions. How being in Ragnar's presence now brings me to arousal almost instantly, how I want to throttle Stone and Nikos and make them stop hating me, how I'd like to find out more from Crius about why he thinks he deserves to be dead by now.

Everything about them is mysterious, and I've discovered things about them I never should have because now I feel partly invested. Okay, more than invested.

Shit. *Clear your damn head, Narah, and focus on the mission only. Not Ragnar and his huge cock, or any of the Viking Alphas.*

Mission.

Sisters.

Freedom.

Exhaling loudly, I stiffen my spine and repeat those words in my head.

Sunlight burns brightly over my head and shoulders, and the woods are different in this section of the forest. The trees are bigger, brimming with huge leaves and red globe fruit, the air smelling crisper and fresher too. We walk through the woods, my hands alight with magic, but there's nothing except beauty in this part of the forest.

"Does it feel like we've left behind the Poisonous Woods?" I ask, taking in the picturesque scene around us. Up ahead I spot a small deer bouncing across our path.

"We are definitely in a different location," Crius agrees.

"Do you sense anything, Narah?" Ragnar asks.

I shake my head and trip over a branch when I let my gaze linger a bit too long on how his dark hair flutters off his face, at how gorgeous he is.

He catches my arm and stops me from tumbling and becoming a laughingstock. "Careful, little fox."

My pulse thunders, and at his touch alone my wolf roars with desire. My breath hitches all the way down to my lungs, and I pull away quickly.

"Maybe walk close to me," he suggests.

Still holding Ragnar's gaze, I struggle to clear my foggy brain. My wolf is there, just below the surface of my chest, sniffing his earthy, musky scent, eager for his attention.

There is intensity in his eyes as he scans my body, and a pulse throbs between my thighs. Goosebumps flare over my skin. I'm more insatiable for him than before, but he stares at me with that same starved need.

In response, flickers of pleasure radiate through me, and part of me wonders if I could possibly drag him away and have my way with him again. But that thought also terrifies me. I'm now convinced whatever he did to me wasn't just a basic bonding to confuse my wolf. Hell, he's confused me too.

But I don't want to deal with that complication right now. Just get through this mission, then worry about the rest later.

"What's going on?" Crius demands, and when I lift my gaze, my cheeks flush, as I'm certain he's sensed my reaction to Ragnar.

Except when I turn to him, he's not even looking at me. His attention is on something ahead of us, and I glance in that direction too.

Amid the trees, there are two burning torches in the distance. They flank a shadowy gateway, and on either side of them spreads out a lofty fence made of twisted branches intertwined like snakes. There are no barriers to enter or anyone else in sight.

I pause along with the men, and silence descends upon us. If this is where the witches live, it's not what I expected. Though in truth I had no preconceived ideas except that it would be bigger. Grander. More powerful.

"So this is where they live, then?" Stone asks.

"I don't know," I answer, and I smell the scent of burning wood from a fire nearby.

"It's probably a maze," Nikos mutters.

"So do we go around it or enter?" Crius asks, all their attention swinging to Ragnar.

He skims his big palm through his hair, his lips pursed, and he looks at me. "What do you suggest?"

My breath catches.

"I will go and scope it out first," I answer. "It'll be safer that way, considering how the last spell went."

"Not happening," Stone snarls in response, and I can't tell if his words come from a place of mistrust or caring that I might get hurt.

"Best you don't go alone," Ragnar affirms, which is not an argument I want to have. If they are going to insist, fine.

I drop my bag on the ground, glad to alleviate the pressure from the bite mark, and that's when Nikos marches right past us. He covers the ground fast with no intention of slowing down.

My pulse thuds in my ears. "Nikos, that's not a good idea." I don't understand his stubborn ass most of the time.

"I got this," he growls, and his arrogance infuriates me.

Rushing forward, I catch up to him. When we are a fair distance from the rest of the group, I glare at him. "What the hell is wrong with you? What if you walk into a spell? Are you still upset about the bear thing? I didn't want to hear your stupid secret, okay, so get over it. Next time, I'll be sure to let you die."

I storm toward the torched entrance, getting really tired of dealing with so many emotions. This isn't the state I want to be in when potentially coming into contact with the witches. Distraction will get us all killed, but these Alphas are driving me insane.

Nikos is next to me in seconds, his shadow casting over me, his fingers curling around my arm, bringing me to a stop. "You're mistaken if you think this has anything to do with that last spell."

I frown, and a strange silence passes between us as my mind quiets, trying to make sense of his words. I only come up with one reason he could be upset with me. "I don't know what to say. Ragnar helped me with my wolf problem."

His jawline clenches. "I'm not talking about you and him fucking, because what you don't know is that we share everything in this pack. So what is Ragnar's is all of ours, which means each one of us will now want a taste. But that's not what I'm pissed at."

I blink at him, dumbfounded by his revelation, and I want to scream because I never agreed to this. "You're wrong, because what happened with Ragnar and I was a one-off thing to help control my wolf."

He laughs bitterly. "Tell me, Narah, how is your wolf reacting this morning to Ragnar? He marked you, didn't he? You know that bonds you to an Alpha whether you are fated mates or not? While you wear that mark, you will always crave him."

I shake my head as panic threads over my mind. After Martell, I'm not ready to get my hopes up and have them destroyed all over again. I wrench my gaze over to Ragnar, who is watching us intently like the other two Alphas are.

"The choice will be yours to allow the rest of us to mark you as well, just as you allowed Ragnar."

The hairs on my nape stiffen. This is happening too fast. I didn't come on this mission to find four partners who will make me pine after them. I have my sisters to find as priority.

"Please stop talking now."

The woods whirl around me while anger rises through me. *That bastard.* This isn't what I wanted, except he said I would no longer pine... or did he mean it was only Martell I'd stop pining for, but in fact I'd start drooling over him? I don't know, but I'm suddenly feeling sick to my stomach. I need to clarify this with Ragnar, I need to hear the truth from his lips. Already I feel queasy that he didn't tell me everything.

When I look at Nikos, he's not smirking, not seeming happy with making me feel like the world should open up and swallow me.

I don't put my faith in any of these Alphas. The more I get to know them, the more I question everything. What Crius said earlier is becoming more terrifying. These four Alphas are broken, and if I let them, they'll take me down to the pits of hell with them.

His brow furrows while my thoughts blur. To find my sisters, I need to track down the witches, then get the fuck out of this place and away from these men. Distance has to be the answer.

A twinge comes from the bite mark on my shoulder, a reminder of my predicament.

"Then tell me," I say, "what the hell has pissed you off? What could I have done now to make you hate me?"

"You think I hate you?" he asks, his soft tone taking me off guard. I'm reminded of our kiss on our first night in the Poisonous Woods, how he left me entranced with him, captivated in every possible way. "You're wrong, Narah. It's the fact that I was never meant to care for you or give a shit if you died. Instead, I question my own decisions to ensure I remained by your side. How fucked up is that?" His shoulders tense, but he never looks away.

Heat seeps into my chest and spreads outward. He wants to be with me to the point of not skipping out on Ragnar's pack? We've clashed from the very beginning, and sure, I've fallen prey to his looks and dominance, and the fact that he is an outcast like me makes me like him more than I should, but his revelation is not what I expect.

I suck in the cool air, shaking my head because he's got to be confused. "No, don't say stuff like that when it's not true. I'm leaving you all once this is over. That was the deal. Nothing else."

Ragnar's words came to mind again. *We may just keep you after all.*

"That's what pisses me off. I don't want anyone, but then you stormed into our lives."

I can't find my voice, unsure how to respond to him. Maybe these woods are messing with all our heads again. It's making us grasp for those near us to avoid admitting that this place scares the heck out of us.

There's no air going to my lungs as I try to process everything. But it's too much, and nothing settles down.

"I need to go," I murmur and hurry toward the open entranceway, needing air, to be alone so I can think.

The pieces around me refuse to fall into place about what I should do, what I want. I'm doing this for my sisters, so then why do I crave these men? Why does part of me not hate Ragnar for claiming me as his, while the rest of me is terrified he'll eventually reject me once he gets sick of me?

A sting flares across my chest, a hurt-filled resignation that I got into this mess in the first place by making a deal with Ragnar to find my sisters.

Nikos steps up beside me without a word, and we're both heading into unknown territory with heavy thoughts.

"Forget about what I said," he murmurs.

"You really think it's that easy?" I wish I could forget the whole damn mission.

He gives me a lopsided frown then turns his attention on the open gateway before us. The towering wall that stretches out on either side and vanishes into the woods sits ominously amid the trees. The open gateway is made of twisted and gnarled wood, the tops of the door spiked with sharp pieces of wood reaching up for the sky. My skin crawls at going in there, but this is what we came here for.

The crunch of foliage sounds behind us, and I twist around to find Stone joining us. "Figured you could use another set of hands but wanted to first give you space to work out your lover's spat there." He cocks a look over to Nikos, then me. His words carry mirth, and I can't tell if he's mocking us or being a jealous ass. That's when I notice the blue glow of his runes from beneath his white shirt, and despite his rudeness, I'm glad to have him by my side as well.

"Okay, let's go inside," I say.

We step over the threshold, and a shiver snakes up my spine. Golden lines of power frantically dance across my fingers, the sharp prickle of magic running up my arms.

"Let me enter first," I tell them.

Inside the doorway, I am faced with another wall made of entwined branches so high that there is no way to easily breach it. On either side of me is a narrow path that is nestled between the two walls. Each stretches out for close to twenty feet, then curves out of sight.

When I glance over to the men who've followed me, Stone flicks his hand for Nikos and I to go to the right and he'll take the left.

We move hastily until we career around the bend.

I pause dead in my tracks, my heart slamming into my ribcage as we stare at an enormous opening that spills into a tremendous open land. There are dozens of small wooden huts, lofty trees with homes built in the sturdy branches, and people roaming about, males and females, along with kids. Families live within the safety of these walls, and suddenly panic jabs into my chest about Ragnar's intentions here.

Magic claws down my back, and my breaths come too fast. There's an invisible force tugging me forward by my chest to enter the grounds and join them, but I dig my heels into the ground, terrified to move.

"Fuck yes, we found them," Nikos whispers beside me. "I need to get the others."

"No, wait!" I say, but he's already sprinting back the way we came, and there's no sign of Stone. A coldness chills my bones.

Something feels wrong. Why wouldn't the entrance to the witches' coven be better guarded? This is too easy... it's a trap. It has to be.

I swing back around to the small village but instead come face to face with someone who wasn't there seconds ago.

A young woman with two black lines drawn across her cheeks and two more across her brow and the reddest curly hair bouncing over her shoulders. She greets me with a darkened smile, but I'm lost in her completely white eyes.

I flinch backward, stumbling away from her outstretched arm.

She steps closer, and her words invade me. "You finally made it."

NINETEEN

Ragnar

Narah doesn't leave my thoughts. She invades every inch of me, and I'm fucking obsessed. I can still feel her soft body beneath me, hear the sexy sounds she makes, taste her on my tongue. She's delicious, and I suspected from the beginning that if I let myself go too far with her, there'd be no turning back.

I knew it, but I couldn't stop. And when I saw the hunger in her eyes, I fell hard. She gave me the gift of being her first, and for that, I will forever be hers. Now I just need to convince her of that.

The line between my mission and Narah blurs with each passing day, and that raises an alarm in my head that I'm losing control.

Helping her with her fated mate problem had been genuine on my part, though another reason had been to eliminate that prick from her head. The thought of him consuming her thoughts and capturing her wolf's attention rips me apart. It drives me to insanity, and if we weren't in these cursed woods, I'd already be on his doorstep, ripping his head off his fucking shoulders.

When she told me he tried to kill her, it seemed an invisible blade had been jammed into my heart, and it's remained there ever since, twisting with my agony and anger growing. Without really meaning to, desire for her seizes me by the fucking balls. With her, I long to claim her until I feel her coming apart at my touch.

For her, I will start a war, sell my soul, lose control. She consumes me to the point of madness, and I crave so much fucking more. Blood rushes through my body, my adrenaline unrelenting.

I'm going out of my mind, and now all I can think about is praying we've arrived at the witches' land to get the mission started. To take ownership of the Savage Sector and then keep Narah by our sides. She reminds me of something in me, the part in my heart that fights savagely to win, and I adore her tenacity, her fiery passion.

My cock twitches for her. After I marked her, something changed between us. It bound us in a way I never expected, and I want more. I fucking need more.

"You okay?" Crius asks, glancing my way. "You're grunting under your breath."

Anger bubbles to the surface, but any response I'd intended is taken by the shrill whistle from across the woods.

I tense and raise my head to the gated entrance up ahead.

Nikos and Stone are both waving us over. My pulse spikes and I'm ready to fight, ready to stop drowning in all these goddamn emotions.

"This is it," Crius coos, practically bouncing on his toes. His jaw clenches, and burning energy radiates from him.

"Calm down," I say, placing a hand on his shoulder. "Save it for when the time arrives. Until then, don't lose your head."

He nods, and when he meets my gaze, his eyes are wild with adrenaline, with his eagerness to be blessed by the gods. My grip squeezes. He's been by my side for so long that I trust him without question. And with the witches, he's our secret plan should shit go sideways. Though I pray it doesn't come to that, as I'm not ready to lose my closest friend.

The thought has me balling my hands into fists. This has to work my way.

We cross the silent woods on long strides, the smell of a fire floating in the air. I scan the entrance, where the other two stand.

"Where's Narah?" I ask, noting she's nowhere in sight. They both look behind them and past the entrance, then back at me.

"She's just inside. But Ragnar, we hit the jackpot. The witches are here, so many of them. Fuck, we've made it to where no one else has." The runes on Stone's chest burn a bright blue.

I clear my throat, my pulse on fire to get this over with, and yet all I can think about is keeping Narah safe. "Okay, so we know the plan. We also keep Narah close. Are you ready to make a deal with the devil?"

"Fuck yeah!" Nikos snarls. Stone nods, while Crius is breathing fast and shallow, his gaze darkening.

"Let's go." I march past the entrance, swinging my attention left and right. No sign of Narah, setting a chill in my veins.

"She was just there." Nikos points to my right, and I dart down a passage flanked by lofty walls made of tightly knitted branches. But my mind darkens as I curve around the bend and emerge in front of an open clearing. Trees and huts line the distance, but my gaze lands on a witch with burning red hair dragging Narah by the arm toward the village.

A possessive snarl rolls over my throat. Over my dead body will they take Narah from me.

I glance over to my men behind me, pointing ahead, and in seconds we charge after them with fire on our heels.

Narah

"Stay down!" The witch pushes me to the ground with unbelievable strength, and I'm no fool to think that's all brawn... she's using her power. My skin ripples, the hair on my neck shifts, and magic rips over my fingers. Even the land trembles under my touch, the whole area a beacon of powerful enchantment.

I clench my jaw despite panic rearing through me at how easily we've walked into a trap. How I knew better but let distractions in the form of four gorgeous Alphas blindside me.

I twist my head back, expecting the red-haired witch to attack me, but instead she's watching four huge figures rushing toward us from the entrance.

My gut hardens at the oncoming force.

My Vikings!

Devastation floods me that this will end badly for them, that they can't possibly defeat the witches. The power I sense is astronomical—how can they defend themselves against such a powerful coven? Initially, I didn't care what happened to them, but now... fuck. Now, I am dying on the inside to think that they are going to end up dead.

Still, they move like lightning, spearing across the open land.

Ragnar leads the charge, and my heart catapults into my ribcage. There is something ferocious, animalistic in the way he moves. It's almost predatory, lower to the ground, each fast step calculated. The three others, just as deadly as him, funnel outward, ready to take out anyone who stands in their way. They are like nothing I've seen before, their presence humming with their own power.

Ragnar's sharp gaze never leaves the enemy, the witch standing before them without fright. There is nowhere to hide when the land is this expansive and exposed, when the coven would sense all intruders. I see that now. With her earlier words to me, I am now more convinced than ever that the reason we arrived in one piece to their home is because they allowed it.

I shove myself to my feet just as the witch raises an arm at the approaching men, murmuring incomprehensible words.

"Stop, don't hurt them!" I yell.

Suddenly the air ripples outward from the witch's hands.

Terror jolts through my body that she'll hurt them, and I pivot in her direction. Without thinking, I charge at the woman, my hands sparking with energy. I call to my power from the deepest pits within me. Dark, menacing, and violent magic whips against my insides, raging to release everything. And that includes my wolf, who snarls for freedom. My skin itches with the force she imposes, with the desperation to come out.

I collide into the witch's back, slapping my hands to the sides of her head, and unleash everything I have. Fire erupts from my fingertips and pours into the woman.

She screams, bucking against me, her hands flinging toward mine.

I groan as power gushes out of me, and I do nothing to stop it with anger pushing me to never stop.

Something sharp strikes me in the middle of the back so unexpectedly, I roar with pain and stumble backward, my legs buckling beneath me. The red-haired witch is on the ground, bellowing with agony, clasping her head, while I cry from my own pain zigzagging across my back.

Shadows cast over me, and I jut my head up to find three females surrounding me, all adorned with similar face paintings, with power and fury in their eyes. They move with speed, not saying a word, while I drive my hands toward them, my power shoving them backward. More came, and I fling my arms, my power burning whatever I touch. They scream and retreat only to be replaced by two more witches.

"Let me go," I yell, thrashing and pushing for release.

I kick and hurl spears of golden magic against them when the icy cold kiss of steel clamps around my neck abruptly from behind. Frantically I grab for the metal shackle, pulling at the collar.

"Take it off me, take it off!" I shout, my body shuddering with rage. Everyone backs away from me, and that's when I see the magic on my hands has flatlined. Dread seeps into my bones that they blocked my power, that I'm rendered useless while they overpower us.

I turn on the spot, terrified, needing to run out of here, but that's when I find the four Alphas suspended in the air by an invisible force. Another witch has them caught in her web. They are clawing at their throats, their faces losing color.

Tears carve a track down my cheeks, and I rush to Ragnar, reaching for his legs. The touch shoots a jolt of electricity into me that tosses me aside. I land on my ass but scramble back up just as quickly, unbreakable anger rising through me.

"Release them," I scream at the group of witches, a collection of males and females all watching with amusement. Black paint decorates their faces too, which is the only element linking them, for they are dressed in normal clothing. Not black gowns as I had imagined. But it is strange that not one of them has dark, burned fingers like me. Not one.

But no one responds to me or even shows a sliver of emotion for the men's plight.

The air hums with their power.

"Please, don't harm them," I plead, hating that I should ever grovel to the witches, yet my wolf growls in my chest, revealing my true nature. These witches are part of who I am, but I don't fit with them, now do I? I am a half-breed, yet the way they look at me is filled with strange wonder and amusement rather than disdain.

"Intruders have no place on our sacred land, especially beasts." A female steps forward, someone maybe in her late twenties, and she carries herself with an authority that has others cowering in her presence. She's taller than me, her hair black as night, cascading over her shoulders in soft waves. The simple dress she wears is the color of violets and follows her every curve. In the center of her brow, she has a black mark in the shape of a crescent moon. Mother once told me covens were governed by a Grand High Witch, and I can only guess that's who approaches.

"But for you, Narah, I will honor your one request." She speaks my name so easily, like it's been on her tongue many times before. But how does she know me?

"I am part wolf like them, so that makes me a beast too," I retort.

"Yes, it does, but I can deal with that when you carry the power we want." She turns to the witch who captured the men and lays a hand on her shoulder. "That's quite enough."

The Alphas abruptly drop out of the air.

They growl furiously as they crumble onto their asses, but nothing holds them down for long, and they are up in seconds. I hurry to their sides, meeting Ragnar's gaze. The trepidation that lines his eyes worries me.

I tug at the metal brace around my neck, but the head witch responds before I can ask. "Stop wasting your time, Narah."

"How do you know who I am?" I demand, a snarl rumbling in my throat.

But it's Ragnar's voice that resonates as he steps alongside me, his presence towering over me. "I call upon the Lupus Pact, the ancient rule of magic between wolves and witches that must be adhered to once invoked."

His words confuse me at first, and I don't know what he's talking about. I've never heard anyone speak of a Lupus Pact.

The witch tilts her head to the side, studying Ragnar from head to toe. "Do you have a name, boy?" she asks, and I can't help but wonder how old she really is with the way she addresses Ragnar as if she is so much older than him.

"Ragnar," he states matter of factly, his earlier aggression tamed. It impresses me how well he controls himself, and I note he doesn't give away details of his pack name or that of his parents. Knowledge is power to a witch.

"I see you are well versed in the old ways, and you also bring two men with you who carry the flame of magic. I'm impressed."

Two? I frown and glance behind me to Stone, whose runes glow blue through the fabric of his shirt, but who is the other? Crius, Nikos?

Crius paces back and forth in a small circle just behind Ragnar, agitated and frazzled like any moment his wolf might spill out. What is wrong with him?

"Then you know that anyone who doesn't partake in the Lupus Pact once announced will be cursed," Ragnar states.

She nods. "This I am. You may call me Lyra. Now that you have my attention, boy, speak your mind, as the reason I'm here does not concern you. It's only the girl I care for, and my patience grows thin."

At her words, Ragnar's arm lashes out across my waist and he drags me to his side, rousing my wolf to rustle for freedom. My heart flutters at Ragnar's touch, at his possessiveness.

"Just so we are clear, she is one of mine," he states, then he lifts his chin, his chest sticking out. "Additionally, my pack and I have claimed the Savage Sector, including this forest, and as part of our rule, we will leave your coven alone. No witch will be harmed under my rule. Do we have an agreement?"

Silence permeates the air. My breaths rush, and my wolf is there, shoving against me to escape, but right now I need my magic instead of her. Panic curls under my breastbone. I had no clue of Ragnar's plan to come in and stake his claim over the land, to force the witches' hand. I wish I had found out beforehand so I could have steered him differently, though I doubt he would have listened to me. Of course, everything seems so much clearer in the aftermath of mistakes.

"Ragnar, you barged in unannounced into my home, so you do realize that renders the truce void," Lyra states, the corners of her mouth curling upward. She's a beautiful woman, but there's darkness behind her deep green eyes.

Her shoulders straighten, and she raises a hand encased in an orb of dark light. With it comes a spark of magic in the air that rubs against my arms, and my skin itches under the shackle around my neck.

"To show you I have no ill intent toward you," she begins, taking a step forward, "you and your wolves can leave unscathed. That does not mean if we ever cross paths again you will be safe from my wrath. You do anything otherwise, and I will skin each of you alive this very second," she threatens, her voice hoarse and loud. "Narah remains with us."

Ragnar barks out a burst of laughter, a mocking sound. "You take me for a fool. I am not here to negotiate, Witch. I am telling you the manner in which the Savage Sector will now be reigned. I am offering you freedom from the hatred and persecution from the wolves beyond this forest. You will no longer need to hide in here like mice. And in exchange, you will not stand in my way. Plus, as I said, Narah is mine and will not be leaving my side," he growls, his arm around me tightening.

"What do you want with me?" I ask Lyra, curious and needing to understand what they see in me.

The woman turns her attention on me, as does everyone watching us in silence. It is unnerving to have so many eyes scrutinizing me, but I swallow past the thickness in my throat and hold my head high.

"You will stay with us as your sister Kaira has done."

My insides freeze over. This is a surprise I hadn't expected. "Wait! M-my sister?" My voice stutters, and I stumble forward, but Ragnar holds onto me by my waist, keeping me locked to his side. "She's here and alive?"

I knew the dead body Ragnar had found wasn't Kaira.

"If that is the case," Ragnar interjects, his grip around me stronger, like he'll fight to the death before releasing me, "bring Kaira forward."

I can't help but fall madly for Ragnar in that moment for being the logical one.

Stone and Nikos move out on either side of us now, creating a wall of us against them, and I'm with them, not on my own for a change.

Yet my breaths choke in my throat, and every emotion I've been holding in pours out, and I'm crying... happy tears that she's alive. Of course I told myself that, but the lingering doubt never left me.

"Where is she?" I gasp, scanning the crowd, half expecting her to run out toward me, to call out my name, to see her crying. My arms shake by my sides. Maybe this is why they allowed us to arrive here. Because of my sister.

"You must make a choice," Lyra states. "Your sister or the wolves."

"Where is Kaira?" I demand, my gaze searching the crowd.

But it's Crius shifting behind us who distracts me, his pacing growing intense, and it's starting to get on my nerves.

"Let me do it," he growls in Ragnar's ear. "They're fucking lying, the lot of them. This is the time." His eyes are fully dilated, his body is jittery while he breathes raggedly.

"Are you okay?" I whisper to him over my shoulder.

He nods and quickly jerks his attention back to the witches, his upper lip curling upward in a silent snarl. I reach over to touch his arm in an attempt to calm him when a spark of electricity zips up my arm from his skin. I gasp and snap my hand back.

And realization hits me. He's the second. Crius also carries magic. How could I have not picked up on it? Why have they kept so many secrets from me?

Ragnar shakes his head. "Hold still, Crius."

What is Crius going to do?

Lyra stands tall, her narrowing gaze on us darkening. She raises her hand, one encased in a black smoke just like the kind on the bears that attacked the men. She's not stupid and must sense something is very wrong with Crius.

A shiver wracks over my body that I know so little about them, that they kept me in the dark. Whatever Crius has planned will bring the witches' wrath down on us all, and there will be no way for me to protect them.

But Crius never stops pacing, and he's scratching frantically.

"Ragnar," I whisper frantically. "What's wrong with Crius?"

"What's your decision, Narah?" Lyra demands, dragging my attention back to her. "You choose your sister or the wolves?"

I swallow hard and look into the depth of her eyes, swearing I see flames behind them. "I asked to see Kaira first."

"And I won't ask again. You must make a decision, or this ends now." The black smoke on her hand ignites into long flames, and the corners of her eyes smile as if she's enjoying this. There is no impatience from her side, only delight in making us squirm.

I tell myself she's bluffing, except I'm shaking and not ready to take such a risk that I might be wrong.

Her command is delivered with finality, and I understand the message beneath her malicious tone, that choosing the witches will mean I never see the wolves again. Lyra will kill them, that is clear. I choke on my breath, and with it comes a reminder that Jae is still hidden who the hell knows where. And I won't leave Jae at the wolves' mercy, lost in the world outside.

My cheeks feel itchy from the tears that refuse to stop falling. How am I supposed to pick between my sisters? I press my lips together, knowing that whatever I decide will destroy me.

My throat seems to close up on me, and when I look back at each of the four men, desperation to save them grips me.

"I don't take pleasure in this," Lyra says with mirth in her voice.

"We are not leaving until you return Kaira. Trust me, Lyra, you do not want to push me on this point," Ragnar promises, his voice heavy and powerful.

Suddenly, a figure is shoved forward from the masses and emerges into the opening before us. Someone dressed in a deep blue dress that falls to her ankles, cinched at a tiny waist, and when I look at her adorable face, her freckles and the short brown hair tucked behind her ears, a cry spills past my lips.

"Kaira," I murmur, my heart beating so hard, it weighs me down. I tug against Ragnar's grip, but he doesn't release me.

I swing my attention back to him. "Let me go." Anger spews from my voice.

He's shaking his head, his brows pinched with a savage anger. "Something's not right."

"What are you talking about?"

It's only when I glance back at my sister that I watch her strolling to Lyra's side, not running to me like I'd imagined, that I begin to understand.

My heart clenches, and panic rears its head as some of the pieces start making sense. She's always carried magic like me, so has she found solace among the witches after escaping the Storm Wolves? But it doesn't explain her behavior now.

I love you, Narah, were the last words she'd said to me before she escaped into the woods. But the confident girl standing before me who wears black lines of magic across her face doesn't resemble my sister. That girl feared Alphas, cried so many nights for our parents when she thought no one noticed, and once asked me if there was a way to burn the magic out of her veins so she could be normal.

"Kaira," I call to her, pushing against Ragnar, the shackle on my neck biting into my flesh.

Yet she leans in to Lyra and whispers, lowering her eyes from me. There's a whimper in my chest, my wolf sensing the ache of my sister's distance. So many questions fill me as I stare at every move she makes, how she seems to care more about impressing Lyra than returning to me.

Fear plunges to my core that they brainwashed her, that she is so far gone I may have lost her. When she glances back at me and approaches, there's a strange grin on her face, one that terrifies me.

"I've missed you," she tells me, but it doesn't sound sincere. Her rejection is more than a brutal slap in the face—it's a savage reminder that this world will break every single one of us.

I shiver as she strolls toward me, smiling. On the inside, I shred to pieces. I only have my sisters left in this world, and I can't lose Kaira. My knees weaken at the thought, and I stand there numb, my brain shooting off instructions, but I can't move. All I can think about is how distant she is from me. I watch her every movement, trying to make sense of every gesture. Flashes of memories from growing up lash into me—her and me hunting in the woods for our meals, us crying after we lost our parents when we thought Jae wasn't watching, how Kaira would fix my hair before I attended the pack meetings and even my mating night with Martell.

But now, her overly-sweet voice makes me sick.

I hear Crius muttering things to Ragnar, but I'm too distracted to pay attention.

"Careful," Stone whispers from my right, while Nikos takes a step forward, expecting the worst.

I search my sister's face for anything familiar, for a sliver of who she used to be. "Kaira, what happened to you?" I murmur, my voice breaking.

"Stop wasting time, sister," she presses, pausing several feet in front of me. This close, she looks older, like she's aged so much in such a short time. "You must bring Jae here too. It's safer than out there. I convinced Lyra to spare your wolves... for now. And she has another offer for you."

"Why are you acting this way?" I ask, my knees buckling at the heartbreak shattering me.

"Listen well, Narah." And that's when I catch a slight tremble in her voice, the giveaway that something so much deeper is going on here, that she may have her hands twisted to follow Lyra's instructions. Behind her, the Grand High Witch waits like a hungry lion, waiting to pounce.

"Maybe there's a way to make you understand why you belong here and not with the wolves. Why you chose the wrong side, sister, and if you don't open your eyes this very moment, you will lose so much."

Her words ring in my ears... there's something so familiar about them, like I've heard them before.

My fingers curl into fists, Ragnar's presence against my side a reminder that I'm not alone in this... except does he really care about Kaira or just gaining the witches' approval of his leadership over the sector?

I shudder, and that's when Kaira's words return like a storm from the vision I had, the one where she had face paintings and said those exact words to me.

You chose the wrong side, sister.

I'm shaking my head, and all warmth has slipped from my body, my heart pounding in my ears. The same devastating feelings fill me as they had in the vision where Kaira wasn't herself, where she had her own agenda, and where she sacrificed Jae by distracting me.

I back away, the nightmare playing out on my mind flooding me with a darkness that tilts the world on its side. Something is broken with this picture, and unease twists my insides.

"What's your offer," Ragnar states, but I pull hard on his hand.

"We need to leave. Now." The words tear free from my lips as a chill races up my spine, because suddenly I don't trust Kaira. This isn't my sister, it can't be. If my vision is any indication of what's coming, then I can't trust Kaira.

"Our mother is still alive, Narah," Kaira says, then smiles. Her words bring me to an abrupt halt. If I thought that finding Kaira alive rattled me, her new revelation punches me in the solar plexus. I can't breathe.

"What did you just say?"

"Our mother is the reason we lost Father, why you were rejected from the Storm Wolves' pack, and why you will always be hunted down for what you are. She is the reason why those in this coven hide in the woods. She left you, me, and Jae at the mercy of the wolves, knowing we'd end up dead under those savages, which is what she hoped for. So what do you think she'll do to us when she discovers we are free from the pack?"

My head swims, my vision darkening in patches. Nausea billows in my belly. This is too much.

Tears sting my eyes at her suggestion that our mother wanted us dead, that her fake death somehow caused our father's. Ragnar holds me upright. I would have fallen over if it wasn't for him.

"Narah, listen to me," Kaira continues. "You and Jae are in danger out there. Bring her here with us. And whatever you do, never let Mother find you."

BROKEN WOLF

SAVAGE SERIES

BROKEN WOLF

Is there such a thing as second chances?

Our mission is simple: track down my mother and find a way to save my sister from the witches. Should be easy, except in our world, nothing ever goes to plan, especially when you're traveling with four sexy, Viking Alphas who are ready to start a war to take ownership of the Savage sector... and me!

The more I spend time with them, the more I feel my mind, body, and soul bending to their wills and desires. This complicates things, especially when my past returns with vengeance.

As if that wasn't bad enough, the dangerously wicked Alphas I've grown close to have been cursed to remain by my side whether they want to or not, making it much harder to trust them.

ONE

NARAH

"Narah, listen to me," Kaira says in a rushed, clipped voice. "You and Jae are in danger out there. Bring her here with us. And whatever you do, never let Mother find you."

My wolf rages within me, begging to steal my sister and forcefully shake some sense into her fighting for dominance.

But I also hate being lied to, especially straight to my face.

My sister should know better, and maybe she does. Maybe that's her intention after all, to make me question her sincerity, because the girl in front of me can't be my sister. This Kaira looks at me with a frozen stare. She's distant and hasn't even hugged me since I found her with the witches. My younger sister used to hug whoever smiled at her back in our town, so something is very wrong with her. And she wants me to bring our youngest sister, Jae, here and put her in danger?

What have they done with my Kaira?

I sweep my gaze across the witches' land, at the amassing crowd, at the High Witch, Lyra. She stands behind my sister like a puppet master, studying me.

Kaira's under the influence of magic, I know she is, and dread bunches up in my chest. She's caught in a spell, just like the cold steel shackle around my neck put there by the witches to suppress my magic. It's the only explanation for her behavior, and I desperately want to snap her out of the haze.

She draws closer, her attempt to appear sorrowful failing. "Sister, please. You did so much to protect us growing up. Now give me the chance to save you." Her hand reaches out toward me, wanting me to take it and come with her.

But my defenses rise.

Ragnar, still holding me, locks his arm around my middle, refusing to let me go.

We shouldn't be here. I feel the magic, the trepidation in my bones. Lyra knew we were coming, she had to know, and unless I get Ragnar and his men out, they'd fight—and die—soon enough. Something in my gut twists and tightens at the idea that they'd die under my watch.

Ragnar came here to stamp his ownership over the land, to sway the witches under his protection, hoping to leverage their power. It really shouldn't surprise me...it's what Alphas do. They fight for territory or women in this broken world, and I hate that females are seen as nothing but objects.

But I'm no fool.

I carry magic, as does Kaira, making us feared by many and wanted by others. Why else would Lyra be so interested in us? She must assume Jae is the same. Maybe by some miracle, Kaira hadn't told her our youngest sister has shown signs of magic. Otherwise, why would they want her too?

I lift my gaze to Ragnar, catching his attention. His face is fierce. He's well versed in the game of negotiations, though even he must know when to cut his losses.

"We need to leave," I say. "Now."

He doesn't protest but gives me a slight nod, which I'll admit surprises me. I expected more of a fight.

"They leave, not you," Lyra barks, green eyes narrowing on me when I turn back to look in her direction.

My heart thumps in my ears because she's crazy if she thinks I'll leave Jae out there alone or deliver her to them. Kaira has been spelled by Lyra, by these witches, so there is nothing to trust about them.

I need to get her out.

I rack my brain and with it comes a solution that I pray works. I lift my head and address the High Witch of the coven with a strong voice. "Ragnar called upon the Lupus Pace, and you corrected him by stating we barged unannounced into your home, making the truce void." I swallow hard as I spin lies on the spot, seeing as I'd never heard of Lupus Pace. But I got the gist when Ragnar invoked it and that it's some sort of protection rite between magic users.

"What are you getting at?" Lyra asks, one of her eyebrows arching, her gaze sharp.

Ragnar's men: Stone, Nikos, and Crius, close in on us, waiting for me to speak.

"That Ragnar's summoning for our immunity stands. I was hauled into your home against my will. I hadn't entered before one of your coven pulled me in, and these men, they are my protectors. They did what they were hired to do and came to my rescue because of your actions." My heart is thundering now, and it takes every inch of strength to not show her how much I tremble on the inside.

"She *was* beyond the entrance," hissed the red-haired witch who dragged me here in the first place.

"Standing in your doorway does not equate to barging in," Ragnar states. "Narah makes a valid argument."

Lyra's lips pinch, while Kaira just watches me like she's not even listening to our conversation. I can't even tell if my sister is aware of what is going on or if she's so heavily spelled that she's waiting for her next command.

I turn my attention to Lyra, holding myself tall. "As such, by the rule of Lupus Pace, we have the right to passage and to leave unharmed."

She strolls toward us, her dark hair seeming to flutter on a breeze that doesn't exist, her violet dress hugging her curves. She pouts her lips and thrusts her full breasts forward. Her gaze is on Ragnar, staring at him, her ruby lips stretching into a smile.

I loathe her even more for the way she looks at him.

"Everything comes at a price," she purrs, her voice sensual and smooth.

A jolt of jealousy spears through me at her attention toward

Ragnar, at the way she pauses near him, running her hand across his chest. My insides burn at the sight.

The urge to reach out and shove her away eats at me. Which I know is insane...Ragnar isn't mine, yet my wolf surges forward, wanting me to lunge at her for touching him. The bite mark he gave me flares over my shoulder, stinging.

His arm remains tight around my waist, his body tensing against my side. But he stands solid, not pushing Lyra away either.

Jaw clenched, he shoots her a sharp glare. "I'm listening."

She grins and speaks a few incomprehensive words under her breath.

My skin prickles, and I steel myself for what's coming our way.

The rest of the coven suddenly starts humming, their eyes shut, except for Kaira. She smirks at us, and a dark flash of something savage glints behind her gaze.

"They're spelling us," I say, shoving against Ragnar, needing to get them out. I desperately grab at the metal shackle around my neck, needing it off so I can access my magic.

With a swift electric snap, my back arches, as do the wolves. My chest tightens. I can't breathe, yet something is building within me.

A sense of fear grips me, and I'm tearing at my throat, my lungs desperate for air.

It feels like I'm being squeezed from the inside out. Energy crackles in the air, dancing along my skin, and I'm convulsing violently.

My lungs contract, and I'm suffocating, scratching at the shackle on my neck.

Suddenly, my throat opens, and I'm gasping for it, sucking in as much as possible. Leaning forward, hands on my knees, I draw in deep breaths while my skin crawls. What the heck had they just done to us?

The men are drawing in heaving breaths, coughing and smacking fists into their chests, trying to get more air.

Crius roars and shoves past Ragnar. He reaches Lyra and snatches her by the throat. "What the fuck was that?" he growls.

Her startled eyes widen, but she instantly throws her hand out and touches his brow. Next thing I know, Crius is flying across the ground like he's nothing but a discarded dead animal. He slams to the ground and rolls a few times before coming to a dead stop.

My heart's thumping at how easily she disposed of him.

He groans and starts pushing himself up. Thank goddess he's not dead.

"You're not the only ones who can bend the rules to suit your-selves," Lyra says, and I hear the smile in her voice before I even turn to be greeted by her lecherous grin.

I really do hate everything about this woman, and each time she glances over at Ragnar, a deeper sense of revulsion comes over me. I feel desperate to do something, like I should be the one to stop her, since I carry magic.

"You can stop all the theatrics now," Ragnar growls. "Speak straight, witch! What did you just do?"

She flicks her hair from her shoulders, seeming rather proud of herself. "You are leaving against my wishes by using the ancient call of protection, but do you think I'm an idiot? What you just felt is a curse I've bestowed upon each of you." She spits the words out, rubbing her neck where Crius had grabbed her.

"Cursed?" I murmur.

"For fuck's sake," Nikos bellows. "What will happen to us?"

My skin pricks at her admission...The bitch cursed us! "For how long?" How the hell do we break it?

"Bring me Jae and I will free you," she explains nonchalantly.

"No," I blurt. "That's not happening. Remove the curse now!" I'm tired of feeling used. It's hard enough living as an outcast with wolves. I don't need a curse from the witches on my ass, too.

"What does the spell do?" Stone asks bitterly, his shoulders curving forward like he's going to lunge at her any second now.

The corners of her mouth curl up. She's loving every moment of our panic.

Crius grabs Ragnar's shoulder, looking pale. "I've got this. Get out of the way."

"No, you don't," Ragnar drawls and pushes him back, shoving a hand against his chest.

Lyra unleashes a sharp cackle. "On our land, our rite is more than words to ensure you don't go against it. Return with Jae before the next full moon, or you'll each suffocate to death at midnight, one at a time, with you, Narah, going last." She meets my gaze. "I want you to watch them die as you remind yourself their deaths are your fault."

I feel sick to my stomach, and I throw myself at her, overcome with blinding-white rage.

Ragnar catches me around the middle and yanks me back, pulling me to his chest. "It's okay, little fox, I know you can rip her throat out, but not now."

Lyra chuckles at his words.

I'm having trouble thinking logically when I just want her to hurt. I'm shaking, tears pricking my eyes at how mad I am.

"Narah," Kaira calls to me, drawing my attention. "Don't be stupid. Bring Jae and save yourself."

But I'm shaking my head, fury digging into me that my own sister isn't on my side, that we so blindly walked into this trap. I should have asked Ragnar more questions, should have done more to dissuade him from trying to make such a bargain with the witches, but everything went to hell after discovering Kaira was here.

"Remove my shackle!" I answer back angrily.

The taste of something metallic on my tongue...magic.

Lyra's whispering something under her breath. She reminds me of a poisonous flower. Beautiful to look at, but her touch is venomous.

The metal around my neck clicks open and tumbles free. It hits the ground with a clunk, and I rub my neck where it pinched my skin.

"I am not the enemy," Lyra says, eyeing the shackle at my feet.

I almost laugh out loud. Does she honestly think I'm that gullible that I'd believe her?

Ragnar starts drawing backward, grabbing me by my arm, his men flanking us, watching for any sudden attacks. "We leave!" he commands.

We've been forced to cower, to retreat, and I strain to hear the words Lyra says to the witches behind her. Just whispered murmurs float on the air. I want to know what she's saying, but we leave quickly.

Our steps are fast as we put distance between us and them. The blow of leaving Kaira is a hard enough shock to hurt. My throat thickens as instinct screams to go back for her and not leave her in the hands of these monsters.

In my mind, all I can picture is Kaira, Jae, and me rushing out of our home in the Storm Wolves pack. Their fear, their panic, and my promised words that we'll meet by the river. But they never made it, and I won't stop until they are both safe with me again.

"Quickly," Ragnar growls under his breath, pushing me forward to the entrance.

"I can't leave my sister," I protest, pulling from his grip.

Ragnar pivots toward me and takes me by my shoulders, staring me in the eyes. "How are you going to do that when she just stood there and watched us get cursed without breaking a sweat? They won't harm your sister for now. But we are in danger."

I know he's right. But my entire life I've been looking out for my two sisters. They are all I had left in this world for so long, so leaving Kaira is like leaving a part of myself behind too.

Tears pool in my eyes, but I can't stop them. Not when my chest feels like it's about to crack in half.

"Let's go."

But I'm drowning in fear. How am I supposed to save Kaira before the next full moon in two weeks?

Ragnar's hand is on my elbow and he urges me to move faster.

I lift my gaze to the exit that looms before us.

An overwhelming sense of being watched has me shivering, and the hairs on my arms raise.

I glance over my shoulder. Lyra and Kaira are whispering, and looking our way. A spike of jealousy, anger, and guilt, pulse through me.

What has that witch done to my sister?

TWO

NARAH

"That went to shit! And now we're fucking cursed!" Crius growls, brushing right past us, but not before he gives me a look like I'm the one to blame for everything that went so wrong.

For some stupid reason, his reaction affects me, and guilt chews on my mind. I'm still shaking at how brutally bad it went with the witches, my eyes pricking with tears for my sister. "Listen—" I begin, but am cut off by Ragnar.

"Not now." He looks back at the witch's territory. "We need to get as far from here as possible first."

Fine, he has a point I guess. We can talk later.

Crius mumbles to himself, mostly swearing, and storms past us, carving his way through the woods.

The four of us are on his heels, almost running. The hairs on the back of my neck are standing on end with the sensation of a predator sneaking up on us.

Sure, I found my sister, and we didn't die. Those are definitely things to celebrate, except we're all cursed now and are walking time bombs. One of my sisters is still with those psychos, which sucks terribly, while my other sister is back in town with Ragnar's guards.

I keep blinking back the tears that want to rush out now that we're away from there. Part of me wants to run back and just force Kaira to leave with me, to let the witches do whatever in the world they want.

Of course, that's not possible, but try telling that to the guilt slicing through my heart, punishing me for leaving her.

Each time I glance back, Stone and Nikos, who follow behind us, watch me. I'm not sure what they want me to say. But they keep quiet too, carrying the backpacks they'd left outside the witch compound. Stone has his blond hair tucked behind his ears, his light-colored beard in dire need of a trim. Whereas with Nikos, all I can focus on are those intense green eyes with flickers of gold.

What are they really thinking? Do they blame me too?

I feel sick to my stomach with what just happened, and now I find myself in the middle of a tug-o-war between Kaira and the witches, these men, and Jae. I should've been more prepared for a trap, and I hate myself for walking so blindly into that hellish situation.

Ragnar sticks by my side. There was something almost comforting in having him stand by me the entire time we confronted the witches, especially when I felt more alone than I had in a long time.

I keep glancing back, praying Kaira changes her mind and comes to join us, that I was wrong, and she's not being controlled by the witches, but when we finally lose sight of the wooden entryway to their land, I give up on that hope.

Crius pauses ahead of us and turns back in our direction, staring at us ferociously, his arms stiff by his sides, his eyes narrowing. He's standing beneath a huge pine tree, the shadows covering his expression, but I don't need to see his face to know he's still furious.

"This wasn't what I fucking signed up for!" he bellows, coming toward us. His deep blond hair whips over his shoulders. Stubble covers his jaw, while the silver rings at the ends of his beard split into two short braids catch my attention. When the sun hits them, they glint, but I can't deny that even when he's angry, he's ridiculously gorgeous. He towers over me, his muscular chest heaving, but today something wild swims in his eyes, like he's lost himself.

He steps right into Ragnar's space.

The air is ripe with fury, and I step aside, not wanting to be in the center of the fight coming.

"Calm the fuck down," Ragnar barks in response, right in his face. "Plan's changed for now, but the result will remain the same."

Crius is shuddering and not having any part of it. He shoves his palms at Ragnar's chest, but the Alpha doesn't even budge. He's solid, and I'll be lying if I say that isn't impressive.

I stare in disbelief that Crius dared to push Ragnar. I've seen men killed for less back in the Storm Wolves pack.

Nikos and Stone close in, both breathing hard, and a chill settles into my skin at being surrounded by these massive men with the look of war in their eyes.

"Crius." Nikos grinds out his name. "Stand down."

But Ragnar raises a hand for them to pull back, which they do.

"Crius," he growls, his Alpha voice commanding and deep, almost to where my knees wobble in response. "Pull your fucking shit together. or I'll do it for you."

I can't look away, not when these two powerhouses are facing off, and in all honesty, I don't have the slightest idea what is going on with Crius. Shouldn't Ragnar be the one more pissed off with how bad things turned out?

Instead, an inhumane growl rolls from Crius' throat, his face darkening with fury, and the powdery wolf smell of a transformation stains the air. Crius convulses, losing control. His skin splits down his arms, white fur spilling out, but he doesn't wince. He only snarls louder. His limbs are stretching, his torso lengthening. These Viking Alphas are bigger than any wolf shifter I've ever encountered. Everything about them is monstrous and terrifying.

"Oh hell, he's losing it," Stone barks, and lunges at Crius. "Get him the fuck down."

Ragnar twists away from Crius and comes back around, attacking him from the side. He pounces at the wolf, wrestling him to the ground.

Crius' jaw snaps at Stone who shoves himself practically in his face, while Nikos grabs for his legs.

My heart pounds in my chest and I slowly back away until my heels hit a tree. I've seen enough Alphas fighting growing up to know this is normal...the whole show of dominance, except what the hell set off Crius? Did he want the encounter with the witches to end up in a bloodbath? Is that why he's so mad?

The feral explosion of growls and yelling pierces my ears, while the three of them wrestle an out-of-control wolf.

I can't even tell what's happening with them all wrapped around one another. But the brutal snarls set my teeth on edge.

A white blur suddenly bursts out of the tangled battle. Crius whips back around like the true predator that he is in his wolf form, blood staining his white fur across his neck and front leg. He unleashes a thunderous howl, his head tilting back, the sound ear-piercing.

A shiver races down my spine.

I suddenly no longer feel safe being anywhere near them, and I glance up to see how low the branch is in the tree behind me.

Stone and Nikos throw themselves after Crius, but my attention is on Ragnar, who's stripping out of his clothes. He kicks off his boots and drops his pants. My gaze falls to his firm ass, at the strength in his legs and the muscles shifting across his back. I know I should be worried, and sure I am, but another part of me is turned on.

Just the sight of him naked burns me up, and my skin tightens, my nipples pebble. A whimper rubs the base of my throat in response. My wolf growls for him. She's stirring awake, pushing me to go to his side.

Down, girl. He's in the middle of a freaking fight...not that it makes a difference to my body's reaction.

Ragnar leaps after Crius, his body contorting and shifting mid-lunge. He snaps into his white wolf form, the shift so fast that I'm left in awe. And I've seen my fair share of transformations back in the Storm Wolves pack.

But none of those Alphas compare to Ragnar. Not even close. He is the biggest wolf I've ever laid eyes on.

I'm locked in place, my stomach churning as Ragnar and Crius come together into a brutal clash.

My head hurts because I don't understand what's going on or why Crius got so mad, but I can't get myself to move either.

The pair tumble across the forest floor, Stone and Nikos watching.

At first, I assume they stand close to know when to jump in to aid their leader, except they're grinning.

They're freaking loving this.

I've never been a fan of Alphas fighting, but even I can appreciate the sheer strength of two powerful wolves in combat.

Ragnar rolls right on top, his jaw snapping down into Crius' shoulder. Blood gushes from the wound, splashing the earth.

Crius half growls, half whines, his body bucking against the bite. Ragnar snarls, pinning him down, his mouth savagely biting into him.

So much blood.

My pulse is racing.

I wince for Crius. He's been an asshole today, but I don't want him to die.

"Stop!" I scream, unable to control myself.

Which was a mistake. Ragnar looks my way quickly, which is just enough time for Crius to knock him aside with a headbutt. They scramble to their feet, but Crius is already heading my way.

He found me.

I whip around and run for my life, because there is no way Crius is coming to me for a hug. Of course I know the rules...never run from a wolf, but instinct has me bolting. I'm not strong enough to stand still while a monster runs at me with savage intent.

Fear pulses through me, and I race madly past the trees when a panicked scream spills past my lips.

I glance back at a terrifying sight.

Crius is leaping toward me in great bounds and is practically on me. But Ragnar is right on his tail, with Stone and Nikos closing in from both sides.

Dread clings to me, and now I'm crying out loud as I run for my life from those sharp teeth. And all I can think about is a stupid fairytale my father told me growing up about a girl in a red cloak who was tricked by a wolf in the woods, how she ran from him and still got eaten.

Is this how she felt? Like she might vomit at any moment?

It's funny the things that go through your mind when faced with death. I think of my magic and how that should have been my instinctual response. But apparently, when in a life-threatening situation, my autopilot switches to run.

My foot catches on a root, and I fall forward.

Terror crashes through me as I hit the ground and instinctively curl in on myself, expecting the sharp cut of fangs to rip into me.

An explosion of grunts and shouting bursts from behind me, making me flinch hard.

I crane my head up and look over to Crius being pinned beneath both Stone and Nikos, Ragnar's jaws latched around Crius' neck, growling.

Submission...he's forcing him into submission. I'd seen Father do this to some of his men when he was the Alpha in charge of the Storm Wolves pack.

Sometimes the raw, primal sides of wolves take over and need a reminder they belong to a pack leader and must submit.

I'm shaking and scrambling to my feet.

Nikos is by my side, taking my arm and pulling a twig out of my hair. "You never call to a wolf lost in a frenzy."

Is that what it's called...frenzy? I prefer to think it's losing total fucking control.

"What's wrong with him?" I can't stop watching the way Crius twitches and fights Ragnar. Stone is still holding him down, ready to intervene if needed.

"Crius just needs a small reminder of who his Alpha is. He's always had control issues, you could say."

I blink up at Nikos, at this gorgeous man with thick, chestnut hair running across the top and back of his head with the sides shaved. A tattoo inked down to the nape of his neck. It's of two snakes entwined and biting the tail of the other.

Based on how strong and powerful he looks, and how he speaks so calmly like this is an everyday occurrence, I can't help but wonder how exactly they lived back in Denmark.

Fighting from dusk to dawn? Chewing on rocks? Wrestling with demons?

"He tried to kill me," I remind him.

"We never would have let him hurt you." His words are raw with emotions I can't read.

"Sorry if I don't fully believe that, but I just had my life flash before my eyes back there." My voice trembles. I'm also still reeling from leaving Kaira with the witches, and everything becoming too much.

He steps closer, and for a moment, it feels like he's going to take me in his arms. Is it crazy that I lean forward as if it's exactly what I want too? He pauses inches away, and from this proximity I can smell that sexy masculine scent that is all him. His eyes are wide like he's not too sure what he should do, and when I look into them, all I can think about is the secret he'd shared with me when we encountered the bear in the woods. How he secretly intends to leave Ragnar's pack, worried he'll be thrown out like he has been all his life. Whatever happened to him to make him feel that way is tragic, and it makes me want to find out the truth of his past.

Each one of us is a broken shell, barely keeping it together. Most of my life, I've felt like I have been waiting for something that won't happen because nothing goes well for me. And today is no exception.

I draw my attention away from Nikos and to Crius who is finally settling down under Ragnar's weight and strength.

Crius shudders, and that scent of shifting fills the air. He's changing back, and Ragnar retreats, heaving for breath, watching him with deadly precision.

In moments, Crius is lying on the ground, naked, blood smeared across his chest and neck.

He gasps for breath, and the sight of him breaks me. The skin around the bite mark is swollen, but the blood has already coagulated and stopped seeping out. But he's struggling for air and quivering.

"Crius," I say, stretching a hand out.

Ragnar lifts his head toward Nikos with a sharp stare. Nikos then steps into my view. "You and I need to go for a walk."

He takes my elbow and we move deeper into the woods, away from the trio.

"What are they going to do to him?" I whisper, not wanting my words to carry back to Crius. Looking back, Stone has his back to me, crouching by Crius, as Ragnar sits close, both blocking my view.

"They'll help him. And he needs some privacy, seeing he's got an ego big enough to blot out the sun."

I understand, I guess, and I let Nikos lead me farther away until we pause in a part of the woods where the trees thin out, and the sun beats down on us.

"Do you sense any magic around us?" he asks, glancing at the woodland that is blossoming with plants and flowers. A rabbit hops practically right past us before dashing away.

"Nothing. There are no spells on these woods to harm us. Maybe we're too close to the witch's home," I suggest.

He shrugs, and I move to settle myself on a rock near several trees, resting for the first time today. It's been go-go-go since the morning.

Nikos is a few feet away, his left knee bent and foot propped up on the tree he's leaning against. He's got his head low, and I can't see his face.

Out of the four Alphas, he's been the most mysterious and the one who keeps his distance from me.

Something tickles my hand, and I look to find a black spider crawling up my arm. In a sudden panic, I fling my arm out and squeal, making a sound I regret instantly as Nikos lifts his gaze in my direction.

I flinch back into a recline once more like nothing happened, even though my heart is thumping. I really don't like spiders.

With him staring at me, the first thing that comes to mind spills out. "What's really wrong with Crius? Why was he acting so weirdly with the witches? It almost looked like he had something planned."

Nikos pushes off the tree and strolls in my direction. Dressed in all black, he reminds me of a prowling panther who notices even the smallest detail before striking first.

Reaching me, he stomps on something just inches from my feet. When he pulls his foot back, I find the spider squished to smithereens.

"Crius agreed to this mission for his own purpose, and things didn't go to plan. So he's pissed."

"What's his mission?" I lean forward. "And he has magic too, doesn't he? Just like Stone."

"That he does. It's very specific." He stuffs his hands into his pockets and glances down at me.

"Why does it feel like I have to drag every word out of you about him? Shouldn't I know who I'm dealing with if we are stuck together for the next two weeks?"

"Tell me something." He crouches down in front of me so we're at eye level. And it's only now that I notice the streak of blood along his jawline. "Did you enjoy seeing Crius losing control? How we had to keep fighting him to keep him from hurting himself and you?"

My shoulders rear back. "What is that supposed to mean? Of course, I didn't."

"But how did it make you feel?" he presses.

"Worried about him. Uncomfortable to see him that way." Just as uneasy as Nikos is making me feel now.

"There you have it. That's how he'd feel with us talking about him." He gets to his feet, his face expressionless, but there's a coldness behind his words. "His story is not mine to tell. I won't take that away from him. But, fair warning, it may be something you won't want to hear, so I suggest leaving it alone."

He turns and strolls back to his tree.

I should have been relieved that he gave me an out to forget about Crius, just like I should do with all of these Alphas. Even Ragnar. Except, I'm already on my feet, following him, and my words are pouring out. "Maybe the reason I ask is because I care. Because if I know someone well enough, I can help them."

He twists back around toward me, and I feel the power he radiates. He may be Ragnar's Second, but Nikos is every inch a powerful Alpha too. He reaches over and gently takes a loose strand of my hair caught in my eyelashes and tucks it behind my ear. The way his gaze dips to my lips distracts me, makes me forget what I'd been saying. A ghost of a smile plays on his lips—everything about him always takes me off guard and draws me to him.

I'm an Omega. He's an Alpha.

In our world, men like him fight to the death to own women like me, and I don't miss the way he stares at me. The way they all stare at me, along with knowing they struggle to hold back their raw, primal instincts. Top Alphas like Ragnar reign over other Alphas, Betas, and Omegas. All Alphas in a pack don't stray from the top of the hierarchy, and are ranked in order of Second, Third, and so forth. It's how it was set up in the Storm Wolves too. How I see Ragnar run his pack.

Betas are the warriors, the work dogs of packs. The Omegas like me are the ones who usually carry no power and are used as breeders. Our heat controls us, draws us to Alphas, except because of the magic in my veins, my heat has never really come out completely.

My attraction to Martell, my fated mate who tried to kill me, was instantaneous, but unlike other girls, I haven't fully come into my heat. Mother told me it was a blessing for us hybrids. No heat meant we had greater control and didn't send men into a craze to claim us.

"I'd think you learned plenty about all of us during the bear attacks." He leans forward and takes another lock of my hair, bringing it to his nose and inhales deeply.

His words have me straightening, and I push his hand away from me. "You hate the fact that you shared something about your past with me? I won't judge you for what you said."

He inches closer. Our bodies touch now, and my breath catches in my throat. "Narah, you have no idea what you've agreed to when it comes to making a deal with Ragnar and all of us. And I'm not trying to scare you."

I swallow hard. "What do you mean?" I desperately want to know what he's talking about. "We all had shitty upbringings, trust me, I understand. Try being an Omega in this broken world where females are commodities, let alone one with powers that can get me killed. Wolves hate witches."

He stares at me like somehow he can do one better. "Everything can get us killed in this world. You might have a target painted on your back, but you had parents who loved you. Mine sold me as soon as they could. So it seems both of us may be no better than commodities, but it doesn't change the fact that, with us, you and your sisters are in more danger than you realize." His voice grows bitter.

The ache in his words messes me up. I knew these guys were just as ruined as me, but what in the world is he talking about? I want to tell him that we're in this together for now, but my chance is stolen by approaching footsteps.

I raise my gaze to three figures emerging from the woods, the men returning, and if I wasn't unsettled before, now I'm scared.

What the hell was Nikos talking about? Of course, now my mind is running rampant with worse-case scenarios.

CHAPTER

THREE

RAGNAR

I march into a clearing in the woods and find Narah standing several feet away, close to Nikos, both of them looking at me as if startled. For a moment, it almost feels like I've caught them kissing.

I made the point of telling my three men that we share every-thing... including Omegas. But seeing Nikos and Narah almost pressed together ignites a searing flame in my chest. She's mine... all mine, and I need her to know this and to understand that the mark I've given her will keep the agony for her rejected fated mate at bay... for now. But the payment for freeing her means she's mine.

I lost my fated mate, too, and accepted that long ago. I'll be drawn to Omegas in heat, but none will lock in with my wolf. It's how our kind works. You have a chance to find your perfect partner, and for the rest of us suckers who never do, or lose them, well, we love with half a heart.

Maybe it's the fact we are both broken that I'm so drawn to her.

Nikos backs away at my approach, and I grab hold of Narah's shoulders, her lips swollen like she's been kissed.

A gasp rolls from her throat, and I soften my grip, well aware that I sometimes forget my own strength. Or the aggression with which I take what I want.

222

"Are you hurt?" I study her beautiful face for injuries from Crius' chase—her porcelain skin, her long slender neck, her large, vulnerable eyes.

I draw in a deep breath, filling my nostrils with the smell of her sex. It's intoxicating, lingering below the surface of her natural sweetness.

I will never understand how her fated mate could have rejected a woman as perfect as her. But if I ever cross paths with him, I'll destroy him for hurting her.

"I'm fine," she says and pulls away from me, her gaze shifting to Crius, who stands at the far edge of the small clearing, arms folded across his chest, shadows darkening beneath his eyes.

"He won't hurt you," I reassure her.

"Sorry if I scared you," he croaks, sounding almost reluctant to apologize.

Though, I'm impressed by his attempt. Most of the time, he doesn't give a fuck.

"I'm not afraid of you," she says calmly.

She's utterly adorable at how strong she holds herself when it had been obvious she was terrified when he chased her.

"Things didn't go to plan, and we didn't walk out of there with the witches' alliance," I address the group, since we are all together and no one is trying to kill anyone for a change. I don't bring up the fact that Kaira turning up with the witches was a massive wrench in our plans.

"You could say that." Crius' voice darkens, and he raises his chin defiantly. I feel for him, but he needs to pull himself together. As much as he's pissed that he never got this big chance for his grand spell, personally, I'm glad it never happened.

I've been conflicted about permitting him to carry through with his intended spell to overtake the witches from the beginning. The risk to himself was too high.

I've lost enough people in my life and I sure as fuck can't lose him too. What he doesn't realize is that regardless of how that went down with the witches, I had a contingency plan to stop him with Stone's help. But the witches' curse and Narah's sister came in just as handy as a distraction.

I clear my throat. "The witches want Narah and Jae, so we're going to use that to our advantage."

"I vote for burning the coven down." Stone spits the words, his chest sticking out, and Crius gives him an approving nod. "That will nullify the curse."

"Our priority is to find my mother," Narah interrupts, drawing all our attention.

"Your sister warned you to stay away from her," Nikos adds. "Are you sure that's the right decision?"

Except, her suggestion makes sense. "They fear your mother for a reason," I say out loud.

Narah's nodding. "She could offer us a way to get my sister back and to overthrow the coven." There is eagerness in her words, and it has everything to do with her needing to find her mother. Narah had told me her mother carried magic too and that both her parents were dead, so her decision to track her down now shouldn't come as a surprise.

"Or we could be walking into a trap and your sister lied," Crius groans. "No insult intended, Narah, but your sister was a fucking bitch and didn't look too happy to see you. So what if she knows that's exactly what you'll do by mentioning your mom?"

Narah stiffens, her shoulders rising. "And what do you suggest?" she snaps, her eyes narrowing on Crius. "That you kill the witches, if they don't get you first? And then what? Every freaking Alpha outside these woods will rampage to claim the land, including taking all of you down. As much as you hate witches, they are the necessary evil that is keeping a sense of harmony over the land. And I won't let you endanger my sister." She stands tall and adamant, her stance clear. She'll do anything to protect her sister, even turn on us.

"I never said we'd kill your sister," he counters.

She's a smart girl, but too easily led by her emotions. Though, it's not too often I see Omegas with such tenacity and bravery. I find it brutally beautiful.

Crius has his hands now in the pockets of his pants, nonchalantly lifting his chin toward Narah. "I don't want you to think I hate all witches. I like you. But I sure as fuck am not going to die by a witch's curse, either. I'll go down as a warrior."

"It's getting really hard to tell," she answers and lowers her gaze. "Your wolf seemed inclined to want to take a chunk out of me."

Tension thickens the air, and I get it. The mission failed miserably. We're cursed, and everyone wants a solution. But as they say in ancient books, *Rome wasn't built in a day*. If this was easy, the witches would have been in alliance with another pack already. So as far as I'm concerned, this is an opportunity.

"We have two weeks," I say, to break the stretching silence. "So, we'll make finding Narah's mother a priority."

Narah's mouth falls open. "Curses can't be removed, you know that? Unless we kill the witch who spelled us."

I nod. "Yet magic can be manipulated to extend the time. I've seen it done back in Denmark. And I didn't come all the way to Romania to fail. That's not even a possibility I will entertain."

She shrugs like she's not sure she believes me. But I intend to prove her wrong, along with my father.

"You're worthless," my father barks. "A waste of my seed, of my time." The man is large and ruthless, destroying everyone in his path. It surprises me he hasn't strangled me in my sleep yet.

Still, his words are punches to the gut, even if I've heard them before. Too often for my liking, and as much as I fucking loath the cold-hearted prick, I can tell his mood by his insults. The day he doesn't curse me is the day I'll end up on a burning boat pushed out into the sea.

"How was the trip?" I sneer and look over to Mother, who sits at the table pretending to eat and is cutting up the sausage on her plate into dozens of pieces. For her, I keep the peace. For her, I try not to antagonize him. When the bastard is furious, it's her who deals with the fury he lashes out.

He pushes up from his seat at the end of the grand dining table, dropping his fork to the plate, which lands with a loud clunk. "Since when do you care about diplomatic matters? Don't waste my time pretending, son. It's not becoming of you."

A growl rumbles in my chest at his hatred.

"Frode," Mother says, her mouth tight. "Please, just sit. Can we eat one meal as a family in peace?"

Father doesn't respond, but heaves heavily, then sits back down with a huff.

"You blame me for Hel," I say, my hands gripping the back of an empty chair at the table. "Then give me the men from your pack to rescue her, to wet the land with the blood from every last Balor wolf. I will claim his land for me... for us."

"No!" Father roars, slamming his fist on the table. The plates and food jump and Mother flinches. "You will fail, and that you stand there and demand war on them tells me you will never be ready to become Alpha. You think with your wolf, not your brain." He growls, the sound reverberating through the room. "Negotiations are set, and in exchange for Hel, The Balor Alpha's son, Nikos, arrives on the morrow. You will be responsible for him. If he dies, Hel's death at the hands of our enemy will rest on your shoulders."

I clench my teeth and shove those memories aside, hating Father with every fiber of my being.

"Grab your stuff, let's move," I order my pack and Narah.

"And our backup plan," Stone adds, causing me to pause as I turn toward the woods. "We destroy the witches?"

"Fuck yes." Crius pumps his fist in the air. "After we get Kaira out, of course."

Narah's eyes grow stormy. She may not like it, but nothing comes out of being nice in this world.

You survive using claws and teeth, with spilling blood. And if you don't, then your blood will be the one to spill.

No one responds, and frustration pinches along my shoulder blades. "Let's go."

Narah turns and walks into the woods. We march after her. I'd fought my entire life, been tortured, told I'll amount to nothing, so my mission to take over the Savage Sector in Romania will be my legacy to prove them all wrong. Then rescuing Hel and having her live in my pack will be the ultimate way I tell my father to go fuck himself.

The woods darken the farther we travel.

After hours of endless walking, there's no trace of magic, not even a trickle in the air. No attacking trees or losing control of our wolves... nothing. About damn time.

The moon hangs heavy tonight. I want to get out of these fucking woods desperately. It feels like I'm constantly being watched. Like there isn't enough oxygen to draw into my lungs, and like I'm being squeezed into a box two sizes too small for me.

"This is a good spot," Nikos says and dumps the backpacks he's been carrying on a flat section of land devoid of trees. The firs that surround us are still like statues. There's no breeze tonight, only the deathly silence of a haunted forest.

We all move on autopilot to set up camp. No sign of animals in this area either, nothing to hunt, so we'll make do with the dried meat, bread, and fruit in our bags.

"Is it just me, or does it feel like everything is frozen in time? I'd kill for a breeze on my face," Nikos murmurs.

"This place sucks," Stone remarks as he digs through a backpack and comes out with a lighter. He drops to his knees in front of the pile of twigs and sets them alight.

"We've been in the worst situations," I tell them.

"Really? Like when?" Crius asks.

"Like being ambushed in Poland by those female warriors."

Stone bursts out laughing, the sound abrupt and echoing around us. It's refreshing to hear laughter instead of sighs and groans. "I'm not sure if I was more worried about them killing or fucking us. Some of them were bigger than me, man. Though, I still think they wanted us as hostages so we could become their breeders. Not a bad way to go, all things considered. But not sure if that's comparable to this mission."

"Didn't stop Nikos from trying," Crius remarks as he dumps more branches near the blazing fire. "It's what got us in trouble in the first place."

Nikos chuckles and shrugs. "When you see an Omega wandering in the woods with no clothes and calling for help, what would you do?"

"Help her, not fuck her," Stone says and laughs.

"Narah, you've been quiet." I turn around to bring her into the conversation. She's kept to herself for most of the trip.

Except she's not behind me.

Frantically, I look around to find her gone.

Panic races down my spine.

"Where the fuck is Narah?"

CHAPTER

FOUR

NARAH

Today was brutal.

I barely keep it together each time I think of Kaira. There is no way in this hellish world that my sister would behave like she had. It's not in her nature, and the farther we distance ourselves from the coven, the more my chest tightens at the thought that I've left her behind. Of course, I tell myself they won't harm her until we return, but what if the spell damages her?

What if, by the time we return, the sister I once knew and loved no longer exists, is too destroyed to ever be herself again? Magic can have horrendous repercussions on those under its influence, and for all I know, she's been under a spell the past two months since we escaped the Storm Wolves pack.

Mother once told me that an untreated spell can spread like cancer, and the longer they are afflicted, the harder it will be for them to ever fully be themselves again.

They'll be broken on the inside, she'd said. *Much like our world.*

Great moon goddess, I miss Mother terribly, and I really hope Kaira is wrong about her. That she had a good reason for having left us at the mercy of the Storm Wolves pack.

The air remains still tonight, and it feels like I'm suffocating on my breath. I'm staring out into the wilderness over the cliff. There's nothing but blackness. I just needed some time away from the guys, some breathing space, and time to gather myself.

Part of me suspects that if I don't get myself under control, that I will stand no chance of saving Kaira or keeping Jae safe. So I need to find a way to cope with everything.

But it isn't long before the soft crunch of foliage sounds behind me, and I twist around. Ragnar marches in my direction, though by his loud exhales, I'm guessing he freaked about me missing.

I want to apologize, to say I'm sorry, except I'm struggling with my thoughts right now.

"Little fox," he says, and all I can see beneath the silvery hue of the moonlight are those haunting blue eyes, his short brown hair framed around his face.

I expect a sleuth of I-told-you-so's and reminders that I shouldn't go off on my own.

"Don't," I tell him, stealing his chance. "I know what you're going to say."

"Is that so?" He takes a seat next to me and drops his arms over his bent legs. Instead of talking, he just sits in silence with me, looking out into the darkness of the land beyond the cliff.

I sense Ragnar staring at me, and I glance over, but never in a hundred years did I expect anyone to be looking at me with adoration. Let alone him. Not after what we went through. Not after everyone's plans failed because of me. And certainly not after I got us all cursed.

There is something deep and alluring in his expression, and part of me wishes that my fated mate had stared at me this way on our first night together. That he hadn't been so drunk that he only wanted to fuck my brains out or freaked out when he found out I was also a witch.

That's the thing about the brutal Alphas in this world. They either want to own and fuck you to breed with you, or they sell you off, discard you.

But no matter how handsome Ragnar is, how many muscles he has, how he watches me like he might devour me, I need to remember who I'm dealing with and what his pack consists of...

Violent Alphas.

"What do you think the world was like before the virus killed nearly everyone?" he asks, turning his gaze to the blackness of space over the cliff.

Quickly adding two and two together, I realize he's trying to get me talking and to calm down. And it works. "I'm going to say amazing. From what I've read in books, things were easier. People were happier. For one, they had endless food they got from places called grocery stores. And they attended parks and fairs with friends."

He's studying me carefully, a smile curling the corners of his lips. "You seem to know quite a bit."

"I love to read. But can you imagine a world where it's safe to just walk down the road and not be attacked by wolves or zombies? Crazy, huh?" I laugh to myself. "Yep, a fantasy world right there. But that shit is long gone. We are the remnants of what was left after the virus killed everyone else. I wish I knew more, like if wolves lived in harmony with the humans back then."

"Whatever happened in the past, we are in a shit place now where zombies are taking over the south, and they are gonna be up here soon in droves," he states nonchalantly. "More reason to set up a sector where people follow one Alpha, and we fight against them. I've seen it done in the Shadowlands Sector successfully."

I feel his touch on my arm, and his warmth swims over my skin, but his words still bother me. "Easy for you to say when you're an Alpha. I don't stand much of a chance of a happy future. I'm an Omega and considered the lowest of the low. And because I'm a hybrid witch, I'm nothing but a target for everyone." I get to my feet, his hand falling away from my arm.

"That doesn't mean we can't continue an alliance after I help you get your sister back."

I adore his confidence, and I'm holding him to his word, but I've also learned that the universe is more reliable in letting me down.

"What do you want in exchange?" I ask warily.

"I'll be ruling the Savage territory, and you need a safe haven, right?"

I eye him carefully and get to my feet. "And in exchange you'll want my magic? Except, maybe that's not what I want."

A flash of hurt crosses his gaze as he climbs to his feet to join me, now towering over me. "So, what is it you want? Look around you,

Narah. There is nowhere you and your sisters can hide. Omegas don't last long on their own. And once word spreads of your magic, you'll be hunted down and killed."

I hug myself and turn away from him, his words sharper than he knows. I've lived with that dread my entire life. "I want to be away from all the chaos and war. I'm tired of being hated for what I am. It's why I've kept my magic a secret for so long."

Half-witches, half-wolves like me and Kaira are worthless. It's why my fated mate rejected me, why I'm now fighting desperately to save my sisters. I've heard of a female sanctuary in Poland, but rumors can just as easily lead us astray and into danger.

Just as easily as Ragnar's offer of sanctuary. He hasn't even taken over the Savage Sector, and the Alphas who call this place home are murderers and would die before bowing the knee to another...let alone a foreigner like him. So, what would they do to me when he makes me use my magic?

It's a disaster waiting to happen. I'll be exposed, hated, and all I want is to slip under the radar with my sisters to survive. I've learned long ago that holding onto any kind of hope that my future will be anything but normal is me being foolish.

His shadow falls over me, and he puts his hands on my shoulders turning me to face him.

My heart beats loudly in my ears as I stare up at him. I hate myself for being so attracted to him at a time like this. Hate how my body leans toward him as if we're drawn to each other.

His hand moves to my neck, holding me in place. "You are mine. You gave me parts of yourself that were truly untouched. That's a gift that I will repay with protection." He traces the pads of his fingers gingerly over the curve of my neck where he'd bitten me. "My mark does more than mask your wolf's desperation for your fated mate. It makes every inch of you mine, and I have no intention of letting you go."

I should shove him away, but instead, I'm losing myself to him. Wanting the things his gaze promises. Everything about him is Alpha, masculine, dominating. There's a part of me that wants his protection for me and my sisters, but I'm also terrified it might be signing a death warrant.

"B-but that wasn't what we agreed. You said…" My breath catches in my throat at what he's saying.

"I said I'd help you, and that's what I did."

I'm shaking and fighting the way my wolf surges through me to get closer to his… and of course, I should have understood. She no longer craves my soulmate, Martell, but now pines for Ragnar. The call is not as painful as it had been for my fated mate, but I see now how submissive I am to my primal instincts.

"I gave you what you wanted, but there was only one way to do that." The sharp, serious expression he sports intensifies as his hold tightens like he's scared I'm going to run from him.

"W-why? Why would you do that? You don't even know me," I whisper, trying to pull away from him while he holds me close.

"Every wolf has a thirst to find someone to call their own, and everything about you makes me want to dominate you. Adore you. Fuck you."

I shudder with that feeling where my body tingles. He brushes the loose strands of hair out of my face. "Thing is that when an Omega gives herself to an Alpha, it doesn't make them powerless. It's a gift they've given the Alpha to be protected and cherished."

My face flushes at words I don't expect or deserve. His hands fall to my waist, and he's close to me. Everything in my mind screams to back away, but my body says *yes*.

I manage to shake my head. "No." I gasp the word as if it's the hardest thing I've ever had to do.

His eyes are wild. "I won't let anyone hurt you ever again." He leans closer to me, his voice deepening. "I won't abandon you, but you need to trust me."

I can't move. Not even if I tried…

His chest heaves against mine, his grip tightening. Fire burns in his gaze, and it awakes my arousal. He knows what he wants, and he takes it. I should loathe him for making me crave him, but how can I when he's eased the ache I carried for Martell?

Instead of breaking away, I relax a little bit and let out a breath.

We're not fated mates. That connection isn't there, but the pull I feel toward him is undeniable.

Suddenly, he's kissing me, claiming me. His teeth tug at my

bottom lip, his fingers twirling in my hair and clenching into a fist, holding me as he licks into my mouth. There are no words for the way he kisses me, the dominant way he's taking what he wants... me.

It's impossible to resist him.

His hands move to the sides of my face, and I'm lost in his kiss. He walks me back until I am nestled against a tree. My heart skips a beat, and I tug on his shirt, fisting the fabric, drawing him closer. The way he kisses me is powerful and overwhelming. For so long, I never knew what I'd been missing by not being with a man like him. How much I've been starved of affection.

I don't even know how long we've been kissing... a minute, an hour, but I'm completely lost, and even if I remembered why I had to pull away from him now, it's too late. The heady smell of desire overwhelms me.

I kiss him back, needing more. Even if my mind demands I back off, I don't think I can. Moans roll out of my throat as his mouth moves to my neck, taking small nips. His hands fall to my waist, and he tugs open the buttons on my pants. Crouching in front of me, he pushes them down my legs in seconds; I step out of them as I kick off my shoes. He moves so fast, sliding my underwear down my legs and off. His gaze pauses on the spot between my legs and licks his lips.

His tongue is on my pussy without warning. A wicked tongue that knows what he's doing.

"Ahh," I moan, my legs quivering as he sucks on me. There's no relenting, this man understands my needs, and he is enjoying himself. He holds onto my hips again, his fingers digging into my skin.

I open my mouth to say something, but only moans spill out. He picks up speed, his tongue flicking over my clit, pushing me right to the edge where I'm beyond control.

I'm there, falling, tumbling into the abyss of a building orgasm. I fist his hair, my cries growing louder when he finally releases me and stands with a growl from his throat.

With rough hands, he tugs me away from the tree.

"I don't want you cut up by the bark when I fuck you."

I desperately fist his shirt and haul him over to me, our mouths clashing. "Make me forget everything," I whisper against his mouth.

"Good girl."

I close my eyes, tilting my head back, and give myself to him. His tongue traces the curve of my throat, his hands on my breasts, squeezing. His words float on the air, "You are mine."

The sounds of his belt unbuckling and his zipper coming down have me eager for him. "Every girl needs a good fucking." His large hands are on the back of my thighs, and I'm lifted off my feet.

Quickly, I wrap my arms around his neck as he steps away from the tree. I coil my legs around his hips, his cock already teasing the heat of my pussy.

A moan spills from my mouth, and he growls. "Fuck, I love the sounds you make."

His mouth finds me, and he kisses me like I belong to him, rough and demanding. He doesn't ask but takes what he wants. For him, it all comes down to control. He's powerful and terrifying, but with me, he treats me like I'm glass.

He pushes into me quickly, the sensation of his cock sliding inside of me, leaves me breathless. He is a very large man and forces himself to fit inside me.

I cry out. He's not taking it slow, and I love it. He cups my ass, takes a deep breath, then drives me against him.

His strength is crazy as he holds me in his arms while standing and fucks me with extraordinary power, his hips rocking into me over and over. The pain he causes, the pleasure he delivers, is indescribable. He picks up speed, his growls filling my ears.

I'm wrapped around him, our bodies plastered together, and I look deep into his blue eyes.

His jaw clenches every time he thrusts into me, and I moan, taking him completely.

"There's something about you, little fox. Something I can never give up." He groans and buries his face in my neck, where I feel his teeth grazing my skin. His sweet words engulf me. No one has ever spoken to me like this.

With those words comes an explosion that erupts within me and drives me over the edge I've been precariously balancing on. And when the burning pressure of his cock swells inside me and pushes against my inner walls, that's when my orgasm tears through me.

My cries are swallowed by his kiss as desire pulses through me, and Ragnar has his own roaring climax. He growls, and I feel his seed filling me, pulsing, and there's so much.

He's tense and holding me tightly, coming for a long time. We're locked in place, both of us united.

His growl vibrates against me.

I close my eyes and tuck my face into the curve of his neck. He's buried deep within me and his bulging knot is tightly fit inside me, keeping us bound. I never understood how knotting really worked, just that it was another way for Alphas to lay claim on Omegas and give their seed a better chance of getting the female pregnant. Lucky for me, I made sure to take a special herb for a month leading up to my ceremonial night with Martell... a herb that aids in me not falling pregnant for a couple of months afterward.

I wasn't a fool to fall pregnant so quickly in a new relationship.

Ragnar has his lips at my ear, distracting me, and he asks, "Are you okay, little fox?"

"Yes," I respond, then he kisses me again, leaving me breathless. We'll be together for half an hour, maybe longer, connected this way until my muscles relax, until his knotted cock unswells, and as crazy as it sounds, I love this bonding time with him.

"I want you to rest now, to let go. I've got you."

We are looking at each other, and there's something ridiculously intimate about having an Alpha's cock locked inside you. Where it feels like I've got the upper hand and he's at my mercy...that's what I tell myself as I lean against him, my arms draping over his shoulders. I wonder why the universe didn't send someone like him to me as my fated mate?

It's only then, when I glance up, that I meet Crius' gaze.

My breath catches in my throat. How long has he been watching us?

He's standing amid the shadows, watching us with a dark expression. And... is that his hand down his pants?

Nothing's worse than waking up with your mouth tasting like you've just been licking dirt.

I chew on my fifth jerky strip, unable to get rid of the funky taste. What I wouldn't give for a bucket of hot coffee. Black, no sugar. And I'm salivating. Another reason to get our asses back into town and out of these fucking woods.

I've had six hours to sleep off the shit-fest from yesterday. Don't get me wrong, I'm still pissed how things turned out with the witches, but like Ragnar had told me, it wasn't the time for me to use my magic. Especially not when it would have meant that Narah's sister might have ended up as collateral damage.

Really, I shouldn't care. I came on this mission with the promise of carrying out a spell that would aid Ragnar in winning over the witches. Of course, it came at my expense, yet Ragnar kept telling me to wait after Narah's sister made her presence known.

But we're going back to the witches, and next time, I won't be holding back. I don't give an iota what anyone thinks, won't let anyone stand in my way.

Chewing on the food, I lift my gaze to Narah stumbling out of the woods and coming toward the campsite. Her hair's mussed and eyes wild. Goddess, she's gorgeous. She's wearing the same clothes as yesterday, tight pants over long legs, shirt, and leather vest taut over the curve of her breasts. Like the rest of us, I'm dying for a hot bath upon our return to town. Preferably with her by my side.

Is it crazy that she's the first thing to have brought excitement to my day?

And now I can't get the image of her from last night being fucked by Ragnar out of my mind. Those sounds she made, the beautiful look on her face as she rode his cock and finally came. One could easily lose their heads to a girl like her, which I suspect Ragnar might be doing.

But it's not my business. These idiots in the pack have their own darkness to deal with. Ragnar and his asshole father. Nikos, the outcast who's forced to live with his family's enemy. And Stone who has always struggled with finding his place in the world and is constantly angry about it. It's like he just doesn't fit in, but I think he's searching for something he hasn't found... a reason to belong.

Don't I fucking know that feeling.

I've accepted my fate and the broken past that I can't undo. Which is why I decided to carry out the spell to help my friends. I've come to peace with that decision... even if it might end in my demise. It's a risk I agreed to take, regardless of the outcome.

I exhale loudly. The dark thoughts creeping forward. My brother's blood on my hands. His death haunts me. I close my eyes, fighting the gaping hole splitting open in my soul. It's ripped me apart, and there is no way of putting me back together again. Not after what I did.

Most days, the smile I wear is all that holds me together.

"Hey, where is everyone?" Narah asks from across the clearing. Her sweet voice slices through my thoughts, and I welcome the distraction. I welcome her. Anything to stop myself from drowning.

I open my eyes and glance over at her. "Meditating."

"Sure." She doesn't believe me, and that's fine. I wouldn't either. But I smile, plastering on the face I wear for everyone because no one wants a fucking sorrowful bastard hanging around with them.

"Come and eat something," I say. "The other three guys are finishing packing up camp and have gone to fill up our water skins."

"Well, that explains why I couldn't find Ragnar."

Exhaling loudly, I stuff more of the jerky into my mouth and reach into the bag for the bread, hoping that might help with the taste in my mouth. My eyes never leave her though, not the way she strolls over, her hips swaying, her hands by her sides while she scans the woodland. There's something so alluring about this girl, even when she looks startled.

Who am I kidding? I love seeing her scared. That is why my wolf went for her yesterday.

I offer her an open bag of jerky. "Help yourself. It'll grow hair on your chest." I smack my lips, to which she rolls her eyes.

"Coffee would be heaven right now." She takes a piece and bites down on it, then pulls at it.

I laugh. "The jerky's a tough sonofabitch."

She wrestles with it but doesn't give up and finishes it. "About last night," she starts, her cheeks blushing.

"You had an amazing time," I answer while grinning. "Did Ragnar not tell you we share everything, and that includes watching?"

Looking mortified, eyes wide, she shrugs. "Sort of worked it out, but it's unusual."

She reaches for another piece of dried meat and glances around the woods, then looks back at me. "Hope you don't mind me asking, but what happened yesterday with the witches and you... you know, afterward?" Her forehead creases, and she's wearing an apologetic look on her face. "Sorry, maybe I shouldn't ask. Nikos told me not to ask you."

Urgh. Of course, he would. I stuff the rest of the food into the bag and zip it up.

"Sometimes I lose control."

"Next time, maybe don't hit the crazy button around me if your wolf sees me as a meal," she teases, smiling. Though, I can tell it's an awkward smile.

"I'm pretty sure if I caught you, I would have either licked you or tried to hump you."

Her mouth drops open, looking partially horrified. "Are you joking?"

I chuckle. "If only I was. My wolf is a horny bastard. Doesn't help that you always smell so delicious." I find myself gravitating to her. She doesn't back away, and I'm impressed by her resolve. "You don't need to fear me. Trust me, there are many things I want to do to you, but killing you isn't one of them."

Her cheeks blush. I adore her innocence. That deep inside, she's wholesome. And while she might disagree, she is not broken in my eyes, but absolutely perfect, just like those kissable lips.

I've kissed my fair share of women in my life, but something tells me once I taste her, I'd do anything to claim her.

And I already have enough crap clouding my head to drag her into the shithole that I've fallen into. So I turn from her, not wanting to complicate things or let her believe I can promise anything beyond the here and now.

She snatches my wrist and says, "You never answered my question. What happened back at the coven? What were you trying to do?"

I don't move but focus on the point of contact where her small hand wraps around my arm, and how such a small hand radiates intense heat. Her fingers twitch like she's trembling. It is ridiculous that such a touch should affect me in any way but draw my attention. Except I'm breathing in her scent while my heartbeat thumps harder.

I turn to her, and she's still holding onto me. Her eyes are swimming in curiosity, and I swallow the thickness in my throat at how easily she makes me forget what she asked me.

"Always keep your tender heart protected, gorgeous girl. In this life, everyone will try to tear it apart for their own gain."

She blinks, confused, and I don't blame her. I have no idea where that bit of philosophical crap just came from. She brings things out of me I never expect, like this overbearing instinct to keep her protected. To ensure the vulnerable girl remains that way for as long as possible.

"I'll take it into consideration," she answers and releases my hand.

I laugh at her tenacity and stubbornness.

"But it's not what I asked."

"And just like your persistence, I am now going to return to packing up because the guys are back." Their scent wafts on the light breeze.

She lifts her gaze just as they emerge from the dense woods, carrying filled water skins.

When she glances back at me, there's a disappointed expression painting her face. I shouldn't care. No. I don't give a shit if she's happy about me dismissing her question. Not at fucking all. Opening up won't serve any purpose but make me care for her more, have her stare at me with pity in her eyes.

I've left a trail of broken hearts behind me because if there's one thing I know, it's that I don't do long-term. I have no plans for a future, and I'm not dragging anyone into my mess. I doubt Narah here is a girl who does anything but long-term commitment.

Against my better judgment and telling myself not to get involved with her more than I have to, I say, "Don't look so sad, gorgeous, or you'll shatter me." I grin at her and move to toss more dirt over the fire's ashes with my foot.

"I know you're scared to open up, but it's not that hard. I mean, I'll start. I'm terrified of bumping into my ex again, scared out of my mind that my wolf will grow so submissive in his presence that I'll hand myself over to him. Then he'll try to kill me again," she says behind me, her voice soft and carries a slight tremble.

Her words touch me, fueling my anger that her soulmate made this beautiful girl so petrified. If I ever find him... he won't even see me coming before I rip him to shreds. What she doesn't know is that she has nothing to worry about from him if we're around.

When I glance over my shoulder at her, she's actually pouting at me. "Narah, babe, I'm doing you a favor by not opening up."

"Is that so?" She arches a thin eyebrow.

I really don't get why she's so persistent. "Yep. If I do, you'll fall head over heels for my charm, and I would hate to leave you broken-hearted."

She bursts out laughing, and I fucking adore her. I'm laughing with her when the others approach.

"What's so funny?" Stone asks.

"Crius told a joke," Narah says, accepting the water skin Ragnar hands her, then drinks several mouthfuls of water.

"Really?" Stone's voice climbs. "Hope it wasn't one of your dumb fart jokes." He chuckles to himself.

Ass.

I get to work, and it isn't long before we're all hiking through the woods once more. A full day passes without a single incident.

"The witches really want your sister, Narah," Nikos states. "Seeing as they've kept us alive this entire trip out of the woods."

He and Narah continue chatting, while I take the lead with Ragnar as we emerge from the forest. The late afternoon sun burns brightly just over the horizon of treetops, the sky streaked in pinks and oranges, while to our right, the sky darkens with the promise of a storm.

"Perfect timing to reach town," I mutter and glance over to Ragnar deep in his own thoughts, his brow pinched. "Where's your head at? Still buried between Narah's legs?" I tease.

He cuts me a sharp look. "Did you enjoy yourself, watching?"

He almost sounds jealous, which isn't like him. "Fuck yeah, I did. You almost sound pissed. Has she made you soft? Get your head on straight."

"My head is exactly where it needs to be."

"Could've fooled me. Looks a little lopsided," I counter, realizing how lame I sound with that comeback. "Anyway, what's our plan tonight? Food, sleep, then—"

"Then we leave at dawn for Black Hallows."

I smirk. "Shit, man, you're going to see *her*."

"Shut the hell up. We're going to ask her for a favor to track down Narah's mother."

Thankfully, I'm not the one who's fallen head over heels for a hybrid like Narah, then intend to take her into a village where Ragnar had to practically promise marriage to the seer living there for information from her when we first arrived in Romania. He hasn't returned since, so this should be a fun trip.

The closer we get to town, the stronger the smells of roasting meat and fire fill the air. My stomach rumbles. Stone is by our side now as we walk along the dirt track, peppered with establishments tailored for Alphas.

Whorehouses, bars, inns, and places to buy almost anything you need. I never thought I'd be so happy to see such a rundown shithole like this. Anything is better than being in those fucking cursed woods, that's for sure.

"I'm so hungry," Stone groans. "Tonight, I'm going to eat one of those suckling pigs all on my own."

"By the size of you, I won't be surprised. And you're getting a gut, man." I poke fun at him.

"Fuck off. I've seen you finish off an entire turkey on your own, so don't even start," Stone snaps.

I glance back at Nikos and Narah strolling behind us. Her eyes skate to mine, making me instantly scorching hot. Of course, I should keep my distance, but I also can't resist playing with her because I'm tortured that way. And really, she's the only thing that seems to distract my mind from everything else, and I like that.

When I blow her a kiss, she shows me the finger, and I suck in a deep breath, turning away, grinning.

We walk right past the inn where we'd stayed the night of our trip and keep trekking to the end of the road to a wooden cottage where Jae is being protected.

We step up onto the porch, only to find the front door ajar. There are no guards out front either, and an uneasy feeling curls down my spine.

I reach over to grab Ragnar by the shoulder to stop him, but he's already barging into the wooden cabin.

He pauses in the entryway, and I don't even need to see it. The metallic tang of blood hits me hard.

My stomach drops, and when Narah starts screaming behind me, my heart splinters into a thousand pieces.

Ragnar steps into the cabin and the massacre that greets us sickens me.

Blood.

Dead bodies.

The furniture turned over, the walls scratched, everything demolished.

"Jae!" Narah is bellowing, and I look over my shoulder at her in Nikos' arms, struggling for release. He's taking her away from the carnage. My chest is hurting from her agony.

"What the fuck happened here!" Ragnar roars, and I rush inside, scanning the place for Jae, praying I don't find her.

SIX

NARAH

"Put me down," I cry, shoving against Nikos, while he has his arm looped around my middle and is lifting me off the ground. He carries me away from the cabin that smells of death and blood, and I scream at him.

It's where we left my sister to be protected, but this is the farthest from keeping her safe, isn't it?

I can't even see straight, not when my insides feel like my heart's burst and I'm bleeding to death.

"Narah, please, just let the guys check it's safe first," Nikos keeps telling me, but I'm so angry, I keep bucking against him to let me go.

I punch, scratch, and pull at the arm he has locking me in place as tears roll down my face. "Jae," is what I keep saying and, "Let me go."

Power surges across my fingertips.

White lines dance over my hands, and Nikos flinches.

"I wouldn't do that if you were you," he threatens, not releasing his hold.

"Then release me," I hiss.

"Narah," Ragnar's voice streams from the cabin, and I shoot him a glance as he marches across the yard toward us. His shoulders are curved forward, his face looking defeated, and I burst into more tears.

Goddess, please not Jae.

My feet touch the ground, but I'm using Nikos to lean against and to stand upright. It's as if I no longer have any bones in my body, and everything inside me aches.

"Your sister isn't in the cabin," Ragnar says firmly.

I freeze, pushing away from Nikos, and stumble to Ragnar. "W-what... where is she?" I'm running before they can stop me.

Ragnar is saying something behind me, but I don't hear him. I race right past Crius and burst into the cabin where Stone's crouching by a man who's gurgling blood.

It takes me a moment to comprehend what I'm looking at. My senses are on overload, while the pungent scent of blood strangles me. More tears prick my eyes. I hate feeling so lost, so petrified.

I swallow hard, fighting the panic as I search the room. Two enormous men are strewn on the floor, their limbs twisted. One has a lethal gash across his throat, his skin torn and ripped as if ravaged by wolves, while a blade sticks out of the chest of the second guy.

The harsh afternoon light coming through the dirty windows makes everything look sickly yellow. I rush through the room, pushing aside turned furniture. "Jae!" When I don't find her in the main room, I dart into the bedroom and bathroom.

Empty.

I spin on the spot in the small hallway and the cabin tilts around me. Of course, Ragnar told me Jae wasn't here, but I had to check for myself. Growing up, Jae had been an expert at hide-n-seek, and I always had to triple-check to find her in the most unusual places. Still, my chest aches so much I can barely draw in breath.

I clench my fists and hold them to my stomach as I fall to my knees and the tears keep flowing. Who took my sister? Fucking men... it's always them, taking any Omega they find for rutting, for breeding.

Darkness swallows me, and I lean forward, crying hard, my entire body shaking while dread races through my veins. The guilt that I left her behind burns through me, stealing my breath, stealing my logic.

She couldn't have gone into the woods with us, but... I can't cope with losing her again.

A hand rubs my back. "Narah," Stone says softly, and he wraps me in his arms.

I fall into them and let him hold me as I cry against his chest, as images of Jae being terrified flood my head.

Stone holds me, stroking my back, and doesn't say a word. I don't know how long I've been crying for when I finally open my sore eyes and stare up at him.

"D-did he say anything about who took Jae?" I glance into the main room to where the gurgling guy now lies dead.

"They were ambushed by six men, but he had no clue who they were. No packs were mentioned, no names, nothing. They attacked earlier today, killed everyone, and took your sister." His voice is grave, and I hiccup another cry that spills past my lips.

"Someone must have seen something. It's broad daylight," I murmur, and I clutch onto this shirt desperately.

"That's what we're going to find out. I promise you, we'll find those assholes and destroy them," he growls. He lifts me to my feet and guides me outside, where I stumble out of his arms, drawing in fresh air.

The first drop of rain lands on my nose. I look up at the tainted clouds smearing the sky, turning the afternoon an ashen color, matching the darkness consuming me.

I bring my attention to the four Alphas standing in the yard, looking as miserable as I feel. Those dead men are their pack members, and their loss must be killing them.

Wildfire burns behind Ragnar's gaze, fury darkening his face. "Stone, take her to the inn," he commands while holding my stare. I'm falling apart, and I can't even find it in me to speak. Then he turns to Crius and Nikos. "You two are with me."

I don't remember moving, but the next thing I know, Stone and I are walking into a room at the inn. It's stale in here, dust covers the tops of the dresser and bookshelf. I keep looking at the bed, remembering the night before we left to find the witches, where Jae and I had stayed up chatting about her trip into the Shadowlands Sector. About how much I missed her. About how we'd never be apart again. I made a promise and broke it almost as fast as I'd made it.

"We should be out there," I say, turning to Stone, who shuts the door behind us. "I need to search for Jae. Maybe she's being held captive in this inn?" My mind is racing, and I'm buzzing with desperation and adrenaline. I want to run from room to room and check for her. I need to find her. Instead, I start pacing back and forth across the room. I even pop into the bathroom and grab a towel to dry the rain from my hair and off my face.

Stone somehow keeps himself calm as he strolls toward me.

Without saying a word, he takes my hand and leads me to the table and chairs near the large window that overlooks the main street below. "From up here, we have a vantage point if anything goes down. Ragnar is a ruthless hunter, and if he tracked down Jae the first time in south Romania with no real clues, trust me, he'll find her again."

I blink, waiting for my tears to stop falling, then turn my attention to the window. Down below, there's a single man sauntering toward the tavern across from the inn. Otherwise, there's no one around.

"Maybe they're long gone," I say. "We should go after them."

"Where to?" he asks, standing right next to me. "Running around frantically isn't the answer. It might feel like the right thing to do, but trust me, it's not. Once we find information, we'll track her. Someone would have noticed six men entering town, and we'll discover who, even if it means burning down this entire town."

I nod, but my stomach remains in knots. It's bad enough that we're cursed, but now we've lost Jae. I never seem to catch a break.

The rain has picked up and hits the window outside. A storm is coming, and I watch the droplets sliding down the glass remembering how Kaira and Jae loved watching drops racing down the windows when it rained. How they'd try to each pick the first droplet to reach the bottom of the window.

My throat tightens, and more tears spill down my cheeks as fast as the rain.

Lightning forks across the sky. Seconds later, the boom of thunder rattles the walls surrounding us.

I fall into my seat, my hands trembling as I hold them in my lap. "I hate to admit it, but I know you're right. I just feel like I'm dying on the inside from doing nothing."

Stone pulls up a seat next to me and we both stare outside where the rain pours down, fat drops plinking against the window.

I turn to him. "I'm sorry about the loss of your pack members."

"I'm going to slaughter whoever did this. They were decent men."

He quiets after that and looks out at the raging storm blowing through town.

I try to make sense of everything that's happened. Kaira. That Mother is still alive. Jae being kidnapped. Sometimes things are just too overwhelming, but then I remember the vision I had not too long ago while I was doing a tarot reading for a client. And my words escape past my lips.

"I think I foresaw some of this danger coming my way," I mutter.

"How?" Stone asks.

"In a vision." I clench my fists in my lap, thinking back to the vision. "I was in the woods, and Kaira was there, wearing strange markings on her face. She was really evil and kept laughing as a great wolf attacked Jae, and… it ripped her throat out." My heart hammers in my ears.

"Do you often have visions?" He shuffles his chair closer to me and curls an arm around my shoulders. I let him draw me into his embrace. I welcome the comfort, the warmth, anything to avoid feeling like I'm being hollowed out from the inside.

I shake my head no. "First time. But it's been on my mind since I saw Kaira with the witches and how different she behaved. And now Jae's gone. Goddess, you don't think the witches did this? Spelled some random guys to go get my sister?" I suddenly feel sick, and I wrap an arm around my middle.

Stone strokes my hair, and he wraps me up. "I doubt it. If they had, they would have eliminated us in the woods already."

I'm nodding, but I'm not sure what to believe anymore. I just close my eyes and let Stone's touches calm my breathing. He doesn't give me words of reassurance, but he stays by my side. His presence alone is everything to me. I grew up not putting faith in anyone but my sisters, and now with these Viking Alphas... They've shown me a part of themselves I never expected. A caring, tender side that has me clinging to them. Who would have thought Stone would be such a teddy bear, especially after I've seen him in battle? He's a savage.

The next hour moves excruciatingly slow. Stone and I barely exchange any words, and mostly that's on me. I'm too busy panicking and staring out the window.

When I spot Ragnar, Crius, and Nikos emerge from the tavern and cross the road toward the inn, I shoot to my feet. "They're coming back."

Stone is already bursting out of the room, I guess to greet them as they wouldn't know what room we're in.

Moments later, all four enter the room.

I leap to my feet, rushing over to them, staring from one face to the next. "What did you find?" The words are out of my mouth before they even shut the door.

Ragnar answers, "A couple at the tavern saw the strangers enter town and go straight to the cabin like they knew exactly where they were going." His lips pinch as irritation paints over his expression. "They said a local man at the tavern apparently spoke with them as they left town, and they had a girl with them."

I gasp, stepping closer, my pulse beating so fast the room is spinning. "And?" I'm holding my breath, unable to inhale until I hear his words.

"No one knows where the man lives, but he's a regular and comes in most days. He's never missed a night for a few drinks. So, we wait for him to return."

His words keep playing over in my head, as desperation blooms in my mind. "That's too much time to wait. One of us should wait for him and the rest of us go into the woods after them. We've all got her scent. Can we follow that?"

"Not with this rain, we can't," Nikos informs me.

I'm shaking, and my fingers play with the hem of my vest, tugging at the loose strands, while I'm fighting to not cry. Heat spreads through my chest, and I stumble back to the window, feeling completely lost. Completely empty. Completely heartbroken.

What choice do I have? I keep repeating in my mind.

I know what Ragnar will say. That we'll run around in the woods blindly, except sitting here waiting, is going to kill me.

My heart beats so fast, the sound of my racing pulse whirring in my ears.

"Narah, I promise we will find her," Ragnar says.

But when I turn to face him, I must have moved too fast because the room suddenly tilts around me, and darkness gathers at the edge of my vision, stealing everything.

The last thing I see is Ragnar lunging for me as my world blacks out.

SEVEN

The fiery blaze licks the cold from my body.

It crackles and spits embers into the night sky, the soft rain doing nothing to put out the flames.

After passing out from the panicked shock of my sister being kidnapped, I woke up and realized that I won't be of any help to anyone if I make myself sick with worry.

So now, I'm standing several feet away from the shore of the river where Ragnar, Nikos, Stone, and Crius push a small boat out into the water. The dead bodies of their pack members lay inside, wrapped in fabric. And as is tradition, they light the boat on fire.

The night comes alive with the inferno, and it draws the locals from town who've crowded around to watch the Viking cremation ceremony for the dead. These strangers whisper in the background to each other as if this were entertainment for them. There are about a dozen of them, all male, and being the only female leaves me feeling highly uncomfortable.

Every time I glance back, I notice three men staring at me lecherously, rather than paying attention to the ceremony. They make my skin crawl.

Ragnar and his men break into a sorrowful song, and I turn back around to watch them. It starts off as a hum and climbs in volume, the tune slow and heartfelt. It touches me in ways I don't expect, my chest tightening, and I swallow past my thickening throat. I don't understand the words, but in my mind, I imagine it's a farewell song to the dead. With it, my gut churns with guilt because these men lost their lives while protecting my sister... for me.

So many lives are lost in this world. My thoughts circle back to Jae and Kaira, and how I never want to say farewell to them in such a way. It would destroy me.

The night seems to be closing in around me; the smoke choking me, the storm growling overhead, and that overwhelming panic surges through me once more.

Deep breaths. I take them in slowly, needing to calm down.

Yet, each time I look at the burning boat, my heart beats furiously. It's a simple fishing boat made of wood and all Ragnar could find at the last minute. Stone had told me they normally layer the dead with jewels before the cremation, but with them having none here, I helped them collect wildflowers to use as a replacement.

I tilt my head up at the black plume of smoke... *it will carry the deceased to the afterlife,* Stone had told me.

The song pauses, and Ragnar steps closer to the water's shore. He begins to speak in a language I don't understand. Maybe Danish or Ancient Norse. But whatever he's saying, my eyes prick at the agony in his voice. The pain of loss.

As hard as I try not to, my mind pictures Jae in the boat. I wouldn't have the strength to give such a speech if I lost her. I'm shaking just thinking about it.

Ragnar falls silent, and he bends down to grab a handful of dirt, then straightens. He tosses it into the water. Each of his men does the same, and then Nikos returns to my side, his eyes glinting against the burning pyre.

"Why did you throw soil into the water?" I point my chin to the river.

He leans in closer, our shoulders touching, and whispers, "In Denmark, it's a symbol to the gods for their blessing to keep those alive with us longer. Would you like to do it and show your respect?"

I nod. "Would that be okay?"

"Of course."

I walk steadfastly to the water's edge and crouch down, scooping up a handful of the muddy earth. It's cold and almost liquid in my hand. Then I toss the soil into the river, where it lands with a loud splash.

I murmur under my breath, "May the deceased find peace in the afterlife. And please... don't ever take my sisters from me." The words stick to the back of my throat and tears collect in my eyes. The hurt and pain of everything we've gone through bubbles to the surface, the memories of them taken from me are like barbed wire tearing across my mind.

I retreat from the river, lowering my head and blinking away the tears.

Nikos stands several feet away waiting for me, and a wry smile crosses his face as I join him. The other three are already strolling toward town, lost in their own grief.

"I didn't even know the men who lost their lives," I say. "Yet I can't stop crying or thinking, what if that was my sister out there on the boat?"

Nikos stares at me for a long while before responding, his shoulders slumped. I'm not used to seeing him this way. He's normally more confident and sure of himself.

"My mother would tell me that death will leave a broken heart, but love will always leave a memory no one can take from you."

"That's so beautiful and sad." I tuck those words away in my mind, needing to remind myself of them on the days when I think I can't go on. And it makes me wonder how much heartache Nikos lives with to hold onto such words too.

He lifts his eyes and gazes out at the river, shadows gliding across his hardened face. "She lost her family to war, then was forced to marry my father for survival. He treated her as well as any brutal Alpha does, but she told me she found her joy when I was born. She still found a way to look at the beauty and positivity in the world amid so much death and chaos. She never forgot her family, even if she watched them get butchered in pack combat. I often think of her when I feel myself falling apart."

I move my hand to his, taking it in mine. We stand in silence and stare out at the burning boat as it floats down the river and out of sight.

"I'm sorry," I finally say, unsure of what you're supposed to say in such a situation.

"Nothing to be sorry about. Fucked up shit happens to every single one of us, and those of us who survive have to find a way to live with it."

"And this is why the world is as broken as it is. All of us have major issues in our heads." I half-laugh at how pathetic that sounds.

"You're definitely right there." His grin warms me, and I'd rather see him smiling than be sorrowful. "Tonight we're going to wait in the tavern for the guy who spoke to your sister's kidnappers, and then we'll find her." His tone grows thick, as if he's fighting his own grief.

"How close were you and those three men?"

"Close enough to have met their parents and siblings."

I nod and lean against him, letting him know I'm here for him. Sometimes that's the best you can do when everything else is falling apart around you. Father once told me that grief is all the love I want to give but can't. It's the built-up agony of not being able to share how much someone means to me.

Rain comes down harder now, as though the universe waited for the ceremony to end. The few locals who stayed to watch the fire are rushing back to town. We stand at the water's edge for a few more moments in silence.

"Let's head back." Nikos' hand curls tighter around mine and he guides us back through the dark woods.

The tension never leaves my body: for the lost lives, for my sister kidnapped, for what's yet to come.

I just need my sisters by my side, and then I'll be the happiest person in the world.

Once we reach the clearing that backs onto the rear of the tavern, I spot Ragnar, who looks back at us from amid the crowd of men that were at the funeral. He signals to Nikos with a flick of his hand, then points to the tavern. The three of them stroll inside. I look down at my free hand, still covered in mud and feeling sticky. I glance around for water and spot a tap just to the side of the tavern.

"Hey, give me a sec," I say and dart over to scrub the mess off my hands, figuring we're probably going to eat.

Nikos joins me, both of us scrubbing the dirt away under the running water, our hands touching, gently pushing each other aside. It's the first time since we arrived back in town that I've remembered I should be wearing my gloves. The top half of my fingers are stained black from magic, but luckily it's too dark for anyone else to see them. Though I'm surprised Nikos isn't freaking out about them at all.

In the woods, he was standoffish, but now he's different. There's a vulnerability to him, his walls lowered for a change. I guess attending a funeral makes people soften.

Without warning, he splashes me in the face.

I flinch and laugh. "Hey, that's how wars start. And you may not know this, but I am the queen of water bombs."

He chuckles. "Bring it on."

The splash of footsteps behind Nikos has me lifting my gaze over his shoulder, half expecting one of the other men coming to find out why we're dragging our feet.

But suddenly there is a rush of movement, a swish of air coming right at us, moving so fast, and I respond too slow.

Three strange men tackle Nikos, and an arm locks around his throat, his knees knocked out from under him. He hits the ground with a growl, and I stumble backward, shock strangling the breaths out of me. Two of them start hammering punches into Nikos' face and gut. He grunts and throws back hits, but he's overpowered fast.

I scream and rush toward them, power already racing down my arms. I don't care how haywire it goes, I'll burn down the whole freaking town if it means these three get the fuck away from us.

On my next step, one of the men swings around, his fist cracking me in the side of the head. It comes so hard and unexpected that I trip over my own feet, literally falling sideways and to the ground.

Burning pain spikes through my head, like my skull's been split in half and my brain is spilling out. I'm convinced that's what's happening as I cry out and reach for my head. But there's no blood.

The world spins around me, everything growing blurry. My head throbs like there's a heart inside it, thumping loudly.

Hands are yanking me off the ground. Pushing against my assailant, I recoil frantically but fall over again.

A shadow is cast over me as my vision comes back. A man stands above me and he shoves his foot down on my chest, pinning me to the ground.

"You're not going anywhere, Omega whore." The man spits the words at me, then sniffs the air. "I'm going to fuck you, then my friends will take their turn until there's nothing left of you."

I'm trembling, terror thundering through me. What the fuck!

That's when I get a better look at the man, at his broad chin, at his beady eyes, at his receding hairline. I recognize him instantly as one of the men watching me during the funeral ceremony. Bastards had been waiting for the right moment to attack.

It's what Alphas in the Savage Sector do. There's no top Alpha to command over them, so it's every man for himself. Each female is an object, whether she's with another man or not.

"Get the fuck off me," I wheeze, barely able to draw a breath from how heavily he presses down on me.

Lifting my hands, not even hesitating for a second, magical sparks leap from my fingertips. I shove my palms against his legs.

White zapping lines jolt up his legs, curling around them like serpents. He yelps and leaps off me, desperately patting his legs as if his pants are on fire.

My magic goes haywire and strands of power zap wildly from my hands, striking the back of the tavern, turning the whole stone wall black as if it's been burned to a crisp. Bits start falling away, creating tiny holes. Oh, shit.

I risk a fast glance over to Nikos, but all I see is a tangled ball of arms and legs, the growls from him deepen as they relentlessly beat into Nikos. But he gives just as good as he gets, and I can't tell who the heck is winning.

The other asshole is swinging back around and rushing at me madly. The hatred on his face terrifies me.

I scramble to my feet, but his fists collide with my chest.

The pain is explosive, and all the air rushes from my lungs in a tremendous gasp. I'm flying backward and smack into the ground hard. I cry out at the horrific pain sprawling across my chest, swallowing me. I can't suck in air, as though my lungs are frozen.

I lay on my back, my mouth opening and closing, and I smack a hand to my chest to breathe again.

The creep leans over me, laughing. He grabs at my hair with a fist and wrenches my head up off the ground. "Stop fighting, witch, or I'll cut your hands off." He shoves my head back down, and I wince at striking the hard surface again. He tears at my shirt, fabric ripping, the buttons under my vest popping.

Air slowly seeps into my lungs, and I wince while my hands push against him. But he shoves my arms away. He's pulling at the buttons on my pants, my whole body shuddering at how roughly he handles me.

Dread and fury collide within me.

I strike him with everything I have, shoving my hands into his face, kicking him. I lash out, scratching my nails down the side of his face, drawing blood, pulling his hair.

He growls and whacks my arm aside again. "Bitch, you'll be sorry you did that."

The look of death spreads over his face… my death.

He's going to murder me.

My heart thumps loudly in my ears as I crawl backward, dragging my ass away.

He lunges at me with the full force of a tornado, and I scream, jutting my hands in front of me, my skin tingling with magic.

Suddenly, the man flies backward and away from me, shock on his face, his wide eyes looking almost comical. He hits the ground devastatingly and groans in pain.

A huge, white wolf lunges out of the shadows and slams into the man so viciously that even from where I'm lying, I hear the crack of bones, the painful exhalation of air from crushed lungs.

I'm on my feet in moments, my pulse racing, but I can't move away. I freeze in place, staring at the wolf tearing into the man, claws and teeth shredding flesh, creating a gaping cavity in the middle of his chest.

My stomach rolls at the sight, and I look away quickly, only to discover the other two men lying in a heap of their own blood, their throats completely ripped out.

I shoot my attention back to Nikos in wolf form, destroying these men with such brutality that it should terrify me to my core. But I want him to hurt them, to tear them apart.

I've seen these Viking Alphas in their wolf forms battling the bears. These men specialize in battle. But this... I'm shocked at how easily Nikos rips their lives away without mercy. There is only anger and revenge, and it's beautiful.

He pauses, still standing atop the dead man and lifts his head up, then unleashes a haunting howl into the night.

Other howls in the distance sing back, connecting with him... there are so many out there that I have no idea how exactly my sisters and I will live safely without a pack's protection. I shake those thoughts away and study the massive wolf.

Rain pelts down on him, washing the blood from his mouth down his white fur.

Nikos is a wolf. A wild beast.

Every inch of him.

He's quiet most days, keeping to himself, but I see his true form now. The warrior who lays within, and how, despite everything, he's a survivor.

He turns his huge head in my direction and his eyes show the strength of this wolf, his soul, his heart. His ears are pointy, his teeth concealed, and he steps off the dead man, then makes his way toward me. His body contorts, fur vanishing, and in a few steps, he stands before me in his human form.

Naked.

Sexy as hell.

And so many muscles. He would easily put most men to shame with that ripped stomach, the strong chest, his biceps... goddess, everything about him is hard... including his cock. I gasp. Does that come after making a kill?

I quickly lift my eyes to look at where blood smears across his chest and mouth. Purple bruises under his eye and a bite mark scores his shoulder. A dark mark colors the side of his ribs, but somehow he's got no busted lip or nose.

"You're hurt." My words come out breathless. I'm not sure what makes me more shocked... his nakedness, his injuries, or how quickly he finished off three wolf shifters.

"I'll heal. Are you all right?"

I nod. "I'm fine."

"That fucking bastard, had no right ever touching you. I should have tortured him more, made him regret ever crossing us." His gaze sweeps over my body, pausing at the torn shirt under my vest. He reaches over and pulls at the fabric to straighten it, though with all the buttons gone, it's sort of useless. But the vest holds it in place. It will have to do.

"What you did is just... fearless."

He chuckles, then winces as his eye with the bruise squints. "I've never been called that before."

I slide a hand to the side of his face where he's injured. "Does it hurt?"

"I've had worse. And you know what they say... the more scars you have, the stronger your heart." He has his hands on my waist, and studies me like he might have missed an injury.

"I've never heard anyone say that before," I say.

"It's an old Norse proverb I've picked up, though I'm certain I'm butchering it. Words don't always stay in my head."

"Thank you for fighting for me."

His thumb strokes the skin he's found under my shirt over my hip bone. It sends tingles through me, the strange emotion of adrenaline and arousal tangling into a dangerous mix.

"They came so fast and scared the hell out of me," I murmur.

He's closer to me now, his breath on my face, and all I'm staring at are his lips, bits of blood at the corners of his mouth.

"The fault is mine for not keeping my guard up. This place is full of rogue Alphas and Betas who hunger for Omegas. But I won't let any of them touch you ever again."

His grip tightens, and I gasp. Something flares in his gaze, something primal. His wolf is there, still hyped up from the fight, and now Nikos stares at me like I'm his meal. His reward.

Both of us are bruised, him naked, me shaking, and we're standing in the dark. My heart is thundering in my chest at his touch, at how I can only focus on the point of contact where his fingers crawl across my stomach.

I don't push him away, not when I'm drowning in his attention. My nipples stiffen against the fabric of my shirt, and my mind is screaming to back the hell away as I find myself falling into his gaze. I shouldn't be turned on by any of these men, but each has a pull on me I don't want to understand.

"Back in the woods, you warned me about being with Ragnar and you three," I remind him, hoping it will force some logic into my lust-soaked brain too.

"I never said stay away from me." That cocky expression washes over his face.

Narrowing my gaze, I'm pretty sure he did mention me making a deal with all of them, but my head isn't exactly focused right now.

"I can smell your fear," he tells me, eyeing me from head to toe.

"I'm not afraid of you," I respond quickly, holding myself stiff. Thing is, I am shaking slightly because as strong as I act around these Alphas, they do scare me.

"That's not the kind of terror I'm talking about." He brings his face closer to mine, and for a ridiculous moment, I want to pretend this is real and that I have a man like Nikos in my life. Someone who fights to the death to protect me, whose stare alone has me imagining the dirtiest thoughts.

So much has happened in my life that in reality, I've never had much time to daydream about men. I accepted long ago my role is to be paired with someone I hoped would protect me and my sisters. But what I keep feeling around these four Vikings leaves me confused and constantly aroused.

"Then what kind of terror?" I breathe the words.

"You're scared to let yourself want me."

I roll my eyes extra hard to show him how far from the truth he is, except he laughs at me and my facade crumbles. So, I push myself forward and our mouths crush together. I can't help myself. His lips call to me, and he just saved my life.

His hungry fingers sweep around my back, pressing me tight against him, and he kisses me ravenously. He groans, licking my lips, and I taste the metallic blood of the other Alpha. The fact that I'm tasting it and kissing this hulking Viking excites me.

It's crazy the attraction I feel for this man I barely know. And the primal, guttural sounds he makes are so sexy. Goosebumps cover my skin with the heat building between us.

Flames ignite between my thighs, and I moan at the way his hand slides under my shirt and cups my breast.

"I love your body," he murmurs as he slides his hand down my stomach and pops open the button of my pants. His hand glides under the elastic of my underwear, holding my gaze. "It's perfect."

Something catches in my chest from his touch, from his words. I grew up never being told I was beautiful or anything along those lines. Just that I had to be the older sister, do the right thing, but to hear Nikos say those words has my knees softening.

I forget about everything but this dangerous man who's kissing me again, so passionately, I push closer against him. His fingers slide along my drenched core, and he growls in a possessive way that tells me he wants so much more.

"Your adorable kiss, your wet pussy, melt my heart," he says between our kisses. Then he pushes a finger into me, and I moan, realizing how starved I am for his touch. His mouth is on mine with the kind of passion that makes my skin tingle with electricity. Everything about him has me floating, with all my problems falling away.

When he pushes another finger into me, my world explodes. I clutch onto his shirt, holding myself up, and I'm completely lost to him.

"Do you want this now?" he asks.

I moan my answer, "Yes."

But the grunt that comes from behind us distracts me, rudely interrupting us. Nikos pulls away instantly, and he turns to find Crius standing at the corner of the tavern. It reminds me of him watching Ragnar and me in the woods, and now I'm with Nikos.

Heat sears my insides, and I lower my head, my cheeks burning. What does he think of me? That I screw any man who shows me attention? I shouldn't care, but for some reason, I do.

I'm rushing past Nikos before I know it, and right by Crius, not able to look at him.

In haste, I button up my pants and fix the shirt underneath my vest, while cursing myself.

What the hell are you doing?

I push open the swinging tavern door and instantly spot Ragnar and Stone near the window at a round table already filled with plates of food and glasses of beer.

The room is mostly made up of men, with a few females who look like the kind you hire by the hour.

Men look at me as if I'm the new entertainment, but when Ragnar stands up and whistles, the whole room looks his way.

"She's with me, so keep your eyes to yourself before I rip them out," he growls.

Biting my lip, I hurry across the room while my heart is pounding at his possessiveness. I know the men keep telling me Ragnar shares everything with them, but the way he's staring at me right now leaves me wondering if he'd tear apart Nikos if he saw what Crius had.

"Perfect timing, asshole," I rasp at Crius as I march toward him while he stands at the corner of the tavern. Because of his interruption, Narah bolted from my arms just when I had been ready to fuck her and make her mine.

Now, I'm left outside with Crius, his gaze sharpening at my words. Yet he doesn't bat an eye at the three dead dudes, but then again, I've seen him take out a man for simply looking at him wrong.

"I never said to stop." His lips curl up with his smirk. "I was rather enjoying the show, though it would be better if I wasn't staring at your ugly, naked ass the whole time. But not sure how Ragnar would feel about you pulling that shit with his girl, but you know, you do you."

I pause in front of him, my teeth clenching, and I am dying to smash my fist into his smug face for pissing me off. On the bright side, he's not losing control of his wolf, but he's being his usual sarcastic prick.

"What the fuck, man? We share. That has always been the agreement." Honestly, I'm not certain why I even care. If he wants her for himself, I shouldn't give a rat's ass, but for some goddamn reason, I do.

No female has ever called to me like she does, so I can't deny the rise she gets out of me. All I can think about is pinning her against the wall and taking her savagely, making sure she'll never forget the way I fuck her. How I won't stop until I break her and she begs for more. Her vulnerable edge nearly destroys me, and each time she blushes around me, my cock hardens. So what the hell am I supposed to do with that?

I've just finished drowning in her softness, in her sugary, sex-filled scent. Somehow, I managed some semblance of control around her, or I would already be balls deep inside her, so that's a miracle in itself.

But my desire for her isn't the biggest issue here, now is it? And neither is Ragnar's feral possessiveness over her. I've seen the way he looks at her, too. The issue is that I'm not the only one who wants her. Especially when just watching her is hypnotic, the way she walks with her hips swaying, how she tilts her head whenever she's talking to you like she's utterly absorbed in the conversation. The girl's completely oblivious to the impact she has on those around her.

"Don't know what to say, bruh, but you see the way Ragnar is with her." Crius shrugs nonchalantly like he doesn't give a shit. What a liar. "He's already fucked her twice, bitten her, marked her. Never seen him do that before with another Omega. There's something about her, so just saying, don't get your hopes up that he'll share this one." He almost sounds like he's looking out for me. Crius might be a dickhead, but he has his caring moments.

But going back to his words, I knew Ragnar took her a second time, but I won't lie, it stings like a bitch after I kissed her. Especially after groping the softness of her breast, remembering the way she clutched onto me, making those delicious moaning sounds. She's the kind of woman who brings men like me to their knees, and my blood pumps ferociously to my dick as I picture her wet pussy... if only I got the chance before knuckle-head here interrupted us.

"Are you trying to convince me or yourself?" I snarl in response and walk past him, my wolf still roaring inside me, my lust for her slaughtering me. But I have the willpower to ride this through, because I don't have another choice.

I look down at myself, completely nude and splattered in blood. My concern isn't the nudity in front of others, not when it's second nature for wolves, but more that the blood might be a dead giveaway that I murdered those guys. Not sure Ragnar will appreciate us being attacked during our celebration feast for the dead.

I march right past the tavern and into the inn where our stuff is. By the time I re-emerge, dressed in new clothes and clean of blood, I'd come up with an answer to dealing with Narah. Marking her might be out of the question for now, but that doesn't mean I can't enjoy teasing her, making her blush, and having her come to me. Who says going down on her isn't possible? That's not exactly claiming a girl. And I'm fucking aching to taste her, to have her sit on my face. Then, it's her choice, really. It's not like I can deny the adorable little thing if she begs me for more.

With a grin, I shove the door open and march inside the tavern.

The smell of beer and roasting meats hits me instantly, followed by a pungent perspiration from too many fucking men. The joint is full of Alphas and Betas, most paying attention to half a dozen females serving meals and flirting with them. A red-haired woman in a black slinky dress stands on a small stage, belting out a heartfelt song, which is mostly drowned out by the raucous laughter and voices.

I cross the busy room, swerving around packed tables, and reach ours near the window. I flop down in the empty seat.

Narah sits next to Ragnar. They're all staring at me, except Narah. She has her head low and is stabbing her fork into a roasted potato. She's wearing black gloves to cover her magic-stained fingers because the Neanderthals in this part of the world fear magic instead of embracing it.

Look at us sharing a meal like one happy-go-lucky family.

"What'd you change clothes for?" Stone asks me, always the inquisitive bastard sticking his nose where it doesn't belong. He's Ragnar's cousin and the reserved one of the bunch. Crius gives him a lot of shit, but I'm starting to realize it's his form of showing affection. Crius is damn loyal to the pack and us four, and while Stone is the same, he is also a terrifying fighter especially when he wields his elemental magic. I glance at the ink of his runes that peek out over his collarbone and neck from under his shirt. I remember him once telling me it was a custom that came down from his mother's family to be inked with them at the age of five, even if his father loathed them.

We're an odd group who all have major father issues. Maybe that's the reason we all work so well together, especially under Ragnar's command. He always puts his pack first, unlike our own fathers.

I look over at Stone, who's watching me. Right, he's waiting for a response. So, I give him a lame one. "Why are you obsessed with what I'm wearing?" I answer and reach over to fill my plate with slices of beef brisket, roasted vegetables, and toasted bread smothered in butter. My mouth's salivating.

"It's just a question." He pushes the point, then takes a long drink from his glass of beer.

"I think he wants to see you naked," Crius stage whispers to me, chuckling. "I mean, I don't get it, Stone. Have you seen Nikos' ass? It's nasty."

Narah half-chuckles, glancing up, looking at me through her long lashes, and I'm not sure if I should take her response as an insult, or maybe she's a lot more laid back than I think.

Plus, I appreciate Crius derailing the conversation. He knows Stone as well as me, who's like a dog with a bone when something's got him curious.

Stone gulps down the rest of his deep brown beer and sets the glass on the table, already eyeing the server girl for a refill. "His ass is the last thing I want."

Crius howls into laughter, slamming a hand to the table, making everything on it jump, which has Ragnar shaking his head as he digs into his meal. "I get it. You want cock."

"Just fuck off, both of you," I answer, unable to stop smiling at our usual table conversations, revolving around cocks and getting laid… we just haven't progressed to the latter topic yet. And I'm guessing we won't with Narah in our company.

When the server arrives, she floods the table with more plates of assortments from pasta covered in molten cheese, baked salmon, hard cheeses, and a platter of fruit with nuts dipped in honey.

Narah is already helping herself to the green grapes, coated with the sweet bee nectar, and pops one into her mouth, then another, a drop of honey dripping from the corner of her mouth. Her tongue darts out quickly and licks it up. I'm utterly mesmerized. It's clear I pay way too much attention to this girl.

But I'd have to be a eunuch to not notice such beauty.

Everyone's gone quiet at the table, as I'm not the only one watching the way she's eating the grapes, her lips pressed around each one before sucking it into her mouth. I won't lie, my cock is twitching at the image. And in my mind, I'm suddenly back with her outside, squeezing her breast, drawing her tongue against mine, and inhaling the scent that is all sex.

I'm craving to slide my fingers into her pants and her drenched core, teasing her clit as I make her scream, as she looks at me with those amber eyes. She wants to say no, but can't help herself and pleads for more. I'm desperate to see the honey seeping from her pussy after I bring her to climax, again and again.

My heart is racing, and I shift in my chair uncomfortably.

Goddammit.

She's killing me, and I pull my attention away from her and back to my food. All I'm doing is giving myself a hard-on and blue balls with such thoughts. Still, I can't help but smirk at how close I came and how I'll make her mine one way or another.

Ragnar has his hand under the table, and it's clear he's stroking her thigh. She's smiling up at him with the same look she gave me outside. Fire flares in my chest, but I also know my place and need to pull back before I leap over the table and lose control.

The thing about Omegas is that no matter how hard an Alpha resists, we're biologically drawn to them, so these emotions driving me mad are nature's way of ensuring our race continues, that we rut and make babies. But the part I find curious is the strength of allure I feel for her when she's not even in heat or my fated mate.

I'm worried for her if she ever does go into heat around us because I have no idea how we'll be able to hold back without us killing each other to get to her.

It's why many females aren't seen around. Many are claimed before their heat hits, especially when they meet their fated mate.

It was one reason Ragnar's sister was sent to my pack. Her heat made her ready, and that also made her a wanted asset. Like me, we were both pawns to be traded. According to my father, that would be like hitting two birds with one stone.

"You leave today, Nikos," Father commands from the doorway of my chamber, his shoulders broad, his deep chestnut hair pulled back off his brutally scarred face. His green eyes narrow against the morning sun's rays drenching my room. Mother tells me they are just like mine, but I refuse to believe I share anything with the man who once told me his offspring were nothing but pawns to be used to grow his strength. And that one day, I'll make him proud when my time comes.

I'm on my feet, putting down the book I'd been reading on historic warfare by a tribe called Samurai. "What mission am I to complete this time?"

Since I could walk, I've been training in warfare, so he uses me on missions, which I suspect are mostly to do with getting me out of his way.

His lips thin and turn upward, the conniving expression on his face suddenly worrying me. He never smiles at me, and when he does, it comes with pain at my expense. Last time he looked at me this way, I traveled across the country to spy on a new encroaching pack, only to find myself in the middle of a savage territory war that had shit to do with me. I ended up with two broken ribs and a cracked skull. When I returned home, Father's only response had been, "I hear you fell in battle. What good are you to me?"

But I accepted long ago to live with his cruelty, as have my two older brothers.

"A mission of utmost importance," he answers. "I've found a bride for your brother, Anker, and with it comes peace from the brute Ulv Wolves who are on our doorsteps. We lose warriors daily to war on both sides."

I wait for my role in his latest scheme to become clear.

But before he responds, several of his guards charge into the room and seize me by the arms. I shove against them, my pulse racing. "What the hell's going on?"

Father strolls into my room, his hands resting across his round belly. "I've struck a deal with the Alpha of Ulv Wolves. To create peace between our packs, he will send us his only daughter, and you will be the exchange from our pack."

My stomach hardens. "Fuck no! I won't do this." My thoughts fly to my mother left with him, to Eve, the girl I gave my promise to marry when she came into her heat, which should be soon. She's fifteen, and I'm twenty-one. I've adored her for so long that I don't care if she's my fated mate or not. She's mine.

I thrash against the guards' iron grips. "Release me," I growl.

But Father steps up to me and grabs my hair, fisting it, forcing my head to the side, giving me a sickening smile. "Listen here, you little shit. Blood bleeds into our rivers from all the dead, and your life has finally received purpose from the gods. You will go to the enemy and learn to love them, suck their cocks for all I care, but you make it fucking work as your presence ceases our war."

A deep rumble rolls inside me. "You sonofabitch!" My heart is pounding, and I shake with fury.

Father releases me. "You ever set foot in my home again and I will kill you myself. You are no longer a Balor wolf. Now make me proud," he mocks. With a wave of his hand, the guards haul my ass out of my family home.

I shove against them fiercely when a sharp jab strikes the back of my neck. My world spins suddenly, and my knees hit the ground. Everything's a blur, and the last person I see is my mother, crying, calling for me as I'm whisked away.

That was over three years ago, when my life grew so dim I've never found my light again, and the wound in my soul is still as fresh as if Father's rejection just happened.

I swallow a mouthful of food when a shadow falls over our table. It silences Stone's constant chatter, and I glance up to the barkeeper, wiping his hands on his short apron. "The man you've been waiting for has arrived." He glances over at a guy striding across the tavern. He looks to be in his forties, has a handlebar mustache, and wears a checkered shirt and slacks.

"Thank you," Ragnar says and shakes the man's hand, sliding into his palm a silver coin for payment.

When the barkeeper retreats with a huge grin, Stone and Crius march toward the poor sucker who has no clue what's coming his way. I finish the rest of my beer when Ragnar catches my eye. He gives me a knowing nod, one that states we don't let the man walk away until we get what we need out of him. "Do what it takes," he instructs, then turns to Narah. "Let's leave."

She frowns. "What? No, I have to find out."

Ragnar's on his feet and grabs her by the arm, forcing her out of her chair. "I'll carry you if I have to. We'll find out soon enough, but in case things get out of hand, I don't want you in the thick of it."

Despite her protests, he hauls her out of the tavern. I do adore her feistiness.

When I glance back around, Stone and Crius are practically carrying the guy toward me. His face is panic-stricken, and instantly I know this will be an easy job. He also came in alone, so I doubt he has buddies who'll jump in to fight for him.

I scan the room regardless, just in case.

Crius shoves the guy toward our table, and I kick out an empty chair. "Sit," I instruct.

He slides into the seat quickly, his face pale and eyes widening with that panicked look as he frantically turns his attention from me to Stone and Crius.

"What's this about?" he asks with a shaky voice. "I want no trouble."

"And you'll have none if you answer our questions," I say, taking the steak knife from the table and start spinning it over my fingers. More for effect, but if he pisses me off, he may lose a finger or two.

He sees me staring at his hand and bunches them in his lap. "Please, I never knew the sheep belonged to you, or I never would have taken it."

"Fuck man, we don't want to know about your weird-ass fetish," Crius growls, scrunching up his nose.

He's trembling before I can even grill him.

Stone is groaning. "Shit! He's pissed his pants."

I shuffle backward, not wanting to be near him. "Fucking hell. Okay, let's make this quick," I blurt. "Yesterday, six men left town with a female. And you spoke with them, correct?"

He nods. He's such a weasel-like man with a thin neck that can easily be snapped. "Yes, I-I bumped into them as I left the tavern. The girl looked scared and was crying, but one of the men had his hand over her mouth." He shrugs. "But really, what could I do? It was six against me, and it's not the first time females have been traded or taken, so I didn't think much of it."

I sigh because he's right. Women are commodities, but that

doesn't mean I'll stand by and let assholes get away with it either.

The man's staring at me then glances down at the steak knife in my grasp. "I-if it was just one or two of them, I could have taken them on," he drones on, which are all lies. This guy's a runner, not a fighter.

"Stop shitting your pants, man," Crius says, sitting on his other side. "We don't need you to fight. Just tell us what the fuck they said. Names, anywhere they went. What the hell did they say that can help us find them?"

Stone sits across the table and is leaning forward, staring death into the poor man's soul.

"T-they told me to fuck off and shoved me out of the way. I didn't try to make conversation with them, but I did hear one name." He gasps for air, his chest pumping furiously for oxygen.

"And? What the fuck are you pausing for?" Stone snarls.

"M-Martell. One of them kept mentioning someone called Martell."

"Martell." I choke out the name, and instantly my wolf shoves forward, moaning in my chest as if his name alone has awakened her longing, but I'm shaking with anger, and I glance at the four Vikings who've just given me a rundown of who took Jae. "That fucking cocksucker," I blurt, causing Crius to smirk and nod at my outburst. "I can't believe he took her."

But I also detest how quickly my wolf reacts to hearing his name.

Just saying it leaves a bitter taste in my mouth, and I think I'm going to hurl. He's my fated mate and the man who not only rejected me but threw me off a cliff. I hadn't even spent one night with him before he discovered my magic and abandoned me. Bastard. All because wolves like me who carry magic are cursed.

We're hunted.

Hated.

Destroyed.

And I'm going to shove all that cursed bullshit right up his ass when I find him for stealing my sister. That piece of shit. I'm shaking with anger.

I glance over to the four Vikings in the room with me, knowing they are so different from other wolves in the Savage Sector, and part of me wonders how much that has to be a regional thing. Especially seeing as Stone and Crius carry some sort of magic of their own.

These emotions strangling me aren't like before, and I thank the moon for Ragnar's bite to tame my wolf's desperation over Martell. But still, the fact that a name alone has her stirring worries me. How will she react when I cross paths with him?

I refuse to be weak for him again. To let my body betray me over a man who tried to murder me. I will get my sister back and make him pay. To get my revenge because if he's found me, he'll never stop until he gets what he wants... my death. Because I may be many things, but I'm no fool. As much as that bastard hates me, his wolf will be pining after me too. That's why he needs to find me. Eliminate the problem, and his wolf will get over me, which leaves my sisters vulnerable. I should fear him, but I'm too angry that he's found us.

"I need to go after her right now!" My hands are shaking badly.

"Are you sure about this?" Ragnar asks me. "Traveling in the dark can be dangerous."

Every inch of me is trembling, not because of his words, but that the longer I do nothing, the farther my sister gets from me while in the company of the devil.

"I'm not backing down. You can come with me or stay here, but I'm going. Nikos said they were on foot, so if we're on horses, we should catch up to them, right?"

He rubs his hand across the short stubble across his jawline. "Depends on whether they found transportation, and if they stayed on the same road. But I'm ready to spill blood if you are."

I tilt my head back, meeting his gaze. The man is panty-melting gorgeous, and he's proven it twice, which can distract me horribly. But to hear the determination in his voice, to know I'm not alone, fills me with confidence.

"I love your tenacity, Narah," Crius adds, drawing my attention from Ragnar. "Maybe you can send some over to me. Maybe with a kiss, just like you—"

"Thanks for the compliment, but you definitely are not lacking tenacity," I reply, instantly stealing the rest of his words while my heart hammers louder in my chest. Who would have thought that Crius is such a blabbermouth. But maybe he's told the other two about Nikos and me in the back of the tavern. It doesn't stop the heat crawling up my neck at what Ragnar might think.

Even Stone, who hasn't said a word and stands as still as a statue, studies me like he knows all my dirty secrets, which has me blushing even more.

"She has you there," Ragnar mutters, his voice dark, his attention focused on the window.

Crius runs his fingers down the two plaits of his brown beard, smirking. "Fine, but just so we make it clear. I will fucking bury every single asshole involved in Jae's kidnapping. Your sister's actually decent."

"No one's arguing with you on that point," Stone states.

"I'm just putting it out in the universe before one of your bastards steals my kills."

I snort a laugh at what he's worried about. "As long as I get Jae back in one piece, I don't care who kills them, but I want that bastard, Martell, sliced from throat to groin."

"Oh fuck me, but that's that hottest thing you've ever said." Crius groans, his hand slides down his body and gropes his cock over his pants.

Such a sexy animal, and I can't help but be turned on by him. I have every belief that he's rough in the bedroom, dominating, and rather large by the size of the package he's groping. In truth, I think that about all three of them... big bastards who could easily pin me down and have their way with me. Ragnar's already conquered me, and I can't even say it will never happen again. I know that if he comes for me, I'll melt.

But my head is pounding with worry for Jae, so I straighten my shoulders. "Are we doing this or not?"

"Fine," Ragnar finally answers. "I'll go down and find us some horses. The tavern owner was talking about someone who has a farm nearby. Stone, you're with me."

"I'm coming too if you're going to the tavern," Crius adds. "I'm fucking thirsty."

"Nikos, Narah?" Ragnar asks, an eyebrow arching ever so slightly in my direction.

"I'll wait here," I answer, standing near the bed, not in the mood to be surrounded by loud noises. When I'm so tense, I feel like I'm going to burst out crying any moment now.

"That makes two of us," Nikos responds, gaining a tight grin and nod from Ragnar, and the three of them walk out of the room, shutting the door behind them.

"Looks like it's just the two of us," he murmurs.

I look over at Nikos, the Viking who tempted me behind the tavern, and realize that maybe us being alone isn't such a good thing. He strolls across the room, his chestnut hair long and tied into one big dreadlock hanging down past his shoulders, the sides of his head shaved. His skin is tanned like he's spent his entire life outdoors. He's wearing dark jeans that perfectly fit him, following the curve of that scorching hot ass. Even in a simple, long-sleeved V-neck shirt, he's absolutely captivating. He's a giant. His hands could easily touch the ceiling if he reached up, especially next to me, but that just draws me to him even more.

He flops down on a chair at the table by the window. The faint light overhead flickers like it might go out. I doubt the generators to run this inn are sturdy enough to keep the rooms lit while the tavern blares with light.

"Sit down," he says and pushes out a seat for me with his foot.

He's leaning forward with his folded arms on the table, and they're huge too. There's something extremely sexy about strong forearms. Maybe it's knowing he can hold me in them and I'll feel safe. He has his eyes locked on me, watching my every move as I step closer. But there's something dancing behind them tonight like I'm the deer and he's the starved wolf studying his prey.

Makes me wonder why he decided to be the babysitter tonight... Does it have anything to do with our kiss behind the tavern?

Everything about Nikos is striking, especially when he looks at me as if I'm his meal.

I slide into the chair and pull my knees up, hugging them to my chest. "Do you think Jae will be okay?"

He loses that seductive look, his face taking on a serious expression. "If they wanted to hurt her, they would have done it in town instead of kidnapping her. Means they are taking her to someone or intend to use her for leverage."

Feeling sorry for myself, for Jae, I just sigh and prop my chin onto my knees. "It's me Martell wants, but he took my sister to ensure he gets that." He'll go to any length to get me back, to kill me, to put a stop to his wolf's agony. I should have known this would be the case, but I'd been too busy drowning myself. Plus, I tried hard to push him out of my thoughts for my wolf's sake.

Gold flecks glint in Nikos' green eyes, and I close mine, wanting the sting in my chest for Jae to end. He takes my hand and drags me off my seat, my eyes flying open. I stand in front of him as he remains seated, my ass propped up against the table.

"I'm going to do you a favor," he mutters, his hands on my hips, keeping me in place, his thumbs finding the bare skin peeking out from under my vest.

"Is that so?" I can't help but smile, even though part of me wants to cry that things keep going badly for me.

"Before every fight and hunt, we are taught to find peace with our inner demons. So that when you step into battle, there is nothing to distract you, only the primal rage you hold toward your enemy."

"So, what do you do to clear your mind? Meditate? Train?"

"Find a girl and fuck her brains out."

I might have just gasped, as that isn't the response I expected.

He's smiling, the corners of his eyes crinkling, seeming to love the reaction that drew from me.

"Well, I guess that's one way of doing it. Can't say I've ever tried that, but I can see how it makes you forget everything." I'm rambling and hot all of a sudden under Nikos' attention.

"We started something behind the tavern, and I want more. I want to be with you, Narah. It's that simple."

I struggle for a moment to respond, as my mind is still caught on his earlier words. Finally, I find my voice, saying, "Nothing is ever simple, you know that. And it sounds complicated to me."

He pulls me toward him to stand between his legs, his large hands grasping my hips, and he's eye-level with my chin, his gaze on my lips. "Only if you make it so."

My breathing quickens a little. He might be onto something because I'm completely lost when I'm near him. Captivated by the way his fingers slide across my back under my vest and shirt.

"I want to give you something that I know will help," he breathes the words, leaning closer, his mouth on my neck.

I tremble, unable to move. "And you'll get something out of it too, I suppose."

"Of course. I want to know if your pussy tastes as sweet as your honeyed scent." He presses his face into the curve of my neck, inhaling, his hands flat against my back, pressing me tightly against him. My breasts brush up against his collarbones, and I'm hyper-aware of every touch, every breath he draws.

How am I supposed to respond to such a comment that has me burning up and ignites a fire between my thighs; to have this powerful Viking be so straightforward with what he craves?

His mouth moves to the base of my ear, his lips sending tingles all over my body. I lean further against him, my body betraying me as a shiver of excitement races down my spine and right to my core, where my nerves are pulsing.

"Is this what you want?" he asks.

"I-I…"

His tongue curls my earlobe into his mouth. It's so warm. He sucks on it tenderly, taking small nips, and his lips are like fire. My legs shake while my fingers grip his shoulders, holding on because I am certain if he lets me go now, I'll fall.

"Is that a yes?" he practically purrs in my ear. "Do you want me to taste you and tell you how sweet you are?" His fingers fumble with the buttons of my pants, and I do nothing to stop him.

My face must be bright red by now, but I need this in my life. "Ah-aha," I stammer, and that has him pushing my pants and underwear all the way down my legs. I step out of them, toeing my shoes off at the same time as the coolness of the room finds my skin, and it takes everything to not cover myself.

"It would be rather rude on your part to make a promise and not fulfill it," I manage to say with a confidence I know comes from the arousal flaring through me.

But to stand half-naked in front of this god has me quivering, and my bravery fades fast. Nikos gets on his feet, and near him, I realize just how tiny I am in comparison. It's crazy how that turns me on so madly.

"Narah, babe," he says, unraveling the cord from my vest, undoing it quickly, then lifting my shirt up and over my head. "I need to see all of you. It's driving me fucking insane with need."

My hands instantly cover myself, but he's pulling my arms away from across my chest. "No hiding. You are too beautiful to ever hide your body from me." His strong hands grip my hips, and I'm suddenly sitting on the table.

His mouth is on my neck again as he nudges my legs open with his hand and steps closer. He cages me in with his body.

I tremble, and he cups the sides of my face, drawing me to him, and I kiss him desperately. My mouth crashes against him, and he kisses me back with a bruising hunger, tugging on my breasts. His hand is on my throat, and he guides me back onto the table, ripping from our kiss, fire flaring in his gaze.

He sits on the chair in front of me. I try to close my legs, but he's making a tsking sound as he pries them open. "Don't think about it. Now that I've seen your perfect cunt, you are mine."

Before I can even try to come up with something to say, his mouth is on my inner thigh, and I tense, completely forgetting how to talk. "Just look how pretty you are."

His eyes are not on my face but my pussy. And he gently places a kiss on my lips down there, then runs a tongue up my slit.

I moan. The feel of his mouth on me is the most incredible sensation in the world. I'm buzzing all over, and nothing is as good as having a powerful man lick me.

He widens my thighs, his fingers peeling apart my lips, and pushes his face deeper. His lips and tongue do things to me that have me crying out and my back arching. I grip the sides of the table and hold on tight.

"You are so much sweeter than honey. You are delicious."

I crane my neck up, but he's buried his face between my thighs again, his eyes on mine as he smothers himself with my drenched wetness. He tugs at my lips and licks me wildly.

My cries morph into screams with how quickly he devours me, with the orgasm already racing through me.

"Nikos, I don't think I can..." Arousal bursts through me, and I'm bowed backward on the table, howling the orgasm that tears through me. He doesn't stop and licks me ferociously like he can't get enough of tasting me.

I yell out his name, writhing, my body convulsing, coming hard in his mouth. He's licking everything up, from my pussy to what runs down my inner thighs.

Gasping for breath, I collapse back on the table, smiling, loving how good I feel. And how I want more and more.

"You taste even better than I imagined." He licks the cum from his lips, his chin and nose glistening as he looks up at me. "You are the most beautiful creature I've ever seen, and to claim you is everything to me."

He yanks his shirt off, revealing a wall of muscles, inked tribal patterns run over his bulging biceps. Then tears open the buttons on his pants and drops them. When he stands, I might have gaped at the size of him. Ragnar is very well built, but Nikos' cock... I don't think I can breathe.

"I'm going to fuck you now," he informs me, taking my hand and drawing me up and off the table.

"I-I don't think that's going to fit," I murmur, my heartbeat picking up again, being completely serious.

"It will be fine. I give you my word." He suddenly spins me by my waist to face away from him, then bends me over the table. His strong hands grip my hips as his foot parts my legs. "Open up for me. I'm barely keeping it together. I need to fuck you, to be inside your sweet cunt."

"I never expected you to be so... big," I exclaim.

He chuckles. "Why, thank you, gorgeous." And he enters me swiftly.

I tense while he plunges deeper into me, somehow stretching me wide enough to fit.

My breaths are raspy, and I moan at having something so huge inside me.

His hands are on my ass, squeezing, then he slowly pulls out and pushes in again, but it doesn't last. He's pounding into me so fast that I lose my breath. The friction of our union sends me into panting shudders. The raging heat between us increases rapidly, matching Nikos' thrusting tempo.

He rides me.

My eyes shut, and I'm lost to everything but this moment in time. I begin to quake, low growls rubbing over my throat as he fucks me savagely. And I could swear he's getting bigger inside me, the pressure within me building. He's about to knot, I sense it, the weight of him is incredible.

When he reaches his hand around to my hip to my pussy, my hips give a small jerk. "Come for me, suck down on my cock." With two fingers, he pinches my clit, hard.

I can barely breathe as he violently thrusts into me, making me dizzy. His thunderous growl booms around us, and with the way he grips my ass and his fingers teasing my pussy, I come completely undone for a second time.

I throw my head back, crying out as the orgasm rattles me. While Nikos' huge erection pulses, spilling his seed into me. My climax rocks me to the core. He's tense against me, growling, his cock knotting inside me, expanding against my inner walls to a super snug fit.

Clenching my teeth tight, I float down and worry I might break a tooth with the intensity of that second orgasm.

Nikos swoops me into his arms and lifts me from the table, both of us still connected, and walks us to the bed.

"That was fucking amazing," he moans, followed by a savage growl from his chest where his wolf makes himself very well known.

We fall onto the bed, him deeply embedded in me, his arms wrapped around me as he spoons me.

This is where I feel safe...in his arms.

My chest is light for once, the overbearing weight of all my problems has left me...for now, at least. I twist my head around to see his eyes are still hazy, and I know he's still pumping into me. Alphas produce a ridiculous amount of seed.

He smiles, his grip tightening. "I wish I could sweep you away from this world and find a place where no one could ever hurt you again."

I t's late, the night air sticky, and the heavy moon glows brightly beside the storm clouds.

After the earth-shattering time with Nikos, I'll never forget, I must have fallen asleep because I woke up to find my belongings packed and fresh clothes waiting for me by the bed. I was alone in my room, Nikos gone. From the window, I'd seen Crius down in the street with Ragnar waiting in front of the inn, so I made a mad rush to join them with my belongings. Apparently, they had to wait for horses to be brought from the local farm, which is what took so long. And now Stone and Nikos are collecting the horses from the back of the tavern. I'm still blushing from what Nikos and I did, and I have no idea if Ragnar and the others know.

I feel amazing, but don't want to discuss any of it with the rest of the guys.

I push the strap of my pack higher on my shoulder and lick my dry lips as I stare at the lights beaming from the tavern windows. Laughter and music pour out of the place. During the weeks I've lived here, waiting to find my sisters, the tavern served beer and food, any time of the day or night.

A clopping sound of hooves striking stone comes from my right, and I turn my head. Halfway down the street, Nikos is guiding two horses on either side of him by the reins, and Stone has two behind him. Dark beasts who neigh as if they've been woken up.

I frown at the sight, seeing as I'm a complete virgin when it comes to riding a horse.

But I don't see anyone bringing a fifth horse, which I'm secretly happy about. But getting to my sister supersedes the dread of being thrown and trampled by one of the huge beasts.

"You're riding with me." Ragnar has his arm around my back before he collects my bag.

"Okay," I answer as I watch a huge chestnut mare step up in front of us, shaking her head and scratching the ground with her front hoof. Each guy gravitates to a horse, with Ragnar tossing my bag to Stone to carry as his luggage.

In seconds, Ragnar mounts the horse, straddling her back, and is settled in the saddle. There's a thick blanket behind him, which will be my seat, I guess. Looks easy enough, though the animal is a lot taller than me. Next to the horse, I might as well be a dwarf.

Ragnar offers me his hand. "Put your foot in the stirrup, and I'll pull you up."

I don't hesitate, as I prefer he doesn't know the horse makes me slightly queasy because of her sheer size.

Gingerly, I place my hand in his, then lift my foot to the stirrup. His grip tightens, and I'm suddenly flying up and toward him.

"Whoa." A sliver of panic strikes as I frantically reach for Ragnar. I crash right into him as I swing my leg over the horse.

My ass hits the blanket behind Ragnar, and I clutch onto the back of his coat with a death grip. "Geez, it's really high up here, isn't it?" I gasp, quickly wrapping my arms around his waist.

He laughs at me and pats my hand. "I'll keep you safe."

The five of us are all geared up, and Ragnar nudges our horse forward. My body sways, and it seriously feels like I'm going to slip off this beast any second now. I'm tense, holding on for dear life.

Nikos, the second in command, takes the lead, followed by us, then Stone at our side and Crius at our rear.

If I wasn't freaking out about falling, I might think there's something almost comforting about traveling with these four powerful Alphas. Their protection is undeniably attractive. These aren't things I should be thinking when we have a group of assholes to find, but I can't deny how much my feelings for these Vikings are growing.

We pick up the pace once we reach the edge of town, and my heart thumps harder as my body bumps and slides against Ragnar's back, whether I want it to or not.

My arms remain locked around Ragnar's middle, my body plastered to him, and there is absolutely no way to stop myself from rubbing my breasts all over him on our ride.

"First time on a horse?" he asks, turning his head to look back at me, his eyebrow arching up an inch.

"That obvious?"

"You're strangling the hell out of my stomach, but if it makes you feel safe, I'll suffer through it," he says sarcastically.

"Oh, sorry." I slightly loosen my hold from around his waist, but I'm not letting go completely. Instead, I fist his coat to hold onto something. My hands are sweating like crazy, not to mention my legs shaking from squeezing so hard to stay on the horse.

He laughs louder, and I do love the way he sounds when he's happy... So at least there's that.

"If it's too much for you, Ragnar, I'll gladly take her on my horse," Stone interrupts. "You can strangle the life out of any part of me, babe, if it means rubbing your tits all over me."

I almost choke on my next breath and roll my eyes. "Of course, you will," I jokingly say.

"If Stone gets her, then it's only fair we take turns carrying her," Crius pipes up from the rear. Nikos jumps in too with, "I'm down with that."

Ragnar doesn't say yes or no to their offers, so I reply, "Not sure any of you can do it as well as Ragnar." And the moment my words register, the three guys begin laughing.

"I mean, the way he's riding the horse with me," I correct myself.

Crius is howling crazily now, one hand clutching his stomach, and I'm shaking my head. "Oh, he'd definitely want to ride you again."

My cheeks are on fire.

"Though Nikos was pretty close too, seeing he had his hand down your pants earlier," he continues, and I want to die. But this also tells me the others don't know yet what we did up in the room. Please let it stay that way. I'm not that comfortable talking openly about my sexual escapades, considering Ragnar had been my first.

"You literally suck balls," I snap at Crius, who coughs a chuckle.

"When did this happen?" Stone asks, his eyebrows drawing together. "Why do I always miss out on all the fun?"

"No balls for me, beautiful," Crius utters, smirking. "Only your sweet pussy, if you'll let me."

He grins at me. And yet the whole time, Ragnar has said nothing. I bury my face in his back, wishing I could be anywhere but here with these three asses.

"Ragnar," I begin my voice barely a whisper.

"It's okay, little fox. Nikos told me. Like I said before, there are no secrets between us."

He had? My stomach clenches hard. How much had he told him?

I notice the rest of the guys have fallen quiet, which tells me they are just as curious about what their leader has to say. It also means that Crius said all that shit on purpose to get Ragnar to speak.

And it seems we'll be waiting forever because he didn't take the bait and is not talking. I don't even know why I'm giving so much thought to this. What's the big deal? I slept with Ragnar twice, then with Nikos, desperately wanted to kiss Crius, and daydreamed about Stone. Not that I'm keeping count, but something must be wrong with me. My fated mate wants me dead, and I'm sleeping with dangerous Alphas who I've made a deal with.

I am losing it.

Men are dangerous, Mother would tell me.

And this is why I shouldn't be playing with fire. As much as my body and wolf seem to protest, what will happen after I get my sisters back? I'm not sure yet, but it worries me that these Vikings are about to start a war with all wolves in the Savage Sector. So, do I want to be in the middle of chaos with my sisters? And I don't even know the deal with my mother.

Refusing to think about that right now, I hold on.

I have no idea how long we've been riding; hours, feels like days, but my ass has never been this sore. The men are silent as we travel through the woodlands, following a wide trail, and the only light is the glow of a burning torch in Nikos' hand.

Trees bleed into the night, and I can barely make out the lofty pines on either side of us. There are no other sounds, only the striking of horse hooves against dirt.

A gravelly groan comes from behind us. It's loud enough that we've all heard it as each of us is glancing over our shoulder.

Nikos' light sweeps over the land, barely revealing three figures stumbling unevenly out of the woods and coming our way in their sluggish attempt at running. Their deathly groans have me gasping loudly.

"It's the undead," I murmur, my heart racing.

They're easier to see now as they come closer, in torn clothes, one with a missing eye, skeletal faces, and a woman with half her jaw hanging at an odd angle.

"Fuck!" Stone murmurs. "Let's get out of here."

"There's only three." Crius draws out his axe. "I vote we take the fuckers out."

"And how many more are in the woods that we can't see yet?" Nikos voices my exact concern.

"Fuck that," Crius groans. "I want to destroy something, and they look like fun things to smash."

"Sure thing, Hulk," Stone groans.

"Who the fuck is that?" Crius asks, climbing off his horse. I'm just as curious, what's a Hulk?

"Forget it. You don't read up on anything from the old times."

My eyes are glued on the creatures stumbling toward us rapidly. "Umm, can we please leave?"

"Crius," Ragnar's voice deepens. "We are not doing this now. Get back on the fucking horse."

Holy crap, the air just thickened in a split second.

Crius holds Ragnar's stare for a long moment , not seeming to care that the goddamn undead are coming toward us. Maybe that's his intention, but not mine. I need to be as far from them as possible before I scream and run away like a mad person.

His gaze breaks from Ragnar's, and he leaps back into his saddle. We are off again, the five of us rushing out of there with incredible speed. I'm latched to Ragnar's back, holding on for dear life as I'm jostled about on the galloping horse.

I keep looking back at the handful of additional undead spilling onto the trail. Fear pounds rapidly in my chest. If we had stayed a moment longer, we'd have been surrounded by them. I press closer to Ragnar, thankful he got us the heck out of there.

Wind blows through my hair, tugging on my clothes. Even when I look back, and there's no sight of the creatures, we don't stop. The thing about the undead is that they are relentless, needy things that will cross the freaking country of Romania if they think food is available. So, no matter how far we get, they will continue their pursuit, meaning the quicker we move, the more time we'll have to find my sister and escape before we're attacked.

The undead have never been this far north in Romania before but have plagued the south in the Shadowlands Sector, eating anything and everything that moves. I've heard stories of the enormous hordes that cross the lands, and the only way the wolves survived is by enclosing themselves within lofty walls. Jae had told me about the Ash pack living down there, doing just that, and how they live with the enemy right on their doorstep. The thought scares the hell out of me, but I truly admire those Ash wolves for living amid the dead.

So the fact that we've just seen a small group in these woods is terrifying. How long before the Savage Sector is overrun by them too?

The virus that eliminated civilization so long ago took most humans in Europe. And while normal wolves like us are not immune to the disease, there are wolf packs who are different, such as the X-Clan who are immune. Once we die, we become one of those monsters because we are carriers, so survival is so much more than just living another day. It's doing anything to not end up as one of the undead.

I sometimes wonder what life was like before the virus ravaged the world. Before it killed so many and created monsters. The books I've read show it to be such a magical place with everything you want at your fingertips. Sometimes it's hard to believe that such a place could have existed, especially with how fast it fell.

When Ragnar finally slows our horse to a stop, I instinctively glance back, as does Crius. There's nothing following us that we can see, but that doesn't mean they're not there.

I quickly stare out past Ragnar to find Nikos looking back at us, pointing forward.

Ragnar gives a small nod, and Nikos climbs off his steed. Then he runs down the track ahead of us as silent as the night, vanishing in the dark.

"What's going on?" I whisper.

"He's picked up on something. We'll know what soon enough," he answers in a soft voice. His hand is on mine across his stomach, and he holds me.

No one moves or speaks after that. I draw in a deep breath through my mouth, hating how vulnerable I feel in the middle of the dark woods. We're standing still, with only the dying glow of Nikos' torch, which he'd thrown to the ground.

The wait drags, and the longer we wait, the more my skin pricks. I listen for any sounds, anything that might indicate the undead's approach.

When Ragnar suddenly stiffens, I flinch in my seat. I look out past him and see Nikos rushing out of the darkness, moving as fast as a shadow, not making a sound.

He pauses near our horse, and Ragnar leans low to hear his words. My ears are pricked.

"Found them. They're heading along the valley, sticking to the river's edge. There are only two with Jae. The other four must be sweeping the woods on either side of them to ensure it's clear for their travel."

I might have made a small gasping sound. We found them!

"How far from our position?" Ragnar asks.

"Sixty yards tops. We ride up a bit further than ditch the horses."

Jae! Just hearing that Nikos found her has me eager to jump off the horse and run to her. But, of course, that would be a terrible idea.

"I'm ready," I whisper, butting in on their conversation.

"You heard, Narah. Take the lead," Ragnar instructs Nikos.

And in no time, we're riding forward in silence, my gaze constantly in front of us. I may not see much, especially now that Nikos has left the burning torch behind, but I'm trembling with anticipation.

It isn't long before we come to a stop.

Crius is off his horse in seconds, and he's helping me off mine just as fast, his hands on my hips, his breath on my ear. "Hey, gorgeous. Ready for your ex to gurgle his last breath?"

"Hell yeah."

He slides me down to my feet, and instantly an ache zaps along my thighs, my ass partly numb. I groan softly when I try to step. "Why does it hurt so much to ride a horse? I'm never going to walk straight again."

"That's what she said." Crius sniggers at his terrible joke.

Stone and Nikos are tying up the horses loosely to several trees, and Ragnar grabs my hand. "You're with me."

We run along the trail, me a bit more awkward from how sore I am, when I hear rushing water. We pause at the treeline, and a small clearing reveals the pebbly bank dipping into a river. I stick my head out with the guys, looking to our left, and there, in the distance, a light bops across the river's edge. I can barely make out three figures, but one is definitely shorter than the others.

My heart soars. *Jae. I'm coming.*

Ragnar pulls back, as do I. "Crius, cross the river and track us from that side. Nikos, you do this side. Anyone you find, kill them. Stone, you keep Narah close. Shit goes sideways, you get her the fuck away from here."

"Or, I just zap them," I suggest, raising my hands, but no one is smiling or agreeing.

Instead, Ragnar's gaze narrows down on me, his expression serious. "Can you control the power to not accidentally zap one of us or burn down the whole forest?"

"Well…" I shrug my shoulders. Shit, I hate that he's got a point.

"That's what I thought. Everyone knows the plan. We go now!"

I don't push the issue because he's correct. They've seen enough to know my power is uncontrollable, and I hate that I'm seen as the weak one, but at the end of the day, we are saving Jae. So I'm not going to complain about how we do this.

Crius and Nikos vanish into the night, our silent protectors, to get rid of Martell's men. He'd be with Jae, I have no doubt about that, and I curl my hands into fists.

Stone takes my hand, giving me a sweet smile. "Are you ready?"

"Yes. I want my sister back."

"Good," Ragnar responds. "Let's go." We rush forward, following the river's path from within the woods to avoid being seen.

I bite my lip, suddenly feeling all kinds of emotions. Fear, anxiety, excitement. But I'm struggling to shake off the feeding of dread curling in my gut that things will go sour. This is Martell we're dealing with, after all.

ELEVEN

NIKOS

My wolf pours out of me, bones cracking, skin splitting, while my heart is pounding with adrenaline. It's been too long since I've had a decent hunt. Back home in Denmark, Ragnar, Stone, and I would head out into the wilderness at least twice a week to bring back big game for the family feasts, but sometimes we just hunted down rogue wolves. Cleaned out the woods of the beasts who attacked the locals, stole females, rutted and killed them. I miss hearing the last whimpers in their throats before I choked the life out of them.

It's surprisingly rewarding knowing that I'm doing a good deed for the pack. Hunting is the only time I truly feel at one with the Ulv pack after my father traded me to the enemy. It's why Ragnar and I have bonded so well, why my allegiance will only ever be to him. For him, I'll fight, I'll steal, I'll kill. Even if I still haven't worked out what I'll do with my future.

But for now, I can't think about what's coming, so I raise myself out of the shadows in my wolf form, then spring forward.

Each inhale I take picks up no wolf scents. The air is still tonight. Too fucking still, giving little away.

I glance toward the river and see I'm coming up close to Jae and the two men by her side. The two fuckers on this side of the river have to be somewhere nearby.

I suck in another deep breath, but still no scent. If I was protecting my Alpha in this situation, I'd be up front, ensuring there were no surprises. But that means an asshole is either behind me or very close.

Sliding in between two shrubs, I crouch. Sometimes, just watching and letting myself get in tune with the night is all I need. It's what we'd do while hunting. Choose a prime position and wait.

My eyes are adjusting, making it easier to see in the dark, and that's when I spot movement. It's small but enough to catch my attention.

I lick my lips and remain still.

A figure glides through the woods with almost no sound. He's in human form, which is a huge mistake on his part.

The second he passes me, I lunge out and slam into him unannounced. He hits the ground, face first, my weight on him.

I chomp down on the back of his neck, my teeth slicing flesh. The snap of bone is loud, considering everything's so silent. I do love the sound of breaking bones. The warmth of his wolf's blood drips down my chin.

He's shuddering, bucking, growling.

Save your breath... but on second thought, you won't need it for much longer.

I jerk my head sideways sharply and break his neck. That finality has him slumping beneath me. I let go and lick the blood from my lips, partly disappointed in how easy that was. I wanted a challenge.

Drawing away, I shake myself, needing to track down the other hunter.

But in the same moment I draw in a breath, something solid crashes into me. It comes so fucking fast, color me surprised, but when something stabs under my ribs, something so sharp that I'm stunned, panic flares.

The ache of a blade deep in me has me shuddering. I kick the bastard with my back legs with all the strength I have, a whimper spilling out of my throat from the burning pain spreading across my middle. Hastily, I angle my body away from him, so I'm facing him head-on. My rear is my weakness, but my teeth will destroy him.

Up on my feet, I stumble, and blood drips from the wound, but I stand tall because I've been injured before. It's not my first injury, and it won't be my last.

I lift my head to the fuckhead who's snarling under his breath, gripping the bloody knife in his hand. The world tilts, but I shake my head. I won't let him win.

"You killed my friend." He leans forward slightly. "And now it's your turn. Eye for an Eye, you piece of shit."

Lifting the blade, he comes at me as I lunge for him.

Crius

I stroll through the woods, resisting the urge to whistle. I badly want to do it right now because, let's be honest here, I want those dickheads in the woods to hear me, to come at me. Who the hell has time to hunt them down? We all know how it's going to end, so why should I exert extra energy I don't need to?

Of course, I make sure to stick as far from the river as possible to make noise. I'm not a complete moron.

My heavy steps crunch twigs and foliage, and as if on cue, two men emerge from the woods ahead of me.

I smile to myself. "Are you ready to play?"

They exchange looks, then grin my way.

"Oh, this is going to be fun. I can feel it in my bones." I'm going to make them cry so much for stealing Jae. She doesn't deserve whatever these pricks have in mind for her. And the fact that they caused Narah anguish is going to have them paying in blood.

The predictable duo rush at me. I sigh at how boring they are. I should have known things wouldn't go differently. But I'll suck it up.

I duck the first swinging fist, grab a thick branch off the ground, and launch it at the one guy's head. It hits with a dull thud, and he falls backward. Hopefully, he'll take a while to come back from that.

The second dude charges forward, his fist hitting me right in the nose. The sting radiating up to my eyes like a spider web of searing pain. "Fucking hell!"

He throws himself at me, slamming into me, catching me off

guard. I stumble backward until my back slams into a tree. Shaking the pain from my head, I drive my fist at his kidney, having had enough of his snorting pig face in mine.

I kick him for good measure in the jewels too.

He's groaning and clutching his groin, while I retrieve the axe from my belt and spin it in my hand.

"My turn." Without hesitation, I swing it at the guy, the blade catching him right in the gut. "Ouch, that's gotta hurt."

He gurgles, dropping to his knees, spitting up blood. I shove a leg against his side as I tear my axe free. The man falls to his side, bleeding to death. He'll get no pity from me. The bastard deserved it for touching what doesn't belong to him.

The crack of a twig comes from right behind me. Instinct takes over, and I slam my elbow up and backward, catching the first guy right in the face.

He groans and stumbles back as I turn on him.

"You made a huge mistake coming here, and now it's time to pay the price, just like your buddy has." In my mind, all I can see is Narah and her tears when she found Jae had been kidnapped. Nothing can take away what she went through, but I'll try my fucking hardest.

The man is clutching his bleeding nose, eyes widening at seeing me approach with my axe. He's grappling to grab his knife from the sheath on his belt with his other hand.

"I'm going to kill you, you know," I tell him casually.

"Fuck you," he spits, his blade out in front of him, both hands now holding onto it, shaking ferociously.

"Really, if you're so fucking scared, why are you on this mission?" I tap the flat side of my axe to my chin. "Oh, I know because you have no spine and follow a weak-ass psychopath who's next on my hit list. Now, let's get this shit-show over with."

I need to do this fast because I want in on the action with Martell, the bastard who tried to kill Narah after rejecting her. Ragnar told us all. He holds no secrets from us. But I don't want Ragnar to steal all the fun now. I twirl the axe casually in my hand.

The man's eyes flick from the weapon to me. "Look, please, maybe we can talk about this." His pleas are just noise.

But in a flash, the bastard comes at me, bending low, his blade flashing in the moonlight. He moves fast, growling. My wolf surges forward, as does my anger. I swerve out of the way, missing the blade by an inch, but the thing catches my coat, tearing fabric.

"Bastard." Fury lunges through me, and my mind grows hazy. Madly, I swing at him, my axe swooping down, right into the side of his neck. Blood spurts out. With all my strength, I wrench it out and slam into him with the weapon, over and over, I don't see anything but the beautiful flow of red. My heart is pounding to a tune matched only by the crunch of bones beneath metal.

Now, this... this is me in my element.

Stone

I keep Ragnar in my sight as he slips through the shadows ahead of us. The man is a fucking warrior. I've seen him win so many battles at home, take down Alphas twice his size, and still his fucking asshole of a father refused to give him credit or promise him the throne to his pack. The dick told Ragnar he has to fight for the role with everyone else, and then he'd decide who the true champion will be to take the position.

Of course, that set Ragnar off and ended up with the pair in a physical fight. Not his finest moment, he confessed to me later, but family has a way of fucking you in the head.

The funny thing is that we all strive for their attention and affection, and yet they tend to be the ones who betray us the worst. My father, Ragnar's uncle, is just as cold-hearted, which is why, from a young age, I'd leave the house whenever I could to escape my dad's beatings. Once Nikos joined us, the three of us were inseparable and used to go into the woods hunting to get away from pack politics and the shit that went down.

Look at Narah. She'll risk her own life for her sisters. Her devotion is fucking beautiful, all of her is, and her passion for her family has me wanting to do anything to help her.

I glance out from the shadows to Ragnar slipping away from the fringe of woods and onto the river's shore. With my arm around Narah's waist, we slowly move closer through the woods, following him from a distance. If shit gets bad, then I need to be there for Ragnar, but still keep this gorgeous Omega safe.

When we pause in a spot that gives us a good viewpoint, I lower my gaze to Narah. She's looking at me, her amber eyes bright and huge tonight, her hair as dark as the night falls over one shoulder in soft waves. Everything about her is spectacular. The vulnerability washing over her face, her sweet full lips, the way she blinks quickly when she's nervous. It takes all my strength to not claim this Omega for myself.

Her sweet, fruity scent floods every inch of me, and fuck me, but it's exquisite. Even now, all I can think about is scooping her into my arms and pushing her up against a tree, her legs wrapped around my waist, my cock spearing into her, savoring the intense, unyielding arousal that she rises in me.

See, she's every inch the distraction I don't need at this moment, as keeping my thoughts straight grows harder. Especially when I picture kissing her neck, freeing those gorgeous breasts, and making her scream. I want to feel her pussy clenching around my cock, squeezing me as we lose ourselves in carnal pleasure.

Fuck! *Rein it in, man.*

Everything about her weakens me. And as much as Ragnar has made his claim over Narah, he hasn't exactly told us not to. I've always been one to take what I want, and I will make her mine, even when I know she won't be an easy conquest. But I do enjoy a challenge.

Right now, she's frowning and pointing at us, then Ragnar, implying we should go out there to help. I squeeze my hold on her waist a bit more.

"We wait," I mouth the words, to which she huffs.

I shake my head and remind myself I need to keep focused.

The second I got distracted, I missed Ragnar darting out of the woods and toward the enemy. Now, I watch him move low as any predator does, having tapped into his wolf, and strike one of the men from behind with perfect precision. His arm locks around his throat and tears him backward. In a swift move, the loud crack of the dude's neck says everything. The man falls to the ground as the second one attacks Ragnar.

Tension jolts through my body, the eagerness to join him, to help him. That rush of adrenaline pushes me to dart forward, but I grind my jaw and wait.

Not yet.

Jae stumbles back, and Narah calls her, waving and pulling against me to be seen. I step with her out into the open while my focus is locked on the deadly roll of battle between Ragnar and his opponent. I have no idea which of the two pricks is Martell, but I have no doubt Ragnar will end his life swiftly if he hasn't already. And that can't come fast enough. Prick is long overdue for death.

Narah runs to her sister and hugs her, their happy cries have my chest clenching. I had never planned to feel these things for this Omega, but even now, her sweet scent is in my nostrils. All I want is to hold her in my arms, which says a lot, seeing as I love to fight.

I lift my attention to where the enemy slips free from Ragnar, but my Alpha gets up nimbly and catches the man's shoulder with a clawed hand. Ragnar's partially transformed, a trick I notice he likes to use often. The man pivots and Ragnar slams him to the ground then straddles his chest, seizing his throat. The man has no chance of moving this mountain off him.

I stroll toward them, and the sucker looks at me, desperation in his eyes. He's gotta know he's not going to survive this…or does he think because Ragnar hasn't killed him yet, he has a sliver of hope?

"I have only one question for you. Answer it, and you might just save your pathetic ass," Ragnar snarls.

The man's eyes are like disks, his face splattered with his own blood and pale as snow. "O-okay," he slurs.

"Good, we have an understanding then," Ragnar continues. "How the fuck did you find the girl and my men in town?"

The guy is struggling to draw in breath, and his lips are already turning blue. He's hitting Ragnar's forearm.

"You're choking him," I say.

"Am I?" he answers, never taking his eyes off the man, and I notice he softens his grip a bit. "Speak!"

"The witches," he gurgles. "They told Martell where she'd be."

I stiffen at his admission. What the fuck? The witches played us?

"Why?" Ragnar hollers, shaking the man by his neck. The man's spurting blood from his mouth. He's in bad shape.

"S-savage S-sector. T-they promised the sector."

"What the fuck did he just say?" I snap, but Ragnar only growls, his arm holding the guy bulging with veins and muscles from how hard he's choking him. The man's thrashing, desperate for escape, but we lose him fast. His eyes roll back, and he goes limp.

Ragnar releases him and tilts his head up, unleashing a tremendous howl that has zilch to do with calling other wolves. The sound he makes is primal and vicious. He's furious.

Savage Sector is ours... and that snot head Martell thinks he can take it.

Ragnar gets to his feet, wiping his bloody hands on his pants. "Those fucking backstabbing bitches. I'm going to destroy the High Priestess for playing me, then burn down the whole fucking Poisonous Woods."

"But if they knew where Jae was the whole time, why didn't they just take her themselves? These fuckheads who kidnapped her had gone right past the witch's forest."

Blowing out a loud exhale, Ragnar scrubs his face. "Isn't it obvious? It's not Jae the witches want. It's something else. We need to work that out fast and pray we're not wrong." Then he glances up to where Narah and Jae are watching. His expression is dark, but he doesn't say anything to them. They would have heard everything.

"Stay with the girls. I'm going out to check on Crius and Nikos," he orders.

I nod as Ragnar approaches the water's edge and splashes his face and hands before crossing; the water sloshes against him, coming up to his thighs.

"Everything will be okay," I say to both of them.

Narah's snuggling up against her sister, but the heavy burden on Narah's face matches how I feel on the inside. We've walked in on something with the witches, and they've decided to use us. I just don't know if that makes us the bait in their scheme.

"I'm never leaving you behind again," Narah says to her sister with a soft but firm voice, drawing my attention as she wipes tears from Jae's cheeks.

"You better not," Jae answers softly. The young sister has definitely grown on me since our trip collecting her from the Shadow-lands Sector. Despite everything she's been through, she always finds a way to make a joke of it, to appear stronger even in the scariest of moments. But seeing her now, crying in Narah's arms, shows how vulnerable this young girl is. And she deserves protection from this cruel world... just as much as Narah.

"It's good to have you back," I say to Jae.

"Took your time, you big lug." She punches me in the arm, but I'm not blind to the paleness of her face, to how much less she's smiling now. She must have been terrified.

"Was Martell even with the guys who took you?" I ask Jae, and I notice Narah is too busy staring at Ragnar getting out of the water to pay attention to us.

"Nope. The weasel sent his men to collect me on his behalf. But the men were saying Martell is furious and wants Narah back." She glances over to her sister, her lips thinning like it hurts her to say it. "He's threatened to raze the world and everyone in it to get her."

My hackles rise. "Like fuck he is!" The moment I meet Martell, I'm going to kill him. It's that simple.

Narah

I feel like someone just sucker-punched me right in the solar plexus, and I can't draw breath. I don't want to overthink why the witches lied to us and why they sold out Jae. Was it to make sure we failed our mission? But to not find my ex was an enormous blow. "Martell needed to be here to die today."

Jae nods and hugs me. "I'm just glad you saved me. Let's not worry about Martell right now."

I hug her back and kiss the top of her head. "Me too, sis."

We have enough problems, so eliminating Martell would have been a blessing. But now he'll send more men, and I shake with anger. But, unlike the first time, I have no plans of whimpering in his pres-ence. I'm going to hurt him with every ounce of magic I have.

The crunch of foliage has us all turning our attention to the bank across the river. Ragnar's slapping the water from his pants while Crius is strolling out from the woods behind him, splattered in blood.

I gasp at the sight, my mouth falling open, expecting him to topple over. But instead, he saunters to the river and washes his bloodied axe like nothing in the world matters.

"See you left nothing for me," Crius says loud enough for us to hear.

"Looks like you've had your fair share of fun," Ragnar answers, already making his way back through the water toward us.

But when a groan comes from behind us, I startle and grab Jae, who gasps as I push her away from the sound.

I turn, half expecting to see an undead.

But instead, it's Nikos stumbling out from the shadows, clutching his gut. Blood running freely from between his fingers. He looks up, meeting my eyes, and beneath the moon's light, I see the terror in his gaze and the paleness of his skin. And it scares the hell out of me.

Suddenly, he drops to his knees.

My stomach churns, and I hurry over to him, a chill enveloping me. "Nikos!"

Footsteps close in behind me, along with the splash of water, telling me Crius and Ragnar are running toward us too.

I reach Nikos and drop next to him, my eyes locked on his hands pressing against his middle, and all the blood. Fear has my heart rattling in my chest.

"I'm fine," he groans.

"Fuck, you look like shit," Crius mutters.

"Geez, state the obvious," Jae responds. I adore her so much.

"Great, now we've got two Narahs giving me attitude," he murmurs, almost jokingly.

"Crius, stop being a dick," I say, my insides twisting with anguish. "Go get the fucking horses. Do something. Nikos is seriously hurt."

He snarls and marches back to where we'd left the horses. Stone is on his heels. I can hear their climbing voices but not words, and in moments, both are sprinting to collect the horses. Whatever Stone told him has got him to stop being an ass.

Ragnar gently gets Nikos to lie on his back. "Let's see how bad it is."

"I-it's just a knife wound," Nikos murmurs. "I killed both bastards."

"You did great," Ragnar says, turning his attention to where Niko is holding his wound.

Nikos' skin is sweaty, and he's trembling. Fear drums through my mind of how terribly injured he is, and we're in the middle of nowhere. What if he bleeds to death?

Ragnar moves Nikos' hand from the wound, and a gush of blood pours out.

It feels like I'm drowning in ice water. "Oh, goddess, that's bad." I regret saying that instantly. I don't want to scare Nikos, but I'm pretty sure he knows it himself.

Ragnar quickly takes off his coat, then yanks the shirt up and over his head, so he's bare-chested. He folds the fabric and places it under Nikos' hand. "You'll need to apply pressure to the wound until we can get you stitched up."

Nikos nods, and I jump to my feet, as does Ragnar. "He may need more than stitches," I say. "I don't even know how close we are to a town."

Jae is kneeling beside Nikos, wiping the perspiration from his brow, telling him he better not die on her. Her words are like spears to my heart, and I blink to stop the tears from falling.

"We're not too far from a nearby village," Ragnar explains, the lines at the edges of his mouth deepening, like they do when he's worried. "We just need to be fast and pray nothing gets in our way."

My breath catches in my throat as cold sweat licks over my skin. I hate feeling like I can never catch a break, and now my bad luck has rubbed off on the guys.

"But he'll pull through," he tells me, yet I hear the quiver beneath his words. "We just need to stop the blood so his wolf can heal him."

I'm not sure who he's trying to convince right now—me or himself.

I nod, needing to believe him, or I'll completely fall apart. I have no choice, and I keep looking back over to where the other two vanished, wishing they'd hurry the heck up.

Pain surges through me that Nikos is in a lot more trouble than anyone wants to admit.

There's just so much blood.

TWELVE

NARAH

Overgrown fields surround us. I'm on the back of the horse, clinging to Stone as we rush to get Nikos help. Orange lights glint in the distance like beacons in the darkness—the small village Ragnar promises will aid Nikos.

Of course, I'm skeptical about trusting any other Alphas, and I have Jae to look out for, but what choice do we have? We need to stick together, and if we do nothing, Nikos will die. So, we all push forward, and I pray to the moon goddess.

Please keep us all safe.

Nikos is slumped on his horse, but he's riding next to Ragnar, who holds onto his reins.

Despite the chill setting over the night, Stone's back is like a furnace, and I have no problems at all warming myself against him.

"You okay back there?" he asks, his hand on mine, which are looped around his middle.

"I'm fine. But how does Ragnar know we can trust the Alphas in this pack?"

"They've sworn partial allegiance to him."

I nod even though he can't see me, and knowing Ragnar has some control over the place we're going to fills me with some confidence that we'll be safe. I fall silent after that and listen to the horses galloping like thunder down the road.

I keep staring at the way Nikos sways on his horse and how Ragnar nudges him to not fall unconscious. I keep my head low as we race across the flat land. I don't know how long it's taken us since we left the woods, but we finally slow down, and I lift my gaze as we turn down a path flanked by pines.

We approach a lofty iron gate, with a chain-link fence jutting out in either direction, encasing the pack's territory.

Ragnar has jumped off his horse and is talking to a guard who carries a shotgun. I can't tell if that's for the undead or other wolves... my guess is the latter. Numerous packs have claimed small pockets of land in Savage Sector, but there is no overarching Alpha, so it's each wolf or pack for himself out here.

In moments, the gates open with a metallic groan, and I breathe easier at the lack of trouble. Ragnar climbs back up on his horse, then we are off again.

I glance at the guard as we pass him, and see he's watching us, mostly Jae and me. Does he think we're commodities brought in to offer for sale? How wrong he is, as I'd never let that happen to my sisters or me. I lift my chin as he turns to shut the gate behind us.

We come to a stop in front of a set of stone steps that look worn from weather, pavers cracked and grass growing between them. Two sets of fiery torches flank the entrance and on either side is an explosion of shrubs that look semi-trimmed like someone really tried to make them look manicured.

We all get off our horses as three men emerge from the darkness behind us. For all I know, there could be stables just around the corner, but I honestly can't see them in the dark.

Crius talks to them about a place for our horses to feed and rest, and there's no argument.

Everything's happening so fast my head spins. Jae clings to me, shaking. She's been through so much already; she deserves to feel safe.

Ragnar and Stone have Nikos between them, their arms around his back, and they carry him up the stairs.

I take Jae's hand and pull her in the same direction. "Let's stay close to them."

We're on their heels, my attention alert. At the top of the steps, enormous flat land stretches outward, surrounded by more woodland. The place looks like it might have once been one of those human parks I've read about in books. Except in this space, there are maybe fifty or more wooden cabins with pointy roofs around the perimeter in several lines, and in the middle is a roaring bonfire, spitting embers into the sky.

The guys move swiftly to the second cabin on the right, knowing exactly where they're going. The ground is mostly dirt and pebbles, and to the side of the home, I spot a vegetable garden. It reminds me of being back with the Storm Wolves. My gut twists, remembering a time when I thought we were safe and how that turned out. Might explain why I'm constantly looking over my shoulder, and my skin pricks at every sound.

Crius gives a loud bang on the arched door, and it is opened in seconds by an older man with white hair. He's dressed in brown leather pants and a matching vest with no shirt underneath. And his skin is deeply tanned. His eyes widen immediately as if he's shocked but also pleased with our interruption in the middle of the night. Then he notices Nikos.

"Ragnar, come in quickly." He waves us to enter, and I pull Jae alongside me, both of us glued side-by-side.

"Mihai, it's great to see you again."

Before stepping inside, I notice people emerging from nearby homes to check on the commotion, no doubt, but I duck my head low and enter.

The cabin is surprisingly large. Blankets and cushions for seating steal half the space, which tells me a big family could live here. Along the back wall, there's a fire oven and a table with six chairs, and at the rear is a hallway, which I assume leads to more rooms.

"Place him here." The man shoves aside the cushions to make a clearing for Nikos on the blanket, and the men set him down. I hurry over to them and tuck a pillow under his head.

He's clutching his side, groaning, and my blood runs cold. He's always been this powerful Alpha, so to see him this way is painful. I've lost enough people and have witnessed so much death that my chest constricts at his suffering.

Blood drenches his shirt and hands. It drips over his fingers, and my heart is in my throat. Jae's next to me, clutching me tightly.

"We'll be alright," I whisper to her. She's watching everyone, not taking her eyes off the old man.

"I apologize for our abrupt arrival in the middle of the night. But you were the closest place and friend to call upon for help." Ragnar stands to face the man.

"Ragnar, you can call my pack home." He slaps a hand to his shoulder, then turns his head and hollers, "Lyssa, girl, get out here now. Ragnar has come to visit." Then he faces Ragnar with a wide grin. "Your friend will need stitching by the looks of it." He goes into the kitchen and collects a bucket from a pantry along with a bottle of what I guess is alcohol.

I look down at Nikos. His face is tight, eyes scrunched up. When he opens them, he tries to smile, but it comes out lopsided and painful.

"N-Narah," he begins, but I shake my head.

"You don't need to talk. Just hold on. Someone's going to fix you." My throat closes up, and my eyes prick with tears. I've held it together this long, so I'm not going to lose it now. Jae rubs my back. She's always been good at sensing my emotions, and I should be celebrating that I have her, but instead, I'm worried sick about Nikos.

Crius, who's kneeling across from me, has his hands on the wound, applying pressure. Nikos looks as pale as a ghost. He lost so much blood during the ride here.

"You better not die on me," I whisper to Nikos. "I just started to really like you."

I sense Crius watching me, listening, but I can't hide away in private with Nikos to tell him he has no right to die.

Crius reaches over with his other hand and slides loose hair off my face. "He's going to survive. He's a fucking tough bastard, and he's not going anywhere."

I want Nikos to tell me the same thing, but when I meet his gaze, his eyes are fluttering like he's going to pass out.

"Hold on," I tell him. "Please, Nikos."

Footsteps striking the wooden floorboards have me glancing up to a woman, maybe eighteen or nineteen years old, with flowing blonde hair that tumbles over her shoulders and to her waist. She's frantically tying a blue robe around herself, her eyes blinking away sleep. Her gaze sweeps over the strangers in her home.

"Ragnar," she says softly, like he's the only person in the room she actually notices, and takes quick steps to his side, sticking her chest out.

What the heck?

"It has been too long since you've come to visit. I was starting to get worried you've forgotten me."

"Lyssa," the old man growls. "I'm sure you and Ragnar can get reacquainted later, but for now, there is a man dying on the floor."

Lyssa huffs, and her smile drops. She turns to the man, frowning. "Did you get the alcohol, Father?" Her tone is almost scolding.

"Everything is waiting for you," he replays with a harsh voice and points to Nikos' feet where he'd laid the bucket, bandages, and everything else she needs.

The silence in the room is deafening.

She purses her lips, raises her head, and walks toward us, her eyes on Nikos. "I need space," she snaps, cutting me a sharp look.

Okay, someone has a chip on her shoulder. "I'm staying with Nikos," I answer adamantly. "And I can help you."

"Wonderful idea," her father answers. "Ragnar, let's talk in the kitchen."

Lyssa's hazel eyes narrow in disbelief, but she doesn't respond. Instead, she kneels next to Nikos and pulls back Crius' hand and fabric to inspect the injury.

"Ouch, this looks deep." She scrunches up her nose.

"Are you a healer?" Jae asks while my fingers flip open the buttons on Nikos' shirt, and my thoughts fly to us together, how the slightest touch left me breathless, and how he showed me euphoria so easily that even now, my body tingles. I don't want to lose the chance to do that again, to fall asleep in his arms. So, I pull the shirt down his shoulders, and Jae helps me slide it off him.

"Something like that," Lyssa answers Jae despondently.

Nikos whimpers, and I place a hand on his arm, so he knows I'm there for him. "You're going to be okay," I reassure him, though I have no idea if he can even make sense of what I'm saying.

Ragnar and Stone move to the rear of the room, and the old man serves them a clear drink from a long-necked bottle at the table. Crius sniffs the air and is on his feet in an instant, making his way to others. "Be back in a sec," he says.

"My name's Narah," I say to Lyssa. "And this is my sister, Jae."

"Why are you with Ragnar and his pack? Is he selling you two to Alphas in town?" She doesn't look at me as she speaks, but is dabbing the blood from the injury with a folded-up towel.

Nikos groans, and I squeeze his shoulder slightly.

"We're not for sale," I respond instantly as Jae moves to Nikos' other side and wipes the perspiration from his face. "They're helping me."

Her head juts up, and her eyes flash on me, then over to Ragnar at the table. "What sort of help?"

I shrug. "It doesn't really matter." Telling her anything sounds like a terrible idea, considering my initial impression of this girl. My instincts scream not to trust her and that she seems to have some crazy obsession withRagnar.

Not that I can blame her. The guy is a god and built like one too. After our time in the Poisonous Woods, the witches, them protecting me, and the mark he gave me, one can say each of these men has grown on me. More than I should have allowed, but nothing in my life is predictable now, is it?

But as I watch Lyssa cleaning Nikos' wound and how she keeps sneaking a look over to the men by the table, I'm wondering what exactly her story with Ragnar is. She's extremely beautiful with her porcelain skin, large eyes, heart-shaped lips, and has curves in all the right places. The girl is stunning; I doubt any man could say no to her.

The longer I study her, the more self-doubt hits me. I can't compete with her. I'm nowhere as pretty as her, not with that bone structure, and her breasts made to be noticed. I want to cover myself up in her presence, as I must look like a mess.

It's clear she and Ragnar have a history, and I hate that it stirs a lick of jealousy through me.

"Put your hand here and press down," she says, tearing me from my thoughts. "Make yourself useful. Splash his injury with this." She shoves the bottle of alcohol into my other hand. It smells of over-ripe plums, and it feels like my nostrils are burning from breathing it in. I squint my eyes at how damn strong this is.

Lyssa starts threading a needle, getting ready to stitch up Nikos. The thing with wolves is that they should mostly heal themselves from any injury, as long as it's not a mortal blow, but that means stopping his blood loss.

I press my hand down on the folded towel to apply pressure and lift the bottle to get ready to disinfect his wound.

"Want me to pour," Jae offers.

"No, it's okay. I'll do it," I answer, not wanting her to even see this, but I guess she's already witnessed so many horrific things in this world, even at just fourteen years of age.

"Nikos, this is going to sting a bit. I'm sorry."

He nods, his jaw clenching. Jae hands him a pillow. "Here, squeeze this."

Lyssa is sniggering.

I look at her, annoyed by her rudeness. "What's so funny?"

"You two are doting over this Alpha. Have you two been living under a rock most of your lives? Alphas don't give a shit about us Omegas, so you don't need to pretend in front of me. No matter how hot they are, don't become their slaves. Learn to play the game and always look out for number one. Yourself." She smirks and glances at Nikos, who is too out of it to really pay attention to what she's saying. "So while this guy is too hurt to stop us, who says we can't make him suffer a bit longer, if you get my drift," she whispers so no one else can hear her.

The funny thing is that before I met Ragnar and his men, I would have been exactly the same way, taking any chance to stab an Alpha in the back. And most deserve so much worse, but I struggle to accept that for Nikos.

I'd just been close to crying over him, and now this crazy girl is telling me to torture him.

"While I'd normally agree with you, in this case, just no. I want him out of pain," I state. "I won't let you hurt him more than he already is."

She shrugs. "Whatever."

I shake my head, my heart hammering in my chest that I'd just stuck up for Nikos… just as he'd fought for me when those other Alphas attacked me near the tavern. Surprisingly, it feels amazing.

Would I hurt Nikos? Could I?

Goddess no!

Absolutely, no.

"You two are the ones who'll regret it later," Lyssa snorts.

But Nikos is watching me, shaking terribly, so I ignore her.

"Okay, hold on to the pillow." Jae pushes it into his hands on his chest, and I peel away the towel, revealing the deep cut where the blade went right into him.

Not wasting time, I grip the neck of the bottle and start splashing the clear liquid over the injury. I'd seen Father do this when he'd caught his leg on barbed wire once. He poured a small amount, then quickly stitched it to stop the bleeding.

Nikos hisses, his body convulsing. A growl rolls from his chest. Jae's forcing the pillow into his hands frantically. "Hold on to this," she keeps telling him over and over.

"Hurry, stitch him," I say to Lyssa, my voice climbing more than it should.

But she's taking her time, fiddling with the blue thread. I'm going to grab that needle and do it myself if she doesn't hurry the hell up.

"You can't trust them." She leans in closer, and I shuffle aside, but instead of working faster, she whispers to me, "I mean, Ragnar has promised to wed me, but that doesn't mean he'll treat me fair or that I'll be the most trusting wife." She winks at me, grinning.

I shudder at her words, breathing so hard that stars dance in my vision. Jae is saying something, but I can't hear her over the hammering of my heart. "You're marrying him?" I gasp, when Nikos suddenly bellows.

I look around to find that I'm spilling more of the booze onto his wound and splashing it everywhere.

"Watch it," Jae cries, snatching more cushions from around her to pat Nikos dry.

I set the bottle down away from us, and Lyssa sews his wound. The rest of the men are looking our way, so she finally gets to work.

I shuffle closer to Nikos and hold his hand. Darkness shrouds his gaze, and he's grinding his teeth through the pain. I wince for him, feeling awful for causing him more pain. All I can do while Lyssa sews him up is stare at him writhing on the floor.

Everything about him is rugged and beautiful, from the sharpness of his cheekbones to his chiseled jawline and even those kissable lips. Being next to him ignites something within me. I can't lose him. My hand runs over his brow, wiping the perspiration away.

His chest raises up and down with each rapid breath he takes as he rides the wave of pain, the muscles in his neck corded and tense.

With a snip of the string with her teeth, Lyssa finishes stitching the wound. She grabs the bandages, mainly strips of fabric, and folds one in half several times before pressing it over the stitches. She wraps the longer pieces around his middle. Jae and I help with getting the material under him and back around for Lyssa to tie so it stays in place.

"Done." She gets to her feet and wipes her hands, then takes the bucket of bloody water into the hallway, vanishing.

"Do you think he'll be okay?" Jae asks. I stare down at Nikos, whose eyes are closed and breathing grows heavy, seeming to have passed out to allow his body to heal.

"Of course," I respond with my best confident voice, even if on the inside, I'm asking the same question as my sister. I want to be strong for her, to take the agony from her if I can, even if it feels like my heart is being strangled every time I look at Nikos.

"By the way." She leans over to me, muttering, "I don't trust Lyssa."

"That makes two of us. We need to be careful while we're in this village."

Everything has an alcoholic stench, and I reach for Nikos' shirt, which needs washing.

"I've just saved your friend," Lyssa sing-songs loudly as she waltzes back into the room, drawing everyone's attention. She saunters right toward Ragnar, standing so close to him, she's practically rubbing her breasts on his arm.

I stare, the sight like torture, while a fire burns over my heart.

Jae collects the rest of the bandages Lyssa forgot and goes up to her, interrupting her flirting with Ragnar to hand them to her. Crius makes his way back over to me and takes my hand, pulling up to my feet.

He's close to me, barely an inch between us, and my knees wobble. "I saw the way you were looking at Lyssa," he says quietly. "I don't want you to even let yourself think such things. You are a goddess in my eyes, in all our eyes. She is nothing to us."

"Crius," the old man calls to him, and with a quick smile my way, he returns to the table.

If that's true, why did Lyssa say Ragnar was marrying her?

THIRTEEN

Narah moans, struggling to wake up. I sit by her bed, watching her. She's so beautiful. I'm tempted to crawl under the blankets and fuck her. To take her over and over, to remind her that she is mine.

She stirs and suddenly opens her eyes, staring at me, almost startled. She pushes out from under the blankets with speed. That's when she looks around and gasps, "Where's Jae? Is Nikos okay?"

"They're fine, little fox. In fact, Jae's with the kitchen girls preparing tonight's meal, as she insisted on helping. Something about learning how to cook something other than fire-roasted rabbit. And Nikos is awake, healing. He'll need another day or so."

Softness sweeps over Narah's face, and she collapses back on the edge of the bed. "Is it sad that my first reaction was to expect imminent danger?" She's got her hand over her chest. "My heart is beating so fast right now."

I can't even laugh because I understand that all too well. "If it makes you feel better, I woke up sweating, thinking we were back in the Poisonous Woods." Not to mention I woke up yelling thirteen days. The exact number of days we have left before the curse strangles us. This shit is getting to me.

She laughs. "That place still gives me nightmares, too." I glance at her nightdress that falls to her knees. It's white and made of extremely thin fabric. It takes everything I have to hold her stare and not devour those rosy nipples standing tight behind the material. My intention had never been to claim her when I struck a deal with her initially. I have my own shit to do, but since catching up with her in town after finding Jae, I lost part of myself to this girl.

It seems I stopped fighting my inner demons about letting another woman into my life after my fated mate rejected me, but Narah is different from my ex. She is similar to me. We have darkness in our pasts, and it feels like we're on the same side.

"Come here." I take her hand, guiding her to stand between my legs, and my fingers slide to her waist. She's so soft and small next to me. "How are you feeling?"

"Like I could sleep the entire day." She gives me a wonky smile and yawns.

"Sorry to tell you, but you've already done that."

She tilts her head toward the window behind me, and her cute mouth drops open with shock. She's just too gorgeous. When she looks back at me, I kiss her, needing to taste her sweetness, to hear her moans, to have her breasts against me. If I could, I'd press her into me so nothing could touch her again.

Narah's been through hell, which has made her stronger. I see the fire in her eyes, in her actions, so hiding her away won't work. She's a fighter, so I'll take my spot by her side as her warrior and defend her. I may not know what will happen tomorrow, but I am adamant that I'll make her mine... even if she doesn't know it yet.

She's kissing me back without hesitation, then suddenly stiffens and breaks away.

"What's wrong?" It worries me to see her smile fade.

Untangling herself from my hold, she stumbles backward and sits back on the bed. "I need to know something first," she says, her words shaky, and she's holding her hands in her lap.

"Of course. Anything."

"It's just that my fated mate, Martell, broke parts of me when he rejected our bond. He broke the wings I thought I had to soar with in this world, but his actions brought out my claws. Before I found you, I thought I lost everything and I was at the lowest point in my life. I don't ever want to feel like that again because I trusted the wrong man."

I ease forward to the edge of my seat. "Little fox, what are you talking about?" I get to my feet, my chest tightening, and I sit by her side on the bed.

"I just want you to be honest with me because Lyssa told me you were going to marry her. Maybe it's just her daydreaming that she will be with you because, I mean, look at you. But I need to be sure."

She's doing that thing where she rambles when she's nervous, and it's cute, but her words are like a thorn in my side. Of course, Lyssa would have told her at the first chance she got, and I should have prepared her for it beforehand. But everything happened so fast.

"It's not that simple," I answer.

She's on her feet and turning to face me. "It's actually a pretty simple question. You are or aren't planning to marry her?" She assesses me, watching me for my reaction, but I don't feel guilty when I have nothing to feel guilty about.

But seeing her worked up does bug me.

I get up and walk to her. She recoils from me. "She is nothing to me. Never was and never will be. She doesn't hold a candle to you, little fox, so you have nothing to be jealous about."

She rears back and pulls from me. "You haven't answered my question. And this has nothing to do with jealousy. But maybe the fault is mine. For some reason, I thought you said you cared for me, and I foolishly believed it."

Fuck.

"Narah." I march after her and grab her by the arms before pinning her against the wall, caging her with my body.

She slams her hands to my chest. "Get off me."

"Not until you listen to me. Lyssa is nothing to me. She is the Alpha's daughter, and when I first arrived in Romania, they were the first pack I encountered. I made a deal with them to gain a foothold in Savage Sector, and the only way the Alpha agreed was if I said I'd take his daughter as mine. I had no choice and said yes, but told him it wouldn't happen until I conquered all of Savage Sector."

Her eyes widen, and her chin trembles. Fucking hell. It kills me to see the ache in her eyes.

"I had no intention of doing so. I am biding my time until I gain enough traction that I will overpower his pack." I reach over and place a hand to the side of her face, but she draws from me. A blade might as well be piercing through my chest.

My mother used to say that pain changes people, making them trust less, assuming everyone is out to harm them. But I never wanted Narah to feel that way toward me.

"Say something, gorgeous," I demand.

"I don't know." She blinks, looking away from me, and that stings. "She seemed adamant you were hers."

"I never want to hurt you, but I never said I wasn't a bastard to others. I will do what I need to win over this sector, but one thing I won't compromise on is you. I have nothing to hide from you."

"And what if I was in your shoes? What would you do?" She lifts her head, holding my gaze bravely.

"I'd kill the man," I growl, jealousy erupting through me at the thought. "I can be a jealous Alpha and, little fox, when I marked you in the woods with my bite, I staked my claim. There is no going back for me... I need you to understand this. No one will come between us, no fucking girl, no ex-fated mates."

Her chin trembles. "A-Any man?"

I'm holding onto her shoulders now, and her small hands are on mine, slightly shaking. Does she doubt that I'd kill someone who tries to take her from me?

"As far as I'm concerned," I continue. "From the moment I fucked you, there was no question about what I wanted. You are mine. And I'll do anything for you."

She has this look of innocence that drives me crazy, that tells me she is full of all the best kinds of good and bad. "You may very well be my undoing if you don't destroy me first," I murmur.

"I-I never expected any of this," she says softly. "My feelings are confusing, my past haunts me, and all I ask is for you to be gentle with me. I keep telling myself I shouldn't be drawn to you, but when you say things like that, I stand no chance. But I don't want to be hurt again, Ragnar." The way she looks at me, smiling, gives me the impression she's barely holding back her tears.

Agony spears through my chest, and my lungs are pumping furiously for each breath. "Narah, under different circumstances, I would have told you about Lyssa before we arrived here."

She nods, and I lean in closer to her, stealing a kiss, needing to have her against me to stop the ache pulsing under my breastbone. Her body melts against mine. When we're together, the world falls away and all that remains is us. The desperation to bite her, to make sure the mark sticks harder this time, pulses in my veins.

I want to fuck her again.

My racing heart bangs louder, and my broken thoughts tell me I can't lose her. I'm still reeling from losing my head and heart so fast, but I can't fully take the blame. The growl in my chest has my wolf just as much responsible. He connected with her wolf both times I took her.

A loud knock comes at the door.

"Fuck off," I bark back.

"Ragnar, the pack Alpha, Mihai, is waiting for you to join their meal. Actually, everyone's waiting," Stone states.

"Goddammit." I swallow hard and look at my Narah, desperate to remain with her, convince her she's mine and that no other woman will do. But that's not going to happen. "I have to go," I whisper to her, our brows touching.

"What's going on?"

"When an Alpha invites me for a meal while I'm in his home, it would be an insult to not attend. So, I'll go and play the games." Frustration simmers beneath my skin at having to leave her.

"That's fine," she says and ducks her head under my arm, then crosses the room before opening the door to Stone. "He's all yours."

Something in my gut tells me we weren't finished with the conversation. "We'll talk later." Then I head outside and turn to Stone. "Stay close and watch both her and Jae."

"You got it," he says, and I walk away. With Nikos still injured and Crius out on a hunting mission with the locals to help bring in game for the villagers, a request we couldn't say no to, I guess I'm doing the honorary guest dinner alone.

But all I want is to be buried deep in Narah and convince her I want no one else.

~

"Can you believe you'll be running this pack in the future?" Lyssa whispers in my ear, leaning so close I'm suffocating from her bitter scent.

Her father, Mihai, watches from the end of the long table, his grin wide. The banquet before us is made of large roasts, a variety of baked bread, and hearty stews. Crius will be pissed he missed this dinner, but he'll eat plenty when he returns, and Stone will ensure Nikos, Narah, and Jae all get a good meal. My mouth salivates at the smells, and the dozen pack members around us greedily dig into the food like such an offering is not a frequent event.

I don't remember some of their names, but I don't care. The way I see it, I will take over this pack and rule soon enough, but not the way they envisage. With Narah as my queen by my side, not Lyssa. I am adamant about this... even if Narah needs convincing that she is the only one for me.

"I will, of course, be by your side," Lyssa continues and strokes my thigh. Her touch is grating on my nerves. It's funny how meeting someone who connects with me, with my wolf, changes my perception. On my first arrival to this pack, I had no problems flirting with Lyssa. She is a beautiful woman, but now her touch repels me.

Does Narah even realize what she's done to me?

Mihai raises a cup of wine that sloshes over the rim and splashes the table. "A toast to a most auspicious night, having Ragnar Ulv join us. To the union, we will gain between our packs, and my support, which I pledge to aid you in gaining control of the Savage Sector."

I take my cup as the men around us cheer and jut their drinks into the air before guzzling them down. I follow suit to show my respect, then stand for no reason other than to remove Lyssa's hand from my groin.

"You are the first pack to welcome me into your home, and that will be something I won't forget. Our unity will be of tremendous benefit to us all." I raise my drink, figuring maybe being forced to come to this pack right now might be opportune after all. Father had a saying that's always stuck with me: Keep your allegiances strong, even if it means visiting them for a drink once a full moon. The glint in

Mihai's eyes reassures me he'll have my back when the time comes. And while I won't take his daughter as mine, I will rule his pack.

"Here's to reigning over the Savage Sector!" I unleash a howl, the sound echoing in the long meal hall.

Everyone jumps to their feet, their heads tilt back, and they join my song of success. Even Lyssa, whom, I have no doubt, will easily find an Alpha to take her.

We fall back into chatter and eating when Lyssa presses into my shoulder.

"Hearing you speak like that gave me goosebumps, all the way down between my thighs," she whispers in my ear. "I give you permission to touch and find out."

I swallow the mouthful of venison I just took a bite of and twist toward her. Her blond hair is swept off her face tonight and plaited. Small white flowers adorn her hair, akin to a halo. Her pale eyes never leave mine, and her crimson lips pull into a grin.

My earlier words come back to me. The ones my dad had made about keeping appearances with those you make pacts with, and last time I'd visited, Lyssa shared a secret with me.

"I'd like to ask a favor of you," I murmur.

Her eyes grow in size, and she shuffles closer to me, which I didn't think was possible.

"Of course. Ask me anything." She places a hand on my leg, and as much as I'd like to push away her advances, I may need to play the part a while longer.

"My friend needs your assistance. She's looking for her mother, and you spoke highly of your seer abilities on my last visit."

Her spine stiffens at my words, and she studies me carefully. "If you don't mind me asking, who are those two Omegas? Are you selling them?" There is a flick of jealousy in her eyes, and to tell her the truth would not aid our cause.

"They're family friends." Reluctantly, I reach over and cup her face, my fingers tenderly holding her, my thumb sweeping over her cheek.

She softens against my touch, but I feel nothing at this moment. No attraction, no arousal, no wolf shoving forward, as he had in Narah's presence.

"Will you do this for me?"

She has eyes only for me like there is no one else in the room with us. And I can see many men falling for the beauty in her eyes, but not me.

"Only for you, I'll help."

She leans in quickly and kisses my cheek, then whispers, "Maybe tonight you should visit my room. I'll leave the window open."

I hate leading her on, but when a hand claps roughly on my shoulder, I gratefully pull from Lyssa and turn to find her father behind me.

"Ragnar, come and warm yourself by the fire with me. Let's talk," he announces.

"Of course." I'm on my feet instantly, more than thankful to leave the table, and follow him across the room to the roaring fireplace.

"You've arrived at a good time, as I have given our union much thought." He stares into the fire, his pause telling me this isn't a general discussion about taking over the sector. He wants something more from me.

"You have agreed to take my daughter, and in exchange, my pack is at your disposal to use for expanding your territory. We've already taken over three packs in the nearby lands, and we have four more in sight. But I feel that my leg work and responsibility greatly outweighs yours."

I bristle at his implication, but I swallow back my pride. "I am always on your side, Mihai, so tell me how I can correct this? And don't forget, I have my own pack of at least fifty men too, and my deal with the witches, which will give us an advantage over everyone." I grind my teeth, needing to stretch the truth somewhat. He doesn't need to know the current circumstances with the witches.

"My men are starved of women. For a pack of two hundred men, we have ten Omegas, so you can imagine the trouble this causes. The lands are so sparse of females, and I fear I'll soon have a mutiny on my hands as the men leave to find a mate to claim."

Distant voices and laughter from the table fill the void while my thoughts come to one quick solution. Ever since the virus ravaged our world and killed most of the people, females have become fewer in number and so rarely found.

But on my recent trip to the Shadowlands Sector, I discovered a larger number of females live in the south of the country.

Dušan is the Alpha of the Shadowlands Sector and, on our last encounter, I'd told him I would pay him another visit, seeing as he was having some issues of his own. Seems someone close to him had tried to take over the pack... either way, it doesn't bother me how that turned out. I made him a promise.

"What promise I will make is that I will return to your land with my warriors. If you are not in charge upon my arrival, and this mess hasn't been swept away, I will wipe out all the males on this land, claim the females, and take ownership."

Dušan stands tall and proud. He doesn't get defensive, and already I can tell he's an Alpha I respect. He finally answers, "If I do not reclaim my sector by the next blue moon, I will not stand in your way. But when we do meet again, I propose we make arrangements for our packs to work together."

I glance up at Mihai, who's watching me, expecting a response. I clear my throat, saying, "There's someone I know who can assist. I can get you what you need. Would that alleviate your concerns?"

"At least a hundred Omegas," he demands.

I hold back the urge to scoff at him. He's fucking kidding. "Twenty, and we have a deal," I growl my response. My shoulder blades bunch up now that I need to somehow add a trip to the south with my list of growing problems.

"Sixty," he counters.

"Forty, and that's my final offer. I will bring them to you in a few months."

His brow pinches at my suggestion. "No, my son. You will deliver them within a month if you want to unite with my pack. Otherwise, our agreement is off, and all the packs I'm currently amassing under my reign will end up your enemy."

My wolf's rolling in my chest, teeth bared at this traitor. But I'd do the same in his position... after all, we're all playing to survive.

"Do we have a deal then?" he continues, putting his hand out to shake.

The noose hanging over my head with the witches' curse grows tighter. It's a risk I have to take. Lyssa will hopefully give us directions to Narah's mother, and I pray to the moon goddess that she will be our answer to eradicate the curse with those witches. Maybe even the ability to take them over. We have less than two weeks for that, giving me two more weeks, if I survive, to pay Shadowlands Sector a visit.

Fuck!

I growl under my breath, but know there's no other way around this. I need Mihai and his growing pack, as they will all be under me to help gain more packs under one umbrella. And that means making sacrifices now.

I shake his hand. "Deal."

FOURTEEN

STONE

I shut the door to the bedroom, where Jae is fast asleep. She's exhausted herself after helping in the kitchen, but I haven't seen her smile that much since I met her. The poor thing is dying for some kind of normalcy. I'd gone to find Narah, but she's not here. The small cabin they've given us for our stay means we don't all get a bed. Crius crashed on the blankets near the window, snoring like a dragon after his day of hunting.

Nikos is across the room from him, also snoozing, though he's twitching like he's having a nightmare. On the bright side, he's healing. Soon we can get the hell out of this town and go find Narah's mother. Somehow. I pin my hopes on Ragnar sucking up to the Alpha's daughter and seeing if she can aid us with her seer power. The girl's lost her shit over him and is so smitten, it's kinda sad. Glad it's him and not me having to let her down.

If it wasn't for Narah, Ragnar wouldn't hesitate to take one for the team and sleep with Lyssa to get her to do our bidding, so I am curious to find out how he pulls this off. We've all witnessed how he looks at Narah, and the thing about my Alpha is that he's fucking loyal to those he considers family.

I kick Crius' boots. He crashed fully dressed.

He groans until I kick him again.

"What the fuck, man?" he snarls, opening just one eye.

"Where's Narah?"

He rolls onto his back and opens the other eye. "She said something about going to wash her clothes or something. Now fuck off." He turns away from me and is snoring again in seconds.

I head outside into the cool night, my attention caught by two men near the blazing fire in the middle of all the homes. It makes me wonder if it's something they keep running all the time or not, as that would take a lot of effort.

Reaching the men, I step into their line of sight. "Evening," I say, with some semblance of respect, instead of just demanding they answer my question right away. Hey, I'm trying.

They lift their chin in my direction, not bothering to even respond. Well, so much for that respectful shit.

"Where's the washroom?" I go for something simple, figuring they might understand it easier. They don't seem like the brightest bastards in the shed.

"It's the cabin farthest to your left, right next to the baths," one man grunts, then turns his back to me to keep talking to his friend, who looks my way. "You're after the black-haired beauty with the fuckable ass?" He grins, revealing a missing front tooth. "She looks easy."

His friend chortles, and fuck, these two are pissing me off. They could only be talking about Narah.

A possessiveness rises within me and claws at my chest. I struggle to not shove him into the fire for speaking about her that way, though I am half tempted... except that might ruin our diplomatic standing with this pack. Some days I wish I was more like Crius, who'd have both men already burning.

Instead, I do it my way. I lash out and snatch the man by the throat, then haul him toward me. His friend comes at me, but I punch him square in the nose with my other hand, which has him reeling, backing into the fire. He squeals. Idiot.

I turn to the asshole in front of me, who's growling. He throws a jab into my gut, but I feel nothing when I'm rolling in rage. "You don't get to look at her ever again, speak about her, breathe near her, nothing. Understand? To you, she doesn't exist because she's already claimed. You cross me, and I will rip your fucking heart right out of your chest out next time I see you."

"You son of a—"

I headbutt him even though my runes burn across my chest, my wolf raging through me to rip open the ground, so he falls into the pits of Hell itself. Instead, I shove him out of my face before I give in to my power. He's crying and grasping his bloody nose.

"Fucking pussies," I call after them as they retreat, rubbing the soreness on my forehead from where I struck that asshole. But it's worth it to remind those two of their place.

When I find the washroom empty, I pop my head into the baths just to be sure because if I don't find her, I'm tearing down every damn cabin until I track her down.

Except, once inside, I can't believe my eyes. The gorgeous girl I've been searching for is standing naked with her back to me, sticking her hand into the water of the round wooden tub she's clearly about to climb into. The tub reaches her thighs in height, and she's bending over enough that my cock hardens in a second flat.

My eyes are locked on the sight of her firm, round ass, long legs, slender waist, and—fuck me—but I need her to turn around before I go insane. But I'm not fooling myself. Since spending time with her on our trip into the Poisonous Woods, she's messed me up big time right inside my chest. Could be that I haven't found anyone serious or my fated mate yet. Or that I'm completely blinded by her beauty, her fiery nature, or that she's a survivor like the rest of us.

But who the fuck cares right now. That's not what I want to think about when she's naked. I'm wearing too many clothes. My cock hurts at how hard it is. I need her. All of her.

There's no one else in the room, and as she climbs into the tub, I shut the door behind me. The bang echoes a bit too loud. Narah yelps and falls into the bath, sending a cascade of water sloshing out over the edge. She goes under, then comes gasping back up, her hair slicked back, and stares at me with those doe-eyes, startled.

My attention locks on those perky tits of hers that bounce from her sudden movement, not covered by water, and she completely undoes me.

"What the hell, Stone!" She quickly covers herself and dips lower, so only her head sticks out.

"No use hiding, sweetheart. Already saw everything, and it's fucking delicious."

"Ha, you did not. Wait, are you spying on me?" Her cheeks are beautifully red and damn but I love seeing her this way. The way she gasps, her eyes dilated, the veins in her neck pulsing.

I stroll toward her, unbuttoning my shirt.

"Hmm, what are you doing?" she gasps.

"What does it look like? I'm going to take a bath."

Her gaze narrows on me. "Well this tub isn't big enough for two." She glances at the other two tubs and points to one across the room in a corner. "Go to that one. Looks big enough to fit you, but first, you need to go request hot water."

"Oh, don't you worry, sweetheart. I'll fit." I smirk as I slide the shirt off and drop it to the floor behind me while I pause and toe off my boots.

"I'm serious, Stone. Don't you dare come in here, or I'll drown you."

I burst out laughing, and the urge to fight this vixen while we're both naked has my cock twitching with an unbearable need to finally take what I've been wanting since I first saw her.

I've been meaning to tell this beauty that I intend to claim her as mine. After all, the four of us share everything, and that includes Omegas. Especially Omegas.

And tonight, I have every intention of treating her as my queen, lifting her into the heavens until she looks at me like I'm all she's ever desired. Maybe later, I'll treat her to a foot massage while I feed her grapes with my mouth.

She's still covering her breasts, and liquid fire shoots through my veins.

I unbuckle my pants and drop them. I always go commando.

Her gaze lowers, and her mouth might have just opened into an O shape.

"You like this, don't you? Of course, you do."

She swallows loudly, and no longer tells me to leave.

The thing about Narah is that I've seen the way she looks at me, how her breaths catch, how her scent changes to one of arousal in my presence. No matter what she might say, on the inside, she knows the truth. She wants everything from me, and I intend to give it.

I climb into the tub with her—it is round and can easily fit three people. It's how they're designed—but Narah's at one end, still hiding those gorgeous breasts from me.

"Don't fight this," I say. "Sometimes, following your instincts is not such a bad idea."

I dunk down into the warm embrace and splash myself with water, along with my face and, run wet fingers through my hair. It feels amazing.

"You lost for words?" I ask.

"Just curious why you think you can just get into the bath with me, and it be okay?"

My eyes drag across her body under the water, to where she has her legs bent, and back to her chest. "Because I needed a wash, and you looked inviting."

She snorts a laugh, yet her chest is heaving and, despite her words, she studies my body too.

"Do you like what you see?" she asks.

"Of course I do. You can't tell? But how about we stop talking about this and let me show you that you are mine and what that means."

She smiles sweetly at me, and sometimes it's hard to tell with Narah what she's really up to. "Is that so?" She lowers her knees in the bathtub, revealing her gorgeous breasts and pink nipples.

Reaching down, I grab my dick and squeeze it, imagining it's her tight pussy. I moan under my breath, then move through the water toward her, both of us at eye level.

I love the panicked look in her gaze; it skyrockets my adrenaline.

When I pause in front of her, she grins, then in a sudden movement, she tosses water right in my face. I blink through the cascade, only to find her twisting around and rushing to climb out of the water, that gorgeous ass bending over.

So what's a man to do? I lunge after her, grabbing her hips, and I shove my face into her ass. Resisting is futile, so I give her what she craves. Me.

My tongue laps out and strokes between her cheeks, taking her hungrily. My fingers dig into her sides, and I lick her, dipping lower, needing to taste her juices, her sweet scent already engulfing every inch of me.

She moans. I love the way she responds to my touch. Instead of pushing me away, she holds onto the padding that winds around the top of the tub and lifts her ass higher.

"You look fucking amazing. Now open your legs wider for me, sweetheart."

She does as I ask, and I'm rewarded by the most mesmerizing sight of her soaking wet pussy, pink and swollen with how truly turned on she is, despite her actions. She glances back at me with those burning amber eyes blinking at me, her lips parting with her rushed breaths.

"Keep being such a good girl, and I'll reward you." Then I bury my face between her thighs again and take what's mine. I suck on her lips, tongue fuck her hole, unable to get close enough. I want her all over my face, so I smell and taste only her.

I ravage this gorgeous peach, slurring and licking. Her growing moans only drive me wilder. Her hips rock and she pushes against my face, wanting more and more. Adorable.

So I pull back and get to my feet. "I need to fuck your pussy," I say.

"Please, Stone, yes."

"That's my girl, you're doing so great."

At my words, her body trembles, her pussy lips are plump, her need dripping down the inside of her thighs. I love nothing more than a woman wet from arousal. Begging me for more.

I palm my cock, and the agony of need hurts. My balls are so tight too. I shift to stand closer behind her.

"Do it," she urges me as she waits for me, so open.

I growl, grabbing her hips, my cock finding her juicy slit. I roar and slam into her, her pussy gripping my dick with each thrust. She's so tight... this is fucking heaven. Here I thought I'd take her, but it turns out, she sent me there just as quickly.

She's moaning, rocking her hips back and forth to meet each of my thrusts. I hammer into her hard and fast, claiming her. And just as her cries grow wilder, my own climax builds, I pull out of her. Much to her anger as she straightens and turns on me with a frown, fire in her eyes. Her tits bounce; they are spectacular.

"What the hell? I was so close," she snaps.

"I know," I smirk, and I reach out and grab her by the back of her neck, roughly hauling her against me. "Come here. I want to watch your face when you scream." My hands glide down the back of her leg, and I lift it, placing it around my hip, opening her up for me.

My dick slides between her folds, and she's pivoting her hips to accept me, to swallow me. Her eyes roll back in euphoria, her hands clutching my arms. I guide myself into her, then wrap her other leg around me, and I slide completely into her where I belong. I grunt, my hips already stuttering in and out of her.

She's making these hot noises as I thrust into her little cunt because I have no control, and I've been waiting so long. I growl, my body tensing, my balls so damn tight they might have gone up into me.

That's when movement out the corner of my eye catches my attention. I turn to find a man, maybe in his thirties, opening the door and freezing on the spot in shock. The look of pure arousal covers his face as he realizes this might be the luckiest moment of his pathetic life... seeing me fuck my queen.

He stands there, enjoying the show, and I keep on plunging into my babe.

When she realizes we are being watched, she gasps and tries to move, but I hold her in place, taking her harder. "You're not going anywhere," I mutter to her. Then I swing my attention to the pervert. "And you! Get the fuck out of here before I shove your cock up your ass. Oh, and shut the door behind you."

He rushes out, slamming the door shut.

"How could you let that man watch us?" she whispers between gasps.

"It didn't turn you on?" I ask.

She shrugs.

"Thought so." Then I fuck her hard, take her, returning to where we'd left off. Her breasts rub against my chest as she rides me, her arms looped around my neck. A man could easily lose himself to a girl like Narah... if I hadn't already done so.

Heat ignites between us.

"You'll take it like the good girl you are."

At my words, she suddenly screams, her body quivering, and that sweet pussy strangles my cock. She brings me the most delicious agony, while my heart beats in my chest like a drum and my own orgasm hits me. It comes so hard; it rocks through me, my erection swelling inside her tight little core. I roar with the pressure of her being so small, but it's everything I demand... she is everything to me.

Her orgasm sends me over the edge and I growl as I burst inside of her, flooding her with my seed, pumping. I hold her, both of us, on a different plane. Nothing but pure elation.

I don't even know how long I've been floating. I finally open my eyes, and my cock is deeply embedded in her, knotted, still jerking seed into her. And I find her smiling at me.

My heart bangs in response at how she makes me feel. How the smallest reaction has me falling deeper.

"Good girl, and just so you know, you're all mine."

She laughs, gripping me as I kneel slowly, then take a seat in the tub with my back against the side. Narah straddling my lap, both of us connected, and to have my knot in her, to force us together, is all I've wanted.

"I keep hearing that from each of you guys. But, I mean, you can't all own me?"

I kiss her for the first time tonight, claiming her mouth, licking her lips. "Why not? Back in Denmark, sharing a mate is not uncommon, especially when Omegas are so scarce."

"Makes sense, but also leaves me feeling greedy. To have four of you is nothing I ever expected."

"And finding a girl like you is nothing I ever dreamed of, but here I am fucking you and telling you that you're mine. That you're such a good girl, and I'll take you over and over."

She blinks at me. "You wanna hear something strange?"

"Go for it."

"I don't know why, but I really get turned on when you say that stuff to me about being a good girl."

I laugh. "Oh, I can tell, babe. You have a little kink for receiving praises, and it's fucking hot."

Her mouth partly falls open. "Is that even a thing?"

"Sure is, and I love saying those things to you. It drives me nuts."

I adore this girl so much. She settles against my chest; she rests her cheek in the curve of my neck and her soft breath flares across my skin.

"Tell me about yourself," she says.

"Sure, what do you want to know?"

"Anything and everything."

I settle back, my arms around her, holding her close. "I grew up in a household that was constantly at war. If my father wasn't arguing with my mother, he was beating me. So I spent as little time as I could there."

"Where'd you go?"

"Mostly, Ragnar's house, since he's my cousin. Plus, their home is a mansion compared to everyone else's home, and they had rooms to spare for nights I didn't want to leave. Not that it was calmer there... Ragnar's father is the Alpha of the Ulv Wolves, and a bastard as much as my dad. Once Nikos moved in with Ragnar's family, the three of us bonded quickly and would do anything to get away from wolf politics." I shrug. "We did a lot of hunting in the woods and went away for weeks at a time to escape the pack."

"I'm so sorry. My father was the most amazing man, treating me and my sisters like we were his world. But the Storm Wolves Alpha killed him, blaming him for my mother escaping, then nothing ever felt right again." She falls quiet after that and wraps her arms around my middle.

"Anyway," she says after a little while, "let's not talk about depressing shit." She traces her finger around the inked runes on my chest. "Tell me more about these. What can your magic do?"

"There is magic on my mother's side of the family; they can tap into the power of runes. At the age of five, my mother had them inked on my skin along with a ritual to open me up to elemental magic."

"Wow, that's really young."

"They say the younger you are, the stronger the power. Though, I'm not so sure about that. It took me years to learn the basics of just getting a plant to fold over. Even then, it's nothing compared to what you can do."

She scoffs. "What I saw you do in the Poisonous Forest was not nothing."

"You're too sweet to me." And I steal a kiss. When she moves, her muscles constrict around my cock, and it only awakens the excitement. I doubt I'll ever have a limp dick again.

She smirks at me and squeezes her pussy around my cock again.

"Oh, be very careful, sweetheart, because you're about to raise hell, and I'm ready to go all night."

She sticks her tongue out at me, teasing, and in her eyes, she's begging for more.

FIFTEEN

NARAH

"Narah," Ragnar calls my name the moment I step out of the communal mess hall after filling up on porridge. It's a larger cabin than the rest of the buildings in the pack compound. Jae is still inside with two girls she's made friends with. They are similar in age, and it warms my heart to have my sister smile and laugh for a change. She's been forced to grow up too quickly, so if I can give her a few days without worry, then I'll do it.

The raucous voices behind me in the mess hall booms, and I'd almost forgotten how secure it feels to be part of a pack, knowing you are never alone to face whatever this world throws at you.

Ragnar is sauntering past other cabins and coming my way, his mouth widening into a grin like he's got a secret he's about to share. He's wearing cargo pants, combat boots, and a V-neck, short-sleeved tee. Everything about this man is dangerous and handsome.

Guilt turns in my gut after what Stone and I did last night in the baths, but to be fair, the way I am drawn to each of these men is unlike anything I've ever felt. It's different from the attraction I had to Martell—that was purely animalistic and my wolf driving me. Except, what these four Viking Alphas do to me is on another planet. They arouse me with a single word. They make me care for them, and they look out for me. The only people to have done that for me before had been my family.

I feel myself slipping deeper for each of these four men, and with each passing day, the knot of guilt in my chest tightens. I need to speak to Ragnar about this and tell him about my attraction. Even if I don't know if my future will be with them, I need to be honest.

"Morning, little fox." Ragnar takes my hand in his, our fingers interlaced, and he draws me into a stroll.

I swallow the words I want to tell him, unable to voice them right now... at least, so his beautiful smile doesn't fade away. "Someone's in a good mood today," I say instead.

"I might have found a solution to tracking down your mother."

"What? Are you kidding me?" I pause, then I'm throwing myself at him, embracing him.

His powerful arms wrap around me, and he kisses my brow. "There's a seer in town who's agreed to help us."

I pull back, staring at him, completely blank on what to say.

"We should be ready to head out later today," he continues. "Nikos is up and about, his wound almost healed."

"Thank you," I gasp, still lost for breath, that this might be the solution. "This means everything." I pray my mother isn't as dangerous as Kaira implied. I don't even let myself go there with my thoughts. This has to work because, otherwise, I don't know how we're going to get my sister from the witches or eradicate our curse.

He urges me with our linked hands to walk again. "The seer agreed to speak with you this morning and try to find your mother."

"Okay, I'm ready. I don't know what to expect, but I'm assuming it's some kind of reading?"

We come to a stop outside the wooden cabin we'd gone into on our first night of arrival, where the pack Alpha lives, and I glance up at Ragnar, my brow pinching.

"She's waiting for you inside." He pushes open the door.

"She?" And when I turn to look inside, I find Lyssa sitting at the table in their kitchen, waving. She's got her blonde hair pulled tight in a ponytail and wearing a navy-blue hoodie and jeans.

"Hey, Ragnar," she purrs, not even acknowledging me, batting her eyes at him.

I want to roll mine, but instead, I whisper to Ragnar, "Are you sure you got this right?"

He's half-smiling like I made a joke. "Yes, now go." Then he nudges me in the back, and I stumble inside. The door shuts behind me, and I just stand there awkwardly. Silence. Lyssa watching me. The strange smell of burning herbs. I nervously fiddle with my gloves, wishing this was anyone but her.

"If you don't want to do this, that's fine," she snaps, curling her hand around her ponytail as she starts to get up.

Except, if Ragnar is right, then who the hell cares who the seer is, right? As long as I get my answer.

"You're a seer?" I ask and close the distance between us, sliding into the seat across the table from her. She sits back down.

There are two items placed between us. A blade and a small drawstring pouch the color of night. I eye the weapon, not too happy about what that might mean. I'm really not into sacrifices.

"Some call me that, but really it's just an ability from my mother's family. All the women in her bloodline have a touch of divination. She used to have visions of the future, while I can sometimes find lost things."

Part of me toys with asking her more about her mom's ability, considering my vision with my sisters still baffles me. In truth, it terrifies the hell out of me that it portrays a future that will devastate me.

"But tell me something, how did you lose your mother?" she asks, looking at me with her head tilted to the side like I'm a complete moron and somehow misplaced a parent.

I slump back in my chair, not falling for the jab. "She left one day and never came back."

Lyssa watches me as she empties the small bag onto the table. Half a dozen black and gray stones roll out. All of different sizes and shapes. There are no markings on them. They could just be regular pebbles from the garden, for all I know.

"Ever think she doesn't want to be found, then?" She quirks a thin eyebrow. "Sometimes when someone's energy is hiding, I can't see them."

"There has to be a reason she left, and I need to find out," I answer, not intending to give Lyssa any more information. Did I mention I don't trust the girl?

"Give me your hand," she says and places hers on the table, palm side up.

I look down at my hands in my lap, at the sandy-colored gloves I'm wearing, and how this isn't going to work. Maybe this was a mistake after all? Mother... the word wells in my mind like a heavy stone. For years, I've dreamed of finding my mother, and this is my chance, but I don't feel comfortable showing Lyssa what I am.

"Is there another way?" I ask.

She blinks, her brow furrowing. "What do you mean? I just need your hand. I'm not going to chop it off."

Her direct aggression always annoys me. "It's just that..."

"Are we doing this, or are you wasting my time?"

I swallow loudly and start pulling the glove off one hand, nerves twisting in the pit of my stomach. Tensing, I slowly lift my hand with my fingers stained black from under the table, and I wait for her comment.

She gasps, then studies me with her narrowing gaze. "What happened?"

"I upset some witches," I murmur, lying through my teeth.

She's silent for a while, then scoffs. "Yeah, I'd believe that. You are annoying." Then she grabs my hand and puts it palm up on top of hers, studying the lines.

My throat is parched. I'm surprised she says nothing more, seeing as it's more common for witches to have black fingers, just as my mother had. Perhaps Lyssa believes me for real... or she doesn't, and this will come back to bite me in the ass.

"I know you have a thing for Ragnar," she mutters suddenly, catching me off guard.

My spine stiffens, and I go to pull my hand back, but she grasps it hard. "I don't blame you. He's the ultimate Alpha, you know, and I haven't seen what he carries in his pants." She smirks. "But I bet it's going to be huge, and we're going to make so many babies."

Heat burns across my chest at her words. "Look, I didn't come here to talk about your obsession withRagnar."

She barks a laugh. "You believe that's what's going on?" Her fingers dig into the side of my hand, and I swallow the pain. "Do you think you are somehow special just because you're family or whatever lie he made up? I've seen the way you watch him, how he watches you possessively. No family members look at each other that way." Her hand constricts mine further, and I clench my teeth. Her nails are like blades going into my skin. "So, tell me the truth. What the hell have you been doing with my fiancé?"

I breathe faster, everything in my mind pulsing with the banging of my heart. My mind races for a reason she'll believe. Bitter jealousy can make even the most reasonable person paranoid as hell.

"I don't know what you're talking about," I say calmly, trying to pull my hand free, even if it feels like she's ripping it off. But a fiery anger brews in my gut from her hurting me, and I can't help myself. "Maybe the real issue is that Ragnar is not that into you."

A harried wildness flares behind her eyes. Next thing I know, she's gripping the knife from the table and slashing the blade across my palm before I can even react.

Pain explodes, and I scream, pulling backward, but she's holding on with an iron grip. "Hold still, you'll survive," she growls. The knife drops from her hand and hits the table with a thump. Then she takes the stones and places them into my bloody palm.

The sharp pain has me jumping each time the stones hit my wound, and I wince at how badly it hurts.

Then she turns my hand sideways and all the stones tumble onto the table, stained with my blood.

I'm finally able to yank back from her and cradle my hand. "You're fucking crazy, you know that?"

She gets to her feet and grabs a kitchen towel from the counter before throwing it in my face. "I don't like you for going after my man. But I understand. He's a pack leader, and when he rules Savage Sector, you want to be safe. Just like the rest of us."

Her words don't carry venom, but a sense of pity for me. If she knew the truth, she'd be clawing my face off.

She takes a seat back at the table and crosses her legs. "You're lucky Ragnar's helping you, but don't get any ideas. He's got his pack, go choose one of those men."

I blink at her, holding back the crazy laugh in my head at how I'm struggling to accept that I am attracted to all four of the Alphas. I wrap my bleeding hand in the kitchen towel to distract myself.

Lyssa studies the stones on the table, and I start to wonder if she really is a seer or pretended just to warn me off Ragnar.

"Narah, there's someone for everyone out there, and perhaps the person for you is a Beta. Have you ever considered that? Not everyone can be with the best."

"What are you talking about? Omegas can't mate with Betas." As my mother once told me, Alphas lead. Omegas are for rutting and making babies. While Betas are the fighters, the work dogs of the packs, they can't get an Omega pregnant. Only Alphas can.

She shrugs like she knew this all along, but used it to mock me. I really dislike her, even knowing she'll be devastated when Ragnar rejects her.

"Do you even know what you're doing with the divination, or are you wasting my time?" I ask, tucking the kitchen towel corner under the wrapped part, so it doesn't unravel.

"Hush," she says, leaning closer to the scattered stones covered in my blood. Then she glances up at me. "Don't be angry with me. Be angry with the shitty world and with the Alphas who rule it. I know you're trying to survive, I get it."

"Don't patronize me, Lyssa. You say you're going to help me, but all you've done is slice up my hand, then insult me. You know nothing about my past or my issues, so don't pretend you do while you're living safely in this perfect pack protected by your father."

I'm shaking at how angry she's got me.

She reels back in her seat, eyes narrowing. "You want to know the truth? Fine, I'll tell you." Her voice turns dark. "My father deemed me too old to sell to any of the nearby packs for their Alpha leaders. And those neighboring Alphas are all in their sixties or older, and they only want girls the age of your sister. So, then my father decided he was going to give me to the men in this pack as a reward for doing a good job. To share me as they pleased because we don't have enough females." Her words tremble now, and my heart clenches. "I am nothing to my father. I'm a pebble in his shoe. So, when Ragnar came and agreed to claim me, he saved me. I jumped at the chance to escape." Her chin is quivering as she blinks the tears away.

I deflate in my seat and feel like the worst person in the world.

"Lyssa, I didn't know." I reach over to her, but she rears back. "Don't give me pity, just your understanding that I'm doing anything I can to survive and not end up as a sex slave to those desperate men out there. I had nothing, and Ragnar gave me something to hold on to."

I sink in my seat, tears welling in my eyes. The ache that rips through my chest has me close to choking on my breaths. I've been so distracted by my problems, that I just assumed the worst of Lyssa.

"Forgive me for my words," I say softly.

She shrugs and sniffles, then glances down to the stones. "I can see where your mother is."

I straighten in my chair, my heart fluttering like crazy. Mother's alive! "You can? Where?"

She's pointing at two stones next to each other, which means nothing to me.

"I'm going to need a bit more information," I say.

"The Wolf Mountains," she replies with a yawn. "Your mother is there, nestled between them in the valley."

I know exactly where that is... well, I've never been there, as it's far, but the Wolf Mountains overlook a big section of the Savage Sector. I want to yell with excitement, but I'm also torn about Lyssa's predicament. I just hope she's not lying about my mother.

Lyssa gets up from the table and sweeps the stones into her hand before dumping them into the sink, where they clang against the metal.

"You can go now."

I'm on my feet. "Thank you for your help, and for telling me about your situation. Us females are treated like garbage by so many men, so we should look out for one another more. I promise I'll do what I can to help you."

She half-smiles at me over her shoulder. "Just stay away from my man, and all will be fine."

My stomach cramps up because I can't promise that when I know he doesn't want her. I turn on my heel and walk out, needing desperately to speak to Ragnar.

SIXTEEN

NARAH

As soon as I step into our cabin, I find Stone stuffing his clothes into a backpack. "Where's Ragnar?" I ask, looking around for any sign of Jae or Nikos. Nothing.

Stone glances up at me, his eyes smiling. "Morning, sweetheart. He's waiting for us down by the horses with the rest of them. We're leaving."

"Now?"

He nods and drops everything to make his way over to me. His hands instantly cup the sides of my face, and he kisses me in a way that makes me almost forget what I wanted to speak to Ragnar about. My toes curl in my boots, and I return the passion he showered me with last night, parting his lips, taking his tongue into my mouth. And suddenly, I'm back in the baths thinking about how he ravaged me, leaving me begging for more.

When he finally breaks from me, and I find myself leaning in for more, he says, "Jae's packed your belongings. We should go before they send a search party for us. I was supposed to collect you, but had to grab my stuff first." He goes to get his bag and throws it over his shoulder.

That's when I notice Jae's bag is still in the room, along with her coat and her heavy boots. The urgency to see her flares through me. I've lost her twice, and I don't plan on doing so again.

Stone crosses the room to open the door. "After you, my queen." He sweeps his hand for me to exit the cabin.

His words leave me giddy because no one has ever called me that. I won't lie; I love the sound of it. "Thanks." I step outside and quickly cross the lawn toward the stone steps leading out of the village.

"I hear you may know where your mother is," Stone mentions as he shuts the door and follows me.

"Where did you hear that? I just finished talking with Lyssa?"

"Ragnar," he answers and catches up to me. "He's convinced you'll know the answer and has already arranged for our departure from the pack to find her."

"Oh, okay. What if that hadn't been the case?"

"But Lyssa did tell you, didn't she?" he asks with an arch of his eyebrow.

I nod. "The Wolf Mountains."

"Then he was right."

The confidence they hold in Ragnar is incredible.

"So you knew Lyssa is a seer?"

"Yep, and she's completely obsessed with Ragnar."

"Yeah, well, there's a story behind everything, before you judge too quickly."

He glances at me with narrow eyes. "Where's that coming from? The other day, you looked ready to murder the girl for flirting with Ragnar."

"Well, that's because I didn't know the full story." He takes my hand as we saunter past several locals who only stare at us in silence. I use the walk to give Stone a quick summary of my chat with Lyssa and the shitty situation she's in.

"Fuck me, I had no clue, and I bet neither did Ragnar." He squeezes my hand slightly and draws me closer in a protective manner that's really growing on me.

"Whatever happens, we need to help her."

"We will," he assures me and lifts his head as we rush down the main steps from the village.

It's only when we reach the bottom of the stairs that I spot the rest of our gang and my sister, along with Mihai and a group of his men. Everyone's here, including our four horses. The pack Alpha is talking to Ragnar, his arms flailing about as if he's proving a big point.

Jae is waving at me to join her. We walk over. "Thanks for grabbing my things, sis."

"Always got your back." She smirks.

"But why is your stuff still in the cabin?"

"You see, when I spoke to Ragnar, he suggested it might be safer if I stay behind, and I'm going to move in with my new friends until you return. They're sisters, and their mother is super kind to me. Plus, Ragnar made the Alpha swear to keep me protected, or he'll personally hunt him down if anything happens to me."

Unease rolls through me. Being slightly annoyed that she asked Ragnar not me, I say, "It's just that I said I wasn't going to leave you behind again. Thought we'd stick together from now on." I push her hair behind an ear.

She hugs me, and I loop my arms around her, not wanting to be far from her. "Can I be honest with you?" she whispers and draws me away from the group while Ragnar and the Alpha are still talking.

"What's going on?"

Her shoulders drop when she looks up at me, and her arms hang slack at her sides. "Narah, please don't hate me. I do want to find our mother, but I'm also scared of what you'll discover. For so long, it's been easier to tell myself after she left us, she was killed. But what if she left us on purpose? What if..." her voice trails off, and she glances down.

"First, I could never hate you, and second, don't even think that," I say as her hitched breaths sting me. The same doubt has haunted me from the day Mother left us with the Storm Wolves. But having my youngest sister struggle with such fear rips me to shreds.

Lyssa's words return to me... *Ever think she doesn't want to be found?*

What if Mother doesn't want to see us? What if Kaira was right, and she's a danger to us?

I stare at Jae, and my heart cracks at her agony, while she bats away the tears glinting in her eyes. I swallow the heaviness claiming me, and in front of Jae, I try never to show my fear.

I lift her chin with my fingers. "Listen to me. She left us because she had no choice."

She shrugs, her mouth pinching to the side, staring down at her empty hands. "I want to stay here until you return. I'm tired of being scared and running."

Her words rattle me, and my eyes prick. "Oh, Jae." I hug her, wrapping her up in my arms. "Of course. If that's what you want, that's fine."

She doesn't move for a long time, and my heart hammers at the tremor in her voice. How can I make her join us after what she's been through? In the last couple of days, I've seen my younger sister again. Youthful. Happy. Excited about life.

And as much as it kills me, the best thing I can do for her is give her what she needs.

I kick myself for not being the one to acknowledge this. I guess I was too selfish, I wanted her close to me, so I can keep her safe, but it's not about what I want. She has to find her happiness.

"Please stay safe, and don't trust anyone." I reach down to my boot and pull out the small blade I always keep with me, handing it to her. "Anyone comes to hurt you, you stab them in the throat or eye. Then run."

Her gaze softens, filling with an inner glow. "You know, I *can* look after myself, but I'll take the knife." She hastily accepts it and tucks it away into the back of her pants.

"Are we ready to go, Narah?" Ragnar asks from behind me.

I meet his serious gaze and nod. My men climb up on their horses. I give Jae one more hug, wishing I could keep her safe for eternity. Protected from this horrible world, but not sure if I can do that forever.

"You're suffocating me," she chokes out, then laughs. "You better go."

"I know. Love you."

"Love you too."

I release her as her two friends approach her, and Jae's already giggling with them. She'll be safe, I tell myself. She has to be.

When I turn toward my men, it's Stone up on his black horse

waiting for me to join him while the other three are riding toward the front gate.

I accept his outstretched hand, and I'm pulled up onto the horse behind him, where I clasp my arms around his middle.

"You ready to go, sweetheart?"

"Yes, and no."

He pats my hands and nudges his horse, then we are trotting after the others. I take a quick glance back and blow Jae a kiss.

"I told Ragnar about your reading with Lyssa," he tells me. "And he got instructions on the quickest way to the Wolf Mountains from Mihai."

"Thank you." I press my cheek to his back, my throat choking up about leaving Jae behind and about our mission.

"Now hold on," Stone instructs. "We're going to try to reach the mountains today. Mihai believes it should only take us a few hours."

Please, Moon Goddess, let everything go smoothly for a change. Please.

A FEW HOURS have morphed into half a day, and we're only just approaching the mountains. Right now, we've come to a stop near a river that leads us directly to the valley between the Wolf Mountains. They're monstrous and tower over us, the sun close to vanishing behind their peaks. The horses are grazing in the pasture behind me. Beyond that, the field seems to have grown out of control with what looks like tall corn stalks. I've already told the guys we're collecting a bunch before we leave.

Crius is lying flat on his back next to me, his hands behind his head, and he's got a long grass stalk sticking out of his mouth. He glances over at me, squinting against the sunlight. "You know if it wasn't for the rogue wolves, the zombies, and the constant war over land, this might be a decent world to live in."

I take a seat next to him in the grass, staring out at Stone and Ragnar chatting by the river, at least twenty feet away. Nikos isn't too far from them, still eating the rest of the cold stew we'd brought from town. I don't blame him... he's a huge guy, and he's healing, so if he eats all our food, so be it.

"The old world must have been incredible," I reply to Crius. "Like, can you imagine each person having a car to get around? I bet they were nothing like the rust bucket I've seen my old Alpha drive."

"If it was me, I'd get a Harley-Davidson. Been reading about them since before I grew up, and it's been a dream," Crius says, and I smile, meeting his gaze. "Something about them gives me a hard-on." He chuckles to himself.

When I don't reply, he asks, "What? You got a strange look on your face."

I twist around to face him, drawing a bent leg between us. "That's probably the first time you just sounded... normal."

He eyes me, then pushes upright to a sitting position. "Normal? Getting hard over a bike? What have I been before this? A crazed lunatic?"

I half-laugh, gaining myself a raised eyebrow, but I shrug. "You're usually acting all macho, telling the guys you're better than them, but it's nice to have more of this side of you. Where I get to see what you like and how much bikes turn you on." I stick my tongue out at him.

He smirks, studying me like he's trying to read my thoughts. There's something dangerously addictive about having these wolves' attention on me.

They're an obsession. And I always want more, like I can't get enough.

"What?" I gape.

"You're cute in the things that you find fascinating about me. There aren't that many happy memories from my childhood, and I'm happy to share those with you if it keeps you smiling."

"Now you're teasing me," I say. "Of course, I want to know more about you."

He leans toward me, eyebrows furrowing. "Are you being serious right now, or are you fucking with me?"

"Why are you so shocked?"

Crius pulls back and folds his arms over his bent knees. "Because no one ever asks me about my past. They're just the ugly, broken memories."

My pulse spikes and I reach over, placing a hand on his arm. "I'm not like everyone else. I mean, how messed up is my life? My fated mate tried to kill me, my mother might have run out on me, my sister sided with witches, and on top of everything, I still have no idea how to properly control my magic. Now, that is fucked up." I leave out the part where I'm falling for four men, and my heart is slowly tearing apart, wondering how I'm supposed to deal with that.

He scoffs, turning his gaze to the river ahead of us when he speaks. "I'll do you one better. I killed my brother, and it wasn't an accident. And he was the greatest brother in the world."

My breath hitches and might have stopped briefly as I process his words. I'm searching my brain for any response, any kind of comfort, but I'm stumped. I want to desperately ask him why, but I don't think he wants to tell me until he's ready.

I just squeeze his hand slightly. "I'm sorry."

"Nothing to be sorry about," he groans, and I feel his arm tensing. "I did it, and my time is coming." He abruptly pushes to his feet and marches down to the river.

A sinking feeling in my stomach has me drowning. What did Crius mean by 'his time is coming'? What happened between him and his brother?

It's like every time I check under a rock, something dangerous bites me, and with so much weighing down on me, I'm struggling to not worry about every freaking person I've crossed paths with.

I regret saying anything to Crius.

A frigid cold swishes across my arms, and I hug myself.

Mother comes to mind again, as she has for most of the trip.

Will she bundle me in her arms or pretend she doesn't know me? It's been so long since she left us with the Storm Wolves that she might have forgotten what I look like. Am I ready to face her after Father was murdered, and I blamed her for leaving us?

My knuckles turn white from how hard I'm curling them into fists; at the dread of what to expect, terrified she'll hate me.

A horse neighs behind us, the sound almost startling, followed by the other mares. I twist around to watch all four horses bolting right into the wild cornfield, vanishing from sight.

I'm on my feet in seconds, as is Nikos. "The horses," I call out, but when I turn back to the other three men, the blood in my veins turns to ice.

They're racing my way, panic scribbled over their faces. And from across the river, a swarm of undead is plunging into the water, scrambling right in our direction.

I shudder, my heart thundering like a storm.

Fuck. Fuck. Fuck.

"Run," Nikos bellows, already yanking his shirt off. "Change into your wolf. We'll be faster." He's yelling his orders at me while my gaze is glued to the sheer number of creatures scrambling up on our side of the river. They rush awkwardly, stumbling, but they're fast.

Fear strangles me, and I can barely draw breath into my lungs. We're in an open field. No trees to try to climb, nothing but land. We are so fucked.

My skin crawls at the way they rasp, their teeth clattering, arms reaching out for us. Their inhuman sounds leave me trembling. Torn clothes, hands of skin and bones, broken limbs, missing skin.

I recoil, my stomach rolling, and unable to even think straight. There are so many.

"Narah, get fucking running," Ragnar yells. He's thundering toward me while the others are all transforming.

I spin and run, my feet hitting the ground hard. Panic slams into me. I burst into the field of corn, and only then do I notice something dark shifting through the stalks on my left. Something else is in here with us.

My thoughts fly to the horses... except the shadows rushing about are not that big.

Figures are shoving through the long stalks. The sound of teeth gnashing carries on the wind, and the vibration of magic races through my veins. My legs pump, my boots striking the ground as I shove past the corn.

There's movement from my right, and one of the undead is coming so fast and unexpected that a cry spills past my lips.

I raise my hands, magic tingling across my skin, when Ragnar crashes through the field like a truck. "Run!" He's still in human form, and when I whip around, I trip on something. I hit the ground hard on my knees, and I scramble to get back up.

Ragnar has my arm, and I'm flying forward before I know it, out of reach of the creature. The Alpha grips my arm and hauls me alongside him.

All around us, the stalks are shaking, shadows everywhere. And then I see one monster amid the corn stalks. It has an empty eye socket, sunken cheeks, and lips long ago worn away.

My skin crawls.

"You need to transform, you'll be faster." Ragnar's words race as fast as he runs with me by his side. We sprint, and the other three men have already taken their wolf forms, sticking close to us.

It takes moments for me to stop being so freaked out, and I call my wolf forward. But just as I do that, an undead with only one arm bursts toward us, right in our path. The dislocated bony jaw that half hangs from his face makes me sick.

Ragnar roughly wrenches me out of the monster's path.

My head swings left and right. Fear is surging through me at how fast things went bad.

Another comes at us quickly, and the five of us gather together. Crius charges at an undead. He slams into the thing, bringing it down fast, then flinches back, not even wanting to bite into the decayed flesh. I can't blame him.

But when more figures arrive, my worst nightmare comes to life. Shadows crowd in around us, their groans and clacking teeth like a song of death. There are so many of them... I lift my hands, needing to draw on my energy, no matter the risks.

Stone shifts back to human form instantly. He's naked and kneels, slapping his palm to the ground as he calls to his magic, having the same thought as me. Power licks along my skin, and the sensation brings my own power forward, stronger.

Two creatures burst out of the field and attack him.

I scream, lunging to help him.

But Ragnar charges at the monsters quicker, as does Stone.

Angry power flares through me in waves, biting into my skin. I'm shaking, but for a change, I don't try to stop the surge. Instead, I throw my arms out into the field, picturing my power hitting every last zombie, tearing them apart.

I funnel my thoughts into the undead, into my magic, into somehow gaining some control of my power.

Power shoots through me in a cruel, painful snap, throttling me at the core. White electricity spikes out of my hands, forking in a dozen directions from both hands. It zigzags uncontrollably through the field. It's hard to tell if it's working when all I hear are the men behind me shouting something and the monsters surrounding us groaning and clattering their teeth.

A sharp ache digs into my chest, deepening the longer I draw on magic.

That's when I notice the creatures that came for Stone now convulsing on the ground, my white lines of power skewed through their chests. Something lofty catches my attention from behind me, and I whip around.

Stone has built an enclosure around him and the men made of twisted roots pushing up from the earth, completely encasing them in a dome.

But my magic strikes his protection regardless of what I intended, turning the roots it touches to ash. Holes punch through the structure, and looking back at me through them are my men with terrified eyes.

They're scared of me! That hurts a lot.

The burned smell of my attack intensifies, and only when I look down do I notice that the black stains on my finger have spread up to my knuckles.

Panic has me screaming, and I flinch back, shaking my hands. The magic fades instantly, just like the world around me.

I fall and hit the ground, completely lost.

SEVENTEEN

NARAH

A soft touch strokes my cheek, waking me, and the memories fill me. Of undead attacking us in the field. Me falling over and passing out. My wolves being in danger.

My heart thunders loudly in my ears, the terror swallowing me. A cry spills from my throat, and I scramble to my feet, magic already crackling over my fingers.

"Whoa," Crius cries out, recoiling from me.

But a burst of my power already shoots across the room and strikes the white wall of the room I'm in, burning a hole right through the painted stone.

"Narah!" Crius' voice booms, and just as quick, the power rushing from my hand flatlines.

I stumble on the bed I'm standing on, gasping for air, trying to understand what's going on. "W-Where am I?"

My head spins because I'm no longer in the field but in a strange room.

Crius' face has blanched as he stares up at me. "Nothing's going to harm you," he says, offering me his hand. "You're safe. So, you wanna come down from there, magic girl?"

I don't move at first, still waiting for my thoughts to catch up, for the sleep to fade from my eyes.

"What's going on?" I gasp.

I accept Crius' hand, and he helps me down.

"We're at a small inn in the mountains. The undead are no longer a threat, and you are with me." He studies me, searching my face and body like I might have injuries. "Are you hurt?"

I shake my head, hating how disorienting it is to wake up here when my mind is still buzzing from the attack in the field. And from not understanding what happened.

I glance down at the blue tee I'm wearing that's wrinkled and falls halfway down my thighs. It hangs off a shoulder, and I assume belongs to one of the guys. "Did you undress me?" I reach down and feel through the shirt that at least I've still got my underwear on.

He grins at me. "Don't worry, I didn't strip you completely, even if I was tempted. But I will admit, I did squeeze your tits."

"Wow, you groped me while I was unconscious." I'm not too sure how I feel about that.

He shrugs. "I'm not passing up the opportunity when I've been dying to do it. Your body is fucking stunning. And you will be mine soon enough." His voice darkens, and I have no doubt he means every word. "Plus, I give you permission to do anything you desire to me anytime I am sleeping or passed out." He winks.

"Well, how about going forward, no one gropes anyone unless they're awake?"

He shrugs, and I can't tell if he agrees or not.

Plus, I'm not sure if I should be blushing or slapping him. Instead, I push the thoughts aside and glance around the room at the wooden bed and bedside table. At the burned hole in the wall still smoking, and the acrid smell lingering. Shit. There's not much else in here, but I see the blue sky outside through the glass door to the balcony.

"Where exactly are we, Crius? What happened after we were attacked? Where are the rest of the guys?" My confusion hurts my head, and I hate not knowing what's going on.

"Everyone is safe. You are safe." He crosses the room and opens the glass door to the small balcony. A gust of fresh, cool air rushes inside and whooshes through my hair. "How about I show you?"

His eyebrow arches as he beckons me to join him, so I step forward.

Out on the balcony, I glance down at the enormous expanse of land stretching out as far as the eye can see. And woods in every direction.

"That's where we came from, isn't it?" I point ahead.

"Yep. Now, lower your gaze, gorgeous." Crius places a hand across my back, and I grip onto the metal railing as I do so. It's a long-distance down, making my stomach queasy. There are trees all around us like we're hanging out of a balcony on the side of a cliff.

When my attention drifts to the land at the base of the mountain, the cornfield comes into view. Except, something's odd about it. I lean forward, squinting at the small black patches dotting the entire field.

"What in the world are those?"

"Your beautiful magic," Crius coos. "Those charred spots are where each undead stood the moment your power zapped them out of existence. You burned them to ashes, babe." He turns toward me, but I can't stop staring at how many black markings there are. My pulse races, my breaths coming too quick. There are at least fifty of them... maybe more.

"That's got to be a mistake," I mutter, mostly to myself. This can't be right. The sheer magnitude scares me because how can I control such things?

"Narah, your magic is fucking epic." He throws his arms into the air, making a huge circle with them to exaggerate his point. "I've never heard of a witch doing this. Do you know what this could mean if you gained a better handle on your power?"

His enthusiasm only terrifies me further.

Crius slides an arm around my waist and draws me roughly against him, face to face. "I'll be honest, when I saw what you did, it both scared me and got me fucking hard. You are a powerful witch, Narah, and intimidating. And once we brought you here, I jerked off thinking about how sexy and strong you'd been out there, eradicating those creatures."

I cut him a sharp stare, not even sure what to do with that information. Though, I won't ignore that compliment he gave me. "Did you jerk off while you were groping me?"

He barks a laugh. "Do you think I'm that much of a monster?"

I refuse to answer that right now and instead say, "It has to be some mistake. I don't have that kind of ability."

His eyes widen. "Babe, did you see the carnage you left down there? You did that."

"But what about you and the guys? I didn't know how to stop the magic from attacking you as well."

"Well, that's the risk we take by being with a lethal girl like you… but Stone's magic protected us. Each time your power burned down his shield of knotted roots, he built another. You know what was interesting, though? That even after you passed out, the power kept trickling out of you like you'd generated so much magic, it had to escape your body. I'll be honest, I've never heard of that happening before."

"Goddess, I'm a freak. I never wanted this." I try to pull away from him, but he holds me in place.

"Don't say that shit. You've been given a gift. You just need to learn to manage it, that's all."

I blink at him, his expression serious, and say, "I'm really trying, you know, but until I left the Storm Wolves pack, I hid my ability. My mother taught me almost nothing about using my magic."

"Well, then, lucky that we've reached the Wolf Mountain town. Now, we can start searching for your mother, if this is where she's hiding. But I think you're going to like this place. It's built on the side of a mountain."

I don't even know what to say. I'm still hung up on what my magic did. How is that even possible?

"Wanna go see the rest of the crew? They'll be excited to see you're awake. But I have one request before we go."

"What is it?" I'm not sure I can take any more surprises just yet.

Crius is grinning widely, and even before he asks, I suspect it's going to be something wild, based on the feral look in his gaze. It's not too different from the expression he had when he busted Nikos and me behind the tavern. "Can you promise me that when I fuck you, you're going to tickle me a bit with your magic? What you did out there was just mind-blowing. And I need to feel it." His pale hazel eyes keep me frozen in place as I try to decipher what he's just asked me.

"You want me to hurt you?" I gasp at the words.

The corner of his mouth curls up. "Just a bit, honey."

Well, shit, I was not expecting that, or for his question to send a tingle down my spine with how adamant he was that we'll sleep together. "I mean, I don't want to kill you."

His sexy grin curls his lips once more, then he pushes a stray lock of hair off my face. "We're talking about a small zap," he pants against my mouth. Then he's kissing me, so deeply, so desperately, that I soften against him, convinced our souls have just merged. His lips have me buzzing, and every stroke of his tongue sends a delicious tingle through my body. How is he doing that? I need more, more, more.

My hands reach up and tangle in his dark golden hair. He moves fast, his mouth ravenous, his hands sliding down to my ass, squeezing it, pushing me against his erection.

"I've wanted to kiss you for so long," he murmurs, then dips his mouth to my neck, inhaling my scent. He's licking me in long strokes, sending my whole body into delicious shudders.

He devours my neck as he walks me back up against a wall, all the while kneading my ass in a way that feels so good. His hands roam over my body, fingers pulling at the elastic of my underwear, and in seconds, he has them ripped off me.

Deftly, he brushes his fingers between my thighs, and my entire body heats up. I moan as he teases me, never going high enough to fully satisfy, but driving me insane with lust. His other hand is under my shirt, cupping a breast, pulling at a nipple, and there's nothing gentle about the way he does it. I'm shivering with arousal because I suspect having sex with a man like Crius will be rough and wild and fucking amazing.

I don't even understand how quickly we moved from me almost zapping him, to having him now hump me against the wall. But I notice I'm also not pushing him away.

A loud knock comes at the door, and we freeze.

"If you don't open up, I'm breaking this down," Nikos shouts as he rattles the locked door.

And I can't help but laugh at the irony of Nikos interrupting, just as Crius had outside the tavern.

"I'm going to fucking murder him," Crius whispers against my lips. "Want me to throw him off the balcony? Then I can bring you to the most intense orgasm you'll ever experience."

"He's not going to give up, you know." It's not exactly the ideal situation, considering I still haven't had a chance to talk to Ragnar about my relationship with each of the men.

"I can work with that," Crius admits, and starts kissing my neck again, but I know he'll do something crazy, so I slip out from under his arm and search for my underwear. They're lying on the bed, ripped.

"Crap."

"You don't need them for now." Crius tugs my shirt up and slaps my bare ass. "Though we've bought new clothes, seeing we lost all of ours with the horses. Including some underwear for you."

I moan in the best possible way, then go to the door to stop Nikos' constant banging.

When I open it, the frown he wears morphs into a smile. "Hey, beautiful. It's good to have you back." He grabs me by hand and wraps me in his arms, my cheek pressed to his chest. He's rock hard and radiating heat. Why does it feel so incredible to be in his arms?

"Don't pull that stunt again. It fucking scared the hell out of me when you fainted," he whispers.

"Don't be such a baby," Crius states as he strolls past us. "And Narah, I've found you a new pair of undies."

My cheeks burn up, and I turn to see him swinging my black ones in his hand.

"What the hell?" Nikos growls.

I snatch them from Crius and give him an evil stare. "Seriously?" I quickly step into them and slide them up my legs, both men watching intently, wanting to catch a quick peek. Instead, I turn away from them and flash them my ass before I tug my underwear the rest of the way up.

"So." I face them in the narrow hallway, gripping my hips. "Where the heck are the other two?"

"Sweetheart," Stone calls from behind me, and I twist my head to see him waiting for me from several feet away near another door. "We're over here."

I can't help smiling and rush over the floorboards on bare feet, realizing I should have probably found more clothes to put on, but what's done is done. And I have this feeling that if I return to my room, Nikos and Crius will end up in a fight and someone will go over the balcony.

Stone waves me in and grabs my ass, which I ignore, on the way into a room twice the size of the one I woke up in. It has a separate bedroom and a main room. Fancy.

I meet Ragnar's gaze.

He's on a couch in black pants and a matching shirt, his muscles bulging against his thin fabric. He sits with legs spread wide, an arm across the back of the sofa, and he's huge, taking up a good portion of the seat. "Are you feeling better?" he asks, not moving right away, and is it bad that my first thought is wanting to climb on top of him, straddle his lap, and pin him down, so I can trace all those muscles with my tongue?

I blame Crius, of course, for getting me hot and bothered. Instead, I go and flop down beside him on the sofa. "Confused. Crius showed me the cornfield. It's so freaky and doesn't feel like something I could do." I tuck my legs under me while the other three men hover in the hallway for some reason.

Ragnar's hand cups the side of my face, his thumb running across my lower lip. "There's something very special about you, Narah. And I don't think you're just a witch, which I've said before. What you did out there is extraordinary."

"Yeah, extraordinarily terrifying." I study my hands and how my fingers are now completely black like they've been singed. "This isn't right, is it?"

When I lift my head, he's scanning my hands too. "I've heard it said that magic needs balance. Energy used must be taken from somewhere and then replaced. Stone draws his power from the earth, an abundance, but if he takes too much, it wears him down." Ragnar collects my hand in his. "Maybe with you, it's similar."

I lean into his side, tucking myself under his arm as he wraps it around me.

"Stone told me what Lyssa said to you," he murmurs.

I perk up. "And?"

"And I had no idea of her situation." His brow furrows at his words.

"But you'll fix it, right? Find her somewhere safe to escape."

His response is immediate. "When I take over Savage Sector, yes, but not beforehand. I need Mihai's allegiance."

"Of course." I frown and collapse back against him, knowing that means playing up the pretense of him being her fiancé. It's fake, but it still ignites a viscous flame in my chest. My stomach churns at how desperately Lyssa believed Ragnar was her knight in shining armor, just like in the old human fairy tales I've read.

"Are you jealous, little fox?"

"Ha, you wish." In fact, I am burning up with jealousy, but I keep it to myself.

He laughs. "Like I said before, you are mine and I don't need anyone else. But while we're on the topic, tell me, Narah, what's going on with you and my men?"

I don't move, my heart is racing and my throat is suddenly dry. I should look up and read his expression, but I remain attached to his side. I grew up ingrained with the notion that a woman has one man. That's how soulmates worked. Except this is something else. I've already found my fated mate, and he rejected me.

Blushing, I lick my lips and say, "Sometimes I don't understand my own feelings. Maybe even less than my magic. That's crazy, right?"

He gives no response, and I reluctantly pull back. He's watching me carefully, his face stoic, and it's hard not to be distracted by this handsome man next to me.

"I told myself that I have to find my sisters, and then we go our own way. But then... things started to feel different."

"How so?" he asks evenly.

"When I gave myself to you in the woods, something shifted in me, and I knew then it might have been a mistake going there with you. Now, I can't stop thinking about being with you, and yet I want nothing to do with the war you intend to bring to the Savage Sector."

"War is inevitable to achieve peace."

I huff at his stiff responses and questions. "Stop being so diplomatic and serious. You're freaking me out," I blurt. "Just tell me. Are you pissed that I'm attracted to your men as well as you? Or because I let them fuck me, and that I keep thinking about a ridiculous notion of having four men in my life?" I rub a hand over my chest to soothe the ache settling there from the hard expression sliding on his face.

Then I rub my sweaty palms down my shirt.

"Shit, Narah, do you even know what you've done to me? I share everything with my men, but when I met you, something inside me broke." He pushes to his feet, leaving me on the sofa. "I actually thought this might be my second chance after losing my fated mate. That I might find that one special person for me." He pauses several feet away, standing tall, his arms hanging by his side, while my heart shudders and I can't breathe.

Those pale blue eyes see right through me. Those lips I've craved from the first time they touched me call to me again.

He is gorgeous and protective, and I crave him. But the deep splintering pain in my chest comes from the disappointment on his face, his mouth pressed tight.

"You've been through so much. As we all have," he continues.

I really hate where this is going, even if I had every intention of raising this topic with him. But now backpedaling seems like an amazing idea.

"I thought maybe you might feel the same way after I marked you and our wolves connected." His tone sharpens, and that stony expression slides over his face again.

Getting to my feet, I go over to him, noting the other three guys still in the hallway, and I know they're listening in on our conversation. Maybe it's for the best, as this involves them as well.

"This feels really weird," I say. "I mean, you were my first guy ever. I gave you all of me, and I know zero about men. Yet, around all four of you, something comes to life inside me." I take his hand and place it over my heart. "It's crazy that I'm even standing here, arguing this point, when all I should do is keep my focus on rescuing my sisters, not losing my head and heart. But that's what I seem to be doing. I can't help myself because there's something I need from each of you. Something that I crave, that I'd kill for to keep you all safe. So, I'm not sure what I can say to make you understand."

He sighs and doesn't respond for a long pause. "I should have known that you would rip me apart," he mutters, pulling his hand away, but his words irritate me.

I step after him. "Look, I'm sorry this hasn't gone exactly to your perfect plan. But nothing has gone to my plan either, and I'm making do. I'm sorry I'm drawn not only to you but to your men as well. Trust me, none of this is what I had in mind when I asked for your help with my sisters. But I also need you to know that I don't belong to any of you unless I choose to, and I won't be treated as an object for all four of you to fight over. I'd rather walk away than create a war in your pack."

Silence sticks to me like tar, choking the oxygen right out of my lungs. Heat sears over my face and neck. When had I gotten so brazen to stand up for myself so forcefully?

"For someone with no experience with men, you had no issues fucking mine. So I'd say you know exactly what you're doing," he growls under his breath.

Anger rises through me at his response, at the bitterness in his voice. I never asked to fall for these wolves, but that's my mistake.

"Don't worry," I snap back, my throat constricting, my eyes stinging with tears at his hurtful words. "I hear you loud and clear. I won't ever touch you again. I screwed up by giving you the impression I was only yours." My entire body is shaking. I still hadn't made up my mind about being with all the men, but at the mention of maybe losing one of them, it set my nerves on edge. A possessiveness came over me that he'd stand between me and them. And what he doesn't understand is the length I'd go to for him to stay by my side too. But I can't do this now.

I stomp toward the doorway, shuddering with anger, my eyes pricking. And I'm furious at myself. *Men are monsters. They always hurt you,* Mother used to say, and I never understood what she meant until now. First Martell rips me apart, now Ragnar.

Heavy footsteps hit the floorboards behind me. Next thing I know, Ragnar's hands are on my waist, and he's pushing me around to face him. A feral snarl rips from his throat, a primal animal sound, his wolf prowling behind his eyes. "I understand perfectly well."

I fist my hands and slam them into his chest as he walks me backward. "I hate you for speaking to me that way." A loose tear slips out and rolls down my cheek.

My back crashes into the wall, he grabs my throat, then kisses me so hard that I know it's going to bruise.

"Is this what you crave from all of us?" he asks.

"Fuck you!" But I kiss him back, regardless. Maybe I'm weak because he takes away all my inhibitions and shakes me to my core.

I tilt my head as he drags his lips down my neck. He releases his grasp and roughly tears the shirt down my shoulder. Then he bites into the soft curve of my neck, his teeth tearing skin.

I cry out and throw my head back, closing my eyes as his lips clamp around the bite hard, one hand on my breast, the other gripping my arm, keeping me in place. The feel of him dominating me sends a blanket of arousal through me.

I need him all over me, to take me savagely, but that comes with a price. He will need to share me.

Yet, he wants to inflict pain, to make me hurt for the pain he's feeling. I grab his brown hair, bringing his face up to mine, and our mouths clash in an angry, messy kiss.

"Um, Ragnar?" Nikos calls from the doorway, breaking the thick tension in the room. "There's someone here to see Narah."

I stiffen and break from Ragnar's kiss. My lips already feel puffy and sore when I speak. "Me?"

"Bring them in," Ragnar growls and steps away from me like he knows who's coming, but his eyes never leave mine. "Little fox, we'll finish this later."

I stumble on my feet; the wall catching me, while my heart bleeds as I see the true hunger and possessiveness he has over me. With how much he's struggling to share me with his men. And I don't know how I'm going to fix this.

EIGHTEEN

A woman steps into Ragnar's room.

The first thing that catches my eye is the teal-colored dress that flutters around her legs with a golden ribbon wrapped around her waist. Hair as dark as the night and cascades over her shoulders, rosy lips smiling with deep creases at the corners of her mouth. But when I look into familiar eyes, I lose all feeling in my body.

They're amber... a mirror image of mine. Just like the high cheek-bones, the narrow nose, the way she stands, unsure where to put her hands, so she fidgets with the ribbon and then her hair.

My breath catches in my chest.

I choke on my tears.

"Mamma," I whisper. It's all I can manage as my body shudders. I try to come to terms with who's standing before me, who I had assumed for so long was dead, who I thought about daily, and every small thing she'd ever said to me is imprinted on my mind like a torn map through life.

I cross the room so fast that I'm hugging her in seconds, sobbing hard.

"Narah, I've missed you so much." She embraces me, stroking my hair, and I'm suddenly a child again, desperate for her to tell me everything is going to be alright. That she's here now, and I no longer have to stumble through life like a blind fool.

Somehow she smells just as I remember her... like flour and sugar as if she's been baking something sweet. I squeeze my eyes shut and remember how safe I felt growing up, how she tucked us into bed, told us stories, made sure we never saw the ugly side of life. I miss those times. Which is ridiculous because everyone grows up eventually. Some just do so sooner... like I had to.

When I finally pull back to really look at her, she's wiping her wet eyes too. I can't help but notice how much older she is now. Thinner too, her skin is not as smooth across her neck, but the way she looks at me is the same. It's full of adoration and leaves me feeling loved. All I can think about is how many years I've lost with her, and it's close to impossible to stop the tears.

"I've been waiting for the day when I could finally see you again," she says in her sing-song voice and offers me an awkward smile like she wants me to forget that she left us all alone. "And look at you and how much you've grown. How are Jae and Kaira? I'm sure they are so much taller now." Pain etches on her face as she speaks of us, and it destroys me to hear the quiver in her voice as it's clear she's putting on a brave face.

"Jae's safe for now. We left her with friends and Kaira..." I glance down momentarily. "She's with the witches in the Enchanted Woods who've spelled her."

She sighs heavily. "Ragnar told me about Kaira being used by the witches as leverage to control you, along with the curse they've put on you," she answers softly. "You've all gotten yourself into some mess."

I fumble with the shirt, easing it over the bite mark Ragnar gave me near my neck, wishing I wore something more suitable than a wrinkled men's tee. That's when I glance around the room to notice he's left me alone with my mother, but the door remains open.

"How did you find me?" I ask.

"Your friend, Ragnar, found me. He was asking around for someone to help him with a curse, and it turns out he was looking for me specifically. How did you know I was here?" She walks to the balcony glass door and opens it, letting in a light breeze that flutters through her hair and dress.

I follow her outside. "A seer told me where you'd be."

Her mouth thins like she's not a fan of my response. "I would have found you, eventually."

"Yes, but maybe I need your help now." The way she's almost disappointed that we tracked her down irks me. "Why haven't you come for us? And why did you leave us at the mercy of the Storm Wolves? We were only kids. Even after Father was butchered, you never returned. I was so young and cried every night, terrified." I lick my dry lips and blink back tears, my mind swimming with so many more questions.

"Narah, I'm so sorry you were forced into that. I hate that you and your sisters endured such pain." She pushes loose hair out of my face. "But I didn't have a choice. I made a heart-wrenching decision to protect you three. I don't know if you can forgive me, but I hope one day you will."

"Then tell me, please, so I understand why you abandoned us." Something inside me twists, and I suck in a shaky breath. Suddenly, I imagine I'm back with the Storm Wolves with my sisters. We're kneeling by Father's grave after he was brutally killed. Our fingernails were packed with dirt, our hands filthy because no one would help us dig a hole for him, so we did it ourselves and buried our father just outside the pack grounds.

I can't stop shaking. Those memories I've kept hidden for so long now rip through me.

Mother turns toward the field, her hands white-knuckling the railing. The wind whips at dress and hair. Yet, I don't feel a thing but the numbness that carries me to a place I've avoided for years, and now I am drowning in the past, in sorrow, in heartache.

"You need to know what you are first," she begins. "We're not witches, Narah. Our bloodline comes from an extremely powerful sorceress. We possess a hereditary gift for performing magic that gives us the ability to use unimaginable power."

"Sorceress?" I've only read about them in ancient books, which were mainly fictional stories. And they were mostly just magic users, from what I could gather. "So, what's the difference between that and a witch?"

"Witches cast a spell with objects and sacrifices. They call to the elemental energies around them. But you, my dear," she turns to face me, "you can conjure magic instantly. It's why witches fear us and want us dead. We have the ability to destroy them if given the chance. But that means catching them when they're vulnerable and not shrouded in spells and charms to protect themselves. It's nothing compared to what a sorceress can do."

I lift my hands, staring at my black fingers. "Well, my attempt at magic hasn't exactly gone to plan so far."

"That is because you're drawing power from within you. In desperate times, we may need to pull magic from our souls, but that comes at a price. You're eradicating your life source by using magic this way. It's dangerous—you can never undo the damage."

I blink at her, wanting to cry. I had no idea until now what I'd been doing. "I don't know any other way. You never showed me."

Her gaze softens. "I promise I'll make it up to you. I'll train you how to take energy from those around you, and—"

"Wait... Say that again. You are draining other people to use magic?" A shiver zips up my spine at the thought.

She nods. "Energy doesn't manifest out of thin air, Narah. It must come from somewhere. A sorceress' power lets her take energy from humans, from shifters, from witches, from any living thing. Animals are too small, and you'd hurt them, so I don't recommend that. You don't take enough to kill people, but it will usually knock them out for days or even weeks, depending on how much you deplete them."

There is so much to digest that it still hasn't registered that I'm a sorceress. It doesn't really mean much to me right now.

All I can focus on is where I draw my power.

Her shoulders square, her expression firms. "So, to answer your earlier question, I was found by the local coven while I snuck out one night with your father to catch a wild turkey. The witches caught us, and when I attacked them with the power I drew from your father, it gave me enough energy to kill one of them. The rest ran... but I knew they'd return. They always do, just as they had when they killed my mother and grandmother."

She lowers her gaze, and the grief on her face has me reaching over to take her hand in mine. "It's okay."

"No, it's not. I made a horrible decision I would never wish upon anyone. Stay and protect my three girls, knowing the witches would return in large numbers. Or leave the pack and draw them away from you, well aware that the Alphas would punish your father for losing me. Omegas are too precious to let go," she says sarcastically.

I swallow the lump in my throat and squeeze her hand as a tear slides down her cheek.

"We could have all escaped together," I suggest.

She half-snorts. "And be on the run from rogue wolves and witches with three young Omegas? We wouldn't last long. The Storm Wolves pack was the safest place."

My heart pounds harder at hearing that she knowingly sacrificed Father to save us. I pull back, unable to get enough air into my lungs while bile scrapes the back of my throat. I'm going to be sick, and my head pulses. I've waited so long to know the truth about why she left us, but it hurts so much more than I ever thought.

"I need to sit down for a bit," I murmur and step back inside on wobbly legs, then crash on the couch.

I grab a small cushion and hug it to my chest, rocking on the spot as Mother joins me.

"I don't blame you if you don't forgive me for your father's death, for leaving you and your sisters. At the time, I did what I thought was best for you three. You have always been my priority."

While I remain quiet, my head buzzes with the news of what I am, what it means, and how we can save Kaira. With it comes the heartache of the past of my father's death, of Mother making the decision that set all our futures into motion. Each time I think about it, I feel sick to my stomach.

"For too long, I stayed away for your own safety, but now it's my turn to fight for you. I have always loved you three and thought about you every day."

"I have so many more questions," I say. "But maybe not right now." I rub my brow where a headache is forming. With it comes me trying to make peace with the past because I hate the excruciating sting burrowing through my heart.

"Of course. But first, let me remove the curse the witches have placed on you and your wolf protectors. How does that sound?"

I perk up, even if I'm wondering where she'll get the power to help. From us? "But will the witches know the curse has been tampered with?"

Her lips pinch to the side. "Depends on how they did the curse and if they linked it to them, so the short answer is, maybe. But I can set a protection barrier around you and the wolves for now. That will stop them from detecting the broken curse."

"That would be perfect." I pause for a bit. "It would have been wonderful to learn all this from you when I was younger, but I know why you didn't."

She smiles tenderly. "At midnight, come to the rear of the village in the woods. Ragnar knows the location. Tonight we will remove the curse, and then we can share a meal together. I will cook your favorite. Chicken stuffed with fruit and nuts."

I half-laugh, half-cry at words I've only dreamed of hearing again. "You remembered."

She crouches in front of me, her hand on my knee. "I have never forgotten. I've cried so many nights over losing my family, so to see you again is like a miracle."

I sniffle, and she gets to her feet.

"Alright, I have lots to prepare then." She clears her throat and pushes her dark hair out of her face. "I will see you and your friends soon." Her grin is bright, and my chest beams with a joy that is tearing me apart.

She leaves the room, and any hope I had of not crying is completely lost. I'm bawling in my hands, the emotions shredding me over a past I so desperately wish I could change.

Despite that, for once, it seems like the stars are aligning and everything is going my way. So why do I have a bad feeling gnawing in the pit of my stomach?

Ragnar

Narah's crying, and it fucking guts me to see her this way. A nerve twitches under my eye at the heaviness sinking deep within me, just like it had earlier when she threatened to leave. Fuck! I'm not strong enough for my heart to bear such a loss. Not again.

I'd lost my fated mate, and I was never meant to find anyone else to replace her. Then Narah broke into my life and destroyed everything. She's all I think about. All my wolf craves.

But sharing her? It shouldn't leave me vulnerable.

I need to be careful, I keep telling myself. It does no fucking good, though, because I've fallen head over heels for her. My wolf isn't helping here, either.

Images from my past rise of my fated mate...

"Ragnar, this isn't going to work," Eisa says, holding her chin up bravely. Her eyes are red like she's been crying, and even her quivering chin shows me how much she's struggling.

"What are you talking about?" I growl, but even that comes out croaky as my chest is cleaving in half. I grab her arm, but she wrenches it free and recoils from me like I'm a beast she fears.

"It's over, okay. Don't make this harder than it is. I don't love you. I tried, I really did, but..." She lowers her head, strawberry blonde hair tumbles over her face as she heaves for breath.

"But what?" I snarl. "It's Ven, isn't it? I've seen you two spending more time together, and I assumed you were friends... except I was a fucking idiot, wasn't I?"

"Ragnar, please don't..."

"Don't what?" Rage roars through me. I march up to her and rip the bag out of her hand, and toss it across the room. I grab her arm and haul her to my side.

"You want to hurt me?" she pulls against my hold. "Go ahead if it'll make you feel better. But it won't change my decision."

I blink at her but don't release her. "Have you forgotten we're fated mates, that if we part, your wolf will pant for mine for eternity? I gave you everything..."

She shakes her head, tears squeezing out from the corners of her eyes. "I-I know how to mask the pain," she stutters, ripping out of my grasp. "I'm sorry, but I can't do this. I love someone else."

I'm shaking, the room tilting around me.

I'm roaring on the inside while my fists clench, knuckles turning white. Fury fills me, controls me, drowns me in the darkest pits of my mind.

"Where the fuck is Ven?" I growl, storming out of the room.

Eisa's behind me, grabbing my shirt and pulling me backward. "Ragnar, no, please don't."

I shove her off me, and she stumbles back into the wall of the hallway. I see nothing but rage simmering so close to the surface.

I'm going to murder Ven.

Nothing hurts more than watching Eisa love another man.

I shake the past from my mind, studying Narah, hugging her knees to her chest. How does she expect me to share her? I've been patient this entire time, knowing my men flirt with her, but I had no clue she'd developed feelings for them. That pit of darkness swells inside me once more at the thought that I'm not her only one.

I remain rooted in the doorway to my room, wanting to encase this woman in my arms, to keep her all for myself, to call her mine, mine, mine. Swallowing the thickness in my throat, all I can think about is someone else fucking her, and it burns me alive.

Tensing, I clench my fists.

I don't hate my men—I never could—so now I'm left in an impossible situation. Is it all that different from what I'd heard Narah's mother tell her about choosing to sacrifice their father to protect his daughters?

Is that going to be me? Lose her, or learn to accept she will never be completely just mine?

Narah slides her feet underneath her ass on the couch, curling in on herself. She's so small, so fragile, yet unimaginable magic fills her veins.

I step into the room, and she looks up, quickly wiping her tears at my approach.

She doesn't say anything at first, but unspoken words hang in the air between us. Our earlier argument is a thorn in my side. Except, I'm not here to talk about that. Not now, at least.

"Are you okay?" I sit down beside her, elbows resting on my thighs, and glance over my shoulder at her.

She stares at the empty doorway, then at me. "Guess you heard everything?"

"I did."

"Believe it or not, some of these are happy tears." She gives me a wonky smile and wipes at her eyes. "I found my mother. Yay." A tear escapes her eye, and I catch it as it drips off the edge of her jaw.

"Family is fucking complicated," I say to her. She's absolutely beautiful, even with her red-rimmed eyes, her pink cheeks and nose. The ache of losing her is going to ruin me.

She makes a strange huffing sound. "Just when I thought my life wasn't horrible enough, and I was sure it couldn't get worse."

"Your mother made an impossible decision. While you can't change the past, you can celebrate what you do have now."

She inhales sharply and licks her dry lips, then looks at me with bravery in her amber eyes. "How do you begin to forgive someone you know got your father killed on purpose?"

Ghostly memories curl under my breastbone and squeeze, leaving me numb all over. My past has devastated me, and I haven't yet worked out how to make amends with it, so who am I to give advice? "I wish I could give you words of wisdom or something comforting, but maybe try forgetting how you feel and focus on what you deserve."

I'm not sure she believes me, with the narrow gaze aimed my way. That's her decision. We all have demons to live with, monsters who destroy us. And she has to decide if she'll run with her demons or let them consume her.

NINETEEN

Night seeps into the woodland around us, fraying at the edges of a large pond. We're in the middle of the woods behind the Wolf Mountains village, and overhead a billion stars explode across the heavens, glinting through the gaps of the canopy. I've always found nighttime beautiful, but tonight I'm jittery and keep fiddling with my hair or clothes.

The four Alphas take their place on either side of me, staring ahead at the water. Only a few words have been exchanged between us on the way to meet my mother, the tension between Ragnar and his men twisting my anxiety into knots.

I blame myself, and while the conversation between Ragnar and I had to happen, I'm not so sure this was the best timing because look at us now. We're about to remove a curse that might signal to the witches we've broken their spell. They might hurt Kaira, or they might declare war and come for us. Who the hell knows? Yet, Mother promises me she'll mask the detection somehow, but what if it doesn't work? Magic is fickle at best.

This is why I need my head screwed on without distraction.

"Okay, so what do we need to do?" Ragnar asks my mother in a gruff voice.

I twist around to where she stands behind us with one hand

holding a blade, and another a bag of what she called herbs. She's in a scarlet robe, which I assume is for theatrics, but with the knife glinting in the moonlight, I'm having flashbacks to Lyssa cutting my hand. Sure, it healed fast thanks to my wolf, but I'm not a fan of being randomly cut again.

Shadows thread around us amid the lofty trees, animals call in the night, a howl sings in the distance, and owls hoot. There are so many sounds.

"Take your clothes off," Mother says softly.

I blink at her, not completely comfortable with this, but it doesn't seem to be bothering the men, who are ripping their gear off, and in seconds are butt naked, now all facing her. They stand proud with everything on display. Mother doesn't even look at them, but she opens the bag of herbs.

"Take a pinch and place it under your tongue."

"You need help undressing?" Crius leans down to my ear to ask.

I smirk, knowing it's exactly what he'd like, but I shake my head, wanting to just get this over with. I strip down, the cold against my skin covering me in goosebumps. I can't help but wrap an arm across my chest.

Mother's in front of me, smiling, as I stick my other hand into the pouch.

"Are you sure this is going to work?"

"Trust me. I've removed hundreds of witch curses." She's so confident that I take the herbs and place them in my mouth. They are gritty under my tongue and taste like peppermint.

Mother drops the bag to the ground, pulls her sleeve up to her elbow, and without hesitation swipes the blade across her forearm.

I hiss, knowing the biting pain all too well, while she just smiles like it is nothing.

She moves in front of Crius first and dabs two fingers into her blood, then runs it across his forehead, down his nose, mouth, chin, and onto his chest.

"Enter the sacred water."

Crius twists and howls as he hurls himself into the water, head-first, the splash striking the back of my legs. I roll my eyes. She sends the rest of the men into the water in the same manner before returning to me.

She marks me; and the blood is warm against my skin. "I can't tell you how happy I am to have you back in my life. There is so much I need to teach you and show you." The corners of her eyes crinkle deeply.

The urge to mention that she should have looked for us earlier lingers. But, like Ragnar suggested, I focus on what I deserve, not the bitterness that refuses to leave my gut over Father. Mother's help will ensure we're free of a curse, and she can help us get Kaira back.

In my head, it sounds too easy because nothing ever goes well for me, so I have to believe this will work.

Her eyes glisten as she takes my hand with her blood-stained one and leans in, whispering. "Narah. Are you sure you can trust these wolves you're with?"

I stiffen, and a sliver of panic claws at my chest at her unexpected words. "What do you mean?" I glance back at the men swimming around in the water, chatting quietly, though Ragnar is keeping to himself.

"They look really familiar to me, and not in a good way," she continues softly. "My mind's just not as good as it once was, and things are not so easy to recall these days. But I'm not getting good vibes from them."

"They've protected me until now," I whisper.

"I'm just saying to be careful, Narah. Something is not right with their energies."

Her warning bends in my mind, and a shiver snakes up my spine. After everything I've been through with these wolves, with the way I am drawn to them, this is the last thing I need to hear.

"Quickly now, get into the water." She nudges at my shoulder to get moving like she hadn't just dumped a bombshell on me.

I step carefully into the cold water, the ground pebbly and sharp under my feet.

Yet my stomach hurts worse from her words, and I wish she hadn't said anything in the first place.

I slosh through the water, going deeper. When I glance up, the men have gone quiet and are watching me carefully. I move faster and dunk under the cold embrace of the pond.

I meet Ragnar's gaze instantly. He's several feet away, and looking at him now leaves me torn. Part of me wants to swim over to him, another part is drawn to the other men, while my head reminds me of our unfinished argument. And now there's the warning Mother put into my head too. After this, she has to tell me what it means before it makes me go mad.

We're all just bobbing heads in the pond at midnight, treading water, and I face Mother. "It's really cold in here. Can we get started?"

"Yep, my balls are shriveling back into my body," Crius barks.

Mother steps into the water with feet bare and pauses. She murmurs something under her breath and claps once. The sound echoes in the woods around us, and silence falls over us.

My skin ripples as I wait.

Stone is suddenly sucked underwater, then Nikos.

I frantically splash to get to them, a small cry escaping my lips.

Ragnar rushes toward me, wild fear in his eyes, when he's also claimed. Wrenched under so fast, he's gone and only bubbles float to the surface.

"Mother, what are you doing?" I cry out, my words ragged.

I turn to Crius frantically, water sloshing around me, when something suddenly grabs my ankles.

I'm yanked underneath.

Terror grips me, my heart thundering against my ribcage.

I flail my arms wildly. It's too dark in the water, too murky to even make out my hand out in front of my face.

I battle to release my legs from whatever holds them. My lungs burn for oxygen, and I'm kicking crazily to free myself. I reach down desperately, finding vines bound around my ankles. They're so thick, so tight. I claw at them, but there's no way to tear them off.

Terror floods through me. Death is all I can think about. The terrifying notion that perhaps my mother lied to me... that I walked right into her trap. That we'll all die out in this pond and no one will ever know. Kaira will die with the witches, and Jae... she'll wait for me to never return.

Liar... please don't let my mother be a liar.

Pressure builds inside me, the ache in my chest, my head is close to bursting.

I can't hold on.

Magic gushes out of my body so fast that it rattles me. But at the same time, the sting of suffocating is too much. Too fucking much.

My mouth gapes open to desperately suck in air out of instinct. Water rushes inside, and my mind blackens in seconds.

Next thing I know, I'm kneeling on the bank of the river, coughing my lungs out.

It hurts so much that I'm crying from the agony. Crius lands in a heap right next to me, as if he's been scooped out of the pond and dumped there. Like me, he's coughing and throwing up water. Ragnar, Nikos, and Stone are the same. We've all been yanked out by magic, choking on the water in our lungs.

Every inch of me is exhausted like I've been walking for a week straight. If I closed my eyes now, I'd fall asleep.

I lift my head to my mother, who's farther from us now in the woods, maybe twenty feet, closing the cloak around her. She has a small lantern by her feet, and yet something looks different about her. Maybe it's the shadows?

"What did you do to us?" My arms tremble, I'm barely able to hold myself up.

"I removed your curse, Narah. Just as you asked me. And you know there is really only one way to eradicate someone else's curse." She pushes her dark hair off her face, and that's when I see her clearly. Where there were once wrinkles on her neck, now her skin is smooth and firm looking, her lips full, the creases from her eyes gone. She's younger, just as I remember her as a child.

What the hell?

I push myself up on shaky legs, unease curling in the pit of my stomach. "What does that mean?" I repeat louder as the men rise up beside me.

"It's not a big deal, sweetie. After a day of rest, you'll be back to normal. But each one of you is now curse free, so you're welcome."

"What the fuck! Answer Narah's damn question straight!" Ragnar growls, his chest puffed out.

She makes a huffing sound, her upper lip curling up and over a perfect line of white teeth. "Fine. You had to die for the curse to be removed. Then I brought you back to life. It's not a big issue. There is a very small chance you will experience side effects, but it's unlikely they will happen."

"The fuck! Side effects?" Crius bellows. "You've made us into zombies?"

Mother chuckles loudly. "Don't be ridiculous. I brought you back to life with your soul intact."

Fear replaces my earlier hope that things will finally go well. "H-how... Oh, shit. How can you say that's not a big issue? You didn't even tell us you were going to kill us."

Bile rises into my mouth like I'm going to be sick.

She bends over and lifts the lantern. "Would you have agreed to the ritual if I had? Come into the house when you've dried and dressed, then I'll explain everything. I've left some towels on the ground here." She glances down by her feet, then starts strolling down the path back toward the village, her lantern swinging in her hand.

"Fuck that," Stone snarls, studying his body like something might be missing.

Crius is checking out his cock, as if that somehow had been affected, while Nikos is heaving for breath, his face red with fury.

"She had no right," Stone snaps. "I've heard too many horror stories of what happens to people who come back from the dead. Fuck!"

I can't even defend my mother when I'm shaking with anger, trying to make sense of what she just did to us.

"Did you see how much younger she looked?" Ragnar asks. "She fed on us."

I chew on my lower lip, shaking violently, my teeth chattering. *Goddess, what has my mother done?*

"And I hate being played!" he roars.

I stare at the dark path Mother took, shaking my head. "But she wouldn't. She's helping us." I'm hugging myself tighter when Crius hands me a towel to dry off.

"Open your eyes, Narah," Ragnar growls. "She used us. How do we know for certain the curse has even been removed?"

I swallow hard, then clench my fists, stilling the tremble. "I'm going to find out the truth." Fury has me hurrying to collect my clothes and I dress quickly, even if I'm still soaking wet, and it's almost impossible to pull on my pants this way. But my pulse is a war drum.

I run after her, not bothering to wait for the men. I have to know the truth if it kills me.

A howl slices through the night air, then again, closer this time. It comes from behind me, and I can only imagine it's one of the men... or maybe a local. I don't care. I'm sprinting past the trees and ducking under low-hanging branches.

A blood-curdling scream pierces the air from up ahead.

My stomach drops as I imagine Mother falling over or something.

I sprint madly, my heart beating in my throat as a cacophony of shouts and growls erupts farther behind me. It's loud and terrifying. What the hell's going on? Are there men fighting?

But I won't stop... I can't.

Around the next bend, I come to a sudden, gut-wrenching stop.

Two black wolves are in my path, tearing into someone who's sprawled on the ground. The savage sounds of tearing, slurping, growling fill the air.

Then I catch a glimpse of her face beneath the beasts.

My knees weaken.

"Mamma!" I scream.

Magic catapults from my hands in seconds, jutting outward, striking the animals in the sides, throwing them off my mother in an explosive flash.

I sprint to her side, my knees scraping the dirt as I land on them. She's on her back, her chest and throat completely torn out, blood gushing. And her eyes wide open.

I cry out, my heart shattering like glass. I grip her arm, and every inch of me has gone icy cold with dread. It brings back horrible memories of burying my father, and I can't do this again. Not again.

"Please wake up. I can heal you. Anything, just don't die on me."

Without warning, strong hands grab me by the hair and wrench me backward.

I scream and fall back on my ass.

I snap my head up and am staring at the face of the monster who tried to kill me. Terror smothers me.

Martell!

His face twists into hatred. "See you very soon, Narah." His fist flies at my face and strikes hard.

Darkness claims me instantly.

FATED WOLF

SAVAGE SERIES

FATED WOLF

Everything I've been taught my whole life has been a lie...

Hate is a cruel word...but finding out what my mother has done... what's she's hidden from me is unforgivable.

Add to that, the four men I've let into my life have been keeping secrets from me too.

I have a few truths of my own to reveal that might change everything between us.

With the threat of war darkening our world and my ex fated mate on our heels, I don't see how we can survive if we let the past break us apart.

Can I find a way to forgive them before it's too late and I lose everything?

ONE

"I don't give a fuck if you're in pain or crying," Martell barks, his stale breath brushing over my face. "You are not getting away from me this time."

Lowering my chin into my chest in desperation, I refuse to let my fated mate see my tears. He lost the privilege when he threw me off a cliff. He shattered my existence the moment he rejected me, separated me from my sisters, and I've been on the run ever since.

Now, look at me. I'm back with this monster, who the universe decided deserved to have my wolf crave and to share my heart with. I never understood how the wolf goddess could have paired me with such a loathsome man, how we have nothing in common, yet our wolves call to one another. Even now, mine whimpers within my body, knowing who stands in front of us.

I hate Martell, but I hate my body more for wanting this asshole. My chest sticks out to him for his touch, making me both sick and aroused.

My toes barely scrape the cement floor of the basement with my wrists tied to chains over my head. This motherfucker has me impris-oned, and I'm trembling with anger.

For the dozenth time, I reach deep inside for my magic, for the power Mother said made me a sorceress, but it's as though all my magic has been scooped out of me. I'm empty, and an empty ache flares in my gut that it's all her fault. She took my power before Martell's wolves killed her, so how can I ever find out the truth?

He grabs my chin and squeezes, his fingernails digging into my flesh until I groan. Pushing my head back, he studies me with a leering look in his eyes. His short, dark hair is parted on the side, and he's grown a dark beard since I last saw him.

His hostility toward me hasn't changed, though.

"You don't deserve me as your fated mate," he growls, then sniffs me, his nostrils flaring. "Especially a cursed like you who's let other Alphas rut her. I knew you were a fucking whore."

"Fuck off!" I never asked to be born half-wolf, half-witch and never wanted him as my fated mate. Thing is, being cursed makes me the lowest of scums in the eyes of most wolves. I'm not a pureblood wolf shifter or full witch, so I'm an outcast in both worlds.

Martell sneers, his lips curling away from his yellowing teeth. A mountain of strength towering over me, his eyes are dark as the pits of hell. He's not the most handsome man, not with his thin, dried lips, oversized head, and his twisted features when he scowls. Apparently, when it comes to fated mates, what matters to our wolves are carnal connections.

"You think you can hurt me?" I say, finding my courage. "Let me go, or you'll regret ever touching me," I snarl. Maybe it's foolish, but I'm no longer the meek girl he once knew. The ache of finding my mother again and being betrayed by her, then losing her, has changed me.

In the past, I pretended to be someone different, someone who was meek and obedient to the Storm Wolves, but that person is long gone.

Fragments of the past flood my thoughts, raising my anger further—my mother dying at the hands of Martell's wolves, me being kidnapped while my sisters remain in potential danger. Ragnar comes to mind, as do the other three men who I've grown too attached to lately. I don't even know if they are alive, but I grind my teeth, needing to believe they aren't dead. I blink the tears away, knowing that letting myself drown in pity and panic will get me killed quicker.

Martell seizes me by the throat, pulling my face closer to him while my whole body shudders.

"You think you're in any position to threaten me?"

His grip tightens, and my breaths lock in my lungs. I writhe against him as my chest burns up from the despair to breathe again. With adrenaline, I kick out my bound feet, striking him, but he doesn't react. He holds my gaze like the monster he is while darkness feathers the edges of my vision. The way he studies me is reminiscent of the rogue wolves who see women as only to be used for rutting. I live in a deadly world where we are possessions to be sold and used.

Magic... that's the only thing that could give me a slight advantage against Martell. The one thing I don't have.

"It's time to right some wrongs," he murmurs.

I jerk my head up to look at him, dreading to find out what he's talking about.

"Initially, I intended to kill you, but I might have been a bit rash. I have a better use for you, my little slut. My men are starved of females, and seeing as though you spread your legs to any cock, well then, I'll toss you to my men."

My stomach tenses, my head spins from the lack of oxygen, and his words are a dagger shredding my heart. I'll take my own life before I let him or any of his men touch me.

"How does that sound?" He arches a bushy eyebrow.

I thrash in response, needing air. It's all I care about.

He abruptly releases my neck with a growl.

Gasping for air, I greedily suck in air into my empty lungs while he snatches my hair and forces my head to nod.

"G-Go fuck yourself," I wheeze.

"This filthy mouth of yours is new, Narah. Something I'll have to fix."

This asshole is a real piece of work. His words fill me with dark thoughts while air saws in and out of my lungs. I try to blink as my heart thunders as if someone's punching me in the chest. On our first night together, I craved his attention, to have him want to know everything about me and promise me the world.

I'd been foolish, not knowing any better.

The way he looks at me now belongs to a man who's unhinged,

unstable. Still, my wolf cries for him, and I know his wolf does as well. I see it in his eyes, but he doesn't seem to care.

The bite mark Ragnar gave me to suppress my wolf's pining does nothing to keep my wolf's hunger at bay any longer.

I imagine dragging my fingernails across Martell's face and the pleasure I'd take. Once again, my wolf snarls against me. She's confused and lost to the mate bonding, but if she knew better, she'd want to rip his throat out, too.

"I will never give you anything." My words are barely a raspy hiss as I still struggle for breath.

He lifts a blade in his hand, and my muscles tighten. In my blurry vision, all I can focus on are his perfect teeth as his lips twist in warn-ing. The tip of his blade skims across my collarbone, scraping skin, tearing it. Flinching, I bite my tongue to stop from screaming. He fists my shirt and rips it open, then makes quick work of cutting it off me as he strips me. I wrench back because his blade nicks flesh as he slices material until I'm left only in my underwear and bra.

"Nothing you do will change that you're a fucking pig," I cry, my whole body trembling, teeth chattering, while loose tears fall down my cheeks. I hate to show him any weakness, but the emotions pouring out of me are fueled by rage, by how much I want to hear Martell wail in pain.

He lets out a dark laugh. "Don't kid yourself to think you have any sway over me. My wolf might long for you, but my disgust for you revolts against the bond." He raises his knife in a flash, then slashes across the top of my chest.

I scream while the sting burns. The thought has my heart thump-ing, my wolf growling against me.

"I want to speak to Lovis," I manage between the sobs with as much steel in my voice as I can muster.

"That old fuckwit is dead," Martell scoffs. "I took his place as head Alpha of Storm Wolves. He won't save you... no one will."

His response rattles me. Not that Lovis was a good man, but growing up, he had shown me sympathy and would have been a better man to negotiate with.

"I will never be yours."

"I never wanted you," he snaps.

My wolf whines at his words.

Narrowing my gaze on him, he backhands my face. Stars blind me, and I lurch backward from the strike. The sharp pain reverberating through my skull never ends but pulses across my face. I cry out louder and feel the shackles around my wrist loosen.

He's removing the chains around my wrists.

The sting across my face and my chest have me collapsing to the ground when my legs give out. It's a strange sensation to feel as if I might have a concussion after that one hit but still have my wolf whine for this asshole. Shaking my head to clear my vision only makes the room spin faster.

"I have a surprise for you," Martell states with a promise to make me suffer. He crouches and slices his knife through the ropes binding my ankles together. "Not that I should bother telling someone as pathetic as you, but this will bring me more enjoyment than you."

On his feet, he snatches my hair, fisting it. Agonizing pain sparks across my skull, and I grab his hand to ease the pain while clumsily scrambling to my feet. My stomach squeezes as I stumble after him. Injuries will heal, but I can't control my wolf's mating bond while we're close, how my wolf moans for him, or the heartache curling around my heart.

Father once told me fated mates were a gift from the moon goddess. To find our perfect match in a world flooded with despair is the beacon of light everyone seeks. How can I believe that when mine is ready to literally throw me to the wolves?

Martell drags me through a dark hallway, and I punch his arm, screaming for release, but my voice only echoes around us. In his hurried rush, I trip on the stairs we're climbing, my knees strike the sharp edges, and the pain ripples up my legs. The bastard never ceases despite my cries.

Moments ago, we were in the dark basement, but now bright light stings my eyes. Standing on the front porch of his home, close to fifty pack members, all male, crowded in the dusty yard. They're frozen in place, their attention pinned on me.

The sight strangles me, and breathing is close to impossible.

Martell shoves a palm to my back, and I lurch forward but catch myself from going down the steps. The hunger in their eyes devours every inch of my body. Martell fists my hair and moves to stand alongside me, looking at his men.

"As I promised you, I have brought back the slut who abandoned us," he roars.

Except he's lying, isn't he? He must not have told his pack he threw me off a cliff to die because he knows they'd turn against him if he did. Females are scarce in our world, so most males will never find a mate or someone to rut. As much as we're hated, we are a necessity. If they discover he attempted to kill me, they'll turn on him.

Just as the last Alpha of Storm Wolves killed my father, blaming him for my mother running from the pack.

I glare at Martell. While screaming the truth would bring me joy, I'm also not a fool to think his men would believe me over him.

"Narah has committed a crime, and for that, I reject her as my fated mate," he crows. "So, she will soon be yours to share. Too many of you are denied a female, and this is my gift to you. No man should ever be without a female to rut."

The men hoot and bellow like wild animals. I want to scream and run from the pack I once called home. The place I grew up with my sisters, where my parents kept us safe.

Martell tightens his grip, and I yank against him.

"I'll die first," I hiss.

"You are too precious to die." He grins with his teeth showing.

Trembling, rage pulsing through me, bile scratches the back of my throat at his sugary words.

A wind blows past me, like invisible hands tearing at my hair just as hard as Martell pulls, and the world shifts around me. Staring at the ravenous males has my skin crawling, and a sense of defeat flares over me.

One push from Martell, and I'll be attacked.

"Give her to us," a tall man calls out, then licks his chapped lips. "We'll take her off your hands."

I instinctively step backward.

Martell snarls, and I shudder as desperation overwhelms me. Perspiration runs down my back, and a frantic sensation floods my veins. Looking at Martell, I implore him to have mercy.

"Don't do it. I can be of help to you." My self-loathing at begging this monster leaves me sick to my stomach, but sometimes, desperation makes you weak. Even a snake recoils when in danger, waiting for just the right moment to strike.

The men grow rowdier, and I can't stop trembling.

I loathe Matrell... despise him. He's the epitome of hatred, yet in his presence, unmerciful energy floods me, reminding me we're fated mates.

Raising his chin to his men, he responds, "Prepare for a celebration tonight. She will be yours officially after a ceremony."

I shake all over and wrench against his hold. My heart thunders, and my palms are slick with sweat as panic carves through me. The sick asshole promised me to his pack, and they're salivating. I yank my head back, needing to get out of here, to find a weapon, anything...

Seconds pass, but they feel like hours before Martell swings me around by my hair and drags me back into the house. I barely sense walking or the pain he's causing me. I'm too close to crying uncontrollably, unsure how much more I can tolerate.

Ragnar. I bellow for him in my mind to come for me, to bring carnage to Martell and his pack.

The basement smells of damp and mildew when he swings open the door. He shoves me inside with a hand at my back, and I stumble forward, tripping on my own feet before I fall to my knees.

"You're right," he snarls behind me with a venomous voice. "I need something from you, and if you don't want my men to rip you apart tonight, you'll do everything she says."

Wait! She?

My stomach sinks as panic rises. Twisting my head around to face the doorway, a young woman, dressed in dark riding pants and a buttoned-up jacket, walks into the basement. There's no missing the black mark at the center of her brow, marking her as a witch, just like others I'd seen. I have no idea who she is or why she's here, only that her presence means danger.

"Hello, Narah," she sing-songs and shuts the door behind her, closing Martell out.

"What do you want?" I hiss through clenched teeth.

The dark forest is bare of enemies. The ones I have found are dead, and I'm shuddering with rage that they ambushed us. I'm an idiot for letting my guard down... so fucking stupid.

Night surrounds me, lofty trees bleeding into the blackness, and everything remains deathly still as though I've found myself in a vacuum of darkness. Shit escalated fast and caught us off-guard. The wolves emerged from the shadows, their numbers tripled ours, but we turned into monsters, slaughtering every one of them, yet it wasn't enough. They were just a decoy for what they really wanted.

My Narah.

Fear flares in my chest, and darkness slithers under my skin.

Catching a hint of her scent—the most fucking delicious scent I've ever smelled—I abruptly veer to my right. It vanishes fast. Hell! I sniff out other wolves who'd been here, all male, but the smell barely lingers on the light wind, swallowed by the pungent sting of blood left by the dead.

From the first time Narah approached me in a bar with her proposal to find her sisters, I lost myself to her. I realized later I'd fallen for her, and now I'm left with broken fragments of memories of her, of our time together, etched into my soul.

When I fucked her in the woods, marking her, making her wolf forget her fated mate, I should have known one time with her would never be enough. That no matter what I told myself, I wouldn't be content until I took her as mine. I crave to kiss her full lips, lick the curve of her neck, caress her breasts, and stoke the fire between her thighs.

Breathing hard, I do a loop around the house, following the scents, only to come back to the dead body on the worn track—Narah's mother never stood a chance against the wolves. Her throat was torn out, her life stolen. The gaping wound on her neck still bleeds, with dark rivulets of blood running down the sides of her neck and sinking into the soil. She smells of death already. How long before she turns into an undead?

They wanted her out of the way to get Narah, wanted the danger of her magic eradicated.

The longer I stare at her lifeless body, the more memories flood my thoughts of the fierce battles I'd faced—blood splattered across my face as I ripped the enemy to pieces, their screams and pleas deafening me. My body stiffens in an odd way. Those fights had never bothered me before today. I'd slay and move on. Death has always been part of my life, a moment in time when a soul blinks out of existence.

Death is life.

Words my father lived by, and his father and so on. From a young age, he taught me when you go into battle, you do so as if you're already dead, so you have nothing to fear. In the afterlife, you join those who left too early, and you go into battle with valiant ferocity.

Yet the longer I stare at the woman at my feet, the more I see Narah on the ground, twisted and broken. Is this her, somewhere else?

Something squeezes my heart.

Coldness runs down the length of my spine, and I shiver.

We hadn't been prepared.

We let ourselves be distracted.

We should have known better.

Fuck!

Footsteps close in behind me, and I lift my gaze to see Stone crossing the dark woodland, coming my way. Behind him, the ground is littered with slain wolves. Nikos and Crius are going over the bodies to see if any of the enemies still live. We lost control. I lost myself to rage when we should have kept one man alive to find where they took her.

"Anything on Narah?" I demand, hopeful he found something.

He shakes his head, his stark expression pale, while blood stains his brow, and more blood drips from the long scratch on his neck, which tells me everything. A deep, unsettling ache presses beneath my breastbone.

"She's gone," he growls. "Those motherfuckers stole her from us." His shoulders bunch up, and he's ready to lose his shit again... we all are. No one takes anything from us.

Fear for her life flares through me, smothering me. Having her taken buries me in emotions I never expected I'd feel for her. The hollow in my chest expands from how much I miss her smell, the sound of her laughter, the softness of her body against mine. Even breathing hurts. Over the course of the past few weeks, she's become entrenched in our lives. I exhale loudly with the frustration suffocating me.

Stone clenches his jawline, agitated.

"We'll find her," I say. "I'll burn down this whole cursed world to find her." My hands shift into my wolf, white fur rushing up my arms and long claws extending with desperation. I hold back the rest of the transformation, knowing I need my head screwed on without losing my shit to my wolf. The painful desperation to charge into the woods to search for her like a maniac pummels into me, but what will that achieve?

"Do another round of the woods. Anyone stands in your way, cut them down," I holler. Shaking my arms, my wolf retracts.

"Scents are everywhere," he states what I already know. "The blood all over the woods is throwing us off their scent."

"That's not good enough," I growl. "Find them."

Without another word, Stone turns and pushes back into the woods, barking the order to the other two men.

Scouring the land, I march along the worn track past the house, I assume belongs to Narah's mother. So, where the fuck is my little fox? The air is absent of her sweet scent. Only the acrid smell of magic from Narah's mother, blood, and other wolves fills my nostrils. I know Narah's not here, but I search for a clue which direction they went.

I push into a run once more, taking a wider sweep around the sloped landscape. Wolf Mountains Village sits on the side of a mountain, and I come to a halt when I catch a sight of the open landscape at the base of the mountain.

No movement beneath the moon's gaze below. No sign of the assholes escaping with Narah. Not a fucking thing in sight.

Something unwanted unfurls inside me—panic that she's lost to us.

Tilting my head back, I unleash a harrowing howl with the promise of death to those who dared cross me and take what's mine.

My last conversation with her had been an argument about her fucking my men and that she was mine. Now, the fight strangles me. Hindsight is such a bitch. I'd give her anything she desired to have her back, to keep her safe by my side.

Following the path down to the Wolf Mountains' entrance and returning empty-handed, I quicken my pace. Something in my gut tells me we aren't dealing with random wolves attacking us to steal a female for rutting. The ambush had been orchestrated, and everything points to the Storm Wolves.

Apparently, Narah's fated mate didn't get the message that she was ours. We slaughtered his men, and the bastard returned.

I launch myself madly into the woods, running with the manic beat of my heart, snarling with each heavy inhale. I don't know how long we search the woods, slashing through the forest, trying to pick up anything that might give us a direction they went, but it's all in vain. Gritting my teeth, I come up short, and my chest fills with the rise of panic. We have no leads, no direction to follow.

"Where the fuck can she be?" Nikos roars. His arms are stiff by his side, and he's shaking with the fury glaring in his eyes.

"Storm Wolves took her." Crius cracks his neck, joining us, along with Stone. "I'm certain of it."

"Then we go hunting," Stone's voice darkened, his expression twisted with rage. He knows as well as I do that Narah's in deep shit, and the longer she's missing, the higher the chance that bastard could kill her. Heat pours off Stone.

"And which direction would that be?" Nikos snaps. "We'll go in circles."

Frustration bursts over me. "We can't keep running in circles like this. We may need to split up. First, let's quickly move the witch's body into the house before she turns into an undead and goes ballistic on the locals. We'll tie her up." I may be a bastard, but I won't unleash an undead on the local village.

"She deserves to be burned. She killed us to remove that curse and distracted us," Crius grumbles under his breath.

"Calm down." I lower my voice. "Let's just get this done, then we can get going."

It takes no time to pick up the witch and carry her into the house. I can only assume this is her home, considering the river where she uncursed us backs up to the house.

"She still hasn't changed. That's strange, right?" Nikos states, his voice heavy with a thread of intrigue more than fear.

Stone and Crius have her in their arms, shuffling along the path toward her house.

"Maybe you should carry her then?" Stone gripes.

"You're doing fine," Nikos rebuts. "I just find it weird she hasn't gone all zombified yet."

"I bet she put enough spells on herself to avoid coming back as one," Crius grumbles. "What happens if a powerful witch returns from the dead, anyway? I mean, have you seen any witch zombies?"

"How can you tell if they were once witches?" Stone quizzes.

"Just hurry up," I grit out.

"Yeah," Stone adds. "I don't need her snapping awake and biting my balls off."

Crius snorts, seeing he's holding her feet.

I push ahead of them and open the front door of the wooden cottage. It's a quaint, one-story place made of dark logs. White curtains cover the windows, and it has a small chimney. There are other homes in these woods, but this one is mostly isolated. Entering a small mudroom, boots are lined up on a small wooden shelf, and coats hang off hooks on the wall.

Stone opens the door into the home, sticks his head inside, and makes a hissing sound. He looks back at us over his shoulder, his nose scrunched up.

"Something reeks. It's bad."

Pushing past the guys, the heavy decay of death hits me.

What in the world has the witch been up to? Allie, Narah's mother, appeared like any normal wolf shifter when I first met her in the town, guarded but not threatening. Now, I suspect there is a lot about Narah's mother we don't know.

Beyond the doorway is a large room with a gas oven and wood counter against the wall on the right, then a cozy hearth, where flames flicker and crackle. The fireplace lights up the room, throwing shadows across the wood walls, and something catches my attention. Someone is sitting on the sofa, their back to us.

I stiffen, then glance over my shoulder at my men and whisper, "We're not alone. Set her down and stay guard. Nikos with me." Nikos and I enter the room.

"Hello," I say loudly, irritated. I don't want to deal with this right now, but I need to ensure this is Allie's house before I leave her dead body in here. When there's no response or movement, I exchange a look with my second in command. He shrugs and raises his voice with confidence.

"Who are you? We have some bad news about the witch we believe lived here." Stone gags from the stench but holds it together.

Silence. My skin ripples—something feels off.

Not having the patience for this, I flick my hand to Nikos to round the couch on his left, and I'll take the right. We move hastily and loop around to face the sofa, and I stop at the sight in front of us. An undead man—sunken cheeks, darkness beneath his large eyes, lips so thin they might as well not exist, body so scrawny, his clothes hang off bones—lounges in the seat as if the creature is playing homemaker. White hair is combed off his face as if someone took the effort to brush it for him.

He's staring into the fire, paying no attention to us.

My skin shivers at the sight.

"What the fuck is this?" Nikos grumbles.

"It's not chained up."

"Maybe it stumbled in here," Nikos adds.

"And what? Decided to keep warm by the fire. Why isn't it attacking us?"

"I'll fix that." Nikos draws a blade from his belt, takes several steps forward, and lashes a hand to its throat, pinning him in place to avoid being bitten. The creature doesn't fight him, not even a flinch. These creatures are anything but docile. They attack anything moving, ravenous monsters who kill everything and infect those they bite.

Except this one.

Oddly enough, the man lifts his gaze to Nikos, and call me crazy, but there's life behind them.

Sympathy.

His mouth opens, making a gurgling sound.

Nikos raises his blade. "That's enough of you."

"A-Allie," he gurgles.

"Stop." I lunge and grab Niko's arm as it swings it for the man's face. "Something's not right here."

"You don't fucking say," he growls.

"No, he just said the witch's name. Have you ever heard an undead talk?"

Nikos blinks at me, then glares at the man he's holding by the throat.

"A-llieeee," the man groans, sounding almost mournful.

An idea strikes me, one as simple as observing what will happen if he sees her.

"Bring the witch in here," I order. "Place her in front of him."

Nikos still holds the man by the neck, locked to the sofa, and leans forward. "What is wrong with you?"

"A-Allieeee."

"It's broken," Nikos says. "I mean, what has the witch been doing? Spelling it to not go into a frenzy on her ass?"

"Maybe she's working out a way to combat them," Crius adds as he shuffles inside, carrying the witch with Stone.

He has a point. What other explanation is there?

Placing the witch on the gray rug in front of the couch, the firelight dances over her limp body, illuminating the blood on her cheek and neck. Her skin has already paled. Anyone else would have reanimated.

What have you been playing with, witch?

"A-llieeee," the man screeches, arms reaching for her.

"What the hell's it doing?" Stone asks.

"Grieving?" Crius suggests.

"Let him go," I say.

"You sure?" Nikos asks, his voice firm.

"It's four against one. We can take on one undead if he turns on us."

In a flash, Nikos retracts his hand from the zombie's neck and jumps away from the couch.

Crius chuckles under his breath.

The man throws himself off the couch with unexpected speed, which has me reaching for my blade. *One bite and you'll change into these pathetic creatures.*

On his knees, he leans over the witch's body, bony ridges from his spine pushing against his shirt like an arched bridge, and paws at her stomach.

I exchange worried looks with Nikos. "Is he going to eat her?"

His eyebrow arches.

"Those are odds I'd bet on," Crius blurts.

The man's pulling at her clothes as if he's digging for treasure, his mouth making slurping sounds that sicken me.

"Okay, this is enough," I demand.

"Shit, I don't need to see him feeding on a corpse. Get it off her," Stone shouts.

Nikos and I hurry forward and grab the undead by his shoulders, wrenching him backward, but his strength is extraordinary, and he resists. Partially dragging him off the woman, I see he's grasping to get hold of a vial half sticking out of her pocket. There's no blood, no eating or tearing of flesh.

"Stone," I bark. "Get your ass over here." In seconds, he's at my side. "Grab the vial from her pocket."

He moves at lightning speed, and the man lurches after Stone, bony hand reaching for him. Stone recoils, his back hitting the wall.

"Give it to him," I instruct, and he practically throws it at him.

The zombie snatches the small glass container from a shaky hand. The cylinder-shaped container is filled with what looks like blood, and the man makes a lip-smacking sound that gives me goosebumps. Not much scares me, but these things have me gagging.

We hover around him, watching as he sits back on his knees, tears the cork off, and presses the vial to his lips. He slurps the contents as they rush into his mouth. Eyes closed, he wrenches backward, tapping the base of the vial with his other hand as his tongue laps into the glass container, licking the edges.

Stone makes a retching sound, and the hair on my arms lifts.

An acidic scent of magic slithers around me, coming from the man—something dark, something inhumane, something powerful.

The vial slips from his grip and tumbles across the rug, bouncing several feet toward Stone's boots before pausing. When the zombie arches his chest forward, bones crack, and his whole body contorts.

Nikos gasps, stepping backward. "Do we kill it now?" he snarls.

"Not yet." I need to understand what's going on. We know so little about zombies, aside from how to kill them. What if Allie learned something about these abominations in our world? Maybe how to stop them or overpower them. Better yet, how to control them.

"Pull back," I say to my men as the man thrashes and growls. His face appears unnatural, and when his head jerks up, I notice he's changing. Sunken cheeks puff out, pasty blue skin lightens to a pink color, lips pillow out, and his body grows, filling his clothing.

"What the fuck am I looking at?" Crius murmurs, trepidation shaking his voice. Nothing scares Crius except his own life, so this is new.

"He's coming back to life," Nikos states matter-of-factly, though we don't really know what's going on.

In moments, the man's posture straightens, his chin lifts, and his eyes blink. I might almost believe he might be alive. Almost. He turns to each of us with golden-hazel eyes, his brow furrowing, and appears slightly perplexed. His attention lowers to Allie, then back to me. There's no grief or agony on his face. He's a statue, void of emotion. There's nothing behind his gaze, just a soulless vessel.

"Are you here to help my wife? She needs to keep feeding me," he says flatly, his tongue slipping out and licking a drop of blood from his lip. His voice is barren of any sentiment.

"Wait the fuck up!" Nikos blurts. "This man, this zombie, is Allie's husband? Does that mean…" He stares at me, bewildered. "He's Narah's father?"

"No way," Stone murmurs. "Didn't Narah say her dad was killed, and she buried him on the land of her old pack?"

"That's what I thought." Yet I'm bristling at the sight of the undead man, appearing and speaking like a normal man. He's staring at us, waiting for an answer.

A response we don't have.

My men are silent, which never happens, a testament to how fucked up the situation is.

THREE

Fear is toxic.

It makes you its slave… something I've lived with my entire life, and I hate it.

So, as much as I can help it, I won't show this witch I'm afraid. Growing up, my father taught me card games that included bluffing, and I've mastered the skill since leaving the Storm Wolves. Raising my gaze to the witch in Martell's basement, I show her nothing.

"What do you want?" I demand in a clipped voice.

The woman with deep brown hair tucked behind her ears stares at me, her pale gaze intense. Her features are delicate, small chin and nose, even her ears are tiny. There's almost an innocence about her, which can't be right. Unless she's another of the High Priestess' hostages. I wouldn't put it past Lyra to have cursed the whole coven under her command, just as she has my sister.

"It may not seem like it, but I can be of help to you, Narah," she whispers. Her gaze moves frantically around the basement, then settles on the door before she returns my way.

"I wasn't born yesterday." I snort, crossing my arms across my chest, standing in my bra and underwear. "What do you really want?"

In a flurry, she rushes past me. I flinch and regret my obvious jumpiness, but this woman, who looks to be in her early twenties or younger, doesn't notice. Why would Lyra send her? Her power must be extraordinary.

Several feet away from me, she picks up the scraps of blue fabric from the floor that was once my dress, which was torn off by Martell. I wince at the thought of how he treated me, of his promise to toss me to his men. Clenching my jaw, I want him begging for mercy for all the things he's done to me. Then I'll shove him off a cliff edge.

The faint sound of the witch's murmurs distracts me. I lick my lips, then the bite of magic races down my arms. Letting out a ragged gasp, I retreat from her, sliding toward the door. I won't end up like Kaira—a puppet to the High Priestess—not in my lifetime.

When the witch pivots to face me, I tense all over, expecting a torrent of magic to stream in my direction. Instead, she's holding my dress, no longer in shreds but whole as if it was brand new. Confused, I blink at my clothing, then at her.

"I'm Piper," she says, her jaw ticking as she makes her way toward me and pushes the dress into my hands. "Quickly, we don't have much time." Her hand extends toward the door, and a spark of electricity zips to the entryway and spreads across the frame.

"What did you just do?" I gasp as I slip into the dress. I don't know what this witch is up to, but whatever it is, I prefer not to face it half-naked.

"Sealed it from anyone overhearing us or barging in. You'll have to trust me, Narah."

"Are you crazy?" I force a laugh. "Are you even listening to yourself? Tell me what you want, or more like, what Lyra wants." A low, rhythmic thud pulses in my temples with a mounting headache.

She pinches her lips, and I notice the nervous twitch in her jaw. What is she scared of? This girl carries power, so there is no reason for her to fear the wolves.

"You're right. I am here as commanded by Lyra. You don't know me, but I know your sister, Kaira. I cared for her when she first arrived at the coven. She was a lost girl, terrified, and calling for you and Jae."

My strength wavers, hearing the terror Kaira must have faced after we ran from the Storm Wolves pack.

"Lyra found her being attacked by two rogue wolf Alphas near our woods." She pauses as though speaking about it hurts her, but she never glances away. There is strength in her eyes as if she's seen enough ugliness in this world and has learned to numb herself from the pain. "They left her in a bad way, Narah. If it wasn't for Lyra, she'd be dead now. She saved your sister and brought her to our coven."

I can't find the words to say anything because my mind is having trouble processing what I just heard. My head fills with images of my sister being attacked, abused, torn... I hiccup a breath, and tears well in my eyes.

"D-Did they rape her?" I ask softly, the words like barbed wire in my throat.

She shakes her head. "No, but they cut her and stripped her. Lyra found her just in time."

Trembling, I wish this was just a horrible nightmare. My legs soften beneath me, and I fall to the floor on my knees. I can't get the image out of my head of how scared she would have been, how I couldn't save her from that trauma.

Piper is saying something, and I realize I haven't been listening as I struggled to pull myself back together.

"I'm sorry," she says suddenly. "I spent a lot of time with her, helping her heal, and she talked about you and Jae a lot."

"Yet Lyra spelled her to hold her prisoner," I say angrily.

Piper doesn't respond right away.

"I did everything to help Kaira, but at the coven, I'm always watched. Lyra knows your sister has powerful magic in her veins, the kind that scares her."

I blink up at her. "What does she want from us?" Anger stews in my gut. Our lives are broken and stained because everyone wants something from us. We're possessions to the wolves, a means of power to the witches. Even my parents lied to us.

"She wants you all dead, stupid girl," she snaps as if I should have known. "Lyra insists you are all a different kind of witch. The reason she released you from the coven was she needed to find your mother to destroy her, too."

A shiver passes over my skin. I'm drowning in news that shouldn't surprise me, yet it buries me under its weight. Pushing to my feet, I step away from her.

"I know Martell killed your mother," she admits. "Lyra doesn't know yet."

She'll find out soon. I turn on my heels to face her.

"Why are you telling me this? To make yourself feel better when you hand us over? If you're going to do something, just do it already," I demand, fighting the panic trying to swallow me but losing.

She gives me a strange expression, and her face pales.

"You have no idea how much trouble I'm going to be in." She's playing with her hands, twisting them over one another. "My mission here is to pretend to cast a protection spell around the Storm Wolves' camp from the undead migrating north. It's their apparent reward for their allegiance to Lyra. Except, in truth, there is no spell that can actually do this. But the wolves don't need to know this."

What does she expect me to say?

"I'm not going to report you to Lyra," she finally says, breaking the silence.

"Why? What do you get out of it?"

"It's my only chance to escape the coven."

I eye her carefully, paying attention to her fearful expression.

"You're running from the coven? What about Lyra and—"

"Fuck Lyra. There are more important things in life." She settles a hand over her stomach, rubbing it softly, and I see the small bump she's carrying. "I'm–"

"You're pregnant?" I don't give her the chance to say it. The only pregnant females I've seen are those owned by Alphas, bred, and kept under close supervision. They nest in preparation for the birth, guarded by the men.

"The father is a wolf shifter," she mutters. "I met him on a mission that never should have happened. I barely knew the damn idiot, but he gave me something I cherish, and he promised to help raise our baby. If I stay with the coven, Lyra will have the child killed. Anything tainting pure witch blood is destroyed." She shakes her head, her chin quivering. "I won't give her a chance."

"I'm sorry." I step forward, but she backs away from me.

"I'm not seeking your pity. I'm offering you a chance to escape because I like your sister. Just promise me you'll get her out from under Lyra's spell before it's too late. She won't last much longer."

"Of course." I stand steadfast, even as my head sways.

"Lyra will go ballistic when she hears you escaped Martell's clutches, and when Martell finds out his pack isn't protected from the zombies, he'll turn on the witches. Let them fight it out. More time for me to get the fuck away from the war coming to Savage Sector."

Can I blame her? I'd do anything for my sisters, just as she would for her unborn child. We might be enemies, but our desperation to survive benefits us both.

"You need to leave. We've wasted enough time. You have to run faster than you've ever have before."

"Okay, how do we do this?" I'm ready to get out of here, to find my sisters, to track down Ragnar and his men—to survive.

"There will be an explosion near this building. When that happens, run out of here, understand? Don't stop, just get the hell away from the wolves."

"Understood," I murmur as panic spreads through my chest, reminding me of what's at stake if this fails.

Piper nods curtly and crosses the room in long strides toward the door.

"Thank you," I call out.

She glances at me over her shoulder. "I'm doing this for me, and you're benefiting."

"I know," I say reluctantly. "Thank you for helping Kaira."

She gives me a tight smile, then removes the spell from the door before leaving me locked in the basement.

I pace, trying to process what she said. Pushing back the fear, I have to believe this is real and not a sick joke.

I have no power.

My mother is dead.

Ragnar and his men will have no clue where I am.

I'm pretty much in the worst possible situation and holding on to the hope that Piper's offer is genuine.

Boom!

The force of the sudden explosion seizes me, throwing me off my feet, and I fall over onto my side. The room shakes, dust raining down. Curling in on myself on the floor, my hands covering my head. Shit! Piper wasn't kidding around.

Boom!

Everything shudders harder, and one of the walls in the basement crashes down, taking part of the ceiling with it.

Screaming, I scramble away from the massive plume of dust, but I suck it in and choke on it. I cover my mouth and nose as the dust stings with each breath, but light pours in through the cloud of dust, offering me hope.

This is my chance to escape before I'm buried alive.

The building creaks and groans. It won't stay up much longer. I get up and lunge forward, frantically scrambling over the fallen wall and broken stones. My eyes tear up from the dust. By some sheer miracle, I stumble outside, and pack members are darting wildly everywhere. It takes me seconds to get my bearings, to know exactly where I am in the pack compound.

I swing left and sprint away from the chaos. Running blindly through a vegetable garden, I eye the metal fence ahead—my salvation. My heart pounds louder.

Glancing over my shoulder, pack members are scrambling while others are screaming. No one notices me, so I run for my life to escape through the gap in the fence—the same one I used to leave the pack the first night.

Under my breath, I vow the next time I see Martell, I will destroy him.

FOUR

NIKOS

"This is fucked up," I growl, fisting my hands.

Ragnar scowls at the zombie. We all watched him transform from undead to... whatever the fuck he is now. Semi-dead? Is that even a thing? On top of that, he might be Narah's dad, which does my head in.

"Shit, man, this is so messed up."

I cut my gaze to Stone, who strolls over to the man sitting on the couch. He crouches in front of the undead guy, wearing his stoic expression. He's always the logical one of the four of us.

"My name is Stone. Now, what did you just drink from the vial? A spell to bring you back to life?"

I roll my eyes. "Are you blind? He's still dead. Look at him."

"Nikos has a point." Crius eyes the man who might have filled out and gained color to his skin, but there's only so much repair and patching up on a corpse to pass it as the living. Whatever magic Allie used wasn't strong enough to do a complete job. One side of his face sags, his skin has patches of flesh from his arms are missing, revealing only rotted brown flesh, and he only has one ear.

Clenching his jaw, Stone glares in my direction with a *shut-the-fuck-up* expression.

"I'm not alive," the man says matter-of-factly. "I know I don't have a beating heart, and I only retain patches of my memories. Allie told me these things. She feeds me potions to reverse the virus in my body, but I can never be a complete human again." He smiles awkwardly, all teeth and creepy, but there's a vulnerability that fills me with pity. Ignoring my mind's voice is hard when I see Narah in his face. They have similar facial bone structures.

Picturing her falling apart when she sees her father this way, my gut hardens at the thought of how much it will hurt her.

"Allie fed him the energy she stole from us," Crius gripes. "We died for him."

The man pushes up from the sofa and goes to Allie on the rug, picking her up and laying her in front of the fire. "She's always cold," he mumbles.

There is tenderness in his movement as though this man with no life has feelings. He stares down at her body for a long pause before brushing strands of hair off her face. Blood from her torn throat spills onto the rug, but the zombie doesn't bat an eye. There is no feeding frenzy.

It's a joke just thinking about it.

The zombie straightens his posture and turns to Crius.

"Thanks for your donation."

We watch incredulously as he lumbers past us and makes his way into the kitchen across the open room.

"Donation? Right!" Crius mumbles. "She *stole* the energy from us for him."

"For her husband," Stone reminds him. "Anyway, why complain? What are you going to do? Take it back?"

Crius considers it for a moment.

The zombie in the kitchen makes a racket—banging cabinet doors, throwing pots, opening drawers—searching for something.

"Has he lost his mind?" Crius states. "Oh wait, he doesn't have one." He chuckles to himself.

Ragnar strides over to the guy, and I'm on his heels, leaving Stone and Crius behind to discuss their theories of the undead man.

"I can't find it," he murmurs, tossing plates, herbs, and anything on the counter in his way.

"What are you searching for?" Ragnar asks, standing feet from the man. I'm close in case things turn sour.

"I drank it all," he mutters, his brows pinched together. "When hunger takes me, it suffocates me, and I didn't think I'd need some for Allie."

"So, she has more of the potion in the house?" Stepping forward, I'm ready to tear up the damn kitchen to find it. Then I can bring Allie back, and she can explain what the fuck's going on.

The man shrugs. "I hope."

"I'm Ragnar," my Alpha states. "And you are?"

"Gregory," he whines, his brow furrowing. For the first time, I see the monster behind his eyes, the emptiness, the hunger staring at us.

I tense, ready for a fight.

With a shake of his head, Gregory's hollow expression vanishes. The monster still lives in him, but whatever Allie placed in her potion suppresses it. I see it now.

"After a few days, I'll lose control, but I promised to help Allie find her daughters." He pats his pockets, then shoves his hand into the pocket in his pants and pulls out another, smaller vial filled with more blood.

"Is that more of it there?" I ask.

"Thank goodness I didn't break it. It's for Allie's cursed daughter to drink to remove the witches' curse. Allie would be very angry if I had broken it." He hands it to me. "You better hold onto it for me."

He breaks into another twitching fit and throws himself into frantically searching the kitchen again, breaking the pantry door off its hinges and tossing it aside. The guy has strength, which worries me. Then he pauses and looks our way while holding a long ceramic plate. Is he going to hurl it at us?

I tuck the vial in my pocket, figuring that will come in very handy to know we have a cure for Kaira.

"Gregory," Ragnar says louder to grab the man's attention. "You lived with the Storm Wolves pack. Do you know where they're located?"

The man hurls a saucepan past my head, missing me by inches. "Fuck!"

"Of course, I do," Gregory finally bites back. "Allie and I used to live there." He pauses from destroying the kitchen, lost in his own thoughts, his eyes rolling back. "Allie and I used to be so happy there."

"And your daughters?" I ask, finding it strange he hasn't yet mentioned his three girls.

He lowers his eyes to me, blinking as though he's searching for lost memories, then shakes his head. "I don't remember."

I hear the absence of emotions in his voice. Next thing I know, he moves back into the pantry, tossing containers that break and dried beans spill across the floor.

I exchange looks with Ragnar. He's batshit crazy.

"He knows where the wolves are. We force him to talk, then leave tonight for Narah," I say.

"I'll get him talking, but Gregory has me thinking. Allie performed powerful spells, meaning she might have other curses in the house we could use against the wolves, even against other witches. Take Crius and search the house, see what you can find."

I groan, wanting to get the heck out of this shithole. There's magic in the air, and I hate not knowing what I'm dealing with, but Ragnar is also a man I trust with my life. His instincts are usually spot on, so I nod and march back to the other two.

"Crius, you're with me. Stone, you have Ragnar's back."

With Crius on my heels, we step into a dark hallway that leads us past several doors. The wooden walls are worn, the floorboards creaking under our footfalls.

"We've been delegated to house searching, I'm guessing." Crius cracks his knuckles.

"Ragnar thinks we might find spells to use, and the zombie says he knows where the Storm Wolves live."

Crius halts, gawking at me. "You better not be shitting me."

I exhale loudly and turn to him. "Why would I lie about that?" I pull back my shoulders, where a sharp pain digs, where I keep my stress. Ever since we were tricked into dying, I've been tense as hell.

Crius gives me a deadpan expression. "Because you never tell us the whole truth. You hide things from us."

I frown. "Where the fuck is this coming from?"

"Don't get your panties in a twist. Since you moved in with

Ragnar's pack, you've acted like the odd asshole out and kept to yourself. Even on this mission, you're behaving like a lone wolf."

"Stop talking crap," I bark and push him into the first room, his words irritating me to no end. Inspecting the bedroom, then the other rooms, we find nothing remotely resembling objects used for spell casting.

"Stone thinks so, too," Crius keeps harping, and it's pissing me off.

"So, if you have an issue with me, just say it." I move to stand in his face, heaving for breath. My fuse is about to detonate. After everything we just went through, I'm fuming and need to smash my fist through something—even if it's Crius' face.

"Nikos, we aren't the enemy." He shrugs and smiles cruelly, enjoying taunting me. "The real assholes are your family for giving you away. We're your family now, and I'm just saying to embrace it."

My fists ball—I'm going to break his face.

"What the fuck does any of this have to do with what's going on now?"

His lips thin, and I see I've finally gotten through to him.

"Because of Narah," he barks.

"What? You're making no sense."

He marches over to the last door and opens it to a set of stairs leading to the basement. It's dark as shit in there, and when I join him, a waft of putrid smells hits me, distracting me from the anger raging in my head. My skin itches, and instinct screams to get the hell out, but I know we're going down there, no matter what.

"It smells like death," I murmur.

"You think we'll find more zombies down there?"

"Or something worse," I state.

Crius flicks on the light switch, but nothing happens, and he shrugs. "Worth a try. Give me a sec." He bolts down the dark hallway into the main room, returning moments later, carrying a fire log, one end blazing with a flame.

"Let's go," he says.

I let him do the honors of entering first... just in case we're attacked.

The lower we travel, the stronger the stench. It's in my throat now, and I barely hold back my gag reflex.

"Do you even see what's been going on around us?" Crius pauses at the base of the steps, where I join him.

"Are we talking about the house, or are you still on a deranged tangent?"

"It's Narah," he barks with emotion in his voice, I've never heard before. "We all want her, man. Ragnar lost his shit when he found out she wanted us, too. I've never seen him like that... never seen him want something separate from us."

When he doesn't continue, I'm left speechless... stunned. Crius is the joker in our pack, the guy who makes light of everything to hide his dark past, and when he's not being a prick, he's killing something. He once went ballistic and butchered a small pack of rogue wolves for pissing him off.

So, this is new. It says a lot because I've felt like an outsider my whole fucking existence. I never fit in with my family or with Ragnar's parents, but this pack is the closest thing I have to feeling at home. I'm not as friendly as Crius and Stone, but that doesn't mean I don't consider them family. Far from it. I tense, thinking what I'd do if any of these men was hurt. I'd paint the world red with blood for them... for Narah.

"So, this is what you're getting up my ass for? You're worried Ragnar will make Narah pick between him and us?"

He gives a low chuff and attempts to brush it off as he casts a glance at the dark basement behind him.

My gut hardens as the reality of his ache settles in. Evidently, this has been weighing heavily on his mind to bring it up now of all times.

"She's gotten under all our skins, hasn't she?"

"Yep. I don't want her on my mind all the time, yet I can't stop thinking of her. Something's broken in me."

I chuckle and slap him on the shoulder. "Sorry to break it to you, but you were broken way before Narah came along, friend."

He arches an eyebrow. "I guess." With a grimace, he turns away, swinging the light to chase away the darkness. "Anyway, let's get this done before I hurl from how bad it stinks down here."

"Listen, Ragnar will see reason," I say, stepping deeper into the room. He has to, or he'll have three major problems on his hands. I'm not walking away from Narah, and I doubt the others will, either.

"The guy lost his cool the other day with her," I state. "When he slammed her up against the wall, I was about to jump in and tear him off her, but when they kissed, I realized there was so much more going on between them than just his words. They have shit to sort out. Hell, we all do. He has trust issues from his past fated mate. I mean, this is the first time I've seen him show any serious interest in anyone."

Crius pauses to hear me out.

"Narah isn't just another Omega to rut," I mutter. "She's special to each of us. We have to keep our unit tight, her included. She's all of ours, not just one of ours."

He coughs, then looks over his shoulder with a shrug. "You're not such a bad bloke, you know. We ought to talk more often, buddy." He goes back to scanning the basement.

"Thanks? I guess." Apparently, that's the end of the conversation, and we're now closer friends. It's the first time Crius has opened up to me about anything, so there's that.

Though I will admit, Ragnar's outburst with Narah pissed me off, and his words still roar through my mind.

For someone with no experience with men, you had no issues fucking mine. So, I'd say you know exactly what you're doing.

That was a shitty move on his part. The hurt on Narah's face stung me because we've always shared, so for him to turn on us caught me off-guard.

Moving into the darkness, I shove the thoughts aside, following the glow from Crius' torch.

"The smell stings my nostrils." Crius gags, which has my reflexes kicking in. I drag my shirt up over my mouth and nose. Taking short, shallow breaths, we hurry because I need to get out of here. "She has bodies down here. It's making me sick."

Fast footsteps move us around the room. I kick something and look down at the arm near my foot. Ice floods my veins, and I snatch the torch from Crius, who's swinging it in the wrong damn direction. "Give me that."

Sunken eye sockets, skin pulled over bones, the dead man is sprawled across the grotty cement floor. How long have they been down here?

Crius gags like he's about to hurl out his guts as I lift the torch to illuminate the rear of the room.

"Holy sweet wolf goddess."

Decayed bodies are piled on top of each other, maybe two dozen.

"Wow, Allie is a closet serial killer," Crius barks.

"Locals." I swallow the bile rising to my throat. "Don't you think it's strange they aren't zombies? Or that she drained us, but we came back to life? What about these poor suckers?"

"She drained them and didn't waste her power to resurrect them. Think about it." Crius snorts. "Then no one could accuse her of murder. I bet this would have been us at the bottom of that lake if Narah hadn't been with us."

I grimace, knowing he's right. Catching the whisper of a footstep and sensing movement behind me, I whip around to find Stone standing behind us. His eyes are huge as he's clearly seen our discovery.

"Is that what I think it is?" he asks, staring at the piles of bodies.

"She's a psychopath." Crius marches out of there. "And you guys think I'm crazy. Fuck, even this shit is beyond me."

Stone steps closer, his face pale, eyes darkening. "We can't let Narah know about this under any circumstance. It would destroy her."

I wince internally, knowing he's right, but secrets have a way of festering.

"I'm certain she knows her mother is a bitch. The woman killed us all, including her daughter, without hesitation and gave our energy to her dead husband."

"Yeah, but this takes it to a new low. Fuck, Nikos. She butchered innocent people for a man who can never be alive."

"She's doing this for more than just her husband. There has to be more to it."

"Perhaps. Anyway, Ragnar needs to see this."

"I know." Marching back upstairs, my pulse is sledgehammering at the grisly discovery. I have no issues with death when it comes with a worthy reason. I don't know Allie well enough to assume she's a complete nutcase, but I've been proven wrong in the past.

Crius and Ragnar are already chatting, and by the grim look on

Ragnar's face, he knows. They march downstairs past us, and something cold presses in my veins, knowing this news will destroy Narah. To find out your mother was butchering people is not something to take lightly.

Stone marches to the kitchen, where Gregory is still flinging things around. The guy has no brains, so why would Allie kill people for him to come back to her? I shake my head.

Heavy footsteps move in the hallway, Ragnar and Crius returning. Ragnar's expression darkens, and when he stares at Gregory, then back at us, the same confusion crosses his face.

"There is no way Allie butchered all those people only for him to be in that state."

Across the room, Gregory wrenches the broken pantry door into his arms and slams it into the wall, growling with frustration.

"Guy's losing his shit," Crius murmurs and smiles; he's enjoying the show.

"There's more to this," Ragnar states, and we all migrate to stand in front of the fireplace. "He told us Allie was using him to break into the witch's compound. Whatever she gave him to drink has given him the ability to command zombies. The dead listen to him."

"No fucking way." My gaze shifts from the man still going apeshit on the kitchen, then back to Ragnar. "Okay, guess that explains the dead in the basement. So, what was her plan? Unleash the zombies on the coven and destroy them?"

"It's a damn good strategy," Stone murmurs. "Think about it. Gregory's been dead for years, right? So, she's been mastering her potion for a long time, and I bet she's left a trail of dead bodies everywhere she's gone."

"This gives us a new direction." Ragnar runs a hand through his hair, staring into the crackling fire. "I have the location for the Storm Wolves, so that's our first point of call. We're going to save Narah. After that, we'll drop her off with Jae, then we're off to kill us some witches."

"What about him?" I ask, pointing my chin at Gregory. "Don't tell me we're dragging him along?"

Ragnar shakes his head. "We'll lure him to meet us near the witch's woods in a couple nights with the promise of Allie's potion."

"Okay, so we have a new plan." Stone claps his hands in a gesture of readiness. "Let's do this."

"I'm heading out to find us horses," Ragnar states. "Find a way to calm him down. Also, see if you can salvage some food from the kitchen for our trip."

I want to roll my eyes when Crius throws himself on the couch, closing his eyes to crash, and Stone follows Ragnar out the front door.

"Great."

"Have fun," Crius mocks.

"Thanks, asshole. By the way, I hope you enjoy lying on a zombie couch where a dead man has been sleeping and bleeding."

He jerks to his feet in an instant.

I chuckle, moving into the kitchen, my thoughts consumed with the urgency to collect Narah. For Martell's sake, he better hope she hasn't been harmed. Otherwise, I'll tear him limb from limb.

FIVE

STONE

Murder flares in my mind.

Savage. Furious. Untameable. As do all the creative ways, I'm going to kill Martell. Hang him by his cock. Skin him alive. Feed him to the undead, one bit at a time as he watches. Even then, it won't be enough for what he's done to Narah.

He's stolen her from us.

Claimed stake over Savage Sector with the witches' influence.

I hate the notion of him being her fated mate, of touching her, even speaking with her.

Fucking bastard has declared war.

The douchebag has no idea what's coming his way.

The four of us race through the field like the horsemen of the apocalypse, and we're about to rain hell down on his pack. Hooves pounding the earth, we've been riding our horses for most of the night and half a day. We stopped here and there, but we're not moving fast enough for my liking.

Narah's in danger and needs us.

I'm not the kind of person who obsesses over things. Not like Crius, who gets hung up on things and can't shake them off.

Then again, I'd never met anyone like Narah, who burst into my life like a hurricane, destroying everything I believed. We faced hell together, and she's become everything to me. An Omega who dominates my thoughts, who's etched herself into my body. When I close my eyes, I can smell her honeyed scent, hear her laugh, and taste her on my tongue.

There's no denying what's happened to me.

She's my perfect little obsession. Something I've fought to tame, telling myself once I fucked her, I'd get it out of my system.

Shit, that backfired and shot me straight in the fucking heart and cock. After tasting her, my world spiraled out of control. Now, I'm drowning in desperation to find her, to fuck her brains out, to wrap her up in my arms so no one will ever hurt her again.

The four of us charge forward, barely saying a word while we ride. Nothing exists except saving Narah. Ragnar leads the charge as we follow worn paths for the sake of the horses, but we'll also need to rest again soon to not wear them into the ground. The woods are thick around us, which makes it easier for us to be ambushed. Out in the field, we could see anyone before they attacked. Here, we're at risk, especially with the undead now lurking in this sector.

"We'll rest up ahead," Ragnar calls out over his shoulder, pointing to something in the distance.

I'm at the rear of our charge and can't see shit in the distance.

Racing forward, it isn't long before we emerge from the woods into a small clearing drenched in sunlight. The guys are moving their horses toward a small creek when a scream rings through the air. A faint cry for help that's all-female.

My heart slams into my ribcage, and my mind is going at a million miles an hour at what I'd heard. I leap off my horse and run toward the sound. I don't know if the other guys heard it, but I'm seeing red fury.

"Stone," Crius yells out after me.

Something in me bellows to keep running, to follow my instinct. I'm on high alert, praying it's Narah but also scared I'll find her close to death—broken. The panicky side of my brain doesn't help, trying to slow me down, but I push forward, crushing shrubs as my ears prick to hear the sound again.

Sniffing the air, I pick up the scent of wolves. Male. Alphas.

Not waiting, I bulldoze back into the woods, where the scent takes me. Right now, I only have one mission.

Narah.

Sprinting forward, I duck low branches and weave around trees. When another cry comes from my left, I pivot sharply in that direction. I see shadows shifting in the distance, maybe three figures, hard to tell, but I bullet toward them, my mind going crazy.

My heart is ready to burst out of my chest.

I careen around a large tree, skidding across the foliage, and come to a dead stop. A growl hangs heavy in my throat at the image before me as my gaze roams the sight of three men crouching over someone.

"Get out here, asshole," one of the men barks at me.

I'm lost when she turns to me. Bright amber eyes find me, a whimper on her lips.

I can see Narah clearly on the ground, her back pressed to a tree, terror bursting from her teary eyes.

"Stone." Crying, she frantically reaches out for me.

Finding her has the world turning back into place for me, the universe back on its axis, and my hollow emptiness flooding with life. I hadn't realized how much I'd shriveled away from the fear that I'd lost her, that she'd been taken from me. Such an obsession is a cruel thing to experience. It turned me into a monster, and the constant agony I'd lose her thudded in my chest like thunder.

"You're safe now," I say to the woman who's my everything, my dreams, my future, *mine*.

"Did you hear me?" another guy snaps, shoving a fist into my arm, distracting me. "Piss off."

Snapping around, fury blinds me. I left logic somewhere in the mountains. All that echoes in me now is my beast. Rage burns me alive as I watch as these fucking weasels turn their attention to me. I'm going to destroy them and will fucking love it.

Heaving for breath, my wolf shoves forward, except that's too easy. No, I want to use my hands to feel every strike. I'll make them scream, to beg, to grovel. Except it's too late. I can barely feel my body now, riding high on the adrenaline to break them. Knowing that I have the power to destroy them, the ability of a god to take life sends me into a frenzy.

A howl bursts from my mouth, seeing nothing but carnage. I'm seething that these pieces of shit think they have a right to touch my Narah. Completely losing my shit, I lunge at them.

Blood. Screams. Snapped bones.

I see nothing but the three faces that I will demolish. Fists, teeth, fury. I give it all and take everything from them. Blood fills my mouth, and I spit out a piece of flesh as snarls erupt from my mouth. I will rip these Alphas apart.

I can't think, can't remember, can't stop.

Images of Narah's face, her tears give way to my madness.

I grab a sucker by the shirt and slam a fist into his face, over and over, then lift him over my head and hurl him at another guy. A punch strikes my back, and I snarl with fury. Pivoting on my heel, I kick the bastard in the gut. If I had my magic, I would have finished off these bastards already, but in truth, I don't want the easy way out. I want to crush these rogue wolf shifters with my bare hands.

I rush after him to finish this. His groans and cries are white noise, and it's irritating me. Grabbing him by the throat, I rip it out with my bare hand. Blood splatters across my face, and I sneer. Throwing myself at the other two, I dance with their death. One of them is changing into his wolf but stands no chance against me. I hurl myself at him, taking him mid-change, slamming into him until there's nothing but a broken body left.

Whipping back around to the third asshole, he's clutching the ear I ripped off him with my teeth. As they say—more like I say—there's no rest for the deplorable, so I attack, finishing him. Having him share my breathing space is not acceptable. His limp body drops to my feet.

I swing around, heaving for breath, and a sharp snarl rips from my lungs when I don't find Narah near the tree. Movement from the woods ahead reveals she's cradled in Ragnar's arms, Nikos and Crius crowding close, holding onto her, captivated by her. While I breathe easier that she's safe, a pang of jealousy strikes at not getting her in my arms first.

When they turn in my direction, there's no shock at the three assholes I just eliminated, and I shouldn't expect any. That's how our pack works.

We kill to keep each other safe, no judgment, just expect we'll do whatever it takes.

The shattering sensation that I almost lost Narah slips into the darkest recesses of my mind, and I step over the bodies to reach them.

"Thanks for leaving some action for us," Crius mutters, except with the way he's studying Narah, I'm not sure if he's more pissed I took all the kills or that she's not in his arms instead of Ragnar's.

"You were amazing and a little terrifying," she says, grinning at me. Pulling at the ripped fabric that's slipped down her shoulder, she breaks from Ragnar's arms. Her face is dirty, those huge eyes glistening with remnants of tears. "I thought I was going to die."

She rushes toward me and slams into me despite me being covered in blood. Her small arms coil around my chest as I bring mine across her back, then kiss the top of her head, wishing I could push her into my body, so no one could reach her ever again.

"I heard your cry," I explain. "There's no way I'd let you die, beautiful."

Ragnar pats me on the shoulder, then squeezes. "You heard something the three of us didn't, so amazing work." There's genuine appreciation on his face.

After the shit that went down in the mountains with him and Narah, part of me wasn't sure what to expect, but for now, things are calm between us. What comes later, we'll deal with then.

I look down at my girl. "So, guessing you escaped Martell."

"You know me." Her lips pinch to the side in a lopsided grin. "Nothing will hold me locked up for long."

"Well, I'm glad you're safe now." Nikos stands super close, his gaze meeting hers. "I really had my hopes high on finally meeting Martell."

"Get in line," Crius barks with a laugh. "He's mine, and you can have the scraps."

"I never thought I'd enjoy anyone arguing so much about who gets to kill my ex-fated mate." She wipes the blood from her cheek, and I hold her tighter. "I still can't believe you're here," she murmurs. With the way she looks up at me, then to the other guys, in her eyes, I see the terror she must have felt.

"Why didn't you use your magic against them, sweetheart?" Ragnar asks.

She twists in my arms to face the group, and I hold her against me, not ready to release her. When she raises her hands, I take several moments to understand what we're looking at.

"The black is gone from your fingers," Ragnar says, reaching over and taking her hands, studying them. "How?"

"Apparently, with my mother's cleansing of our curse, it reset things inside me. Including my magic, which I can no longer access." The ache in her voice stabs through me. With a deep inhale and a call to my power, I concentrate...but I feel nothing. Not a single thread of magic.

Fuck.

I look at Narah, who watches me. "I don't have my powers either. I can't feel them."

The edges of her mouth downturn. "I'm so sorry, Stone. I think my mother drew a lot of *our* magic into her." Instead of anger, there's only bitterness and sorrow in her words. Being mad at a dead person is never simple, says me who's internally fuming that she stripped me of my magic too.

Mother told me magic can never be taken away. It will always be inside you, even if dormant, so perhaps it's time that we need for our abilities to grow in strength once more? It better work or I'll be losing my shit because my magic comes from my mother's bloodline. A connection I never want to lose.

"I'm sorry for your loss. We've placed your mother safely in her home, so we can return to bury her," Ragnar says, then takes her hand and pulls her from my arms.

I hold back the growl in my throat at discovering my power is gone and knowing we're all shaken by how close we came to losing her.

"Let's get you cleaned up by the river, then get moving," Ragnar says. "We're not safe out here." He lifts his head, and our gazes clash. Then he smiles his gratitude, giving me a knowing nod of how much this means to him, but I did it for all of us, for me, not just him.

My wolf growls in my chest that she's mine—all mine. As Ragnar walks her out of the woods, I notice Crius and Nikos also watch her just as possessively.

"We need to talk," he tells her, something that has me following them closely, as do the other two, needing to know where everything stands between us.

Don't get me wrong. It's crystal clear in my head. She will continue to be mine, regardless of what Ragnar decides. How things between us play out all comes down to him now.

"Maybe not now," she says softly. "I want to check on Jae, and I want to stop feeling like I'm constantly scared and running for my life. I'm exhausted."

"We'll take care of you, Narah." He wraps an arm around her waist, drawing her to his side.

I keep silent for now. This time isn't about me. It's about what *she* needs.

We all make our way to the creek, where we left the horses, and I know it's going to be a long ride back.

SIX

NARAH

"Narah." Someone shakes my arm, and I pull away. It takes seconds for my thoughts to catch up to me, to wake up and remember where the hell I am. My brain is sluggish.

I slip open my eyes, and my vision blurs, the world slightly tilting around me. It's dark outside, and I glance down from the horse I'm still on top of. We've stopped, and I'm still hugging Ragnar.

A rush of memories overwhelms me, coming at me like a tornado.

Martell.

The pack turning on me.

My mother... her death.

Rogue wolves attacking me.

Stone killed them, and their blood and cries had pierced the air. I cheered for Stone, wanting those assholes to suffer. If he hadn't come for me, I would be dead. I know that it makes me a horrible person to wish for someone's death, but there are some loathsome people in this world who do not deserve this life.

Rogue wolves span through the forests in Savage Sector since there's not one dominant Alpha who has taken charge of this territory. The numerous smaller packs are vicious and will kill anyone getting too close to them... either that or they're taken out. Every other Alpha and Beta end up becoming rogue, attacking who they find, especially females to rut. Thing is, we're low in supply as men outnumber us at least ten to one.

So, having someone like Ragnar reign over this sector would benefit so many, even if it is a ginormous feat for him.

"You fell asleep," Ragnar says, patting my arm, stealing me from my thoughts.

"You slept like a log," Crius murmurs with a grin. "I've never seen anyone crash on a horse."

"I was exhausted and must have passed out." Meeting Stone's gaze as he steps toward the horse, I accept his help to dismount the charger. "I'm surprised I didn't fall off." I attempt to laugh, but it comes out raspy and strained as sleep still clings to me.

"I held on to you the whole ride." When Ragnar climbs off the dark horse, I look around and notice where we are. The open field, the gates in the distance manned by guards, and the set of stone steps that lead up to the wolf pack—where we left Jae. I perk up, excited to see my sister. I check out the men, who are still studying me, waiting for a response. "Okay, I crashed for a long time. My body needed the rest."

"I'm pretty sure we thought you were dead at one stage." Stone laughs. "Ragnar had to stop so Nikos could check your pulse."

"You did not," I rebut, shocked I slept through all that.

"Until you snored." Crius barks a laugh.

"Wow, I'm not sure now if I wanted to be saved by you lot." I stick my tongue out at them, which gains me tight smiles. I can't even express how incredible it is to be back in their company. Warmth blooms through me because I missed every one of them, more than I assumed I would.

Right now, there's something tense going between them, or maybe I'm still spaced out. The last time we were together, I had a huge argument with Ragnar, so I assume it has something to do with that.

"We need to celebrate, and my throat's dry as the desert. Let's get the horses to the stables, then I can drown in beer," Nikos says, his eyes only on me.

I struggle to believe how far we've come and how much they've grown on me. With a sexy wink my way, Crius helps Nikos round up the four animals, and they walk them into the night in the opposite direction.

Ragnar and Stone take position on either side of me as we head up to where the pack lives. Stone's fingers slide into my hand, and our fingers interlace. There's incredible warmth in his touch. I hold on to him, never wanting to let go.

"I want to see Jae first," I say, unable to keep the smile off my face. Just knowing she's safe and doing well is all I need.

"Of course," Ragnar says. There's a bit of awkwardness in the way he looks at me and the tightening of his jaw when he notices my hand joined with Stone's. He wants to say something but is holding back, though I know it'll come later. It's written on his face.

We reach the top of the stairs to the pack's homes. They spread outward in every direction, and more huts sit around the circular perimeter. There are at least fifty wooden buildings, and in the middle, a bonfire roars, crackling with embers and illuminating the darkness.

Several pack members near the flames are looking our way, and more guards are peppered around the place. Ragnar promised me the Alpha of this pack protects his females and that Jae would be safe. I have to believe that's the case, or I would never have left my sister behind. Now, I want to see her that much more.

Recognizing the guards, Stone lifts his chin toward them with a nod. Ragnar gazes over his shoulder, then back at me.

"Narah, I need to advise the Alpha of our arrival, arrange for a meal and place to sleep for us all, then we need to talk."

There's finality in his tone that he won't let this go, but there's kindness in his face. He's worried about something, which makes me uncertain.

"Okay, fine."

He turns and leaves without another word. I watch him walk away and blend into the night, hoping his anger from our last argument has been tempered.

Stone's hand in mine squeezes lightly. "You doing alright?"

I shrug. "I'm just not sure what he's thinking or really where we stand."

Stone's brow pulls together in frustration. "He's dealing with a lot of rejection from his past. He told you his fated mate rejected him, as did his own father, and after all this time, the scars haven't fully healed."

"He still has feelings for his fated mate?" The thought slips out, and I regret how jealous I sound. Especially considering I'm struggling with my own fated mate and my wolf being drawn to him.

Stone turns to face me and gives me a soft smile, his hands running up my arms.

"He struggles to trust. He once told me he could never love again, that losing a fated mate broke him and made him incapable of finding anyone else to take her place."

I can relate so much to this.

Stone leans forward. "Do you have any idea the impact you've had on each of us? How over the length of working with you on what was meant to be a straightforward mission, we've all ended up losing our heads over you? Each one of us is broken, Narah, maybe beyond repair, and for me, something about being with you helps put part of me back together."

"You aren't broken. Everyone is redeemable." I blink at him, and he just grins, not arguing my point, which tells me how much he doesn't believe me. Despite that, I find myself distracted by his smile. He has the most incredible smile that weakens my knees.

To say the past few weeks have been crazy is an understatement of how insane my life has become. Never in my wildest dreams did I expect to find myself in this situation—four men vying for my attention, and I want them to agree to share me. I yearn to hold and protect them from their past, just as they do with me. Maybe I've lost my mind, or maybe I've finally found the one thing to fill the hollowness within me.

When I look back up at Stone, he's staring at my mouth with a hunger in his eyes and doesn't hide it when I catch him.

"I missed you," he admits. "I was going ballistic, not knowing if you were safe. We all were. Ragnar would be crazy to do anything other than sweep you into his arms and accept us all in your life. Otherwise, fuck him. I'll steal you for myself."

I laugh, not used to men being so possessive of me. I'm the girl who'd lived mostly isolated from the rest of the world.

There was a time when my life was anything but exciting—routines to keep my sisters safe, to put food on the table, hoping when my time came to find a fated mate, he'd be kind and protect us. Well, that life went to hell in a handbasket.

Yes, my life is now a lot more complicated, and I'm in huge danger, but I've found something I never thought I would—a craving for real happiness with four Alphas. Except things aren't exactly smooth between us right now.

"You are ridiculously adorable when you pout." Stone's voice breaks me from my thoughts as he draws me into a walk in the opposite direction Ragnar went. "Come, let's get you to your sister. I also want to hear everything about how you outsmarted Martell and slipped away. Please tell me it involves him crying like a baby in pain."

I laugh, wishing that had been the case.

"It was more like luck. There was a witch with the Storm Wolves, and she basically helped me escape."

His gaze narrows. "What did she want in exchange?"

"She felt bad about how horribly the High Priestess had treated my sister, and well, I was in the right place to help her leave the coven. So, it benefited both of us." Relaying a short rendition of what happened, his eyes were glued to me. His attention falls to my chest, and with the way his brows pull together, I know he's not staring at my breasts.

"He did this to you, didn't he?" His thumb gently runs beneath the cuts Martell had inflicted, and I nod, the injuries still tender. His gaze darkens, and his shoulders stiffen. "I'm going to murder him for touching you. Fuck, I'm so sorry we didn't find you quick enough." He holds my hand tighter and with his other arm, drags me toward him with obviously no intention of ever letting me go.

"Main thing is I got away. He's more psychotic than I thought, but I didn't really know him. What I felt for him...still feel for him, is only animalistic instinct." I sigh. "I hate that I'm tied to such a monster and crave him when I would die before letting him touch me. Tell me that's not messed up."

"You want fucked up? Welcome to our pack. You're the perfect fit for us."

Something about those words, about me fitting in, floods me with warmth. I've only belonged with my sisters, nowhere else, so the smile that touches my lips overwhelms me with a strange happiness. Have I actually found where I truly belong?

Stone just grins at me and wraps his arm around my waist. "How about I show you how good I am at reminding you how perfect you are for us?" His hands dip down over my ass, and it amazes me how quickly my body burns up.

My wolf, on the other hand, snarls in protest. She and my body are at odds, and it's exhausting, but I won't become a slave to her instincts—not anymore.

I reach up on my tippy toes and place a kiss on Stone's lips. "Behave."

Except that action triggers him. Growling, he presses one hand into my back, the other threading through my hair. "Fuck, Narah," he curses against my mouth, looking ready to claim me. "You are going to kill me if I don't fuck you right away." The hard, thick ridge in his pants hardens as he rubs my back in small circles, his hand fisting my hair and holding me in place for the taking.

I missed this possessive side of him. Things have been getting wilder between us, especially considering the last time we fucked was in this very town. Now, he's driving me crazy with the way he holds me, tempting me to lose control.

Movement from my right has me noticing a local in the distance, walking past two homes, watching us.

"Uhm, it's probably not a good time," I whisper against the seam of his lips.

"Your sister is sleeping," he says, clearly thinking I'm referring to Jae. "All the lights are off in the home where she was staying." He glances at the hut several feet away, where night swallows the property. Not a single light is on, but what about others who are outside?

"I need you now," he purrs seductively.

Is it selfish of me to even contemplate this or more selfish to consider waking up the whole family so I can tell Jae I'm back?

My lips pinch as I glance up at Stone. This is definitely a huge progressive step for us, openly talking about having sex and being touchy-feely. Everything about him has my stomach fluttering.

Perhaps being kidnapped by Martell has changed the dynamics between us.

"Just you and me, sweetheart." He kisses me, slowly and passionately, the kind of kiss that makes me float and rips the world out from under me. It leaves me vulnerable and remembering why I'm so heavily drawn to him. Damn him, I don't think I can ever do without such a kiss again. It's sweet, firm, and all-consuming, taking me like a storm that dominates everything in its path. He holds me locked to him, our bodies flush. His tongue sweeps into my mouth, the gesture possessive.

Hearing the creak of door hinges, we turn our heads just as a man in his late forties emerges from the home where Jae's staying. I pull from Stone, who grabs my waist and draws me back to stand in front of him.

"Don't go too far, just yet," he whispers in my ear, and when I feel his huge erection cradled against my ass, I understand he's trying to conceal his bulge from the man at the front door.

"Can I help you?" the man says, blinking sleepy eyes.

"I'm Narah, Jae's sister, and I came around to see her. I know it's late. Maybe I can just take a quick peek at her?"

He studies me for a long pause, then nods. "Oh yes, sorry, I didn't recognize you at first in the dark. She's sleeping, but you can come in."

Stone's hands on my waist soften.

"If it's not too much hassle, I would love to."

"She's been talking about you non-stop." He opens his door wider to a room lit by candlelight. "Everyone's asleep, so please be quiet."

"Of course." I step forward.

"I'll be out here," Stone says, already retreating when I glance at him over my shoulder.

With a smile, I turn and hurry into the house, excited to see Jae. I hated being away from her, so I'm ecstatic she's safe. The house is cozy, with small rooms and wooden walls covered in hanging dried flowers. We move into the tight hallway to the first room, and he carefully places his lit candle on the small table just inside the room.

"She's in the cot next to the window," he whispers.

I peer into the room as the light from the candle behind me steals some of the darkness. Blinking, I stare at three small cots in a tiny room, and to the right, Jae is curled under a blanket. My heart soars, seeing her safe and sound, as are the other two girls in the room. She and Kaira are all the family I have left, and I'll do everything to give them the life they deserve.

"Narah," her voice croaks.

Making a small gushing sound, I hurry over to her, excitement pulsing through me, and kneel next to the cot. When she pushes to sit up, rubbing her eyes, I can't wait and hug her.

"I missed you, Jae," I whisper. Her body is so warm from sleep when she hugs me, practically draped over me. Then she breathes heavily. Wait... has she fallen asleep?

"Jae?"

She flinches and pulls back, moaning softly.

"That's good," she mumbles. "Did you find Mother?"

Something pinches tight in my chest as an image of our mother flashes through my mind—dead in the woods, her throat torn out by Martell's wolves. Before I left Jae here, she told me she preferred if I didn't find our mother, and I understood her worry. Sometimes, the truth was more terrifying than what our minds may conjure up.

"Let's talk about it tomorrow. It's late, and I'd hate to wake up the other girls in the room."

"Mhm." She pulls back and slides back under the blankets, her eyes already sliding shut.

"Sweet dreams, sis." I tuck her in and kiss her brow. "I'll see you in the morning."

She's breathing heavily again, so I slip out of her room.

"Thank you," I say to the man who looks half asleep. "Sorry for disturbing you. I can breathe easier now, knowing she's okay."

His gentle smile and caring eyes remind me of my father, staring at me knowingly before he gave me words of wisdom. I used to roll my eyes at him, but now I hold on to his words with dear life. They're all I have left of him.

The man clears his throat. "Just behind our house, we have a small bathhouse we share with the neighbors. There's hot running water for the showers, and my wife has some clean clothes on the shelves." He looks at me, then rubs a thumb over his own cheek.

I imitate him and find dried blood on mine, then notice how much blood is splattered on my torn dress.

"Well, thank goodness for the night, so Jae didn't see me like this." I offer him a wonky smile. "Thank you."

"Jae is a wonderful girl who just needs time to be young. She's seen too much in her time, hasn't she?" His brow furrows, and I don't take it personally.

Everything my sisters and I have been through resulted from others' actions. I nod, wishing more than anything I could take those away from her and Kaira.

"Thanks again for looking after her."

He nods and opens the front door.

Looking around as I step out into the night, Stone is nowhere to be seen. A cold wind blows past, swishing through my hair, and I decide I'll take the man's offer. I move around the house and find a smaller wooden hut and go inside, where an oil burner lights up the bathhouse. A wooden tub is on the left, an open shower on the right, and across the back are timber shelves with towels and various folded clothes. Closing the door behind me, I hurry to the shower and flip it on. It makes a clunk, and I flinch as water spurts out in small gushes. To my surprise, it's warm at my touch, and I want to cry with joy. A warm shower is precious and rare.

Stripping, I drop my dirty clothes and jump in under the spray. Hot water strikes my skin, and I moan under my breath. Grabbing the bar of soap I find on the small shelf on the wall, I scrub the blood off me, lathering every inch of my body, scrubbing all the blood off my body, then wash my hair. Finishing my speed shower, I turn off the water, not wanting to use it all up. I ring out my hair over my shoulder, realizing I didn't grab a towel from across the room. Water stings my eyes as I grope for a towel I hope is hanging on the wall just outside of the shower. No such luck. I swing around to hunt for one, and a shadow falls across me. I tense, a squeak breaking the silence when I find someone else in the room.

My eyes widen in shock.

"H-How long have you been watching me?" I whine.

The corners of Ragnar's mouth lift into a sinful grin, enjoying the impact he has on me. Normally, I'd have a witty response, but right now, it's stuck somewhere in my libido, especially since I can't control my gaze from wandering over his spectacular body.

"Long enough."

Completely naked, casually standing feet from me, his head tilts to the side, and his lips part as he takes in a sharp breath at my nudity. By the looks of his erection, he's been having a good time watching.

I gasp as I feel heat climb through me, curling around and swallowing me. My hands snap over my body, more out of instinct since this man has seen me naked before, and I'm torn between running to grab a towel and letting him stare all he wants.

Says me, who can't keep my eyes off him—a chest carved out of stone, abs all angles and curves.

His bicep flexes as he runs a hand through his hair, and butterflies burst through my stomach the longer I stare at this beautiful man.

He's perfection—tall, broad, and lust gazing behind his eyes.

My attention lowers down his body once more because I have no self-control. His cock is hard, sitting upright, and the long vein that runs its length bulges. Of course, he's huge, yet seeing it again reminds me of the anaconda I'm dealing with.

His hand dips lower, following my stare, and wraps around his thick cock. He palms it and hisses, making his intentions for me clear.

I might have just moaned and squeezed my legs together at the sight.

"Wh-What are you doing here? How did you know I was here?" I say all in one breath, surprised I can even form words.

All my rational thoughts vanish, losing myself too fast, especially under his gaze. I love the way he stares at my body, even if it scares me that I'm not good enough compared to his fated mate. I can't get Stone's words out of my head about Ragnar's struggles to forget her. In my mind, she's extravagant and a sex goddess. I tell myself his connection to her comes from their wolves but try telling that to the green-eyed monster inside me that wants to claw her face off.

"I followed you in here to talk, but then..." He runs the back of his hand across his mouth in a gesture that implies he's drooling. "I forgot what we were going to talk about."

My body tightens, hyper-aware of every move he makes as he strolls toward me, his cock bouncing with each step, hypnotizing me. I never thought I'd be drawn to such a huge cock.

"Make yourself busy and grab me a towel," I state, putting more sass in my voice, figuring if he comes any closer, I'll lose all control.

He keeps his eyes on me and stops right in front of me. *Oh my, did his cock just touch my stomach?* I might have gasped.

"You won't need one," he rasps, his voice gravelly and so sexy. Taking my hands, he lowers them from across my body. "Don't hide your body from me. It's so beautiful, and I want to see every inch of you."

My body thumps with arousal, his heat enveloping me, and that devastatingly sensual smirk completely undoes me. Even my wolf, who's been betraying me with Martell, silences as though she knows a *real* Alpha stands in our presence.

Ragnar lifts my hand and presses the tip of each finger to the soft cushion of his lips, then kisses them. He studies my body, my face, all of me. My cheeks are warm, and my pulse races in my ears. With him,

I feel incredible and invincible, as if I am allowed to be adored, as though I mean the world to him.

"What did you want to talk about?" I ask meekly while the pulse between my legs throbs. I yearn to lean in and feel his lips against mine, to feel every inch of him on me.

"All I can think about is how I'm going to fuck you up against the walls, how your screams will tell everyone you're mine." His hand slides down to my shoulder. "Do you know how hard it was watching you run your hands across your gorgeous little body in the shower and not join you? How much I want to sink my cock into you."

I'm stunned at his admission, though I really shouldn't be. Since I escaped from the Storm Wolves, I've noticed the struggle in the men's eyes when they stare at me, between tension and unbearable lust.

"First," Ragnar says, drawing my attention back to him. "I want you on your knees, sucking me off," he commands, pressing down on my shoulder. "I need you to memorize my taste, to remember how my cock feels in your mouth. Tonight, I'll imprint my mark on you again, and it's going to fucking stick." Ragnar's scorching hot words are a whisper across my lips.

With him, I never really know what to expect. Tonight, he's in a darker, teasing mood, provoking the tingle inside me that started the moment I spotted him watching me, the itch to have him claim me... all of me. Even if my wolf pined within me for Martell, twisting around my heart like barbed wire, my body demands Ragnar.

With a mind of their own, my knees soften as I lower myself in front of him, his cock in my face. He's big, thick, and long. Everything about him is impressive. I might salivate, even if I'm new at this. That hypnotic scent, a light musk, envelopes me, and his sex floods me. It's captivating.

"Does this mean you're now willing to share me with your men?" I say, confidently lifting my gaze to him.

Through hooded eyes, he looks at me, then scratches his chin.

"This has nothing to do with them," he growls, catching me off guard.

Okay, that's still playing on his mind.

"I can still smell Martell all over you, and it's driving me fucking crazy. I'll remove every inch of him from you and remind your wolf who you belong to. Tonight, I want you to submit to me." His hand slides to the back of my head and pushes me toward his cock. An incredible cock at that.

Focus, Narah. I'm struggling to think straight when I'm face-deep in his groin.

Ragnar is rougher tonight, darker, and maybe I shouldn't give in to him so easily, but looking up into his eyes, I know we both need this to patch things between us. What he offers me is pure bliss and an escape.

Curling my fingers around his shaft, I tighten my grip slightly, and he jerks in my hand, his skin on fire and full of rock-hard heat.

Suddenly nervous, I admit, "This is my first time doing this."

"Then we'll go slow." There's ruthlessness in his voice, a dominance to claim me, to make me his, and goddess forgive me, but I crave him to where my brain fogs.

Gripping his cock, I bury him in my mouth, and an excited buzz travels the length of my spine. Surprisingly, he's warm in a comforting way. He tastes slightly salty and sweet, hard to pinpoint any flavor, except to say it's extremely pleasant.

I suck him, listening to his sharp inhale, which has me tingling all over. Bopping my head up and down, I sense his body stiffening and know I'm doing it right. His hand tangles in my hair as he guides me slowly forward, pushing himself deeper into my mouth. He hits the back of my throat, which closes as my gag reflex kicks in. Pulling him out of my mouth with a pop, my eyes water. I blink up at him, gasping for air. He runs his thumb across my cheek, soothing me.

"Just take a long breath and relax, little fox. Work your throat into accepting me. Now, open up for me, and let's try again."

With his hand on my jaw, I draw him back into my mouth and close my lips around him. Working my throat around him, I gradually take more... and remember to breathe. I flatten my tongue beneath his shaft while holding on to his strong thighs.

He moans, his hand on the back of my head, and works himself deeper into me. He feels perfect in my mouth, soft but firm. I suck on him, stroking him with my tongue, and work my throat to take more of him.

"I love seeing you this way... on your knees with my cock fully in your mouth. It's such a beautiful image."

The urge to release him and make him beg me for more is tempting. His hips jerk forward, but he keeps his hand on my head. He needs to hold on to control, to dominate me, even when it comes with extreme pleasure.

As much as I'm sitting on the fence with him forcing me to remain under his command, fiery arousal pools between my thighs with my growing desire. It would be easy to walk away from him if he wasn't so sinfully gorgeous and didn't drive me crazy.

I glide one of my hands underneath his balls, pushing up and cupping them. His growls are all the consent I need to keep going as I suck and massage him.

His hand tightens on the back of my head, fisting my hair, his breathing racing. I never pause because there's something in me that seeks his approval, to know I pushed him over the edge with my actions.

"Enough," he hisses and pulls out of my mouth. Gazing up at him, I lick my lips, and he takes my arm, bringing me to my feet. His face is flushed with desire.

"Let me finish," I say, reaching for him.

He takes my hands in his. "I'm nowhere near finished with you, but tonight, I'm not going to come in your mouth. Tonight, I need you to come all over my cock." He smirks, and there's wickedness behind his eyes.

His puts fingers under my chin, tilting my head back, and he leans in. My heart beats quicker. Drawn to him, I move forward, lifting myself on tippy toes to reach him, and our mouths clash. I inhale a desperate breath, and he kisses me roughly. My lips will be bruised in the morning, but still, I press myself closer, holding on to his arms, longing for his touch, for him to claim me. I can't stop my body's reaction.

Taking my elbow, he draws me out of the shower and moves us to the middle of the room, where the floor isn't slippery with water. Feet from the door, he crouches in front of me, and the thought of someone walking in on us plays on my mind, and that perhaps I should find something to lock us inside.

His mouth suddenly wraps around my breast, and I forget everything. He suckles on my nipple, pulling at it until it hurts in a way that has me moaning for more. There's no pause as he follows the same assault on my other breast, sharp teeth on the nipple that I know he will leave marks.

My hands brush through his hair and fist it as my pulse thumps louder in my ears. The wanton desire within me builds, and the sensation is intoxicating. He has me losing control as the heat pools between my legs. Taking a leaf out of Ragnar's book, I push him down my body, needing him where I'm aching.

He laughs darkly as he lowers to his knees. Scooping an arm behind my knee, he puts my leg over his shoulder, opening me up.

"Fuck! I love the way you smell. I'm going to ruin your pussy experience for anyone else, and you'll never forget me. Afterward, I'm going to fuck you up against the wall so hard, you'll still feel me a week later." He pushes his face between my legs, locating my throbbing clit.

I moan, holding onto his hair as his tongue laps across the seam of my pussy, pushing between the folds. I'm soaking wet, which he devours. Squirming against him, he ravages me, and I'm shuddering from his words, from how roughly he eats me. Ragnar's unrelenting, forcing me onto his slippery road, where I don't think I'll ever forget the things he does to me.

At that moment, my wolf whines, but I'm tired of her protests, exhausted of that pining in my body for Martell. I want it gone, and Ragnar offers me a way out.

Sucking my inner lips, he pushes two fingers inside me, thrusting so hard, I'm on the verge of losing myself. I grind myself against his face, holding on.

"Oh God, don't stop." My body shakes ferociously at how hard he fingers me.

He glances up at me, his mouth glistening.

"*I* am your god, Narah," he growls. "You'll worship me. You'll beg me for more and spread those pretty legs for me whenever I demand it."

"Ahhh," I gasp as he fingers me hard, never pausing. His grin is pure evil, knowing I am at his mercy. When he presses the flat of his tongue to my pussy, flicking my clit, my body tightens, and an avalanche of arousal crashes through me. I thrash as I come completely apart over his mouth. He buries his face against my pussy, sucking, taking it all.

I'm shaking, my legs weak, a scream streaming from my throat. He's the only thing holding me up. The sensation is mesmerizing, leaving me a complete mess, heaving for breath and my pussy pulsing. Losing track of time, I have no idea how long I've been quivering, coming down from my high, but it feels like hours, the most blissful hours of my life. Of course, it's more like minutes, but I'm smiling, glowing.

Ragnar lowers my leg from his shoulder, and I'm unstable on my feet, but his grip on my hips steadies me. His fingers press into my skin, heightening the sensation that still courses through me. He rises before me, broad and so intimidating.

"Have you ever tasted yourself, Narah?"

I shake my head. "I'm not exactly experienced with these things."

"Oh, you are doing incredibly well."

His chin and mouth shine with my cum, and there is a slight moment when I'm proud to see this powerful Alpha with my cum on his face.

"I want to taste myself on you," I purr in a husky voice.

He kisses me without ceremony, our lips dancing in their own carnal show. I taste myself on his mouth, on his tongue. It's light, almost sweet, and a bit spicy, the scent making me heady. He pushes against me, rubbing my cum all over my mouth, cheeks, and jawline.

"It's kind of sweet."

"You taste like honey, Narah, sweet nectar, and I want it all over me," he rasps, then licks his lips. Powerful hands fall to my hips, down to the back of my thighs, and I'm off my feet in seconds. Wrapping my legs around this strong man's waist, I loop my arms around his neck to hold on.

With one hand on my backside, he grips me as though I weigh nothing. His other hand slides between us and grabs his cock, sliding it across my slick and finally pushing his tip into me. I arch against him, pressing my breasts against his bare chest, feeling already how much he'll stretch me.

"Are you ready for me?" he asks as if that's even a question when I'm drenched and moaning for him.

"Good, I'll take that as a yes. I'm going to fill you with my seed and replace every molecule of Martell's scent on you. After this, there won't be anywhere you can go without me finding you."

I blink at him, breathing fast. He's a furious monster, jealous as hell that Martell was next to me. I tense, better understanding the truth of how obsessive this Alpha is. I should be annoyed and shove him away, yet I stare into his gaze, ready to give myself to him over and over.

"I'll take it all, Ragnar, just fuck me." I push the other thoughts out of my head, knowing they'll come back to haunt me later. Right now, I just want Ragnar to steal me away from this world and make me forget about Martell.

A heavy growl rumbles from his chest as he presses into me without pause, without taking time to fit inside me. I cry out, my body tensing as he drives into me to his hilt, and I'm gasping for air. Fuck me, but I feel every inch of him crammed into me, pushing against my inner walls.

The room sways as he takes me hard and fast. My fingers dig into his powerful muscles across his neck, rocking up and down on his erection as he jackhammers into me.

His eyes cast down momentarily to my bouncing breasts, then back up at me with his delicious grin. The muscles in his neck clench, holding my stare while staking his claim wildly.

In my heart, I am utterly lost to this man. I don't know when I fell so hard and became faithful to him, but I know I won't bend about picking him over the other men. It breaks me to think about it, and I need to make him see sense.

Deep down inside, I know if he doesn't agree, it will destroy me.

"I'm crazy for you, Narah," he pants.

I know he means every word, and it touches me somewhere in my chest. When I kiss him, it's addictive, and I'm hungry for him—just how he makes me.

Our tongues tangle, and I cling to him. When I come up for air, a moan spills from my lips as my body grows tight with the escalating climax peaking within me.

He pauses for a few moments as I catch my breath, then walks us toward the wall, still thrusting into me. I don't know how he's managing it, but his stamina and strength are insane. Even if he's not exactly walking straight, it's super impressive.

"I'm close," he growls, his shoulder crashing against the wall to hold himself, his whole body shaking.

"Whoa," I gasp from the impact, but he's too far gone. He roars, his explosion ripping through him. Turning his back to the door, he holds me and thrusts his hips.

Fire bursts within me as I feel him pulsing inside me. Screaming and shuddering against him, I feel him come inside me, filling me with his seed. His lips are on my neck, pinching my flesh, and his breaths grow faster.

I'm panting, my pussy soaked from his fucking. His hands slam against the door behind me, and I'm holding onto him to not fall off. He's desperate and wild, and the animalistic sounds he makes are my new addiction.

Then he bites down on my neck.

"Oh, shit," I call out, pinned in place by him. The beautiful agony of his teeth breaking skin, my body tears apart as my orgasm rips me to shreds, and another wave of carnal desires crashes over me, rocking me at my core.

I feel him growing inside me, thickening. He's knotting, ensuring he fills me to the brim, keeping me captive under his spell.

"You are mine now," he snarls, his voice and gaze darkened from how far we've fallen. Blood smears his lips... my blood.

Wood breaking sounds around us, loud and unexpected. Next thing, the door behind Ragnar gives way, ripped right off its hinges, and smacks to the ground. We fall with it, and I scream out of pure shock. Ragnar crashes, hitting the flat door with his back, with me locked to him. I bounce against his body, but he holds me tight, holding me safe.

It only takes moments for reality to check in and for us to realize we're lying outside the bathhouse on a broken door, and we're not alone. Two guards stand nearby, just as surprised as we are, their orb-like huge eyes taking in the sight.

Heat blushes across my cheeks, and I tuck myself against Ragnar, who pushes himself to a sitting position, his arms coiled around my back. He twists his head to the stunned guards.

"What the fuck are you looking at?" he bellows. "Fuck off before I rip your eyes out of your sockets."

The men scramble out of there. Even with my heart beating at a million miles an hour, when I look over at Ragnar, he gives me a wonky smirk, and I break out laughing. He growls, and his body stiffens.

"My little fox, keep constricting my dick like that, and we're going to be locked together all night long."

He's stuck inside me, his cock engorged, and right now, I have a bad case of the giggles.

"Guess that's a problem we'll have to deal with."

EIGHT

RAGNAR

It's been over an hour since I fucked Narah, and I can still feel her.

Even as we sit outdoors on a log by the bonfire, I can't get her out of my head.

The softness of her body against mine, legs snaked around my hips, and my cock buried deep in her sweet cunt, are imprinted on me. She'd been dripping wet, and her taste and smell had invaded me. Even now, my fingers tingle with the memory of her gorgeous tits in my palms.

By the stunned look on her face, she hadn't expected me to bring her to her knees in front of me. She was beautiful, her eyes dilating, her breath catching in her throat when she looked up at me. It scared her how much she wanted me. I saw it in the way she covered herself, then greedily sucked my cock.

I liked her looking scared and defeated before me.

Fucking someone as perfect as Narah is a distraction I've permitted myself when I should have known better. When I should have taken what I wanted and not looked back.

Although did I even have a choice? I doubt it. She has a body made for sin, and every time I look at her, I want to bury my cock and stay inside her, to feel her pussy squeeze down on me. Her cries for more still suffocate me, weaken me, so how the hell am I meant to deny that?

I'm not ready to leave her side. I'd craved her since we got her back, and the first thing I did was get laid, figuring I'd get it out of my head. Of course, it did fucking nothing. Half the time, I trick myself into believing *that* shit works—get into her pants and not deal with the other shit in my head.

Now, this stunning creature watches the bonfire in front of us while the moon glows heavily across the landscape. She's enjoying a roast ham and cheese sandwich. It took two hours for my engorged cock to go down, and by the time we emerged from the bathhouse, the other guys had all gone to bed. So, I had some food quickly made for us.

Stuffing the last bite into her mouth, she brushes away the crumbs from the dress she'd found in the bathhouse. I'd have to arrange for Stone to fix the broken door in the morning. He's the handy one in our pack.

"I don't think it worked," Narah says quietly, and if I wasn't watching her, I might have missed her words.

"What's that, little fox?" I turn to face her, swinging a leg over the log, straddling it to face her.

She places her empty plate on the ground near her feet and pushes her wild, dark hair out of her face. The wind's picked up, sending the fire into a flutter and tossing embers into the air like fireflies. Narah stares at it in amazement, then glances back at me.

"What we did, you know?"

Is she blushing? Across the bonfire are several locals. After we broke the bathhouse's door, she became jumpy around the Bane Wolves in this pack.

There's something utterly enjoyable watching every movement Narah makes. She rubs the crumbs from around her mouth, and I consider leaning in and licking them off her face. Tucking her hands under her legs, she stretches out and wiggles her toes toward the blaze's warmth. Her legs are long and toned, and she's on the thinner side, something I'll need to rectify.

Perhaps I enjoy her too much, which might explain why she has me in her trance. I doubt she realizes how deeply she has her claws in me or how much further I wanted to push her during sex. I crave to see her tied up and completely at my mercy. Images of how beautiful she'd look send jolts of desire straight to my cock.

Next time for sure.

I shake my head and focus on what she said.

"You mean me fucking you?"

Her eyes widen with shock. "You gotta say it so loud? Why not scream it for everyone to hear. Geez, I bet they're already all talking about us breaking the door."

I chuckle, adoring the threads of innocence she holds on to.

"Okay, you're going to have to elaborate because I have no clue what you're talking about."

She pauses and pulls a bent leg between us as she swivels to face me, then her gaze drops.

"Your mark... I don't think it worked." Her hand raises to her neck, where my bite blushes pink on the side of her neck.

"What do you mean, didn't work? Of course, it did." My brow furrows.

She exhales loudly. "My wolf still pines for Martell. I feel her, even now, stirring within me, whining. I hate the longing that rises in me. I hate the bastard, yet my chest squeezes with grief at being so far from him. Last time you marked me, I felt the change almost instantly, but now, there's nothing there."

Her words hit me like a ton of bricks. How the hell didn't the mark stick?

I watch the way the bridge of her nose wrinkles and close the space between us, shuffling closer. With her bent leg cradled against my groin, I push the loose strands fluttering across her face, needing to fix this.

"Let me try something," I say, placing a palm against her warm chest. My wolf surges forward, just as he had earlier in the bathhouse, eager for a connection, desperate to bond. Closing my eyes, I sense her wolf's vibrations, fast and aggressive, not what I'd expect from a wolf connected to mine. I tense, not understanding what I did wrong.

"I don't understand how," I say, lowering my hand to my side. "It should have worked. My wolf called to yours."

"Ever since my mother cleansed us, I feel as if I've lost bits of myself." She swallows, then sighs. "I tell myself it'll just take time, then I'll be back to normal, but I still don't have my magic, and my wolf is craving Martell stronger than before. Plus, I don't know how to tell Jae about our mother. I'm toying with saying we didn't find her and leave it at that. I mean, to find something you've lost, then have it stolen again is heartbreaking. I can't do that to my sister."

"That's a lot to carry on your shoulders, Narah." My chest aches, thinking about how much thought she's given to all the problems, adding to the growing burden that I still haven't told her about her father. Is that something she needs to worry about on top of everything else? If I don't tell her and she finds out, will she hate me?

"These are things you can't control, but once a witch, always a witch, Narah. I've never heard of one losing their powers."

"What if I'm the first?" The corners of her mouth deepen with worry lines.

It troubles me to see her this way. I reach over and stroke her cheek, running a thumb over her sweet lips that deserve to smile more often.

"Back home in Denmark, there are witches who carry dormant power, which activates later in life."

"How?" she asks with a hint of desperation.

"Usually, a traumatic event or being in life-threatening danger can trigger it."

"Great," she sighs and seems to sink in on herself. "Both things happened to me and still nothing. What if I'm really broken, Ragnar? What if I can never do magic again?" Her brow knits in frustration.

"You will always be my Narah. Nothing changes who you are, how you behave, and what you do. You told me most of your life, you had to hide your powers, right?"

She shrugs, then nods. "Yeah. I know what you're going to say, that I survived without it before, but that's not the point. Kaira remains with the witches, so how am I supposed to save her now with no magic?"

I straighten. "We'll find a way to bring your powers back. If one witch helped you escape Martell, we'll find others to assist us with your sister." Though I have plans to take them out without Narah knowing. In two days, Gregory will meet my men and me by the Poisonous Woods where the witches are.

The high priestess bitch dies first. Then I'll bring back Narah's sister.

If all goes well, Narah may never need to know about the grisly fact that her mother resurrected her dead father from where Narah had buried him.

She sighs again. "My mother told me I wasn't an ordinary witch. Our family line makes me a sorceress."

I tense, knowing all too well about sorceresses. I understand how dark their magic is and that they draw their energy from other people, depleting them to death. I've heard stories about them but never met one.

Worry flares in Narah's expression, and I think back to everything I'd witnessed from Narah's mother.

Draining us to death.

Dead villagers in her basement.

Her father brought back to life.

Here I assumed she used powerful potions and spells to do it, which begs the question—what was Gregory drinking from the vial that looked like blood? I have a terrible suspicion he drank Allie's blood, which would be infused with magic she siphoned from poor suckers like us. Is that why we, and the dead in the basement, didn't come back as undead? Her magic affected us differently, just as it had flatlined Narah's powers.

"I will not be like my mother," Narah says abruptly, pulling back her shoulders in a defensive move.

"I never said you would be."

"Yet you look at me as if I'm a monster." Her eyes narrow in on me.

"That's not true." I shake my head. "I look at how brave you are after everything you've been through."

"Stop bullshitting me, Ragnar. Just say it as it is. My mother was a fiend, who drained people. For all I know, she's killed a bunch of others."

Well, she's not wrong there, but I say nothing. That won't help her cope with the reality of what her mother's done.

Narah turns from me and stares into the flames, which reflect in her amber eyes. I can almost see her mind working overtime, going through every memory, trying to make sense of her missing magic. I let the silence sink between us, but it isn't long before she's twisting her head in my direction.

"I don't really want to talk about this anymore if that's okay. Anyway, you wanted to talk to me?" Her words are clipped, and she's pulling away from me.

"I did. Before the shitstorm hit us, we didn't end up on good terms."

She studies me, and I'm not sure what she expects me to say. That I'm sorry? That I'm absolutely smitten with her? That it turns me into a jealous sonofabitch, even of my own men, who are like the brothers I never had? They are family, yet I burn up when I see them flirting with her, touching her. It kills me that Stone and Nikos have fucked her, and I know Crius is vying for his chance.

I clench my jaw, torn in half by how shitty I feel.

"I've never felt this way about anyone, let alone four Alphas. I know you have some things to work through from your fated mate leaving you. Stone told me; please don't be mad at him. I opened up to him about us first." She's talking fast, sounding nervous.

"I'm not upset. They all know about my past." I'm more annoyed about her not coming to me to talk about her issues.

"Yet you don't trust them to be with me?" Her voice is soft, and there are heartfelt emotions behind her words, not accusations.

Ignoring my mind's voice that tells me Eisa, my fated mate, promised to be mine, too, I just look at Narah. She could be everything I need. Someone to replace the gaping hole in my soul I'd resigned would remain barren. But what stops her from one day deciding I'm not good enough? That one of the other guys is all she needs?

It's fucking eating me alive that I have such thoughts, and I hate myself. I'm a damn Alpha and about to bring war to the Savage Sector to claim it as my territory, yet I'm pining like a love-struck teenager that I'll get hurt.

Get your fucking head together, Ragnar.

My wolf snarls in my chest to wake me back to my senses, to see the beauty in front of me and not destroy the only chance I have with her. Sure, I'm an asshole. Part of me isn't sorry because I refuse to let anyone ruin me again, but the other part of me craves to let go of the past.

"Everyone tells me time will change me, but it's done nothing so far," I admit. "I know you want us to share you, but I'm struggling with that idea. I've shared everything with my men, but I've never met anyone like you, and selfishly, I want you all for myself."

She doesn't say a word, but her expression conveys disappointment. Her eyebrows pull together, and I regard her curiously. She cares that much about my position on this? I'm drawn to her like a moth to a flame, can't stay away if I damn try, so there's reassurance in seeing this isn't an easy situation for her either.

I clear my throat. "You're mine, Narah, but if bringing you happiness means accepting sharing you, then..." I take a deep breath that rattles all the way down to my lungs. "I'll have to find a way."

Her smile melts me. She reaches over, hugging me tightly.

Now, I know what's going to happen. I have to keep my word to Narah, and I owe it to myself to finally break away from my past and forget my fated mate, who rejected me.

Then why the fuck does it feel like I've made a mistake, and I'll never be able to walk away from this if I don't win over Narah?

"I promise, they won't mind if I go fishing with them," Jae insists, sitting across from me in the pack mess hall. It's big enough to fit most of the Bane Wolves pack comfortably, though it's late morning, so there's hardly anyone there. Well, except for my sister and her new friends, plus a handful of people somewhere behind me in the room.

Without a word, she lets go of my hand and turns to her friends, who are taking their dirty dishes to the front. Throwing any waste in the bin, they place their plates with all the other dirty ones in buckets.

"The pond is on their pack land, so it's safe." Jae shrugs. "I know it's lame, but I want to go with them. They make me laugh. You can come, too." Jae looks at me, hopeful.

I can't really blame her for wanting to hang with her friends and do normal things. She missed out on so much of that. Back at Storm Wolves, for her own safety, she spent little time with other kids. Too many desperate men leered at her as if she was food, and it creeped me out. I wanted her safe.

"It's not lame at all. Sounds like fun, and I'd love to join you, but I have a few things to get done today," I say, my thoughts already pivoting toward finding Ragnar and talking to him about how we're going to rescue Kaira. No distractions or emotions like last night. I just want both my sisters with me. After that, I'm not too sure where we'll go. Getting my head screwed on right with Ragnar and his men is priority. Things are volatile, simmering as though they might explode.

"Really?" Jae jumps to her feet from the wooden bench and collects her breakfast plate from the table. "Thanks, Narah. I'll catch us something for supper." She is so giddy, bouncing on her toes, and I love seeing her like this.

"Your friends' mother is going with you, right?"

She nods. "There are several families going and all their mothers as well. I swear, it'll be safe."

"Of course, it will. I want to hear all about it when you return." A pang of guilt stirs in my chest. I'd love to join her, but I need to find the men and find out when we're going to rescue Kaira. Then, if I have time, I'll join Jae for some fishing.

She squeals and comes over to hug me, bits of egg spilling on my lap from her plate. I just laugh and wipe the mess off faded jeans as she runs to her friends.

Leaving the mess hall behind, I stroll through the sunlight. By the time Ragnar and I returned to our hut last night, the other guys were snoring like bears. I fell asleep in Ragnar's arms, and in the morning, the hut was empty. I had seen none of them since.

When I step out from behind a wooden hut, I spot Ragnar. He's half turned away from me, in close conversation with Lyssa, the pack Alpha's daughter. It takes me off-guard, especially when she winds her arm around his, and he doesn't push her away.

My eyes bore into them as fire erupts in my chest, and the truth pummels my mind. Her father threatened to give her to his men as their mate because there weren't enough females to go around. So, how much different is her monster of a father from Martell?

When Ragnar agreed to take her as his mate, it was a purely strategic decision on his part to gain this pack's support in his attempt to take over the Savage Sector, a decision made before he knew I existed, and now things are completely messed up. I can't hate the girl for trying to survive, yet I want to rip them apart.

Her blonde hair drapes loosely over her shoulders, and she's in a white dress that hits across her thighs with frills across her low neckline and short sleeves. She keeps pouting her ruby lips like a damn frog. I can't ignore how beautiful she is. High cheekbones, crystal-like eyes, and ample breasts, she rubs against Ragnar's arm. Her faint giggle fills the air at something he said, but from my angle, I can't see his face, let alone hear what they're saying.

I'm dazed and burning up with red-hot anger. My head and instincts are warring, and the only solution is to find Lyssa another man and get her the hell away from mine. A ridiculous and impossible idea, seeing I know no one in this town.

They are standing close, and I'm inches from bursting toward them. Instead, I do one better and retreat, then rush frantically around the back of the hut and come up on the other side to be closer to them. I'm desperate like that, it seems.

I dart to an apple tree that towers between two homes, dangling with heavily laden branches, red globes everywhere. They smell so sweet and heavenly, but I ignore the temptation and tuck myself behind the trunk before peering out to watch Ragnar and Lyssa.

They're feet from me, and I'm shaking all over, my insides set aflame.

"Ragnar, it will look suspicious to Father," she purrs, still pouting.

My insides burn hotter.

Ragnar looks at her dismissively, then tilts his head to the sky, releasing a sigh.

"That won't work for me."

On the bright side, he's not drooling all over her, but that doesn't stop me from holding on to the tree digging in my claws as if it was Lyssa.

"Well, you'll have to. It's not that hard to have one dinner with your mate. You've been gone from me so long, Ragnar. I miss you." She bats her eyes at him.

His nostrils flare, and he looks away, a mask of pure hatred sliding over her face.

"It's because of her, isn't it?" she snarls. "I smell her all over you. It's disgusting that you show interest in a half-breed you brought into our home. She's a mongrel."

I catch my breath. *That bitch!*

Ragnar swings back toward her with a growl, and she recoils, realizing she's pissed him off. He closes the distance between them in two steps and towers over her, heaving for breath. Arms tight by his side, I expect him to strike.

"Enough, Lyssa! Narah belongs to me, and that's not going to change."

Her grin drops, and she glares as Ragnar turns to leave once more.

"One word from me to Father, and you'll lose your allegiance with the Bane Wolves. You need to forget her."

He pauses and looks over his shoulder at her with pure hatred.

"If you do, you'll become the whore of this pack at your father's word."

Her shoulders rear back, her face pale as milk. With her chin high, her eyes flash to him with a threat.

"That's a risk I'm willing to take. Are you willing to do the same, Ragnar?"

I swallow hard, and despite my earlier words, I really hate her. Sure, desperation makes people do unforgivable things, but that's no excuse.

Expressive blue eyes narrow on Lyssa. "One meal," he grits through clenched teeth.

Shit, is he kidding me?

"Good." A smile unravels over her lips once more. "Now, Father wants to see you. Shall we go?" She's so sickly-sweet, I feel sick to my stomach.

I only see red as she sways her hips in his direction.

Stepping out from behind the tree, fury flashes in my mind. I lunge after her just as someone grabs me from behind by my waist and turns me away from them.

CRIUS

"Put me down," Narah hisses.

"Calm down," I whisper in her ear, her back flat against my chest as I swing us away from Ragnar's direction. The moment she lunged for him and Lyssa, I knew what would happen. Our witch had grown possessive of Ragnar and would have ruined months of work cultivating a relationship with the Bane Wolves.

"Let me go!" She thrusts against me.

"Hush now." I tighten my arm, locked across the front of her shoulders. "Ragnar knows he's yours and that you're powerful enough to fight for him, but not on this, my little hummingbird."

"All of you may be alright with this, but I'm not."

Her words trigger something. Ragnar means a lot to me as well, but if she keeps brushing that gorgeous ass, we're going to have a problem.

I came into this mission for Ragnar for one purpose—to help him gain his territory, so I can attain my warrior entry into Valhalla. The path is simple as fuck, and I know Ragnar hates my plan, but I agreed to join him for that sole purpose—which he accepted. You see, he has this way of making you completely loyal to him and collects followers like zombies are drawn to the living. The guy has a heart of gold, even if he's terrifying as shit when he's furious, and that's a hard quality to find in people in this damned world.

Narah isn't any less impacted by him.

I hold on to her, trying to make her settle down when I shouldn't give two fucks, yet I find myself captivated. I'm having thoughts about stripping her down and showing her what she's done to me. To let her experience a high like no other. To get her out of my fucking head so I can refocus on my mission. To not let my attraction to Narah or other doubts seep into my thoughts... doubts put there by Ragnar, who keeps trying to imply I should rethink my plan.

"Crius, let me go," Narah gripes, her threat darkening, something I'm particularly fond of.

"I love it when you're angry. Have you ever had hate sex, Narah?"

She scowls as she glares at me over her shoulder, eliciting a burst of laughter out of me.

"I'll take that as a no. When you're ready, I'll show you. You've never experienced anything like it, but I promise you'll scream for more."

"I-I don't know what you're talking about." She glances to where Ragnar walked off.

"Oh, you'll find out," I murmur under my breath.

She looks back at me, and I'm convinced she heard me. Good.

Keeping her against me, it's not hard to see how beautiful she is—fiery amber eyes, full lips I want to bite, and an ass I crave to fuck. I'm fully aware, of the four of us, I'm the only one who hasn't plunged into her cunt, but I've seen the way she studies me, smell her arousal when in my company, and our time is coming. I'll make sure of that, a fleeting thought that passes my mind each time I see her. Lately, my wolf has been growing louder in my head about claiming her.

When she finally calms down, I release her, and she stumbles from my arms before coiling around toward me. The ache on her face touches me. Seeing Ragnar with Lyssa kills her, and even though Ragnar hates the girl, it doesn't change Narah's hurt.

"It's going to be okay," I suggest, moving toward her. "I promise."

"I just hate all the bullshit politics being played here," she mutters. "There's no way I'm okay with Ragnar having a meal with her... She's not his fucking mate." Her eyes widen.

I adore how passionate she is. Hell, it's giving me goosebumps. I want her to get this fired up over me one day.

"Sometimes, we have to do crap we loathe for the greater good."

She sneers at me, looking ready to sucker punch me in the face for daring to say that. Who is this lioness who has been coming out of her shell? Damn, I love this side of her. She might have appeared meek at the beginning of our mission, but I'm starting to see she had us fooled.

"There's a feast tonight," I explain, taking her back into my arms, though her hands snap up and press against my chest. "We're all invited, so what is the harm of Ragnar sharing one meal with her in our company? The pros are we keep relations strong with her father and have a safe place for your sister while we prepare to go into the Poisonous Woods." The moment the words left my mouth, I realized I'd said the wrong damn thing. Fuck.

"Tomorrow?" she says, her eyes brightening.

"More like the day after," I lie. Ragnar will have my balls for telling Narah our plans. He didn't want her on the mission. *Nice job, Crius.*

"Ragnar needs the Bane Wolves to build his reach and strength to take over Savage Sector," I say softly, leaning my face to hers. "It's gorgeous that you're jealous, but tonight, you'll need to rein it in."

"I'm not sure I can do that." She glowers at me, and I love her all moody and mad.

Without warning, I kiss her, crashing my lips against her, and catch her off guard. She tenses against me, but she's not shoving me away. I leave a trail of kisses across her cheek, then bury my face in the curve of her neck. Inhaling deeply, I drown myself in her spicy, sexy scent. Lips on her warm neck, I kiss and bite, torturing her skin.

"Crius," she mumbles. "We shouldn't be..." Her words turn to moans... and there it is. She fucking wants me just as much as I crave her.

Her shivers against me have my hands falling to her waist, fingers digging into her sides. Just as quickly as I started, I pull back and lick her taste from my lips. She has that stunned expression that turns me on more than she'll ever know. I'm the wolf, and she's my lamb. I love this game.

"Why'd you kiss me?"

"Isn't it obvious?" Sliding my hand down her arm, I pull her hand and press it against my groin over my jeans. My hard cock twitches under her touch, and she doesn't flinch. She holds onto me for a long moment, not backing away, and for the first time, I feel fucking vulnerable and needy. Shit, what the hell is wrong with me?

She lightly squeezes my erection, and I hiss. It feels so good. Then she draws her hand away, smirking, well aware of what she's done. I moan, needing it back, and my wolf coils in my chest, shoving against my insides.

How easy would it be to shove her against the wall, rip off her clothes, and fuck her brains out? The earlier anger vanishes from behind her eyes, and a new look replaces it—desire. She might not say it, but I know she wouldn't push me away if I claimed her now. It's tempting.

"Tonight, we can give Ragnar a show," I suggest, toying with the idea of what I'll do to Narah to drive her insane with arousal. "Make him see what he's missing out on, and if he stops being a dick, he can join us." My words come out without thinking, well aware Ragnar will lose his shit, but when have I ever been to a party that doesn't end in death or sex?

"I'm already one step ahead," she says. "Ragnar already said he'd find a way to accept sharing."

Wait!

"He actually said that?"

"Yep." She gives me a tight nod and slips from my arms. "So, there's no need for your grand plan. I don't even know if I'll go tonight." She makes a hasty retreat toward the mess hall.

Well, color me fucking surprised with Ragnar. Old dogs can learn new tricks after all.

Crius waves at me from across the grand hall to join him and the other two guys.

They're seated at the farthest possible table, tucked away in the shadows. Rows of long tables with benches are arranged in the room, all pointing to the front where there's a U-shaped table, headed up by the Bane Wolves Pack's Alpha. My gaze finds Ragnar instantly on the Alpha's right-hand side, then Lyssa.

I might be foaming at the mouth with jealousy, seeing her all dolled up in a sapphire green and gold Renaissance gown with a low-cut bust line, her blonde hair falling over her shoulders in soft waves.

I'm wearing a dress Jae borrowed from her friend's mother. I'm not exactly traveling with a bag of clothes, and I've never owned a gown. Looking down, my dress is simple, in a deep burgundy color that cinches at my waist, with long sleeves that ruffle at the wrists and a straight bust line. I pulled my hair back into a ponytail with a few loose strands framing my face. I thought I looked attractive, but next to Lyssa, I might as well be wearing a hessian sack. A deep ache settles in my gut at how awkward I feel.

Ragnar keeps pulling at the high-collared black shirt he wears, looking out of place and uncomfortable. Deep brown hair sits over his shoulder tidily as though he put effort into looking his best.

When he catches my eye from across the room, his lips curl into a smile, and his sky-blue eyes light up. Of course, that's when bitch face notices and reaches over to paw his bicep, releasing a fake laugh.

If I rolled my eyes any harder, I'd lose them somewhere in my head, so instead, I march through the filled room to the back corner. Crius said not to make a scene, and this was for the greater good.

Yeah, well, *my* greater good is all for my sisters. For them, I'll do anything.

Every other seat is taken in the hall, and guards in black uniforms pepper the room, watching. The air thickens with wolf scents, and my wolf stirs, whining at being surrounded by so many Alpha and Beta men who leer at me as I pass them. Their desperate smells invade my nostrils.

Candelabras hang from the arched ceiling, a display of fanned-out swords graces one of the walls, while tapestries of wolves in battle fill the other walls.

My three men smile as their gazes moving up and down my body. I won't deny their attention helps my self-confidence.

"Why are we sitting all the way back here?" I slide in next to Crius while Stone and Nikos sit across from us.

"We had a bet," Nikos says. "And this spot won."

"Do I even want to know what you bet on?" I reach for a breadstick from the wicker basket in the middle of the table and bite into it.

"You," Crius adds, his hand sliding across my lower back. "It was unanimous that you wouldn't want to be close to Lyssa without wanting to gouge her eyes out. Plus, with us having our own party at our table, we didn't want to torture Ragnar any more than he already was."

"Wow, you make me sound so jealous," I mutter, a soft warmth spreading over my cheeks at being so obvious.

"My hummingbird," Crius says, his hand sliding across my back, which felt amazing. "If I hadn't been there to stop you today, you and Lyssa would have gotten into a huge catfight. While I would have loved to watch you kick her butt, this isn't about what you or I want."

"You surprise me, Crius," Nikos responds with a sarcastic smirk. "Since when do you give a fuck about not causing chaos?"

He shrugs and reaches over for a breadstick too. "Ragnar needs this to work. We're not exactly swimming in options."

We all turn and look at Ragnar. Lyssa is leaning against him and staring up at him like a puppy dog while he's in deep conversation with her father.

"He's fuming," Stone states. "Look at how much he's sweating."

"I bet she's feeling him up under the table," Crius adds, and I glare at him for putting that image into my mind.

Nikos howls with laughter. "About time he took one for the team. Most of the time, it's one of us doing something ridiculous."

My glass empty, I spot a jug of wine on the opposite edge of our table beside Crius. The image of me accidentally spilling it onto Lyssa's lap makes me giddy.

"My mouth feels like it's drier than a desert. Can I have some wine, please?"

"Allow me." Crius pours wine into my glass and hands it to me. "Here you go."

"Thanks," I mutter and return to glaring at Lyssa.

Crius turns his attention back to Nikos. "Like the time you got dressed up as an old hag to get us into a pack. Man, I almost pissed my pants when that guard tried to feel you up."

"Wait, what happened?" I ask, caught up in their conversation while the three of them howl with laughter and chug back wine from their metal jugs.

Surprisingly, I find myself partially enjoying the night, listening as they tell stories from their battles in Denmark, even though I keep glancing across the room at Ragnar. I play with the idea of leaving the dinner party and making a quick escape. Just seeing her draped over Ragnar hurts.

As plates of sliced meat and roast vegetables arrive at our table, I ask the guys, "What's the occasion for tonight's gathering, anyway? I mean, the hall is packed, but not everyone from the pack is here." Including all the kids, elderly, and mothers. Men fill the room, outnumbering all other groups, and I won't deny it's slightly unsettling.

"A celebration of Ragnar's return," Stone explains sarcastically.

"He and Mihai are making plans tonight on how they'll conquer the Savage Sector."

Mihai... must be the Alpha's name. I just hope whatever they discuss involves rescuing Kaira since I haven't had a chance to catch Ragnar all day to talk.

I swallow a mouthful of what tastes like venison and follow it up with crispy potatoes soaked in dripping butter, which melt on my tongue. It's been too long since I enjoyed a hot roast meal, so I dig in and enjoy every last crumb, including the dessert of bread pudding, all while the guys drink and exchange embarrassing stories about one another.

A loud clapping from the front of the room catches my attention.

Mihai stands from his chair, and the chatter in the room dies down. He's an older man with trimmed white hair and deeply tanned skin. He's wearing dark pants, a fitted white shirt buttoned to his throat, and a jacket hangs on the back of his seat. Despite looking older, muscles fill his shirt.

"Tonight is an auspicious occasion," he begins. "A new beginning for the Bane Wolves. Living in the Savage Sector has always come with its challenges, and for our survival, we need to fight to hold our footing in this world. Daily, other packs encroach closer onto our lands while more undead migrate north. We need to take action before it's too late." His jaw clenches as he talks, but in his eyes, I can see he truly cares for his pack. Everyone hangs off every word, their eyes glued to their Alpha. Mihai half-turns toward Ragnar and slaps a hand on his shoulder.

"We have joined forces with Ragnar, our northern friend, and his pack. His immense help with the witches and rogue wolf packs will be invaluable, and just as important is that he will join my family once he officially mates with my daughter, Lyssa. They will be the new generation to guide us into leadership and survival."

An explosion of cheering and clapping ensues in the room.

While I'm glaring at them, Lyssa throws her arms around Ragnar. Fire flares through me, my muscles tensing at the sight. *Mating.* What the fuck does that mean? One meal he'd promised her.

Crius' hand slides from my back to my thigh as he leans in close to me. "Mihai's words are empty. We're just biding our time to get the upper hand."

"If you say so," I mumble back, feeling ice cold.

The other men's eyes are still on Mihai, while my heart thumps so hard, it might burst out of my chest and fly away on wings.

"I promise," Crius whispers. His breath across my cheek and his hand sliding under my dress through the high slit on the side warms me.

"Crius." I push against his arm, and he gives me a heated glance.

A young male server, who must be a Beta to be working as a server, arrives at our table to clean up. Alphas wouldn't be caught dead working such menial jobs. They're given to Betas, while we Omegas are used for one thing—rutting and breeding. That's how our cruel world is divided. Three types of wolves, all abiding by a hierarchy and accepting their roles, even if many don't agree with the unfairness. It's utter crap that an Omega is seen as nothing other than making babies by Alphas, while Betas are the inferior wolf and often treated as slaves to Alphas. The only people it doesn't suck for are the Alphas who fight tooth and nail to hold status. The rest of us do our best to just survive.

"Are you finished, miss?" the Beta asks, pointing his chin at my plate and distracting me from my thoughts.

"Yes, thank you." I reach up to give him the plate. Of course, that's the exact moment Crius' hand slides between my legs, brushing against the thin fabric of my underwear.

I gasp loud enough to have the Beta glance my way. My cheeks flush with heat, and his touch awakens my wolf. On cue, she's groaning in my chest for Martell. I fucking hate him, but she holds a candle for him, not knowing any better.

Crius' fingers remain locked under my skirt while he grins at the poor Beta, who looks so confused. Crius leans in, his mouth on my ear.

"Open your sweet legs for me. Let me show you how you'll forget Ragnar right now."

"Have you lost your mind?" My body shakes as I stare at him incredulously. "We're in a room with wolves." I push against his hand, but he's like steel and unmovable.

"Don't make me ask you again. I'm not above dragging you out of here over my shoulder, making it clear to everyone that I'm taking you outside to fuck you. Then I promise you, we'll have an audience."

"You wouldn't," I hiss.

"Don't test me. You've been on my mind all day, thinking about how you groped my cock and our kiss. No one will see us. With so many damn wolf smells in here, we'll be fine."

"*You* forced me to touch you," I snap.

An evil grin splits his mouth, revealing a line of white teeth. He wriggles his fingers across the apex of my thighs, and every small caress sends a jolt of arousal through my body. It doesn't take long for liquid heat to soak my underwear. I hate myself for being so weak when these men push me to my limits.

He presses so close against me, I couldn't slide a piece of paper between us if I tried, while my breath wedges in my lungs along with my whining wolf.

I'm staring into his eyes, and he's grinning.

"Shall we?" he asks.

"You're an ass," I growl. Tingles race down my spine that I'm even contemplating it, knowing he'll carry out his threat.

"And you're aching for me," he whispers. "Now, open up and look at me. I want to see the moment you melt and come undone all over my fingers."

Frantically, I look around. Stone and Nikos are oblivious, their backs to us as they stare at Mihai, who's still talking.

I must be crazy, widening my legs slightly, thankful my dress is long. I give him my best death glare when he pushes the scrap of material of my panties aside. Shivering against him, our eyes lock as his fingers slide across the slick seam of my pussy. Barely able to catch my breath, I'm startled. His hand is on me... in my panties... at the pack gathering. I bite my lip, refusing to make a sound, but my widening eyes give me away. The reaction on Crius' face is lustful.

He glides his finger between my folds, and a flaring need consumes me. My nipples tighten to hard points and push into the fabric of my dress. I give him my best death glare, or at least attempt to, but when his finger applies pressure to my clit and rubs me, I moan. Gripping the edge of the table, suddenly, I don't care that there are dozens of people in this room who could glance our way and see his hand under my skirt.

"You're a very brave girl, Narah," he whispers in my ear.

Am I brave or just someone who is constantly horny for these men and can't seem to say no to them?

He adjusts himself next to me. "Scooch forward a bit," he asks. Crazily, I listen to him and do just that.

There's no warning before he pushes two fingers into me. Arching in my seat, I pull my lower lip between my teeth, biting down to stop myself from moaning. It feels incredible, and every inch of me is bursting to scream and let my body ride the wave he's forced through me.

"You haven't told me to stop, Narah," he teases. "Why's that?"

I blink at him, my brain foggy, my body buzzing.

"Because you threatened me?"

"It's not like you to give in that easily. You know what I think? You've wanted me from the beginning."

His fingers work their way in and out of me, his thumb on my clit, making me lose my mind. What were we talking about again?

"That..." I trail off as he fingers me faster. "Crius," I breathe his name so softly, I have no idea if I made a sound.

"Is this how you like to be touched?"

He's fucking with my brain.

A shadow falls over us, and I stiffen, glancing up, half blushing, half about to scream with an orgasm.

It's the Beta guy again, placing several plates of fruit, nuts, and cheeses on our table.

"Eyes on me," Crius whispers in my ear, and I lift my attention to him, holding his gaze. "I've waited a long time for this." His fingers move in a different way, and my hips rock, and my breaths are heavier.

Clutching his arm, my nails dig into his flesh, but his fingers never pause. The way he stares at me with his evil grin dares me to lose control. I see it in his hungry eyes, his greedy fingers driving me over the edge.

My skin tightens, and my body is on fire.

One whimper from me, and his fingering destroys me. My mind

explodes, and my body shakes. I arch my back, keeping my mouth shut, which is close to impossible as a climax rocks through me. Pleasure digs deep within me, completely ruining me as I come on Crius' hand. My walls squeeze him, and every movement he makes, his thumb never ceasing to tease my clit, heightens the sensation.

He holds me close as I twitch uncontrollably, and I bury my face in his neck, the cry strangling me coming out against the heat of his skin.

"You are beautiful," he whispers. "So much more than I ever expected when you climax."

When I finally settle down, my head spins from how intensely I came. I've never felt it burst through me like that. Crius withdraws his fingers, and my body sways as I lift my head from his neck and realize we have an audience after all. The Beta's face is red, his mouth gaping open. It's clear he knows exactly what had just happened to me.

"You've had your show, now fuck off," Crius growls, sending the server scurrying out of the hall.

When I twist around, Stone and Nikos are leering at me with primal hunger in their eyes, and in the distance, Ragnar's looking our way.

Did he see everything?

Crius brings his fingers to his mouth and licks them clean, smirking. "Delicious."

"Whatever the hell I just witnessed, I want in," Nikos states, while Stone nods frantically.

I'm still coming down from my high, and the earlier need consumes me. Despite being watched and knowing they'll never let me forget this, there is no way I can deny that was fucking amazing.

ELEVEN

RAGNAR

"Ragnar, just one dance," Lyssa drawls, her eyes batting with desperation.

Every time she touches me, my skin crawls.

The girl's touch shouldn't revolt me. She's beautiful, and when I first entered the treaty deal with the Bane Wolves, I considered her a good mate for fucking and breeding. There was no love or longing between us, and that hasn't changed. The decision was made when I first arrived at the Savage Sector from my home in Denmark, and I was eager to establish a foothold in Romania.

Now, I'm a different man, and my sights are set on my little fox, Narah. She sits in the rear of the room with my men, and I would have to be a fool not to see Crius enjoying himself with her, pushing her. My muscles tense, and my hands stiffen by my side. The guy knows exactly how to press a girl's buttons, and it takes every inch of strength not to storm over and rip him from her side.

Except I've made her a promise, haven't I? Fuck.

My men are like my brothers, and Narah has become my fascination. Who am I kidding? I'm fucking obsessed with her, lost to her, and there's nothing I wouldn't do to keep her by my side, even go against my instincts.

"Ragnar, are you listening?" Lyssa pesters me.

461

I shake my thoughts away, then glance at her.

"A meal was all I offered you," I shoot back and climb to my feet. I've had enough of being a damn monkey on show for everyone. All this time wasted. Mihai and I could have been working on plans to take over Savage Sector, determining which packs we'd attack first and which we would try to win over without resorting to combat. I'm suffocating between him and Lyssa, both putting on a show to their people.

I question if it wouldn't be a good time to educate them on the undead migrating to this sector and teach them how to fight the new threat instead of placating them.

"Ragnar," Lyssa pleads, reaching for my hand, but I leave her behind, needing fresh air.

Before I even make it to the door, Mihai is by my side. He sets a large hand on my shoulder, pausing me in my escape.

"The people are scared," he says in a hush. "Let them see some merriment in their lives, some hope. I have arranged for a band, so everyone can dance, with you and Lyssa taking the lead. Watching you enjoying yourself, they'll be less afraid."

I grind my back teeth. "Maybe they should be terrified."

I take a step forward, and the hand on my shoulder tightens.

"I'm not asking, Ragnar. This is something my pack needs. After this, we'll make plans and maybe discuss once more the number of females you'll bring me. Forty is low... maybe I can sweeten your deal for more females."

My body tenses and I want to squeeze the life out of Mihai for pressing me to dance with Lyssa, for wanting to negotiate our agreement. I have yet to travel to Shadowlands Sector and convince Dušan, the Alpha there, to sell me forty Omegas, and I'm not prepared to budge on that number.

I lift my gaze to Narah, who's laughing with my men, and a different kind of rage unleashes. The wolf inside me rages that we're not with her instead of playing politics. He's been drawn to her since the first time we met at a bar, where she approached me for my help with her sisters. At first, I put it down to her being just another beautiful face, even if my wolf was crazed around her. In hindsight, I see it was easier to ignore the obsession she's become.

"One dance to get everyone else in the spirit," Mihai buzzes in my ear. "Then you and I will head to my office. Bring Nikos, too. It'll be good to have another strategic viewpoint."

Keeping my eyes on Narah, I remind myself as much as I want to say fuck it all, I can't forget the bigger picture. There won't be a welcome party if I return to Denmark, not after I left the country in what my father would consider a disgrace by simply walking away from him.

Let's be honest; he had no plans to hand his pack over to me. The bastard would live forever to ensure he never lost power. Remaining under his reign would end with me murdering him, so I left.

I have every intention of showing that prick I don't need him. That I can build a future for myself in the Savage Sector. Then I can rescue my sister, Hel, who Father sold to our enemies to marry their warlord. Clenching my teeth, I look back at Narah. She always makes me forget how savage this world can be.

Sacrifices—we all make them, even if this shit infuriates me.

I turn back toward Mihai, who smiles and pats my shoulder. The urge to break his arm in several places might bring me joy, but I opt to play his game. I grew up in a pack where no one could be trusted, and if you didn't manipulate others, you were as good as dead, so this is nothing new to me.

"Fine," I murmur.

"Good man," he says as I lift my gaze to Lyssa, who's already rushing toward me eagerly. I take a deep breath and remind myself... it's just one fucking dance.

CRIUS

"Are you kidding me?" Narah murmurs under her breath, her eyes glued on Ragnar and Lyssa on the dance floor.

They look so damn awkward, I almost burst out laughing at how she's practically strangling him. She's wrapped around him, her cheek attached to his chest, while he's only holding onto her shoulders.

One way or another, he'll have to deal with Lyssa and her father.

I'll admit the dance surprises me. Ragnar does everything with purpose, so I trust there's a good reason behind it. Especially when he was cursing her like a storm before we arrived at the hall.

Nikos had left to join Mihai, who summoned him for a strategic talk after the dance, and Stone was strolling across the room to track down a server for more wine.

I turn back to Narah, only to watch the precious little thing running across the room and bursting out of the hall. She's so mad at Ragnar, it makes me grin. Her emotions are explosive.

Hell, this was going to blow up.

I jolt to my feet and take fast steps right behind her. Someone has to defuse the situation, so it looks like I'm the man for the job. Drawing in the fresh air, the cool breeze washes over me. There's movement to my left, and I catch the flash of her burgundy dress disappearing behind a hut and take off after her.

Catching up to her, I think about how I'd love to chase her down in a real cat-and-mouse game and make her all mine once I capture her. Even now, the way her sweet ass moves with her fast steps consumes me. Her scent from fingering her remains in my nostrils, the smell as delicious as she tastes.

A small tease that's nowhere near enough... not even close.

She rushes down a dirt path, which will eventually bring her to the town's lake.

"You can stop now." I grab her arm as I reach her. When she swings around to me, she's scowling, and her eyes glisten with tears.

My heart shudders at her pain.

"Lyssa means nothing to Ragnar. I'll stake my life on it," I say, feeling compelled to convince her. Taking her hand, she rips it away. There's more than jealousy on her face.

"I'm so furious with myself," she finally admits. "I've become so damn weak. The way I reacted back there is stupid, but if I went back inside and saw them, I'd be no different. My plan was to rescue my sisters, then I went and got feelings for Ragnar, for all of you damn Alphas. Now, look at me. I'm shaking with anger because I'm jealous." She lowers her gaze as though her words strike a chord.

She is absolutely stunning, even more so because she's angry for liking us.

"Wow, that's actually the nicest thing you've said to me," I say sarcastically.

She doesn't bite back, marching to where the town's lights fade behind us.

"Why are you out here, putting yourself in danger if you're so worried about protecting your sisters?"

"I'm furious at myself and at how easily I let emotions control me. That's how you get killed in this world."

"So does walking in the woods alone at night."

She cuts me a glance. "I've got you with me, don't I?"

"I can only do so much against a horde of zombies." The thought has me glancing around, aware we're still within the confines of the Bane Wolves' territory, fencing all around. I've also seen first-hand accounts of how relentless these fuckers are when it comes to reaching their next meal.

"See over there." She points ahead of us through a small clearing between several fern trees. "There's a lofty wire fence, and it looks untouched to me. I think we'll be safe."

I squint through the dark, and the metal fence catches the moonlight. "You've been here before?"

"Ended up joining my sister on a fishing expedition with a few families."

Silence beats between us.

"Caring for us doesn't make you weak, Narah. It makes you a fighter."

"My father once told me people who have nothing left to lose are the most dangerous. I don't consider myself a fighter or strong, more of a survivor."

"What do you think a survivor is? The strongest people because nothing stops them." Her words bring her father to mind and how he's now undead. I am remorseful about keeping secrets from Narah, but Ragnar made us promise not to upset her with what her mother has done. I've always been a man to speak honestly and say it as it is. While I understand why Ragnar made the call he did, I would have already told Narah the truth if it was my call.

"How about we head back to our hut?" I suggest as worry flows over her expression once more. "There are several pillows in there you can punch and pretend they're Lyssa's head."

"That actually sounds like fun." The moonlight reflects in Narah's amber eyes.

"Done." I stick out my hand, which she gingerly accepts, then we walk to the small home on the edge of the village we've been given for our stay.

Though, to be honest, my suggestion is completely selfish. Ever since I enjoyed her pussy, my cock hasn't gone down, and I intend to have her all to myself for a few hours.

"By the way, that dominating thing you did at the party was a dick move," she says, not looking at me.

"I didn't see you complaining, and that was just the beginning."

Her huffs break into a laugh.

Challenge accepted.

Not that I need much motivation. Her scent remains lodged in my head, teasing me with what I need to achieve my peak. When she had no real resistance at the party gathering, I knew then she'd have me worshiping her. I'm ready to make her wildest dreams come true as long as it involves me.

"It's still a dick move," she grumbles and pouts.

Something savage, primal, comes over me, an intensifying need that is all-consuming. This walk is taking way too fucking long. I pivot around to step in her path, my hands falling to her hips, and lift her off her feet, then walk her back so fast, she has no time to complain. Pressing her against the closest tree, I can't help but smile at her shocked gasp.

Her hands snap up, flat on my chest, but a little too late. She's already mine.

"You like me? Fucking fantastic, Narah. Now, how about we do something about that?"

"Put me down," she growls, pushing against my chest.

"There's my Narah. I want you angry and take out your fury on me. I'm going to fuck that tight pussy until you forget your own name." Pressing my body to hers, I hear her heartbeat thumping faster. Such a beautiful sound.

Not wasting a second, I drive my hand up her dress. With a single snap of my fingers, I rip off her underwear and shove the scraps of fabric into the pocket of my pants.

"Crius... shit!"

"Game's changed, my hummingbird. I'm in charge now."

She swallows hard, staring at me, not quite believing I have her caged and bare.

"What do you want to do, fuck me? Your cock is hard, and your balls are hurting after your stunt at the party," she bites out. "Maybe you deserve to hurt."

"Good, keep going," I snarl as my wolf thrusts forward, urging me not to stop. I want her to use me as her punching bag. This is what she's been demanding with her actions. "Get it all out of your system, and when you calm down, I'll show you what a goddess you are." I don't waste a second and press my knee between her legs, spreading them for me.

"Tell me, is this what you want?" I shove her dress aside and unbuckle my pants with one hand. My cock jolts to attention upon release, and I hiss at how good it feels to unleash him. Pressing the tip to her drenched cunt, I meet her gaze. She's slightly panicked and looks around at the houses in the distance. There's no one around, and even if they were, I'd tell them to piss off. I'm not letting go of my delicious treat.

Still, she doesn't tell me to stop. Panting, her hands grip my shirt as her pupils dilate with lust.

"You smell fucking incredible," I growl against her neck as the tip of my cock teases her entrance, and it's killing me. I crave to feel her wrapped around me, sucking me down.

"I wanted my first time with you to be gentle, but I can't wait much longer, Narah. Ready?" I groan.

"Fuck you, Crius, for making me want this so badly."

Laughter bursts from my throat, and she stares at me with lust in her eyes. Oh, she has no idea what I have in store for her.

"I'll do my best to not tear you in two."

Her eyes widen, but I'm already pressing into her while guiding her legs to wrap around my waist. Once I have her in position, placing a hand on her back so the tree won't scratch her back, I sink into her, tight walls squeezing around me. I want her stretched. Her nails dig into my shoulders as I move in and out, quickening my thrusts.

"I want every inch of you," I say, breathing heavily

"You can have me," she moans as her head falls to my shoulder. Her eyes flutter, and she shivers in my arms as her pussy tightens around my cock.

Fuck me, she's everything I crave.

Pulling her away from the tree, I cup her ass with two hands as I bounce her up and down on my dick. Her lips are on my neck, and she bites down into the tender curve, her chest arching against me. I howl as her sharp teeth sink into flesh, driving me to madness. Pain and pleasure are my thing. My cock twitches as the heightened climax claws through me, but it's too fast. I'm not even close to finishing with Narah.

Sliding out of her, I lower her to her feet, and her dress tumbles down to cover her gorgeous offering. Tucking my cock back in, it hurts to trap him back in my pants.

She gives me a wonky look. "What are you doing?"

"I don't want to knot in you just yet. I intend on fucking you a lot more before we go down that path." Not waiting for her response, I take her hand and rush us across the village at ultra-speed, and we're in the hut before I can say, *let's get to fucking.*

Kicking the door shut, I reach for her dress, and my wolf's claws extend just long enough to rip the dress off her body. She gasps as shreds of red fabric cascade, unveiling a body I'm about to worship.

"Shit, that's not my dress," she groans.

"I don't give a fuck. Now, come over here." I seize her arm and spin her around to face away from me, then bend her over the arm of the couch.

She cries out at how fast I move her, which only makes me grin. Impatient and my erection straining, I rapidly strip from my clothes and kick them aside, then turn to my girl, who's starting to get up.

"Don't move." Running my hand up her spine, I force her back down. "I want your ass high and your legs spread. Tell me how much you want this, Narah... beg me for it."

When she doesn't respond but narrows her gaze at me over her shoulder, I slap her adorable ass, then grab and grope it.

"Ouch," she cries, and I love the sound she makes.

"You are so beautiful, Narah, but that's not going to mean I'll let you off easily."

"You know what I want," she purrs, her grin devious.

"Say it." I squeeze her ass cheek as my thumb brushes small circles of her rear entry.

Her body shivers, and her hips rock, pressing against my hand for more. She's drenched, making my thumb slippery. I slip the tip of my thumb into her ass, just enough to tempt her, and her moans bring me off-the-chart pleasure. I palm my cock with my other hand and push a bit more into her gorgeous little ass.

"Crius," she begs.

"Ah, there it is. Let me hear it."

"Fuck... fuck me like an animal. Make me scream."

"Oh, my hummingbird, that's it," I growl and reward her by fingering her ass.

Her scream is mesmerizing.

My dick throbs at the sight of my thumb going in and out of her rear, of her swollen, wet pussy on display as her legs spread wider. She's ready... so damn ready, I can't wait another second.

I slip between her legs, drawing my thumb out of that gorgeous hole. Gripping my cock, I guide it to where it belongs, sinking back into her cunt. She grips me tightly as her glistening lips swallow my cock.

"Narah," I gasp when she squeezes her walls around me. Adjusting slightly, I hammer into her, slow to get a feel for her. When it comes to doggy style, I can reach much deeper inside her.

"That's it. Fuck me hard."

Gripping her hip, my other hand curls around her hair and pulls her head back just enough, it's the kind of pain that gets her off. I rock into her, forgetting where one of us starts and the other ends. I never would have guessed my little bird likes to be pounded this way. The sounds of slapping echo around us, but her cries are louder.

"Oh My Fucking God!" she screams, which only pushes me faster to the point that with each thrust, the couch moves across the floor.

Hearing a gasp to my left, I twist my head to see Stone walking into the hut, his mouth gaping open and lust already bulging in his pants.

"What the fuck?!" he blurts, breaking my perfect rhythm.

Narah tenses beneath me, then turns her head toward Stone as he shuts the door behind him.

"You bastards left me all alone in that boring-as-shit party to have sex? That's just cruel." He's already ripping off his clothes. "For that, I'm joining in."

"That isn't why I left," she gasps, breathing heavily. "But yes, come over here, big boy."

Stone practically rips his pants off, then struts toward us, his cock hard. Narah gawks at him while I'm still deep inside her.

"I'm not a crossing-swords kinda guy, so if you can deal with that, join us." I have no issues sharing with the three other guys, as long as the focus is Narah.

Stone moves to stand next to Narah and cups her face. "You're such a good girl, aren't you? And you're going to be rewarded now. Come climb me like a tree." Stone glances at me. "You good to take her from the rear?"

"I want this," Narah purrs, looking at me with pleading eyes. How can I resist that look?

"Sure, just waltz in here and take over," I growl at Stone. "You're just lucky I'm so fucking horny right now, I'll do anything to push my cock back into our beauty."

"You owe me this for ditching me at the party."

"Damn, what are you, five years old?" I gripe, slipping out of Narah. Slipping an arm under her stomach, I lift her to her feet.

"When it comes to sex with my sweetheart, I don't give a fuck what you call me." Stone tenderly pulls Narah to stand in front of him, both of them naked, face to face, and they kiss.

Sure, I'm fucking mad he's acting like a dick, but Narah's enjoying herself, and ultimately that's what I want, right? Besides, this is just the beginning. Now that she's opened the flood gates, so to speak, about our sex life, she has no clue what's coming her way.

The way she scorches me with her body has me prowling toward her. Narah draws me to stand behind her, sandwiched between Stone and me, in the middle of the room.

"I want you both at the same time."

"That's my girl." Stone lifts her off her feet, and she wraps her legs around his hips.

With a smirk, I step closer to my girl, pressing my chest flush to her back, with my cock cradled against her full ass. I embrace her and take her full breasts with both hands, kneading them, my fingers lavishing her nipples, pinching. She likes a bit of pain with her arousal.

She turns her head toward me, her eyes full of desire, and I claim her mouth, tasting her sweetness. Pressing my tongue to the seam of her lips, I demand her surrender. I crave to dominate her, to let every inch of me consume her.

She stiffens, moaning, and I realize the greedy bastard who interrupted us is pushing his cock into her. My competitive nature plunges through me, and I seize my cock, positioning myself at her ass.

"You ready?" I whisper against her mouth.

"Please," she moans. Pinned between us, she makes small impatient sounds.

I run my tip over her drenched ass before gently pressing into her, then find the perfect rhythm with Stone. She's so wet and ready to go.

She clenches her muscles at first, squeezing me. Stone hisses, feeling the same sensation.

"We'll take it slow at first. Now, let us in," I say.

"Do you like this?" Stone mutters.

"I'm ready to explode and can't get enough. Of course, I blame Crius for bringing this wild side out in me."

I laugh. "The blame is mine, and I'll own it."

"I adore the full of lust look in your eyes," Stone adds. "You are perfect like this, dripping over my cock. You are doing so well."

Bracing herself, we all shift slightly as we find our standing position. With my powerful arms, I hold on to her ass while Stone grasps her hips, and we slowly push back into her until we find the right positioning between us. Locked in a lover's embrace, Narah pinned between us, we thrust harder, falling into a pattern that has Narah crying out for more. She's absolutely stunning during sex.

"Where the hell is Ragnar now?" Stone mutters between thrusting and Narah's sweet cries. "He needs to see how perfect we are when we share."

"He'll find out soon enough." I try to catch my breath as we thrust faster, and the build-up tears through me.

Narah's body shudders, her back glistening with sweat, while Stone's chest heaves for air. Then she convulses in our arms, screaming as an orgasm claims her.

When she squeezes my cock, I roar with how much it hurts, how incredible it feels.

Stone snarls and his eyes flutter back.

"Don't you fucking lose control," I bark. "She needs to climax at least three more times before we flood her with our seed. Don't you fucking knot," I growl.

"Three, are you crazy?" she murmurs.

"Chill, buddy," Stone rasps. "I have control."

Holding on to my girl, wrapping her in my arms, I pull out of her and draw her off Stone's cock. Her legs wobble, so I lift her into my arms. Stone follows us to the bed, never taking his eyes off Narah, who's still high from her amazing climax.

I lay her on the bed and push the hair out of her face. Her body is heaven—bouncy tits, curvy hips, and a pussy I'm dying to suck. "You're so sexy." Climbing in next to her, I glide my hand along her jaw as Stone throws himself alongside her on the bed, making the whole damn hut shake.

My cock pulses, and adrenaline thumps in my veins.

"Catch your breath, gorgeous, because I want you to ride my face," I tell her.

"I'd like that." She smiles, looking from me to Stone. "Ragnar was my first, so I never knew being with two men could be so incredible. So, how about this? I ride your face while I suck Stone's cock?"

"Fuck, yes," Stone bellows.

I take her into my arms and pepper her face with kisses.

"Tomorrow, you won't be able to walk straight by the time we're finished with you."

She grins and kisses me quickly on the lips.

"Is that a promise?"

TWELVE

NARAH

Sleep clings to my mind. It's too early for anyone to be up, so it's alarming to wake up and find myself alone after falling asleep in Stone and Crius' arms.

And the first thing I feel is my wolf, sitting in my chest heavily, furiously snarling at me for betraying our fated mate.

I grind my jaw, so exhausted from this shit.

The cool air brushes through my hair just outside the hut, and morning frays at the edges of the horizon, painting the sky in oranges and purples. It's spectacular. I might enjoy it more if I knew where all the guys had gone and my wolf would chill the hell out.

Last night, I sensed Nikos joining us. Ragnar had been there too, but he kept to himself, mostly. I'd been too tired to make a big deal of it.

Where would all four of them go before dawn?

I continue down the dirt path toward the mess hall, figuring they might be early risers; at least, that's what I tell myself. Something feels off about the day, and it's barely started. Night still has shadows surrounding the village, though locals are already milling about the village.

"Look what the wolf dragged out of bed," Lyssa gripes as she steps into my path from behind a home.

I sigh heavily. She's the last person I want to face right now as I stifle a yawn. I'm not awake enough to deal with her, especially when she looks immaculate with her hair pinned off her face and cascading down her back. What time did she wake up to look so perfect? I quickly run my fingers through my hair since I haven't had a chance to comb it.

"I asked you a question," she whines, folding her arms across her chest.

"In fact, you didn't. You made a stupid remark that isn't even correct. It's 'look what the cat dragged in.'" I blink at her while she scrunches her nose at me as if I'm wrong. "Listen, I don't know what you want, but I'm not in the mood." Sidestepping her, I groan under my breath.

Apparently, that gives her the opening she needs. She snatches my arm, her nails digging into flesh. I spin toward her, tugging my arm from her grip.

"Don't think I didn't hear you screaming like a slut in your hut last night, being fucked like the whore you are."

I rear my shoulders back, my mind thinking about how crazy Crius and Stone drove me, how they'd brought me to orgasm three times. Had I been so loud, others in the pack heard us? Shit.

With the way she's glaring at me, instead of embarrassment, anger climbs through me.

"It was an incredible night, one you'll never experience." I hate being bitchy, but Lyssa is pushing my buttons when I have zero patience.

"Ha," she bellows. "I know you're jealous of Ragnar and me, so you fucking his men makes you so desperate. He spent the whole party with me."

My response flew out of my mouth before I could stop myself.

"And he spent the night with me."

Her mouth drops open, and she slaps the right side of my face, dragging her claws across my cheek. The pain is sharp and stings like hell.

Instinct kicks in, and I sweep my arm up, knocking hers aside, then kick her knee, leaving a dirty footprint on her white jeans. Better yet, she loses her balance and tumbles into a mud puddle next to the path.

I touch my throbbing cheek and come back with spots of blood on my fingertips.

Goddammit.

I should laugh in her face, but I can't bring myself to do it. She looks pitiful enough as it is, and the fact I know why she's behaving like this makes it harder. Ragnar needs to tell her the truth because things are getting out of hand. And while he's at it, he can tell me what the hell is going on between us.

"You fucking cow," she snaps, pushing herself up off the ground, her white pants covered in mud. She sneers at me, her upper lip curling and a death stare behind her gaze. "I've actually been nice to you. Hell knows why."

I roll my eyes hard. She has no idea what 'nice' means.

"I haven't told you the secret Ragnar's keeping from you since I felt sorry for you, but after that move, you can forget it."

"I don't care what you have to say." I turn to leave, clenching my jaw.

"Ragnar was meant to kill your mother," she announces, and I can hear the smile in her voice at how much pleasure it gives her to tell me this.

I pause, trying to make sense of what she's saying, but a dozen or more questions pop into my mind, and a cold flare rushes down my arms. I turn around to face her once more, my stomach flips with unease as though it knows something bad is about to happen.

"What do you mean?"

I stand several feet from her where she's slouching on one leg, her hands deep in the pockets of her pants.

"Having the Alpha as my father, I hear a lot of things."

"And... what did you hear?"

She smiles, and I really hate this girl.

"Months ago, he told Father about meeting a hunter from Storm Wolves, who offered him a decent payment to hunt down an older female. She ran from her husband and three daughters, and their pack wanted her back at any cost. After you came to town, I started digging around about you. When I found out where you're from, I put two and two together. There aren't many families blessed enough to have three daughters. When I asked Ragnar, he didn't deny it."

My heart races at her words while my mind frantically tries to piece the past together with her reveal. At that stage, I doubt Ragnar knew my mother carried magic. Otherwise, the Alpha of Storm Wolves would have killed my sisters and me long ago. So, yeah, he might have been asked to do it.

"Why are you telling me? I know, for a fact, he didn't complete his mission."

She strolls toward me with a leering expression.

"Whether he actively hunted your mother down and perhaps never found her isn't really the issue now, is it? It's that he never told you about it, did he? So, how can you really trust him? What other secrets has he kept from you? Like, did you know he has plans to secure Savage Sector, then go save his sister, who was married off to another pack?"

I lift my chin, hating what she's implying.

"I don't have time for your stupid games, Lyssa." Turning on my heels, I march out of there, simmering at letting myself listen to her and that Ragnar didn't tell me. My breath catches as her words fill my ears.

"Relationships aren't based on selling your body, Narah. It's about trust and not hiding secrets."

"Fuck off," I growl and put more distance between us. I march out of the village, down the steps toward the entry gate, needing to be as far from her as possible.

If Lyssa put it together, surely Ragnar did, too, so he knew who my mother was when he met her in the Wolf Mountains. Same with his sister. I know it's not crucial to our mission, but I was a fool to think I meant enough to him, that he'd share important things about himself. I shouldn't care, but it weighs on me. Damn Lyssa, I'm letting her gaslight me. So what if Ragnar didn't tell me? They aren't exactly details that would have come up in our conversations, and Lyssa is only causing trouble.

Raised voices catch my attention from the gate farther to my right between the guards and someone on the other side of the closed gates. The man is wearing a wide-brimmed hat that sits lopsided on his head and a thick coat that hits mid-thigh, and it's done up to his throat. It's peculiar since the weather isn't cold enough to be so warmly dressed up.

"Ragnar," he says in slow motion and loudly. "I'm here to see him."

He's alone behind the gate, and I'm curious to see who he is.

One of the guards marches in my direction, not paying attention until he lifts his gaze and sees me.

"Oh, it's you," he says haughtily. "Have you seen Ragnar? Be a good girl and go collect him. He has a visitor," he orders me.

My skin crawls at the degrading way he speaks to me.

"I don't know where he is. I'm searching for him, too."

The guard huffs and curses under his breath before storming past me.

I find myself stepping toward the gate out of pure curiosity, along with Lyssa's words that linger on my mind about me not knowing Ragnar. Light footsteps take me closer when the man looks up in my direction.

Amber eyes—just like mine—look back at me.

My feet pause and seem to glue themselves to the ground while my whole body runs cold.

Daddy?

My pulse thunders in my temples.

Am I seeing things?

He's dead... he has to be dead.

I buried his body near the Storm Wolves compound. I cried for weeks. I sat by his grave, talking to him.

"Goodbye, Daddy," I whispered to the fresh grave, well aware that I would carry this moment with me for eternity. An ache in my heart that will never find closure when I doubt I can ever truly accept he's gone. Taken from us because our mom ran from the pack.

Kaira and Jae are kneeling beside me near his grave, crying softly, while Storm Wolves' members walk past us, not paying their respect. No one does, even though he had once ruled this pack as their Alpha. They go about their normal lives while I mourn how lost I feel in this world. How much I hate everyone, except my two sisters. They are all I have left.

Drawing them toward me, we hug as they whimper, their tears soaking my dress. I can't stop crying. Closing my eyes, the breeze stirs across my teary face as I hold my sisters close, unsure how I'm supposed to face another day without my dad.

I'm suffocating on the inside because this can't be real—it can't be—yet I force my legs to move and rush to the gate.

"Miss, do you know this man?" one of the guards asks.

I grasp the metal gate, staring into familiar eyes.

"Is it really you?" My voice chokes with tears.

"You look so sad, girl," he says, his expression unmoving, though it's hard to see since his hat shades half his face.

"Daddy, is that you?" I ask stubbornly, annoyed he's not reacting to seeing me. Has it been that long? "It's me, Narah." My words hang between us, and my mind races. The only undead are zombies, and he's behaving like one.

He blinks, then stares at me blankly. There's something odd about him; his skin a few shades too pale. Tears keep springing to my eyes the longer I stare at him in disbelief. Reaching out to touch him, to make sure I'm not imagining him, he pulls back from my touch.

"Is this man your father?" the guard asks, but I ignore him.

"Daddy, do you recognize me?"

He shakes his head. "Should I?"

I pull back, stumbling a few steps, my chest feeling as if it's being carved in half. It has to be a mistake. A man who looks identical to my father but is not him. All the broken parts inside me float to the surface—the agony, the loneliness, the heartache.

I'm a wreck, staring at this man who shows no emotion.

A horse's neigh from behind me startles me. I flinch and whip around to see Ragnar walking a large black horse toward the gate. He's dressed for travel in his leather jacket zipped to his throat and riding boots. Behind him are the other three men, each of them with a horse... one for each. It's clear as day, they had every intention of leaving the pack this morning.

Without me.

The other guard from the gate charges up alongside them. "That's him," he says, pointing to the gate. "He's asking for you." He glances at Ragnar, then walks back to his post.

"Narah, what are you doing here?" Ragnar studies me like I'm the last person he expects to find standing here as if I've caught him doing something he shouldn't.

I'm shaking from the overwhelming sensation that I'm about to discover something I don't want to hear. My breath speeds up, and I stare at Stone, Crius, and Nikos, and that same guilty look appears on their faces.

My heart pounds in my chest, and the thought crosses my mind that I made a terrible mistake letting Ragnar and his men become the center of my life. I try very hard not to think about him betraying me, but it's close to impossible.

Ragnar looks past my shoulder to the man I swear is my father. The man who's now calling out his name and confusing me.

"Just tell me, is that my father?" My voice shakes, and tears spill from my eyes. I'm barely holding it together.

"Yes, but it's complicated."

I don't hear anything else before I'm crying, completely wrecked. My world is spinning, and my chest squeezes with agony I never wanted to feel again—grief, mourning, and deception. With it, a sense of betrayal sinks through me that perhaps Lyssa was right.

I don't really know Ragnar.

THIRTEEN

NARAH

"Please, tell me, what's going on?" I plead with Ragnar in a choked voice as he takes me aside by my elbow, as far from the gate as possible. I look back to where Nikos is talking to my dad, Stone and Crius flanking his sides.

Why doesn't my dad recognize me? What's going on?

All I can think about is that I'd buried the wrong person back in Storm Wolves.

I turn back toward Ragnar, and my anger flares. I've had enough of dragging this out. Tugging my arm from his grip, I dig my heels into the supple soil.

"Enough, Ragnar. What the hell is going on? Why is my dead father here? Why doesn't he recognize me, yet he's asking for you?" Shaking and hugging myself, everything in my world feels broken beyond repair. "How long have you known that my dad is alive?"

Ragnar sighs, and there's darkness in his expression as though it pains him to respond.

"Just tell me, please. I can't live another moment not knowing."

"Oh, Narah. This is hard for me to say, but you need to know the truth." He reaches a hand out to me, but I brush him away, my shoulders rising as I'm torn in so many directions.

"Just fucking tell me already. And while you're at it, you can tell me why you thought it was your decision to keep such a secret from me. He's my father. Shouldn't I have known?" Ranting, my anger and frustration pour out of me. If my heart wasn't already broken from Dad's death and more recently, losing my mother, it is now. Seeing my father guts me into tiny pieces. I'm barely holding it together, and the tears refuse to stop falling.

Ragnar's brow furrows, his lips pinching. "I tried to protect you, Narah, but you're right. I should have been upfront."

"Yes, you should have." Despite looking into his eyes and seeing the pain behind them, I'm too angry to care about anything but the truth. No matter what it is, I can take it.

"Okay, Narah." He sounds downhearted. "After your kidnapping, we discovered what your mother has been doing to gain her power."

I blink at him. Ice fills my veins before he even speaks, suspecting what he'll say.

"She's been killing the local villagers in the Wolf Mountains, draining them of energy to feed her magic. Power she used to revert your father from his undead state to what you see out there." His chin points to the gates.

I mull over his words, but I'm numb. I didn't expect the part about my father.

"Sh-She brought him back?" Turning toward my father, he's talking to Stone, his arms almost animated. "She fed him magic, so maybe his memory will come back as he keeps healing, right? Then he'll remember me," I murmur under my breath, my chest squeezing so tight with the hope I'll have Dad back.

"Narah." Taking my hand, Ragnar forces me to face him and stares at me with pain. "She killed dozens of people. We found their bodies piled high in her basement. And your father is not back to normal. Unless he's fed a constant supply of energy drawn from other people, he'll revert to his zombie state. I don't know how many days he has left like this."

Silence hangs between us, and my head is spinning. Mom killed all those people to bring back my dad. "Why? She missed him?" I whisper to myself, barely able to manage words. I'm shaking, trying to process everything. *If she was lonely, why did she leave Jae, Kaira, and me at the mercy of the Storm Wolves?*

"I think she took him from his grave years ago and kept him in his undead form in the basement of her home. I found worn chains bolted to the walls under her house. Then she killed enough people in the village without drawing attention to herself. She fed her empowered blood to him, but he's missing a lot of memories, Narah. He doesn't recall you and your sisters."

He takes my arm; a good thing when my legs soften beneath me. He holds my weight until I find my footing, hating how much I struggle to breathe from the news. I feel like I've lost my father all over again.

"This is why I didn't say anything. Your mother intended to use your father to break into the witches' coven and rescue Kaira. His existence is temporary, but it seems while under the influence of the power, your father can command zombies."

"So, what?" I abruptly snap. "You thought you'd go without me to rescue my sister and be the hero?" I'm shaking with anger the more I learn. "Would you have even told me about my dad if I didn't bump into him out here?"

"It's not like that at all." His shoulders shoot back, but he's not furious, he just looks remorseful. "I don't want you hurt, especially with you not having your power."

"That wasn't your decision to make," I cry and pull free from him. "This whole time, you knew my father was alive and that my mother was a monster, yet you pretended like nothing happened."

"I'm sorry, Narah, but your mother *was* a monster. She killed so many innocent lives and cursed them not to return to life as the undead, but still took their lives away." He squeezes my arms slightly, almost a declaration of his feelings, except I'm not ready to hear his heartfelt apology.

I pull away from him, resigned he can't change his actions, but that doesn't mean I'm ready to forgive him. Not when my chest aches, grieving all over again for my father. So much time has passed since I lost him, and now he stands there as if all my pain was in vain. I hate my mother for bringing him back, and I hate Ragnar for hiding this from me, but most of all, I hate myself that I still mourn him after all this time. For a long time, I blamed Mom for Dad's death, and now, thanks to her, I get to experience it all over again.

"What do you want to do?" Ragnar asks from behind me, his words flat and broken. "Do you want to join us? Will that make you forgive me?"

"I will join the mission," I state adamantly, twisting my head toward him. "And while we're being honest with each other, you want to know why it's better nothing more happens between us?"

He doesn't respond but stares at me as if he's stopped breathing.

"I'm not too different from my mom. We are both sorceresses, and she told me how to use my power. My power comes from draining people, too. That's where my ability comes from, so as you can see, I'm a monster just like her. With my power, I will hurt people, but without it, I am useless to you."

I don't wait for his response but march across the lawn to the gate to reach Nikos' side, drawing him aside. I'm shaking so hard, I can't walk straight, but I use every inch of strength to hold myself together.

"I'm joining you to rescue my sister, but you need to give me a quick moment so I can tell Jae I'll be out for the day."

He looks at me heavily, wipes a tear sliding down my cheek, and glances up at Ragnar, somewhere behind me, then he gives a tight nod. "We'll wait."

Stone and Crius watch us, but I figure Nikos will fill them in, and I make a hasty retreat into the village. Frantically, I clean away the tears from my eyes, not wanting Jae to see that I've been crying. I just need to tell her I'll be gone for a day, maybe two, but in case something happens to us, I need to ensure the family she's staying with can look after her.

Blinking back fresh tears, I step up to the front door and knock.

You can do this, Narah. Just stop crying.

WE'RE ON HORSEBACK. Me on Stone's horse with him while Dad is on the back of Crius' horse. Their horse neighs and pauses now and then, well aware something unnatural is on his back. I don't blame the poor creature. Even Crius looks stiff and uncomfortable.

The village is behind us, and we're trotting along the dirt path, me bouncing behind Stone, but I hold on tight in order to not fall over.

I can't stop staring at my dad, who's alongside us. When he meets my gaze, he gives me a weak, awkward smile. We're strangers now, and I can't stop crying when all I want is to have him recognize me, hug me, and tell me how much he missed me. For too long, I cried for him, missing the easy way he laughed, the stories he told us, and the way he loved us.

I'd dreamed of this moment when he'd miraculously come back to us, but not like this... never like this where he stares right through me. It isn't fair to be left alone to carry all the memories, all the hurt, all the emotions for us both while looking into the face of the man who's left me broken and alone in this world.

My life has been a litany of disasters. Maybe I'm one of those people who is meant to always hurt. The old saying that time heals is a lie. It's nothing more than life distracting you from the pain. My crushed heart will never repair.

Ragnar is taking the lead of our charge. My emotions are so jumbled up over him and his men. There's no doubt about the attraction I feel toward them, that they are constantly on my mind. I crave their support and know Ragnar and his men are sorry, but there's been so much tension between us lately.

Is it the right decision to walk away once I have my sister? The thought only multiplies the heaviness in my chest. But can I be with someone who hides secrets from me?

I tuck myself against Stone, my cheek pressed to his back, and blink back the tears, needing to pull myself together. He strokes my hands looped around his middle as we move through the woods quickly, with no one speaking for a long while.

A sharp sound fills my ears, and I perk up to Dad whistling. We're in an open field with the edge of the woods at our rear, far from the village.

"What's going on?" I ask, then notice movement in the woods. A figure emerges from behind a lofty pine, stumbling forward, lurching. I shift my weight on the horse for a better look, and I'm staring at an undead. My stomach curdles.

Ragnar said Dad could command them, but it still fills me with dread, and I tighten my hold on Stone.

"Um, why is he calling the undead now?"

Once more, my thoughts are stolen when an ocean of zombies emerges from the woodland. I shudder and press myself against Stone, instinct screaming for me to run. Stone stiffens against me.

The undead creatures rush toward us in their lopsided, broken runs, some with arms outward as if they're rushing to their feed. Us! There has to be close to two hundred. Shit!

"Maybe we should get moving," I suggest.

Dad whistles at them once more.

"Fucking hell," Crius blurts. "Tell me you're not about to feed us to them?"

"Why would I do that?" Dad answers, straight-faced, genuinely confused by the question. "We need them to save Allie's daughter."

His words stab my heart. He really doesn't remember us.

"I have a shortcut to the witches' compound that will take us there faster," Dad explains. "We need to go now, and they'll run after us."

"Are you sure this will work?" Ragnar is his usual stiff and commanding leader, void of emotions, although when he glances at me, there's a dark pain in his eyes. We haven't exchanged a word since we left the village, and maybe that's for the best. There's too much going on right now to get into another argument.

I swallow hard and look away.

STONE

THE TENSION IS through the roof, and to add to the whole shit fight with Narah and Ragnar, we now have an army of undead chasing after us like wolves being delivered to their feed.

This wasn't our initial plan. Narah's dad, Gregory, was supposed to wait for us near the edge of the poisonous woods after he'd showed us the shortcut around the woods to reach the coven, hoping we entered the compound first and found Kaira. It'd been straightforward.

Then Gregory unleashed the zombies on the witches.

I pray to the moon goddess this new plan works.

Narah clings to me as we race across the open plains. Ragnar, Crius, and Narah's father take the lead to reach the witch's coven, a passage Allie had discovered after tracking the witches' movements. And to think, we spent so much time going through the thick of the poisonous woods the first time when we could have shaved off a full day in our travels if we had known this shortcut.

Entering an adjacent forest, which looks like a dead end with a huge rock face mountain in the distance blocking our path, I'll guess we'll find out soon enough. I'm dubious as fuck, but then again, I'm trapped with the zombies trailing behind us. Even though they've fallen a bit behind, they're still following. I'm not afraid to admit each time I look over my shoulder at the horde, my gut squeezes.

Too late to fucking worry about that shit when we're neck-deep in crap already.

We're going to battle, but not the kind I'm used to. For a change, we're not doing the killing.

I just hope Gregory is right about this, along with not snapping back into full zombie mode on us.

If I had any say in this, I'd call this a close suicide mission because if anything goes wrong, we're fucked. This is why I supported Ragnar that Narah shouldn't be with us right now. Narah is stubborn and tenacious, and after the argument between her and Ragnar near the gate, there was nothing that would stop her from joining us to collect her sister.

She holds onto me tightly, her gorgeous tits rubbing up and down my back with every bump, and I love having her this close. Even with the two breaks we took to rest our horses and let the undead catch up with us, she stayed mostly on her own.

Gregory leads us toward a wall of overgrown bushes, which he tramples with his horse to reveal a tight passage between the rock mountain and forest. Well, I wasn't expecting that. Once we emerge, we travel for another few hours through heavy woodland with a thick canopy overhead. So far, there's no bite of magic over my skin either.

Finally, Crius stops near a thicket of pines, and Narah's father climbs off the horse. His body is twitching, reminding me of his crazed state when he was tearing apart the kitchen. Without more magical blood, how long does he have before turning into one of them, and we're left with an onslaught of the undead.

I tense at our situation, more so because Narah's with us.

With the sun descending, flooding the woods with shadows, our presence is easily concealed, so there's that.

Narah slides off my horse, and I turn to take her hand, helping her. "You'll feel a bit sore from the long ride."

She half-smiles as she stumbles a bit to catch her footing. Ragnar caught us up on their conversation about where Narah's power really comes from. In truth, all magic comes from somewhere. It doesn't manifest out of pure air.

I draw mine from the elements around me, from nature. Narah will find a way to work with what she's given once she learns to gain back her power, which I doubt she's lost. It's inside her; she just needs to bring it out. Her mother's spell suppressed our power, and it's not as if she's around to ask how to fix it.

I hop down from my horse and stretch my back, my bones cracking. "That feels amazing."

Nikos is at my side. "I'll take your horse. We're releasing them a bit further away. Let's hope they don't go too far."

"Thanks." I pivot toward Narah, who's rubbing her thighs, which would be sore. "Hey, listen," I begin. "I know things are complicated right now, and they suck, but there's no rush to decide on anything. I'll always be by your side."

Her breaths deepen as she turns her head to take in everyone moving toward Ragnar.

"That means a lot. I just have a few things to work through." Her eyes are still red and puffy.

I wish I could put her up in a tree to wait out this mission. Instead, I say, "Stay close by my side. If things go to shit, I'll protect you, but you need to listen to me. Understood?"

She nods without hesitation. Narah's no fool and understands the danger we're all in.

Wrapping my arm around her back, I draw her to my side, the

urgency to tuck her away safely hitting me like a torrent, consuming me.

In silence, we join the rest of the group.

"From here, we're on foot. Woods are too dense for horses to pass," Ragnar fills us in. His chin lifts to the passage between two bowed trees, revealing a tight dirt track in the woods that I assume was often traveled by the witches.

Over my shoulder, the first wave of encroaching undead shifts through the woods like shadows. Dread zips up my spine, and I hold Narah tighter against my side.

"Once the undead arrive, there will be no stopping them," Narah's dad says. "Stick close to me, and they won't touch you. Plan is to have them barge into the coven. Then we find Allie's daughter. Once the undead begin feasting, their frenzy will be impossible for me to control, so we must leave."

"That instills me with no confidence," Crius groans.

"I'm not sure I like this plan," Narah mutters, concern on her face, and I agree. "We're putting Kaira in danger. There has to be another way."

"We stick to the original plan," Ragnar states. "A few of us sneak into the compound to find Kaira, and once we give the signal, Gregory will unleash the undead on the witches." He stares up at Gregory. "Can you hold them back for that?"

"I can try," he admits, more uncertain than he sounded at Allie's house.

"Not try," Ragnar demands. "You must."

Silence falls between us until Gregory gives a noncommittal nod.

Fuck, this is going to go bad, isn't it?

"I'll take the lead with Nikos. Crius, you're in the rear with Gregory. Stone and Narah, in the middle. No talking. Let's go."

I nod and look down at Narah, whose face has paled.

"You okay?" I whisper.

"Yep. I'm ready to save my sister." Her voice is shaky, and it's clear she's terrified.

Her bravery impresses me, but I won't let anything touch her. I'll fight every single fucking zombie to protect her. Looking behind us into the darkening woods with so many shadows now moving, that anxiety rapidly climbs through me.

"Um, can we hurry, please?" I'm not ready to get close and personal with zombies.

We fall into formation and speed forward. Each time I look behind us, the shadows of undead are closing in on us. Echoes of their gurgling sounds and their rapid footsteps have me rushing, instinct pressing me to run. I keep Narah in front of me. Sensing movement to my far left, I twist my head to see the first zombie scrambling over the overgrowth, making a shortcut right for us.

"Fuck," Nikos bellows.

"Gregory," I snarl, but the man is already pushing to stand in front of us, whistling, which doesn't stop them. The undead teeter on the spot, snapping their jaws, appearing to fight the instinct to rip into us. More appear behind him, and I don't care what Gregory says. I don't trust that he can keep us safe.

"Change of plan," Gregory announces, his body shuddering once more, his voice crackling. "They're a lot harder to control than I initially thought. Run. We need to get them into the coven before they turn on us."

"Are you fucking with us?" Nikos growls.

"Run," Ragnar snaps, shoving us all to hurry ahead of him.

I grab Narah's hand, and we run. A tremor races down my back, then shudders in my belly and my chest that we let ourselves get into this fucked up position. We must be the dumbest people in the world to have listened to Gregory.

Up ahead, there's no sign of an entry to the coven, and panic strangles me. I search the trees as we sprint past for any low-hanging branches I can throw Narah onto.

Fuck.

FOURTEEN

NIKOS

Nobody listens to me!

My gut instinct was off the charts the moment we found Gregory in Allie's home, then add in the dead bodies, and my alarm bells rang like sirens. I should have made Ragnar listen to me, should have forced the point. Making a deal with zombies is asking for our death.

Case in point—we're running for our lives from the undead and rushing toward another enemy, the witches.

Just fucking great!

I stick to the rear with Ragnar to fend off any of the fuckers if they get too close while Crius and Gregory take charge. Stone protects our most precious cargo—Narah. After her confrontation with Ragnar at the gates, things blew up, and now we're all feeling the aftereffects, the growing tension between them. Where does that leave the rest of us? Up shit's creek, that's where.

Pounding the earth with fast steps, the shadowy cloud of undead draws closer. They're on our heels, their chattering teeth, their groans right on the back of my neck. My skin crawls, and I'm running on pure adrenaline. I sure as fuck won't get eaten alive by these creatures.

"This way," Crius calls out, waving at us to take a sharp turn up ahead.

I lift my head to him, and I'm right there, scrambling forward. The path brings us to an arched passage between two bent trees to an open field. The woods are so closely packed together, they're impenetrable. I throw myself through the arch right behind Narah and Stone.

Crius grabs my arms and hauls to my right. Stone does the same with Ragnar, and we're all tucked in behind Gregory, who whistles at the undead charging into the field toward four-foot walls made of twisted branches that span left and right as far as the eye can see. Beyond the wall lays the coven.

"We need to get in there and save Kaira." Narah's frantic voice sets off my panic. If I wasn't already tense as hell, now I'm about to burst.

"Gregory." Ragnar nudges his shoulder. "*We* need to get in there now before the zombies kill everyone. Move."

The man nods, but I don't miss how much he's twitching, how one of his eyes blinks twice as slow as the other. How much time do we have before he turns on us and loses control of the undead?

We're on the run once more, alongside the lurching zombies. There's nothing like being scared shitless that there are actually undead standing feet from us. Clothes hanging off their emaciated bodies, bones visible through gashes and wounds, missing limbs, empty eye sockets, their groans climb with their hunger.

They'll announce their arrival to the witches, but with how fast they're moving, the attack will still be a complete surprise to them.

The more I look at them, the more I wonder what we're unleashing on this coven.

Are we any better than Allie?

She had kept Gregory alive a lot longer than the witches had Kaira. Considering Gregory knew exactly where we had to go to find the witches and what to do, I'd say Allie had plans to take out the witches on her own. For all I know, she could have had plans to take over the wolf packs as well. I'll never admit this to Narah, but perhaps her mother's death wasn't such a tragedy.

"This way," Gregory barks, steering us to the right while the undead move forward like a raging river, slamming right into the wooden barricade. The few who first hit the walls are attacked with bolts of blue electricity that spark outward, striking their bodies, magic meant to kill anyone who touches the wall.

Falling over, the undead get up just as quickly, but the more they ram against the wall, the more the structure creaks and bows forward. They pile on top of each other, building a mountain for others to climb over.

My gut twists in on itself at how relentless these assholes are.

Slipping farther to the right, just out of sight of the creatures, I survey the surrounding perimeter. All clear.

"We get in there from here," Gregory commands and slaps his hand against the wall.

I expect him to get zapped, but nothing happens.

"The zombies have tripped the spell, and while the witches deal with them, we hurry inside."

Taking Narah's arm, her eyes are huge, and the poor thing's shaking.

"I'll help you over." I squeeze her hand slightly.

"Thank you," she answers softly, looking completely lost.

Stone and Ragnar are already scaling the structure, using the intertwined branches as hand and footholds. Crius shoves Gregory up the wall; the man isn't exactly steady on his feet right now.

"One of the other guys will catch you on the other side," I instruct Narah. "Don't take off until we're all over. Understand?"

"Okay."

Grabbing her waist, I lift her and place her on my shoulders, her legs straddling the back of my neck. What I wouldn't give to be in this exact position but face first in her sweet pussy—life goals. I fight harder to make sure we all survive to achieve them.

"Stand on my shoulders, gorgeous." Stepping up to the wall, I press myself face-first to the structure. "Pull yourself up and over." Next to me, Crius has his hands on Gregory's ass, shoving him up. I might have laughed if I wasn't high on adrenaline and panicked at how vulnerable we are.

Holding onto Narah's legs so she doesn't fall over, she awkwardly gets up, then steps off me and scales the rest of the way to where Ragnar's half dangling over the wall. He hauls her up and over. I exchange glances with Crius, who dusts his shirt, then tosses his plaited dreadlocks out of his face and scowls at me.

"Nice that you got pussy smashed up against the back of your head while I had smelly zombie ass in my face."

I half-chuckle. "Says the guy who got pussy last night while I was stuck talking strategy with that old fart. You won this round, my friend."

"Race you over," he suggests, and I pounce on the chance, scaling the wall like a spider, not shy of whacking Crius in the face with my foot. Growling, he throws himself into me, and we tumble over the top and inside the compound, with him crashing against me.

"Fuck!" I groan, having landed on my back. "Get your fat ass off me."

Crius grins, knowing he won that round and offers me his hand. Taking it, I'm on my feet in seconds and dusting my pants, only to see we're alone.

"Where the fuck are they?" I ask.

"Looks like we're on our own. Let's go witch-hunting."

NARAH

CHAOS.

That's the only way to describe the situation.

Undead rush madly through the coven's land, the witches' screams are terrifying, and the heavy stench of magic fills the air, its power biting into my skin. Death against magic. That's what's happening, and we still haven't found Kaira as we dart into the third cottage.

Ragnar and Stone go first to knock anyone out while Dad keeps the zombies away. I'm next to him and keep glancing up at him with a stupid urge to just hug him. It's absurd, especially now, of all places, but my eyes tear up each time he looks at me. I don't need that kind of distraction.

A scream catches my attention from the open lawn in front of the cottage we're in.

Frozen in horror, I watch as a group of zombies plow into two older women who are casting a spell, then swallow them in their feeding frenzy. I knew what would happen, but seeing it leaves me tortured.

I don't know who is good and who is bad. Or are there any good witches in this coven? According to Mom, they all wanted us dead. How can I defend that when I'd seen firsthand how much they wanted my sisters and me dead?

Needing to find Kaira, I whip around to see Stone is cleaning his bloody knuckles on the curtains, and Ragnar is about to punch the life out of a man who's on his knees. There are two other men already on the floor, unconscious.

"Stop," I call out, impatient to find my sister. "Not yet."

"I told you to stay outside," Ragnar roars.

After a gasping exhale, I hurry to the man Ragnar is holding by the throat, and Stone has his hands pinned at his back.

"Kaira," I mutter. "The new witch the High Priestess took in recently. Where is she?"

His blue eyes are huge, knowing if he makes one move, Ragnar will finish him.

"The main hut at the end of homes with a pointy roof." His eyes shift to his left to indicate the direction.

I pull back. "Thank you."

Ragnar smashes his fist into the man's face, sending him sprawling onto his back, but I'm already sprinting out of the house.

Ragnar has Dad, and Stone follows me. Sprinting past the zombies and homes, we see witches fleeing their homes while others are chased down by the undead. We run down the path that runs between the two rows of huts. Dad's whistle carves a path for us amid the sheer number of zombies everywhere.

Ahead, a dark, wooden home with a pointy roof comes into view. I move faster, although it feels as though I'm moving in slow motion.

Kaira, please be there. Please.

There's no delay. Stone goes first, plowing the door open with his shoulder. The wood splits open, and we're inside a large room with a table and cushions on the floor. The scent of burning herbs fills the air, but there's no one there, so Stone charges into the back room.

"Where's the High Priestess?"

"Here," Stone bellows, and we're running, my heart in my throat.

Shoving into the right room, I wrench my gaze over to the large cage.

It's not the High Priestess we find.

It's Kaira.

She's inside the cage, huddled, hugging her knees, not looking at us.

A choked breath escapes my throat as I throw myself onto my knees by the cage.

"Kaira." Tugging at the metal, I find a lock on the large door. "We'll get you out, I promise." I yank at the locked door again, my pulse beating in my ears while I want to scream. The bitch has been keeping my sister caged up like an animal.

She looks up at me, her eyes cloudy but doesn't react. It's as though something has been switched off inside of her, and she's just waiting to be reactivated.

Seeing her this way, a sharp ache slices through my heart.

"Stand back," Stone demands.

I retreat quickly as he slams a rock into the lock. Three strikes later, the padlock breaks away, and I frantically rip the door open and drag my sister out. Stone picks her up, cradling her in his arms. She slumps as though she has no ability to stand on her own.

"Kaira." I cup her face, forcing her to look at me, to remember me.

All I see is emptiness when I look into her eyes.

"What's wrong with her?" Stone asks.

"I think the Priestess has been treating her like a puppet."

"Here, give her this to drink," Ragnar announces, producing a vial filled with something red from his pocket. "According to your mother, it's a curse eraser. She intended to use it when she ambushed the witches with your dad's help."

I blink at the small vial Ragnar hands me. The last time Mom healed us, we died, and I lost my powers.

"Is it safe?" I whisper, while outside, a new onslaught of screams ring in the air.

"What choice do we have?" Ragnar says with urgency. "She takes it now, and the Priestess can't awaken her if she finds us, or she doesn't, and we pray we don't cross paths with the Priestess as we escape."

My stomach hurts, and my head spins. I don't want Kaira harmed, but I also can't have her reawaken to use her powers against us. Seconds feel like hours as I feel the men's eyes on me, their expectations for me to decide. Pulling the cork out of the vial, I lean against my sister.

"Kaira, I need you to drink this for me. Alright?" I place the lip of the vial to her mouth while Ragnar holds her jawline and opens her mouth. What looks like blood slurps into her mouth. It smells rotten, but Kaira swallows it, showing no reaction to the taste, then suddenly, she's convulsing in Stone's arms.

My stomach drops, and I cry out, "Kaira, no, please, no." I grip her arms as her eyes roll back into her head, then she goes completely slack in Stone's arms. "Please, please, Kaira. Don't you dare do this to me."

FIFTEEN

CRIUS

"Fifteen zombies," Nikos states, sticking his chest out like a rooster, standing on the roof of a hut across from the one I'm on.

"Get over yourself. I'm already at twenty-one."

"Fuck off, you are not."

I glance down at the trail of dead zombies in my wake. The animated ones are pawing at the walls of our huts but have no idea how to climb up here on their own. Suckers.

Many of the witches have run. They're not even bothering to cast magic in their fight to save their family because one wrong move and you're eaten. I'd do the same if two hundred undead were unleashed on me.

Nikos and I are on our own without Gregory nearby, and the zombies turn on us, so we change tactics and hunt them as we search for our crew.

"I barely see twelve," he chimes.

"Keep telling yourself that. Anyway, can you see the others from up here?" It's getting on my nerves that we haven't found them yet.

Nikos doesn't respond. He's glancing out in the distance at a dark house with a pointy roof... something the rest of the huts don't have.

"Does that look like Gregory?" He points up ahead to someone who could be him in an argument with who I swear is the High Priestess. My hackles rise, remembering our last encounter when the bitch put a curse on us.

Gregory's sudden cry catches on the wind.

"We need to get to him now." I back up a few steps, then run and hurl myself over to Nikos' roof. Landing, the wooden planks groan under my weight. I nudge Nikos. "If you had your powers, you could call to the elements and give us an upperhand to finish this quickly."

"You think it's not on my mind, too?" Nikos had told us not only Narah's power was gone, but his as well. In fact, the small touch of power I have—nothing even close to what Nikos or Narah have, but something specific which can only be done once—is useless now. I feel nothing within me, no spark of magic. We've been wiped clean by Narah's mother.

"It fucking sucks balls," I growl. "And why we're having to do this old school—fists and steel."

Nikos nods and looks down at all the undead next to his hut.

"See those three huts in front of us," I say. "We're going to jump across them, then run for our lives to Gregory. You ready?"

With a grin, he whips around and sprints to the edge. Propelling himself over in a great leap, he sticks a perfect landing. Asshole.

I chase after him, and we don't pause, needing to put distance between us and the horde. Slamming down on the lawn in front of the last hut, we bolt across the open area toward Gregory. The chattering teeth of the creatures chasing us grow in volume, and there's movement all around us. My gut tightens at the sight.

A spark of magic erupts from the High Priestess, striking Gregory in the chest, and white light curls around his chest like a lasso.

Panic strangles me. Nikos growls, knowing exactly how much shit we're in if Gregory dies.

We come up behind them fast, and I'm close enough now to see the scratches and even bite marks on the priestess's neck and arms. She's been fighting zombies and will become one soon. I don't even want to find out what a powerful High Priestess zombie would be capable of.

Seizing the blade from my belt, I give Nikos a knowing look. He's gripping a knife in his hand as well.

Time to spill blood.

With newfound adrenaline, I throw myself behind the witch, who's wobbling on her feet as Gregory drops to his knees. I can only see the whites of his eyes now.

Hell.

He's almost gone from us, and we have undead on our heels. Their moans escalate, and their pounding footsteps pummel the earth. Fuck me.

I launch myself at the priestess, exhausted of this shit, Nikos right at my side. Slamming into her back, one hand crashes down on her shoulder to hold her while the other drives my blade into her back, thrusting hard to pierce her black heart.

She shrieks, half-twisting, half-arching in my grip, and the zap of her power strikes my shoulder. I bellow from the burning sting that digs down to my bone as if I'd been struck by lightning. Tossed backward, I hit the ground with a groan.

At that same moment, Nikos jumps on the Priestess' back and in one swift move, slices his blade across her throat. Blood spurts over Gregory's face, and the white lines of magic around the man disappear in a crackling snap.

The High Priestess drops to her knees, then falls to her face, and her body self-combusts. One minute she's there, the next she bursts into a puff of dust that swarms the others who stand on the porch.

"Whoa, what the fuck!" Scrambling to my feet, I hold my shoulder, still stinging from her magic.

Narah and Ragnar dart out of the hunt, followed by Stone carrying someone in his arms. We all witness something that makes no sense.

The dead witch cloud of ash floats directly for them, and they bat it away.

"How the fuck did that just happen?" I mutter, then notice Nikos' by Gregory's side, holding him upright.

All around us, zombies are standing and watching, almost in a frozen state.

"What are they doing?" Ragnar asks, his voice shaken, and I can't blame him.

Not much scares me, but I'd just seen a witch turn into dust before my eyes, and now this...

My attention swings to Narah, who runs to her father, kneeling near him and grabbing his arm. I can't hear what she's saying, but she's crying. My chest tightens at the sight, yet the faint groan of the monsters who've suddenly paused is scaring the hell out of me.

How much longer before they attack us?

Ragnar moves to them while I join Stone, who's carrying Kaira. They found her. Perfect.

"We need to leave like yesterday," I grumble under my breath.

The creatures in front of us only all have eyes for Gregory as if they're somehow stuck.

"The moment he turns, we're all fucked," Stone mumbles.

Not waiting another second, I hurry to Ragnar's side and lean in, whispering, "We gotta go now. Gregory's gonna change any second now."

He cuts me a look filled with dread and nods. "You, Nikos, and Stone head back the way we came. See if you can find our horses. We'll be right behind you."

Narah's crying, grasping onto her dad's arm, but he's shuddering. My heart breaks that she has to say goodbye to her father for a second time. That shit destroys a person. I want to be the person who picks her up and reminds her she is loved... Fuck did I just say the L-word?

"Go," Ragnar growls, and I back away, Nikos joining Stone and me.

We carve our way through the mass of zombies, every hair on my body on end.

"This is fucking freaky as hell, man," I mutter.

"Go faster," Stone says, moving so quickly, Kaira bounces in his arms.

Glancing back quickly, Ragnar is lifting Narah into his arms as she reaches for her father. Her cries pierce the air, and my insides shred at the tragic agony she's going through. Ragnar sprints toward us with her clutched tightly in his arms.

Her dad is lying on the ground, still shuddering.

Time is against us. Nikos and I spring ahead faster, and it isn't long before we burst out of the coven into the woods we'd used to get here.

By some miracle, our horses are in the distance, eating grass in an open patch of land beneath the sun. Surveying the land, I notice a group of figures deeper in the woods, rushing away from our direction. Witches.

Thank fuck. Considering they lost so much today, we are the last thing they care about right now. Maybe later, they'll seek revenge, but not today.

By the time we get the horses reined, I heave for breath. Without a word, Nikos and I get everyone loaded, tying Kaira to Stone's back so she doesn't slide off the horse, then we're off.

My heart's galloping, and I haven't been happier to leave a place. We ride in silence until the woods are a blip behind us. Still, no one stops.

A nagging sensation is prodding my mind, telling me it was too easy. That there is no way, the High Priestess would go down that fast. I keep picturing her self-combusting into dust. Is that a thing witches do when they die? Doesn't seem like it to me.

I want to celebrate her death, yet instinct screams something is very off. The more I think about how she died, the more I'm convinced it's not the last time we'll see her.

SIXTEEN

NARAH

I sit quietly beside Kaira's bed. She's groggy as the pack healer, Flora, tries to get her to drink an herbal concoction. Even though it smells like soil and grass and resembles dirty water, Kaira gulps it down.

Flora is curvy, has red curls, and smiles a lot. The moment she walked into the hut with a huge smile, I felt certain she'd heal my sister. Some people just have peaceful natures, and this woman is the epitome of calm. I already like her.

Sitting on the second bed, only a foot away from Kaira's, Jae's curled up against me, hugging a pillow and watching everything. She burst out crying the moment she saw Kaira and hasn't left her side since. Neither of us has. I've been crying from sheer happiness to have her back. We've all been through so much.

"A couple of days of bed rest, then I'll come back to check on you," Flora says to Kaira, who nods. "You're just exhausted and malnourished, which means eating lots of food to gain your strength back. You need to put some meat on your bones, dear."

"Thank you," I say to the healer while Kaira weakly smiles. I walk her out of the hut, where I whisper to her, "So, she'll be back to normal in no time? You didn't sense anything else strange about her?"

"No, she's just tired." Flora's smile is beautiful and reassuring.

"Nothing else out of the ordinary. If anything changes, let me know. She's on the mend. All she needs now is nourishment and lots of love."

"That I can do." Giving my thanks, I shut the door and turn back to my sisters. Jae has crawled into bed with Kaira, and they're chatting softly.

Seeing them together, images of the past flash through my mind, reminding me of a simpler time when ignorance had indeed been bliss. Where just being home with my sisters was all I ever wanted.

So much has changed since then, but for tonight, I let myself focus on my sisters.

I hurry to them and sit on the edge of the bed, staring at my sisters and smiling. I've wiped away the dark marks on her brow from the High Priestess, but there are still small smudges around her eyebrows. When she's better, I'll run her a bath.

"How are you feeling?" I ask, brushing a strand of hair stuck to her clammy forehead.

"Like I just ate grass." She smacks her mouth and licks her teeth. "That stuff was nasty."

Holding on to Kaira's arm for dear life, Jae giggles and stares at her sister as though she can't bear to look away in case she vanishes. My heart melts seeing my sisters so close.

"It smelled pretty bad," I say, my heart beaming at how normal she appears. Gone is the crazy in her eyes, and I don't sense any magic around her. "Want me to bring you some food? Hot tea? Anything?"

"Everything I need is right here." Her hand clasps mine, and she shakes her head. "I just want to be with you two. Just stay with me. When I was under the spell, it felt like I was trapped inside myself, and no matter how much I screamed, no one heard me. So, I thought about you two and all the adventures we'd been through to keep me from losing my mind."

I snort, and Jae laughs. "I'm not sure I'd call living with the Storm Wolves an adventure."

"Well, there was that one time you caught and released the rabbit in our house, and it took us half a day to catch him," Jae reminds me. "Then we found him chewing on your underwear."

"Ah, yes, I forgot about that." Like so many other things recently,

I've been too preoccupied with surviving and saving my sisters. A thread of sorrow flares through me at how easily I forgot how to enjoy the small things while I've been on the go for months. With Kaira back, maybe that can finally change.

Kaira just smiles as Jae talks her ear off. She looks pale, with dark shadows under her eyes. My chest tightens each time I picture her trapped in that cage. I wish more than anything I had my power to make the High Priestess suffer for what she's done to my sisters and me.

I should take solace that she's dead, and we never have to deal with her again. I try not to worry about the way she died. I've heard of powerful witches dying in mysterious ways, which has everything to do with how much magic they draw within themselves. Lyra seemed like a power-starved priestess.

She's gone. That's all I care about.

Sidling closer to Kaira, I join their conversation. I never want this moment to end.

Having my sisters back makes it bearable that I lost my father a second time. I've decided not to tell my sisters about him coming back to life. There's nothing from that ordeal that will benefit them but might scar them for life. This world has ruined us enough, and if I can spare them some of the horrors, I'll do it.

Just as Ragnar has attempted to do for me.

RAGNAR

"The witch isn't dead," Crius chimes in, then gulps down several mouthfuls of beer. "We all saw it. People don't explode into dust, no matter who they are."

"There was that one time back home when the witch turned someone into dust," Stone mutters. "So it's not implausible."

Crius' mouth pinches to the side. "We're talking about death, bruh, not a fucking spell. I mean, you, Ragnar, and Nikos got a whiff. What do you think? Did you feel anything magical at the time?"

"I was too busy trying not to choke on it," Nikos croaks. "It was nothing but ash."

"Didn't feel like magic," Stone says. Reaching for the sliced meats and cheese from the platter of food on our table, he builds himself a small tower before stuffing it in his mouth.

I shake my head. "The priestess is gone, but let's keep a close eye on each other and the girls in case something feels wrong."

Crius shrugs. "It feels wrong already. Think about it. Those of us who had magic ability lost it, thanks to Allie. That could be why we're not sensing anything."

"More reason to be careful," I state and help myself to bread smeared in butter and honey. "Anyway, tonight's about celebrating that the wicked witch is dead, and we saved Kaira. Tomorrow, I'll start putting into place actions with the Alpha Mihai to claim nearby territories and packs. We have to move fast before Martell discovers he's lost his connection with the witches."

"And before the witches gather to retaliate," Nikos murmurs.

"Valid point," I answer. "Tonight, let's get drunk and be merry. This is a tremendous win for us."

"Narah should be with us," Stone says, his mouth downturned.

Her absence chokes through me as well.

"Agreed, but her sisters need her tonight. More reason for us to have another celebration." I raise my jug of beer, and the men all do the same. "Skál," we say simultaneously and cheer before gulping down our beers.

"More," Nikos bellows, calling over the barman.

The men break out into a conversation, mostly about Crius declaring he killed the largest number of undead at the coven. His competitiveness is admirable, though I've noticed a change in him over the past few weeks. Starting this mission, his jokes were spiteful and dark, and he constantly spoke to me about when he could finally carry out his magic, an ability he could do only once and would result in him dying. That's how his power worked. He drew extraordinary magic from the earth, but in exchange, he had to pay with his life.

Crius had been in a dark place for a long time after the tragedy with his brother. It wasn't his fucking fault but his parents'. He wouldn't listen to reason and, for a long time, sought his own end. So,

I promised him coming on this mission with me would be an end fit for a warrior to enter Valhalla. My intention had been to get him to change his mind and never let him go through with it. For the first time, I'm seeing that hopeful change in him.

Narah is responsible. I've seen changes in all of us since she joined us. She's made us better men. To know she's impacted someone as broken as Crius to where, for weeks, he hasn't asked about finishing himself off is an enormous step.

We've all become entangled, and my heartache of sharing Narah is a burden I'll need to overcome because I can't break Narah's heart, my men's, or my own.

NARAH

Two nights later, Kaira is almost back to her normal self, though she becomes exhausted and short of breath if she does too much, so she's homebound. Jae convinced me that she and Kaira should spend tonight at her friend's home, and when I spoke with the girl's mother, she was more than happy to have them.

That leaves me with a night off, and for once, I don't feel as if my life is hanging in the balance. Well, if I ignore my pining wolf, who has been relentlessly whining for him the last few days.

Sitting near the window in the tavern with Ragnar, red streaks the sky as the sun sets. We're alone, but the others are joining us after running a few errands. Ragnar sinks deeper in his seat, watching me across the long table with an unusual, mischievous expression.

"What's that look for?" I ask, taking a sip of my fruity, red wine.

"You're beautiful." Gone is his dark, broody, serious expression. Now, there's softness in his eyes, blue as the sky after a spring shower.

"Well, you've been too busy to see me the last couple of days, so you might as well enjoy what you've missed." I poke my tongue out at him.

He laughs, throwing his head back, and I completely adore the sounds he makes. My whole body responds—nipples tightening, knees weakening, and my thighs pressing together to heighten the tingle deep in my core.

Of course, my wolf stirs and makes me uncomfortable as she shifts within me, protesting my attraction to Ragnar. Only one wolf exists for her—Martell's. I wished I would have eliminated my ex-fated mate and got him out of my system once and for all.

Leaning on the table, Ragnar places his strong arms crossed on the table in front of him, distracting me. He oozes masculine sexiness, and my pulse quickens every time I look at him.

"A lot has happened since we were alone and really talked, and we didn't exactly leave on the best terms."

"So, now you want to talk about it?" I meet his eyes, determination bubbling through me not to be upset with whichever way the conversation goes. For a change, things have gone well for me, and I need to hold on to those high spirits. I've suffered and grieved enough.

"Yes," he answers, sitting there with the hard line of his jaw and his captivating smile.

"Okay, what do you want to talk about?" I'm already listing things in my mind, but I want him to steer this conversation.

"I never should have held back information about your father and what we discovered about your mother. You were right. It wasn't my place, though I only wanted to protect you, Narah." He reaches across the table and takes my hand, his thumb stroking in small circles. "I'm sorry you had to go through the grief of seeing him in that state. I wanted to keep you safe from that."

My heart eases as his sincere and heartfelt words calm the ache from my loss. My fingers curl around his hand, holding on to him, and my chest tightens as he stares at me. Fuck. It's overwhelming and warming that he apologized. Lately, we've clashed, and I worry things won't work out between us. The thought devastates me.

"That's not on you. It was a decision my mother made. Goddess knows why she did, but I'm not angry with you about it anymore." I bite my lower lip, and my thoughts spill out. "Maybe I overreacted. I mean, I don't want to tell my sisters about my father coming back or what my mother was doing. I want to protect them and understand why you held back that information from me. I kind of lost my mind when I saw my dad."

His hand squeezes mine. "It doesn't ease the pain, but you're not alone."

"Thank you," I murmur softly. "I'm almost embarrassed at how quickly I snapped." My cheeks warm up.

"I just need you to understand that I would never harm you. I would burn down the world to keep you by my side, Narah," he says without hesitation. "You need to learn to trust me."

"I will. Right now, even from across the table, you're too far away."

With the most delicious grin, he stands and moves to sit on the bench next to me. My heart constricts, having him so close, our sides touching. His hand sweeps across my back, holding me near. I love being in his arms, keeping me warm and safe.

"I don't want to argue with you again," he said, rubbing my back. "It fucks up with my head too much." Leaning in, he buries his face in the side of my neck. He licks my ear, then whispers, "And it's been really difficult. I've been dying to fuck you."

My underwear are wet almost instantly. I try to speak, but a moan spills from my lips instead.

He pulls me impossibly close to him. "Now, where were we?"

Every part of my body is heightened, and I fight hard not to climb him like a tree as he strokes my hip. My wolf, who's mad at me, growls in my ear and makes for an interesting experience.

"I need things from you, too," I say when I find my voice. Around him, I have no control of my body. Maybe what I need is a huge distraction like Ragnar to ignore my wolf.

"I know you want me. I'm turning you on right now... I can smell your arousal." He takes my other hand and places it on the growing bulge in his pants. "I need to fuck you."

"Now?" I gasp in shock, yet I'm startled at how easily I keep my hand over his cock and give him a slight squeeze, making him hiss with desire.

He laughs, sounding so confident, while I'm drowning in how much I crave him but also want to confirm where we stand.

"And what about your men?" I slip my hand from his cock, well aware anyone in the room can see us.

"I have no desire to fuck them… only you."

I try to turn to face him, but he holds on to me tightly.

"What about *me* fucking your men?" Holding my breath with anticipation, I wait for his response.

He licks his lips, and there's a hard shiver in his voice when he speaks.

"I have trust issues, Narah." He pauses. "After my fated mate rejected me, I've never felt anything for another woman. She left me for another man, and that shit has fucked with my brain for a long time. So, when I saw you with my men, I tried really hard to accept it, but I fell for you too hard and fast and couldn't cope with having you in their arms and not mine."

I study his hard face, and my breathing accelerates hearing the ache in his voice.

"I'm not your fated mate or theirs, but it doesn't mean I can't be drawn to all four of you." My heart's hammering in my chest, wishing the universe had fated me with Ragnar, not Martell.

"Yeah, I know, but jealousy is a dangerous poison once it hits your bloodstream. After I marked you with my bite, my wolf deemed you ours."

"So, how do I help you?" I swallow the lump in my throat, glancing up at him just as my wolf lifts her head within me, unleashing her pining for Martell. I grind my teeth, needing that asshole dead and out of my wolf's head.

Ragnar says nothing right away, leaving me uncertain. Maybe he's coming to terms that I'll work through this with him.

Looking over my shoulder, he smiles at someone, and I twist around to see Nikos walking inside to join us.

"I have an idea of how you can help me," he whispers in my ear as Nikos approaches us. Suddenly, I have a feeling that his plan is going to take Nikos and me by surprise.

SEVENTEEN

NARAH

"I want Nikos to fuck you," Ragnar states as he closes the door inside our hut.

I blink up at him, convinced I misheard. "Wait, did I hear you right?"

He strolls into the room, his focus on me, where Nikos and I are standing near the couch.

"We talked about trust, Narah, and how hard that's been on me. My men are my family, and if I am going to share you with anyone, it's them. First, I want to watch and see firsthand how I react, to know that I can do this without losing my shit."

He sounds frantic, and I want to know how he'll behave watching Nikos fucking me. Will he go ballistic? I stop myself from asking. I don't think I want to know and prefer to believe it won't get to that stage.

I glance over at Nikos, who's smirking and unbuttoning his shirt. He slides it over his round shoulders, revealing muscles on a tanned chest that has my knees weakening. The tattoos on his powerful arms and even those on the shaved sides of his head have me intrigued, and I make a mental note to ask him what they mean.

The man is enormous, built like a mountain.

He sweeps the dark dreadlocks—twisted across the top of his

head like a mohawk—over his shoulder. My stomach flutters crazily as this stunning, half-naked man waits to have sex with me. His gaze trails down my body and fills me with confidence I only gain in the presence of my four men. My pulse quickens, and I draw in a sharp breath at the reality that we're doing this.

Nikos unbuckles his belt, then winks at me, and my underwear is instantly drenched. Nibbling on my lower lip, I stare at this Viking god as he opens his zipper and drops his pants, then kicks them aside. Scars litter his body with an especially long one across his chest, which only adds to his rugged and sexy-as-fuck look. When my gaze falls to his heavy cock, hard and ready, he grabs the base and palms it a few times. A growl rumbles in his chest as his eyes darken with lust.

"Let's do this," he snarls.

"Oh, I see. Talk about romantic," I say sarcastically, still stunned at how thick Nikos is, and we've barely touched. Not that I can talk with how wet I am.

"You want romance?" Nikos mutters, smiling slowly. "I'll strip you with my mouth. How does that sound?"

My knees weaken. He's not a man to waste time, focusing on what he intends to claim—me.

Twisting my head, I find Ragnar sitting comfortably on a chair near the door, legs parted, his arms in his lap, watching intensely.

"Is this what you want?" I ask him.

"Yes. He's going to fuck you until you come," he says with a husky voice that makes me wonder if he's not turned on at the thought. Well, that was promising, accepting me with his men.

My cheeks are burning up. "You're going to just watch?"

"I just ask one thing." The corners of his lips curl upward as he reclines further into his seat, shadows falling over his face. "Your mouth is made to take *my* cock." His eyes glint. "No blowjobs."

"Deal, but I can eat her pussy?" Nikos responds eagerly, moving behind me. Heat pours off his body, as does his shadow.

"Anything you want," he answers with a surprisingly calm voice.

"I think I get a say," I murmur as Nikos' large hands tug on my dress. In one deft move, he rips it off me, leaving me in my underwear. A shiver dances over my skin. Nikos isn't a patient man. His now clawed finger curls under the elastic of my panties at my hip and tears them off so easily, they fall away in shreds. Then he presses his chest against my back, towering over me. My nipples pucker at the sensation of his fingers gliding down my arms.

"I'm going to take such good care of you." My eyes remain on Ragnar, watching from the shadows. There's nothing left to the imagination as I stand naked before him.

Nikos's touch trails to my breasts, cupping and squeezing. He pinches my nipples, tearing a moan from my throat. Stepping around me, he blocks my view of Ragnar.

"You are stunning. You smell so good–like sin—and it's been too long since I spread you with my cock."

Arousal courses through me as his hands cup my face, and he kisses me like an animal. Hard and savage, he bites and licks me, reminding me who is about to fuck me. Nikos may be Ragnar's second in command, but the man is a dominating opponent and likes to stake his claim. The way he's kissing me, he's making sure I never forget him.

I'm going to be bruised tomorrow, yet I want more. I claw at his shoulders as his scent burns me up with desire.

He breaks away from me so fast, I stumble from his absence.

"One moment, my beauty." He strolls across the room to do who knows what.

My gaze lifts to Ragnar, who hasn't moved from his seat, hasn't said a word, but I hear the sharp, ragged intakes of his breath. A shiver of delight licks between my legs. I've never had anyone watch me have sex before.

"Is this what you want?" I ask, squirming under his attention.

"Not yet." Ragnar's voice darkens to a rasp. "I haven't heard you scream."

I smile, knowing I won't be able to help myself when Nikos starts. Nikos is an incredible lover, and I'm panting for him. What will Ragnar do? Join us or go ballistic?

There's a scratch against the wooden floorboards, and I turn my head to find Nikos dragging a whole damn table from the back of the hut to where I'm standing.

"What's going on?"

"Ragnar needs to see all of you." One last push and the heavy table is behind me. "Now, come here, gorgeous."

Hungry hands fall to my hips, and I'm suddenly sitting on the edge of the table, the cold kiss of the wood beneath me. He's kissing me once more, and my pussy tingles, starving for him.

Nikos growls as he leans down, taking mock bites from my neck, followed by a long lick where he's pinched my skin. Making his way to my breasts, he falls to his knees to worship me. Drawing a nipple into his mouth, he works his tongue in light circular motions before flicking it.

I arch my back against his touch, my cheeks flushing wildly at the fire erupting through me, and mewl like a kitten. He makes his way to the other breast while his fingers trace my heated pussy. Desperate, I tilt my hips to give him easier access.

Ragnar's gaze never leaves me, and my skin ripples with goosebumps to have him just sitting there, staring.

Nikos releases my breast from his mouth and guides me to lie back. His hands curl around my ankles, bringing them up and prying them open. I feel the low rumble of his possessive growl in my bones, a sensation that leaves me panting, that such a powerful man reacts to me.

I peer down at my body while he stares at my pussy, holding my thighs apart for Ragnar to see everything.

"You are pure seduction." He slides a finger between the seams of my drenched lips. "I've never seen such a gorgeous pussy." He presses a finger into me.

I can barely breathe, my whole body buzzing. Without hesitation, his mouth is on me, stroking me with light flicks.

I arch, moaning. "That's it, right there. Faster, please."

He watches me with a smile in his eyes, enjoying making me beg —he loves this.

His tongue flickers over my clit, and every nerve between my legs tingles. I hear the quickening of his breath, and when he replaces his fingers with his tongue, I know he's enjoying every second.

My hand falls and slips down to Nikos' mohawk as his face pushes deeper, nose grinding against my clit. I moan with the pleasure shuddering through me as his tongue is deep inside me, finding all the right places to make me shudder helplessly. His finger plays with my ass the whole time, teasing me relentlessly, so when he adds a finger, I scream with pleasure.

The man's a beast. Sucking and grazing me with his teeth, quickening his pace, I lose all control and thrash, completely out of my mind. He made me come so hard, I can't think or move, just gasp for breath and grin. That was fucking amazing.

The smacking sound of his lips and tongue lapping me up is fucking sexy. When Nikos gets to his feet, I glance at Ragnar. His chair has fallen onto its side, and he's pacing behind Nikos, a wild animal, trying to hold back.

I meet Nikos' gaze, and his mouth and nose glisten with my slick. He steps aside as I lay on the table, splayed wide for Ragnar.

"Ragnar," I call to him, but he shakes his head, not even looking at me, and my stomach sinks.

"Fuck her already," Ragnar roars.

I can't make out if we're torturing him to a point where he'll never come back to us or if he's fighting his demons.

"Let me know what you want me to do, Narah." Nikos grips his cock, the tip shining with moisture from his precum. "I'm craving to fuck you, but I need to hear it from you first."

My attention swings from Nikos to Ragnar as they turn toward me.

"I want you both," I answer truthfully, stretching my hand out to my tormented Alpha. It kills me to see jealousy twisting his features.

"She's all of ours," Nikos tells him, his eyes sparkling with the arousal and impatience pulsing within him.

"You want us both?" Ragnar asks with a croaky voice, a thick eyebrow arching. The corners of his mouth look as if they might curl into a grin.

"Yes, now. Get over here," I order him. "Please."

He hesitates, and I tense, ready to get down and go over to him. To my surprise, he squares his shoulders and strolls over, though his face is hard to read.

"Come with me," he says softly. Tucking his hands under my body, he lifts me off the table and gently lowers me to the bed, then strips.

Resting on bent elbows behind me, I watch as he peels his top up and over his head. His body is carved of stone, angles and valleys of muscles everywhere I look. When the boots and pants come off, he's erect and bulging. He wants me, no matter how much he's struggling with his thoughts.

"Come to me," I say.

Nikos remains near the bed, his hand on his cock, watching me with hunger in his eyes. I want to give Ragnar the chance to take the lead until he's comfortable.

Pushing against the bed, he lies over me, presses my legs open with his knee, and positions himself between my spread legs. The tip of cock graces my entrance, and I feel his eagerness.

"I want you… crave you," I purr.

"I'll give you everything you need, Narah." His lips curl into a smirk, then he thrusts into me unceremoniously. I arch against him, my muscles straining, my body quivering. Another thrust, pushing harder and stretching me wider. "Fuck, you're so tight."

Ragnar growls as he plunges his cock deeper. Pain flares, and my body jerks beneath him. His eyes are only on me, he takes me savagely, and it's more enjoyable than I would have expected. He's lost to the frenzy of dominating me and making me his.

Gasping for each breath with each thrust, I turn my head to Nikos and stretch my hand out. "Join us."

Nikos hesitates, and darkness slides over his face as Ragnar rolls us onto our sides, my back to Nikos.

I gasp at the fast movement, my heart hitting the back of my throat.

"Get on the damn bed," Ragnar growls at his second in command, then winks at me, leaving me gushing.

"Does that mean…" I whisper.

He nods. "I'm going to make this work. I can't ignore how much Nikos adores you, and I won't take that from him."

The bedsprings groan as Nikos joins us, moving to lie close behind me. His fingers spear through my hair, turning my head so I'm looking over my shoulder at him. He steals a kiss as his thick cock settles between my asscheeks.

"About fucking time," Nikos growls.

The three of us shift, finding the right position to make it comfortable for each of us. Ragnar is buried inside me, waiting for Nikos.

"I'm rather enjoying being sandwiched between you two." My body's on fire, and when something thick pushes into my ass, I stiffen.

Nikos works himself into me slowly, but that barely lasts. Ragnar holds me, one hand on my hip, the other nestled under my head. Our legs are a tangled mess, and somehow, our bodies perfectly join.

Caged between two Alphas.

Two cocks deep inside me.

I moan, wanting to be fucked by them.

Our movements find a rhythm after a few trials, then they plunge in and out of me. I shiver as these men claim me as their own. Their hands are all over my body, their mouths on me, licking, kissing.

My legs are weak, and I doubt I'd be able to hold myself up. Nikos sucks my tortured neck while Ragnar kisses me, his tongue sliding into my mouth. They leave me dizzy and flying high as my heart beats faster against my ribcage.

"You guys are bastards," Crius' abrupt voice streams across the room so suddenly, I startle. "From now on, I want to be invited to group sex."

We pause our manic fucking and peer up at Stone and Crius, who are watching us with huge eyes.

"So, sharing is back in the cards?" Stone asks, already toeing off his boots and pawing at his shirt.

"You could say that," Ragnar says with a smile in his voice. Gone is the strain.

He's giving me everything I want.

"Well, you all owe me," Crius blurts, peeling off his clothes.

"Hey, wait," I say, slightly alarmed. "A girl only has so many—"

"Holes," Stone finishes with a smirk. "I'm happy with taking turns, sweetheart."

There's no stopping them, and now I've got four naked guys climbing onto the already squished bed.

"We're going to break the bed," I say, breathing heavily as Crius tosses the pillows aside and crawls to my face, peppering me with kisses.

Stone's at our feet, his hands snaking up my legs.

"There are a lot of cocks in this bed," Ragnar murmurs, sounding slightly annoyed and closing his eyes briefly.

I burst out laughing.

"Isn't it me who's supposed to worry about that?"

Nikos is purring across my neck as his cock slips in and out of my ass, unable to help himself.

We're a bundle of lust, arousal, and excitement.

"Since we're all here,"—Ragnar's jaw twitches—"I want to remove Martell's mark on Narah. My bite alone didn't work, but four of us might do the trick." My breathing grows irregular as Ragnar's eyes fix on me. "What do you say?" He slips out of me, and I immediately miss him.

Falling into their arms had made me easily ignore my wolf's whines, but giving it thought stirs her awake. I hate her pining, and I've had enough of feeling anything but hatred for the asshole.

"Yes," I breathe, bracing myself and trying not to feel suffocated.

Nikos withdraws his cock from me.

"Let's do this then." Rolling onto my back, surrounded by these gorgeous Alphas, I smile. "Take your pick of where you'll bite me." That's all it takes. The men find their perfect positions, and anticipation licks through me.

Nikos nuzzles my neck.

Ragnar licks the softness just above my pelvic bone.

Crius slides down, his tongue leading a path to my breast as he shuffles to my side.

My gorgeous Stone kneels between my legs, looking like the luckiest man in the world, his mouth on my inner thigh.

I swallow hard, my heart beating ridiculously fast.

Trapped by four wolf shifter Alphas, submitting to them.

What have I gotten myself into?

They kiss me, then I feel the sharpness of teeth on my flesh. They bite into me without mercy, and I scream, not expecting it to hurt so much.

Canines sink into flesh, and my wolf growls in response to their assault.

With the deep ache comes arousal I didn't expect, and right on its tail, an electric bite pinches across my skin. I thrash and jolt beneath the guys.

"Stop," I bellow. Something's wrong. Oh Goddess, I have to stop this now.

Sparks of blue light jump from my body and leap out, striking my men.

Silence flatlines between us.

Shouting and panic replace the earlier harmony. The men scramble off the bed in a manic rush, all except Crius.

"I knew your magic would feel fucking amazing. I need more while I'm fucking you."

Truth be told, I love his devotion, but the other three worry me.

Wild, huge eyes, stricken with terror, stare at me incredulously, confused and startled.

Vision blurring, I fight against the fear that I hurt them. So far, none of them have fallen over dead, and they have no injuries, though I don't like the way they're staring at me with fright.

"What just happened?" Ragnar demands.

I take a deep inhale, attempting to come to terms with it myself.

"Bad news is that my wolf still pines for Martell," I say, pulling myself up, attempting to appear as calm as possible while naked and aroused but also startled.

"Good news is, you've brought my magic back."

At the dinner table in the mess hall, Jae is giggling and whispering to Kaira, who's smiling. She's still healing, and my heart expands with the amount of love I have for them.

I didn't have the courage to tell my sisters about our parents. I chose the cowardly path, saying it had been a mistake, and we never found our mother in the woods. I convinced Jae the information Kaira had received about our mother from the witches had been wrong. I feel horrible, but I'd be bawling my eyes out right now if I told them the truth. I'd do anything to protect my sisters, even carrying the burden of the truth.

My men bring us platters of food from the kitchen. I gawk at them—muscles, ruggedness, and their heavenly, masculine, and sexy scents fill my nostrils. How did I get so lucky? How often does someone get to see their fantasies come to life? For once, everything worked in my favor. I have my sisters, my men, and my magic back.

My attention remains on the men as I nibble on my lower lip, remembering the other night in our hut. I have never been more turned on in my life than having four Alphas trying to fuck me.

"Careful there, Narah," Jae says sarcastically, snatching my attention. "You're drooling down your chin."

I cut her a raised brow, then stick out my tongue. "You should focus on serving the orange juice, sis." That's another thing I haven't spelled out for my sisters—my tangled relationship with the four Alphas. My gut aches, thinking how I'll say out loud that I have four boyfriends.

Don't get me wrong, I'm not embarrassed. Fuck, I want to scream the news from the tallest hut that four men want me, but these are my sisters, and I don't want them to be confused.

"Food's up," Stone announces, setting a wooden platter bursting with cuts of roast and crunchy potatoes drenched in butter in the middle of the table. The aroma has me salivating, and I reach over to steal a small potato wedge before popping it into my mouth. It's hot. Fuck is it hot. I frantically fan my mouth and try to chew it without burning my tongue.

Nikos laughs and sets down a basket overspilling with bread rolls and a bowl of churned butter. More food and drinks are set down around us.

Jae's on her feet, passing the plates around, and I catch Kaira staring at nothing, looking lost. If she was back to her normal self, she'd be stealing the food and being a chatterbox like Jae, but she sits quietly, and her face remains pale. What is she thinking? She watches everything with a child-like curiosity.

Time. She needs more time to heal after the ordeal the High Priestess put her through.

"You going to dig in?" Ragnar asks, nudging me in the ribs as he climbs onto the bench next to me. Crius takes my other side, both mountain men pressing against me, while Stone and Nikos cage in my sisters.

"I still can't believe we're all here like this," I say, smiling. "It's a dream come true."

"That deserves a cheer," Nikos calls out, and everyone grabs their drinks as I take my beer-filled glass.

"Skál," he kicks off, lifting his drink, beer splashing over the rim and down his fingers.

I smile ridiculously and lift mine, along with everyone else. "Skál," I call out in unison before clinking our glasses and taking a long drink

"Can we eat now?" Jae asks, already piling her plate with food. "I'm starving, and with so many wolves at the table, I don't think we have enough food."

I laugh at the comical evil eye she gives each of the guys.

"There's more where that came from," Stone murmurs. "You won't starve, little one."

With everyone else, I lean in and fill my plate. Even Kaira joins in, which is a relief. At first, no one talks as we dive into our meals, all of us starving by the sounds of lips smacking, the tearing of meat, and the clanking of knives on the metal plates.

"So, I'm curious," Jae says in that mischievous voice, and I know she's up to something. "How long will we continue to have four Alphas as our guards? They must have cost you a fortune to hire, sis."

Crius chuckles the loudest as he drops a stripped bone to his plate before stabbing his knife into another piece of meat from the main platter.

"You still have a smart-ass mouth on you, just as I remember," he says. "If you must know, your sister has been struggling to pay us what we're really worth, so we're taking it in other forms."

My mouth drops open. He isn't going to say what I think he's going to say.

"Crius," I hiss.

He waves his hand holding the piece of meat in my face to shut me up.

"Yeah, and what's that?" Jae asks curiously and arrogantly. The girl hasn't changed a bit, and I adore her for it.

"You will clean our clothes and our room for months to come," he finally states, and I burst out laughing.

He had me going there for a moment, but I should have known better. My sisters know every excuse under the sun to get out of doing chores or cleaning.

"Is that so?" Jae huffs. She bites into an ear of barbecued corn, eyeing him with a death glare.

Kaira's eating and smiling at the conversation but not saying a word. A niggling unease uncoils in my chest. Maybe tomorrow, I'll have the healer take another look at her.

"Well, you know what I think," Jae interjects while I moan under my breath at how tender the meat is when it falls apart on my tongue. Next to me, Ragnar gives me a soft smile as he fills my plate with more food. Stone and Nikos are shoving food into their mouths like beasts. I guess everyone's hungry today.

"Go on," Crius eggs her on, then bites into his steak.

"You like my sister," Jae suggests, her cheeks blushing.

I adore how innocent she is while attempting to be tough.

"Narah is *my* mate," Ragnar interrupts, and I stare at him with my heart pounding in my chest at the words I've wanted to hear from my real fated mate for so long. Even my wolf's pining for Martell doesn't throw me off because my heart melts for Ragnar.

"And mine," Crius pipes in.

"Mine, too," Nikos adds.

"Count me in," Stone says.

My sisters' eyes bulge out.

"Well, guess the cat's out of the bag," I say to break the silence. "I was going to tell you both tomorrow, but hey, it's out now."

"You have four boyfriends?" Jae's eyeing me like a hawk. "But you already have a fated mate... Martell." Her brow pinches. "How do you all sleep in the same bed? What about Kaira and me? If you're now officially her new fated mates, will you protect us, too?" She keeps on rattling off questions.

Before I can respond, the men all speak simultaneously with their own variation of how our relationship works, how sharing is commonplace among wolves, how fated mates are not the only chance at love. The more I listen to them, the more I grin wildly at how much thought they've given this.

My sisters aren't freaking out but considering their ideas. I'm surrounded by family talking about my awkward-as-hell love life. This is a lot more entertaining than I would have ever imagined.

As they all chat and laugh, I catch Kaira's gaze.

She's silent, sitting with her hands in her lap and looks at me with an intense look that raises the hairs on my arms.

"Are you okay, sweetie?" I ask.

Her throat moves when she swallows, and she takes a few moments to answer.

"Yeah. I'm fine." Then she returns to eating and joins the conversation.

Something uncomfortable stirs within me... something doesn't feel right.

I lower my gaze and tell myself it's just my paranoid imagination. Tonight is about putting the past behind us.

That's exactly how I want to spend the rest of the night with my new family.

RAGNAR

Coldness from the new day blasts my face and rips at my clothes.

I slow my horse after a frantic race across the field. Over my shoulder, there's no sign of the undead we'd spotted in the distance. They're becoming more commonplace in the Savage Sector, and it's fucking alarming.

My skin crawls as I'm reminded of the tightly enclosed compound in the Shadowlands Sector to keep the zombies out. How long before they swarm everything here, and we have to lock ourselves up behind walls?

"Colt's the leader of the pack we're visiting first, and he's a fucking weasel," Mihai growls under his breath, dragging me from my thoughts. The Alpha of Bane Wolves rides beside me through sparse pine tree woods while his men stay wide to ensure there are no surprise attacks. Nikos takes the lead while Crius remains at our rear.

"Good to know," I reply. "What's Colt's weakness?" We're heading out to visit nearby packs to gain their loyalty.

"Women mostly. He runs the next largest wolf pack after mine, and he's desperate. He has only five females in a pack with close to one hundred males." He casts a glance around us at the sound of twigs snapping. A deer bounces through the woods, away from us. "Unfortunately, he's a weasel and untrustworthy."

"So, we offer him some of your forty females but don't deliver until he's completed his mission."

Mihai cuts me a sharp look that could skin me alive. "The forty women you're bringing me are for my pack alone," he growls.

"So, what's the plan then? Promise and don't deliver?" I sneer. I may be as callous as the next Alpha, but in this world, everyone watches, and no one forgets, so I always try to keep my word.

"Not everyone is going to survive *our* takeover of the Savage Sector." Mihai shrugs, a look of disdain washing over his face. "I would think you of all Alphas would know because of where you're from."

I clench my jaw, knowing too well that everyone sees northerners like me as barbaric, but we're no different from the monsters in this country, killing at any chance they can take.

I give a low chuff. "Those in my hometown may be ruthless bastards, but we keep our word."

"Good," Mihai barks. "Then I trust you will keep yours and bring me the forty bitches you promised before the month's up. If you can get more, do so, and I may forgive you for the shit you've pulled with my daughter." There's fury behind his gaze.

I'm fuming on the inside, ready to gouge out his eyes. Mihai pushes me with his uncouth words, and I want to tear his fucking head off. I cast a glance at Mihai's men, who flank us from deeper in the woods, watching us.

One command from me, and my men and I would destroy them. I'd take pleasure in ripping out Mihai's tongue for daring to threaten me. We are far away from the pack and could easily blame their deaths on the undead. No skin off my nose if they die... well, except I need the fuckhead, who has sway over some of the local packs.

Since the damned virus destroyed the world, sectors have burst with male-domineering Alphas who want two things—territory and females—and trust only those in their sectors.

Not strangers like me.

I swallow the rageful words pushing at my throat and lift my attention to Mihai.

"I gave you my word, didn't I?" I snap, my voice darkening. I'm already in a filthy mood. Better we didn't talk, or one of us wouldn't return to the pack.

"You are a manipulative son of a bitch," he gripes. "I get it. Pussy is pussy, and if it wasn't for our damned primal cravings, females would be nothing more than slaves, never to be seen, but we're talking about my daughter."

"Like I said, there's no problem." I tamp down the anger boiling inside me.

"Have you fucked her yet?" he growls abruptly, catching me off guard.

My shoulders rear back, and I snap that time at the ugly bastard. "That's not your business."

"I know you haven't. She told me, crying about you bedding the scrawny wolf girl you brought into my pack. Feed Narah to one of your men. They look sex-starved. Your focus is Lyssa. Remember that."

Hate shifts through me, cold and deadly, and my knuckles turn white, gripping the reins. I crave to shove my fist into his face and rip his spine out for talking about Narah that way.

You need him to take over the Savage Sector.

Fuck! Fuck!

I grind my back teeth.

His beady gaze is on me, expecting to get a rise out of me. Cockhead.

"Narah is not an issue," I hiss through clenched teeth, the words shredding my throat like barbed wire. "What I do before I complete my deal with your daughter is none of your fucking business or hers." I hold the bastard's gaze.

"Do whatever you need." His mouth curls into a menacing grin. "Fuck the girl until you get it out of your system, but you're mating with my daughter. Break our arrangement, and I'll kill you and your men. Better yet, get rid of the girl, or I'll do it for you."

My muscles twitch, and a growl tears through my chest.

"Don't threaten me, Mihai, or this will end only one way." I hold my voice steady, even if my wolf roars within me. "You burned to ashes. We made a deal, so I'll see it through, but you will uphold your end of the fucking bargain—sway over the large packs to our loyalty, and I step into the position of Alpha for Savage Sector. Otherwise, I will destroy your whole pack."

His upper lip thins over sharp canines.

That had been our deal, but the bastard has his eye on a bigger prize. From the beginning, I knew he would be a problem, but I hadn't planned on killing him before I took over reign.

NINETEEN

A distant wolf's cry startles me out of sleep.

"Ragnar?"

I look around the hut but see no sign of my men. They hadn't returned last night from their mission to win over the local pack, and I miss them terribly.

Harsh orange sunlight streams through the window, and I rub my eyes. Pushing my legs out from under the blanket, I'm convinced they'll arrive back today. My throat is as dry as sand, and I'd kill for a hot brew of coffee from the mess hall.

My head is spinning, and something already feels odd about the day. Coffee will help. It should help.

Standing on my bare feet, the floorboards are cold to the touch. Jae's soft snores fill the room as I turn my attention to Kaira's cot across the room. Worried, I blink the sleep from my eyes. I quickly cross the room and peel back the messy blanket to find a pillow underneath. No Kaira.

There are no other rooms in this hut, so I can only assume she's gone out to the toilets. Not loving the idea of her going out there alone in a pack crammed with male Alphas and Betas, I quickly change out of my flimsy nightdress. Once in baggy pants and a long-sleeved shirt, I step into my boots.

Stifling a yawn, I shut the door behind me. The morning cold wraps its icy claws around me. Winter is getting closer. How long before the snow starts, and it's freezing? I need to speak with Ragnar about where we'll stay as winter approaches.

Once upon a time, I used to dream of taking Kaira and Jae as far from the Storm Wolves as possible and finding a perfect place to live alone, a safe haven. Maybe I've been too naive or just foolish—no such place exists in our world.

Survival requires strong Alphas. As Ragnar carves out his own territory in Romania, I have to ensure my sisters are out of danger from the war about to break out.

No wolf bends the knee to an Alpha without resistance.

Especially to a foreigner like Ragnar.

So, chaos will ensue between the packs before anything improves. Not to mention how the Storm Wolves will play into this.

That thought awakens my wolf, filling me with a weak whine of longing. The agony she carries for Martell weaves through me. It's a strange sensation to both hate and yearn for someone, against your better judgment.

Wrapping my arms around my middle, I follow the winding, worn path toward the bathhouses. Only a few Alphas are out and about, mostly guards. The smell of porridge cooking in the kitchen floats in the air, and my stomach grumbles.

I pass a dozen homes, about to swing toward the bath huts when the spectacular sky calls to me. Billowy red clouds shine on the horizon as though someone had painted them with blood. It's beautiful in a haunting way. I turn away, but not before something else grabs my attention...a flowing white nightdress.

Blinking, I pause and realize it's Kaira, standing with her back to me in the woods by the river. She crouches by the water, seeming to wash her hands. Her spine pushes against the thin fabric of her dress, her back curved forward, looking so frail, my insides hurt. But with it, ice starts somewhere in the pit of my gut and lingers inside me—a worrying, gnawing sensation that something looks wrong.

Is she sleepwalking and forgot where the bathrooms are? She hasn't walked in her sleep since she was a child.

I shake my head, and the rhythmic beat of my heart picks up its pace. In haste, I cross the open grounds, leaving behind the huts, reminded of the last time I'd been here nights ago with Crius.

Back then, butterflies had burst through my stomach, beating their wings at the emotions he aroused within me.

Now, I'm scared half to death that something is wrong with Kaira. After everything, she deserves peace. *Please let it be nothing.* I swallow hard, my fingers dancing across my middle as I hurry closer.

"Kaira," I call out, needing to know she's alright.

Silence. She doesn't respond. When she finally pulls herself up, I reach for her shoulder.

She's cold to the touch.

My sister slowly turns toward me, a smile in her eyes and licking her lips.

I'm not sure what I'm looking at—the twisted expression on her face, the blood splattered across the front of her white nightdress.

Or the monster I see lingering behind her glare.

Fright slams into me. I've seen this look on her face... but it can't be.

Please, please, let it be a mistake. Please don't let her still be under the High Priestess' spell.

"Kaira..." My voice cracks as my throat thickens, and I fight to still the tremble in my arms. "What have you done?"

Part of me doesn't want a response. I'm not sure if I can take it after everything we've been through after losing our mother and our father twice. I hate the feeling growing within me, hate how it makes my heart race, and hate that it makes me feel vulnerable and think the worst.

Deep inside, I know the truth, and it shreds through me.

Kaira has never been herself, has she?

I fucking knew something had been up with her. I knew it!

I stiffen, and the dance of my wild magic bites down on my arms, and my mind spins. Memories of things Mother taught me about being a sorceress mean nothing when anger and unease hammer my insides.

Kaira's eyes seem to be darker. "Don't worry, sister, this isn't my blood." Her voice is different, like it was before—she's still possessed.

"You're not my sister," I hiss. "How the fuck are you still under the spell? Lyra's dead," I mumble, my hands curling at my sides. The spark of magic dances across my knuckles and feels like barbed wire slicing into my flesh.

I grit my teeth, furious.

"Who said I'm under any spell?" she answers with a wry smirk. "Besides, I think we can call a truce, don't you? And to show you I mean every word, I've done you a favor and removed one of your obstacles." Her piercing stare turns away from me, making it clear she wants me to look in the same direction.

I follow her line of sight to the woods running parallel to the river.

That's when I see Lyssa.

A sob breaks past my throat, bile stirring in my empty stomach.

Lyssa is nailed to a tree trunk. Her lifeless head hanging forward. Her arms are pinned to the tree over her head, and the front of her body is slit open, neck to groin.

Blood stains nearby trees.

I'm suddenly bending over, hurling up bile, every inch of me swallowed by terror. Throwing up an empty stomach hurts, as though someone is gutting me from the inside out, but it doesn't compare to what Kaira... no, what the High Priestess has done.

Fragments of memories slip into my mind—Father back home and the way we'd found him after the Storm Wolves finished beating him. Broken bones and so much blood, he was unrecognizable. If it wasn't for the tattoo on his chest, I could have easily pretended it was someone else.

Terror pulses through me, and I fight the panic rushing over me like undulating waves.

I wipe the mess from my mouth and straighten up, facing Kaira.

She's laughing, her head thrown back.

I'm so livid, I can't see straight.

My hands shoot outward, white lines of magic flashing from my fingertips. The kind I haven't felt for weeks and that makes me feel whole once more. I don't give a fuck where I draw my magic from, as long as I end her now.

Kaira moves with such speed, one second, she's in front of me, then she's at my back, her taloned hand wrapped around my throat, the other digging fingernails into my chest, right over my heart. A bite of magic encases and engulfs me, tightening around me, keeping me locked in place, and making the rest of the world appear hazy, as though we're encased in its cocoon.

I scream with excruciating pain, my magic vanishing in an instant, having nothing to do with me.

"The only reason you're not dead is because of Kaira. The bitch has a strong hold and is fighting me. Thanks to her, you still breathe."

I'm shattered, absolutely devastated. She's possessed my sister this whole time? Bile churns in my gut, knowing I let her spend all that time with Jae.

"What do you want?" My words are barely audible because of her grip on my throat.

"While your sister won't let me destroy you or Jae, I know your enemy wolves are coming for this pack and will rip you to shreds." She cackles in my ear, and I shake with fury. "Besides, I know exactly where to find your mother now...Gregory was very cooperative once I got into his head. She's all I've ever needed—even if dead. She holds the true power I seek. You and your sisters were merely my stepping stone."

I struggle against her magical hold constricting around me, and my breath locks in my lungs.

Her words are like blades, piercing through me, knowing we'd been used this whole time. My sister was abused by the witch just to get to our mother. Untameable fury rises through me, and my wolf shoves forward with a dark anger.

"I'm sorry I can't kill you," she purrs. "But I'll leave you with something just as destructive."

At that moment, I shift, my wolf shaking and emerging.

Something hard strikes me in the back of the head, pain cracking across my skull. My eyes flutter upward, I'm falling, and the world darkens.

"Narah," someone's frantically calling my name and shaking me.

My thoughts bleed into each other, but something stronger comes over me. The smell of sexy, masculine males floods my nostrils and swallows me—so beautiful, so delicious.

Yet the terror of Lyra's return destroys me.

All while a fire blazes over me as if I've been set on fire.

I open my eyes to all four Viking men staring down at me, and my heart races. Ragnar cradles me and sets me on my feet, then tucks me against him so protectively, I gush.

I might enjoy it more if the world would stop spinning as I peer out across the grounds, finding no sign of my sister.

"Why do you smell different?" Stone asks, his nostrils flaring as he sniffs me.

"Fuck, you smell delicious. I could eat you up," Crius purrs in my ear.

Nikos has his hands on me, his eyes morphing into his wolf's with a feral hunger burning behind them.

"I feel strange," I murmur to Ragnar, the earlier fire now racing through my body as if I'm about to self-combust. "I think Lyra did something to me. And she's back. She possessed Kaira this whole time... and the wolves are coming..." I ramble, gasping for air.

"Narah," he growls possessively, not seeming to hear my words. The sound he makes has my knees buckling. His hand slides across my lower back, and a moan slips past my lips. My panties are drenched instantly, and I fall into his arms.

"What the hell is wrong with me?"

His nostrils flare once more when he inhales my scent, and his eyes flutter backward, almost losing himself. His grip tightens while fear pummels me.

"Fuck, we're in huge trouble." His voice deepens. His men are all around me, smelling, touching, and licking me. "This is the worst possible timing, Narah. You'll attract every male in this pack instantly, every male anywhere near you in fact. They'll kill us to get their chance to rut and breed with you. Your scent will drive them insane. Drive us insane."

"Wh-What do you mean?" I gasp, my blood running cold.

"You're going into heat."

CURSED WOLF

SAVAGE SERIES

CURSED WOLF

They were once my enemy...Now I'll burn down the world to save them.

There was a time when I believed I'd never find love. That females like me were only good for one thing.

After all, my fated mate had rejected me, then tried to kill me.

I'm just not that lost wolf girl anymore. I'm stronger and have a few secrets of my own.

Now my ex-fated mate has returned for me, ready to destroy the bond I have with my four Viking alphas.

Yet he has no idea the lengths I'll go to protect those I love...

Four alphas growling, ravenously pulling at my clothes, their animalistic cravings drive me to madness. I'm just as starved, kissing them, holding them with my life, needing everything they promise.

"Mate. Heat. Mine," beat into my head between the pounding pulse of my heart in my ears and the burning ache between my thighs, an ache that terrifies me. I try to rationalize it's due to the recent trauma of discovering my sister Kaira was still possessed by the coven's high priestess. She'd lied to us, infiltrated our pack, and endangered my younger sister, Jae.

Except now, something's wrong. Something was broken inside me when the witch touched me with her magic. I can't think rationally and can barely breathe from the blaze burning me from the inside out.

"Please," I plead to Ragnar, grasping his shirt, unsure what's happening, yet I can't get close enough to him or the other three alphas surrounding me. They're so close, yet not close enough. I cry out, the sharpness thumping in my chest with a need that will destroy me.

"You're in heat," Ragnar growls.

Desperately grabbing at my men's shirts, the madness inside me grows as though I'm being swallowed by darkness.

Heat. Of course, I know what it means, but when Ragnar says the word, it makes so little sense.

I'm not in heat. I can't be.

But I don't exactly have a decent track record of good luck. Is that what Lyra did to me?

Another heavy pulse of fire burns through me, the slick between my legs seeping down my inner thighs.

Goddess...

"Please, I need you. Make it stop," I cry out, my body tightening. Strange anticipation stretched across my stomach as fear grips me.

Ragnar grabs me, and I plaster my body against him, trembling. Grasping his arms so hard, my knuckles turn white, I whimper to feel him all over me, to have him strip and take me to ease the hunger inside me. I can't tear my gaze away from his lust-filled eyes.

Everything about him is mesmerizing. His scent embraces me—woodsy with a hint of his wolf, and beneath it all, ladened with pheromones that make me want to drop to my knees and take his cock in my mouth.

"Coming into your heat right now is the worst timing, but we'll take care of you, little fox." Ragnar runs his fingers under my eyes, catching the stray tears. My knees barely hold me up, and the other men keep me up. They're sniffing me, their mouths on my neck and arms, their wolves growling. I feel them all, their masculine scents drowning me, the hard cocks in their pants grinding against me.

Strong arms wrap around me, and Ragnar has me off my feet. I press myself against his chest as he cradles me. Curling my legs around his waist, instinct makes me rock against his hardness.

"It hurts so much," I whisper, crying and desperate for this huge man.

"I'll take care of you. I know what you need," he coos, walking us deeper into the woods, farther from the pack homes, where we'd been given residence. Where we brought both my sisters for protection. Now, instead of hunting down the witch inside my sister, Kaira, I was dying to be fucked.

I can't think straight. The overwhelming starvation feels as though I'll be turned inside out if I don't connect with Ragnar soon.

My emotions are wound tight, and I can't even process logic, can't think beyond the cloud of lust in my head.

"We need to do this now," Crius says, following behind us.

"I've got this," Ragnar growls, impatience in his voice as his fingers dig into my hips with urgency.

Pressing me against a tree, his kiss melts me. My tunnel vision only sees Ragnar in front of me at first, and the things he does to my body by a kiss alone have me begging for more. Then I feel his mouth everywhere, devouring my mouth, my neck, his tongue leaving strokes that cover me with goosebumps.

He tears at my flimsy top, the fabric ripping easily and exposing my breasts, the primal instinct behind his growling breaths driving me insane.

"You smell so fucking delicious, I can barely stand it. My cock hurts." He lowers his head to my breasts, sucking a nipple into his mouth. Grasping his shoulders, I moan when he tugs hard on my nipples, and his tongue flicks them. He holds me with complete control, his force hard, as though nothing could snap him out of his trance.

I glance up to find Crius standing feet from us, his eyes foggy with lust, his cock already out of his pants, and he's palming the thick, heavy flesh.

"You're killing me," he mutters. "Your smell is strangling me. It's so sweet, so fucking perfect. I want it smeared all over my face."

I stretch my shaky hand to him just as Ragnar tugs down on my pants, leaving me completely naked and vulnerable. He growls, and there's no pause as he plants himself on his knees, his mouth pressing against my pussy. His tongue is unrelenting, sweeping across my slick folds.

"Sweetest thing I've ever tasted, little fox." Then he pushes my legs wider and drives two fingers into me.

My cry is closer to a howl. Crius is at my side, his mouth making its way to my breasts, while my gaze is locked on Nikos and Stone, hurrying toward the village. I can't even think about the danger we're in or how to get out of being in heat, but when they look back at me, an ache burrows through me that they aren't by my side, but I get it. They need to protect us for now.

Especially when I'm close to exploding if someone doesn't fuck me soon. I spear my hands through Ragnar's deep brown hair. He's barely putting a dent in the fire consuming me. Fisting his hair, I push his head back.

"Please," I beg. "I need you both inside me. I can't stand it any longer."

Ragnar's on his feet, licking his glistening lips, his eyes on me like a predatory wolf. He and Crius exchange a knowing look and strip in seconds.

Two large cocks point in my direction, I'm literally salivating. I normally would hunger for them, but this is different. It's a raw desire that tightens around me the longer they keep away from me, as if we're magnets meant to be locked together. Any distance causes me unbearable pain, as though someone has my chest cavity open and is holding my heart away from my body...and I need it back.

The men are mine, and I need them just as much.

"I can't wait," I repeat and throw myself at Ragnar. My hands cling to his shoulders as I climb him, my legs curling around his hips. His hands grasp my ass and lift me with ease.

"Narah," Grabbing me, he lifts me against him.

Feeling the hardness of Crius' cock against my ass, I'm sandwiched between their steaming chests. They are fire beneath my touch while I'm the lava in our volcano about to explode.

"We have you," Crius purrs in my ear as his cock slides across my ass crack, over the slick that has me completely soaked. "You're so ready for me," he adds, his finger pushing into my ass.

I stiffen as my desire billows.

Ragnar's tense as he holds me tightly to him, his cock slipping into my pussy.

"That's it, please... more," I plead.

Crius takes the cue and replaces his finger with his dick.

I'm way beyond breaking point, and my breath is catching in my throat as both men fill me with their huge cocks. It's primal, a savage hunger that needs fulfilling.

My wolf whines for the connection, and I can't help but think how horrible it would have been if the heat had come over me near my ex-fated mate. The thought of Martell gives me jitters, and I curse myself for even letting his name enter my mind while two men I adore are fucking me.

They push all the way in a bit too roughly, distracting me, but I'm not going anywhere. I'm pinned between these gorgeous men who fill me, stretch me, and slide their hands all over my body.

"Are you okay?" Ragnar asks as Crius whispers in my ear, "You're so tight. I love the way your ass sucks down on me."

"Take away the hurt, please."

"Yes, yes," my alpha growls, his eyes heavy as he stares into mine, rocking his hips into me and back out. Crius picks up the rhythm, and the friction of their rubbing ignites a fire.

"You're so wet," he purrs.

My breath hitches as I bounce up and down on two cocks, my breasts jiggling. I love the way they stare at my body, the slapping sounds we create, and how I'm completely at their mercy. Euphoria stretches within me, my moan shuddering as they plow deeper. Gasping for breath, I cry out for more.

I've never felt so high, so sensitive to every touch, or so horny.

"Ragnar, Crius..." The rest of my words came out in a long moan. It felt so good to have them grinding their dicks inside me, their balls slapping against me.

"That's it, take it like the good girl you are," Ragnar groans.

Moving faster, I love how we're in tune with one another. I grow tenser, knowing what's coming.

"I'm close."

"I know," Ragnar confirms, as though he's in my mind. His lips graze mine before he claims my mouth with unbelievable passion. He's a man who loves to dominate, and that's how he kisses—as if he owns me. His tongue pushes between my lips, and wrangles with my own, both of us finding the same beat as they fuck me.

Crius has his mouth on my neck, sucking, demanding more.

My senses are reeling, my body humming between them and squirming with the building pressure.

"Don't hold back," Ragnar moans against my mouth. "Let go. Release the pain."

There's no pause as I buzz from the orgasm running through me. They work me as I completely fall apart, shattered. They continue ramming into me. My heart pounds, and my screams are stolen by Ragnar's kisses.

Crius is in my ear as his fingers dig into my hips. "You're so incredible. Your body is Nirvana to me."

Their animalistic sounds only drive me crazier as I float on arousal, my clit thumping, my nerves wired. I don't know how long we remain locked that way, but when I finally open my eyes and my men withdraw from me, I breathe easier.

Gone is the tightness constricting me, the pain, along with the hunger that made me an utter mess at the mercy of lust, but something feels different from the other times we'd enjoyed sex.

"Why didn't you both cum?" I ask suddenly.

"You have no idea what I'd do to explode in your sweet cunt." Ragnar cups the sides of my face. "But we don't have the liberty of knotting in you now. That will come later."

Crius holds me against his chest as Ragnar grabs up his shirt off the ground, dusting it free of leaves.

"So, my heat is gone for now, right?" I ask, desperation clinging to my voice.

"That's hard to tell," Crius explains, his arms around me possessively. "Once an omega's heat is triggered, she will randomly have episodes, building more intensely. Anything could trigger it. Gorgeous girl, did your mother never tell you about going into heat?"

The past was a painful wound that felt permanently open and hurting. I grew up with a mother who cared for us, kept us protected, and told us nothing about the real world. Nothing about how to fight for survival. I like to think her decisions had everything to do with having a genuine concern for us, but after discovering she wasn't dead after all this time and resurrecting our father to keep him as a zombie puppet, I'm not sure what to believe anymore.

Crius watches me, waiting for my response.

I half-laugh and make a strangling sound at his question.

"My mother always said I wouldn't have to worry about going into heat because I wasn't a full wolf. What I learned was from hearing others talking about it in the pack, which was limited to the female being locked up with her fated mate, sometimes for weeks."

For a long time, I didn't understand what they were doing behind closed doors. I was young and naive until one of the women died. During her heat, I discovered she didn't have a fated mate, and something was broken in her. So, a few of the men took turns rutting her daily, and in the end, she died because of how rough they were with her. It terrified me, and for a long time, I thanked the moon goddess that I wouldn't have to endure it.

Now, look at me—drowning in heat and feeling completely lost.

Crius' tender touch on my arm lifts me out of my mood.

"It's okay, we can help," he whispers.

"I-I don't think this is true heat. The high priestess, Lyra, cast a spell on me just before you arrived." I practically spit out her name as if it was dirt in my mouth. I hate her so much. "The bitch forced me into heat."

Anger flares through me at how bad our predicament has become. I give the two men a fast rundown of what happened—how I'd found my sister Kaira by the river, how the witch had possessed her from the time we left the witch's coven. Then there was Lyssa. The witch had killed the pack alpha's daughter.

Dread hitches all the way down to my lungs. I stare deeper into the woods, where Lyssa's dead body had been strung to the tree. I can't see her from our location, but I know she's there, and the hairs on my arms lift. I try my hardest not to picture her. She'd been sliced open and left to die there.

My heart thunders with fear because her father will no doubt blame us... the newcomers to his pack home.

"Put this on," Ragnar says, his expression as grim as I feel. With their help, I tug his shirt over my head and down my body. It falls to my knees, and I'm swimming in it, but I'm not naked. Ragnar tore my tee, and my pants were soaked from my heat. In truth, my body still hums as if the arousal doesn't want to let go of me.

To distract myself, I talk about what I learned from the high priestess.

"She's after my mother, even in her dead form, not my sisters and me. Lyra is headed to her house in the mountains." The longer I talk and recall Lyra attacking me, the more I shake with fury.

The men just stare at me, their faces blanching.

"What the fuck is she going to do with a dead body?" Crius blurts.

"And no insult to you, Narah, but your mother's house gives me the creeps."

I don't know what to say since I've yet to visit my late mother's home, but his words leave me covered in shivers.

"There's more," I continue, despite having so many of my questions left unanswered. "Lyra said *my* enemy wolves are coming for this pack to kill us. She was talking about Martell," I manage. His name is like acid on my tongue, and I hate the sting of trepidation he stirs in me.

"Sonofabitch," Ragnar snarls under his breath, combing a hand through his hair.

"We know he's doing deals with the witch, so she must have somehow sent a message to them about us being here," Crius says what I'd been thinking.

I let out a long exhale. "We're in huge trouble, aren't we?" My voice grows shaky as I stare from one man to the other.

Frustration flares behind Ragnar's eyes, and he releases a deep sigh, confirming my worst fears.

Crius' jawline twitches.

"We're in danger out here. You need to leave this pack," Ragnar states.

I blink at him, my stomach churning with unease, while my head plays catch up on what happened before I lost myself to heat.

"What do you mean, leave?"

He pulls back to zip up his pants, standing in front of me bare-chested and absolutely stunning, and partly ignoring me for a long pause. Crius hurriedly pulls on his clothes, his brow furrowed with clear trepidation.

"What do you mean?" I repeat a bit louder.

"Narah," Ragnar starts, taking my hand in his. "Your heat can return at any time, and the moment other alphas are near you, they will kill each other to get to you, to rut you over and over. We need a way to explain to the pack alpha that his only daughter has been butchered, and it wasn't us."

"Jae..." I grasp his arm, trembling as panic slides through me. "I need to get Jae, then we'll leave."

"Narah." Ragnar takes my hand, his thumb gently rubbing the

back, and while normally, it might coax me into a false state of calm, now I'm too terrified to be anything else.

"I'm not going without her," I reiterate.

His lips pinch tight, and I know there's an argument on his mind, but it's lost when the thump of heavy footsteps approaches us from the huts.

Nikos and Stone are running in our direction, one of them holding a duffle bag over his shoulder. They're moving with the speed of being chased and are with us in moments.

My stomach lurches.

"We gotta go now," Nikos snaps, and I see the worry in his eyes. "Your scent's reached the homes, and there are men staggering out of their beds, starved to find the source."

"B-But, I'm over the heat for now, so I can sneak in and get Jae."

"That makes no sense." He looks at me, confused. "That's not how it works. I can still smell you," Stone says.

"She doesn't know much about going into heat," Crius adds, then lowers his attention to me. "Even outside episodes, omegas still emit a faint scent that will call alphas in close proximity to her."

"But I can't leave Jae behind," I murmur, my chest constricting.

"She'll be safe" Stone reaches for my hand, and I soften against his hard chest. I hear the pounding of his heart matching my own. "We'll make sure of it, but she won't be protected if you get yourself killed."

"Ragnar," Nikos states almost with a warning. "There's no time to waste."

"Nikos and Crius, you take Narah to her mother's house in the woods," Ragnar says with a growl in his throat. "If you see the witch, keep your distance until we get there. Stone, you and I will try to salvage this clusterfuck, then escape with Jae and meet them in the mountains."

My head reels with his plan, with how many things could go wrong.

Suddenly, the sound of voices comes from the direction of the huts, and I stare at where several men are roaming about. How long before they come this way and find the dead body? Before they attack to get to me?

I'm devastated. Lyra has possessed my sister, and now we're leaving Jae behind again.

Ragnar gives Crius and Nikos instructions while Stone hands me fresh clothes and boots to change into. I do so quickly, my hands shaking.

"You'll be alright, you'll see. So will your sisters." Stone's reassurance gives me something to hold on to, a piece of hope.

I can't fall apart now.

I haven't come this far to allow a lunatic high priestess and an obsessed ex-fated mate to destroy my life. I have my magic back and four alphas on my side. Sure, I'm still unsure how to control my power, but I'm not exactly going empty-handed into battle.

Ragnar and Stone are at my side, kissing me before leaving.

It's all happening too fast.

"Please tell Jae I love her and why I had to leave." My voice chokes as I fail miserably to stop the tears. My chest hurts so bad. I'm not ready to run again. I just got my sisters back, and now everything is destroyed.

Nikos is suddenly at my back, scooping his arms around my waist.

"It's time."

CHAPTER

TWO

RAGNAR

"This is new for me," Stone barks with humor as we stride across the woods, leaving them behind. "I'm usually dragging bodies into the woods to burn them, not taking them into homes." He chuckles.

"I'm surprised you can find anything funny right now." I glance over at him. He has Lyssa's body slumped over his shoulder. It had been a bitch to get her down from where the witch pinned her to the tree, let alone considering she was split neck to gut. The High Priestess is a fucking psychopath to butcher this girl so severely. We'd done our best to wrap her up in Stone's shirt to avoid her insides from falling out any more than they already did. Stone had also jammed his blade into the back of her head, right into her brain, and cut the nerves back there. We didn't need her coming back as a zombie while carrying her.

We live in a world where wolves fight wolves for land and women and where we all fear the walking dead, who plague every country with the virus that destroyed civilization a long time ago. Now those of us who aren't immune to the undead are carriers, meaning we die and come back as one of the fuckers. So burning, removing the head, or severing the nerves connecting the brain to the spinal column ensures they don't reanimate.

547

I shake my head clear of the creatures I hate and look at Stone, who holds onto Lyssa without squirming. Lines of blood drip down his bare chest from the corpse, but it doesn't bother him.

I should feel some remorse for the girl, but in truth, I don't. I never liked her when she was alive, so why would I like her after death?

Everything I feel has been taken up by Narah. My little fox has entranced me, her scent still in my nostrils, and my cock strains from not releasing inside her. Her body... a fucking goddess. Hair, a chestnut reddish color and silky to the touch, calling me to twist it around my fist as I ram into her from behind.

I remember the fear and innocence in her eyes as she lost herself to heat. Her hunger drove me to the point of losing my mind. Her scent, the softness of her skin, and her cries to be fucked went straight to my dick.

Everything about her is sexy, delicious, and vulnerable. She completely undoes me, and half the time, she has no idea she's doing it. No woman should have such power, but for Narah, I'd fall to my knees and worship her. A jolt of awareness runs down my spine at how entangled our lives have become.

I have no idea why the universe had given her and me different fated mates when it's clear we're meant for each other. I crave to get back to her, sink my cock into her cunt, knot inside her, and flood her with my seed. To remind her she belongs to me. In one of our last conversations, I'd agreed to share her with my men, but that didn't stop me from reminding her I crave to have her submit to me.

Stone laughs, mostly to himself, dragging me out of my thoughts.

"It's either laugh or go on a rampage after that lunatic, Lyra. What witch is capable of killing this way?" His chin points at the body over his shoulder. "We're dealing with something psychotic. Even with all our magic combined, I worry it's not enough against her."

I see the desperation and dread in his eyes, and my pulse beats frantically because he's right. I wonder if Narah's power is strong enough to combat Lyra's. My little fox still hasn't fully harnessed her abilities, and I had hoped we would have time in this village for her to do so, but we'd been tossed into the fire and were out of time.

"I don't know, but whatever Lyra wants from Narah's dead

mother has to be worse for us. So, we finish this quickly and race after our team into the mountains."

"Agreed." Stone nods. "Whatever we need to do, you know I'm up for it."

He's the brother I never had. Like me, his relationship with his father was savage. Beaten, dishonored, never good enough for having the ability of magic, something men shouldn't harness, according to his old asshole father. Maybe that's why Stone and I connected so well. We think alike, hunt the same way, and when it comes to loyalty, I trust him with my life.

We approach the great hall, where I'd last seen Mihai, Alpha of this pack and Lyssa's father, enter this morning. A boulder sits on my chest from the news I'm about to deliver and what his reaction will be.

The last few days, we'd visited neighboring packs to gain their loyalty and agreement to aid us in winning over the Savage Sector. Of course, each prick demanded something, and by the time we finished, I was tempted to eliminate the lot of them. None of them are trustworthy, but I understand warfare and that the larger the numbers on your side, the more likely it'll ensure triumph. So, I shut my mouth most of the trip and resisted the urge to tear their throats out.

Shoving open the door to the hall, my gaze lands on Mihai. He's at a table beneath an arched window, with a spread of food in front of him, chatting loudly with several of his men who are sitting at the table, enjoying their meals. A young man is playing music in the corner too, but the conversation and tune stop at our entrance.

"I apologize for the interruption, but I have tragic news," I state, watching everyone in the room for their reaction.

Mihai lowers his fork to the table, his gaze studying me, but his eyes follow Stone, who marches into the room to the closest table near the wall. He gently lays Lyssa on the table on her back, her arms and torso tightly wrapped in his shirt, tied with his sleeves. Blood seeps through the material, and more of it stains Stone's shoulder, dripping down his chest. He's not perturbed. We'd been in many battles that left us bathing in our enemies' blood.

Mihai makes a strangled cry, and he's on his feet, the table in front of him flying forward, plates and food flung into the air. His men scramble out of the way in the chaotic mess.

"Lyssa," Mihai groans, his voice cracking. Since meeting the man, I had never seen him show much emotion beyond anger. Now, he's at his daughter's side, leaning over her, the painful sound of sorrow filling the suddenly silent room.

The sound of a parent losing a child is never an easy ordeal to ignore, and I'm not a complete bastard not to feel the stabbing ache in my chest for his loss.

Father once told me major changes are preceded by death. When it came to Mihai, I wasn't sure how this would end.

When he finally jolts up and turns on his heel, the glare in his gaze hits mine.

"Who the fuck killed my daughter? Was it you?" He points at me, his chin trembling, tears crowding his eyes. He stomps across the room, his body trembling.

I don't move, standing tall in front of him. He's in my face, the wild, panicked look behind his eyes making him unpredictable.

"I asked you a fucking question. She smells of magic. Why?"

Swallowing slowly, I answer with a calm voice, holding his stare.

"We found her pinned to a tree by the river, gutted. By the time Stone and I arrived, there was no one around, but you're right. She reeks of magic. On our recent trip, I mentioned how the Storm Wolves have made a pact with the witches against us."

"What are you saying? A witch came into my home and killed my daughter? That makes no fucking sense. Why her? Why the fuck not go after you or me?" His face glows bright red, fists curled by his side.

I clench my teeth, stilling my urge to shove him out of my face.

"I've heard word that the Storm Wolves are on their way to your pack as we speak. Don't you see? You're a threat to Martell. He wants to rule the Savage Sector and eliminate all those who oppose him, and your daughter was his way of sending you a message to back the fuck off."

I hated lying since I prided myself on sticking to the truth, which I tried the best I could, including warning him he had the enemy on his doorstep. I also had no plans to reveal that a dangerous witch possessed Narah's sister, who we had brought into his home. That would be suicide.

Running a shaky hand over his face, blinking quickly, he stares at his daughter, then back at me, trying to accept the tragedy.

I wait silently.

Fear happens when you feel yourself losing control over a situation or a person. It's when something is taken from you, and you want to destroy everything, but you know nothing you do will bring back the one you lost. That's the look flaring over Mihai's face.

He releases a growl, which sounds more like a wounded groan. Turning back to his daughter, he tenderly pushes strands of hair off her brow.

"She just wanted to find her mate and settle down. She was so excited for you to finally give her that, Ragnar, but you couldn't even do that, could you? You had to make her last memories of you fucking that scrawny wolf girl you brought into my pack."

His voice is brutal and angry, and my wolf stirs inside me in response, but this isn't our fight.

Stone shrugs when I glance at him, then lifts his chin to the door behind us, indicating we should leave. Maybe leaving Mihai to grieve will be best.

The alpha suddenly whips back around, and the air crackles with the same fury that dances in his eyes.

Stone steps closer to me when he sees the change in the man's demeanor. I'm not scared. It's more what he'll do about our partnership and agreements that bothers me.

He barks at his men to take Lyssa to his chamber, then says, "Prepare her for cremation. I want the whole pack there. Everyone!" he bellows.

His men nod and hurry to remove his daughter without a word exchanged.

Mihai's face darkens as he turns to us.

"I will discover the truth of what happened to Lyssa, and if you lied to me, I will hunt you down, Ragnar, and skin you and your men alive. I will then pay your family in Denmark a visit to deliver your corpse to them and watch the agony on their faces, as you have done to me."

The man is falling apart, grief ripping him to shreds, so he needs someone to lash out at. Normally, I'd kill anyone for such a threat, but I will warrant him this leniency.

His shoulders bunch up as he turns back around, throwing the tables around once more like a mad man.

"I change my terms," he snaps in my direction. "I no longer feel like a generous man, and part of me can't help thinking you've been taking advantage of me. You brought me my dead daughter, so what do you expect me to think?"

"We didn't kill her," Stone mutters with a growl. "We are the messengers who found her in this state, saving you from finding her out there pinned to the tree."

"Shut the fuck up," Mihai blurts. "This is between Ragnar and me. You can fuck off out of here."

Balling my fists, I hold back from shoving them into his face for talking to one of my men that way, but Stone can look after himself.

He licks his lips, eyes narrowing on Mihai, and through clenched teeth, hisses, "Only reason you continue breathing is you lost your daughter today." Stone pivots on his heel and storms out of the hall, the door slamming shut behind him.

"Why you keep such an irreverent alpha in your pack is beyond me."

My jaw tightens as I take a step forward. "You mentioned something about our terms of agreement changing?"

Would it be such a tragedy for this man to lose his life on the same day his daughter did? My fingers tremble with urgency to eliminate him, and my rustling wolf demands we finish Mihai. With it comes the reminder that he's opening doors for me to more packs to join our fight and also ensure the ones who've agreed continue to do so.

"Yes." He lifts his head, and coldness slides behind his gaze. "I don't enjoy having things taken from me. We both know how much your success in claiming this sector depends on me, but I need more."

"More what?" Irritation runs through me. "Women? Time? What the fuck more could you want?" My shoulders rise, and my control over my anger slips.

He leans forward, his lips in a permanent sneer. "If you continue to want my help, you will bring forty Omegas for my pack in seven days," he bellows in my face, spit flying in every direction.

I feel the sting of his fury, but despite the sorrow in his glistening eyes, I'm too damn pissed to give a damn care.

"And seeing that I lost my daughter, you will give me your first-born child."

For the first time, I'm lost for words, and as much as I attempt to remain serious, I burst out laughing.

"What the fuck?" Okay, that completely took me off guard.

Anger twists the bastard's expression, his gaze blazing with fire as he heaves for breath. If he's going to attack me, bring it on, then I'll have a reason to smash him into the wall.

"First, I have to travel south of the country for the women, and there's no guarantee they are available yet, so I need more time. Second, what the fuck? That's not going to bring back your daughter." Besides, I have no intention of having children anytime soon. Taking over a sector and inciting a war isn't a place to raise children. When the time does come, I will destroy Mihai before he even touches anything that belongs to me.

"I don't fucking care, you sonofabitch," he barks. "Accept the deal, or you can get the fuck out of my home and lose all the allegiances from the packs we've connected with."

My jaw ticks as rage flares in my mind, knowing I'm wedged in a corner, and the fucker knows it. It's the only reason I'm here. I'm not worried about the child thing as it won't happen, but the forty females will be a problem.

He growls, and all I want to do is hit him over and over. To make him bleed and hear him plead for me to stop.

A sharp whine sounds in my chest from my wolf, who knows it's a mistake, but I haven't come this far to have it all thrown away because this asshole is mourning his daughter.

Before I came to Romania, I told myself I would do anything it took to win over the Savage Sector. Any fucking thing to show my father I wasn't the waste of an alpha he thinks me to be. Everything to have a territory that allowed me to return home and claim my sister, Hel, from the tyrant husband my father forced her to marry.

Without a nod, I reluctantly growl, "Deal." I turn to march out of there before I rip his fucking head off when he calls my name, causing me to pause.

"Don't think of going anywhere tonight. I have a large pack from the west visiting. They would be perfect to join our team, and they want to meet you. Besides, I'm sure you wouldn't want to miss Lyssa's cremation." His words are bitter and vindictive.

"Fucking sonofabitch." I curse under my breath and leave him behind.

Now, my mind tears between playing sycophant to this bastard and racing after Narah.

THREE

"Four on the left, go," I yell at Crius.

Gripping his axe, he cuts across the field, heading for the three stumbling zombies coming our way. Narah's behind us, hopefully safe.

I pivot to my right, a knife in each hand, and unleash a war cry as I lunge at the two ahead of me. They're fast, not staggering like so many I've seen, and by their scrawny, hollow-cheeked frames, I'd say it has everything to do with them starving and desperate.

Coming down on the first one, my blade sweeps across the air, whistling as it bites across the creature's neck. The lack of blood gushing out confirms how hungry these undead really are. Kicking him in the gut, knocking the lump of shit off his feet, I swing around to the second zombie and go crazy on him with my blades. I don't want the fuckers touching me, but with so few of them in our travels, I'm enjoying the fight.

Three, two, one... he drops to his knees, his head tumbling off his shoulders, joining his friend.

I hoot just as Crius shouts from across the field, "Four down, and I'm in front again."

Narrowing my attention, I turn in his direction. "Asshole," I mutter under my breath. I ignore him and let my gaze sweep the grounds for any more enemies.

It's clean. Only lofty pines circle the field in the distance, mountains soar around us, and the river gurgles at my rear.

I turn in the direction where we left Narah and find two zombies strewn on the ground about twenty feet away. The dead things are twisted and seem to have smoke rising from their bodies. I hadn't seen those fuckers approach, but it seems our girl used her magic and polished them off with no trouble.

She's sitting on our duffle bag, her legs crossed in front of her, smirking rather proudly.

My heart thumps. She's absolutely gorgeous—long hair fluttering in the breeze, her leather vest over the loose shirt following every curve of her breasts.

"I'm impressed." She claps. "You finished those two in record time. Maybe you deserve a reward." She blows me a kiss that has my heart squeezing.

"You seemed to have done well yourself." I eyed the creatures fleetingly, then turned my attention to her.

My initial instinct is to rip her clothes off and bend her over. I'm still riled over Ragnar and Crius fucking her when her heat struck. My cock has remained hard since drawing in her deeply sweet smell that reminds me of ripe strawberries. I want to devour her, lick her all over, and spread her pussy with my cock.

A smile tugs on her lips at my approach. My perfect little wolf girl ignites a blaze inside me, and I doubt she has any idea.

"Beat you," Crius chuffs, coming toward me like a storm. He leaps on my back, and fuck me, he's heavy.

"Shit, man." I stumble on my feet from his momentum as he tries to lock an arm around my neck. Wrestling against him, half laughing because I'm going to get him good, my feet slip out from under me. We fall forward, and Crius might have screamed like a girl. I hit the river, icy water swallowing me instantly.

Shoving Crius off me, I push upward. When my head breaks the surface, I suck in air and shake the water out of my face. Crius bursts out of the water in a dramatic show. The guy always strives to be the center of attention, and as much as it pisses me off that I got shoved into the river, I laugh at his theatrics.

"You two are the clumsiest guys I've ever seen," Narah states from the bank of the river, standing with hands on her hips, smirking.

She's a goddess, and I can't stop staring at her beauty, at those amber eyes studying us.

"I beg to differ," I mutter. "It's that fat ass over there who shoved us into the water."

"You needed to wash the undead blood off you, so what does it matter?" Crius glides on his stomach toward Narah. "Now, your turn to get in, beautiful."

Her eyes widen, and she back peddles. "I don't think so. Besides, we're sitting ducks out here, especially with all the noise you two are making."

"I'll make you deal. Come in the water, and we'll stay quiet."

She arches an eyebrow, surprised at his suggestion. I doubt anything should surprise her when it comes to Crius.

"Better yet, you two get out of the water. We need to get a move on." There's a somber tone to her voice, and of course, she's right. Our break was merely to eliminate some creatures in our way.

Dragging myself out of the water, my clothes dripping and heavy on my body, I groan while Crius dives back under the water. I strip, peeling off my wet shirt, not wanting to be slowed down if we are attacked again. Pushing the dreadlocks from my mohawk over my shoulder, wring out the water. My boots are filled with river water as well, but I can live with them being wet. When I drop my pants and step out of them, I lift my head.

Narah's a few feet from me, looking me up and down, her mouth hanging slightly open. There's lust in her gaze, and her nipples harden, pushing against the fabric of her clothes.

My cock twitches, thick and growing harder. It comes from having sex on the brain all day. My reaction to Narah is as honest as anyone can ask for, and I'm proud to show her the effect she has on me.

"Well," she mumbles as her cheeks heat. "You're so big. Isn't cold water meant to cause, you know,"—she pinches her fingers together —"shrinkage?"

"I can't speak for other men, but I have no shrinkage problem."

She swallows loudly and turns away shyly.

My heart's pounding as more blood rushes to my dick. I laugh at her response, trying my best to close down the horny side of me, dying to get out. I'm so fucking turned on, and being naked isn't helping the situation.

Crius splashes behind me, so I assume he wasn't privy to our conversation, or he'd be here in seconds, cock in hand, asking to compare sizes. Wouldn't be the first time.

Snatching my clothes off the ground, I walk over to the duffle bag, and Narah follows me. The flush on her cheeks deepens, and she's nibbling on the corner of her mouth. The fragrance of her pussy floats on the breeze and fills my nostrils—delicious, mouth-watering, and seductive. My head screams to walk away, to remember where we are, but my body refuses to listen. When it comes to my gorgeous wolf girl, I'm rendered utterly useless. I crave to hear her gasping out in pleasure and panting as I bring her to orgasm.

The bulge of my cock doesn't help the situation.

"Please don't judge me," she says quietly, taking a few steps toward me. "I still feel the fire in my body, and I'm burning up. The moment I saw you and Crius fight, I struggled to think about anything but fucking."

My cock lurches, and I reach out to her urgently.

"Is your heat rising again?" What I know of Omegas in heat is once it begins, it stays with them until it hits its peak, which can be days for some Omegas, weeks for others. The insatiable hunger to be fucked comes in waves, hitting them out of the blue, and outside those episodes, they constantly yearn for sex. The smallest thing can set them off.

With the lust swimming behind her eyes, my nudity has added to her already aroused state.

"It's not as intense as before, but I can't get it out of my head."

"What do you need?" Drawing her closer, I hold back the groan, thinking of all the things I want to do to her if she gives me permission. "I'm here for you."

"I-I want to suck your cock."

My balls tingle with explosive desire, and my head spins. I can't say yes quick enough.

"Of course.... yes... please."

Laughing, she falls to her knees. "Was hoping you'd say that."

I might have just gone to heaven. Those were the last words I expected to hear from her.

A moan rolls from her throat as she wraps her thin fingers around my shaft and strokes it a few times.

I grunt with approval and steel myself since there's nothing to lean against. She looks up at me with vulnerable eyes and bats them, teasing me. Then she presses the tip of my swollen cock, with a bead of precum, to her mouth. Slowly, she pushes it past her ruby lips and wraps them around my hardness, then licks the underside as she draws me in deeper.

Fuck me... I almost cum just at the image of her swallowing me. Where did she learn that tongue trick?

My ears perk at the water sloshing behind me, and I know Crius is getting out. He's no doubt worked out what's going on here, but I don't care, not as my girl sucks me off. The squelching sound of her bobbing back and forth has me growling while she moans, seeming to have the time of her life.

"The fuck," Crius snarls, except as he steps around into my line of sight, still in his dripping clothes, he's grinning like the dirty dog he is. "How did I miss out on this?"

"You had your turn—" I growl when the tip of my cock hits the back of her throat, working to get me fully into her mouth. I'm not a small guy and for her to get that much in already is a feat in itself.

"Sexy as fuck." Crius stands there, gawking.

"Fuck off," I growl.

He smirks, then he moves a few feet away, grabbing the duffle bag.

Eyes back on my girl, I jerk my hips, holding onto the back of her head as she works me faster. Watching her take all of me, even when her eyes tear up, is mesmerizing. It's the hottest thing I've seen in my life and sends excited shivers down my spine.

"That's it, suck my cock. Keep going," I snarl, my voice raspy and ragged.

She stares up at me, her eyes burning into me. My balls tighten as the ache builds up, then I lose it.

I growl, grunt, buck, and take in rapid breaths. I'm deep in her mouth when she swallows me, gulping down the ribbons of cum I flood her with. While my cock pulses, it doesn't knot. Thank fuck, something inside an Omega's pussy triggers our knotting. I love blowjobs too much not to have them.

Her eyes widen as she accepts me, not trying to pull back. My body spasms, and I'm close to losing my mind as I empty into her.

I slip out of her mouth, and she stays kneeling in front of me, wiping the corners of her mouth as if she's just eaten the best meal of her life. Her smile is everything, giving confirmation she enjoyed herself. Falling to my knees in front of her, I slide her hair off her face.

"That was beautiful, a gift I will never forget."

"I love the way you taste." Her breaths are fast and loud as she licks her lips. "I can't explain why I needed that, but I feel better, more relaxed."

I collect her into my arms, kissing all over her face. Breathing into her hair, I adore her scent. My hands fall to her small waist, holding her close.

"Coming into heat means the smallest things can trigger you into a state of arousal. I should have known better than to strip in front of you."

"Well, you are irresistible, even in clothes." Her lopsided smile makes me adore her even more. She runs her fingertips across the lines of my tattoos and around my chest and biceps, her touch feather-soft.

Is it possible to be so infatuated with someone you're not sure if you could breathe if you lost them? Or am I feeling something so much more for her?

"How do you know so much about Omegas while I know nothing? Have you been with Omegas in heat?"

She stares at me desperately, and my memories flash about the family I grew up with, who then gave me to Ragnar's family in exchange for his sister. I shuffle through the past, only to be reminded of a family who never loved me but saw me as an instrument to further their hold over their territory.

"When I was younger, my father's second wife went into heat, and it was chaos. At first, everyone could resist her, but her heat cycle stretched over several weeks, and no matter how much my father rutted her, her scent still drove the other Alphas in the house crazy. She couldn't help the hunger she felt, and when my father found her sleeping with two of his guards, he lost his shit." I don't mention the part where rage consumed him, and he butchered all three right then and there.

Narah blinks at me. "So, I'm going to be constantly in lust... until what?"

"Normally, when an Omega goes into heat, her body is preparing itself for breeding."

"Shit." Her eyes bulge, and she makes a strangled, gasping sound. "But I'm not..."

"I don't know how your heat works since it was brought on by my magic or if Lyra cast a faux heat. For now, all we can do is find her and get her to remove the spell."

"I hope you're right." Her gaze catches mine, and there's terror behind them. "My mother said half-wolves like me couldn't go into heat because breeding... I'm not ready for that. Look how terribly I've done looking after my two sisters." She's breathing heavier, a stricken look in her eyes.

Dragging her into my arms, I kiss her brow as she quivers against me. "We'll get this fixed. I promise you. Until then, you remain near one of us at all times."

If I could remove her worry, I'd do it instantly.

A shadow falls over us. Crius is eating an apple, the crunching ripping me from my thoughts.

"I couldn't help but overhear you. Now, what you're saying is the sight of us naked will render you irresistible to our charm? Interesting." His evil grin splits his mouth, and I roll my eyes, knowing exactly what he's thinking.

"Keep it in your pants. This is about what Narah needs, not us triggering her," I snarl, baring my teeth at him to back off.

"Says the guy who practically wagged his dong in her face."

I give him my best deadpan expression, which he ignores.

He pulls out another apple from his pocket and hands it to Narah with a smile. "Something to freshen your mouth, gorgeous." Then he looks at me with something dark behind his eyes. His posture changes, stiffening, shoulders squaring, and my gut clenches as if something bad has happened.

"We need to get going," he instructs. "There's movement at the end of the field with a larger group of zombies. We can evade them if we move now."

The elation in my body fades, and in the blink of an eye, panic rises through me. I'm on my feet in seconds, lifting Narah with me. I rush to get changed, pack our wet clothes, and we're on the move once more.

For the rest of the day, Narah's all I can think about. My cock twitches each time I glance at her mouth, imagining it wrapped around my cock. I have no idea how I'll make it through the night.

Omegas in heat affect Alphas with their pheromones. We turn into starved, horny bastards, and the longer we stay with her during this phase, the more we lose ourselves to our primal needs. Normally, that wouldn't be a problem, but in our current situation and our focus on Narah, we could become sitting targets to anyone who wants to kill us.

We've gained a line of candidates wanting to fill that role.

CHAPTER

FOUR

STONE

"One more night and we'll be with Narah," Ragnar murmurs under his breath, looking at me, though I wonder if he's saying it more for his own benefit than mine.

Narah has been a temptation for us from the moment we agreed to help her with her sisters. We all stare at her like hungry wolves, remaining in the shadows where Ragnar ordered us to stay until desire became too much.

We were supposed to treat her as off-limits, only a business venture—nothing more. Look how well that went. Each one of us has tripped over our own feet to make her ours, to put our dicks in her, including Ragnar.

Now, she's joined our forces to take over the Savage Sector, and we've dedicated everything to keeping her safe. That's why I'm close to bouncing in my skin to get the fuck out of this town and catch up with the others.

Dangers lay everywhere.

Instead, we're playing games with Mihai. I told Ragnar, one word from him, and I'd execute the Alpha, then we lay claim over his pack. I'm still waiting for him to give the command, my wolf eager, ready to eliminate this prick who treats us as boot-lickers.

The wind whistles past my ears, and in front of us is an enormous blaze in the middle of the town. It warms me, even from where we're standing at the back of the crowds. The pack has shown up, paying respects to Lyssa's death. Mihai finishes his eulogy, then begins to sing. Everyone around us joins in the sad, slow ballad, which speaks of mourning.

My chest squeezes, hearing the pain in their voices of losing one of their own. It also brings forward worries about what I'd do if we lost Narah because we were with the Bane Wolf pack instead of with her. I quiet the thoughts before I become a fucking mess, determined not to let that come to pass if I have anything to do with it.

Through the masses, I watch as several men push Lyssa's wrapped-up body into the fire, and it isn't long before the flames engulf her. I thank the moon goddess that the wind isn't blowing in our direction from the fire.

The longer we stand there, the harder my pulse pounds through my veins to run to Narah. The whole situation is fucking annoying. What has to be an hour later, everyone moves toward the mess hall for drinks, and Mihai is nowhere to be seen.

I clench my teeth. "Where the fuck is he now?"

"We track him down and get this done," he growls, shadows gathering in his eyes.

Speaking of assholes, two guards march up to us, animosity crawling across their expressions. The dark-haired one stops in front of Ragnar.

"I'll take you to Mihai. His guests have arrived."

"About time," I grumble and take a step to accompany my Alpha when the other asshole, a tall, lanky prick, jabs a hand out, practically slapping it to my chest.

"Not you," he barks. "Only Ragnar."

Anger flares and I react before I can think. I grab his hand and twist until I hear the satisfying snap of bone. He wails, and I smash my fist into his face so he shuts the fuck up. Blood explodes from his nose, and he stumbles backward, tripping over a hole in the ground.

I whip around to face his friend. "No one fucking touches me, and I don't leave Ragnar alone." The dark-haired man studies me for a long pause, then nods. Smart man.

We're moving again, leaving his friend behind to cry.

Ragnar doesn't say a word, and I know he's just as edgy as me tonight.

We enter a large hut and find ourselves in a hallway that spears out in two directions. Flaming torches in metal brackets on the walls throw shadows across the stone structure.

"This way," the guard states.

We march after him into a room with one round table and chairs. Crossed swords and tapestry adorn the walls, and an enormous medieval chandelier flickers with lit candles.

Mihai's on his feet, as are the three beefy men dressed in fur coats. Ragnar moves forward for his introduction, and I retreat, my heels hitting the wall near the doorway. I've been to enough of these to know the drill. Sit back and try not to fall asleep.

Their conversation replicates previous meetings with other packs, with them peppering Ragnar with questions about Denmark and how they can build allegiances with his family pack as well. I'll give Ragnar credit. The man knows the fine artwork of steering people into believing what he wants while hinting at the possibility of giving them what they want.

After an hour, beers are brought out while they tell tales of great battles their pack had won. I decide to slip out mostly to pee and stretch.

I head into the bushes behind the hut and unleash my huge snake to pee. Fuck, that feels good. Been holding onto it for too long. Draining myself, I tuck it away. Hearing whispers, I freeze and turn to see who's talking. I'm concealed in the shadows and don't move to avoid giving away my position. Two figures stand behind the large home, and my ears perk up to listen in on their conversation.

"Why the fuck haven't you told Mihai?"

"Keep your voice the hell down," the second guy growls. "Have you seen the shitty mood he's in? I'll do it after his meeting."

Silence.

I roll my eyes at the two dumbheads.

"It's a mistake. He's going to go ballistic that you didn't tell him earlier. He'd want to know you saw the bitch who killed Lyssa."

The fuck! A shiver races up my spine. Someone saw Narah's sister kill Lyssa? They'll never believe that the girl had been possessed when she attacked the Alpha's daughter. Dread pounds in my head. This could destroy everything we've been working for. They could turn on Narah and her sisters and have the whole pack after them.

Fuck. Fuck. Sonsofbitches.

Fists clenching, I suck in a ragged breath and lunge out of the woods straight for the soon-to-be-dead assholes. Snatching the first prick by the back of his neck, he yelps, jolting at my sudden appearance. There's no pause as I snatch the blade from my belt and slice his throat with one swift swipe of my knife.

The other guy is yelling and running away, and panic strikes me. I dump the first asshole on the ground and charge after his friend. My heart thumps as my thoughts race with one thought—stop the fucker before anyone else sees us. Urgency bleeds into my veins, and I pound the ground as he reaches the doorway.

"No, you fucking don't." I hurl my blade at him, the knife spinning, hilt over the tip, through the air. It slams into his back, sinking into his flesh with the force of my throw. His knees buckle, and he falls face-first to the dirt in front of the closed door.

Fuck me, that was close!

Scrambling like a madman, I grab his ankles and quickly haul him to the back of the hut. A fast scan confirms no one saw, yet my pulse pounds in my head. I make rapid work of dragging them both into the woods, coming to a small cliff's edge. Darkness steals the view down below, but who cares? As long as these assholes are hidden.

The man stabbed in the back still groans. Yanking out my blade, I slap a hand over his mouth to cease his cries and crouch down by his side.

"Here's the thing, dickhead. I can save you, but first, I need something from you. I hear you saw something this morning you shouldn't have. Who else have you told?" Keeping my voice calm grew harder by the second. I remove my hand from his mouth.

"N-no one." He groans like a wounded boar.

"Don't lie to me. Did you tell your family? Your wife, perhaps?"

His face twists with pain as blood dribbles from the corner of his mouth. Looks like I punctured something major with my blade. Too bad for him.

"I'm n-not mated," he groans and coughs up blood. "I t-told no one."

Wasting my time made me furious, so I put him out of his misery with a blade to his throat. Then I sever the nerves at the back of the men's heads and shove them over the cliff with my foot. The dull thud when they hit the ground is all I need to hear.

Cleaning my blade on the grass, I tuck it away and use the grass to wipe any blood on my hands. To be certain I'm not covered in blood, I run my forearm across my face to be safe, then march out of the woods.

Feeling fucking wired, I storm around the building, surveying who's around and what homes are close enough to have seen anything. When I'm convinced I've eliminated a possible disaster waiting to happen, I stroll back into the stone building, praying their meeting is over.

The bunch of them are drinking beer and chortling.

Clenching my teeth, I step back in my position against the wall. Ragnar glances over at me with a look in his eyes that asks if all is good.

Giving him a tight shake of my head, I hope he understands we need to leave. I've known this man for a good part of my life, and he can read me like a book.

Finishing his drink, he sets it down with a bang to get everyone's attention, then stands and gives his lame excuse of needing to get up early. Finally, we're leaving them behind but don't exchange a word until we're outside.

"What's going on?" he asks, deepening his breath.

"A pack member spotted Kaira killing Mihai's daughter this morning."

"The fuck!" he stops dead in his tracks, turning on me like a venomous viper.

"I dealt with it. He was talking to someone else, and they're both dead and over a cliff at the rear of the town."

Panic is in his eyes, and I can't blame him. "Did you ask him who else knew?"

"He said no one, but that doesn't mean shit. A dead man will say anything to survive. I suggest we leave this pack tonight."

"Fuck. Okay, collect our stuff and Jae. I have to tell Mihai I'll be gone for about a week. I can't have the fucking weasel think I ran off on him and betray everything I've worked for." He jerks around on his heel and hits the ground with brutal steps as he races back the way we came.

I glance around the open land with homes around the perimeter and the fire blazing in the center. A handful of guards remain near the fire, talking and not seeming to pay me attention.

The earlier shiver runs up my arms again. Our perfectly laid plans could completely unravel if the dead prick told anyone else.

FIVE

CRIUS

My heart thumps in my chest as my hips slam forward, plunging my cock into my sweet girl's cunt.

Narah is gorgeous, bent over with her back to me. I adore hearing the sounds she makes. It's selfish, but I love her being in heat. I'm in heaven, every inch of her scent saturating me, and I never want this to end.

After a full day of traveling, the night brought the cold. When we reached a small rogue town offering a room to rent, we decided to rest. No one asked questions, and we were left alone. With the undead out there and Narah's heat, we had no choice but to check in for the night.

She grabs hold of the side of the couch she's leaning over, her sweet ass in the air, legs spread. My balls tighten and buzz when I glance down, watching the way my huge cock spreads the pink lips as I slide in deeper. My girl is leaking, making it easier to glide in and out. With her body going through the wave, her insides are on fire, and I feel it on my cock each time I thrust.

Faster. Faster against her pussy.

"You are fucking everything to me," I call out as I plunge my long length into her hole.

Glancing to my right, where Nikos sits in a chair, giving me the death glare, I grin. The bastard is writhing against the thick rope I used to tie him to the chair—his arms behind him, his ankles restrained, even his mouth. I don't need to hear his filthy words while I'm enjoying my girl.

Laughing is a lot more difficult when you're pussy deep and being squeezed into a state of Nirvana.

"Don't look at me that way," I say to him. "She's gone into heat, and you deserve this after you got a blowjob and left me hanging. I'm doing you a favor and giving you a front-row seat to the show."

Purring, Narah looks over her shoulder at me, her cheeks flushing, sweat collecting on her brow. Lust clouds her eyes, and I know she's struggling to focus on anything but the pleasure devouring her.

"I'm going to take my time, Narah, and give you exactly what you need."

Nikos thrashes, the chair jumping, but I don't have time for him, not when I'm humping Narah. She wriggles her ass, demanding more.

"Tell me this is what you want. Scream it out."

"Don't stop," she groans. "Harder."

Reaching forward, I curl my hand around her hair, fist it, and gently pull her head back.

"I'll give you everything, my greedy girl." I take her with force, just as my beauty requested. My vision blurs as I let myself go wild. We're rocking so hard, the couch slides back and forth with our fucking.

Looking at me, she mewls, and her body slightly jolts. She's close, and my cock squeezes tight, the end already swelling into a knot.

I want her exploding with me, both of us screaming. I'm so fucking close. I rub her clit with my finger, then pinch it. She shudders beneath me, suddenly tenses, and she's convulsing. Her screams are beautiful as her cunt squeezes my cock. With me growing and her constricting, the squeeze is unbearably delicious.

"More," I growl, joining her tune as I burst, cum spurting inside her. One hand is on her ass, the other tangled in her hair, as wave after wave of my seed pulses out.

Narah's making the most delicious sounds, almost bird-like chirps as she floats down.

Knotting inside her and flooding her is intense, and my breathing is rushed. I couldn't stop if I tried. She's my addiction.

After a short time, I calm down, and she's panting beneath me. The heavy fog of her heat has softened, and the air in the cabin is that of sex. Releasing her hair, I run my hand down her spine, her skin soft and tender. Wrapping my arms around her middle, I lift her.

"How are you feeling, my little bird?" I ask as she leans against me.

"I'm still buzzing." She giggles, sounding slightly drunk, and it makes me grin. "I had no idea an orgasm could be better. Everything feels a hundred times more sensitive, more heightened."

"You were incredible," I coo, lost to how soft she felt as she arched against me. "I can so easily lose myself to you." I embrace her, knowing she's mine until the end of time, until my last dying breath.

"We'll take it slowly," I whisper to her, taking my time, already feeling how soft her body is from exhaustion. With me still locked in her pussy, I take her weight, pressing her back to my chest, her ass cushioned against my groin, and turn around.

Nikos stares at us with huge eyes. I forgot about him. My bad.

"Guess you're free to go now," I say, walking Narah right past him, her head lolled back against my shoulder. I tug the knot at the back of the seat, the one I'd tied for easy release. He can undo his ankles and mouth gag.

By the time I get into bed, Narah is cradled in my arms, my knotted cock embedded in her, and she's breathing heavily.

"I'm so tired," she whispers.

"I'll hold you, gorgeous. You're safe."

"It's almost like I'm floating," she says, her voice soft, already drifting away to sleep.

Nikos is on his feet, growling like a damn bear, ripping his gag off, and turns toward the bed in the back corner of the large room.

"That was a dick move," he scolds in a low voice. "A fucking great show, but you're still an asshole." Cracking his neck, he strolls toward us.

Narah's breathing is labored, her body slumped against me, and she's out like a light.

"You've exhausted her," he says softly as if worried he'll wake her.

"What other way would you have it? Now, you're gonna join us or gawk? Whatever you decide, blow out the candles."

I turn my attention back to Narah. How beautiful she felt in my arms. I don't remember the last time I let such happiness into my life.

I'd never thought I was capable of love, never thought it was a possibility. My past is a horrific mess, something I couldn't live with for a long time, and it has broken me. Something I wanted never to remember, and there was only one way out.

Using the one ability I have meant if I used it in battle, I'd go out as a warrior in a final explosive end—something Ragnar opposed. I've known it from the beginning, yet I still came on this mission with him. Maybe a part of me had desperately wanted his help... I don't fucking know.

Now, look at me. I'm smitten and completely ready to give my heart away. Hell, I'm still broken, but those rough edges don't feel so sharp anymore. I don't even recognize myself.

"I think I'm falling in love with you," slips past my lips and floats to Narah.

Narah

Waking up to the soft murmur of words, I open one eye, not ready to move from under the blanket's embrace or get out of bed.

The voices grow heated, and I'm intrigued, so I open the other eye. Crius and Nikos stand across the room, talking in what they must think are hushed whispers, but with all the growling, it sounds more like two dogs about to break into battle.

Of course, my thoughts fly to us being trapped by zombies, Lyra finding us, or a dozen other scenarios. I seem to have enough enemies now that my fear is warranted.

"Are we in danger?" I croak, the bedsprings squeaking as I push to sit up.

Both men twist to face me, the darkness on their faces fading, replaced by smiles. I blink at them, unsure what's going on.

"You're awake, good," Nikos says, strutting across the room. He's dressed in jeans and a loose Henley top, looking as sexy as ever. Sitting next to me, he pushes loose strands of hair behind my ear. "There's no danger. How did you sleep?"

"Like a log. I didn't know how tired I was."

"We had a big day yesterday, and you experienced two heat episodes. Those will wear you out quickly."

My cheeks burn at the mention of heat, even after everything I've done with the guys. I can't explain how intense being in heat feels, except that my body completely rules me, and it just wants these men —their cocks—and it startles me how starved I am.

"It's just so new to me. The sensation is overwhelming."

"Someone as vulnerable and gorgeous as you shouldn't be in a place like this while in heat. Last night, when you were sleeping, I couldn't help but think such beauty and perfection mingled in a dark and filthy place was wrong. We'll fix this, you'll see."

My heart thumps harder with his sweet words. This powerful man, who's always been standoffish and broody, stares at me with a flare of fire in his eyes–completely opposite of the harsh, cold gaze when we first met. He no longer locks down his emotions, and he's grown on me to where I doubt I could bear to lose him.

"Bruh, you were watching us sleeping? Creepy," Crius blurts, stealing the moment as he joins from across the room.

"I watched Narah, not you. Never you," he throws back, grinning and coaxing a giggle from me.

They're adorable when they quip, but I'm left curious what they were chatting about when I woke up. Catching Nikos staring at my mouth, my heart skips a beat. I hold the blanket tighter to my chest, not out of cold, but worry the smallest thing will trigger my heat. I love all the sex, but there's only so much a girl can take in such a short time.

Besides, my mind is thumping with so much worry for Kaira, who's possessed, and for Jae, who has no idea what's going on but is on the run with Stone and Ragnar. I can't wait to speak with her and put her out of her worry, knowing she'll be scared out of her mind.

Crius flops down on the bed, making the bedsprings creak again. His lips press against my shoulder, so warm, so inviting, as his hand slides around my bare waist. "You fell asleep quickly last night," he murmurs, cradling me. "It was beautiful, but we're going to need to leave soon."

I nod, watching the intensity on his face. "Are you sure everything's okay?"

"Absolutely," Crius adds. "But we should leave soon."

Leaning forward, I embrace them both, inhaling their addictive scents—musk, pine, and wolf. "I can't thank you both enough for looking after me." My stomach grumbles for food, and I frown, trying to remember the last time I ate.

"Are you kidding?" Crius pulls back with a slight pinch on the bridge of his nose. "I'd fight an army of zombies to keep you safe. Anything for you." Suddenly standing, he twists away. "While you get ready, I'm going to get us breakfast." He marches out of the room before any of us can respond.

It takes me a second to work out what just happened, then I burst out laughing.

"He had an erection, didn't he? He's insatiable. You all are."

Nikos chuckles. "As are you." He kisses me, and I lean in, wanting his touch, his warmth. He carefully pulls away from me, and I groan, pawing him to come back.

"You're so warm," I whine.

"And you're a temptress," he says in a low, firm voice.

I hold on to his hand to keep him by my side.

"What's going on?" he asks as if bracing for an unpleasant conversation.

"What were you and Crius arguing about earlier?"

Nikos sighs, his shoulders curving forward. "Nothing important."

He starts to get up again, but I squeeze my hand slightly, holding on.

"I have a right to know if it impacts me."

"Crius is worried," he says, sitting down in front of me. "I'm worried about how we're going to deal with Lyra when we catch up to her. Neither of us wants you to confront her, but we don't stand a chance. Crius suggested he could use his power, except he's only able to draw a large amount like that once, and it would most likely kill him. His power is so intense, the one time he tried to use it, he barely survived."

I gasp, and my chest squeezes. "Then no, he can't use it."

"That's what we were arguing about. He'll do anything for you,

Narah, but he needs to understand we're a team now, and we all need to survive this." His lips press together. "He absolutely adores you. I've never seen him this way with anyone before. I told him to think about a future with you, not to give his up for yours."

Hardness settles in my chest at the thought he'd do anything so stupid. "I'll speak with Crius." I need him not to play the hero this time.

With a serious expression, Nikos' gaze never leaves me, most likely trying to work out what I'm thinking.

"We just have to keep a close eye on him." I throw my arms around Nikos' neck, embracing him and pressing closer. "Thank you."

My pulse is frenzied, and my body is a live wire. I don't know if I should cry or beg Nikos to make love to me. I'm so messed up right now.

Large hands, hot as fire, run across my bare back as he embraces me, holding me tightly. It covers me in tingles, and warmth rushes to my face. I look up at Nikos, at this rugged, tattooed Viking, and my heart thumps louder. I trace my fingers over the rune-patterned ink on his shoulder.

"I'll always take care of you, Narah. I'll destroy the world if it puts a smile on your face, but I know your temptation is my weakness," he says. "Unless we get you dressed, even a man as strong as I am will break."

A fire curls low in my stomach, my mind filling with all the naughty things we could do. As the sensations perk up, I quickly pull away from Nikos.

"Yep, you're right. I gotta get ready and take a super-cold wash." Pulling away from Nikos, his eyes lower to my breasts. I climb out of bed and saunter to the bathroom. When I glance over my shoulder at him, he's staring at my ass.

"Narah, you're going to destroy me."

We've been traveling nonstop for most of the day.

Panic thunders in my chest the farther we travel up the mountain path. Lofty pines suffocate the mountain, and shrubs pepper the terrain, as do fallen logs and branches. With the sun already dipping behind the crest of the hill, the night is crawling over the landscape. The few weak torches dotting the dirt path barely do anything to cut through the coming dark.

Nikos holds my hand and draws me up the steep path. Crius takes the lead. Ragnar, Stone, and Jae should be behind us, or perhaps they passed us when we stopped for the night. I don't know, but I pray they're safe.

One step after the other, I keep pushing, even though my thighs sting, considering we've been climbing for what feels like hours. Muscles quiver the farther we travel, and it has everything to do with the anxiety knotting in my stomach.

My thoughts spin out of control. What is Lyra doing with my sister? Are they in my mother's house? What are they doing to her? Are we too late? What if we can't stop her?

I clench my jaw, needing to shut down my thoughts before I freak out. I don't need to be hyper-wired up. I'll need to concentrate to use my magic.

Nikos' large hand around mine squeezes as though he can sense my tension. He glances at me with a tight smile, catching my gaze.

"Should we rest?"

I shake my head. "Let's just keep going."

By the time we finally reach the top of the mountain, where the path spears out in several directions, I'm breathing rapidly. Each direction vanishes into the woods, and there are small orbs of lights bouncing in the distance, telling me the local wolf pack is out and about with lanterns or torches, going about their lives.

I've lost the idea of what normal feels like. It seems all I've done is run since escaping with my sisters from the Storm Wolf pack.

The wind doesn't blow, the trees are still, and there are no bird sounds. Tension sparks in the atmosphere tonight, as though the night knows something's wrong in these woods.

We're in the Wolf Mountains village, which sits mostly on the side of a mountain. There is no one-governing alpha in this territory. It's a place for anyone to take residence, regardless of status. It might very well explain why no one went on a mad hunt when people started disappearing in the village. All those poor victims my mother killed and locked in her basement to drain their power.

My skin crawls, and I fight the urge to recoil from this place. My mind fills with what I've been told about my mother's basement holding the dead people she drained. Am I ready to see that? I hesitate, staring at Crius sprinting down the path ahead of us. Nikos tells me we're waiting until Crius checks if the path is clear.

"What do you think Lyra wants with my mother's body?" I whisper.

"To siphon her power, I guess. Your mother was using her blood mixed with magic to reanimate your father, so it could be blood. Although so much time has passed, I don't know if there will still be magic in your mother's body."

Staring as Crius darts back toward us, I chew on my lower lip, convinced Lyra knows what she's doing and that there's something she needs from my mother that will make her more powerful.

"Path ahead looks clear." Crius waves for us to follow him. We leave behind the smell of food cooking and the bopping lights, yet I fail terribly at leaving behind my trepidation.

Despite the woods shielding us, the sharper cold bites into my skin. I pull the sleeves down my arms and remain close to Nikos, who radiates warmth, yet nothing warms me up.

When we finally hear the familiar gurgle of the river that runs across my mother's property, my ears perk up. I can't stop the memories pushing forward of my mother removing our curse by drowning us, then fed off our energy. That's how important I was to her. She killed my men and me despite the small chance we might not come back or return as zombies.

With Nikos' hand on my back, I remind myself I'm in a better place now and push those hurt emotions aside. They won't help me.

An owl calls across the night, and I flinch.

Nikos glances down at me, smiling. "It's okay."

"Not sure I'd say that." Regardless, we keep moving and soon catch up to Crius, who's stopped ahead of us.

"What's going on?" Nikos asks quietly.

We emerge to an open yard, cleared of trees, where the river comes into view about twenty feet away. My mother's house sits in the shadows like an oversized wolf crouched low.

I can't move—don't want to move.

I stare at the wooden cottage made of timber logs. Darkness yaws from within the windows, and there's no smoke curling up from the chimney. It's silent...too silent. No sign of Lyra or even any of the neighbors. Mother's house is completely isolated, and I suspect this was exactly why she selected this location.

Shivers run up my spine to be standing across the yard from where she'd been living for so long while my sisters and I were stuck with the Storm Wolves. She left us alone and in danger. Her words flare in my mind, bringing me no comfort.

I don't blame you if you don't forgive me for your father's death, for leaving you and your sisters. At the time, I did what I thought was best for you three. You have always been my priority.

I can't stop the sensation of betrayal squeezing my chest. Fisting my hands by my side, I draw in a deep breath, needing to remain focused to save my sister. Mother is dead. Nothing can bring her back to change the past. The longing for what could have been doesn't leave me, so I turn to both my men, my new family—my future.

"What do you think? Maybe Lyra hasn't found the place?" I ask.

"Or she's come and gone," Nikos suggests.

My stomach turns, and coldness echoes in my mind that we've missed them.

"I'll scope the house," Crius says, removing the handheld axe from his belt and easily spinning it in his hand.

"Maybe we should stick together? What if there are traps or zombies hanging around from my mother's kills?"

"There's only one way to find out, gorgeous. I promise I'll be careful. Besides, you're not stepping foot inside until I know it's safe. Until then, Nikos will keep you protected."

My mind floods with Nikos' words about Crius prepared to use his powerful magic—one use, and it'll be the end of him. Unfurling my fist, I reach out for his hand.

"Please, nothing heroic. She's powerful, and I need you alive."

His gaze lifts to mine, and there's a slight pause before he nods, understanding the meaning behind my words. Or perhaps it's a wish on my part to cope with the panic making me shake. Crius leans toward me, kissing me on the lips. My insides twist to think anything could happen to him, and something comes over me—desperation and the need to be honest. Grabbing his shirt, I draw him closer.

"I think I'm falling in love with you, too," I whisper.

One of the reasons I slept so incredibly last night was because of Crius' sweet words—a deeply emotional confession I've wanted to hear my whole life.

He faces me, and there's a spark in his eyes, followed by a smile curling on his lips. My cheeks grow hot.

"I heard what you said last night." The heart-warming sensation he brings me curls around me.

"I promise I'll return. You've just made my whole fucking year." He chuffs, and my heart lunges. I reach to bring Nikos over, not wanting to leave him out.

"I know it's the wrong place, and maybe I'm being over dramatic and worried, but Nikos, I'm going to just say it and hope I'm not embarrassing myself. You've grown on me, and I love you, too."

His breath hitches, and I think his gaze might be glistening. Suddenly, I'm in his arms, and he's kissing me.

"I fucking love you to the stars and back. For so long, I wanted to make you understand how much the smallest moments you spend with me mean the world to me."

He kisses me again, and butterflies are bursting in my stomach, beating their wings. Both men are now with me, and I'm bathed in their affection.

Nikos kisses my nose and murmurs with a grin, "Of all the places to have a conversation that will stay with me for eternity, it's here."

We all laugh quietly and pull ourselves together. Fear has a way of bringing out emotions I never intended to share, yet I don't regret a thing. Perhaps I've been keeping back my emotions for too long.

"Let's get you two out of view and in the shadows," Crius says, unable to stop touching me or looking at me with that cheeky grin. Nikos is at my back, holding me tight.

The three of us shift off the worn path and move quickly to the shadows of a cluster of trees. A few steps in and an electric buzz zips up my legs. It comes so fast, I don't have time to scream. I spin to Nikos and Crius, both with huge eyes and faces blanched, and like me, they're not making a sound.

Something's crawling up my legs, but the darkness smothers me, feathering at the corners of my eyes. Panic rocks my insides. Desperation claws at me, but it's all happening so fast, we lose our chance to react. In seconds it consumes me, making my pulse thump in my temples. As much as I try to scream, to move, to call my magic, it comes too late.

My world vanishes in a heartbeat.

"PASS THE CINNAMON," Nikos calls out frantically.

I hear the panic in his voice from across the cottage, and I can't help but giggle. I know he and Crius are in the kitchen, cooking up a storm. If I'm not there, the place will resemble a disaster zone once they're finished creating breakfast.

The sweet aroma of pancakes has my stomach grumbling. I woke up starving, which got the two men jumping into action.

Groaning, I push to my feet from the chair and release a long exhale.

Lately, I've been so slow, my two husbands won't let me do anything in the house. What's a girl to do? Milk it for everything it is.

A breeze swooshes into the room from the open French doors, lace curtains fluttering like undulating waves, flooding the room with the golden glow of sunlight. Outside, the meadow stretches to the creek, yellow flowers freckling the lawn.

Perfect... like every day. It feels as though we live in heaven. The three of us—a perfect little family.

Most days, the longer I look outside, the more a strange sense tickles the back of my mind. A feeling of emptiness fills me, the kind from forgetting something, and nothing I do helps me remember it. Yet it sticks to my mind like cobwebs, a reminder something isn't quite right.

Shaking the thought away, I wander into the hallway where daisies from the garden—a wild rainbow of creams and reds and candy pinks—fill a vase on the side table, flooding my nostrils with the sweetest floral scent. Photos of us three adorn the walls—hiking through the mountains, swimming, fishing—everything we've ever done.

At the doorway to the kitchen, a tightness stretches across my stomach, and I groan, rubbing the spot until it settles. I pause to catch my quickening breath.

"Narah, why aren't you in bed?" Crius rushes to my side. He's covered in a dusting of flour, not to mention it's streaked across his cheeks like war paint. He slides an arm across my back, his other on my large belly, and the moment he strokes me, I feel the kick of our baby.

My eyes go wide. "Did you feel our jelly bean?"

"Oh, Narah." Dropping to his knees, Crius kisses my enormous stomach, his eyes glistening as he murmurs soft whispers to our unborn child.

Nikos is there, wearing slacks and only an apron, and takes me in his arms, his kiss on my neck. "You smell divine, but you need to be off your feet. You're due any day now."

"I'm bored and don't want to be alone."

Suddenly, I'm in Niko's arms, and he sets me on a chair by the kitchen table. Crius brings a small stool and lifts my feet up on it. Next thing I know, they're bustling about the kitchen and bringing me a plate of pancakes, maple syrup, and juice. There's chopped-up fruit and freshly beaten cream as well, and I see they're still cooking.

"This is incredible," I murmur.

"Well, dig in," Nikos insists, leaning his back on the counter and watching me. This man, with bulging muscles and tattoos dressed in a frilly white apron and the one swimming in flour, his long hair looking more white than blond from the mess, are my world.

Seeing he's waiting for me to eat, I cut into the pancakes and take a bite, moaning as the fluffiness melts on my tongue. "Divine. I definitely need more."

"We're on it," Crius announces, sending me an air kiss.

Both of them are back at it, bickering about who flips the best pancakes, and I notice they have two frypans going, competing.

If there's such a thing as Nirvana, I've found it.

Swallowing my mouthful, I glance out the open back doors into the backyard. Fruit trees sway in the light breeze, and the sky glints like it's made of jewels. I catch sight of an apple dropping from its branch, a big red fruit, and I can already taste its sweetness on my tongue. Salivating, I'm on my feet and slowly waddle past the back door into the yard. My toes wriggle in the grass as I make my way to the tree and pick up the fallen apple. It smells delicious, and I take a crispy bite out of its flesh.

Juices fill my mouth, dribbling down my chin, but with it, a strange sensation rises through me once more. I've definitely forgotten something, but it's more than that. The taste of the apple reminds me I don't belong here. For a few moments, I'm a stranger standing in a gorgeous landscape. It makes no sense. My clothes aren't right, and I don't know this cottage. The flowers smell sickly sweet, and a distant wolf howl sings in the breeze. A longing squeezes in my chest.

A thread of something comes to me as I stare at the apple... a memory of a river, of me soaking wet, of—

"Narah!" Nikos' voice slices through my thoughts. Gone are the memory and sensation, and I turn to him. "Is everything alright?"

I blink at him as he emerges from our beautiful white cottage home.

His smile has me grinning as I make my way to him, dropping the apple behind.

"Yes, everything is perfect."

CHAPTER

SEVEN

RAGNAR

"Are you sure about this? What if they've been caught by the undead? What if—"

"Enough," Stone cut Jae off. We were all trekking up the mountain with barely any light for guidance. "I know you're scared for your sisters, but you need to trust us."

"Yes, but—"

"No buts. Crius and Nikos are warriors," Stone continues. "Nothing will happen to Narah. I give you my word." When I glance back at them over my shoulder, she's glaring at Stone.

"Just remember, I saved you from a zombie attack earlier today, so I get a say in the plans. I'm a contributor now."

Stone snorts. "Screaming, 'watch out,' isn't saving me."

"Oh, so I should have let it bite your ass?"

I laugh to myself.

"Should a girl your age use such language?" Stone's persistence in never giving in to her constant arguing is amusing and admirable. He's relentless in proving his point with Jae, and Jae won't have any part of it.

"So, I can fight and kill the undead, but I'm not allowed to say ass? Ass. Ass. Ass. What are you going to do about it?"

"I'll stuff your mouth with dirt, for one. I'm pretty sure Narah will

583

approve. In fact, I remember her telling me I could do anything to teach you some manners." Stone laughs. "Ouch," Stone suddenly moans. "You pinch so hard."

I chuckle to myself. He's keeping her occupied and not crying for her sisters, as she had already done twice on this exhausting trip.

We finally reach the top of the track on the mountain, and I turn, letting the duo catch their breath.

"We're close now," I say. "Let's hold talking to a minimum. We don't know what we're going to find."

Jae runs her two pinched fingers across her mouth and does a small twist at the corner to signify she'll keep it zipped. The girl is a handful, yet when I look into her eyes, I see Narah and miss her terribly.

My heart speeds up with the thought of what we'll do if we don't find Jae's sisters. If the situation was different, I would have left Jae with Mihai's pack and not put the young girl in danger. Of course, that bitch high priestess had to kill Lyssa, making my life more complicated.

It's past midnight, and the moon is high and bright, doing nothing to eliminate the surrounding shadows. After the two groups of undead we encountered and the enormous one we bypassed without being seen, every movement has me jittery as fuck. We might as well be back in Shadowlands Sector, where these fuckers were crawling all over the place.

I glance into the darkness, convinced if zombies are near, they would have already attacked. It doesn't ease my restless nerves. This morning, I knew the day would be a fucking beyond belief, and we weren't near finishing it, considering there's a high priestess on the loose in Kaira's body.

"So, what's the plan?" Stone whispers.

"I'll take the lead. Stay close behind until we know what we're dealing with."

Stone nods once, and we're on the move. Night swallows the woods, the breeze absent, and only the crickets sing and frogs croak. I cross the worn path amid the trees, a skill needed when hunting. Behind me, Jae's footsteps pat the ground, but Stone's steps are as silent as the night.

Anticipation tightens my gut. We're going in blind, but we'll make it work. We always do.

Once I reach the home that belongs to Narah's mother, I survey the land and the river, then turn to the house. Not a single light, no sound, unease scrapes its tongue along the back of my neck. When I turn toward Stone and Jae, I become aware of something strange off the path and next to a cluster of trees not far from the house–dark shapes sway from the trees like giant bats suspended from branches. Unable to make sense of what I'm looking at, goosebumps race up my spine.

"Stay here," I whisper and step toward the tree, my pulse thumping in my ears. My wolf is right in my chest, sensing the danger.

The shadows grow darker and more prominent the closer I move. What the fuck am I staring at? I pray it's something stupid and a play of the dark, except something inside me shudders. I can't put anything past the witch—especially when the hairs on my arms stand upright like they always do when there's magic in the air.

Darkness bleeds into everything, and only when I reach the edge of the tree do I pause and glance up. Feet are the first things I see, heavy combat boots, scuffed and worn, and attached to them are long, strong legs. Fuck me—bodies are dangling from the tree.

A hard breath, followed by a raspy inhale, and my head still spins to make sense of it all. Stepping around the tree, I notice the glint of silver in the streak of moonlight—an axe hooked on a belt.

Crius' axe.

My heart thunders as the realization sucker punches me in my solar plexus.

Three bodies hang from the tree, and panic squeezes me.

I can't breathe, but I'm already madly scaling the tree. My lungs are on fire as I picture them tied by their throats. My muscles tense as I shove myself higher until I reach the axis where branches stretch outward and come face to face with Crius—eyes shut, head slumped forward.

Desperately, I grab for him, only to notice he's not strung up by a noose. His torso and arms are tightly wrapped in wooden vines.

"Cirus." I shake him. But he's not moving. I press two fingers to the side of his neck and feel the pulse of his heart, slow but present.

Twisting, I struggle to move with limited foot space. On another branch is Nikos, and farther up, Narah dangles, shrouded in darkness. From my position, I can only see her feet.

"Stone," I call out just as I wrench out the blade from my belt. Without waiting for him, I hack at the first vine holding Nikos. A branch snaps forward, smacking me in the face, and I'm thrown backward. My boots slip out from under me, and I lurch. Arms flinging outward, I claw at the tree to catch purchase.

Thump.

Landing on my back, a sharp ache races across my shoulder blades.

"Fuck," I groan, lying there for a moment, catching my breath. My head pulses with pain, as does the strike across my brow, which still stings like a fucking bitch. Goddamn tree.

Stone is suddenly there, staring down at me with a grin and offering me his hand.

"Forgot how to climb trees, old man?"

"Fucking tree's cursed." With his help, I get to my feet and dust myself off. "Gods, how long have they been stuck up there in the tree like that?"

Before Stone gets a chance to check out the tree, Jae yelps, and Stone's instantly at her side, plastering a hand to her mouth. She points up, and he gives a guttural snarl.

"Fuck me!"

Next thing I know, he steps up to the tree and places both palms and his cheek against the trunk, listening to something.

Jae moves next to me, trembling. "Narah's up there, isn't she?"

"I'm afraid so." I hold her near, scanning the grounds and the house, my eyes lingering on the front door. I want to go in there and make sure we are alone. I feel vulnerable out here, an easy target.

"Stone, what's the verdict?" I ask, lowering my voice.

When Stone finally stops hugging the tree and turns to us, the runes across his collarbone and chest glow a bright blue, showing through his clothes.

"It's a trap spell to capture anyone who approaches the house. Lucky for us, these kinds of spells are a one-off thing when cast."

"Can you remove it?"

He arches an eyebrow. "Who do you think you're talking to?" He's cracking his knuckles.

"Without hurting them?" Jae blurts, the smartass taking the words right from my mouth.

"Now that, I can't promise, but I'll try. Every magic speaks differently. Now, step back."

"Well, try your best not to kill them," I snap as tension curls across my back.

"You got it." Most of the time, I appreciate Stone's aloofness, but sometimes, it sends my anxiety into overdrive.

Taking Jae's hand, we move back toward the path, keeping Stone and the tree, as well as the house, in my line of sight.

Stone turns back to the tree, and his soft murmurs carry on the breeze. He's had an affinity with nature since birth. It runs in his mother's bloodline, and the runes she had inked on him at a young age work as an activation dial to access his power.

His magic comes from the land, from family, and isn't as powerful or as varied as that of a witch, but it's fucking impressive. The things I've seen him do still blow my mind. To think his father rejected him because of the runes. In the Alpha's fucked-up mind, men didn't harness magic. It was a female ability.

The first time Stone accidentally used his power at home, his father broke two of his ribs and tossed him out of their home. Stone had only been eight years old. My family took him in, and we grew up together as brothers. Not that my home was a prime example of family happiness, but he had food and a roof over his head.

"Will Narah be okay?" Jae tugs on my sleeve. "I mean, why are they tied up in the tree? Is something feeding on them?" She's blinking a lot, and her eyes glisten.

"If anyone can find out, it's Stone. Whatever happens, we'll deal with it." I rub her back. "My mother once said when I let bad thoughts into my head, I was giving the universe permission to make them a reality. Instead, think of the positive things you want to happen."

"So, what am I supposed to do? That's all I can think of now."

I laugh softly. "It'll take time, but trust me, it works."

Suddenly, the earth shudders under my feet, and Jae presses herself to my side. Holding her, we take a few steps back. Stone's still facing the tree, his hands on the trunk, but the air's changed. It feels charged, lifting the small hairs on my nape.

One moment we're watching, the next, the ground shakes hard, the tree sways, and the branches shake. All I can do is watch in horror as the three bodies of those closest to me swing wildly. My heart lurches to the back of my throat.

"You know what you're doing?" I call out. Stone doesn't respond, but I trust him. Fuck, I do, but magic is an unpredictable bitch.

He's suddenly thrown backward, but Stone's never one to stay down and is back on his feet in seconds. Blue magic dances from his hands and stretches outward, coiling around the trunk. The tree hasn't stopped swaying.

"Oh God, I think it's trying to climb out of the ground," Jae mutters, her body tensing against my side.

She's right. Roots jut out of the ground all around the tree and seem to be rocking out of the foundations.

"What are you doing?" I call a bit louder. "Please tell me it's not a repeat of those attacking trees in the Poisonous Woods."

"I've got this," he hisses. "The only way to end the curse is to kill the tree, which means cutting off its life force." He's basically digging the tree out of the ground.

The cold dread of fear twists in my gut that this could put Narah and my men in greater danger.

"Okay, you heard him." As much as I feel hopeless, I need to trust Stone.

Drawing Jae a few steps away, we wait and watch the three of them sway from the branches. With the tree halfway out of the ground, there's a loud crack.

The branch Crius is hanging from drops, and he hits the ground. I lunge toward him with a blade in hand. Crius moans, but the damn vines remain tight around him. Grabbing the axe from his belt, I slash at the vines running from the tree to him, needing to sever the connection. The branch might have snapped, but evidently, it's not enough.

The more I dismember, the more Crius shoves against the restraints. I'm hacking madly when I hear another splintering of wood, and Nikos is thrown to the hard ground. A final chop and I sprint over to Nikos.

The whole time, Stone's murmuring words, his eyes fluttering backward, his eyes completely white.

Nikos is awake, swearing like a beast and thrashing. "Narah. Get Narah," he growls at me.

"Crius," I yell out.

The guy's stumbling toward me, unable to walk a straight line.

"Give it to me. I'll do it. Go get Narah."

Nikos' eyes bulge when Jae takes the axe, but I don't have time to argue.

With most of the tree out of the ground, I dart under the tree, frantically chasing a swinging Narah. My heart's thumping, the air thick with magic. A growl slips from my lips with urgency and frustration.

When the thunderous snap of wood resonates, a jolt of panic strikes me. The branch with Narah swings left behind the tree. I charge in that direction just as the branch breaks away from the tree. I jerk my arms out and lunge to where she's coming down.

Her terrified cries suddenly fill the air.

She hits me hard, driving me to my knees, but I grasp her with all my strength and lean backward to take her weight, anything to not drop her.

My little fox feels so warm against me and so much bigger, which tells me more vines are tied around her.

"Hello there, gorgeous. I've got you."

"Ragnar?" she groans, then winces.

Standing, I rush out of the shadows into the open. I quickly place her on the lawn, and Jae's there, giving me the axe.

Something looks wrong.

She's crying with pain, and her body's wrapped in the vines, but why are there so many around her?

Frantically, I cut the vines, with Jae, Nikos, and Crius on their knees, pulling at the massive mess.

"We're here," Nikos says.

Crius is cooing something about a jelly bean, but I'm not paying attention. Finally, I hack the last connection, and we rapidly tear away the vegetation.

I freeze, startled.

Narah's on her back, whining, her hands clasping a massive, round belly.

I had expected to find her bruised and hurt from being tied so tightly... but no one could have prepared me for this. No one.

"Oh my God, Narah," Jae blurts out. "You're pregnant!"

EIGHT

RAGNAR

"Sweet Hell, I'm still pregnant," Narah cries out in shock, staring at her belly and rubbing it. "I can't see my feet."

"That's what you're worried about?" Jae mutters. "How did you get so big, so fast? Did you swallow a whole pig?"

"Jae," Stone warns in a deep voice, then turns to me with a furrowed brow. "But seriously, angel, did you eat something that didn't agree with you?"

I'm by her side in seconds, an arm around her back to support her as she rubs her lower back. Her shirt keeps riding up across her midriff, revealing her round stomach. Confused, my head hurts, trying to come to terms with this.

Yet my dick is rock hard at her curvy body and how gorgeous she looks. I'm completely captivated.

"Narah," I say, my voice cracking as I stare deep into her eyes. I'm so overwhelmed, I don't have words. She presses herself closer. My heart swells that she's carrying a child, and my knees actually wobble. Am I ready for this?

"This is kinda scaring me. I'm not exactly ready for this," Narah admits.

"I have you, little fox. We all do, and we're going to get through this together. I don't really understand how you could be so pregnant, so I need you to help me."

Her large eyes burn a bright amber, and her hair is messy with small twigs in it, but her touch is like silk. My hands itch to strip her and explore how beautiful she is with her baby belly. When she groans and holds her side, I swoop her into my arms.

"You need to rest." I carry her to a small wooden bench by the river and away from the house.

"Whatever spell we triggered, it sent all three of us into a dream state," she explains, as the others quickly follow.

"It was freaky as fuck," Crius mutters. "I was a damn kitchen maid making pancakes."

"Wait! What?" I blurt, and Jae laughs.

"We were cooking pancakes for Narah because she was pregnant," Nikos details.

"And I woke up in a strange bed," she begins. "I was pregnant and living in a small cottage. In my head, I knew it was my home, and I was happy there, living with my two husbands. But something felt wrong, as if I knew things weren't right, but my head was so fuzzy. It's so confusing."

"All I remember was how excited I was that you were having our baby," Nikos says, sidling up next to Narah on the bench.

Crius moves behind her, stroking her shoulders and smiling down at her, completely smitten.

"I'll be honest, seeing you this way turns me on," Crius purrs.

"Ew, gross," Jae blurts out. Crius only shrugs and kisses Narah on the top of her head.

The obsession in their eyes for Narah ignites a flare in my chest, carving away at my heart. I'm not jealous, but I feel like I've missed out on a moment that means so much.

"Well, if it was a dream, why in the world am I still pregnant? I mean, it can't be real, right?"

She's not as big as some pregnant women, but for her small size, she has a perfect baby bump. Call me insane, but it suits her perfectly. Her breasts, I notice, are much larger, and I love every inch of them.

"Stone, any insight into what we're dealing with?" Nikos asks.

Stone seems to be as shocked as I am, staring at Narah in disbelief. He makes his way to her, falling to his knees.

"Narah, you are so beautiful, and no matter what, I will take care of you and the baby. Anything for you."

"Geez, has everyone got baby on the brain? You're all acting so weird," Jae says. "She's freaking pregnant when she wasn't yesterday."

Narah's lips pinch tightly as she fumbles to pull her shirt down over her belly.

"So, is this a spell that needs to be removed, or is it actually happening? It feels real and really terrifying."

"Well." Stone rubs his mouth with the back of his hand. "Something could have gone haywire since you were already spelled to go into heat, then the trapping spell put you in a trance or coma, so there was definitely some overlapping magic. Crossing magic never plays up."

"So, what? I'm pregnant and almost due in the span of one night?"

"Impossible." Jae chuffs.

"I can only guess. I've never seen this before." Stone sits up from his heels in front of Narah, taking her hand against his chest. "Whatever it is, we'll know once we find Lyra."

"I'm going to guess the baby's most likely mine," Crius declares out of the blue, "I was the last one to f—" His words flatline as they land on Jae, who's giving him a death glare.

"Or Ragnar's," Nikos adds. "You were both with Narah the same, and you don't need to knot in an Omega to make her pregnant. It's not foolproof."

"Oh, this is so gross. I'm going to have nightmares for the rest of my life. Please stop talking about it." Jae covers her ears.

"Let's focus." My gaze lingers on Narah's breasts, so I tear my attention back to her face. She's smirking at me, and my balls tighten at how absolutely gorgeous she looks. I swallow, trying to think of what I was about to say as my pulse throbs in my throat and her sweet, nectar scent teases my nostrils.

"We need to go inside and check the house for Lyra. Stone, you'll lead this with your magic. Narah isn't—"

"I'm not sitting back. She has my sister." She holds out her arm. "Help me up. You know you can't take her down on your own, and this needs to end tonight. Sure, I'm as huge as a whale, but I'm not any less deadly."

"Is it safe to use magic during pregnancy?" Nikos asks.

Narah shrugs, and Stone runs a hand through his hair. "I've seen pregnant witches back home use it without issue."

"As have I," I respond. "I don't think it would affect the baby." An arm around her back, I lift her with ease, holding her against me. "I don't want you to get hurt, but maybe you're right about us going in together. Crius, Stone, Nikos, check the perimeter around the house, see if you can look into the window for any activity."

With a quick nod, Stone takes the lead, followed by Nikos and Crius.

Narah's stomach is so warm and comforting against me. I never thought about being a father or having my own family. There's too much for me to conquer, and now the universe has thrown me a massive curve ball.

The shock has left my mind buzzing, yet excitement sparks across my chest that Narah is carrying our child. I don't even care if it's mine or Crius'. We're one unit, one family, and it's ours. My thoughts are churning, spinning on themselves, and I desperately want to touch her stomach.

"There's way too much lovey-dovey stuff." Jae rolls her eyes. "I'm going down by the river, but I have one question. This will make me an aunt now, right?"

"I guess," Narah answers, sitting back down.

"Yes! Technically, I'm an adult."

Before either of us can correct Jae, she's moving to the river's edge, where we can see her clearly.

"Are you okay with this?" Narah asks. "You're staring at me strangely, and when you first saw me, you paled."

"Of course, I'm okay. I won't deny I'm still reeling, but I would never leave you. You're in this position because of the decisions we all made."

"What if it's not a spell, and well, I have an actual baby? Goddess, how can this be happening to me? I feel awkward even talking about it. We're just getting to know each other, figuring out how to make things work, and now this." She looks down at her stomach, rambling like she does when she's nervous. "I'm scared, and you've all been dragged into this." She draws in a heavy breath, then winces, her hand in the middle of her stomach.

I move my hand next to hers, and a tiny kick taps my palm. My heart thrumming, I grin, thinking about a little life inside Narah.

"Narah. I felt it."

"Jelly bean. It's what we call it in the dream state."

"I want to have this child with you." I smile, buzzing all over with an inexplicable warmth and an overabundance of emotions. "Our child. Our jelly bean. I never thought I'd want this, but feeling the kick..."

She leans against my chest, and I hold her, well aware how terrifying this must be for her. I glance back at the house, noticing the men are returning quickly. With a whistle, I grab Jae's attention and call her back with a flick of my hand.

"My little fox, we just need to get through tonight, then we'll work out our next steps. You are the priority now. You and Jelly Bean." Kissing her soft lips, her breasts are absolutely tempting. Before I lose myself, I get to my feet.

"What'd you find?"

"Not a sign of life. Unless she's in there sleeping, we don't know until we go inside."

"Then we're doing this," Narah says, getting up with Jae's help.

"Okay, we move in and keep Narah and Jae between us at all times."

There's no hesitation. We're all ready to deal with this.

Narah

One day, I'll wake up and not face life or death scenarios. Today has to be the strangest day of my life, and I just want it to be over.

Dealing with witches comes with dangers, but ending up pregnant takes it to a completely different level of insanity.

I'm nineteen, and I hadn't expected to have a baby until I was at least in my middle to late twenties, and that was if I found an Alpha to protect us. Sure, I have four of them, but we're in the middle of chaos and nowhere close to being able to have a child. We don't even have our own home where we could care for a newborn.

Going back to the Bane Wolves pack is a possibility, but I haven't even spoken to Ragnar about the outcome when the Alpha found out his daughter had been slaughtered.

So what do we do? Live in my mother's home? I grimace at the thought that she killed people in this house, and I don't have it in me to stay here.

"Are you okay?" Jae asks, sidling next to me as we wait for Nikos to break in the front door.

"I'm okay, considering." I give her a lopsided grin. "What about you? I haven't even had a chance to talk to you and tell you everything."

"Stone pretty much told me everything." She shrugs and looks at Stone, who's at my back, grinning and listening to our quiet chat.

"I know, but you're my younger sister, and I should be looking after you." I take her hand in mine, slightly squeezing it. "I shouldn't put you in danger."

"Is there such a thing as somewhere with no danger?" she asks, sounding so much more mature than she should.

"I promise you, sweetheart, we'll find a place to call home soon."

She hugs me, and I hold her against me, wishing I could hold her safe forever, and that scares me. Look at the horrible job I'm doing with my sisters. What will I be like with a baby? An ache settles in my shoulders, thinking I will be a bad mother. What do I know about raising a child, anyway?

"We're in," Nikos whispers over his shoulder, drawing my attention. Slowly opening the door, he and Ragnar move in first, and we're right on their heels.

I shake off my thoughts, knowing this isn't the time to worry. I have enough troubles on my plate.

Inside, the house is so dark, I can barely see my hands, let alone anything else. In moments, a flame flickers to life from the candle in Nikos' hand.

"Where'd you find that?" I whisper.

"I remember seeing it on a shelf in this room last time I was here, and I always carry matches." He hands a candle to Ragnar and another to Stone, and I assume that's all there is.

We leave behind the hallway and enter the main room with a massive fireplace on the left, illuminated by Nikos. He's moving quickly through the room with the other two, searching to see if we're alone. Crius remains at our back, with his hand on my waist. His touch is so warm, and it's comforting to know he's there for us.

The more rooms we search, the more it becomes apparent we might be alone after all.

My pulse is racing regardless as I hold Jae near my side. She doesn't say a word, but she knows this is where our mother lived without us. In a place so run down, there are holes in the wall, part of the ceiling has fallen away, and the kitchen is a gutted mess with things thrown everywhere. The place is destroyed, and I don't know how it got like that, but it's startling to see it.

Mother's obsession with bringing our father back to life—without being a zombie—has cost her dearly and us so much. The sting of seeing him alive, knowing so many lives died for him, still tears me up. I loved seeing him but knew it wasn't right.

My throat thickens with emotions, but I can't fall apart, especially not in front of Jae. Holding her hand, I draw her even closer to my side.

"You okay?" I whisper.

"Yeah, for sure. This place is a mess."

Our steps head down the long hallway when I notice a faint flicker of light under the door to my right. Panic twists and turns inside me like pincers. I tell Jae to catch up with the others at the end of the hall. Grabbing Stone's hand, I point to the light skimming the base of the door.

"We go in there," I whisper, opening myself up to my magic. I do my best to focus on not drawing power from within me and putting the baby in danger.

"Let me go first," Stone murmurs back, the blue glow of his runes piercing through his shirt.

My breath hitches as he pushes open the door. A dim light greets us from somewhere in the basement. Of course, that's where Lyra would be.

Shivers dance up my arm, but I push the fear aside. Following Stone, we creep down the stairs. My hands buzz with the call of magic, despite not calling on it, and I feel it tingling along my fingers. Breathing deeply, I concentrate on only drawing energy from around me and more specifically, Lyra. If it knocks her out, we can tie her up long enough to stop her from attacking us.

We reach the base of the stairs, and while Stone goes right where the light shines brighter, something calls me from the left. The sensation of pin pricks runs up my left hand, and I turn in that direction. Barely a few steps in, I freeze on the spot, my breaths hitching.

In front of me, Lyra, still in my sister's body, is hunched over my dead mother's body, her mouth gaping open, a glowing yellow light racing from my mother's body and flooding into her mouth.

Terror shudders through me. All I can think is she's going to kill Kaira, that my sister will never be the same again.

Anger flares in a heartbeat, and the cruel heat consumes me, leaving me burning up. With it, desperation pummels me. Without pause, I unleash the floodgates of my magic.

Yellow light radiates across Lyra's back and zips toward me. It floods me, filling every pore, feeling as if someone's scraping thorns over my body. I steal her magic, her darkness, everything she has.

Suddenly, she jerks up and twists in my direction.

Startled, I stumble backward, and a rush of breath, hard and fast, speeds past my lips, and the acid taste of magic fills my nostrils.

"You've come to die," she growls, sounding more like an animal.

Fury pummels me, and I picture my sister, terrified and trapped.

With that single thought, power tears out of me, covering me with the feel of static running over my skin. It spears outward from my hands just as Stone calls my name from behind me. Blue beams of light strike Lyra so hard and fast, I couldn't stop if I tried.

Shaking, I fall to my knees.

The High Priestess bellows, and her yellow magic bursts from her hands, but unlike mine, it goes outward in every direction, engulfing everything in sight.

Panic tears through me that she's going to kill us all, that we'd made a mistake coming in here.

For those few seconds, I am convinced this is the end.

This is where I'll die.

Startled awake, I look at a white ceiling drenched in sunlight. For those few seconds, I'm convinced I'm back in my coma dream—the small cottage with my two husbands, enjoying the perfect little life without a worry in the world. With it comes a selfish relief that in that cozy home, I'm safe, but I've left others I love behind.

With a groan, I roll onto my side, glancing out the open window that brings in a cool breeze. Outside, the trees sway, and I still have no idea where I am.

A sudden tightness in my stomach stabs across my side. Right, I'm still pregnant. All my thoughts rush through my mind—the witch possessing Kaira, me finding her in the basement with my dead mother, and me attacking her with my magic. Someone must have carried me upstairs after I passed out.

A spark of terror envelops me, and I can't raise my hands to my face quick enough. There's not a trace of black on my fingers, and I exhale loudly with relief that I hadn't drained energy from myself and harmed the baby.

It's strange how worried I am when a day ago, I wasn't pregnant or even thinking about having children. There's something so different about suddenly sharing your body with a gorgeous little angel, but the memories of my time living in the cottage offer a fake sensation of being pregnant for the full term.

Pushing up in an awkward move of arms and legs, feeling like a turtle on its back, I stumble out of bed. Glancing down at myself, I'm wearing a long shirt and nothing else. Someone changed me after I blacked out.

"What are you doing up?" Jae shrieks from behind me.

Twisting around, I find her in the doorway, hands gripping her hips with a stern expression, and I laugh. "Get over here, you," I say, ecstatic and over the moon that she's safe. Considering she's not panicking yet, I hope that means good news after last night's events, where I evidently blacked out.

She runs across the room, closing the distance, and is at my side, hugging me around my belly.

"I was so scared you were hurt, I barely slept last night. In fact, I was lying next to you, hoping you'd wake up, but of course, you do when I pop out to use the bathroom."

"I'm okay," I say with brazen confidence. "Where's Kaira? Are Ragnar and the others here?"

She takes my hand and brings me back to the bed. "Take a seat."

Unease travels up my spine. "Is it that bad?"

"I don't know." She shakes her head. "We've been waiting for you to wake up so we can make sure you're safe."

"Okay, I'm here. Tell me," I ask impatiently, sitting on the edge of the bed, then shifting a few times until I find a comfortable spot. Once I'm settled, Jae flops down next to me, touching my stomach and smirking.

"On a side note, I'm so excited to be an aunty, but last night, I realized I didn't ask you if you were happy about it. I mean, I would be freaking out if it was me, but you seemed okay to be pregnant. Those men out there were going all baby crazy over you, with Nikos talking about building a cradle with wheels to carry the baby around. I never thought I'd see a Viking warrior go all gushy." She giggles.

Her words have me grinning like silly to hear they're just as excited as I am.

"The truth is, I'm still getting used to it. I love it, but it's left me shell-shocked, and it's the worst possible timing."

"Is it ever the right time?"

I grin and run a hand over her long hair across her forehead, making a mental note I need to trim her hair as soon as things settle down.

"Guess not, but this is really a bad time with all the stuff happening."

"I know, but whatever happens, you have us, and this little bub already has six people who love him or her." Her lips form an O shape, and her eyes are just as round. "What if you have twins?"

"Okay, you're giving me heart palpitations. Let's not say that right now. I'm trying really hard not to even think about how I'm going to give birth without a midwife." Wrapping an arm around her shoulders, I hold her against me. "But you're right. We'll always have each other. No matter what, we'll be together. We'll all live in a huge house with a large kitchen and a garden out back. You and Kaira will have your own rooms."

"What about the guys?" she asks, smiling. "I just don't think there's a big enough bed for all five of you, plus the baby."

"Didn't I mention that as aunty, you get babysitting duties, including the little one sleeping in your room?" I tease, ruffling her hair.

She cuts me a narrow gaze. "I'm not saying no, but we'll see about that."

A comfortable silence falls in the room, and I finally ask, "So is Kaira free of the High Priestess?"

"Not quite, but she's safe. Last night, after you used your magic on the High Priestess, you basically drew her energy into you, then knocked both of you out. She's still inside Kaira, but she's tied up and inside a protection spell, so she can't escape."

"How can she still be stuck?" I sigh heavily, the chill of the news hardening in my chest. "I did everything I could to get rid of the witch." Part of me worried we'd come too late, and whatever Lyra drew from my mother had permanently fused her with my sister.

A tremble rushes down my spine at the thought we might never free Kaira.

"Stone has been reading Mother's books all night to see if there are any spells or information about how to exorcise someone." She chews on the corner of her lip.

I know she's scared. She doesn't have to say it, but I hear it in her voice. I don't intend to put more fright into her.

"We'll find a way. Nothing is ever permanent." Coaxing a smile from her brings me a flutter of hope we can save Kaira.

The clatter of something heavy hitting the floorboards resonates, and I look toward the doorway. "What's that?"

"Crius and Stone are attempting to put together the broken table and chairs so we have a place for breakfast. Ragnar and Nikos have gone to the local pack market to get food."

Slowly rising to my feet, Jae places a pair of sandals in front of me to step into. I don't ask whose they are and just wear them.

"Where's Kaira?"

"In Mother's bedroom. She's still unconscious, but Stone is keeping a close eye on her. You know, it's weird being here. I know Mother lived here, but to me, it doesn't feel like her." She shrugs. "Maybe I was too young when she left us to really remember her." There's heartache in her chest.

How could there not be? When I first found out Mother had excluded us from her life, I was hurt and jealous. It pains me to see Jae brushing the hurt away when I know deep inside, she's upset.

"I love you, Jae." I drag her into my arms. "We're all the family we need. I'll always be here for you."

When she finally wriggles free of my embrace, she wipes her eyes and smiles.

"Come see what they've been creating."

Following Jae into a hallway, I blink at what I see. Huge holes puncture the walls, the ceiling is half broken, one beam hanging down, and I have to step over a gaping fissure in the floorboards.

"Hmm, I don't remember the place looking this bad last night, or was it so dark, I missed it?"

"Ah, yes," Jae says over her shoulder, then hops over another hole. "When the witch attacked you last night in retaliation with her magic, it went haywire and basically ripped through the house. I'm surprised it's still upright. It shook like crazy after you passed out. You should have seen the chaos of the four guys running around madly to save you and imprison the witch."

"Wow, I missed out on all the fun," I say sarcastically, coaxing a laugh from Jae.

Despite the craziness of my life, there's a calmness in the air today, which I appreciate. I'm not sure I could take too many stressful days.

Entering the main room, Stone and Crius are standing back, evaluating a round table and an eclectic collection of chairs, stools, and upside-down wooden crates for seats. When they turn in our direction, the elation spreading across their faces has me tearing up.

"Angel," Stone blurts out, rushing over to me, as does Crius. I'm in their arms faster than I can say hello, and suddenly, I'm off my feet.

"You're awake," Crius coos, running a hand over my brow as if checking my temperature. "And you're looking well. How do you feel?"

Stone has me sitting on a cushioned high-back seat by the table, then they both drag chairs to sit on either side of me while Jae grabs me a glass of water and sets it in front of me.

"Relaxed and like I've slept for eternity."

The men stare at me as though they can't get enough of me, their hands all over me. I think about how scared they must have been all night with me passed out, and this is them dealing with that dread.

"You had us worried to death. We had to do something to keep ourselves occupied," Stone explains, glancing at the table.

"This is where my axe came in handy," Crius adds, grinning wickedly.

"Wait, you made this table from scratch?" I ask.

"Are you mad? Of course not," Crius says. "I chopped the uneven legs so it stopped wobbling."

Jae's bursting out laughing. "You should have heard how much he swore as if it was the hardest thing in the world."

The creak of the floorboards has us looking up. Ragnar and Nikos enter the room, carrying a large box. It seems like a lot of food for breakfast, but there are six mouths to feed... seven, actually. Thinking of Kaira, my chest aches.

"Narah," Nikos says, rushing over to set the box on the table. Jae is already pawing through the food.

Ragnar's at my side in moments, nudging past Crius to lean in and steal a kiss. Then he peppers my face, and I'm in heaven. When did I get so lucky to have these men in my life? Nikos also takes a kiss, then, of course, Stone and Crius do the honors, and I'm left burning up. Despite the pregnancy, a level of arousal still lingers in my body, just not as intense as before.

After giving me a rundown of what happened after I passed out, mirroring Jae's explanation, we all sit around the table. The men are broad-shouldered, and nothing is ever big enough when it involves all four, so it's a tight squeeze.

"Well, what's to eat? I'm starving." Crius hands out plates he must have found in the kitchen, which still resembles a murder scene.

"The selection of food to buy at the market was limited," Nikos says. With Jae's help, he places a large bag of peaches and grapes on the table, followed by what resembles a mountain of fried flatbread. "These are Romanian and filled with all kinds of ingredients. Some have potatoes, others meat or cheese. They're called plăcintă or something like that and smell delicious."

Everyone collects a round flatbread easily larger than my head.

Stone serves me, and I discover mine is filled with meat and green onion. The moment it touches my tongue, I might have died and gone to heaven. Still warm, the savory taste is incredible. Taking another bite, noticing I'm not the only one who's fallen quiet and tearing into the food, I smile. It's great to finally have some food in my stomach.

"Tell me there's more in the box," Crius mutters with a mouthful while reaching for a second piece.

"Got you covered," Nikos answers. "When we ordered fifty pieces, we may have made the Beta's day at the market stand. It's why it took us so long. We had to wait while they cooked them all. Figured if we eat the meat ones, we can take what's left and the fruit on our trip."

"We're leaving?" I almost choke on my flatbread.

Ragnar looks at me, his lips pursed. "We need to talk about our next steps. We're not safe here. Martell knows this is your mother's house, so how long before he turns up when he doesn't find us with the Bane Wolves?"

I blink at him, the food in my stomach sitting heavy. One day of normality, of not feeling scared for my life, is all I ask for.

"We can't risk you getting hurt right now," Nikos adds.

"So, where can we be safe?" I ask, putting the flatbread down and wiping my oily fingers on the kitchen tea towel we're all sharing.

Ragnar swallows the food in his mouth, and every eye is on him. I can't tell if the rest of the group knows about this decision, but I'm certainly in the dark.

"Our priority is your pregnancy, Narah, and that means getting you to safety. That might mean we all travel south into the Shadowlands Sector."

I gasp loud enough to draw attention to myself.

"I'm so confused. Didn't you want to take over Savage Sector? Why aren't we just hiding low elsewhere for now?" I drop my gaze to my belly, which is covered in crumbs. "I don't think I have it in me to travel that far. Then there's Kaira. What's the plan? Drag her with us while a psycho high priestess still possesses her?" My head's spinning. I don't mean to come across as difficult, but my patience isn't exactly cooperating.

"I've thought about that. Hear me out," Ragnar says and takes a deep inhale. "I know the Alpha in Shadowlands Sector, and he's a man with strong morals. From what I've seen, he's not corruptible. We lie low until you give birth. Your safety is more important to me, and I'll deal with Mihai somehow." He pauses, giving me the chance to respond, but I'm still not sure how I feel.

"The Alpha's Omega, Meira, is the most incredible girl, who I adore. She saved me when I was stuck there. I know she'll help us," Jae says, bouncing in her seat.

"So, how do we get down there?" I ask.

"Carriage," Nikos says. "There are roads and those willing to take passengers at a cost. We hire one of them, and hopefully, you're off your feet for most of the trip."

"And Kaira," I ask.

Ragnar runs a hand over his mouth, and I see this is a topic of concern in his eyes.

"I had a thought, which is controversial," Ragnar says softly. His eyes lock on mine, then he twists toward Nikos. "Go collect some water from the river and take Jae with you."

"What, no," Jae protests. "I want to hear this."

Nikos stands and yanks her chair away from the table, with her in it. "You'll hear all about it later, trust me."

Jae sighs loudly, rolling her eyes. "I always miss out on all the fun." She drags her feet as she follows Nikos outside.

Clearly, whatever he has planned, he doesn't want Jae to know, which sets off my trepidation.

"I'm worried whatever Lyra took from your mom has made her more powerful, and nothing we do will remove her from your sister's body. The longer we leave them locked together, the greater harm could come to Kaira," Ragnar explains in a serious tone.

"So, what do you have in mind?" I ask, fumbling with the kitchen towel in my lap.

"Do you remember how your mother cleansed us of the curse? She completely reset us."

"Are you insane?" I rear back. "You want to kill Kaira?" I get to my feet and pace up and down the room, going over the chaos Mother caused us. "She drowned us in the river behind her house, drew our energy, then revived us with magic. Yes, we were reset, but at a huge risk we might not make it or that we'd turn into zombies."

Ragnar's lips grew thin.

"I don't know if it'll work. What will happen to Lyra?" I pause at the end of the table. Crius and Stone haven't said a word, but I see the dread in their expressions, too.

"I guess she'll be evicted from Kaira's body, and with nowhere to go, she'll perish," Ragnar answers.

"There's a lot of guessing. What if I accidentally draw her into me?" Shaking, I sat on a stool, placing a hand over my belly.

"We use an object to focus the energy, so that doesn't happen," Stone speaks up finally. "I've seen witches do it to eradicate dark spirits."

"This isn't what I want," Ragnar says, moving over to sit by my side and taking my hand in his. "But we don't have another solution. We need her out of your sister before it's too late and before she attacks us."

My chest rises and falls quickly with shallow breaths while my pulse thunders. So many thoughts blur in my mind, and nothing I can think of offers a way to remove the witch.

"I'm terrified for my sister... and for us."

"I'll help you." Stone comes to my side. "I can't use your kind of magic, but I will do what I can to protect us all."

"The sooner, the better," Ragnar reminds me.

The urgency drums louder in my skull.

I stare at Crius, who's been too quiet. "What about you? What do you think?"

He licks his lips and gets to his feet. "I fucking hated the idea when Ragnar first told me. What we went through was horrifying, and I wouldn't wish it upon anyone, but I don't see another way out of this fucked up situation. That bitch has her claws in Kaira, and using the curse removal and the river may be the only way to rip her out."

I want to admit the solution might work, but I'm scared out of my mind. Ragnar wraps his arm around my back, but instead of comfort, I break down and cry. My emotions are all over the place, and I can't seem to think. He holds me against him, his warm breath on my cheek as his hand rubs my back.

"It's going to be okay," he tells me as the other two join in, embracing me. "I would never suggest anything that would harm your sister."

"I know. It's just scary, and I'm feeling stupid emotional right now." When I finally come up for air, these three crazy men, who I've fallen so deeply for, are there to greet me with warming smiles.

"How does a foot massage sound?" Crius asks. "While you think it over?"

I laugh at him as more tears fall. "I think my tear ducts are broken."

Grinning, Ragnar takes me in his arms, not showing any sign of letting me go, and kisses my wet cheeks.

"Cry all you need. We'll be here to catch every tear," Stone says, pushing my hair aside.

"Okay, now you're making it worse by being so sweet." I'm laughing as Jae and Nikos return.

"So, what did I miss?" Jae asks. "Is someone going to fill me in?"

Taking in a deep breath, I slowly release it. She's not going to like it, but we're out of time and options.

TEN

NARAH

"You can't," Jae repeats for the tenth time, tears flooding her eyes. "You're going to kill Kaira," she rasps, her voice choking. "I can't even wrap my head around doing that to her."

Holding her trembling hand, I fight the urge not to fall apart. My insides are crushed at seeing Jae so distraught.

"It's only temporary, then I'll bring her back," I desperately try to explain to my sister. I don't think I would have the strength if I had to explain this to Kaira as well. I'm praying she'll be back with us soon enough, and all of this will be behind us.

Right now, Jae's staring at me with tears in her eyes, and it's ripping me apart to see her agony. I would have preferred she wasn't brought into any of this. She's already seen so much ugliness in this world, but to have her witness the cruel decision we have to make, the risk we're taking with Kaira is destroying me.

"Come with me." Taking her hand, I draw her down the hallway to Mother's room. My pulse speeds up, seeing Kaira tied to a chair, which is chained to the bed. Rope is wound around her middle and ankles, her arms behind her back, and her head slumped forward. A thick circle of salt surrounds her, along with crushed herbs and a protection spell Stone found in one of my mother's books.

Kaira has been this way since last night, and I trembled to see her in such a state. Every inch of me burns with guilt, but what else could we do? Lyra was dangerous. One mistake could let her escape, and one of us might be killed.

"I hate this so much." Jae softly sobs. "I just want Kaira back. She doesn't deserve to be tied up like a prisoner."

"I know, but we can't find any other way to remove the witch from Kaira's body. My magic didn't work, so we have to try Mother's method. It burns me to see Kaira like this, but what happens if we don't remove the witch possessing her? Who will she kill next?" My throat chokes, and I fight the urge to cry, trying to be strong for Jae.

She just sobs into her hands. I bring her into my embrace, stroking her hair and cooing, "It's going to be alright. You'll see. I bet if Kaira could have a say, she'd ask us why we haven't already done the spell and freed her."

Jae hiccups and looks up at me. "She would do that, then make us feel guilty. She's always so impatient. I'm just scared for her. I don't want to risk her life, but I can't stand seeing her this way."

Every word squeezes my heart, and my throat thickens. I clear it, then murmur, "Just think, when this works, she'll be so shocked to see me in this state. Remember that time she told us she wanted to have ten kids?"

Jae giggles, wiping her eyes. "And they were all going to be girls because she wanted a pack made up of only female warriors."

A beat of silence passes between us. My thoughts fly to Kaira's fierceness, and I know she's fighting and will never give in to Lyra.

Jae's lips pinch to the side, and I reach over to dry her cheeks of tears.

"I think we should do it. She'd want that."

"Whatever you feel comfortable with, sweetie." I have to be strong for both my sisters, but I'm so full of guilt and fear, I worry that I'll crumble inside and out. I don't have a choice. I have to do this for Kaira and all our sakes.

Jae gnaws on the corner of her fingernail, and I tenderly take her hand and lead her out of the room.

"Let's get our sister back."

"Okay. Please just don't let her become a zombie."

"Of course," I say confidently, though, on the inside, I'm quivering. I have no idea what I'm doing, but if I've proven anything to myself, it's that I'm incredible at winging things.

Nikos

"How do we get stuck with all the fucked-up jobs?" Crius whines as he and I maneuver Narah's mother out of the basement, where we moved her the last time we'd been in the house.

Her body is dead cold and already in a state of decomposition. Fingernails and teeth have fallen out, and she reeks. The musty stench of rotting flesh has me on the verge of gagging each time I inhale.

"Just hurry the hell up. I'm taking all the weight down here." My arms strain at the bottom of the stairs, with Crius in the lead.

Heaving her up each step, he groans. His fists are white from gripping the bedsheet we'd rolled her in.

By the time we make it to the hallway, she slips from my grip, and her feet thump onto the wooden floors.

"I don't know why you're complaining. I'm carrying most of the head and torso, and it stinks. I think she might be reaching a liquifying state." Crius stares at the wet patches on the bedsheet.

I don't even want to think about it, or I'll puke all over her.

"Just fucking pick her up, and let's get her outside. Then I'm scrubbing my body with a wire brush." I bend and wrench the fabric once more, and we hurry through the house toward the back door.

Stone and Narah had discovered her mother's curse removal spell and paired it with another spell to remove spirits from possessed people. For that, a body was needed to expel the spirit into and a talisman that evidently would draw any nearby spirits to it like a magnet. Apparently, Lyra's spirit should be snatched into the dead body, then vanquished almost instantly.

Patching the spells together terrifies me, but we're not exactly swimming in options to save Kaira.

Once in the yard, the afternoon sky grumbles with dark storm clouds, promising rain. Following Crius, we make a fast stumble to the riverbank and dump the body. I groan, stretching my back, while Crius crouches by the water's edge, frantically washing his hands. My skin crawls just as much.

Twisting around, I find Stone and Ragnar in a heated discussion with Narah. Jae's sitting on the lawn closer to the house, tearing at the grass and wiping her eyes.

"Is she alright in this location?" I ask out loud to Narah, pointing down to her mother.

"Perfect," Stone answers. "Can you partially unwrap her?"

I cringe, and Crius is by my side, patting my back.

"Thanks for taking one for the team."

"Asshole." Hastily, I tug at the fabric, touching as little of her body as possible. The sight is revolting. Once done, I make a hasty retreat over to the others and see that Crius has joined Jae.

"Okay, so what's the next step?" I ask, wanting this over with.

Narah looks up at me, her face flush, her lips pinched tight, beyond stressed.

"I think we're almost there. We just need to bring Kaira out. Once we begin, you and Crius untie her and get her into the water."

"Okay." Nodding, a jolt of fear runs up my spine. "That's assuming she won't wake up and go feral on us, spelling our asses, right? Is there something we can do to ensure she doesn't awaken?"

Narah's face pales.

"That's why we need to do this fast," Stone explains. "The moment she hits the water, Narah will cast the spell. It should go quickly from there."

"You make it sound easy," I say sarcastically.

"Hopefully, it will be," Ragnar adds, his brows pulled together. Goddess, it's worse than I thought. They're petrified this won't work.

"I'm ready," Narah states bravely. "I can't keep going over it. It's stressing me out." She's huffing for breath, and I worry about how worked up she's getting and if casting such a spell will put any pressure on her pregnancy.

In our dream state, it felt as if she was due any day, so does it apply to real life? She's waddling when she walks and puffs when she moves around too much. In any other situation, I'd have her lying in my arms and taking it easy, but as the only sorceress among us, she is our own savior, and there's no reasoning with her when it comes to saving her sisters.

Narah rubs her belly, and my gut clenches. Answer is to get this fucking spell done and pray it works. When I look over at Jae, she's crying. As much as I'd like to take Jae away from here, the stubborn girl already made it clear she's not leaving. So, we all need to be extra alert in case the witch inside Kaira attacks. Reluctantly, I turn on my heel and march toward the house.

"Show time, buddy," I call out to Crius. "We need to bring Kaira out."

Crius leaps to his feet, cracks his neck, and marches in after me. "I'm ready."

In the bedroom, we stare at Kaira, still slumped in the seat.

"What's the best way to do this?" Crius asks, holding his axe in his hand.

"We leave her in the chair. I'll take the back, and you pick up the two front legs."

"Right..." He cuts me a deadpan look. "So, I'm in the firing line should psycho witch come back."

"Only fair we take turns. I carried the legs on the last one. Now you take one for the team."

"Fuck you. Let's flip for it."

"Not happening," I say, but he already has a coin out of his pocket.

"You calling it?" He lifts his gaze just as he flicks the spinning coin in the air.

"We're not flipping," I repeat louder.

"Fine, I call heads."

I roll my eyes as he catches the coin and slaps it on the back of his hand. I can't help myself and lean toward him. I don't trust him not to cheat. The moment I see the coin, I grin.

"Tails. The front feet are yours. Now, stop dragging this out."

"Fuck." Crius glares my way with a half grin. "Next shit job, I get to choose what side I'm carrying."

"Works for me. Now, get cracking. I want this done. Narah needs to rest. She looks ready to drop off her feet."

"I was thinking the same. Jae's all kinds of messed up. She's so stressed, I worry about her state of mind if this doesn't work."

"It's gonna work... it has to." Mentally, I scramble for something to shut down the terror of what we'll do if things turn to shit, how to protect everyone if Lyra awakens and attacks.

"Okay, you ready?" Crius asks after using his axe to lacerate the rope that chains the chair to the bed. The mood becomes somber.

Nodding, we get Kaira and the chair in our grasp. In silent prayer, we move like the wind outside and make a mad dash for the river. My heart's pounding, and by the time we reach the river, I'm drawing in shallow, raspy breaths.

Ragnar is by my side in seconds, knife in hand.

Narah and Stone stand a few feet behind us, and the prick of magic is already tainting the air. I feel it licking the back of my neck.

Ragnar doesn't waste a second. He makes fast work of slicing the ropes around Kaira. Crius and I are there, catching her as she slumps forward and right out of the chair.

Every hair on my body stands on end.

"Quick, dump her in the water," Ragnar commands.

We don't need to be told twice. We haul her into the water, Crius and I each holding an arm. On the count of three, we push her into the water. My chest twists with agony, knowing this is Narah and Jae's sister, but I want the witch inside her dead.

Kaira's body splashes into the water, sinking at first, then bouncing back up and floating face down.

Behind me, Jae's having a panic attack, screaming that she's drowning.

That's the intention.

Ragnar grabs my arm and drags me away from the river, but ice has filled my veins the longer I stare at the girl we're drowning. Rubbing a nervous hand over my mouth, I try my hardest not to shout that this is fucking wrong. I know it's not, but instinct is bellowing in my head that nothing about this is right. Jae's sorrow is a blade in my chest, twisting in my heart. These three sisters have grown so much on me, they're part of my life now.

Clenching my teeth, every instinct in me demands I rush into the water to rescue Kaira, but I do the hardest thing ever. With heavy feet and an even heavier heart, I walk away.

Kaira may be the one in the water, but I'm drowning on the inside.

I came to a stop where I have a vantage view of everyone, ready for any attacks.

Narah unleashes a loud groan, her hands jutting in front of her.

The air between her and the river ripples. It sparks, and a jolt of electricity runs up my arms from the static.

My heart rages in my chest as I swing my attention to Kaira. Every eye is on her when suddenly her body is sucked under the surface.

Jae gasps loudly and rushes toward the river, no doubt to save Kaira.

I twist to lunge for her, but Crius is already on it, swooping her in his arms. Sobbing, she beats her fists on his chest as he carries her back to the house.

My chest is close to bursting. I swallow my past dried throat and notice tears running down Narah's face as she casts the spell.

I don't move. None of us do, given the hellish situation.

Seconds are all it takes before Kaira abruptly bursts upward, her head and shoulders breaking the river's surface, a scream in her mouth, arms splashing wildly.

I flinch, my heart in my throat.

Jae's screaming behind us, and Crius snatches and rushes with her into the house.

I step closer to the river, but Ragnar lifts his palm for me to stop.

Focused, Narah's not moving, and Stone's chest glows with the blue runes. When I feel the tremble of the earth and see the rising roots from the ground and the river, creating a spiked enclosure around Kaira, I understand he's keeping her trapped in case the witch escapes.

I'm not sure if it will contain her, but Stone's magic controls the elements beyond movement, attacking and restraining someone if needed. We're counting on it.

Kaira's sucked back under, the water thrashing, wild waves splashing the banks from the commotion someone her size couldn't make.

It tells me we're dealing with the High Priestess, and my hackles bristle. Still, as we watch her fighting the magic drowning her, part of me can't help but pity her.

Memories flash of Narah's mother doing the same to us. I'd never been so scared in my life.

Ragnar's gaze darkens when he glances my way. He's worried. Fuck, we all are.

Suddenly the splashes cease.

It's silent... too silent.

No one moves, but my pulse is racing, and I'm tense as fuck. I wrack my brain for how long we were under, but I don't remember. At the time, it felt like an eternity.

In a flash, a haze of yellow light zips out of the water and hurls toward Narah, Stone, and the dead body.

Stone throws himself to protect Narah, but in the same heartbeat, a thunderous roar bursts from the river. I lunge for Narah as I twist my head toward the river.

"Run!" Ragnar shouts.

A wall of water has risen from the river, towering over us, and it's coming down fast.

Panic has me scrambling, but it smashes down on us so violently, so fast, it feels like I've been run down by a fucking mountain. My shouts are drowned out as my legs wash out from under me. I swoosh with the current that tosses and twists me. Flinging out my arms and legs for purchase, I try to find a way to the surface. Holding my breath, I spin out of control, losing track of what's up and what's down.

She's fucking with us. The witch is distracting us!

Next thing I know, I'm hurled and spat out, hitting the ground and rolling until I whack into a tree. I groan from the pain zigzagging down my leg from where my hip struck the tree. Every inch of me is drenched, and I'm sucking air into my lungs. Eyes open, it takes me seconds to work out what the hell's going on.

Stone got Narah in a tree, both of them perched on a branch and mostly dry, while Ragnar and I are left floundering like fish out of water.

Narah's safe, and that's what matters.

"What the hell!" Ragnar growls, getting up on his feet. Water has drenched the surrounding woods, dripping from the house's roof.

Sprinting to the river, my footfalls splash the soaked ground. Kaira is lying at the bottom of the riverbed on her back, coughing up water.

My heart soars with adrenaline.

Not waiting, I hurl myself in after her and drop to my knees. Hastily, I twist her to her side, rubbing her upper back so she can throw up any water she swallowed. Water rushes over my bent legs and Kaira from farther up the mountain, so I quickly sweep her up and pray she's not possessed.

I keep studying her face for any signs she's taken, but she's too busy coughing. There's a strange innocence to her expression I haven't seen on her face. Since I met Kaira, she's been under Lyra's influence, but something feels different now. I can't explain it, but I don't feel magic around her.

Ragnar's at the river's edge. Leaning down, he grabs my arm and helps me up the sloppy bank. My other hand is around Kaira.

"She looks normal," I tell Ragnar, whose brows are pinched, scrutinizing the girl's face. I don't blame him since we'd already been tricked by the High Witch.

Kaira finally calms down and hiccups, whimpering Narah's name.

Narah's down from the tree now, Stone attached to her side and both of them staring down at her mother's body.

Something dark curls up from the magic talisman attached to Narah's mother's chest, a wisp of smoke tugged away by the breeze. Everyone watches as it disperses like ashes—there one moment, then gone.

"Please tell me Lyra is dead now," Ragnar mutters. He's drenched, his hair plastered to his head, but he doesn't care.

Narah's panicked face swings in my direction, her eyes locking on Kaira at my side. With tears and a smile, she squeals as she awkwardly hurries toward her sister. She's at my side in seconds, hugging Kaira, and I step back to give them space.

"Narah, when did this happen?" Kaira asks, touching her sister's pregnant belly.

Narah laughs and hugs her, telling her she'll explain everything later.

I assume Lyra has been eradicated. The heavy sting of magic no longer lingers over my skin or in the air, which I take as the best news in the fucking world. My chest clenches at the emotions curling around my heart.

Kaira's back. I can't help grinning, knowing it brings Narah boundless happiness.

"Stone," I call to him, and with Ragnar, the three of us come together.

"She's gone," Ragnar confirms. "As far as I can tell, that wisp we saw was the wicked witch vanquished."

"And the river bursting its banks all over us?" Ragnar queries while wringing water out of his shirt.

"Her last attempt," Stone confirms. "But you can feel the difference. The air is lighter. She's definitely gone."

"Fuck, yes." I nod. "You can see it in Kaira's face, too."

A beat of silence passes over us, the three of us breathing easy for a change, and it has everything to do with us being unable to believe we might have actually destroyed that fucking bitch.

"After that," Stone begins, "I need to get blind drunk tonight. I have never been more terrified that something would blow up in our faces."

"Kaira," Jae's suddenly yelling from across the yard and running to her sisters. Her cheeks are drenched.

I might have choked up to see the three of them together.

Crius strolls over toward us, running a hand through his hair and staring at the yard that was completely destroyed by the river. His footsteps slosh in the water, and his brow furrows.

"Do I want to know why the river is all over the lawn?" he frowns. With one look at the three sisters, then down to their mother, he knows we've succeeded. He cheers, doing air punches.

With a deep inhale, I stretch my back and suggest to the pack, "We should hold a burial ceremony for their mother, get it finalized."

There's a moment where all four of us stare around, still amazed something went our way for a change. Since arriving in Romania, we've constantly been fighting, constantly going backward. This is a big success, and I'll take the damn win, considering everything we've endured leading up to this point.

Crius is telling a story about the time he got caught in a flood and how he saved a whole village. I laugh at his dramatic stories, but when I glance at the girls, Narah's looking at me with a smile that melts my heart.

For tonight, at least, we'll have peace in our souls.

ELEVEN

NARAH

Today, we're leaving the Wolf Mountains, and it's bittersweet. We buried my mother in the backyard last night. I've remained in my bedroom this morning, feeling a strange pull to the house. In my soul, I feel that once we leave, I won't return. My wolf stirs restlessly inside me, eager for us to leave. She hates it here, hates the smell of death, but the emotions run deep.

There's so much pain and agony, too many memories I need to leave behind. I have to help my sisters deal with the trauma they've been through, and this place is not healthy for any of us.

I've made up my mind but still haven't left my room.

Our carriage is booked, and we're ready. My sisters, who've been inseparable since we rescued Kaira yesterday, are with the men at the local market, picking up supplies for our journey. Ragnar is planning a small detour with Nikos to visit the Bane Wolves Alpha, Mihai. He mentioned something about gaining more time for an errand he promised to run for the Alpha. The two will catch up to us on horseback on our way to Shadowlands Sector.

This chaotic shift in our lives has everything to do with my pregnancy and having no idea when I'll pop. Like everyone else, I'm praying it's after we reach Shadowlands and hoping they have midwives to help me. I'm panicking about giving birth.

Is it strange that I feel both terrified and excited to meet my little jelly bean? For so long, I've had love only for my sisters, then these four Norse warriors, who crashed into my life, making me fall head over heels for them. And just when I thought I understood my emotions and how deeply I felt about my new family, something little came along that made me realize how much more love I have to give.

Staring out the window at the woodland, my hands are on my stomach. The baby has been moving all night, leaving me uncomfortable. Smiling, I look down and whisper, "I don't know who you'll be yet, but I know you will be my world."

The floorboards creak behind me, and when I turn around, I find Stone standing in the doorway, rubbing his fingers along his short beard. His golden hair, as bright as the sunlight outside, sits messily around his face and over his shoulders as though he's been running his fingers through it. Blue eyes as deep as the ocean smile at me.

"Are they back yet?" I ask.

"Not yet." Grinning, he shakes his head. "Based on the long shopping list you gave them for supplies, they'll be there for a while."

"I might have gone overboard, especially for food items." I laugh, remembering I wrote it while I was hungry.

"Good luck to them finding everything." He pushes into the room, strolling toward me. "This might be the last peaceful moment the two of us can be alone for a while." He kicks the door shut behind him, eyeing the bed with the most delicious expression.

I smile widely. I love how turned on my men are, how they are as insatiable as I am.

"I see. What do you have in mind?" I tease.

"I want you to beg me," he says, peeling his top up and over his torso in slow motion. He's all angles and curves, muscles everywhere. The man is solid, and my body tightens with arousal. Stone is an Adonis, and he's all mine.

"I want your hands all over me," I try to say seductively but end up giggling, feeling silly. "I can't do this. Look at me. I'm an elephant, and you look like a god." I shrug. "Just feeling a bit insecure, I guess. I'm so tired of wearing men's shirts, but they're the only things that fit me right now." Blushing, I feel like I've ruined the mood.

Glancing down at my hands, which look just as swollen as my

ankles, I turn back to the window, struggling with the emotions battling inside me—exhilaration about my newborn and the loss of self-confidence about how I look.

"You are absolutely beautiful, Narah." Stone is at my back, his body pressed to mine, and he's burning up. He kisses my shoulder. "You have no idea how much I love seeing you pregnant, how attractive you are."

He presses his erection against my ass, and I adore knowing I still turn him on.

"Every inch of you has me hypnotized, and babe, you have all four of us drooling with how much bigger your breasts are. I wake up every morning with a hard-on, thinking about them. Don't deny me this. I need you."

I twist back around, and his hand caresses my chin, drawing my mouth to his. His kiss is magic. Fire and hunger burn me up. Stone kisses me as though he's cherishing me. There's no rushing, no aggression, but something he's imprinting on his mind. It's addictive to be adored in such a way. His tongue sweeps across my mouth, a growl in his throat, and when he breaks away, I'm breathing heavily.

"Don't go too far. I miss you," I purr, running my hand down his hard chest.

There's fire in his eyes as his hands tug at my shirt, up and over my head, before he tosses it aside, only to find I'm completely naked underneath.

The way he studies me up and down, licking his lips, completely undoes me. It brings a delicious ache between my thighs, a powerful, lustful ache. My wolf rises to the occasion, purring beneath my skin, which in turn coaxes a purr from my throat. Heat swallows me, and my body trembles.

"You are beautiful. Your body is a goddess'. I don't know how much longer I can wait to slide into you." Focusing his gaze on my breasts, he squeezes them. They are huge and sensitive, but his touch eases the ache. Unable to help himself, he leans in and takes a hard nipple into his mouth.

His tongue is crazy wicked, flicking me, and I tremble. He delivers just as much loving attention to the other one. Already drenching wet, the groans in my throat grow louder.

He releases me from his mouth, but his hands never release my breasts. Squeezing them, he pinches the nipples between two fingers as he stares at me.

"I love seeing you so turned on. The sounds you make have my cock hard as a rock. Everything about you makes me wild."

My reply comes out as moans while heat pulses between my legs. Dirty thoughts swirl through my head of all the things I want Stone to do to me. I would never have thought I could be so horny while pregnant or that Stone could be so aroused.

"I think it's unfair that I'm the only one naked," I complain, pawing at his pants.

Lifting me into his arms, I laugh at how easily he carries me before he sets me on the bed on my back.

"I want you on your hands and knees, which should take a bit of pressure off your back," he explains while popping open the buttons on his jeans.

Stone is absurdly good-looking—rugged, sexy, and addictive.

I'm too distracted to move. I want to see all of him, and on cue, his cock pops out. He's thick, swollen, and enormous, sitting upright toward his stomach, the tip already coated in clear, sticky precum. By the looks of it, the gorgeous hunk has been horny for a while.

My core tightens with anticipation, knowing what's coming. In slow motion, I roll over and climb onto my hands and knees. Stone is at my side, his sweet kisses on my back as his fingers trail down my spine and lower to between my thighs.

I tilt my head back, groaning as his fingers slide over my pussy, driving me crazy.

"I've been dying to fuck your sweet cunt."

I moan at how incredible his fingers feel sliding over my slick entrance, making his way to my clit. Every muscle responds to his touch.

He climbs onto the bed with me, and the mattress bounces under his movements. Moving effortlessly, he kneels behind me and gently spreads my legs.

"Wider, babe."

I obey, already drawing in a long inhale, completely intoxicated by his scent, by his very presence. He pushes a finger into me, and I purr. "Yes, please more." The pulse between my legs has me gasping.

"I love the way your pussy sucks my fingers, greedily drawing me in."

"I've been craving you," I murmur, riding his finger until he pulls out, and I growl in protest.

"Is that so?" he says, pressing the tip of his cock to my entrance.

I steel myself as he strokes his huge cock across my pussy, pushing the tip in and out, teasing me.

"Is that how you're going to play me?" I ask over my shoulder, wiggling my ass. "I can just as easily tease you."

The sexiness in his gaze covers me with goosebumps.

"You want my cock that much?" Hands gripping my hips, he slowly pushes into me, making himself fit.

My pulse beasts harder, my body tingling. Of course, he's right, but I'm not going to tell him that. Not when I need this more than I realized.

"Narah," he growls, pushing into me. "I'll always take care of you."

I gasp with pleasure, heat bursting through me. Then he pauses.

Looking at him over my shoulder, I ask, "What's wrong?"

"How deep can I go? I don't want to hurt you or the baby."

I exhale, trying to think of all the things I learned about being pregnant, which isn't much. Most of the women back in the Storm Wolves pack talked mostly about sex and comparing men.

"I've heard it's okay to have sex during pregnancy, and as long as it doesn't hurt me, we're good."

He stares at me, unsure. "Just to be sure, I won't do anything rough or go too deep, okay?"

Part of me wants to protest, especially with him buried halfway into me, but I absolutely adore how caring he is.

"Please don't stop. Keep going," I beg, giving us both what we want.

His devious grin makes my breath catch in my throat. Pushing in and out of me, I'm drowning in raw desire and crying out from his sheer girth. The stretch is exhilarating, my breaths shaky and racing.

Moving faster, his breathing picks up, and my body aches for the release building inside me. The filthy, squelching sounds we each make as he buries himself into me are beautiful, coming faster and faster.

I whimper and pant.

"You're so tight, so wet." His fingers are suddenly on my clit, tapping it, and the sensation makes me delirious.

I moan, gently bucking against him when he draws out of me.

"Why did you stop?"

He throws himself onto his side next to me. "I want you to lie in front of me, facing away. When I knot inside you, I want you in a comfortable position."

Dancing on the edge of desire, my eyes tear up, and I blame it all on my emotional state.

"As long as you promise to stop pausing. I was so close." I give him a comical frown, and he rewards me with a light slap across my ass.

"Get down here," he purrs.

Snuggling in his arms, his body spooning mine, his cock glides along the slick. I moan at how good it feels, especially when pushes his huge cock between my soaking pussy lips and into me.

"Come here," he purrs, one arm under my neck, supporting me and wrapped around my chest, the other on my hip. "I need to get back into your little pussy, then I want you to come all over my cock."

Oh, damn. "If you keep talking that way, I'll come instantly."

He laughs, then his lips graze my shoulder as he pushes deeper into me. I curl my leg up and over his leg, giving him easier access. He pumps into me harder. He's close. I feel him tensing inside me and his panting breath on the back of my neck.

He cups my breasts, squeezing them with one hand, toying with my nipples, while I slowly lose my mind. Rocking against him, I'm burning up.

Stone growls in my ear, suddenly pausing. He pushes in me, and I feel him thickening, growing, his cock swelling with his knot. His fingers slip to my clit and stroke in circles as his warm liquid spills out of me.

"Come for me," he snarls possessively.

His touch and words trigger me, and my arousal blooms and bursts. I cry out, my body quivering with the orgasm that floods me.

We're locked in a lover's embrace, breathing heavily, taken by pleasure.

He keeps pumping, seemingly proud of the sheer amount he's producing by the pleasuring sounds he's making. The man is gorgeous, and he wants me. Something I'm still coming to terms with after everything we've been through.

"I feel your sweet pussy sucking my cock, drinking me," he says, his breath on my neck, then kisses the tender skin below my ear.

Despite being locked in me from his knotting cock, his pelvis still gyrates against me as he pumps his thick, white cum into me.

I gasp, rocking with him, taken by the way he holds me possessively. Every touch, every rub of our skin ignites a wildfire between us. My wolf groans in my chest, awakening to the connection Stone and I have. She calls to his wolf, still bound to him by the bite mark he gave when my four men marked me to bring back my magic.

She's rising, craving him when she normally pines for Martell. This change is huge, but it's hard to make sense of it when my toes curl and my body quivers with an incredible climax.

"Narah," Stone whispers, peppering my neck with kisses, breathing heavily. His hand on my hip tightens with hungry need. "Having you cum is the most beautiful thing I've ever seen. Can you hear our wolves recognizing one another? Since our first kiss, I knew you'd ruin me for anyone else. But this...our mark from the other night when we all claimed and bit you, marking you as ours and removing Martell's connection."

His words leave me elated. This is what I've dreamed of since running from my fated mate, and Stone is saying it's finally worked? I want to scream with happiness, but I end up moaning when he squeezes my breast.

"You will always be mine," the Alpha growls. "Whatever happens, you will be mine forever." His heavy, hungry breath washes over my ear with the words, "I love you, Narah."

I twist my head over my shoulder, my heart blooming with the words that have my heart racing. I fight back the happy tears and manage to choke out, "Oh, Stone, I love hearing that. I love you so much."

He's given me everything, and I know if we can overcome the

dangers, all my dreams will come true, and I will have everything I ever wanted.

We kiss in a perfect moment of bliss, and my heart sings to know I will grow old with these incredible men. It's a simple thing, but to me, it means the world.

I feel the baby kick, and I quickly grab Stone's hand, placing it over the spot. Another small kick, and when I look at him, his eyes light up, and his smile makes me imagine him chasing our child in the yard, building a treehouse, and all the small things I never had growing up and all the love I want for our baby.

"I'm so excited to meet our little jelly bean," he purrs.

For these few moments, I find my happy place and know whatever fight comes our way, we'll overcome it. We have too much to lose now if we don't.

Cold rain soaks me, and my clothes stick to me like glue. I run my hand over my stubbled face, dislodging the droplets stuck there, not that it does any good.

Crius is charging ahead of the two-horse carriage driven by an older man we'd paid well in gold coins Ragnar took from his father before leaving Denmark. The coachman sits on a bench at the front of the carriage, mustering the horses along the worn path. The four-wheeled vehicle rattles and creaks. The carriage is worn and has seen better days, but the three sisters inside are protected from the elements, and that's what matters.

I catch Narah watching me from inside, her hand on the glass pane, her eyes glinting with a smile. Jae pops her head up behind her, sticking her tongue out at me, and I laugh.

The girl is trouble and reminds me so much of Ragnar's sister growing up. Always opinionated, his sister, Hel, would stick her nose in all of our business. Although I wish I could have done more to help Ragnar keep his sister protected from her forced marriage into Nikos' family, I have taken Narah's sisters as my own family and will protect them with my life.

Blowing Narah a kiss, I nudge my heels into the horse and hurry forward until I'm lined up with the coachman. Despite his bowl-like hat pulled down low on his thick head, wisps of white hair flutter out from beneath. His black coat is buttoned up tight around his throat, and he twists his head in my direction with a raised eyebrow.

"The rain's remained light," he tells me with a raspy voice that says he's smoked cigarettes most of his life. "As long as it doesn't get heavier, the wheels shouldn't get bogged in the mud."

"How much longer until we arrive at our first stop?" With the sun sliding behind the surrounding mountains, night will consume us in an hour, tops. We'll be sitting targets for the undead since we won't see them coming from a distance. The small groups we pass are too far to pay attention to or catch us.

Jon, the driver, draws in a hissing breath. "Maybe in an hour or two, we'll reach the tavern."

I nod, my muscles tensing. "Get us there in an hour, no longer."

He cuts me a dark glare. "I can't control the weather, son."

"Get us to the tavern in under an hour, and I'll double your payment."

The coachman's shoulders square, the mention of money interesting him greatly. "You got yourself a deal." With a snap of his reins, he whistles to his horses, and suddenly, we're moving fast.

Sly bastard.

Rogue Alphas roam the woods, desperate to hunt down any Omega to rut. It's in our DNA to crave females, and right now, we're carrying three Omegas, with only Crius and me to protect them. I can't risk us getting caught. I have no trouble fighting, and I'll use my power, but if we're attacked, how can I completely keep Narah and the baby unharmed?

Ragnar and Nikos made a detour to the Bane Wolves to deal with Mihai, and for all we know, that could go to hell fast. Like us, they will have to find a way to stay alive and eventually catch up with us.

Especially since we'll most likely reach Shadowlands before them, and while the Alpha of that sector, Dušan, was amicable to our presence after we helped him, Ragnar left him with a warning before we parted.

What promise I will make is I will return to your Shadowlands land with my warriors. If you are not in charge of your land upon my arrival, and this mess with your brother fighting you for ownership hasn't been swept away, I will wipe out all the males on this land, claim the females, and take ownership.

Now, we're about to barge into his home with a pregnant Omega... without Ragnar.

Fucking great.

Crius

Frustration bore a hole through me.

Night billows around us, its claws stretching across the landscape.

Whatever Stone told the coachman, we're now moving at lightning speed. About fucking time. The flashlights tied to the horses' reins will light the path ahead of us, but those two lights will be close to useless once darkness comes.

Jon wouldn't answer where he got the flashlight batteries from. Anything from the old civilization is close to lost, but there are other packs and supernaturals in this world who harness unimaginable technology. They also keep it closely guarded and kill anyone who gets too close.

I've seen it first hand back in Denmark when Ragnar's father sold Omegas for weapons, ammunition, and whatever the hell he needed to give him an upper hand against Nikos' family.

Ragnar and I have discussed technology often, along with being smarter about who we align ourselves with. The small packs in the Savage Sector are dead weight, but I get what Ragnar's doing. With the witches out of the way, he needs the packs combined into a powerful force to eliminate that dickhead Martell or any other prick who decides to rise to power.

Regardless, I wouldn't want to be in Ragnar and Nikos' shoes right now, dealing with an Alpha whose daughter was just murdered.

"We should be at the tavern in an hour," Stone calls out as he rides up beside me.

"My ass is so fucking sore, and it's getting dark. We're sitting ducks riding like this in a straight-line formation."

"You want to travel in your wolf form?" he asks with a rise of his thick eyebrows.

"Well, think about it. Tie these horses to the carriage, and they'd move faster, then you and I can cover more land to check for dangers. We're in the fucking woods, Stone, and the girls aren't safe."

"I've been thinking the same. My skin's crawling with unease. Something isn't right out here."

"We're being watched," I say. "I feel it in my bones. I need to get off this fucking horse and into wolf form to find who it is."

Stone's expression is stoic, but with the hardness of his eyes and the way he stares out into the dark woods around us, he knows it's better to attack first.

I inhale sharply and lick my dry lips.

With a single nod, he falls behind me, and we ride side by side behind the coach.

I'm itching to get out there, to shake off the feeling we're not alone. With a whistle, I glance back to see the carriage coming to a stop, so I slow down and turn back to join them.

Stone's in deep conversation with Jon, and I'm just too jittery to deal with the Beta wolf shifter. I hop off my horse and hand the reins to Stone.

"I'm heading out ahead of us."

His brows scrunch together. "I won't be far behind you."

With quick steps, I reach the side door of the carriage, and I'm greeted by the three worried faces. Opening the door, I stick my head inside.

"Nothing to worry about," I explain, needing them not to panic. "Stone and I are going into the woods in wolf form from here. With the carriage using all four horses, we can move faster. We're less than an hour from the tavern." I'm talking fast, already yanking my shirt up and over my head, then tossing it into the empty spot on the cushioned seat.

"Are you sure everything's alright?" Narah asks, her gaze traveling across the surrounding woods. "I can try to help."

I shake my head, staring from her worried expression to Jae's and Kiara's. They remind me of bunnies—so small, huddled together and vulnerable.

Reaching to take Narah's hand in mine, I kiss her fingertips. "You are better off in the carriage so we can move faster. Just hold on, and we'll be enjoying a hot meal in no time." The smile I offer feels wrong.

Although a lie, I prefer to think I'm stretching the truth. I lean forward and place a hand on her belly, her body radiating extreme heat. "How are you and the baby feeling?"

"It's kicking like crazy," Jae says. "I don't think it likes the bumpy ride."

"While I think it's enjoying it," Kaira adds with a small smile. Like Jae, Kaira also has an innocence about her. In truth, I hadn't met the real Kaira until now.

"You might be onto something," I say to her. "When my mother was pregnant with me, she traveled the country in carriages and ended up giving birth to me in one."

Narah makes a strangled sound. "The poor thing."

"You'll be okay." With a kiss across her knuckles, I give her a soft smile. "I promise. I'll deliver the baby myself if that's what it comes to. I once watched my mother help one of our maids during her labor."

She grimaces, not looking convinced by my offer.

"If we had the time, I'd climb in there with you, but give me an hour, and we'll get the chance. Okay, gorgeous?"

She nods, and I reluctantly step away from the doorway. I strip from my boots and pants, toss the clothes into the carriage, and shut the door.

Calling to my wolf, he responds instantly, tearing out of me, skin splitting, bones stretching, fur spreading over my changing body. In the span of only seconds, I'm a wolf, darting into the woods.

Behind me, I spy Stone helping the coachman connect the two riding horses to his carriage. He won't be long, but while they're sitting out in the open, I need to find out what the fuck's causing my instincts to go off.

Paws pounding the ground, I push deeper into the woods, sniffing the air. Nothing, yet my skin still itches. So, I backtrack and decide to do a fast scan of the woods on the other side of the path.

Bursting out of the woods, I startle the coachman, who gives out a yelp at my sudden appearance. Without hesitation, I sprint across the passage in front of them and dive into the other woods, but not before I see that the horses are all tied up, and they're ready to get a move on.

Fucking fantastic.

Breathing heavily, I dart forward, my nostrils flaring, drawing in a scent that stops me in my tracks. Heavy musk, fur, and the tinge of something electric jolts up my arm—the sensation I get from other Alphas.

Here I thought we were dealing with the undead, but in truth, other wolves were following us. Rogue bastards who don't belong to packs roam the woods, attacking anything that moves, and if they get a whiff of our Omegas, they'll follow us to Hell and back.

That was another reason we kept the girls closed up in the carriage—to prevent their Omega scents from floating on the breeze, especially Narah's since she still carries her heat.

This is why we're with them—to destroy any fuckers who think we're easy game.

Throwing myself in the direction of the scent, I rush madly, excited about fighting. I need to eliminate the anxiety I've been holding onto. All the shit with removing the curse from Kaira and the High Priestess took their toll. I'm a damn fighter. I deal with things by tearing them apart, and I felt utterly useless, sitting back and doing nothing while magic solved the problem.

The stench of other Alphas strengthens, and my pulse races as fast as my paws. Hearing the crunch of twigs behind me, ice slides over my nape. Someone snuck up on me?

Fuck. Fuck. Fuck.

I pivot abruptly just as a black wolf crashes into me. A new smell floods me, and I realize there's more than one party. Excited to tear into someone, I let my guard down.

We hit the ground, and I fight brutally, teeth and violence on my side. Rolling across the ground, I tear into the asshole's shoulder just as he latches onto my arm. I growl in his ear, then latch onto his neck.

Fury bleeds through me, tightening my chest, and I see nothing but red. In one cruel bite, I rip out the side of his neck, tearing out sinew and muscle, the blood warm and thick. I don't stop there. Straddling his chest, I go to town on the prick, my heart beating frantically in my chest.

There's something rewarding about taking a life from someone who fucking deserves it.

A snap of foliage at my back has my ears pricking, and a piercing growl shudders through me. There's no wasting time, not when I'm having too much fun.

I twist around and hurl myself at the asshole who thinks it's okay to sneak up on me. The gray timber wolf's eyes widen, lips peeling up and over sharp canines. I use his shock to my advantage. A second is all I need to get the upper hand. It's how battles are won. A slight hiccup on the enemies' part, them tripping, anything to distract them. In war, you use any fucking thing to win.

I slam into the bastard, driving him back into a tree so hard, all the air rushes from his lungs past his mouth. My teeth are on his jugular before he can react, and in seconds, he's slumping by my feet. Well, that was too fucking easy.

Another crunch and I flip around, a snarl on my throat, every inch of me alert, but instead of another fucker, it's a huge white wolf, about my size, stopping feet away from the first dead Alpha.

Stone makes a groaning sound, protesting that I didn't leave anyone for him to play with. I give a small yip and trot over to him, purposefully knocking my shoulder into his.

Several guttural growls darken behind me, and the hairs on the back of my neck rise.

Twisting around, I count six wolves spread out around the woods, blazing eyes on us. Anger spears through my veins to think so many pricks have been chasing us. Each one of these soon-to-be-dead Alphas had their eyes on my Omega—my Narah—and for that, they will fucking die, just like their buddies.

Glancing at Stone, his head is low, ears plastered to his head. Works for me. Three for each of us to destroy sounds like good odds.

In a heartbeat, we charge the wolves, fury dancing in my mind that they will pay for ever thinking they would touch my angel.

THIRTEEN

My father used to say when it came to battle, you should avoid the strong and target the weak. He also said to defeat your enemies on the field before they reach your home and rise for battle before the sun to seek victory.

I hated the man, but sometimes, he offered gold nuggets of wisdom that surprised me. Even though he failed miserably as a father and husband, he excelled in warfare.

His words came to mind the moment I stepped foot into the Bane Wolves' pack territory. Standing inside Mihai's home, the heavy stench of death assaults my nostrils.

Dead bodies.

Blood splashed on the walls.

Broken limbs.

The echo of screams seeming to linger on the whistling wind outside.

Mihai was lying on the bed on his back, one leg hanging off the edge of the mattress as though he was mid-struggle when someone came in and murdered him, driving a blade into his heart. The black hilt of a standard dagger protruded from his chest, surrounded by a wide patch of dried blood. The poor fucker has been killed in cold murder. His mate lay near the door, face down in a pool of blood.

Since arriving at the pack minutes ago, we'd found bodies strewn everywhere. Mostly Alphas.

My heart squeezes at all the useless death.

Drawing in a sharp inhale, the coppery smell reveals another scent—wet fur infused with heavy perspiration, something I recognize instantly. Curling my hands into fists by my side, I growl, the deep sound cutting across my chest.

These poor men died at the hands of a fucking piece of work who came here searching for Narah, my men, and me. It fucking burns me up with fury.

An Alpha has also been building his army, and he's just declared full-out war.

Martell.

Guilt claws at me at the destruction he caused to this pack. He ripped them apart, removed their leader, Mihai, and eliminated their warrior Alphas. With war comes casualties, but fuck. Mihai was an asshole, but I wouldn't have wished him such an undeserving death.

Grinding my jaw, I stand there, feeling useless and knowing my attempt to take over the Savage Sector had led to this massacre. But would it have gone any other way—with or without my intervention —if Martell intended to take over the territory?

Who the fuck knew, but that didn't diminish the mountain of anger surging through me.

I move over to Mihai's side and gently close his eyelids, whispering, "Maybe the gods take pity on your soul and find you a place in Valhalla."

We leave the home behind just as Nikos marches toward me across the open land, his face sour and his brows pinched together.

"Only a handful survived," he growls. "The survivors said it was Martell. That shithead needs to die, Ragnar. He's killed so many fucking men in this pack. Only saving grace was most of the Omegas and children escaped with Alphas, who got them out to safety. They're hiding in nearby mountain caves." He moves closer, roughly running his hand through his hair. "To be honest, I know we need to help the pack, but I'm even more petrified for Narah, out there with Martell's men on the loose."

"You think I don't feel the same way?" An invisible hand fists around my heart. "With her carrying our child, she's our priority… even over claiming the Savage Sector." I'm partially surprised to hear my own words, but Nikos nods in agreement.

For years, I'd had one goal—take over the Savage Sector, finally show my father I wasn't the waste of space he'd labeled me, and provide a safe haven for my sister after I collected her from her forced marriage.

"We're still taking ownership of Savage Sector," I reconfirm. "But it's taking a backseat to Narah. Then we'll hunt down that bastard and make him and all his supporters pay, even if I have to do it with my bare hands."

"Agreed," Nikos growls, his upper lip curling over sharp canines. "I'll be right there by your side, cutting those fuckers down. Martell will hurt for everything he's done to Narah."

With a raspy intake of breath, I turn to the land around us, to the dead, to the few stragglers coming out of homes, looking devastated.

"What's the plan?" Nikos asks.

"This pack has been demolished. Those left behind will be easy pickings with no Alpha to rule over them." I lick my dry lips, the morning air frigid on my skin. "I will claim the Bane Wolves' pack as mine, and we'll get everyone back into their homes. Then we'll pay a visit to the nearest pack and get them to send warriors to guard them until I return."

"They'll ask for a big price," Nikos states.

"And they'll have my undivided loyalty when I take over the Savage Sector, giving them first pick of a new land in the territory." Their Alpha had spoken about needing more space for his growing pack, so I prayed my offer worked.

"Fine, but we do this fast. It's killing me to be away from Narah. I don't want to miss her having our baby," Nikos says, his voice dark, and I hear the frustration in his voice.

My gut hardens that I'm delaying joining Narah and protecting her, but I can't leave this pack to be picked off by other wolf clans, rogues, or the undead.

I keep telling myself, a bit longer, but I'm wound up so tightly, wanting to say fuck it all and go to Narah, I'm ready to explode.

Nikos watches me, waiting for direction, and looks fucking

annoyed. His face is tight, hands clenched. He's dying to get back to Narah as much as I am.

"Tonight, we depart for Shadowlands Sector," I snarl. "I have no idea how Dušan will react to having two of my men and three Omegas just turn up on his pack doorstep without me there."

"Then let's get this pack fucking sorted." Nikos' mouth thins. "The quicker I get to Narah, the better I'll feel."

FOURTEEN

NARAH

The carriage bounces beneath us, and I'm doing my best to sit comfortably, which feels impossible with a huge belly. We rush past the darkening woods, trickles of rain running down the windows as the last streaks of sunlight brush the treetops like streaks of blood left over from a great battle.

Crius and Stone shifted into their wolves, vanishing into the woods, and had been gone for too long. My heart's drumming louder in my ears, and panic sits under my breastbone like a time bomb. What could be taking them so long? I peer out the carriage window as the landscape flashes past.

"It'll be okay," Jae reminds me for the tenth time. "Those guys are beasts. Nothing will happen to them."

Turning back, I lean into my cushioned seat, my hands resting across the top of my stomach. "I really hope you're right."

Jae nods, smiling with confidence I wished I possessed right now. Kaira's sitting with her legs bent beneath her, watching us and looking spooked.

"You should have seen them when we traveled back from Shadowlands Sector," Jae says, bouncing in her seat when we hit a pothole. "They were machines and worked well as a team, eliminating everything in our path without hesitation. Ultra-competitive Crius made killing the undead and rogue wolves into a game. To be honest, they were seriously scary to watch, but I knew they were on my side. So, I have faith they'll come through. You'll see, Sis."

I smile softly, knowing she's correct. I've seen them fight first-hand, and it's impressive.

"I guess I'm just worried for them, for us, for my little jellybean." I glance down, then back up at my sisters, who are smiling and staring at me as I rub my belly.

"It feels as though I've been asleep for ages and completely missed out on so much of your lives," Kaira adds. "Listening to you makes me feel as though I've been left behind. I don't even know what you both went through."

"Oh, Kaira." Jae throws her arm around our sister's shoulders and drags her against her side. "I'll catch you up on everything, but you were never left behind."

Kaira's sitting with Jae in the seat in front of me, facing me, and I take her hand.

"We love you, and you have the rest of your life to be part of everything we do. Trust me, I would do anything to forget the craziness of the past few months."

Kaira's lopsided grin makes me giggle. She's always so adorable and grew up competing for attention from our parents or from me over Jae. If Jae and I disagreed on anything, Kaira made herself the peacekeeper. Now, when I look at her, she seems timid and scared. I have to help her find herself once more, but it will take time for her.

Thinking back to those times when we lived with the Storm Wolves, when we had no clue what lived outside the pack, we assumed we would be forever safe there. Those naive days were simpler, but ignorance also gets you killed faster.

"I don't remember much of what took place once Lyra possessed me, but back in her coven, she revealed why she hated us so much," Kaira suddenly confesses, gaining my full attention.

"And? What did she say?" I ask impatiently.

"You've been holding out on us all this time." Jae fake hits her in the arm.

Kaira's smile warms my heart, and I love seeing her opening up more.

"Well, apparently, before our parents got together, Father and Lyra were a thing."

My mouth drops open. "Wait! What?" I'm sure I misheard.

"No way. He wouldn't have dated a psycho. No, we would have known about that," Jae rambles, her face paling.

"Would we, though?" I voice. We recently discovered how little I know about our parents. "They kept so much from us, so I wouldn't put anything past them."

Jae shakes her head in disbelief. "And?" she prods Kaira's arm again. "Keep going."

"Our mother had fallen in love with him. You see, he was dating them both at the same time, and when they found out, it was full-out war for who would claim him. Mother cast a spell on him to make him completely infatuated with her, then they vanished, and Lyra was left heartbroken. Oh, and Mother also spelled Lyra by siphoning a huge chunk of her magic, making Mother more powerful and Lyra weaker."

"Are you kidding me?" I'm lost for words.

Jae's shaking her head, blinking at Kaira in disbelief.

"I know," Kaira says, her eyes huge, then she shrugs. She's had long enough to deal with the news and accept our mother might be a far more horrible person than I ever suspected.

While my head is running rampant, learning this new information, I'm trying to piece together things that never made sense to me —why Lyra hated us and why she was desperate to get to our mother, even in her dead form.

Did she want her magic back?

I think about how Lyra slipped into Father's mind when we were at the coven to rescue Kaira. She said she easily gained information about where Mother was from his memories—they'd had a connection. For the short time before he died, she could have easily restored his memories to bond and find out everything our mother had done.

I'm dumbfounded. Then the horrible thought hits me—I now understand why our mother never came back for us at the Storm Wolves.

She didn't really want us, did she? With Father dead after she left, she'd been working all these years to bring him back for herself—without a care about what happened to my sisters and me.

I still have so many more questions, but I doubt Kaira has the answers. After losing our father, I told myself I would move on and not let our mother's actions bring me more anxiety. I'm sick to my stomach, and I'm breathing heavily, my chest tightening to think Lyra had been driven to be the crazy woman she'd become. To have someone you love stolen from you... Goddess. It would make me insane, too.

How could our mother have done that?

"D-Does that mean our parents didn't really love us?" Jae's voice cracks.

My eyes prick with tears, hearing her heartache and from my mixed emotions.

"Of course, they loved us," Kaira answers and smiles my way, as though saying she'll take this one. "Why would they have three kids if they didn't love and adore us?"

"But if Dad was under a spell..."

"Jae," I begin, my voice soft, my insides shattering. "The spell was to make him fall deeply in love with Mother and most likely, forget Lyra, but it had nothing to do with the love he had for us. That was real." My throat thickens because I don't know who I'm trying to convince more, her or me. I want to cry but won't in front of my sisters. I have to remain strong for them.

Kaira squeezes Jae in a hug as I hold her hand.

"All that matters is that we're together. You two aunties will need to show all the love and attention to our new family member." I glance down at my stomach, then back up at them with a genuine smile. My grin isn't forced, despite learning the terrible truth of the things our mother has done. I won't allow her decisions to bring us down.

"Family isn't just those related by blood." I take Kaira's hand as well and hold on to both my sisters. "It's those who love us more than our own real family ever did. Those who put us first, who never stop fighting for us. We have each other, as well as my four Alphas. They have fought by my side so hard to rescue both of you. Pretty soon, with little jellybean joining us, there will be eight of us in our newfound family. We'll find a home, somewhere we're safe. I give you my word... things won't be as chaotic as they are now."

I try not to think that the baby will be anything but a healthy wolf shifter, but at that moment, doubt spreads over my thoughts.

I got pregnant under a spell, while wrapped up in tree vines and experiencing a strange, induced dream. Does that mean I'll give birth to a half-breed baby, part tree or some kind of monstrosity?

My heart beats faster, and I'm suddenly sweating, thinking about that nonstop. I can still feel the baby stirring, but it all happened so fast. I can't let myself panic, or I'll lose my mind.

"Are you okay?" Kaira asks.

Lifting my gaze, I nod as they both come forward, and we hug while the carriage jostles us about. I need to calm my mind.

The baby will be okay... jellybean has to be okay. There's no other option.

She's my baby.

Stone

After destroying those fucking rogue Alphas in the woods, we catch up with the carriage and run alongside them until we reach the tavern. All five of us spend the night in a broom closet of a room—something I wouldn't mind if it was just Crius, me, and Narah. With Jae and Kaira with us, Crius and I slept on the floor so the girls could take the bed. We leave at the crack of dawn. The path in the woods is long, but we finally arrive in the Shadowlands Sector.

I quickly notice two things.

First, there are few undead roaming these woods, unlike the many groups we encountered back in Savage Sector. Second, we haven't run across one rogue Alpha or Beta in the forest.

Dušan, the Alpha of the Shadowlands Sector, has kept his back-yard clean of undead and wild wolf shifters. I also haven't seen any guards watching us. So, either I've been distracted and not seen them, or the Alpha is confident of his safety. Then again, as we move closer into his territory, the carriage comes to a pause where the dirt track ends, and we all look up at the lofty wall that surrounds his pack compound in the distance.

The woodland opens up to a piece of land I recognize from the last time we traveled here. We reached Shadowlands Sector on an errand for Narah to find her sister, Jae. The three sisters had been split up once they escaped from the Storm Wolves, and our job had been easy—find Jae and, in exchange, Narah would use her magic to help us overtake the witches in the middle of the Poisonous Woods.

I almost laugh out loud at how that task had snowballed into chaos and changed our lives forever. Look at us now!

We're about to have a baby!

The compound in front of us looks more like a medieval castle. Lofty stone walls with crenelations across the top spread outward, encompassing the enormous fortress. I'm impressed by how well the Alpha has securely set up his pack home. A steadfast fortress lays inside, along with huts for the pack members. I read up on the location, and in ancient times, it had been called the Râșnov Fortress, where knights lived to protect the locals against invaders from nearby countries.

Now, the Ash Wolves call this place home.

Watch towers dot the walls, and I see movement in the one ahead of us. Two men step outside on a small veranda of the tower, with guns pointed in our direction.

"Fuck," Crius mumbles. "Want me to deal with this?"

"No." I'm well aware his attempt might lead us to war against the pack we need help from. "Tell the others to remain in the carriage. I have this," I mutter under my breath, then step forward, raising my hands in the air.

"My name is Stone, and we are returning friends of Dušan," I call loudly. "My Alpha, Ragnar, and a few of us visited here months ago when you were dealing with some unfortunate takeover troubles." The kind that came in the form of Dušan's brother trying to overthrow him for the position of top Alpha and taking over his pack.

In this world, you couldn't even trust your family, which is why I've forgotten mine. My newfound family with Ragnar and his men has replaced what I lost. Now, we have Narah and her sisters joining us. For them, I have to make this work.

When the two guards only whisper to each other—standing too far for me to hear their words—frustration flares.

"I'm sure if I could speak with Dušan, he'll accept our visit. How about you collect him?"

The dark-haired man raises his head in my direction. "You're not welcome. Leave. I won't warn you again."

Grinding my teeth, I calculate how many seconds it would take me to rush to the wall, scale it, and wring the prick's neck. Instead, I grin and take a step closer.

"Dušan arranged this meeting, so we are here at your Alpha's request." I stretch the truth and bend it every which way I need. Fuck them.

The asshole's head raises to someone behind me just as the soft tap of footfalls on the grass has me twisting my head around. Narah and her sisters join me, with Crius behind them, shrugging— meaning he failed at controlling them. I growl, but it's too late.

The guards' eyes roam over the females, their interest piqued, then sniff the air for their scent. Thank the Moon Goddess, Narah's pregnancy has helped block her heat, or these men would be already fighting us to reach her.

"You're here to trade Omegas?" the guard barks.

I recall Jae telling me, when she'd spent time in the Shadowlands Sector pack, she discovered the Ash Wolves traded females with other packs for merchandise such as guns and supplies. She insisted the pack only sent the Omegas to Alphas approved by Dušan.

Let's be honest... this is a fucked-up world, and everyone is out for themselves, but if so-called approved Alphas help Dušan sleep at night, that's his demons to deal with.

"Yes," I finally answer, figuring once we get in front of Dušan, I can explain the situation and not deal with these fucking monkeys. "Now, call your Alpha, or better yet, take us to him."

They chat to themselves again, and I glance down at Narah.

"You should have stayed in the carriage. I don't want you to get hurt."

"My back hurts, and I can't sit down any longer. Besides, I'm pretty sure we just helped you." Her sweet grin has me adoring her, which is wrong when I'm annoyed that she doesn't listen to me even to keep her safe.

Crius scans the grounds for anyone sneaking up on us.

"Return in two days," the guard states. "Dušan will be available then."

"Fuck that," I snap, a snarl in my throat. "What do you expect us to do? Park outside your walls while undead roam around?"

"You can't stay here. You'll draw the undead's attention. Fuck off and return in two days." He shouts, lifting his rifle.

I swear to hell, I'm going to break his face when I get the chance.

"Meira," Jae suddenly calls out. "I'm Jae, Meira's sister. I'm certain you will get your ass kicked by Dušan if you deny his fated mate's sister into the compound."

I glance at Jae, her chin high, her shoulders squared. Looks like I'm not the only one great at spinning lies. The little girl's a firestorm, and clearly, I made a mistake not utilizing her knowledge from her time with this pack.

"Hurry up," Jae reminds them. "Or you will find yourself with an Omega out here about to go into labor. Then every damn undead will hear her screaming. Take us to Meira."

"Jae, you would make a wicked warrior," Crius whispers.

Behind us, I catch sight of our carriage driver, not moving from the seat as he watches this unfold. He'll have to wait around until we're ready to head back. Though after hearing the guard talk about the undead being drawn to the commotion, I note the frantic way he's scanning the woods behind him.

"Stay there," the guard yells at us, then turns and climbs down a ladder on the other side of the wall before vanishing.

Turning to the team, we gather. Kaira hugs Jae while Crius holds Narah from behind, taking some of her weight off her feet.

"Quick thinking, Jae," I say, reaching over and ruffling her light brown hair, which dances across her shoulders.

She pushes my hand away. "Hey, don't make me look weak."

I laugh softly to avoid being overheard, then lean over and kiss Narah's cheek. "How are you feeling?"

"A bit sore all over, but I'm okay. Just hate that we're out in the open."

"How about I carry you back to the carriage and get you off your feet?" Crius asks, but she shakes her head.

As Jae and Kaira chat quietly, I don't know how much time passes, but it feels like hours.

Finally, the crunch of grass sounds behind us, and I turn just as half a dozen guards appear from around the corner of the compound wall, with a young woman in charge. Deep chestnut brown hair flutters over her shoulders with her approach. She's dressed in black jeans, boots, and a folk-style white shirt with red embroidery around the v-neckline. The woman is beautiful with flawless skin, though nothing compared to my Narah. My heart thunders just thinking of her.

Five foot two or three, this woman is tiny, looking even more so next to the beefy guards surrounding her. I recognize the two Alphas by her side. Lucien stares at us as if he's playing out in his mind everything he'll do to us if we touch his girl. He's in a checkered button-up shirt, dusty jeans, and cowboy boots. Brown hair sits messily around his face as if he'd just been running. The second beefhead looks like a mountain, and I remember him well—Bardhyl.

Like us, this Alpha comes from Denmark and has Viking heritage. Long, blond hair is tucked behind his ears, his shoulders are broad, and bright green eyes scan the intruders in his home. His shirt sits lopsided around his neck, and I note he's barefoot, telling me he rushed to see us.

Kaira makes a small squeaking sound, her eyes bulging at Bardhyl, but I can't tell if it's intimidation or loving what she sees. Too bad because if I remember correctly, these Alphas, including Dušan, are Meira's fated mates.

"Meira," Jae calls out and is suddenly running away from us and toward her.

Meira rushes from her men toward Jae, and they come together in a tight embrace. They laugh, then pull apart, holding each other's hands and smiling. Jae points at her sisters, catching Meira up on what's going on and who's who.

I see the heartfelt emotions between them on their faces. Whatever these two have gone through, it was life-changing.

With Crius embracing Narah, we all approach the team, with Lucien and Bardhyl stepping into our path. Their gazes roam over us, and by their tight expressions, they recognize us.

"Where's your Alpha, Ragnar?" Bardhyl's gravelly voice demands.

"A day's travel is behind us. We faced difficult circumstances and had to leave earlier."

As if understanding, his attention sweeps past me and lands on a very pregnant Narah.

"Hi," she says shyly, waving at the guys.

Heat flares over me at seeing how absolutely gorgeous she looks. My mouth opens to introduce her, but Jae's voice cuts me off.

"Narah, this is Meira, who I told you about. She saved my ass so many times and took me in. She's an angel." Jae drags Meira by the hand over to Narah to be introduced, stealing my moment. Kaira's with them, and I'm on the outside of the group with Crius, Lucien, and Bardhyl standing awkwardly. The guards keep their distance.

I turn to the Alphas, feeling as if we've all been kicked aside. "So, is Dušan around?"

Lucien shakes his head. "He's out for the day. He'll return tonight."

Silence. I'm seething that the asshole guards tried to push us back two nights.

"You traveled the whole way in a carriage?" Bardhyl asks, reaching for conversation while the girls talk up a storm. "What's it like? Up in the Savage Sector?"

"Full of fucking undead. Seems they're migrating north," Crius butts in. "Thanks for sending them our way," he smirks mockingly.

"You better be prepared and build some big walls around your pack home," Lucien adds, scanning the stone wall that looks newly built around their home.

Grasping the strength not to joke that we have yet to lay claim to the Savage Sector, I just nod with a tight grin. I draw in a sharp breath, knowing if Ragnar and Dušan were here, we'd already be inside the compound, most likely eating. I could eat a whole boar right now. My gut groans at the thought of roast meat.

Meira suddenly turns toward us, smiling radiantly at her two Alphas. They stare at her like she's their sun, captivated by her attention.

"Narah's gonna give birth any day now," she says sternly. "We have to get her inside." She looks at me with kindness, and I can see why she and Jae bonded so easily. They are so similar with huge hearts. "Any friend of Jae is our friend. Come inside before night arrives. I'm sure you have a lot to tell us."

"That we do," I respond. "She needs to be off her feet, and she's starving right now." Narah narrows her gaze at me, and I wink back at my gorgeous babe.

Meira nudges her men into urgency, and we're ushered quickly toward the compound.

Narah slips her hand into mine, and she looks up at me cheekily, whispering, "Nice move. Using me as your excuse to be fed."

I chuckle and lean in for a quick kiss on her forehead. "You have no idea how starved I am."

She rolls her eyes as we make our way toward the entry gates.

The guards guide the carriage driver inside the protection of their twelve-foot fences, along with the horse-drawn carriage.

Looks like there's no turning back now. I shuffle through my mind for an explanation, well aware I have no intention of mentioning Ragnar's demand for forty females once he arrives at Shadowlands Sector. Though there's nothing that says I can't ask a few questions about how they collect and trade Omegas before Dušan returns.

I'd have to ask without the women overhearing. No sense stirring up that hornets' nest if I don't have to. Narah will kill me if she finds out what Rangar promised, and it could put her sisters in danger of discovering the reason for our trip.

FIFTEEN

RAGNAR

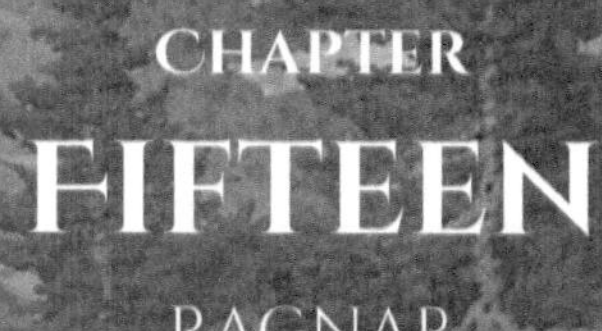

We've finally arrived.

I catch my breath as I climb off the horse and clasp the reins in my fist. The Shadowlands Secret compound stands like a mountain before Nikos and me.

Darkness swallows the landscape as the breeze whispers in my ears, and my heartbeat is pounding. We'd raced here on horseback, pausing only to change horses in nearby towns to avoid riding them to death. For the entire trip, I kept searching the woods, worried I'd find the carriage broken down or attacked and my little fox in danger.

I'm fucked up like that in the head, always expecting the worst. Growing up, I'd told myself believing the worst would happen meant I would never be disappointed. I now see how toxic that was and how much my father impacted my life.

So, I hold on to the thought that Narah will be alright. Though, standing at the front gates of the Ash Wolves' home, my chest constricts that we won't find her here.

Nikos bangs a fist on the lofty front gates. He looks as battered and bloody as me, though our injuries are minor—bruised ribs, cuts, things that heal quickly for us. Most of the blood belongs to the numerous rogue Alphas and Beta males who attacked us. Surprisingly, it wasn't the undead who caused us trouble, but these fucking starved wolf shifters who live like wild beasts in the woods, charging at anyone to steal everything from them. The bastards got some good hits in, but we also left them as corpses in our wake.

A scuffing sound from overhead has us both raising our gazes to the guard looming on the watchtower, gun in hand and smacking his lips, staring down at us.

Lifting my chin, I state, "I'm Ragnar, Alpha of the Savage Sector, here to speak with Dušan." It's the middle of the fucking night, and my skin crawls, knowing we're out in the open, easy targets.

With another smack of his lips, the guard clears his throat, taking his time to respond.

"He's been expecting you."

Hearing those words, I breathe a huge sigh of relief. My gorgeous girl has arrived. Whatever state they were accepted by the Alpha, I'll sort it out now that we're here. Eager to get inside, we watch as the guard takes his time getting down to open the gates.

"Would it look bad if I smack this fucker around the head a bit?" Nikos whispers under his breath.

Cutting him a smile, I shake my head and hand him my horse's reins just as the gates open with a screeching wail. The man waves us inside, and we step into an opening engulfed by shadows. Nikos brings the two horses, and another guard steps forward to help him.

In no time, we're following a worn path up a hill toward the compound. An open field of grass, shrubs, and trees flanks our walk. It's refreshing to see that within the walls, the wolves can run free and feel safe from the undead.

For a long time, the Shadowlands Sector had been buried under an army of undead, and to many, it had been seen as a cursed land. It still amazes me that wolf shifters survived and made a life in this part of Romania.

Silence permeates the night, with only the occasional wolf howl in the distance. We pass an open courtyard surrounded by huts as we make our way toward the stone fortress that rises out of the darkness.

The men take our horses to the stables, leaving us alone to approach the building. Nikos strolls by my side, glancing around as much as I am.

"This place brings back memories of home," he whispers. In truth, it appears completely different from where I grew up in an open village, where the perimeters were protected with magic against our enemies and the undead. Though I suspect he may be referring to his place of birth—before his father sold him to my family in exchange for my sister.

The compound gives me ideas of what I will need to build once I finally claim Savage Sector as my forever home with Narah and my pack. If the undead remain up north, perhaps simple fences weren't enough. What Dušan had created here is genius.

Speaking of the man... he steps out of the front doors of his castle, meeting my gaze with his steel gaze. He wears jeans and a wrinkled shirt, showing he'd dressed hastily. We must have drawn him from sleep.

The Alpha always struck me as a reasonable man, so even if he looks irritated, he wasn't a fucking asshole like so many of them. Besides, for him to meet us on his own shows trust and that he knows where Narah and my men are for the moment.

"Dušan, I wish I could say we're meeting under better circumstances."

His icy blue eyes pierce Nikos and me, especially the splattered blood over my clothes. When he steps forward, I close the distance between us. This is his home, which means he holds dominance—especially if I want his help.

"Ragnar, it's good to see you've arrived." The breeze sweeps through his inky dark hair, which sits messily around his face and over his shoulders. It's grown wilder since I last saw him. "I always keep my word. Any pack in trouble is welcome in my home," he states loudly and takes me into a strong embrace, slapping my back. "Your pack's visit is unexpected, though. Evidently, since our last visit, you've found yourself an Omega and got her pregnant."

I laugh. If only he knew the truth of the chaos I'd endured since we last met all those months ago.

"I have much to tell you. This isn't the way I'd intended to pay you a visit, but sometimes, fate has a way fucking with us."

"You're not wrong there." With another slap to my back, he nudges me inside his home.

Light from the fiery torches sitting in brass brackets on the walls blinks against the stone building. Our footfalls echo around us as I trail after him down a corridor. We take a set of curved stone steps and emerge into a dimly lit foyer with tapestries of wild wolves in battle hanging from the walls.

"Your pack has been fed, then sent to rest in our guest rooms," he states, strolling alongside me. Nikos remains at our back, and a guard follows him.

"You are too generous," I state. "At our last meeting, things weren't exactly easy between us." A time when we came to collect Jae, who'd been lost and somehow made her way down to the Shadowlands Sector. It was chaos when we got here—undead running amok, Dušan restrained and fed to the zombies by someone in his pack. Of course, we saved him, which, in hindsight, was the best fucking decision I'd ever made.

"On your last visit, you could have taken advantage of my situation and eliminated me to claim my pack, but you didn't." He gives me a look of understanding. "For that, I am forever grateful. Besides, Meira would have my balls if I didn't treat her friends with anything but hospitality." He grins and runs a hand through his hair, pushing the loose strands off his face.

"I'm all for not creating chaos in my life by disagreeing with my Omega." I bark out a laugh.

"You got it. Anyway, I'll show you where everyone is before we sit down to talk. I assume you'll want to make sure they're all okay."

I nod.

"Absolutely," Nikos answers behind us, gaining an approving grin from Dušan.

We reach the first door, and the moment Dušan opens it, thunderous snores escape. I instantly know Crius and Stone are in there, growling like dragons. The light behind us stretches into the room, revealing two large beds with bulky shapes under the blankets. Stone's lying on his stomach, with his leg hanging off the mattress. Crius is lying on his back, with his axe near the bed as though he'd fallen asleep gripping it. That sounds like him. By the smell of perspiration and sweet wine in the air, I'd say they experienced a fun night.

Nikos scoffs. "Tell me I'm not stuck in there with those two."

Dušan shuts the door and chuckles. "Don't worry. You have your own room." While he shows Nikos to the next room along the corridor, he suggests we pay a visit to their showers first. "We have running hot water."

Nikos' eyes widen. "You better not be fucking with me. The cold showers I've taken lately nearly froze my balls off."

I'm blown away by the large communal bathroom. An oversized bathtub, which could easily fit twenty people, takes up a big section of the room Or four Alphas and an Omega—the thought sends a buzz down to my cock. I savagely miss my little fox.

"Well, this is my stop, if that's alright." Nikos glances my way with a raised eyebrow. "I stink like a corpse, and the promise of hot water is too much to refuse, even for me."

"You're good." I pat his shoulder. "Go for it."

Leaving him behind, I ask Dušan, "Where's Narah?" We walk past more guards, so it's good to see there's protection.

"Just ahead. I gave you a bigger room."

When he opens the door, my heart is beating faster to see my gorgeous girl again and ensure she's safe. I stick my head in to find her in the middle of an enormous king bed, with the sheets tangled around her, the way she always sleeps, hogging the entire bed and blankets. She's breathing deeply, and as eager as I am to join her, I step back and shut the door.

"Okay, let's go talk before I fall asleep on my feet."

"Good," Dušan agrees.

We make our way back the way we came, past the balcony into a grand room, which looks as though I've stepped back into another timeline. The place might have existed before the virus ravaged our world. Light bulbs twinkle from brass light fixtures, and staring at them, it takes me a moment to realize they're not candles but electric. It's been too long since I've seen such luxury. Back in Denmark, we had running electricity and water, something my father had arranged with the use of magic from the local witches—when he wasn't killing them. Everyone had been disposable to him.

Hatred unfurls in my chest, but I force myself to release the thoughts. It won't do me any good thinking of him.

Dušan laughs, distracting me and drawing my attention to him staring up at the light fixture.

"I do a lot of trade with other packs, especially with the X-Clan. They are extremely well off and have an abundance of technology, so I make the most of my relationship with them."

"Smart idea." I'm envious, yet it makes me more determined to secure Savage Sector and create a home for my family. More reason to keep my relationship with Dušan strong.

We approach the fireplace, where two brown couches face each other. Bookshelves line the walls, filled with old books, and moonlight spills through the window.

"Are you hungry?" he asks.

I shake my head. "I crave more than anything a hot wash, then my Omega pressed up against me."

"I understand. It's way past midnight, so I won't keep you long." The Alpha reclines in the middle of the couch, arms by his side, legs spread. He stares at me, waiting for me to explain how the fuck I ended up on his doorstep with my immediate pack and my pregnant Omega.

So, I gave him the lowdown on what I'd endured in taking over the Savage Sector, our dealings with the witches, Martell's rising forces, and even Narah possessing magic. I had no intention of entering this Alpha's land and being untruthful about the things that mattered to him. I trusted him to be fair and suspected he was the kind of man who wouldn't take lightly to being tricked.

I have too much to lose not to reveal the truth, and what I need is an ally.

I omit a few things, like the ordeal with Narah's parents and how magic got her pregnant, since I don't see them as critical and are unnecessary details for him. Additionally, I left out the mention of forty females. With Mihai dead and the pack now under my rein, his demands are no longer a problem.

"You've taken on a lot." Giving me a reassuring nod, he leans forward and rests his elbows on his thighs, staring at me. "It seems as if I was your last resort escape plan. What are your intentions in Shadowlands Sector?" His gaze settles on me, and there's silence in the room with the underlying question of if I'm here to claim his pack.

"You're right," I admit, leaning back, showing no aggression. "I found myself in a tight spot. Martell is hunting us down, and after he killed the Bane Wolf leaders, I couldn't risk Narah's life and our unborn child. I find no shame in running when the time calls for it. I am here for the purpose of safety for a short time, nothing more."

Dušan stands and goes over to one of the shelves, where he picks up a glass decanter and pours honeyed liquid into two glasses. He hands me one, then takes a seat.

"You look like you need a drink."

"Fuck, yeah."

"So, you need a haven for your Omega to safely give birth. Then what will you do?"

Lifting the glass to my mouth, I inhale the rich sweetness of honey and charred wood from the whiskey before I press the rim to my lips and drink it in one go. No heat rushes down my throat, only a caramel, spicy aftertaste. It's delicious. Setting the glass on the table between us, I meet Dušan's gaze.

"I would be indebted to you for your help with Narah. All I ask is for her and her sisters to remain here a while longer when we return to finish off Martell. In exchange, you'll have my unwavering loyalty. We will be neighboring packs, and there will be no war waged from my end. We will welcome your pack to my land anytime."

He swirls the whiskey in his hand, then takes a sip. "Only if you succeed in removing Martell, right?"

I grin and move forward in my seat. "Everything I do is with the intention of succeeding." I suck in a harsh breath, more concerned about how Narah will react to me leaving her behind, but I won't put her in danger, especially with a child who will depend on her. "I ask for your generosity to seek refuge at your home for a small time."

"As I mentioned, my home is open to you for as long as you need it. I do need two things. One is an agreement that once you secure the Savage Sector, I will have clearway to travel through your land anytime to easily reach the northern countries for my trades."

"You got it," I confirm without hesitation. "What else?"

"If anyone in your pack harms my pack or I discover your visit is anything other than security, I won't hold back from eliminating them. Anyone who stands in my way will face the same fate."

My exhale is shallow, but I agree just as quickly. "I have nothing to hide from you, but I do ask if you find something you disagree with that I'm informed first to avoid action taken from a misunderstanding."

Dušan sips his whiskey.

"I am merely extending you the same grace you did on our last visit." Then he's on his feet. "As such, I'm calling for a blood oath to seal our agreement."

I stiffen, well aware a blood oath is an agreement that should either of us break, the one Alpha automatically claims dominance of the other's pack and Omegas. This comes in the form of attempting to take over each other's packs during my stay here.

Dušan is not an idiot, that much is clear. On our last visit, I threatened him, and as much as I hate the notion, right now, he has my balls in a vice. With Narah so close to birth, I can't risk having her anywhere else.

Grinding my teeth, I study the Alpha, who isn't grinning, telling me he's not enjoying this, either. I don't hate the guy, but fuck, I loathe making such deals out of pure concern that no one can control fate. Lately, she's been a fucking bitch with everything going haywire.

"So, do we have a deal?" he asks.

I swallow my pride and get up. "Yes, deal. I have no intention of bringing any harm to your Ash Wolves."

"Good. I'd prefer to think this is the beginning of us trusting each other for future dealings."

I can't help but laugh at his words when I've just agreed to a blood oath.

"Agreed. Let's do this."

Against my better judgment, I have no other option, and if there was an Alpha I'd willingly do such an agreement with, it's Dušan. The things I heard from Jae about his loyalty and how he treats his pack give me nothing but appreciation for him.

He crosses the room and grabs an empty glass along with a sharp blade. Once he's set the glass on the coffee table between us, we take a seat across from each other and lean forward.

"To put you at ease," Dušan begins as he lifts his hand and the blade over the glass. "Once everyone from your pack leaves my home,

I'll burn the proof of our blood oath." He slashes the blade across the meaty part of his palm, not grimacing once, then curls his hand into a fist and lets the blood drip into the glass as he hands me the knife.

"I'd appreciate that." The sharp bite of the blade cuts across the top of my palm. Dušan moves his hand back, and I add my blood portion to the oath. We then shake on it, our blood mingling. The oath is more than proof in a glass—it is entrenched down to our wolves.

My wolf rouses, grunting in my chest with acknowledgment, though he growls against my decision. However, I'm no longer the man I once was. I have more than my pack and land to worry about. I have a family and a newborn on the way. For them, I'd risk everything —even my life.

"We've agreed to a blood oath between our wolves," Dušan states. "If the oath is broken, our wolves will also honor the agreement— your pack and Omegas will bond to me. And should I harm your family, you will own all that I dominate."

"Agreed," I growl, shaking his hand as more blood drips into the glass before we pull our hands back. He gives me a rag to wipe my bloody hand, then does the same. I take that as my cue to leave, which is for the best as irritation curls in my chest.

"Thank you for taking us in, Dušan. I will not forget your generosity," I say, not wanting him to think I'm bitter. That's not how partnerships are formed, and this Alpha holds a lot of power and connections I can use.

"Good night, my friend," he says with a yawn tugging at his mouth.

I see myself out of his room, shutting the door behind me. Cracking my neck, I breathe easily. I have no issues with Dušan, but it's not in my nature to play the submissive in any relationship.

Narah's beautiful face swims in my mind. I miss her terribly, but my pulse is on fire, and I need a few moments to remind myself why I'm out here, why biting my tongue and living with Dušan's threat is a necessity. So, I stroll onto the outdoor balcony that sweeps outward in a circular motion.

He has his family to protect, and I have mine. I stare down at my cut, where the blood has already coagulated and stopped bleeding.

Tilting my head, I stare at the immense woodland. It's barely indistinguishable from the night, with only the silvery glow of moon-light brushing the tops of the canopies giving away the forest. It's quiet outside, but there's war in my mind. I clench my jaw. I'd planned every goddamn move in taking over Savage Sector for a long time, and not one thing has gone to plan. Things have definitely moved in our direction, but in ways I never expected.

I left Denmark to establish my own pack and will not return home until I've completed my plans. Despite the death we've encountered so far, I suspect it's only a fraction of what's to come. I have no idea what chaos Martell will create or how many packs he'll destroy if they don't bow down to his dominance.

And I can't do a fucking thing about it, which leaves me furious as hell, shaking with anger.

A storm's coming, yet with our baby on the way, for now, all I can do is remain low. I'm thrilled to become a father, even if it's the worst fucking possible time.

Family has always been something I've wanted... down the track, and not until I've set down roots in my own territory. However, if I've learned anything since leaving Denmark, it's that nothing ever goes to plan. The universe has her own agenda, and right now, she's bringing my family's plans forward.

I'm fucking ecstatic and can't stop thinking about holding our little bundle. I don't care which of us four is responsible. With Narah as the mother, the baby might as well be my flesh and blood. We are family, regardless. I fucking adore every inch of her and can't wait to meet our baby.

My priorities have shifted, but the long-term goal is still in sight.

I peer into the woods, frustration and adrenaline surging through me at the same time. Somehow, I have to make everything work.

Narah

The soft indent of the mattress behind me wakes me, and with a single inhale, Ragnar's masculine and wolf scent washes over me. I smile to myself that he's finally arrived safely.

He slides into the bed and comes up behind me, his large hand working up my thigh and gripping my hip. The thick ridge of his cock presses up between my asscheeks. That single touch is all it takes for my body to shudder and ignite the heat that's been lingering just beneath the surface. An inferno licks between the apex of my thighs so fast, it leaves me dizzy.

"I missed you," I whisper into the night, attempting to twist around, which is impossible since he's plastered to me. His body is burning up, and he's already rocking his hips against me, ready to go.

"I've thought of nothing but you."

The warmth of his kiss on my shoulder sends a buzz over my body, and it doesn't take long for me to feel the slick of my arousal drenching me. My nipples harden at his touch.

"But right now, little fox, I need to fuck you," he whispers the words against my neck. "It's been a shit of a day, and all I've thought about was taking you into my arms and sinking my cock into you." His arm slides under my pillow and neck, embracing me. He squeezes one of my breasts as his face presses into my hair, breathing deeply. "You smell like sex, and I'm starved. You're perfect, made to fit against me."

I groan as he guides his cock between my thighs, and I shift my legs apart to let him in.

"Babe, I need to hear your words that you want this," he growls. "Talk to me. Are you alright?"

"Yes," I moan. "I'm sleepy but suddenly extremely horny as I feel my heat growing."

He unleashes a groan and guides the tip of his cock to my entrance.

"Heat, you say." There's no ceremony or teasing me before he pushes his huge cock into my pussy. "I'll fuel your fire," he purrs in my ear, the blaze from his body scorching with mine. He rips the blanket off us, and I tremble against the ferocity of his hunger. "You're so fucking beautiful. Your pussy is soaking wet and so tight for me. Every inch of you is made for me, my gorgeous girl. Now, be a good girl and let me fuck you."

His praise makes me whine for more. My body rocks with his movements as he pushes deeper into me, forcing himself inside. I feel every inch of him as he presses farther in. He pinches my nipple as his teeth graze the skin on my neck with the promise of pain I crave.

I'm floating on the sensation of my Alpha's cock stretching me.

"I need this so much," he growls.

I fist the bed sheet as he fucks me hard. Lying on my side is comfortable since there's no pressure on my huge belly, making it easier for him to pump in and out.

"Your pussy's squeezing my cock so tightly. Fuck me, I love you. The way you get so wet for me, how hard your nipples get, how delicious you smell. And your breasts are so big. I fucking love them and want them all over me."

The sensation of his sliding in and out of me drives me crazy with desire. I close my eyes, giving myself to him, letting him fuck me just as he needs me. This moment is more about him. I crave to give him everything. I feel him all over me, his thick cock wedged deep inside me.

He pinches my nipples, tugging on them, giving me the ache I need. I shiver at being taken by him without pause.

"Ragnar," I groan. "I'm so close."

He snarls as he assumes he needs to pump into me faster. Our breaths race as the bed rocks beneath us.

"Come for me, baby."

Desperation for more leaves me aching, and I cry out, shuddering in his embrace. He thrusts his hips as he fucks me, over and over, holding me tightly against him.

My exhales came out in gasps. "I'm so close. Ragnar…" The orgasm barrels into me, stealing my words, and I keen as I shudder hard.

"Scream it all out," he grunts in my ear.

My toes curl, and stars dance at the back of my eyes. I bellow my pleasure as euphoria sweeps me away without mercy. I shake and howl, loving the sensation of floating, as though I no longer feel my body or my mind, only the delicious climax that rushes over me, the orgasm building as if it's never going to end. Caught up in the sparks swallowing me, I embrace how good it feels.

"I love you so much, Narah," Ragnar softly growls. "You will always be mine."

I feel him slipping out of me, and I miss him terribly, leaving me feeling empty.

"You come so beautifully, and I'm going to lick it all up."

His words dance in my ear.

I shake harder from the lust claiming me, and his promise only turns me on more. I vibrate against him, the intensity of my climax longer, deeper than any I've experienced before.

When I finally settle down and barely catch my breath, I collapse against Ragnar and twist my head toward him. Perspiration runs down the side of my face, which he catches with a finger.

"You didn't knot," I say on a rushed exhale.

"I'm not done with you yet," he whispers, peppering my arm with kisses. "I have to taste you. I'm going to clean you with my tongue first, then I'm going to lick your boobs. I've been dreaming about them. When I fuck you after, we might break this bed."

"Oh." I grasp his arm that's wrapped over my chest. "Is that a promise?"

He laughs and leans down, kissing me, his tongue sweeping into my mouth. He's rough tonight, taking what he wants, and I love him like this.

"I'm going to make you come at least two more times before I knot inside you. I hear orgasms are good for pregnant women."

I laugh. "Did you just make that part up?"

"Perhaps." He laughs and unfurls his arms from around me, then slides farther down the bed and guides me to roll onto my back. Spreading my legs, he kneels between them.

"You are so beautiful pregnant, Narah. I'm constantly turned on seeing you this way."

"I think you're talking too much," I tease, then nibble on the corner of my lower lip, adoring the way he studies my body. The smile curling his mouth melts my heart, and with the single look that destroys me, he leans between my legs, kissing my inner thighs and making his way deeper.

I know we're guests in the Ash Wolves' castle, and I should be quieter, but with Ragnar's breath already blowing across my drenched core, I don't care anymore. Losing myself to what he's offering me, I inhale the thick sex-filled air, every inch of me responsive to every touch.

"I need you," I murmur, throwing my head back on the pillow, my legs spread wide, about to float back to heaven. I am forever ruined by my four men, and I wouldn't want it any other way.

"I know, little fox," he answers smugly.

Then his tongue runs the length of my pussy, and I completely lose myself in this man's mouth.

SIXTEEN

NIKOS

"Are you alright?" Narah asks from across the long table in the Ash Wolves' mess hall, which is quiet and empty today. She stares at me cheekily, her fork piercing a cherry tomato, eyes narrowing on me while a tiny grin teases the edges of her perfect mouth. Someone's mischievous this morning.

Dark, chestnut hair drawn into a high ponytail, her eyes are as fiery as the blaze roaring at the other end of the room. I slept in and discovered the rest of the team had gone out hunting with the Ash Wolves for fresh game. Turns out, I wasn't the only one who stumbled in late for breakfast.

"Couldn't be better," I answer. "I slept heavily last night once we arrived, enjoyed another hot shower this morning, and now I get to share breakfast alone with my sweet peach."

"Sweet peach, huh?" She grins at me, looking more adorable than ever. "Where did you sleep last night if I was so sweet? Only Ragnar came to me."

"It sounded to me like you were more than happy with just Ragnar. Most of the night, in fact," I tease, remembering being woken up by her screams of pleasure. "But do you want to know the truth?" I say, leaning forward and lowering my voice.

"Sure." She pops the tomato into her mouth.

"I lay in bed, listening to your delicious cries, beating on myself until I came so hard, I howled out your name."

A spot of pink taints her gorgeous cheeks. I adore how she reacts to me. It's a mesmerizing feeling to know I impact her in such a way.

"Well, I guess we both had an incredible night then, though I would have preferred you joined us. I was worried to death about you and Ragnar."

"You have no idea how much I missed you." Stretching my legs under the table, I wrap them around hers, trapping them. "My hand was a poor imitation of what I wanted to do to you." The way she looks at me with a sinful smile sends a jolt of arousal straight to my cock.

"So, everything went well with your visit to the Bane Wolves?" Her abrupt flip of conversation throws me off, especially with my head drowning in arousal. Thinking about all the dead bodies we'd found in the pack or how many of the deceased we carried for burning is not something I want to think about any time soon. And under no circumstance will I be revealing any of it to Narah. With her pregnant, Ragnar and I agreed to keep what Martell did to the Bane Wolves to ourselves, so we don't bring her more stress and worry.

We'll deal with that asshole, but for now, I need to clear my head of those horrific images imprinted on my mind.

"It all went to plan," is all I say, then smile to distract my beauty and distract myself with her captivating face.

Untangling her feet from between mine, she suddenly gets up. With a devious grin, she steps away from the table and makes her way to the doorway. She's wearing a loose yellow dress with short sleeves, and the moment she opens the door, the sunshine peers right through the fabric, making it translucent, revealing her beautiful figure. I'm absolutely obsessed with her curves from being pregnant. I never imagined I could love anyone as much as I do Narah. Her carrying a baby has made me adore her so much more. I know I would die for her.

Looking over her shoulder, she says, "So, are you coming?" She blows me an air kiss, and my heart strikes harder against my ribcage.

"I sure hope so," I mutter under my breath. Jolting to my feet, my fork falls from my hand to my plate with a loud clatter. I can't get to her fast enough and hurry after her outside of the mess hall. She rushes ahead of me down a path, and I'm done flirting. My cock's hard as stone in my pants, and just watching the way she strolls has my pulse racing.

There are several locals walking in the courtyard we pass, Ash Wolf pack members, who stare our way inquisitively. I do the polite thing and nod while attempting to twist my hips away from them. They don't know me, and here I am in their home with the biggest boner in the world. Besides, I'm certain by now, word has spread around the compound about visiting pack members, hence all the attention.

Catching my wolf girl, I close in behind her just as she reaches the edge of the courtyard that's surrounded by huts.

"Narah, you're killing me right now." I do a quick sweep of the yard and notice we aren't exactly alone, or I'd have her on her hands and knees, her panties off in seconds. That's how starved I am. I press my hardness flush against her ass, adoring how soft and warm she feels.

Breathless, she twists toward me and pushes up to reach my mouth. I slide a hand behind her back to support her and claim her mouth. She's so warm to the touch, and the small sounds she makes are an aphrodisiac. Her breasts are crushed against me, her nipples hard, and I'm losing my mind with how much I need her.

She breaks away from me, her eyes burning with lust and her sexy as fuck scent fogging my senses. While pregnant, she may not go completely into heat, but it's enough to drive me wild. The fragrance of her arousal has me reaching out and pulling her body back to me.

"I need to have you now... I can't wait." The sight and smell of her... something grips my heart so hard, I can't breathe. Swallowing to calm myself does nothing. She's in my head, in my senses, and I've waited too long to slide into her pussy.

"Not here," she whispers in a rushed breath, her eyes wild. Fuck, I love when she's turned on, her breathing races, and she's barely holding on. "Let's go back to your room."

"No, I won't make it. I need to feel my cock deep inside you." With her hand in mine, I draw her along a dirt track between two wooden huts to the open forest beyond them. I love that the compound has its own woodland within the walls.

We quickly leave behind the main part of the village, and we're finally alone. The land ascends slightly, and the trees are denser, meaning more shadows. When I find a flat piece of land crowded with trees and ensure we're by ourselves, I turn to my beautiful girl and draw her into my arms.

Our mouths clash, coming together savagely, our hunger primal.

Her eyes are closed, and I adore how she lets herself completely fall into the moment. The air is fragrant with her scent, deepening my hunger for her. Running my fingers through her hair, I hold her close to me, knowing I can't get enough.

Birds sing around us, the breeze cools against my nape, and the most beautiful girl is on my lips. I don't give a damn who sees us. I'm so intoxicated, so far gone, all I see is Narah. She breaks from my lips, breathless, her cheeks pink.

"I didn't know anyone could get so turned on while pregnant."

"This is how I prefer you, lusting for me, your sexy scent flooding my nostrils." Her pulse flutters beneath my touch. "But most of all, I love that you're dying for me."

"Maybe you should just stop talking." She fists my shirt and drags me back to her mouth, and an inferno ignites between us.

"I need you now," I growl, not waiting a moment more. My cock throbs, aching for her as I fist her dress and wrench it up to her waist. Slipping my fingers into the band of her panties, I slide them down. Our kiss breaks as I fall to my knees to glide them down her legs. She steps out of her underwear, and I bunch them up, stuffing them into my back pocket.

Just as quickly, I wrench my shirt off and lay it on the grass. In seconds, I'm on my feet and lifting my princess off her feet, gaining myself an aroused laugh. I lay her on her back on my shirt. The ache in my body lingers. My wolf is snarling to put an end to the hunger that claims us. It's a good pain, a fucking delicious one, but there's only so much a man can take.

"Come to me." She beckons with a curled finger. Her lips part on a moan as if the thought of me devouring her has her already close to the edge.

"Don't start without me," I quip, laughing as I fall to my knees in front of her, wasting no time pushing up her dress for the most beautiful view in the world. She's drenched, glistening from how turned on she is, and my cock strains at the sight. A growl of impatience bursts from my chest as my fingers dig into her inner thighs, pushing them wider, then I look up at my girl. "Are you sure this won't hurt?"

"I promise it will be so incredible, I'll forget everything else."

My little one rocks her hips, and I can't wait another moment. Shuffling closer on my knees, I lean forward just enough not to put any pressure on her belly.

She arches her back, showing me everything, and as her Alpha, I'm about to take it all.

My fingers grasp her hips as I plunge into her perfect, tight pussy. She constricts around me, but I take my time, pushing in and out, watching the way her greedy pussy sucks down my cock. I want every second of my life to be like this.

She's my obsession.

Made for me.

Her body.

Her cries.

Her heat curling around my balls.

I find my rhythm and work my way faster. I don't go as deep as I'd like, not wanting to hurt her, but it's enough to tease us both.

Sometimes, I wonder if I deserve someone as spectacular as her. I struggled to belong anywhere my father sold me to for peace. Fuck. I've been struggling with my identity ever since. But with Narah, there's a... belonging.

She stares at me with sexy eyes and hungrily calls my name. Her body reacts to every touch, every word. I growl as I thrust inside her, and she arches her back.

"You're doing so well, taking my cock," I growl, loving how sopping wet she's become.

Absolutely entrancing.

I tug at the neckline of her dress, needing desperately to see all of her. A breast pops out, topped with the prettiest dusty pink nipple. It's hard as she writhes against me. Freeing the other one, I grab the nipple between my fingers, working it. Her moans wash over me as she cries out in mindless lust.

"I love you so much." I breathe heavily with each plunge. "You are my world, Narah."

"I love you, Nikos," she moans.

The sounds she makes are a song to my ears. She starts vibrating against me, then shudders. Her pussy clenches around me, and her excited screams set off my own chain of events, but I'm not ready yet. I have so much more in me before I'll knot and make her mine. I don't want to rush this.

Grunting, I hold on to her hips as she squeezes me hard.

"You will always be mine. Always."

As her body shakes, I love watching her come completely undone under me. She gradually calms as I slowly move in and out of her. When she makes a soft whining sound, I pause, a slight panic coming over me. I pull out more, ensuring I haven't in any way hurt her.

"Is everything alright?"

"Something just feels like it popped inside me." As she speaks, a flush of liquid gushes from her pussy. Her eyes are huge with panic. "Something's happening."

I leap to my feet, knowing what's going on.

"Your water broke. You're going to have a baby." My mind races, my heart thumping, and I don't know where to start, but seeing the fear on Narah's face smacks into me like a bulldozer. She's terrified. I have to get my fucking shit together. I'd love to pace and freak out that I'm about to have a baby, but I remind myself my sweet girl is the one doing all the work.

Rushing to her side, I push down her dress to her knees, then lift her into my arms and cradle her against my chest.

"I have you."

"I'm not ready yet, Nikos. This can't be happening yet."

Fear flares across her face, and while I may feel my chest squeezing, I need to be strong for her.

"I'll be with you the whole time. I promise. We're going through this together." My pulse thunders in my veins as I rush back to the castle, my head in a million places about the best place to take her.

When I glance down at her, she's smiling, and there are stars glinting in her eyes.

"We're going to have a baby," she murmurs in disbelief.

"I'm so excited." And slightly terrified that everything won't go well. As I reach the main entry into the castle, Meira strolls outside, holding a wicker basket as though she's about to head into the meadow and pick flowers. The moment her gaze clashes with mine, she drops the basket and runs to us, her face blanching.

"What happened?" she demands.

"My water broke," Narah responds with a wonky smile, as though she's burdening Meira.

"Oh, my goddess," Meira snaps, and I see the slight tremor of anxiety on her face as well.

I'm guessing this is her first time helping someone have a baby.

"Where do we go?" I ask.

"I've had one of our guest rooms turned into a birthing room just in case this happened." She wrings her hands as her words come fast. I can tell she's nervous, but she's so sweet and helpful.

Narah holds my arm, smiling but crying. "I'm scared but excited."

"Me, too, gorgeous."

As we rush up the stairs, Meira barks at everyone we pass to get the nurse and orders towels, hot water, disinfectant, and a bunch of other things I don't think are needed. I'm guessing she's as overwhelmed as we are.

The room we enter is large, with a small bed, a bedside table, and a large table to the side, piled with towels. Setting Narah on the bed on her back, I push the wild strands of hair from her brow.

"Everything's going to be fine. You'll see. Don't worry." I'm rattling, and she laughs at me, reaching up to take my hand.

"Take a breath, Nikos. You won't be any help if you hyperventilate and pass out on me." Her stare softens, and she kisses my knuckles.

"I'll be back," Meira states, then marches out of the room.

Lost to my Narah, I'd completely forgotten she was with us.

"Do you think I broke your water?" The first thing coming to mind rushes out of my mouth.

"I doubt it. When it's time, it's time."

When she scrunches up her face and squeezes my hand, I freeze on the spot.

"Narah?"

"It's…" She rubs her belly. "Just a tightness around my belly caught my breath."

It isn't long before Meira bursts back into the room with an older woman dressed in a green dress and an apron. Did Meira bring in the kitchen chef?

"This is Lily, our doctor, nurse, midwife, and anything we need." Meira's words are heavy with her ragged breaths.

"Hello, Narah," Lily says with the softest voice and the kindest smile I've seen in a long time. "I'm going to have a quick look to make sure things look alright and how far along you are, okay?"

"Of course," Narah says.

"Now, bend your knees up and open them for me. It's uncomfortable right now, but trust me, soon you won't care." She laughs at her own joke, even though the rest of us aren't laughing. We all look harried as if we've had ten cups too many of coffee.

I hold on to Narah's arm while Lily inspects her. Meira comes in and shuts the door, fiddling with the new bundle of towels she brought into the room.

"Oh, you are doing wonderfully. The baby really wants to come out, it seems," she says, catching our attention. "You're already five centimeters dilated. It shouldn't be long before you go into full labor."

"It feels like the baby wants to come out now," Narah gasps as she tries to push her dress down to cover herself. I help her, then sit up on the bed next to her, holding her close.

"Not yet, but soon," Lily says, then turns her attention to Meira.

"I can't wait to meet our baby," I say, trying to distract Narah from the ache she must be feeling. "I don't mind what we have as long as they're healthy and get your beauty. Oh, we haven't decided on what to call the baby yet," I say, finding myself doing that panic talk. My adrenaline is soaring with excitement.

"Figured it's something we can all decide once we know what we're having." Her eyelids look heavy.

"How about I get behind you and hold you against me?" I'll do anything to bring her ease when the contractions hit.

"I'd like that," she says. "I want you next to me the whole time. I hope the other three come back soon, so they don't miss out."

"I'm not going anywhere." I help Narah sit upright, holding her weight, and frantically toss the pillows off the bed. Meira wraps an arm around Narah's back while I get onto the bed behind her, shuffling to straddle her, my legs curling around her hips.

"Okay, I have her." When Narah tenses and groans in pain, I collect her in my arms so she can lean her back against my chest, letting her grasp my arm and squeeze the hell out of it. I'll survive, considering what she's going through.

It feels like she only breathes a minute or two before another one comes, and she digs her nails into my arm. I soothe her while Meira runs a cool towel over her brow.

"We are actually going to have a baby," I whisper. It feels surreal because it's happening so fast.

I don't know how long we stay like that, but it feels like the entire day. Still, the rest of the crew hasn't arrived. I'm cramping up, and my arm is numb from how hard she grips me. As her contractions come quicker, she puffs for air.

"I think I need to push," she murmurs.

"It's not time yet." Lily checks Narah once more.

I go to move away from behind her, wanting to see all of this and welcome my baby into the world.

"Feels like a huge mountain is pressing down on my pelvis, worse than—" She stiffens against me, clasping her stomach and crying out, still grasping my arm. Today may be the day I finally lose an arm.

Meira has the towels and buckets of hot water nearby.

I lose track of how much has passed when Lily finally says, "Okay, Narah, start pushing."

"Did you hear that?" I say. "It's time, sweetheart. Let's push." My heart thunders as I wipe Narah's perspiring brow and her neck. She's been in pain for hours now, with still no sign of the rest of our pack from their hunt.

"I don't think I can do this," Narah screams. "It hurts too much and feels like I'm being ripped in two." Her huge watery eyes plead with me.

I lean in closer, my chest constricting hard. "Sweetheart, you can do this. Deep breaths like we've been doing, okay? I'll breathe with you… in and out."

"I can't." She's gripping my hand to death, and I might be screaming with her very soon.

"It's only a bit more. You've got this." She gasps, trying to breathe, and I feel her sag against me. "There, your contraction is slowing down, right?"

A second later, her whole face scrunches up, and she starts panting again.

"There's no stopping it now," Lily says from between Narah's legs. "The baby's already coming. I just need you to push for me." She pulls back, holding onto Narah's bent knee, joining us in the breathing techniques, as is Meira.

"Nothing is normal about this much pain!" Narah's crying and her eyes are wild. Her anger is slightly terrifying.

Lily doesn't seem fazed. "Okay, deep inhale, then let's push."

As I wipe Narah's forehead, she gives me a death stare… I did this to her. Well, I definitely had a part, regardless of who the actual father is.

After a long moment of pushing, then crying more, she collapses back on the bed, exhausted and gasping for air.

I turn to Lily as Meira speaks softly to Narah.

"Is this supposed to happen? She's so tired."

"Every pregnancy is different," she explains while focusing on Narah. She frowns, and there's heaviness when her shoulders slump forward.

"Okay, we try again," she instructs.

My sweet, gorgeous girl never gives up despite her pain.

After a long attempt, she collapses once more, tears drenching her cheeks. Grasping my arm, she draws me closer.

"Nikos, what if something's wrong because of how I got pregnant? What if—"

"Narah, don't think that way. We all felt the baby kick, and he or she is coming out."

She cries harder, and my chest is breaking in half. I feel lost, broken. My whole life, I've faced problems with a pragmatic approach —get in and fix the problem—but this is different. I'm dealing with our emotions, stress, and the horrible thought she might be right about this not being a normal birth. It lingers in the back of my mind that the baby won't survive. I scold myself for even thinking that shit, yet my throat thickens at the thought.

"Nothing bad is going to happen, but I need you to just push a bit more, sweetheart." I hold on to Narah, stroking her, kissing her, telling her it's going to be okay. "Please do it for me."

She sniffles, and I reach over to steal the tears drenching her cheeks.

Trying again, Narah grunts as she pushes hard, then a sudden explosive snap of power erupts from her fingertips as blue lines of magic flare from her hands.

Meira and the midwife rear back.

"It's okay," I explain. "Her body's under shock, so her magic will be impacted, too."

When the baby still doesn't show, the midwife starts to gently prod Narah's stomach.

"I feel the baby has turned, but something is blocking it from coming out."

Giving me a look, she points her chin to the door, then walks out.

My gut hardens at what she'll tell me.

"Narah, I'll be back in a second, I promise."

Her eyes are wide. "Nikos."

Meira is right at her side, talking to her, distracting her.

In the corridor, I shut the door and turn to Lily, my heart galloping in a marathon.

"What's going on? Why isn't the baby coming?" I ask rapidly.

"Sometimes, the baby gets stuck." She shakes her head, which doesn't fill me with confidence. "It could have the umbilical cord wrapped around it or something else. We need to hurry because, at this stage of labor, the child is in danger."

"Okay," I say with a shaky breath. "What are our options?"

"We cut the baby out, but there's a huge chance Narah may not survive, even with her fast wolf healing."

"That's not an option," I state instantly.

"If I push down on her stomach, it's a bigger risk to her and the baby's lives." She pauses. "The only other thing... My grandmother used to say feeding blood to a pregnant woman puts her body in a fighting state. It might help push the baby out quicker while her wolf tries to deal with the foreign blood in her system. That's why we feed after an attack. We're in a heightened state as our body reacts to foreign blood in our system."

I don't even know how to make sense of that, but at this point, I'll try anything.

"And this works?"

"I've never done it myself, but my grandmother swore she saved several women's lives this way. Otherwise, I don't know what else to do. I only know so much about childbirth."

"Well, then we'll try it. If it doesn't work, we'll cross that bridge when we get to it." A shiver crawls up my spine. I fucking hate this situation.

Nodding, her lips thin, Lily's face has lost a lot of color.

My breaths rush out raspy, and the weight of making such a decision buries me. Nothing can happen to Narah, but she will be beyond broken if we don't save the child. Dread rears through me, but I won't let Narah down. She's the one in pain, so I suck it up and march back inside with Lily.

Narah's huge, watery eyes meet mine. "What's going on?" She groans, clutching her belly. Meira remains by her side.

"Gorgeous girl, we think the baby might be stuck, but we have a solution."

"What is it?" Fresh tears fall down her face, but she's listening, a desperate hope flaring behind her eyes.

"You have to drink some blood. It might trick your body into thinking it's fighting an invader in your body, and it might release the baby easier. You can have mine."

She blinks at me, then looks at Lily. "That's going to work?"

"Of course," I say, sounding more confident than I feel. I'm a believer that sometimes our own mind blocks us. So, if Narah thinks the pregnancy is fake, she could be her own worst problem here.

"Alright, we do it then," she murmurs.

Meira watches me, confused, then hands me a blade from the table with the towels. Then she goes to speak with Lily as I hastily swipe it across my wrist. The bite of metal stings, but I'd take all of Narah's pain if I could.

"Drink as much as you can, okay?" I instruct her, lowering my bleeding wound to her mouth. Blood is nothing new to wolves. "Back home, we made a blood wine brew for celebrations. It was said it strengthened and awakened the warrior inside anyone who drank it."

"Wh-What happened when you drank it?"

"Well, my adrenaline pumped through me so much, I was bouncing off the walls." So, maybe the midwife is onto something about the blood.

Grabbing my arm with two hands, her mouth latches onto my wound. She takes the blood into her mouth, her tongue licking the wound, while her huge eyes stare up at me as she remains lying on the bed.

"That's it, beautiful." Offering her a smile, I maintain my gaze with her, needing her to know she's safe with me. "Take as much as you need. We'll make this work."

She just stares at me, making slurping sounds as blood seeps from the corners of her mouth. Suddenly, she flinches and shoves my arm from her mouth. Her eyes grow wide as her body twitches.

Panic folds around me, and I grab hold of her. "What's happening to her?" I bellow at the midwife.

She and Meira are on Narah's other side, holding her down by her arm and leg.

"Her body is adjusting to the blood," the midwife says shakily.

Narah cries out, and everything quickly goes to hell as she screams.

The midwife scurries to the end of the bed and takes her position between Narah's legs. Meira paces in a panicked state, and I hold Narah slightly upright as I tuck pillows behind her.

This has to work because there are no other options. Losing Narah or the baby is not even something I'll consider.

"The baby's coming," the midwife yells, which sends Meira to grab the towels.

I take every breath with Narah, but she's still in so much pain. I can see it on her face, and yet my beautiful girl never pauses. She fights so hard, already loving her baby unconditionally.

Moving on pure adrenaline, I can't even feel my body. Fear claws at my insides, and the room seems to spin from my blood loss. When I look down, I find more blood dripping onto my pants and the floor from my cut. Blood taints everything. Rapidly, I grab a towel and roughly wrap it around my arm. Meira's at my side, using a ribbon from her hair to tie the towel to my forearm.

She's as terrified and as pale as a ghost.

"Thank you." Twisting back around to Narah, her eyes seem to be glinting with a golden glow. It's her wolf... and something so much more.

Her power.

Blue threads of magic run across her fingers, and I'm worried about what it means for the baby.

"I see the head," Meira calls out, standing shoulder to shoulder with the midwife, bent forward and ready to receive a new life into our world.

"Narah, you're doing it," I say, my chest on fire. I want to yell and cry that it's working, but I don't dare move from her side.

She pushes, and I join her in breathing. The harder she works, the more her magic seems to go haywire, now taking loops above us. The lights overhead flicker, and the power leaves singeing marks on the ceiling.

A sense of urgency comes over me—her ability is building. I'm not the only one who keeps watching the magic. Meira does as well.

We keep going until Lily calls out, "The baby's out."

Wrapping the tiny bundle in a towel, she hands it to Meira, who quickly accepts and takes it to Narah. Lily returns to Narah, then glances at me with a furrowed brow.

"Narah's bleeding a lot."

My heart hurts, but then a snap of power spears outward, coming right for Meira, the midwife, and me.

Meira screams, but none of us have time to react.

Magic strikes my chest, a sharp, burning hot spear piercing me. I groan, clasping my chest as a shadow feathers across my vision. The last thing I see is Narah's panicked face as she reaches for me. My legs crumble out from under me, and I fall, darkness inhaling me.

SEVENTEEN

CRIUS

"Fuck, I need to get out more," I grunt, pushing the dead deer slumped on my shoulder higher. It smells of blood and meat, and I'm starving. Considering we rarely saw undead animals stalking the woods, it didn't mean they didn't exist. So, to be on the safe side, we decapitated it, which helped reduce the weight. These bastards weigh a fucking lot.

"Tell me about it." Stone is carrying his own catch. We're helping out the Ash Wolves and also paying for our stay. "I'd almost forgotten what it felt like to hunt for food rather than survival. And no, it's not the same thing."

I cut him a glare, but he's too busy staring ahead at the compound that rises in front of us as we emerge from the woods. He's tense, we all are, but this hunt is what I needed. I've been ready to climb walls from all the built-up energy, and the only way to sate that is a good hunt or fucking.

Dušan and Ragnar take the lead, getting along like a house on fire. This hunt was beneficial for our relations with the Ash Wolves. Ragnar excels at making connections. Me, I want to hunt and smash my fist through things, and when I'm not doing that, I crave to fuck. Narah and the last time I claimed her tight, pretty pussy come to mind. Arousal spun in my mind, and I knew what I'd be doing when I got back to the compound—track down my gorgeous girl and strip her, then take her until she screams and squeezes my cock.

With that thought, I pick up my steps, quickly catching up with the others. Stone is on my heels as I arrive at the main gates, where we're greeted by several pack members waiting with a wagon. I dump my catch into it. We've caught seven, which will easily feed a large pack for at least a few days.

With the afternoon sun beating down on my shoulders, I grin, more inspired than ever to create a home like this for Narah. With everyone walking up the dirt path toward the town center and castle, I can't help but move faster, eager to wash up and collect Narah into my arms. Footfalls crunch behind me, and Stone is suddenly at my side, moving just as fast.

"You're in a rush," he comments, the corner of his eye lifting. "Going anywhere specific?"

"Fuck off, Stone. I'm going to see Narah first."

"Not like that, you're not. You're covered in blood."

I want to punch him in the face but look down, and he's right. Crimson is splattered all over me. A quick wash is all I need.

"You can't talk," I say.

Stone has dried blood plastered to the side of his face from his battle with a boar he tried to catch, but he got his butt kicked.

He runs a hand down his face, then lunges into a sprint toward the castle.

"Asshole." I charge after him, closing the distance fast. Nudging his shoulder as he reaches the doorway, I shove him out of the way and sprint inside, laughing maniacally. I dash for Narah's room, hoping she's there, even in my state. Just to be the first to see her and steal a kiss. Bursting into her room, I rush into her bedroom, only to find it empty. My pulse spikes as disappointment comes over me. As I swing back around, Stone skids into the room and crashes into the door frame.

"Where is she?" he gasps as his gaze sweeps across the room.

"Maybe with her sisters?" If that's the case, I definitely have to wash up first so I don't scare the girls by being covered in blood. Plus, I stink.

"I just found out that they've gone into the woods to pick fruits with a group from the pack," Stone explains.

I sigh.

As if on cue, Stone retreats from the room, speeding toward the bathroom, and charges inside. I do one better and rush into our shared room, snatch fresh clothes, and dart out after him into the adjoining bathroom.

Bursting inside like a lunatic, the place is busy, and everyone's staring at me, bewildered. There are three females in the tub, completely naked, and I fight the urge to lower my gaze to see their tits. I'm a fuck who has no control, and it's instinct to stare at females, but they don't come close to Narah. Pushing past the large spa, I nod at the three Alphas I pass, well aware of what's about to happen in that bath. Fucking lucky bastards.

That's going to be me soon. I reach the door that leads me to the shower cubicles. I find Stone by following the trail of blood pooling around the drain in his shower. There are no doors, but we're alone. Setting my clothes on a dry bench, I dive into the first cubicle and switch on the water. I groan at the combination of how incredible it feels to have running hot water and the sting on my arms and back from where I gained wounds in the hunt. I take the world's fastest shower. Stone and I switch off our waters simultaneously, then towel off.

"You know, she'll only be able to take one of us in her state, so be prepared to sit back and watch," Stone promises.

Laughing, I throw myself across the tiled floor on bare feet and drag on the clothes. The pants stick to my legs, which aren't completely dry. Hopping about on one leg, I watch Stone button his jeans, and adrenaline pumps in my chest. No way is he going to win. I yank the jeans up, grab my tee and run out with him at my side. The mad rush is met more by stares, which is only compounded when we get jammed in the doorway to leave the bathroom, locked shoulder to shoulder.

"Stone," I growl, and those in the spa laugh. I elbow him to push myself forward and sprint. Realizing I don't know where Narah is, I rush to her sisters' room just in case they have returned early, only to find it empty. Stone's there in seconds, bulldozing right into me and sending me careening sideways into the wall.

"Fuck, man," I bellow.

"You wanna play? I'll show you who'll win." His lips thin, and he hunches his shoulders. The guy's not joking.

Good. I love a challenge. I narrow my gaze at him.

"Fine, I'll tear apart this whole fucking castle to find Narah first, and if I win, you'll leave us the fuck alone."

"Deal. And if I get to her first, she's mine."

Clenching my teeth, we fist pump, something he's been doing lately after seeing another pack use it as a greeting. I think it's dorky but don't give a fuck, so I entertain him.

Then he's gone, and my bare feet pound the stone floors as I searched every room for Narah, taking every corridor, then the steps up to the balcony, figuring I might see her outside. The sun's descending, but that doesn't mean she's indoors. Upstairs, I sprint down the barren hallway, eyeing the balcony in the distance, when a familiar smell catches my attention.

I skid to a halt, inhaling the air deeply.

Blood dances on the air, and with it, Narah's sweet nectar smell. My chest rises and falls rapidly. Is Narah in trouble? Goddess, the baby!

Following the faint scent, I dart along the hallway, turning down a corridor, then another. I come to a stop in front of the door where the strangest smells suffocate me. I don't pause to knock, pushing the door open, and I freeze.

My gaze clashes with Narah's watery eyes.

She's in bed, blood staining the bedsheets, her mouth, and dress, clutching something tiny to her chest. It's wrapped in a towel and making gurgling sounds. Shock pierces me. She had the baby! I can't move because I don't know where to look—at my gorgeous girl with our baby or the three bodies strewn on the floor, unmoving.

Nikos, Meira, and an older woman I don't recognize.

My heart squeezes, and terror shreds me at the devastation. Did she drain the three of them for the baby?

"Crius," Narah calls for me desperately, ripping me from my

thoughts. Before I can respond, a flurry of wind hits my back when others join us.

"What the fuck!" Ragnar's voice cuts across the room.

Narah

"I didn't mean to hurt them," I whisper, tears flooding my cheeks.

Ragnar growls as Stone and Crius hurry to the bodies on the floor around the bed. Dušan pours into the room, along with two other Alphas, all three rushing to Meira's side.

I haven't moved, can't move. My jellybean is in my arms in a towel, and her eyes are wide open, blue like the brightest sapphires. I had a girl, and I'm happy she survived, but I'm completely destroyed, shaking uncontrollably at the heavy expense.

"I'm sorry," I murmur and hold her closer, feeling as if my world is about to fall apart. "Ragnar, I didn't mean to. It just happened. My magic struck them, and I think it drained them, so I could give birth because the baby was stuck." My words race as my heart booms loudly in my ears. My gaze dips to Nikos—the man I absolutely adore might be dead. "What have I done?"

On his feet, Dušan shoves a fist into Ragnar's chest, catching him off guard, and slams him up against the wall.

I flinch as the two huge Alphas' growls flood the room.

"We had a fucking deal, and you broke it," Dušan booms, his voice explosive. "Meira's not waking up." He jerks his attention my way, his eyes changing like a raging storm, heartbreak twisting his face. "What did you do to her?" his voice cracks with emotion.

I hitch a breath, trying to find my voice. "I don't mean to hurt anyone," I finally answer.

Crius and Stone jump to Ragnar's side, hands fisted, and their fury thickens the air. The other Alphas are there, and a war is about to break out.

"They're still alive," Stone barks. "They're not dead, so everyone needs to back the fuck down."

I squeak out a cry, sobbing. I should have checked, but after they passed out just as I gave birth to my angel, I've been hyperventilating, weak, and exhausted. I assumed the worst when they didn't wake up.

"That's not the fucking point," Dušan snaps. "You promised, Ragnar, if anyone in my pack was hurt, there would be repercussions."

Swallowing hard, I glance down at my fingers. There are no black marks, but I know what I accidentally did, and it still terrifies me that I used my magic on them.

"I would never hurt anyone," I say, desperate to ease the tension about to explode. When I attempt to move, I wince. Everything hurts, and the bed is stained with blood from both Nikos and from me. "Meira tried to help me."

"And look where that got her," he barks, then swings back at Ragnar. They stand toe-to-toe, sticking out their huge chests. "If my Meira doesn't wake up by midnight, you will be sorry you ever set foot on my land." Dušan picks Meira up off the floor, one of the other men collects Lily, and they leave the room.

The moment Crius shuts the door behind them, I turn my attention to my men while Stone and Ragnar lift Nikos from the floor and lay him across the bed lengthwise, his feet alongside me. He's barely breathing, but I can see the shallow rise and fall of his chest. Relief flare that I hadn't killed the man I love.

Ragnar's at my side, wiping my cheeks, then looks down. "So, who do we have here?" he coos as he runs the pad of his index finger gently across her cheek.

Crius and Stone crowd around me as well, each of them eager to see her, kissing me all over.

"Sweetheart, you had our baby," Crius coos.

"You have no idea how much this means to me." Stone holds back tears as he hugs me from the side. "You have no idea how much this means to me. I'm a father. All four of us are. I wanted to be here so much. I'm sorry we weren't."

"In hindsight, it's better you weren't here." I laugh almost hysterically. "Poor Nikos went through a lot and never stopped being supportive. He was perfect, then I zapped him." Sighing, I look at our baby. Staring at that beautiful, innocent face takes away all the pain from the world.

"What did you call her?" Stone asks.

I raise my gaze to meet his, and the three men are watching me. I'm beaming that she survived, but a name hasn't crossed my mind.

"I'm not sure yet." Lowering my gaze to her once more, I murmur, "Every time I look down at her, she calms me. A sense of harmony settles over my mind, and I find myself humming to her. I'd be lost if I didn't have her after everything that happened."

"Harmony," Ragnar murmurs. "That's a beautiful name for her."

"It suits her so perfectly." Crius nods, and Stone looks ready to burst out crying. "She has your cute little nose and lips."

On cue, she lets out what I swear is an approving sound. I might be overreading it, but I don't care. "I think she just agreed, and I adore that name. Now, we need Nikos to wake up so I can stop feeling like the worst person in the world, and we can celebrate our baby."

"He'll be fine," Crius states, looking at him passed out on the bed.

"I screwed up." I sweep my gaze to each of my men. "What if they don't wake up? What if I took too much power? I mean, I had no control over the magic, which makes me dangerous."

"You did nothing wrong," Ragnar tells me, tenderly running his hand over my cheek.

"But Dušan was so angry. What if he kicks us out? And what deal was he talking about?"

Ragnar's brows pull together, his lips thinning. "It was just something he made me agree to so he could ensure the safety of his own pack and family."

I blink at him, waiting, but when he doesn't elaborate, I ask, "What was the deal?"

"Look, you have enough to worry about right now."

"Ragnar." Frustrated, I raise my voice. "I have a right to know." Especially since I might have just blown our chance with the one pack I feel a kinship with, other than mine with Ragnar and the others.

Silence beats between us, then he sighs and gives me the look when he's forced into a corner. "If anyone in his pack is harmed at our hands, he has a right to punish them accordingly."

I gasp. "He's going to hurt me?"

"Like fuck he is," Stone blurts.

"Not happening." Crius stands tall, adamant, and sure of himself that he'll stop the Ash Wolves' Alpha.

"Narah, this is my burden to bear, and if there is any punishment,

I will be the one who bears it. But Dušan is a fair man, and when Meira wakes up, I'm certain he'll see reason."

"I really hope they wake up. I don't want to be responsible for destroying so many lives, including my own, if anything happens to Nikos."

"It's going to be alright." He leans in closer and wraps an arm around my back, his lips on my brow. "You'll see."

I wish I had his confidence. Trembling, I keep glancing at Nikos, willing him to wake up. I touch his legs, giving a light squeeze to wake him.

Ragnar unexpectedly drags his blood-stained shirt up and over his head, leaving him bare-chested and absolutely mesmerizing. Muscles everywhere, he is exquisite. I am completely distracted by this Adonis, who has me swooning, even after just giving birth.

"May I hold her?"

"Of course. Just make sure you support her head."

He tenderly pulls Harmony into his huge arms, tucking her into the curve of his bent arm and pressing her against his chest. She stares up at him as though she knows who he is.

"They say you can see someone's soul in their eyes. Harmony has an old soul. It's why she's so calm. She's ready to join our world, eager for it. I'm going to show her everything. She'll become a warrior... anything she wants." Ragnar smiles at Harmony and makes baby sounds.

I'd managed to cut her umbilical cord, then wrapped her up tightly in a towel. She's still covered in the mess from birth, but Ragnar and the other two pressing in on either side of him don't seem to notice.

"I'm convinced she has my mouth," Crius says. "But as long as she looks mostly like you, she's going to be beautiful. And any guy who even thinks about looking at her will have to deal with us four first."

"No guy will be good enough," Stone states.

I smile to myself, hearing and seeing the affection they hold for our baby. She is going to be the most protected girl in the world.

Lying on a mountain of pillows, my body is still sore, but it's easing, and I give thanks for my fast healing. Though I'm not ready to move, it's a mess between my legs, and I'll need assistance to clean up, but I'd prefer it wasn't my men. I still want to be beautiful in their eyes.

They'll disagree, and I grin to myself at the thought, but I'd feel extremely self-conscious. Instead, I focus on Nikos, whose nostrils are flaring with each deep breath. Slowly, his eyelids peel open, and my pulse accelerates.

"Nikos," I call out, and the others turn to him.

He groans like a bear, scrunches up his face, then pats his chest. "It feels like I'd been run over by a stampede of elephants."

Crius is by his side and yanks on his arm to drag him to a sitting position. "You gave everyone a scare when you passed out like a damsel in distress." Crius grins and gets a grunted laugh from Nikos.

"Right. And shut the hell up." Sluggishly turning toward me, he groans, then his eyes fly open as his mind plays catch up. "Narah." He throws himself at me, his arms coiling around me, and I wince at his weight.

"Stop squishing her to death, you big lug," Stone barks.

"The baby," Nikos almost squeals and frantically looks around until he sees Ragnar walking her over to us.

"Say hello to our baby girl Harmony," I say.

Gasping a strangled sound, Nikos takes her into his arms, and I notice the glint in his eyes.

"Little Harmony, if you knew what we went through for you, you'll never misbehave your entire life."

Crius barks out a laugh. "I'm pretty sure Narah went through most of it."

Nikos raises a death glare at Crius that could scare away the dead. "You have no idea what we both went through."

Stone's eyes open exaggeratingly, but Ragnar hasn't taken his attention from Harmony.

"Don't worry, Nikos," I say. "I know how hard that was for both of us."

He's looking down at Harmony, humming a tune to her, and my heart swells at the sight of these powerful Vikings completely at the mercy of a tiny baby.

The door suddenly bursts open, and a red-faced Jae and gasping Kaira stand in the doorway.

"Oh. My. Goddess. You had the baby," Jae squeals and rushes over to Nikos while Kaira moves to my side and hugs me.

"Are you okay, Sis? We just got back from the woods, and when the guards told us you had the baby, we came running. No one came to tell us."

"It's okay now, but it was an ordeal. I don't want to experience that again for a while, but you have a little niece now. Her name's Harmony."

Kaira's smile stretches all the way to her eyes as she scrambles around the bed to reach the others. As they all stand around Nikos and Harmony, I feel the heaviness of exhaustion coming over me. As my eyelids slide down, someone else enters the room.

I spring them open to see Meira looking around. She cries when sees the baby, then moves closer to see Harmony. Next thing I know, she's coming to me, just as her three Alphas enter the room, looking slightly sheepish.

"Oh, Narah, you were so brave, and you've got a baby girl." Meira gently hugs me.

"I'm sorry I zapped you with my magic. I didn't even—" I murmur.

"No, don't you dare apologize. I don't know what happened, but I woke up feeling fine. Tired, but I'm healthy, and more importantly, you and the baby survived. Seriously, for a while there, I was terrified we'd lose you both. Then I'd have to somehow tell Ragnar that I let you die, and I was scared. Don't ever do that to me again."

The care in her voice touches me deeply.

Dušan asks Ragnar to talk to him in private in the hallway. Once they're gone, I turn to Meira.

"Maybe I should speak to Dušan and explain I never wanted to hurt you. I'm so sorry."

"Hush. When Dušan told me about the deal he made with Ragnar and that he threatened you all after what you went through, you could say I got really mad at him." She glances over her shoulder at the closed door. "I can't blame him, though. He's my life, and he cherishes me, but he wasn't here to see what happened. So, he's out there telling Ragnar that the deal is off, and you're welcome in our home for as long as you want."

Tears prick my eyes. "I'm going to cry again."

"We Omegas have to look out for one another." She hugs me again.

"That means so much. Until I met my Alphas, it was just me and my two sisters in a world ruled by men. I need more Omegas in my life."

"You got it."

I wince from the sudden ache I feel, and she draws back.

"Oh, Narah, how heartless of me. We have to get you all cleaned up. When I last saw you, there was a lot of blood."

"I actually think I'm okay, but I am a mess and could use some help. I'll explain it all to you, but basically, my magic heals me.

"Alright, you got it." She stands and walks out of the room, leaving me confused. Is she coming back?

Jae and Kaira move to my side, both of them hugging me.

"Harmony looks like you." Kaira hops up to sit on the bed next to me.

"She definitely has my nose," Jae says, just as Nikos returns with a grumbling Harmony.

I take her in my arms, and everyone around the bed is just watching me.

"Just so everyone knows, I adore every single person in this room. Our family just got bigger."

Where the air moments earlier felt tense, now it's calm and has me giddy. I've always wanted a big family that stayed together, and I guess that was happening.

Holding Harmony is pure bliss. She keeps staring at me with those deep-felt eyes. We've all gone through so much. I crave peace and want to just lose myself in my family.

Meira hurries back into the room with two other women, including Lily, who looks a bit shaken up. I can't blame her, and no matter what Meira says, the guilt of what my magic did stirs in my stomach. I don't want to be anything like my mother, drawing on anyone's energy and making them pass out or worse.

"Alright, everyone but Narah and Harmony needs to leave the room. The new mother needs some help to clean up and other things." Meira waves for everyone to go, despite Jae groaning loudly.

My men kiss me.

"I'll be right outside waiting to make sure everything is okay," Nikos assures. The love and sincerity in his voice smother me with so much love, my chest shudders. I've never experienced such an abundance of love.

"Love you," I say with a grin. "I couldn't have gone through this without you."

He rushes back to my side, stealing another kiss and whispering, "You and Harmony are my world." When Meira ushers him out as well, he blows me a kiss and strolls out of the room.

For the first time, I feel as if nothing can ever hurt me again.

EIGHTEEN

RAGNAR

A howl echoes in the air from the woods. I'm on the balcony, staring out across the land, the sunlight beaming brightly, while down below, the Ash Wolves are going about their everyday business.

It's been two months since Narah gave birth to Harmony, and we've all stayed with Dušan's pack as his guests. He and I have bonded and come up with several strategies to ensure that between us, we hold complete control over the entire country of Romania. What we need are more Alphas in this world, like Dušan. So, having him in my corner is a huge advantage and outweighs all the fucking roaches of pack Alphas up north.

Like everything good, our time in the compound has come to an end. At least for my men and me. It's time to claim our land up north. I still have some men inserted in a handful of packs up north, unbeknown to those packs. They'll steer the pack in our favor from the inside. I met up with them on my visit to those packs with Mihai, and they are expecting me to make a move.

That time has arrived. For weeks, it's irritated me to wait so long, but I wouldn't have given up the time we've spent with Narah and Harmony.

Oh, my sweet little angel has my heart, and for her, I will fight to the ends of the earth to watch her grow up. She will need some siblings, at least three or four, but I'll have to convince Narah. She's still somewhat recovering from the birth, but time dulls painful memories, and the next time, she'll have all of us by her side every second of the way.

So, for her, for my children, for our future, I have no choice but to claim our land, so we can begin our new lives.

"I was wondering where you'd gotten to," Narah says from behind me.

Turning to my adorable Omega, she's wearing a flowing white dress that seems to glow in the sunlight. It flutters loosely around her legs and gathers in at her waist with a red ribbon. Her sandals tap the stone balcony floor as she approaches with a beautiful smile, her chestnut hair fluttering over her shoulders. She's an image to behold, a maiden who may have just descended from Valhalla with such radiance.

"Morning, little fox." I collect her into my arms, and our lips graze, which is all I intended, but she tastes too sweet not to claim her. Our gentle kisses morph into passion, our tongues tangling. My hands on her lower back press her to me, crushing her breasts between us, and my cock hardens.

"I miss you," I whisper against her lips. "How much longer before I can slide between your thighs?"

She's breathless, and her lips are already darker and fuller from how hard I'd kissed her. "The midwife said two or three months would be best, but there's no pain, and I think I'm ready. I'm so horny and miss your cock."

My cock punches hard at her sweet words, at the tiny moan when she says cock.

"Let's go back to our room," she whispers, lifting onto her toes. Her body, so soft, so delicious against me, is an addiction I can't say no to.

No man can resist her, and I'm sure as fuck not strong enough to say no to such an offer.

Sliding my hand into hers, I turn her around to hurry to my room before I strip her this very second, but one of the Ash Wolves' stablemen appears in my path. On the younger side, he's nervously pushing his hair behind his ears and not holding my eyes. A sniff of the breeze, and I find he's a Beta—they tend to be more nervous and reluctant to face an Alpha.

"Is there a problem, boy?" I ask.

"I've been sent to tell you that your horses are prepped and will be ready at the crack of dawn at the main front gates." With a quick bow, he retreats and vanishes into the shadows inside the fortress.

"What's he talking about?" Narah asks. "Are you going somewhere?"

I swallow hard. I'd hoped to have this conversation a bit later to avoid her being mad at me the entire day. Guess the cat's out of the bag now. Fucking Beta. With a long exhale, I draw Narah to face me.

"Tomorrow, we're heading back to the Savage Sector and finishing this bullshit with Martell. I already have some of my men in place up north. I just need to find that asshole. Once I kill him, I'll take ownership of everything."

She blinks at me, her lips pinching to one side, and I can see the wheels spinning behind her gorgeous amber eyes.

"You make it sound so easy, but I'm ready to do whatever it takes. It's not like we can live here forever."

She's nervous, so maybe what I tell her next will be easier than I expect.

"My Narah." I slide a hand over her warm cheek, and she leans into my touch. "You're not coming with us. I need you to stay here safe. Harmony is depending on you, and I can't risk your life."

She stiffens, and her soft eyes ignite into an inferno. Okay, maybe I was wrong about her taking this in stride.

"What do you mean?" she says, pushing my hand away. "Of course, I'm coming. Remember, I carry magic that can help you, and if I've learned anything from this world, it's that nothing goes according to plan. So, you'll need me."

"I have Stone and his magic, and we have made arrangements for additional backup. This is going to get savage and could result in hand-to-hand combat. I can't be distracted worrying about you."

Her shoulders rear back.

Fuck, I said the wrong thing.

"Narah, that's not how I meant to say it. Fuck. You mean the world to me." I reach for her, but she retreats, anger and pain in her gaze. My chest constricts with a wave of awareness that she'll be pissed with me until I return and make it up to her. This isn't how I wanted to spend my last day with her.

"Yes, that's exactly what you meant. I'm a weakness to you, an inconvenience."

"No, that's not right," I growl and grab her arm, this time with purpose. "You are the most powerful person in my life who can face any danger and overcome it, whose power leaves even me slightly scared. But damn it, Narah, I love you too much to risk you getting hurt when you have Harmony to look after... should something happen to us."

All the color drains from her face. "Even more reason I should join you, so we can protect each other."

"And how well can you control your magic?" I say, a bit too harshly. This conversation is getting out of hand when the last thing I want is to argue. I just wish she'd understand I'm not doing this to ostracize her.

"I've been practicing," she snaps. "You can't stop me from coming." Her adamant tone has me grinding my jaw.

"You'd leave Harmony so easily?"

She pauses, and I see the tears in her eyes. My heart breaks, but when I reach for her, she turns and runs back inside. My insides shatter like glass, and I feel like a piece of shit. Narah's stubborn as hell, but on this decision, I won't bend. I won't relent when there's too much at risk.

No matter how much I try to convince myself, the ache in my chest deepens.

I'll give her time, but she has to see reason, even if it kills me to live in this state.

I'll have the rest of my life to make it up to her.

Narah

Fury pummels into me, and my breath turns shallow. Marching the corridors of the fortress, I absently return a few smiles to pack members I pass. My sisters are watching Harmony as she sleeps.

Ragnar has no right to stop me, no fucking right. There's so much vengeance I want to deliver to Martell, but that's not why I need to do this. It's because I've fallen in love with four Viking Alphas and can't bear to lose them.

Not after I already lost so much.

Death seems to follow me, and I'm scared to hell that one of them will end up killed, and I'd have to live with the guilt that I did nothing. I felt a sliver of that heartache when I thought I drained Nikos to death, and it came close to completely destroying me. That small taste was enough to scare me for life.

At the door, I pause and try to pull myself together. A few deep inhales, and I tug my lips into a semi-smile, the most I can manage right now.

Inside, Jae and Kaira are sitting cross-legged on the bed, facing each other and playing cards. They aren't quiet, which is okay since I want to teach Harmony to sleep soundly with noises around her.

"How'd it go?" Jae asks with her back to me, then turns to me and freezes. "What's wrong?"

"Everything is great." I attempt to blow it off with a tight grin and a shake of my head. "How's Harmony?" I go to stare at her in her crib. She's on her back, tucked in her blanket, looking like the world's cutest caterpillar who will one day break out and become the world's most beautiful butterfly.

"Narah," Kaira says with the stern voice she's been using of late to correct us.

When I turn, Jae's by her side, and they're staring at me with serious expressions.

"You're doing that strange face where you pretend to smile but look more like you're constipated," Jae says.

I roll my eyes. "When have I looked constipated for you to recognize that face? Don't answer that."

They just stand there, ready to pry the information out of me by any means, and I wouldn't put anything past them. Besides, there's no harm in sharing my anger with someone. I'll go insane if I keep it inside.

"Okay, fine. I had an argument with Ragnar."

Grabbing my arms, they drag me across the room to the bed. I sit on one end, and they sit across from me, slouching against the pillows, shoulder to shoulder, as if like this is going to be something juicy.

"So, what happened?" Kaira asks.

With a deep inhale, I let it loose. "Tomorrow, all four of my men are heading back to the Savage Sector, and they won't let me go with them."

They blink, waiting for the punchline.

"What's the problem, then? They want you to stay with Harmony and us," Jae insists. "It makes sense." My sisters turn toward me, wearing quizzical expressions.

"That's the hard part. I can't bear to leave her side and would feel like the world's most horrible mother. But I'll cry with worry every day when the four of them are away. They are going to hunt Martell, and I'm worried they'll get hurt when I could have helped them." Realizing I'm ranting, I sigh and pause.

They crawl across the bed to hug me.

"Whatever you decide, we'll support you," Kaira murmurs, snuggling up against my side.

"I have an idea." Jae latches onto my arm. "Kaira and I can look after Harmony, along with Deborah, since she's breastfeeding Harmony."

I frown at her. I've tried so hard but can't produce enough milk to feed Harmony. Luckily, another woman who's just had a child has agreed to feed my baby girl.

My sisters are still young, and I made myself a promise to give them the chance to enjoy life and not grow up too quickly.

"What?" Jae says. "I have it all worked out. Deborah has a baby, and when she's not feeding, she needs someone to look after her little one during the day. We'll move in with her... oh, and I have a name for our business."

Kaira's laughing. "Go on, let's hear it."

"The Cub Club." She nods with a huge smile. "It's amazing, right?"

"It's actually really clever," I reply. "I love it, but I'm not sure what to do."

"So, with this Cub Club, do we get paid?" Kaira asks.

Jae frowns. "Well, if Deborah is helping us out with Harmony, we can't charge her anything."

"Yes, but this pack is huge, and I've seen other babies and small kids. I'm sure the parents would love an hour or two of peace."

"Hmm." Jae taps her chin with her index finger.

I love how well they work together.

"I'm sure you'll work it out, but it sounds like a good venture. Maybe you should run it past Meira first?"

Jae's eyes light up, and in seconds, they scramble off the bed, put their shoes on, and dart out of the room.

"We'll be back soon," Kaira calls out as the door shuts behind them.

The door closes with a heavy thud, waking Harmony. Crying, she grizzles as I hurry over to her and lift her into my arms.

"Hello, my gorgeous girl. How did you sleep?" I kiss her face, loving the way she smells. Cradling her against me, she quiets down. I move to take a seat on the lounge and run a gentle finger over her face, which she loves. She stares up at me, making me teary to think she is mine.

When I think about my argument with Ragnar, my insides twist, and my stomach hurts because I don't know what I should do.

"I love you." I kiss Harmony again. "If you could speak, I know what you'd tell me to do." With a heavy breath, I push the thoughts aside, hating the straining ache in my chest each time I think about what comes next.

NINETEEN

STONE

We left at the crack of dawn while everyone still slept. With Crius and Nikos, Ragnar and I popped in to say farewell to Narah and Harmony with a kiss, even if they were both sleeping. I'm going to miss them incredibly, but we're doing this for them, for our baby's future.

Since we jumped on horseback at the compound, Ragnar's silence stretches out for most of the trip. He's pissed. Jae told me last night he'd had an argument with Narah because she insisted on coming along, and he denied her.

I understand both sides, but sometimes, a hard decision has to be made for the benefit of the innocent—Harmony. It would be incredible to have a sorceress on our side. I'm under no illusion that we aren't outnumbered, although with half a dozen of Ragnar's men stationed up north and infiltrated into other packs, I feel better that we have eyes on the inside.

We're not going there to declare a world war but to eliminate the bastard Martell before he gets the upper hand. Warfare is so much more than the clash of two powerful armies. Most of the time, the biggest battles are held in the shadows and behind the scenes.

"We're coming up on the tavern," Nikos announces, his attention on Ragnar. Crius flanks the rear of our travels.

My ass is sore as fuck, and I'm starving. We've been riding for most of the day with short stops for the horses. I need a break as night nears.

We've only encountered one group of undead and a scattering of rogue wolves. I expected more, considering what we faced on our way to the Shadowlands Sector.

"We'll stop but leave before dawn," Ragnar answers.

There's tension in his voice, but I can't tell if it's a result of his argument with Narah or being away from the Savage Sector for the past two months. A lot can change in that length of time, and for all we know, we could have completely missed our opportunity to take it over and would have to start from scratch.

We fall silent as the horses' hooves pound the earth with our speed.

When Ragnar comes to an abrupt halt, we all stop. My pulse kick starts into high gear, and I glance around.

"Someone's following us," he mutters quietly, pointing to the woods on his right.

Off my horse in a split second, I dart into the woods on whisper-quiet feet. Nikos slips into the forest farther ahead. The wind's not in our favor, so whoever's here will sniff us out before we smell them.

That just means we need to be faster and not fuck this up.

Darting forward, keeping to the shadows, I'm alert for any sound, any movement. Nikos is silent as fuck—the guy might as well be a ghost as he stealthily moves through the woods.

Surprisingly, I came upon a dirty track. It's narrow and most likely used by animals, but I spot indentations in the ground—horse hooves. The tracks are sharp and well-defined at the edges, and when I touch them, the soil is soft and crumbles away. If they'd been here a few hours or more, they'd likely be hard. These are fresh, and whoever is near is also riding a horse. That eliminates the undead and most likely, the rogues, though I have seen the wild bastards steal horses to ride them across long stretches of land.

Up on my feet, I rush back the way I came to relay my find to Ragnar and Crius. Nikos returns seconds later with similar information.

"Could be a traveler passing by," I suggest.

"I'm not willing to take the chance. We don't know what Martell has changed, what guards he's set up as perimeter around the Savage Sector."

"Fine, then we take the same path," Crius states the obvious. He's off his horse.

Quickly, we walk our horses through the shrub onto the second path. Taking the lead, I hop onto my stead, and we're off, bolting down the track. Cold air rushes through my hair and over my face. I don't know how long we've been traveling, but night has claimed the land, and still no sign of how we pursued it.

When the track opens up to a field that presents the tavern, I slow to a trot before finally climbing off the horse. The place is an over-sized, three-story building made of stone with a wooden veranda out front. Windows pepper all the levels, most of them lit up. The two chimneys on the pointed roof pump out smoke, working overtime, and with it, the delicious aroma of roast comes at me like a sledge-hammer, making me salivate.

"Whoever they are, I'd say they're staying here for the night."

"Go with Nikos and get the horses in the stables for rest and feed," Ragnar growls as he dismounts and hands the reins to Crius. "Then do a check around the place for anything out of the ordinary, anyone who might be working for Martell, guards."

"Got it," Crius grumbles as Nikos takes my horse. The two vanish around the back of the tavern, where travelers leave their horses to rest overnight.

Alongside Ragnar, we march toward the front door. "Are you alright, considering everything with Narah?"

"I feel like shit," Ragnar groans. "I wanted her support, not to make me feel like a shithead. I would love to have her with us, but I don't know what we're facing, and I fucking hate going into anything blind." With a growl, he climbs the front three steps to the wooden veranda of the establishment.

I shouldn't be surprised how much Narah has gotten under his skin, but it's unlike him to let his emotions get to him. He's the cold, calculating one of our team who never lets things get to him. He's the king of suppressing that shit so deep, one day, he'll go crazy from holding it all in. So, it's a refreshing change.

Not that I can talk. I've become a fucking emotional wreck since Harmony entered our lives, constantly concerned when she cries. I swear she sounds like she's in pain, but Narah insists it's normal and that her cries mean she wants different things.

It didn't stop me from waking up to her cries in the middle of the night and holding her in my arms until the early hours of the morning. I never thought being a dad would suit me. I didn't have the best father figure growing up, but that's something I won't let Harmony ever experience.

Inside the tavern are jovial voices, music from a man with a flute, and beer flowing. My stomach rumbles when we walk past a table where a heavy man is tearing into a whole roasted chicken.

I'm drooling at this stage, but with every table taken, we'll be lucky to have an available room for the night. At this stage, I'll be grateful for food and gladly sleep in the stable if it comes down to it.

We cross the large room, pausing at the bar. The white-peppered hair man behind the counter lifts his chin in our direction.

"What will you have?"

"A room for the night," Ragnar answers.

"You're out of luck, my friend. I just gave my last room to a young chap. He's waiting for his four companions to join him, so if they don't turn up, there might be a chance to share the space. There are two large beds in the room, and with so many here tonight, room sharing is common."

Ragnar stares at the man as if he wants to reach over the bar and deck him.

"This chap, did he mention the names of his companions?"

"He mentioned something quickly, but it was difficult to hear properly in this place. Rooster something."

I blink at the man, who's distracted by someone at the bar waving him down.

"Do you mean Ragnar?" I shout to be heard over the raucous crowd behind us, but he doesn't hear me, so I twist my head toward Ragnar. "A trap from Martell?"

"Whoever it is, we're going to find out, then beat the shit out of them, if that's the case."

I turn back to the bartender, who's handing beer to a man two seats down. "Room," I call out to him. "What room is the chap in?"

He glances over. "Twenty-two. Top floor." Then he's gone back to serving his customers.

"Thanks," I mutter.

We leave the tavern behind and march upstairs, ready to deal with whatever the fuck is going on now.

Ragnar

I'm in a shitty mood. The entire trip, Narah's been on my mind—every word exchanged, every regret of how I could have handled the situation better, how her stubbornness drove me crazy.

The cold chill of the dark corridors clings to me as I climb to the second floor with Stone at my back until we reach the door with twenty-two painted in white on the wood.

I strike my knuckles on the door, and a raspy voice answers.

"Open."

Narrowing my gaze, every inch of me tenses, ready for fuck knows what. I don't hesitate to push the door open but stay in the doorway. When I see what I'm dealing with, my stomach drops, and I can't find my words.

"What the fuck!"

"Well, nice to see you, too," Narah says, her chin high. Wearing a black hooded cloak, she peels a fake beard off her jaw.

I don't have to step into the room to smell the stench of mud. I see it on her coat and boots, well aware she'd done it on purpose to mask her Omega scent.

"Why am I not surprised?" I walk into the room, Stone at my back.

"Though it is a pleasant surprise."

"See, at least someone is happy to see me."

I cut Stone a glare, which gains me a shrug. Of course, he'd take her side.

"What about Harmony?"

She pauses for a moment, and a flash of pain clearly shows on her face. "My sisters are looking after her," she says with a croaky voice.

Narah shoulders off her coat and kicks off her boots, and pushes a smile on her face. "They've started a cub club."

"Wait! A what club? What does that have to do with Harmony?"

"Jae and Kaira are moving in with one of the new mothers in the pack, who will help them look after Harmony. Meira is setting up a mother's meeting once a day for them to get together and help each other out, with my sisters taking an active role in caring for the little ones." She pushes her hair off her face. "I'm going to miss Harmony, and this was a hard decision, but I made what I felt was the right one. Harmony has a team of loving people looking after her, while Martell's army outmatches you. Growing up, my little girl will need her four fathers. So, I'm doing my part." Finally, she takes a breath.

"What happens if things go bad for us? Would it be better for Harmony to have one parent as opposed to none?"

"Calm the hell down, Ragnar." Frowning, her shoulders curl forward. "Stop using fear to push your point. I get it, but I don't agree. I'm here because of Harmony. If we don't fight now to ensure the world is safe, what future will she have? And I'm trying really hard. I want to give her the best and yet I feel like I already failed her because I can't breastfeed her. So don't you dare take this from me." Her fury and pain twisted in my chest because stupid me never once thought how much more painful this journey has been for her Narah and her challenge to breastfeed Harmony.

My shoulders curl forward with the ache that I'd caused her, so I give her space. She's a strong woman who I absolutely adore, and I can admit when I've overstepped. "You're right, and I'm sorry."

She shrugs and pushes a smile on her face. "Besides, I'm exhausted from a long trip and don't need your cranky ass right now. All I ask is for your love."

After a long pause where I see her struggling to rein in her emotions, she undresses in front of us by peeling her top up and over her head, followed by the undergarment, putting her beautiful breasts on display. She's kept some of her curves, which I'm completely obsessed over.

When she drops her pants and underwear, standing naked in front of us, she grins. Was this her attempt to make me so turned on that my brain forgets what I was saying?

"I'm going to have a shower." She walks across the door that takes her into the bathroom, and my eyes lock on her gorgeous ass as it moves with each step she makes. Stone's as captivated by her as I am.

At the doorway, she looks over her shoulder.

"I ordered food for us, so don't eat it all if it's delivered early." She slams the door shut.

"So, do you think she's inviting us to join her?" Stone asks.

I laugh, glad to finally find something funny.

"I honestly don't know, but we're stuck with her now. She won't leave, and I have to set things straight with her. How about you go downstairs and order us beers for the room?"

"Right..." He arches a brow. "You have Crius and Nikos looking after the horses, and now, you're kicking me out, so you can go into the bathroom with a naked Narah. I see what you're doing, my friend. Clever." He winks, then slaps me on the back. "Go get her."

Once he leaves the room, I remove my clothes, under no illusion of what I want, but maybe I've been too quick not to understand how much it has affected her. She's also lost her parents, and when she finally finds a family, there's a risk she'll lose it.

Fuck! I get it, and while part of me still prefers she wasn't on this mission, I have to get the fuck over it.

Setting my clothes on the back of the chair, I enter the bathroom. Narah's in the shower cubicle, steam pouring out, which means hot water. I close the door behind me with a loud, resonating clunk, and she turns toward me, her body covered in soap suds, and grins.

"I was wondering how long it would take you to join me. Come to apologize? That's the only way you'll get in here with me."

Chuckling, I step forward.

"How about a truce? I understand why you need to be and I should have made more of an effort to understand your needs. And, it's better if we work together to ensure our baby girl doesn't end up an orphan."

She hurls the bar of soap at me, striking me dead center in my chest.

"That's the crappiest apology I've ever heard."

"I may need some practice." Picking up the soap from the floor, I join her in the shower, the fiery water feeling like it's going to peel my skin away. "Hell, why's the water so hot?"

"It's not hot. Maybe you're just too sensitive."

Laughing loudly, I pull her to my side while the other hand puts the soap on the ledge and turns down the death water. Before she can protest, I lean in and kiss her. She kisses me back ferociously as her hands curl around the back of my neck. Our mouths clash together, and our tongues tangle.

My cock hardens to the point of pain as she rubs her tits over my chest and her hand tugs on my shaft.

"Fuck me," she purrs against my mouth.

Heart hammering, I'm burning up with the need to sink into that gorgeous pussy.

"Are you sure you're ready to have sex?"

"Yes, I really am. It's been torture not having sex for two months."

"Well, in that case, we better do something about it." I twist her around her hips, and she bends forward for me, wriggling that gorgeous little backside. Lowering my hand between her legs, to my surprise, she's drenched. I'm not talking about the shower water, but the silky slick that tells me how much she's longed for me.

"Is this what you want?"

"Oh, yes, big Alpha. Rut me." She grins at me over her shoulder.

Someone is in a smart-ass mood. Raising my hand, it comes down across her cheeks, and she calls out for more.

"Hey."

"Did you enjoy that?" I guide my cock to her soaking pussy, slipping the head into her.

"Oh, yes, but I like this better."

She feels so hot, so right the more I press into her. When I can't take anymore, I drive in deeper, pushing into her all the way.

Purring for me, Narah's hands are against the shower wall. Her hips buck back with each of my movements. I grip her hips as I fuck her, wanting to hear her screams when she's completely at my mercy. This is the perfect release I've craved.

Maybe having Narah join us isn't such a bad thing after all.

Tomorrow will be a difficult day, but until then, I intend to do everything to remember why I fight for the Savage Sector. I may have started with the goal of becoming the most powerful Alpha of Romania to show my father I wasn't the loser he said I was, but my priorities have changed.

Now, I will fight for dominance over the Savage Sector to provide a home and a safe future for my family and my pack.

Death.

The moment we reach the edge of the Savage Sector, it's obvious something had changed in this part of Romania.

No one says a word as we ride down the track as we pass dead bodies. Some are shifters who were butchered and dumped, while others are undead with their heads hacked off. The path through sparse woodland takes us past an undead lying in the long grass, his arm sticking out as if reaching for us. It quickly becomes clear he's in no position to come after us since he only has half a body. I don't look for long because my stomach is already lurching, and the smells are revolting.

Passing another undead, it growls softly as its glassy eyes follow us while blood seeps from his head. Nikos does the honors and puts him out of his misery, which is more about ensuring it doesn't find the strength to come after us.

"I'm certain we've just walked into one of those horror books you used to read, Nikos," Crius says, swinging his axe in his hand.

I've come to realize it's how he deals with stress. As some count beads on a string or curl their hair, he uses his axe as a distraction.

When I first met him, I assumed the mannerism was his cockiness, showing off how strong he was, but I had him all wrong.

In truth, I misread most of them.

We're still getting to know each other, I realize that now, and I'm excited to learn more about them. I keep thinking of Harmony too, unable to get her out of my mind. There's a bond to her I never expected to experience, and the need to hold her against me sits so heavily on me that I want to cry.

But like I told Ragnar, I'm on this mission for her future. To give her something so she will always know how much I love her, and I will do whatever it takes to return to her side.

"Yeah, well, I don't like being the hero in this horror story," Crius blurts, distracting me from my thoughts. "During our absence, I suspect the Savage Sector has seen a bigger influx of migrating zombies than we thought."

"Fucking great. Dealing with one bastard isn't bad enough... now we have two enemies to watch out for," Stone adds.

Ragnar's been quiet, riding alongside me, and I catch him staring at me now and then.

"How are you doing?" he finally asks.

"I'm okay. Just miss Harmony so much, but I also need to do this for her. I'm also a bit freaked out about all these dead body parts, but I knew it would be horrible. But after a long sleep and a big breakfast, I can take on the world." I grin his way, absolutely adoring this man. All four of them are my world, and my heart thunders whenever I think of them.

I think about Harmony and how she slept. The separation from her has been torture. I can still smell her on me, still hear her sweet cries in my mind, and it physically hurts how much I want to hold her and feel her against my body.

"Of course, you feel amazing," Crius responds sarcastically. "You got a hard fuck in the shower, ate most of our dinner, then crashed and stretched across the entire bed."

I burst out laughing. "Guilty as charged. I didn't know the portions would be so small."

"Don't worry, once you crashed in bed, still holding on to a chicken wing, we ordered more food."

"You were so cute." Nikos chuckles. "Ragnar struggled for several minutes, trying to get that chicken bone out of your hand without waking you."

"You were adorable," Ragnar smirks.

A blush slides over my cheeks—I'd fallen asleep so hard and with food in my hand. "I was exhausted." I shrug, unable to defend myself since I don't remember the incident.

Once we leave the woods, we move faster and keep our talking to a minimum to avoid drawing any attention. I keep my eyes peeled for the undead and spot them in the distance, but we're moving too fast for them to come our way.

"Do you notice there aren't many travelers?" I ask Stone, who's alongside me. Ragnar's taking the lead and Crius is at the rear.

"I'm sure they're afraid of the zombies. You saw the compound in the Shadowlands Sector. They only go out for hunting and foraging, but up here, no one was prepared for the wave of undead."

"Maybe it'll work to our benefit," Crius states. I glance over my shoulder at him, riding his steed, shoulders square, and scanning the landscape as he talks. "Less of a chance of dickface Martell traveling to all the packs and terrorizing them."

"Wouldn't that be nice?" I mutter, knowing nothing will stop him. My ex-fated mate had lost his mind. He enjoyed hurting me, and I saw him bursting with arrogance after claiming the Storm Wolves. So, not for a second do I believe he's anything but a psychopath who won't let the undead stop him from taking what he wants.

By the time we reach the Bane Wolves' pack home, anxiety comes over me. On my last visit, my possessed sister killed the pack Alpha's daughter, then I ran away.

"I assume we'll be welcome here, Ragnar?" Since their last visit to this pack, none of the men told me how it went. To be fair, I'd been so occupied, I forgot about it.

"It'll be fine," Ragnar finally answers. "We didn't tell you, but you'll find out soon enough. On our last visit, Martell had killed Mihai and some of his men, so I took over this pack."

I'm stuck for words as a sense of guilt ripples over my stomach. "Oh, my goddess. It's because of me," I blurt out, and with it comes all the emotions, making me sound like I'm about to burst out crying. It makes me feel sick to think if it wasn't for me, those he killed would still be alive.

Ragnar pauses, and we do the same. He turns in his saddle, his eyes half hooded, and I see the rapid rise and fall of his chest.

"Little fox, this isn't your fault. Martell decided to rule the Storm Wolves on his own, as he decided he would claim the Savage Sector. That isn't on you. He would have bullied the packs into submission, and in takeovers, there are always casualties... too many." He pauses, the ache of what happened here painted across his hard expression.

"So, what are we doing here, then?" I ask, trying my best not to let the news get to me.

"Check on the pack, rest, and prepare for our next steps," he says stoically, his warrior persona slipping into place, and I know the tragedy hurts him more than he'll admit.

"Okay, but I still feel like crap," I whine and can't help but feel all those people would be alive if I hadn't brought all my problems here.

But without a word, we're off again. The gates sit open, which isn't a good sign, but no one else is panicking. Reaching the front yard, we climb off our horses.

"Doesn't look like anyone's home." Crius scans the empty field. In the past, we'd always been greeted upon arrival and our horses walked to the stables. Now, nothing.

"Stay with the horses, just in case," Ragnar orders, eyeing Crius, who doesn't protest the command.

The air feels heavy, carrying with it a smell of something stale. Crius grabs my reins and blows me a kiss, his smile a bright light when it feels as if we're about to walk into the devil's den.

The four of us head up the steps, and the place appears abandoned. The roaring fire in the center of the yard is gone. Scanning the grounds, the huts, and the mess hall in the distance, not a soul is in sight.

"Are you sure someone's living here?" I murmur, and shivers run up my arms. What if Martell had returned?

Ragnar stays by my side while Nikos and Stone fan out, moving ahead of us.

"When I left, they had intended to move back into their homes, but they could still be hiding in the caves in the mountains."

"Those poor families and children." My stomach is in knots as I hurry across the grounds. I'll be happy when we leave. This place gives me the creeps, and I keep looking over my shoulder as if someone watched us.

"Think there are people here after all." Stone points to a hut, where the curtain falls as though someone has been watching us.

Ragnar pauses and stretches an arm out across my stomach to stop me. "Let them check first."

Joining Stone, Nikos knocks on the door, then calls out, "Hello... we're not here to hurt you. Ragnar, your new Alpha has returned." When no one opens the door, Stone pushes it open.

And Chaos rains down on us.

Stone and Nikos recoil as undead pour out, one after another. They lurch toward us, greedy jaws snapping, arms reaching for us. Torn clothes barely hang on their thin frames, and their faces are gaunt, their cheeks sunken. One man has only one arm, but to these things, the only thing that matters is eating flesh.

I shudder and retreat as terror rises to my throat, picturing us trapped with no one to help us. My heart clenches tight.

Creatures frantically hurry toward Stone and Nikos, who have their blades out and lunge into battle.

"Go to Crius," Ragnar orders as he jumps into the fight.

I retreat, well aware where there's one—or in this case, five zombies—there are more. Swinging around to run to Crius and warn him, I come almost face to face with an undead—a man with no hair or lips, his teeth and pasty gums all I see—coming right for me. And he's not alone. Half a dozen others quickly stumble behind them.

A scream pours past my throat, and I backpedal, but my instincts have other ideas. One second, I'm trying to find a way to escape, and the next, my hands jut out in front of me, and magic sparks on my fingertips.

All I hear is the pounding in my head as the zap of power snaps outward, colliding with the zombie. He convulses and drops to the dirt ground, his body seeming to cave in on itself, decomposing right before my eyes until there's nothing but dust.

Wrenching my gaze to the other creatures coming toward me fast, I can hear the grunting sound of fighting behind me.

"Ragnar," I call, snapping my attention toward them where two zombies are down, and the guys are in a fight with others, Crius beneath one. Panic rips into me. Not waiting, I hurl my magic toward his undead, along with the other two. The men grunt as they turn toward me in shock, but I don't have time to explain that I'm going to kick all the undead ass. My body thrums with each attack, and as my mother did, I focus on drawing the energy out of them.

I did it to the zombies by the river when we rushed to the mountains to my mother's home, and I'll do it now.

"Narah!" Ragnar sounds panicked.

"Give me a sec," I yell as I thrust my hands out, sucking all the energy out of these fuckers. More of them come out of a nearby home, teeth gnashing, fast feet carrying them toward me. Instead of retreating, I rush toward them as lines of power dance in the air.

Is it bad that I'm enjoying myself?

My body tingles as I turn more of them to literal dust. Stepping forward, my legs wobble beneath me, and I can feel the heat of my magic running up my arms.

"Narah, stop!" Ragnar snaps so loudly behind me, I flinch.

The last zombie collapses into a pile of dust, and I call back my power, surprising myself with how much more control I have now. When I'm convinced no more undead are coming for us, I turn to my men with a bit too much excitement and have trouble standing up. Stumbling, I catch myself, then lift my gaze.

"Don't worry, there'll be plenty—" My words catch in my throat when I find the three staring at me as though they've seen a ghost. Stone's mouth is open, and Nikos is frozen in a strange pose, his hands to his stomach and his face a statue in permanent shock.

"Why are you staring at me that way? You're kinda scaring me." I keep peering over my shoulder, looking for more undead.

"Narah... your skin." Ragnar's voice shakes, which makes me even more scared.

Glancing down at my arms, I scream. Seeing pale white skin with my veins blue and bulging, I rub my arms.

Goddess, what happened to me?

"Make it go away. What's going on?" I cry out as tears pool in my eyes. I'm frightened and so confused as a wave of heavy exhaustion slides through every inch of me. A sudden bone-crushing ache cuts through me, and I cry out as my knees give out from under me. Ragnar catches me before I hit the ground. I'm in his arms in no time, crying as terror bites into me.

"What's going on with me?" All I can think about is Harmony. I have to see her again. I have to!

Stone and Nikos are at my side, touching my brow and arms.

"You're freezing to the touch," Stone murmurs, his voice cracking. "Why would you draw all that dead energy into you?"

"What do you mean?" I blink up at him. "I did it to a couple of zombies a few months ago, and I was fine." Exhaustion comes at me once more, and the world spins.

"Oh, sweetheart," Stone says, his hand on my cheek.

"I look like some kind of alien. Am I going to die?" Trembling, I stare at my arms again.

Everyone looks at Stone for a response.

"Well, when you take energy into your body, it impacts you, and if you draw in something dead, your body will be impacted. It could even kill you if you go overboard."

"Crap, you're really scaring me. Please tell me I'll be okay, and I'll never use my magic on a zombie again."

Just as Stone begins to explain, the world tilts. I grasp onto Ragnar.

"Everything keeps spinning."

In a flash, my world goes dark... dragging me down with it.

CHAPTER
TWENTY-ONE

RAGNAR

Narah's a tiny thing, curled up in bed and breathing deeply. Her skin has warmed up, color returning to her face, and her veins are not as obvious. I've been watching her sleep for the past hour, remembering how she shuddered in my arms, her breaths raspy, and my heart splintered.

If anything happened to her, I'd die, and I couldn't do that to Harmony, which is why I insisted she remain in the Shadowlands Sector.

Sighing, I watch the way her chest rises and falls. How beautiful she is.

Narah's my everything. With her, the world shines brighter, and I laugh more. I now have a purpose and a reason to look forward to my future. Something I discovered about myself only after she came into my life.

So, when she collapsed, we frantically got her to the nearest pack where we had allegiance and prayed Martell hadn't destroyed or taken them over. The Goddess must have been shining down on us— we were welcomed with open arms.

Their medic was startled to see her in such a state, saying she was on death's door. He prescribed lots of rest and food, saying she was suffering from malnutrition. She'd been completely depleted of energy, and while I partly agreed with him that she needed to regain her strength, it was for a very different reason than what he suspected. We let him believe we found her in the woods—a lost Omega—to avoid drawing attention from the Alpha.

Things are tense enough without bringing in an Omega with magic abilities, who used to be Martell's fated mate, into their home.

"How's she doing?" Nikos asks as he enters the room.

"Looking better," I murmur, turning to leave the room. He follows me, gently closing the door behind him. "She's healing fast, but that was a scare none of us expected."

"Fuck, I almost had a stroke when she was pale as a ghost and so lethargic." He swallows loudly. "It's not an image I'll get out of my head anytime soon."

"Agreed." Stepping into the kitchen of the home the Alpha gave us to stay in, Crius and Stone are digging into the wild boar stew, which one of the locals brought us after they saw how sick Narah was.

Half of it is already eaten before Nikos flops down on a chair, grabs a fork, and drags the whole dish over to him.

"I didn't know using her magic on the zombies would impact her so severely," Stone says, then wipes the crumbs from his mouth with a napkin.

"Or that she'd try to take on all the freaking zombies," Crius says, smacking his lips. "Though I'm so fucking proud of her that she had the balls to do that."

"I wonder who the fuck put the undead in those houses," Nikos blurts out, always the astute one. "There's no way they obediently filed into those homes and closed themselves inside. Sure, maybe one house, but not so many. It was a setup."

"Bet it was Martell, leaving us a parting gift. It would explain why there were no pack members on our visit... alive or dead," Nikos explains.

"Martell doesn't strike me as a guy who would clean up the dead he leaves in his wake," Crius adds.

"They're most likely with the Alpha I asked to care for them." I angle my head toward the doorway, convinced I've heard a sound.

"What's our next step?" Niko queries, always the guy to get down to business and one of the reasons why I keep him close on my team.

We're very similar in that respect. "Do we let Narah continue resting and head out to hunt for Martell?"

"She's going to be pissed," Stone says what we're all thinking.

"We'll live with it." I know it will come back and bite me hard in the ass, but the fright I got seeing her close to death was too much to ignore. "That was too close. I'm not putting her in a situation where she would place others in front of her own life."

There's a loud knock on the front door, and I tense. Crius leaps to his feet and marches out there. Moments later, he returns with Lortell, one of my men who had infiltrated this pack. He's lean, taller than me, and has been loyal to me since he'd lost his parents when my father sent both males and females to battle. He lost his family in an agonizing heartbeat, and when he discovered I had every intention of opposing my father, he joined my pack.

I stand and give him a strong hug, smacking a hand on his back, then we step back.

"I heard you were in town, Ragnar. It's been too damn long. I wasn't sure when you were going to show up and was worried I'd have to call this pack my new family." He breaks into forced laughter. "Don't get me wrong. There's nothing wrong with them, and they have three unmated Omegas who have caught my attention, but these Alphas are no Viking warriors."

I remembered now how much Lortell loved to talk. Getting in a word sometimes was excruciatingly painful.

"Fuck yeah, they're not." Crius hoots.

He grabbed a seat, and I joined him at the round family table.

"An urgent matter came up that couldn't wait, but we're back to eliminate Martell, so tell me everything. What's been going on in the sector in the past two months? I need answers before Martell makes a show in this pack, too."

He nods, then reclines in his seat, making himself comfortable. "We've heard the stories about Martell making his way to all the packs with an ultimatum... join his forces, or he'll eliminate them. And trust me, when he comes to your door, it's with a fucking army. So, everyone's fucking caving. What else are they supposed to do?"

Stone leans forward, staring at Lortell across the table. "They'll turn on him the first chance they get."

"Absolutely, but by then, he'll have gained so much power and support from those who will turn loyal, he'll be untouchable."

"We take him out before this happens." My muscles flex as my wolf growls in my throat. In the past two months, the situation has grown dire. I'm under no illusion that he'll make moves to claim the sector, but to hear he'd grown so big this fast leaves me tense as fuck.

"He has a death wish, turning so many against him," Lortell snarls. "So, this pack is preparing, knowing it's only a matter of time before he comes knocking here. I also spoke to the others in our team from different packs. Martell told them to kill you on the spot. He's put a target on your back and on anyone who supports you, for that matter. The bastard has it bad for you. Rumors have spread that you stole his fated mate, which is why he's gunning for you."

Stone bursts out laughing. "Fucking moron. As if his attack has nothing to do with Ragnar gaining allegiance with at least a dozen packs already in this sector."

Lortell shrugs. "Just telling you what's going around."

The more I hear, the harder it is to hold back my aggression. Irritation pulses in my veins. "Where's the bastard staying?"

"As of two days ago, he was in the valley with the Crescent Wolves."

"So, about an hour's travel on foot," Nikos murmurs, shifting his attention to me. "That should be easy. We head out at night, sneak into the camp, find him in his bed, and slice his throat."

"It won't be that easy," Lortell corrects, his lips drawn into a tight frown. "Heard the guy's paranoid as fuck and sleeps with twenty guards around him."

"More fuckers to destroy," Crius growls. "I've never backed down from a challenge."

"Then count me in." Lortell grins, cracking his knuckles. "I'm bored as shit in this pack."

"What do you say, Ragnar?" Stone asks. "I'm ready to knock this bastard off his pedestal."

We came here for Martell, and the longer we delay it, the more time we give him to find us first.

"Let's make it happen," I growl. "We'll leave after supper, collect our men from the other packs along the way, then take out the fucker." Slamming my fist on the table, a surge of excitement soars through my veins. The others join me, the thumps of our fists loud.

"There is no room for failure. Tonight, he dies," I roar, adrenaline lacing my blood. War is not always won by sheer size. Many are fought behind the scenes. Take out the Alpha, and most of the time, the rest will fall.

A scream pierces the air.

My mind racing to Narah, I jolt up, my chair hitting the floor behind me as I rush toward her bedroom. Bursting inside, I find Narah still in bed asleep, not stirring. I could have sworn it had come from inside the house.

Crius, Stone, and Nikos shove into the room and let out relieved sighs.

"Fuck, what was that sound then?" Crius mutters.

"Ragnar, we have a problem," Lortell yells, and my stomach turns to rock.

I shove past the guys and find him at the end of the hallway with the door partially open. Before I take a step forward, I hear Martell's commanding voice. My shoulders bunch with tension, my knuckles white from how hard I fist my hands. Sucking in a sharp breath, I glance at my men, who know full well the demon has found us.

I run toward Lortell, who steps back to let me peer outside. In the far left corner of the compound, Martell is talking to the pack Alpha. Behind Martell are at least a dozen Alphas, big fuckers. Nothing we can't take down, but what lays beyond the open gates has me worried. A wave of his followers, maybe fifty, linger out there, intimidating muscle to scare any pack into submission.

No one's looking this way... yet. Shutting the door quietly, I turn to my men. My gut is tight as hell as I try my best not to show the dread I feel that we're cornered. I wrack my head for an escape plan.

"We need to steer Martell away from Narah." That's my priority. "Stone, you'll accompany her, using your magic to protect her. Whatever it takes. Once we go outside and begin the challenge, sneak her out the back with and get as far from here as you can."

He nods, though the tension in his stance shows me he's wary of leaving the rest of us.

I turn to the other three. "I'm going to call for a Lup Challenge, which he can't deny."

"Are you certain?" Nikos asks, the bridge of his nose scrunching. "This is Martell we're dealing with."

I shudder at the anxiety dancing over my skin. This isn't how I intended things to go, but we have to make do.

"He'll accept, trust me," I snap, the pressure of our situation building inside me.

My men stare at me, dread clearly painted on their faces.

"I know this isn't how we wanted to do this, but when have we ever turned away from an impossible situation?"

"We never walk away!" Nikos snarls, striking his chest with a fist, his shoulders raised, eyes narrowing with his wolf glinting through.

The others follow suit.

"Good. We have a plan. Get your weapons and let's go to war."

They scramble to do just that while Lortell shows me he's armed to the teeth beneath his clothes.

My gaze skitters over to the front door, my wolf in my chest, growling, ready for battle.

We will stand against the greater enemy, even if outnumbered, to protect those we love.

Today is not the day we die.

Moving to the bed, I take one last look at Narah. I push the hair off her brow, and she groans her sleep and rolls onto her back. Studying her for the briefest moment, I imprint this image on my mind to remind me why I'll risk everything for her.

Leaning forward, I whisper, "I'll always love you, my little fox, and I will always be with you." I kiss her lightly on the brow and walk out as Crius and Nikos move in to see her. My heart squeezes so hard, I feel tears pricking my eyes. This isn't the last time I intend to see her or my little Harmony. For them, I have to make this work.

Once my men return, we have no hesitation, no fear. They stand tall, fire blazes in their eyes, and we're ready. Stone stands by Narah's door, and with one final glance his way, I say, "Take good care of our girls."

Marching to the front door, we slip into the yard. The afternoon sun beats down on us as we walk down a pebbled path past houses and the stone fence that surrounds the compound.

One of the guards yells at our approach, then there's a blur of movement as Martell's men emerge from all around us, closing in.

I tense with anger buried deep within me with the instinct to rip their fucking heads off. That will come soon enough.

Martell comes into view, staring directly at me. Our gazes clash, and fury bursts through me.

Tall with short dark hair, parted at the side, his head is held high, and he's built like a barrel. A wild beard coats his jawline, and his thin lips are peeled back over a line of white teeth. He watches us with pure hatred.

His men rush us, snatching us by hair and arms, blades at our throats, forced to head toward Martell. It goes against everything, but I don't put up a fight.

"We come to you as free Alphas," I state. "Not with aggression but to talk."

"Fuck you," Martell barks like the dog he is, a death glare in his dark eyes. "You stole my fated mate and tried to steal the Savage Sector from me. Maybe in Denmark, you allow such deceit and look away like cowards, but in the Savage Sector, we're wolves who'll rip your fucking heads off."

Nikos groans under his breath beside me.

"I don't give a shit what you have to say," Martell continues. "Tell me where you've hidden my Narah, and maybe I'll consider taking pity on you."

Crius barks a robust laugh behind me. "I'm calling bullshit."

Growling, Martell snatches a blade from his side and storms toward us.

I tense when the guard presses the sharp bite of a blade to my throat.

"I summon the Lup Challenge, Martell."

Martell stops feet from me, then howls with laughter.

"I think not."

"Once it's invoked, it must be accepted," I growl. "You and three of your best fighters against us to the death."

Martell picks his teeth with the tip of his blade, then lowers his gaze to me.

"I decline. Now, where the fuck is Narah? You hiding her in one of these huts?" He turns to the men behind him, and with the flick of his hand, half a dozen sweep outward, storming toward the homes.

I grind my teeth, praying Stone got Narah out.

"Now, Ragnar," he spits, "how about we play another game? The longer it takes my men to find Narah, the more of your men I'll kill." He snorts a laugh.

Fury howls through me, my wolf scratching for me to let him out, to rip this asshole apart.

Soon, so fucking soon.

"You're afraid." I provoke him with a grin, looking around at everyone watching, and raise my voice. "The all-powerful Martell proclaims himself as the new Alpha of Savage Sector, yet he's too scared to face the Lup Challenge. What sort of Alpha is afraid to fight for his pack and land?"

"The man you're following is gutless and can't fight. Is that who you want as your leader?" Nikos barks.

"I'm going to gut all of you like pigs," Martell roars.

"Lup Challenge, Lup Challenge," Lortell booms, and to my surprise, the local pack catches on, and it grows louder.

I never take my eyes off Martell. His face is red with rage, and he's ready to detonate.

"Do you accept?" I growl.

Every eye is on him. An Alpha is only as strong as his last successful fight. As soon as the leader loses, those around him see him as easy prey, and all respect is gone.

His jawline is clenched so tight, he's trembling.

Finally, he barks, "I accept the challenge to the death, as evidenced by the Moor Wolves in this pack. You will die today, Ragnar." He lifts his gaze to his guards. "Strip them of their weapons... hand-to-hand combat."

Martell rips his shirt off his back, revealing his huge barrel torso and the muscles clenching in his huge arms.

Grinning, I drop my weapons, watching the bastard turn to his men and point out who he will fight alongside. He picks only beef, mountain-sized men. Works for me. I don't give a fuck what size they are. My men and I have fought worse.

They step up alongside me, tense, their hands curled into fists.

"You ready for this?" I ask. "You know our target. Take him down and fast."

Crius bounces on his toes, a primal hunger in his wild eyes. He had to give up his axe, but the guy was a berserker at heart.

Guards back away from us, and I stand in line with my best fighters. Stone would have made us a stronger team, but his mission is a lot more important and dangerous than ours—saving Narah.

The leader of the Moor Wolves steps onto the battlefield, which is surrounded by pack and guard wolves. The man stands tall, but the dread on his face is palpable. He knows this could go to hell on his playground, and he has no say. He runs a small pack and is not known for having strong warriors.

That's where we come in.

"Today, the Lup Challenge has been called and accepted. The last team standing wins."

"To the death!"

TWENTY-TWO

"Narah, sweetheart, you need to get up now," a soft whisper floats over my mind. Someone is shaking me, giving me whiplash.

My eyes flutter open just as Stone lifts me into his arms.

"Wh-What's going on?" It takes only seconds to jump into a panicked state. Looking around the room, I gasp for air. "Are we in danger?"

"How are you feeling? You're looking much better and no longer resemble a freaky undead." He grins at me teasingly.

As he lowers me to my feet, I look down at my arms and body and discover I'm only wearing a tank top and underwear. My skin's normal, more of a pinkish-white hue instead of freaking white with blue veins.

"I'll explain everything, but you need to get ready. Martell is here."

"Fuck, he's here?" I'm suddenly wide awake. Adrenaline pulses in my veins, pounding in my ears. "Does he know where we are? I'm so confused. I don't even know where we are." I rattle off questions that pop into my head as I quickly grab the clothes from the end of the bed. I hate this surreal confused state. "Where are the others?"

"Just get ready, and I'll quickly explain." Bringing me my boots, he sets them near my feet as I pull on my jeans, jumping up and down to drag them up my legs because, of course, they're skin-tight.

"After you took out the zombies at the Bane Wolves' home, you passed out. We rushed you to the closest pack we had a partnership with, and you've been sleeping ever since. In the meantime, Martell arrived to claim this pack, or he's tracked us. We need to sneak out the back and get out of this pack."

I've never moved so fast in my life, purely on adrenaline and fear.

When I'm ready, Stone grabs my arm, and we fly out of the room toward the back door. I keep looking over my shoulder, unable to spot the others.

"Are they already outside?"

"You could say that," Stone whispers as he slowly opens the door and sticks his head out.

My stomach trembles. The urgency I pick up from Stone worries me. He suddenly swings back inside, shutting the door and locking it. We stand still as my heart beats a million miles an hour.

"Please tell me what's going on," I whisper. I'm trying my best to be calm and not drown in the desperate terror clawing through me.

"The only way for us to escape was for the others to confront Martell to a Lup Challenge, a fair fight between a handful of men from each pack. Ragnar wins when Martell dies."

Blinking at him, my head spins.

"And if Martell wins?" I gasp.

"Narah... nothing you do now will stop the events that have already begun. They're already out front with Martell." He lifts his chin at the door at the opposite end of the hallway.

My heart in my throat, I turn and run down the hallway, barely holding back my tears. Stone's feet pound the floorboards, and I'm in his arms so fast, I lose my breath. "Put me down, please." Tears are already falling, and my throat thickens to the point it hurts.

"Please, Narah. They are risking everything. Don't take that away by not leaving with me." The ache in his voice adds to my guilt.

"I want to see what's going on... please." When he sets me down, I go to the window by the door and move the curtain ever so slightly to peer outside.

In the distance, people are everywhere. In truth, I barely see much because of the trees in my way, but there's definitely something happening. I can hear people cheering and hooting. My stomach drops, and the tears come, stinging and blurring as I picture my three men being beaten to death while these assholes shout for more.

I hate everyone—the world, the Alphas, the stupid games people make. Most of all, I hate that I was so weak, I passed out taking out a handful of zombies.

"I'm sorry, Narah, but we have to go now."

Gasping for air, it takes everything in me not to run out there and help them, but I know I'd fail against so many.

Fingers gently curl around my wrist, and Stone pulls me back down the hallway to the rear door.

"All they have to do is win, right?" I ask, clinging to him.

"It's four against four."

"Four?"

"One of Ragnar's men has been living with this pack. He's taking my place, so Martell doesn't ask where Ragnar's other warrior is."

My head spins out of control. Evidently, I missed a lot while I was passed out.

"I promise when we are safe, I will explain it all to you from the beginning. Okay? Now, I just need you to trust me. We have to get out while they're in the challenge, and everyone is occupied."

Heartache carves its way all the way to my soul, but I begrudgingly nod.

Stepping outside the hut, beyond the small yard are trees and more homes. By the looks of it, there are people over there, but it's hard to tell with all the woodland, which I hope also means they can't see us clearly.

Hooting and shouting come from the front of the house, and it kills me to be running from my men when they are doing everything to protect me.

My breaths coming hard, with my hand in Stone's, we sprint along the back of the huts. Heartbeat in my ears, my mind is too blurry to come up with an alternate plan to go back for my men. The feeling I'll regret this day stabs at the back of my mind.

A bitter breeze whistles past us. Reaching the last home in the long line, we pause to catch our breaths. Stone peers around the corner, then snaps back just as fast.

"Fuck," he mutters under his breath. "Fuck. Fuck."

"What's going on?"

"Martell's men have snuck out of the compound and are climbing back in over the corner where we were going to escape, but that's not the worst." Shadows whip under his gaze. "This is what I was about with the plan, but it wasn't as if we had many options. Maybe Ragnar realized the risk."

"What are you talking about?"

He turns to me, a hardness stiffening his face.

"These warriors are going to get behind Ragnar and surround them. I knew that fucking turd, Martell, would never play fairly."

I fumble with his explanation as he's talking fast and in a hushed voice.

"His men are going to attack my men if they look like they're winning? Of course, he would." A coldness slices through me that Ragnar knew this all along. He'd never make such a mistake.

"My guess is he's hoping the local pack will assist him, but I don't know if they will." Stone swallows hard, as wrecked as I feel.

"We can't leave them! You know deep in your heart we're leaving them to their deaths if they are surrounded."

His shoulders bunch up.

"I'm no longer the scared girl. I'm not running! Fuck, Martell. We're a team, and our family needs us."

Stone licks his teeth, and I know he's thinking the same thing. His gaze suddenly snaps back down to me.

"Ragnar will be pissed at us, but I'm with you. Leaving is a massive mistake."

"I don't care as long as we save their asses." I grin, and Stone steals a quick kiss.

"Let's be their backup."

No more words are needed.

We move like wildfire the way we'd come, and the urgency to be there for my men replaces the fear. Darting between two homes, we come up on the commotion. There are enough gaps between the people standing around for us to see what the hell's going on.

It's hard to work out what I see as the Alphas move with unimaginable speed.

Nikos is suddenly tossed across the ground, and the air is expelled from his lungs. Bruised and bleeding, smears of crimson streak his clothes and his face. He's beaten, and when I see the barbarian stomping toward him, looming over the man I love and grinning, my heart's about to give out.

He raises a fist just as Crius lunges onto his back, punching his head. Looping an arm around his throat, he snaps his neck. The sound echoes in the air, and the man drops to his knees. Crius jumps back as his opponent falls face first to the dirt.

Nikos gets to his feet just as Martell barrels into him, bringing him down with force. Crius throws himself onto Martell, and before I know it, there's a mountain of men battling in a tangled mess.

My head pulses with pain, and with it comes the flow of power that tingles through me.

"Not yet," Stone whispers harshly, his hand on my shoulder.

"Why the hell not?" I snap, jerking my head to look up at him.

"If we interrupt the challenge, Martell automatically wins."

"Who cares? He'll be dead."

"It means Ragnar can never take Martell's packs or land he controls. It would automatically go to his second in command. There are too many witnesses, so we wait. The final blow needs to be delivered by Ragnar."

"I can't wait for them to die," I growl under my breath, loathing the stupid rules Alphas insist on following when we live in a world where anything goes. Blind rage thumps through me, but I hold back, curling my hands into fists.

Remaining in the shadows, watching the fight makes me nauseous. The longer I watch, the more I burn as small tingles of magic prick the edges of my fingers. Just like my wolf, who's growling in my chest, the power is erupting in response to my fury.

Ragnar's thrown harshly onto his back, but he rolls away just as Martell's about to stomp his head. Another man, I don't recognize, throws himself at Martell, and they hit the ground hard. I can only imagine he's one of Ragnar's men.

Martell moves swiftly, snatching the man's neck, and rips his throat out. Blood splashes everywhere, and many in the crowd erupt with vicious cheers.

I flinch and whimper.

Stone grabs me into his arms. "Don't look."

It's too late—I saw everything.

The longer I watch the battle, the more I hurt on the inside.

"I can't stand by and do nothing. One of them could die. I don't care about the stupid rules. I'm going to take out Martell. I need to." Bile hits the back of my throat when I think about all my encounters with him—the hatred, the cruelty, the deaths.

Crius stumbles backward, fresh blood leaking from an ear, one leg of his pants soaked in crimson, and I notice he's limping.

I step closer, but Stone's arm is around my stomach.

"Don't make me use my magic on you because I will," I snarl. "I've had enough of watching this brutal savagery."

A flurry of panic comes over him, but he finally growls. "Fine, but we're doing this my way."

"Yeah, and how's that?"

"I have no idea if this will work, but I don't know how else to stop you. You're going to siphon power from me, then thrust it into Ragnar."

I wrench my gaze from the fight to Stone. "Will that work?"

"In theory, it should. You draw energy from people, so why can't you funnel it back out? It's what your mother was doing with your father. Feeding him her blood and funneling power she drained from others into your father."

Of course, he was right, but I don't want to accidentally zap my lover. My intention had been to just drain as many of the assholes as possible until I most likely passed out again, but the longer I considered Stone's idea, the more I liked it.

"Alright, let's do it. How?"

Stone kneels by a tree and places one hand on the earth. Almost immediately, the runes on his chest glow a powerful, hypnotic blue. They may be our saving grace. His body buzzes all over, and the hairs lift on the arm he offers me.

Taking his hand, the shudder of sharp magic cuts into me, and a whine rolls across my throat from the sharp pain.

"Don't fight it. You're just a conduit for the magic."

I wrench my gaze back to the arena, where Ragnar's on his knees between two monstrous men. They look ready to shift into their wolves but never do. No doubt, another dumb rule. Seeing Ragnar at their mercy slices through me, and I snarl. I've had enough of this torture.

With all my concentration on him, I throw my arm out, and a spark of white light snaps across the ground with such speed, if you blinked, you would miss it. Magic strikes Ragnar's ribs so fast, so hard, it throws him out of both men's grasp.

I lower my hand as they flinch back, looking around to see what happened.

Getting to his feet, Ragnar shakes his head and rubs his side where the magic had burned a hole into his shirt. His head jerks up, and our gazes clash.

I smile and try to move my hands to tell him I gave him power, but I'm certain I look like I'm waving madly. Stone gestures to his runes, then to me, and our Alpha nods.

Glued to the arena, I move closer. As long as I keep my head low, hopefully, no one will recognize me. Stone is pressed to my back as we squeeze through the crowd.

Ragnar makes a wild dash for Martell, who has his back to him. His beefy arms have Nikos in a headlock.

A cry scratches my throat, afraid he's going to snap Nikos' neck. Cirus is on the ground growling while the savage crowd calls for Nikos' death.

Moving with unimaginable speed, Ragnar rips Martell off Nikos, and they fall into a vicious roll across the ground. They move so fast it's hard to see, but I'm certain I see tiny sparks of magic from Ragnar's hands.

No one else seems to notice, or they'd be calling it out.

They come to an abrupt stop, and Ragnar stands, then grabs Martell. His body moves with speed that can only come from magic. Unleashing a thunderous roar, he hurls my ex-fated mate at a nearby tree. The moment the asshole hits the tree, he bursts into flames, and the whole tree goes up in an explosion of fire.

I scream in shock, as does everyone else.

Their panic rings out across the air, followed by shouting and people running in every direction. While everything goes haywire, I notice the group of Martell's men we'd spied sneaking up on the right, charging toward us.

Fuck!

Ragnar had just set their Alpha on fire. Of course, they'd be pissed.

Where moments earlier, the fight was punches and teeth, we'd now show them why we are the true leaders of Savage Sector.

Stone and I push forward.

Ragnar doesn't hesitate to use what power he still has on the river of shifters coming at us from both directions.

Fiery magic erupts from my hands, striking the wall of newcomers. My body trembles from the sheer surge of power I draw into me. It's like warm water trickling over my body. My chest swells as my power leaves me buzzing and bouncing on my toes. Then suddenly, the lines of energy zigzag out of control.

I no longer know who I'm draining.

Panic and fear collide in me, my skin crawling that I'll kill everyone in sight.

I cry out when someone steps up behind me, their hands around my waist.

"You hold control of your power," Stone whispers. "And you can stop now with a single thought."

"Stop!" I cry out.

The power dies instantly, and I gasp out of disbelief as I stumble into Stone's arms.

The tree with Martell still burns, and beyond that, the grounds are littered with bodies, close to thirty unmoving men. It scares me to know how easily I took them out. I want to believe they aren't dead, just stunned, but I don't move to check.

When someone calls my name, I turn to the three men approaching me. They are bloody, bruised, and limping. Behind them, the grounds are bloody and littered with more bodies. Everyone else seems to have vanished.

"Does anyone ever listen to me in this family?" Ragnar teases. "You two were supposed to have vanished."

"Shut up and hug me," I say. "You can thank Stone and me later for saving all your asses."

Laughing, Crius clasps his side, then winces. "I want to know why you didn't jump in before that fucking beast punched me so hard. I'm certain he broke my ribs."

Taking his hand, I bring him closer. Nikos stumbles over to us, his face streaked in blood from a huge gash under his eye.

"Whatever you did to Martell, Ragnar, you will be on everyone's lips for years. Fuck, he deserved to die spectacularly, and you sure delivered."

Ragnar grins, his eyes burning with love when he looks down at me. "No thanks to borrowed power." Taking me in his arms, he cups my face, then kisses me. I push against him, fisting his torn shirt, and let myself finally believe we may have a future that doesn't involve my ex-fated mate trying to kill us.

When we break apart, all my men crowd in around me, and we embrace, holding each other close.

"Today will be remembered for those who have fallen and for us starting a new future. With Martell and so many of his followers gone, there will be few who might oppose my takeover. But first, you and Stone have to teach me that trick of giving me your power."

I laugh, surprised that I feel so incredible after using my power. My mother told me we were unimaginably powerful, but it still stuns me.

"I don't know about all of you, but I say we help the pack clean up their yard, prepare Lortell's burial, then I want to drink and fuck tonight," Ragnar murmurs,

Stone and Nikos eagerly say 'yes,' which leaves me giggling.

"No fair. Let me at least heal first," Crius pouts.

"Don't worry, my friend." Nikos pats his shoulder, which has Crius moaning louder in pain. "I'll prepare a seat so you can watch."

I laugh at their bickering, Stone insisting he knows what they're talking about.

Ragnar's hand slides into mine, and our fingers intertwine. We stare at the flaming tree, then at each other.

Everything we've endured still feels surreal, but I know it won't take long to accept that Savage Sector will be my new home, with my

Alphas reigning over all the packs up north. Being with my soon-to-be husbands—when I finally propose to them—and planning our future is more than a girl like me could have ever imagined. I've come a long way and like to think I more than deserve a happily ever after.

We're standing in the middle of a battlefield of dead bodies, yet I'm bursting with happiness, all those heavy burdens no longer on my mind.

"What are you thinking?" I ask Ragnar curiously.

"Deciding on what sort of mansion to build for our family home. Something high enough for perfect views, with lofty walls to keep out the undead, and a bathroom with a spa to fit all of us at once."

I press up against him. "I see your mind's always in the gutter."

He turns to face me. "Then tell me what's on your mind?"

"Something extremely important."

"Yeah?"

"Yep. How exactly am I going to give my four Alphas a sponge bath at the same time."

Throwing his head back, he bursts out laughing. The first time I heard the sexy sound, I knew he'd be someone special in my life.

Who would have thought he'd end up as my true fated mate?

BONUS EPILOGUE

Surreptitiously, I watch Harmony from the corner of my eye. She's grown up just as beautiful as her mother.

She's chatting with her friends during Mating Night. Like them, she's wearing a white dress that falls to her knees, is barefoot, and her chestnut hair is in curls, tumbling over her shoulders.

In the woods behind our home, every tree is decorated with fairy lights, and every unmated Omega and Alpha from the Savage sector packs are here to celebrate the blood moon and hopefully, find their mate. With the shortage of Omegas in our world, the males outnumber the females ten to one, which is one of the reasons for the Mating Night event.

To control what happens to the few Omegas we have, Dušan, who has a large portion of Omegas, will hold a similar event and will welcome some of our pack to attend.

The longer I watch Harmony, the more I remember the argument we had with her that at only sixteen, she was too young to attend, but our little bird turned up despite our decision. Now, she's across the field from me with other Omegas, with a huddle of young Alphas huddled next to them. They're only a few years older than her, and those pricks are eyeing my baby girl.

She flips her hair out of her face, the red highlights glinting beneath the lights, and even from here, I hear her voice as sweet as an angel's laughter.

My chest burns to see how they all stare at her, and she bats her eyes at them. When I was their age, my father beat me and told me to make a man of myself. I want to give Harmony memories filled with love, not anger. It's why I haven't gone over there and ripped those boys apart.

I stiffen when she catches me staring and gives me the death glare that would scare off a pack of zombies. I hold her gaze, letting her know she'll be grounded tomorrow.

She turns away from me abruptly to talk to the boys.

I growl under my breath, but this is Harmony's special day, so I won't make a scene in front of everyone and embarrass her. Besides, Narah would lose her shit since she had leaned toward letting her attend. Just because my daughter won't listen to me doesn't mean whatever guy she brings home will get away with such behavior. I'll rip his head off.

Footfalls close in behind me, and Crius steps up next to me.

"See how pencil-neck's looking at her? Fucker's staring below her neckline. I'm going to snap him in half," he groans.

"As much as I would enjoy that, we need to stay diplomatic," I explain through clenched teeth.

"I think it's adorable," Nikos states, appearing out of the blue.

"Have you got a screw loose in your head?" Crius barks a bit too loudly, gaining the attention of several parents gathering around to watch their children in the gathering circle. All those eligible had been corralled into an open area with the intention that they mingle. While they remain in the circle of lights, the females are free to speak to any of the males, not having to wait for the male to make the first move. Once they leave the circle, they are under parents' orders to keep their distance. The males are fucking horny, including the younger Alphas, so for the Omegas' safety, they are kept separated between certain ages when they have little control over their desires.

So far, they've remained in small groups with their friends, which makes me ecstatic.

Crius lowers his voice. "She's underage, and no girl of mine will end up with someone who looks like he can't bench press a fallen tree."

Nikos bursts out laughing. Crius hasn't lost his sense of exaggeration over the past sixteen years since we took over the Savage sector.

"This is just a meet-and-greet, so when they come of age, they know who they are fated to be," Nikos explains with a logic that doesn't ease the fire in my chest as I watch the pencil-neck boy going over to talk to Harmony, offering her a single flower he picked up off the ground.

"Gods, she's giggling," Crius groans. "It's a lost cause. Only one solution. We kidnap him and toss him to the zombies outside our pack home."

"Calm the fuck down," Nikos replies, giving a teasing grin. "If Harmony hears you, your life will be hell."

Crius huffs, and I laugh because he's spot on. With Harmony going through her teen growth, she's a beast, and most of the time, we tiptoe around her.

"Last time I looked, we were the Alphas of this entire sector," Crius murmurs.

Crius and Nikos break into a mini-debate while I glance back to the three-story wooden home we built for our family. A garden and fruit trees fill the yard, while in the distance, my pack's huts pepper the grounds. Those who swore their allegiance to me joined my pack and received a home within the safety of the lofty stone walls that keep the undead out. There are only a handful of packs who oppose joining me, but I'm working on changing their minds.

Scanning the grounds, I find my gorgeous little fox with Stone beneath a blossoming apple tree. He's kissing her neck, and she's laughing. She's glowing and absolutely spectacular. Every time I stare at her, my heart speeds up, and it feels like I'm seeing her for the first time—fiery eyes, delicate cheekbones, kissable lips that call to me—then there's the body that sets me alight.

My cock stirs at the sight of her.

Stone slyly slides a hand to her rear, which explains why he has her beneath the shadow of the tree.

The blood moon isn't just an auspicious night for the unmated to find their partner, but also for the rest of us who are dealing with unhinged desires off the fucking charts. I've already fucked Narah twice today to get it out of my system, but considering the way my balls are drawing up with hunger, I'm not even close to sating my urges.

"Stay here and watch Harmony," I order the other two, who are still bickering, as I make my way across the open woodland.

On my stroll toward Narah, I nod and welcome those who've joined our celebration. The food is set up farther to my left, where I spot Kaira standing between her two husbands. The three of them have been inseparable since they found each other in the Shadowlands Sector. Who would have thought the time we spent in that sector after Narah gave birth to Harmony would spark a romance between the three? It's brought her out of her shell, so to speak, after her ordeal with the High Priestess possessing her.

Stepping beneath the blossoming tree, Stone and Narah turn to face me with deviant grins. I laugh before they say a word, well aware Stone was out most of the morning, helping set up for the Mating Night, while I took advantage to have Narah all to myself.

"You know everyone can see you both." Making my move, I take Narah's hand and pull her into my arms.

"I held back," Stone argues. "Otherwise, I'd have her back in the house, fucking her sweet brains out."

Narah rolls her eyes at us.

"You can't talk," I tease, lifting her chin to me. "Who begged me this morning to eat their drenched pussy?"

Stone growls. "I knew I'd miss out on the fun the moment you sent me to help in the woods." He takes Narah's arm and swoops her back into his arms. "That's why she's mine tonight."

"How about we save it all for tonight in our room," she murmurs, lifting her gazes to someone behind me. And when I turn and see Crius and Nikos strolling our way, I bristle. Their expressions are coy, and they're staring at me strangely.

"Who's watching Harmony?" Before I finish speaking, they sidestep, revealing our daughter behind them, pencil-neck boy at her side, and my hackles rise.

Hair shaved on the sides and trimmed short on top, the boy was maybe seventeen or eighteen and stood taller than Harmony. On the skinnier side, for sure.

Harmony meets my gaze, intensity burning behind her amber eyes for me to accept him and not make a big deal. I adore her so much and only wanted the best for my daughter, but I'm well versed in how fucking horny Alphas are when it comes to Omegas. I eye the boy carefully.

While Harmony has her mother's beauty, she's picked up her fierceness from us. Some days, she drives me crazy with her arguments until I give in from pure exhaustion. Like the time she refused to join the other Omegas in a class to discuss going into heat, taught by Kaira, who's become a teacher for our pack. Regardless, Harmony didn't budge, insisting she wasn't ready for that. Well, she has a rude awakening coming her way if she now insists on picking a potential mate.

For the moment, I put on a sugary smile while Narah nudges past me.

"Harmony, who's your friend?"

Crius, Stone, and Nikos close in, and while Harmony grins at her mom, the boy is sweating bullets. Perspiration coats his forehead, and he's unsure which one of us to look at first. I enjoy his discomfort, but anyone who intends to be with my girl needs to stand up to her four fathers.

"This is Dante." Harmony gives a wide smile, and when she looks over at him, something glints in her eyes.

Narah hugs the boy, and when he turns to us, I do the right thing and shake his hand. His eyes bulge the moment I squeeze, but he puts on a lopsided grin. Maybe there's more to like about him than at first impression.

Crius makes a grunting sound, clearly not happy. But this isn't exactly what any of us expected, and yet we all shake his hand. And I'm certain he won't be using his hand for a week, yet he puts on a brave face.

"It's an honor to meet you. Everyone talks about the four Alphas of the Savage Sector with such respect. I only wish one day I can be a fraction as powerful as you," Dante states with such discipline, I'm surprised. Then again, he's staring at us with stars in his eyes, too.

Narah chats with Dante, clearly sensing the unease, while Harmony slides over to me, practically bouncing on her toes.

"So, what do you think?" she whispers.

We move out of earshot of Dante, and Crius responds before I can.

"It's okay. Bit skinny, but you just met him. Don't rush anything… you have time."

"He works out with his three brothers and has joined the hunting team." She frowns. "You should hear how much he admires all of you."

"As long as the admiration is for you, not us," Nikos murmurs as softly as he can. Stroking her cheek, he coaxes a smile from her. He's always had a way of softening her. She and Crius butt heads, Stone is the practical one, and I ended up as the authority and have the final say. Sure, I'd prefer to be her friend, but I also want the absolute world for her, which means it's up to us to teach her.

"Sweetheart, if you're happy, that's all that matters." I interrupt. "There's no rush. You have time to get to know him."

She pinches her lips to the side. "I already know him." She motions her chin over her shoulder to where Stone is chewing off his ear. "I turn seventeen in a few months, and I don't want another Omega to snatch him up. I've seen the way Becky stares at him." She glances at a brunette with curls, who keeps looking over at us.

Taking Harmony's hand, I draw her closer to us. "If Dante is truly interested in you, he won't have eyes for Becky. A man must prove to you he's worth it and fight for you. Don't chase him."

"Ask your mother." Crius nods. "We chased her, even when she tried to push us away."

"You deserve someone who will cherish the ground you walk on," Nikos adds.

She stares at each of us, and I have to say, for once, things are going smoothly, not to mention our advice is solid.

"I'll think about it, thanks." Just as I think she's going to hug me, and I lean forward, she turns and rushes back to Dante's side. "Come on, Dante, let's go get some food. Oh, look, Becky's here."

I laugh to myself at how obvious she is.

Narah turns toward us, Stone joining her. "Did you really just hand out guy advice to a sixteen-year-old?"

"As her fathers, yes we did."

"In today's world, Omegas chase the guys they want t. It's not how it used to be." She smiles beautifully. "But I love you all for trying."

"Not sure I'm a fan of the new way." Crius makes a face. "I loved chasing you, angel."

Narah slides into my arms, and we all gather under the apple tree, watching Harmony mingle with Dante and the others her age.

"Where has the time gone?" Narah says softly, then sniffles. "When did she grow up so fast?"

I wonder the same thing as I watch her laughing with Dante at the food table. How long before she wants to move out? The thought brings possessiveness over me, along with the need to steal her away from the world. She's still my baby, and I'm not ready to let her go.

I kiss Narah on the head. She wanted more children, and we tried, but she could never bear another baby. We later discovered whatever spell the High Priestess had put on her that ended up making her pregnant destroyed her chance of ever conceiving again. She was upset for a long time but learned to accept the universe never wants us to take the easy path in life.

I love her even more with each passing day, and we're blessed with the one child we do have. Besides, I'm convinced Kaira might be pregnant. She has a scent around her that reminds me of when Narah was with child.

"Dante was fangirling hard over you." Crius slaps my back, chuckling.

I roll my eyes just as Harmony releases a small scream. I stiffen, Narah flinches, and Nikos charges forward. Harmony is running across the field to the front of our home, and following her, we see what's going on.

Narah's suddenly calling out and rushing in that direction, too.

Jae's home. She moved in with her husbands, and when she visits, everyone gets excited. Jae faced a lot of hardship after she made it her mission to hunt down the man who killed her fated mate. Somehow, through all that, she found happiness in the unlikeliest of places—the home of her enemy.

Laughter fills the air, something I've wanted for a long time. A family and place of my own, where the pack remains safe and those I love are reminded every day how lucky we all are.

Farther down the road, the front gate to our compound opens, and curiosity has me changing my path in that direction. My gaze lands on long, flowing blond hair, and my pulse races. My sister, Hel, and her husband have arrived from their home on Nightmare Island.

She'd escaped her abusive husband in Denmark, only to find herself caught by another pack and taken to the islands. For too long, I couldn't find her after I heard she escaped from Denmark... until she sent me a message that she was alive and might have met her fated mate.

Everyone I love and want in my life has all arrived, and I couldn't be happier. My heart is close to bursting.

Narah's at my side, exploding with joy, her face all lit up.

"Hel's just arrived."

Before she runs from my arms, I turn her to face me.

"In case I forget to tell you later, this is the life I've always wanted with you. To share it with our families." My heart drums faster because the last time I'd felt this giddy and happy was when Harmony came into our life.

Hugging me, Narah looks up at me with tears in her eyes. "Everything is perfect and how it should be." She pushes her up on her toes to reach me, and our mouths clash with fire, with hunger, with a never-ending love. Deepening the kiss, she digs her fingers into my arms.

"You're mine," she growls against my mouth. "All four of you."

I burst out laughing. "My little fox, you are made for me. Now, let's go welcome our sisters."

Arm in arm, we stroll through a mass of people everywhere, and I wouldn't want to be anywhere else. Okay, I lie. If I had to pick, I'd choose to be with Narah, where my cute, little fated mate can climb me like a tree and have her way with me.

About Mila Young

**Find all Mila young books at
www.milayoungbooks.com**

Best-selling author, Mila Young tackles everything with the zeal and bravado of the fairytale heroes she grew up reading about. She slays monsters, real and imaginary, like there's no tomorrow. By day she rocks a keyboard as a marketing extraordinaire. At night she battles with her mighty pen-sword, creating fairytale retellings, and sexy ever after tales.

Ready to read more and more from Mila Young?
www.subscribepage.com/milayoung

Join Mila's **Wicked Readers group** for exclusive content, latest news, and giveaway.
www.facebook.com/groups/milayoungwickedreaders

For more information...
mila@milayoungbooks.com